To CHAIM ZVI LIPSKAR and the many other friends who helped to make this book

THE RELIGION

Tim Willocks was born in Stalybridge, Cheshire, in 1957 and studied medicine at University College Hospital Medical School. He is the author of three previous novels, *Bad City Blues*, *Green River Rising* and *Bloodstained Kings*.

ALSO BY TIM WILLOCKS

Bad City Blues

Green River Rising

Bloodstained Kings

TIM WILLOCKS

The Religion

VINTAGE BOOKS
London

Published by Vintage 2012

2 4 6 8 10 9 7 5 3

Copyright © Tim Willocks 2006

Tim Willocks has asserted his right under the Copyright, Designs and Patents Act 1988 to be identified as the author of this work

This is a work of fiction. Names and characters are the product of the author's imagination and any resemblance to actual persons, living or dead, is entirely coincidental.

This book is sold subject to the condition that it shall not, by way of trade or otherwise, be lent, resold, hired out, or otherwise circulated without the publisher's prior consent in any form of binding or cover other than that in which it is published and without a similar condition, including this condition, being imposed on the subsequent purchaser

First published in Great Britain in 2006 by Jonathan Cape

First published in paperback in 2007 by Arrow

Vintage
Random House, 20 Vauxhall Bridge Road,
London SW1V 2SA

www.vintage-books.co.uk

Addresses for companies within The Random House Group Limited can be found at: www.randomhouse.co.uk/offices.htm

The Random House Group Limited Reg. No. 954009

A CIP catalogue record for this book is available from the British Library

ISBN: 9780099581291

The Random House Group Limited supports the Forest Stewardship Council® (FSC®), the leading international forest-certification organisation. Our books carrying the FSC label are printed on FSC®-certified paper. FSC is the only forest-certification scheme supported by the leading environmental organisations, including Greenpeace. Our paper procurement policy can be found at www.randomhouse.co.uk/environment

Printed and bound by CPI Group (UK) Ltd, Croydon, CR0 4YY

MORAY COUNCIL
20378023
LIBRARIES &
INFORMATION SERVICES
F

THE RELIGION

PROLOGUE

THE *DEVSHIRME*

THE FÂGÂRAŠ MOUNTAINS, EAST HUNGARIAN MARCHES

Spring, AD *1540*

ON THE NIGHT the scarlet horsemen took him away – from all he knew and all he might have known – the moon waxed full in Scorpio, sign of his birth, and as if by the hand of God its incandescence split the alpine valley sheer into that which was dark and that which was light, and the light lit the path of devils to his door. If the dogs of war hadn't lost their way, the boy would never have been found, and peace and love and labour might have blessed him all his days. But such is the nature of Fate in a time of Chaos. And when is Time not Chaos? And when is War not a spawnhole of fiends? And who dries the tears of the nameless when even Saints and Martyrs lie sleeping in their crypts? A King had died and his throne was disputed and Emperors fought like jackals to seize the spoil. And if Emperors care little for the graveyards they scatter in their wake, why should their servants care more? *As Above, So Below* say the wise men, and so it was that night.

His name was Mattias and he was twelve years old and of matters of Policy and State he knew nothing at all. His family were Saxon metalsmiths, transplanted by his migrant grandfather to a steep Carpathian valley and a village of no importance except to those who called it home. He slept by the kitchen hearthstone and dreamed of fire and steel. He awoke in the dark before dawn with his heart a wild bird in his chest. He pulled on boots and a scorch-marked coat and silently – for two sisters and his mother slept next door – he took wood and summoned flames from the pale pink embers in the hearth so that warmth would greet the girls on their rising.

Like all first-born men of his line, Mattias was a blacksmith. His purpose today was to complete the making of a dagger and this filled him with joy, for what boy would not make real weapons if he could? From the hearth he took a burning brand and stole into the yard and the sharp air filled his chest and he stopped. The world about was painted black and silver by the moon. Above the mountain's rimrock, constellations wheeled in their sphere and he sought out their shapes and marked them under his breath. Virgo, Boötes, Cassiopeia. Lower down the slopes headlong streaks of brightness marked the valley's forked stream, and pastures floated misty beneath the woodlands. In the yard, his father's forge stood like a temple to some prophet unknown and the firelight on its pale stone walls promised magic and marvels, and the doing of Things that no one had done before.

As his father, Kristofer, had taught him, Mattias crossed himself on the threshold and whispered a prayer to Saint James. Kristofer was out on the road, shoeing and sharpening tools for the farms and manors thereabouts. Would he be angry, when he returned, that Mattias had wasted three days' forging? When he might have made fishhooks or a wood saw or a scythe – goods that always found a ready buyer? No, not if the blade were true. If the blade were true, his father would be proud. Mattias crossed himself and stepped inside.

The forge smelled of ox hooves and sea salt, of clinker, horses and coal. The firepot was readied as he'd left it the evening before and the kindling caught with the firebrand's first touch. He worked the bellows and fed yesterday's coke to the flames, coaxing the fire, building it, until burning charcoal lay two inches deep on the tuyère. He lit the lamp, then unearthed his blade from the ashes in which he'd buried it overnight.

He'd taken two days to straighten and harden the steel, six inches in the blade and four in the tang. Knives he'd made before but this was his first dagger, and the requisite skill was multiplied in the weapon's double-edged symmetry and the forging of strength in the spine. He hadn't perfected the symmetry but the edges didn't roll beneath a file. He blew away the ash and sighted down the bevels and found no warp or screw. With a damp rag he wiped the blade clean and worked its either surface smooth with pumice. Then he polished the blade until it gleamed dark blue, with powder of Emril and butter. Now would his Art be tested in the temper.

On the charcoal bed he laid a quarter inch of ash, and on the ash the blade, and watched the colour creep through the steel, turning it face over face so the heat remained even. When the cutting edges glowed as pale as fresh straw, he pulled the blade clear with the tongs and plunged it into a bucket of damp soil. Burning vapours spiralled with a smell that made him heady. In this first quench, by his grandfather's lore, the blade laid claim at its birth to the power of all four elements: earth, fire, water and air. Such a blade would endure. He rebuilt the coal bed and layered the ashes on top, and took the lid from his second quench, a bucket of horse piss. He'd collected it the day before, from the fleetest horse in the village.

'Can I watch, Mattie?'

For a moment his sister's voice vexed him. This was his work, his place, a man's place; not a place for a five-year-old girl. But Britta adored him. He always saw her eyes glow when she looked at him. She was the baby of the family. The death of two younger brothers before they could walk remained always at the back of Mattias's mind; or rather, not their deaths but the memory of his mother's grief and his father's silent anguish. By the time he turned, his anger was gone, and he smiled to see Britta in the doorway, her silhouette doll-like in the first grey rumour of dawn. She wore a nightshirt and clogs and she clenched her hands about reedy arms as she shivered. Mattias took off his coat as he walked over and slipped it round her shoulders. He picked her up and sat her on the sacks of salt inside the door.

'You can watch from here, as long as you stay back from the fire.' The bargain wasn't ideal, he could see, but she didn't demur. 'Are Mamma and Gerta still sleeping?' he asked.

Britta nodded. 'Yes. But the village dogs are barking. I was scared.'

Mattias cocked an ear. It was true. From down the hill came a chorus of yaps and snarls. Absorbed by the crackle of the forge he hadn't noticed.

'They must have found a fox,' he said.

'Or a wolf.'

He smiled. 'The wolves don't come here any more.'

He returned to his blade and found it cool enough to touch. He wiped it clean and laid it once more on the fire. He was tempted to pump the bellows, for he loved the surge of life within the coals, but if the colour rose too fast the core of the steel might weaken and he resisted.

'Why don't the wolves come here any more?'

Mattias flipped the blade. 'Because they're afraid of us.'

'Why are the wolves afraid of us?'

The edges flushed dark fawn, like a deer's coat in autumn, and he grabbed the blade with the tongs and flipped it again, and yes, the colour was even and rising still, with magentas in the spine and tang, and the second quench was upon him. He pulled the blade from the forge and plunged it into the urine. The hiss was explosive and he turned his face from the acrid, ammoniac steam. He began at once to say an Ave. Halfway through, Britta joined in, stumbling over the Latin, and he continued without waiting, timing the quench by the pace of the prayer until he'd finished, then he pulled the smoking steel from the caustic brew and buried it down in the ash box and wiped his brow.

The second temper was done; he hoped well enough. The pungent bite of the piss quench would impart itself to the metal and keep its sharpness keen. Perhaps too, he hoped, the fleetness of the horse would quicken the dagger to its mark. For the third quench, most magical of all, he would take the glowing blade out to the dense green grass by the vegetable patch, and temper it with the newly fallen dew. No waters were more pure, for no one had ever seen them fall, even if they stayed wakeful through the night, and they flowed from Heaven. Some believed them the tears God shed for His children while they slept. Through such cooling dew the spirit of the mountain would bind to the dagger's heart and its purpose would always be true. He pushed a pair of tempering tongs into the coals and pumped the fire until the thickened ends glowed orange.

'Mattie, why are the wolves afraid of us?'

'Because they fear we will hunt them and kill them.'

'Why would we hunt and kill them?'

'Because they kill our sheep. And because their skins are warm against the winter. That's why Dadda wears a wolfskin.'

'Did Dadda kill the wolf?'

Kristofer had indeed, but the story was not for a little girl's ears. Mattias wiped ash from the blade and laid it by the fire. Britta was not to be ignored, he knew, but the blade was where his attention was needed most. He said, 'Why don't you sing me a song? Then the song will be part of the steel, and so will you, and it will be your blade as well as mine.'

'Which song? Quickly, Mattie, which song?'

He glanced at her face and saw her flushed with delight and for a moment he wondered if he had not doomed the blade to be hers forever, at least in her mind.

'*The Raven*,' he said.

It was a song their mother sang for them and Britta had caused much amazement when, at the age of only three, she had piped her way through every verse. It told of a prince bewitched into a raven by a jealous stepmother, and of the princess who risked the life of her only child to bring him back again. Despite dark deeds it was a happy tale in the end, though Mattias no longer believed it as he once had. Britta still believed every word. She started to sing in her high, trembling voice and its sound filled the gloom of the forge with her stainless soul. And he was glad he'd asked her for the song, for as his father, Kristofer, had told him, no man could comprehend the mystery of steel entire, and if a blade forged during a snowstorm was other than a blade forged in the sun – and who could ever doubt that that was so? – then why would a sound as sweet as Britta now made not leave its imprint too?

As Britta sang he put his all into the final tempering. He quenched the handles of the tongs and clamped their glowing jaws along the dagger's spine. Thus he drew the hardness, for hardness is not itself strength. When the spine was a solid dark blue he worked the tang and the ricasso darker still. And to the very tip of the blade he gave a pale blue temper, like the early morning sky on New Year's Day. And all the while he worked, Britta sang her song, and the Raven won the Princess's heart, and in his chest grew the knowledge that this would indeed be a blade to make his father proud. He dropped the heated tongs into the water and took the cool pair. He relaid the bed and spread the ash and placed the blade on the coals with its tip on a lump of raw charcoal. When the cutting edges bloomed the colour of his mother's hair – a fierce, coppery bronze – he'd take the blade to the dew and its moment of truth. He watched the steel as if his place in eternity hinged on it and he didn't hear the sound Britta made when she fell to the floor. He heard only the sudden silence in her song.

He called out over his shoulder, 'Britta, don't stop now. We're almost done.'

And there: the hues were changing, rising like alchemical gold, yet the silence remained unbroken and his gut cried out for the song for he knew, in his bone by now, that her voice would indeed forge one blade and not another, and that truly it was hers as well as his, and that they both had fixed some portion of their souls into the metal, and that in that fixing would inhere the blade's nobility. He turned from the fire, his hand still on the tongs, to find her eyes.

'We're almost done!' he said.

He found her sprawled on the ground.

Her skull was smashed apart like a broken jar of wine. His coat had fallen from her shoulders. Her nightshirt was drenched with something black that gleamed like streaks of treacle through her pale yellow hair.

Standing over her, with the incurious expression of a farmer who'd spaded a mole, was a stocky youth, wispily bearded and half a head shorter than he. He was swathed in a motley of wrappings and rags and on his head was a filthy green cap. By his side he held a short curved sword, clotted with the treacle and strands of Britta's hair. When the youth looked up from the murdered child, his eyes were as dead as stones. His roving gaze held Mattias for no more time than he spent on the anvil and the tools. He grunted a question in an alien tongue.

Mattias stood stranded in the forge's heat yet inside he felt icy and empty. Empty of breath. Empty of will. Empty of each and every feeling he'd formerly known. Some portion of his mind asked if this was how the blade felt in the quench. And if so, which quench? And he took refuge in the fire, where something he did know yet awaited him. He turned and looked at his blade and saw the cutting edges bloom into the colour of his mother's hair – a fiery bronze that crept across the bevels to the dark blued spine. He felt the final temper slipping from his grasp and with it all the magic they'd spun that dawn and with it, too, his father's pride when he saw what they'd created. These things he could not let stand. He clamped the tongs fast on the ricasso and pulled the blade clear of the coals. Then he turned.

The murderer had started towards him and his face betrayed no alarm until he saw what Mattias carried. The bolt of fear that pierced him betrayed his youth, but earned him no mercy. As if of its own volition the dagger lunged forward, the air a shimmer in its wake. Mattias lurched through the first pace with feet as heavy as lead, and through the second propelled by a rage that choked his gorge. By the third pace raw hatred drove boy and dagger both. The youth cried out in his alien tongue and Mattias ran the blade into his gut. Flesh sizzled on steel as he crammed him back against the wall and the stench of burning wool and fat filled his throat and the stones in the twisted face bulged forth in horror. The murderer screamed and dropped his sword and grabbed and screamed and screamed again as the red hot tang stripped his palms down to their sinews. Mattias clamped his left hand across the gaping lips. He leaned into the tongs until their jaws met the heaving belly and the tip of the dagger grated on what felt like bone. And then he prayed.

'*Ave Maria, gratia plena, Dominus tecum, benedicta tu in mulieribus et benedictus fructus ventris tui, Iesus.*'

The youth's gullet convulsed and vomited blood spilled through Mattias's fingers. He squeezed tighter. Blood snivelled from the flaring nostrils and the skinless hands clawed at the tongs and the stocky chest convulsed in futile spasms. The light in the protuberant eyes began to fade and the spasms waned and Mattias completed his prayer.

'*Holy Mary, Mother of God, pray for us sinners, now and at the hour of our death.*'

Mattias felt something pass from the body, something that vanished with a stealth that chilled his marrow. Something that had been and now was gone. The youth sagged, heavier than anything Mattias had ever known. The face clamped in his hand was as pale as putty. Its half-closed eyes were lightless and dull, like those in the head of a pig on a butcher's stall. So this was death and this was killing.

Mattias said, '*Amen*.'

And he thought: *The quench*.

He pulled the dagger free. The blade down to the ricasso smoked black as sin. He let the body fold and didn't look at it again. Amidst the distant barking of the dogs he heard coarse foreign shouts and screams of terror. Britta lay in the doorway, bloodied and still. Something had passed from her too that was no more. In his hand the tongs began to shake and so did his knees. His bowels felt loose and his vision was blurred. He turned to the safety of what he knew. The forge, the tools, the fire. He scrubbed the steaming blade with a damp cloth but its blackened hue remained, and somehow he knew that the blade would stay black forever. The steel was too hot to hold, yet he was loath to plunge it again, for in a world turned upside down his mind clung tight to his Art. He dipped the cloth in cold water and wrapped it around the tang. And then he paused.

From the chaos beyond the forge house door he heard a voice – closer than the rest – shouting out to God, but not for His mercy. Calling, rather, on His vengeance and His wrath. It was the first voice Mattias had ever heard. It was his mother's.

Mattias squeezed the sodden hilt in his hand. The tang's heat was tolerable. The dagger's final quench had not been purest dew but a murderer's blood, and if its destiny and purpose were now other than he'd planned, so too, now, were his own. And he wondered then, as he would wonder always, if it were not his forging of this Devil's blade that had brought this fatal doom upon his loved ones. He searched for the soul with which he'd woken and found it not. He searched for a prayer, but his tongue didn't move. Something had been torn from within which he hadn't known was there until the hole it left behind howled in sorrow. Yet gone that something was; and not even God could restore it. His mother's fury pierced him. In fury – not in sorrow

– had his mother chosen to die. Her fury called him to her side. He walked to the door and stooped to cover Britta with his coat. Britta at least had died whole, with a song on her lips and the joy of creation in her heart. There was an angel in the blade along with a devil. He'd take her with him. He'd take angel and devil both.

He stepped out into the cold and steam rose from the black dagger in his fist, as if the forge contained a shaft bored up from Hell and he were a demon assassin newly ascended. The yard was empty. The heavens at the rimrock's edge were reefed in vermilion cloud. From the village pillars of smoke quavered skyward and with them cries of anguish and crackles of flame. He walked across the cobbles, sick with fear. Fear of whatever vileness afflicted his mother. Fear of shame. Of cowardice. Of the knowledge that he couldn't save her. Of the darkness that had housed itself inside his spirit. Yet the darkness spoke with a feral power that brooked neither refusal nor hesitation.

Plunge in, the darkness said.

Mattias turned and looked back at the forge. For the first time in his life he saw a drab stone hut. A drab stone hut with the corpse of his sister, and the corpse of a man he had killed, inside.

Like the blade in the quench.

Plunge in.

In the kitchen little Gerta lay tangled on the hearthstone. Her features were twisted in bewilderment and her puddled blood smoked foul among the coals. He straightened her fragile limbs and knelt and kissed her mouth. He covered her corpse with the blanket he'd slept in. He plunged on. Across the ransacked room the door hung creaking from one hinge. In the dirt outside was a melee. He stepped closer. He glimpsed the village priest, Father Giorgi, for whom he served at altar on a Sunday morning. Father Giorgi was shouting at assailants unseen, with a crucifix upraised in his fists. A squat figure hacked him in the neck and Father Giorgi fell. Mattias stepped closer. What kind of man would kill a priest? Then he stopped and wheeled away, his mind erased in an instant of all he'd seen.

He blinked and heaved for breath and the forbidden picture returned. His mother's nude body, her pale breasts and thick dark teats. Her pale belly, the hair between her legs. Shame writhed in his gut with the urge to run. Across the yard, beyond the forge, to the woods where they'd never find him. The darkness that was now his only guide and counsellor made him turn back to the door and he looked again.

A horse, pierced with arrows, lay dying on its side, its great head flapping and its eyes rolling wide above the pink froth bubbling from its muzzle. Nearby sprawled a villager, also pierced, as if in flight, and by him Father Giorgi in a widening pool. Across the horse's carcass, as if upon a mattress obscene, lay his mother. Her copper hair tossed as she fought against the four men cursing and struggling to hold her down. Her stark naked skin was marble white and slashed with scratches and blotched with the indigo welts of brutish fingers. Her face was drawn. Her teeth were bloody. Her shocking blue eyes were wild. She didn't see Mattias, and while part of him yearned for those wild blue eyes to meet his own, he knew that the knowledge of his witness would drain her defiance, and her defiance was the last gift she would give him.

Someone punched her in the head and screamed in her ear and she turned and spat in his face and the sputum was crimson. A fifth man knelt between her legs, his breeches pulled down. And all of them shouting – at each other, at her, one with a twisting finger up his nose – in their yammering alien tongue. They were raping a woman dragged half-sleeping from her bed, yet their manner was like herdsmen freeing a stranded calf from a bog: gesticulating, blaming, bellowing encouragement and advice; their faces innocent of malice and vacant of pity. The brute between her legs lost patience, for she wedged her knee against his chest and wouldn't let him take her. He pulled a knife from his boot and pushed up her breast and took aim and ran her through her heart. No one tried to stop him. No one complained. His mother stopped moving and her head flopped back. Mattias wanted to sob – but his breath was frozen in his lungs. The brute dropped his knife and reached for his crotch and he slotted something stiff inside her and started pumping. And someone must have said something funny, for they all of them laughed.

Mattias held back the tears he hadn't earned. He'd failed his sisters. He'd failed his father. His mother's corpse lay violated by beasts. He alone was left standing, dispossessed and powerless and lost. He came to as he realised that he'd pushed the tip of the dagger into his palm. His blood was bright against the crusting filth on his fingers. His pain was clean and true and it cleared his mind. His mother had denied them what they'd wanted even more than her flesh: her surrender and humiliation. The laying of her pride. The desire to be close to her soul overwhelmed him. The desire for death and in death that companionship he treasured more dearly than life. He clasped the blade against his arm where it wouldn't be seen. Without haste – for if the blade was yet warm, his blood was now cold – he waded into atrocity to claim his share.

The first creature shuddered and whooped in a bestial spasm and the others cheered, and he rose to his feet and staggered back with his breeches round his knees. A second beast knelt to penetrate his mother and the other three groped her thighs and breasts to arouse themselves for their turn. All but the second looked at Mattias. They saw nothing but a wretched boy. From the direction of the village came the sound of hooves at the canter and this concerned them more, but the hooves concerned Mattias not at all. The darkness rose within him and he felt free.

He plunged in.

After hammer and tongs the blade seemed delicate as paper, yet he punched it twice through the first devil's back as if his ribs were woven from straw. The creature sighed and his breeches snared his ankles and he dropped to his hands and knees with his arse in the air and stared at the ground between his elbows and panted like a heat-exhausted dog. Mattias kicked him over in the dirt and plunged on.

The second creature grunted between his mother's splayed legs. He knew nothing was amiss until Mattias scraped the cap from his skull and grabbed him by the hair and bent him backwards. Mattias saw a bewildered sense of injustice in his eyes, as of a child dragged unawares from a pot of jam, then he punched the blade through his upturned cheek and pulled it free and punched again and an eye popped forth and dangled from its socket by the string. Working his arm with the rhythm of the forge he ploughed the childlike face with bleeding slits, splashing the heel of his fist in the screaming mask as he stabbed the dagger through teeth and tongue and bones, and through and through the fluttering hands that the man flung up for protection.

Mattias paused and heaved for he'd forgotten to breathe. He looked at the other three devils, and found them watching him agape. A wordless cry escaped Mattias's throat, for he was now more beast than they, and he cast the yowling blind man to the mud. The three backed away on the far side of the horse and one came to his senses and unslung a bow from his back. He fumbled an arrow from his sash and it dropped to the ground. Mattias turned away and looked at his mother and his madness was expunged. He knelt and took her hand and pressed her work-worn fingers to his cheek. The fingers were yet warm with life and Hope knifed his heart. He looked up: but her wild blue eyes stared sightless, and the knife twisted, and he choked into the hand held to his face. The thud of hooves pounded in his ears but he was beyond all the things of this world. From this world, the touch of his mother's hand was all he needed.

His head jerked up to a crash as loud as thunder. The brute nocking the arrow to his bow spun into the ground, his skull dashed apart and grey slop spilling down his shoulders as he fell. The two remaining rapists dropped to their knees amid a drift of blue smoke and they babbled like the crazed as they crammed their foreheads to the dirt.

Mattias turned and saw a sight such as never he'd seen.

A man, though he seemed a god, sat astride a grey Arab stallion, the twin plumed breath from the bores of its nose giving both the look of phantoms in a tale. The rider was young and proud and dark of complexion, with high, fine cheekbones and a beard like the blade of a spear. He wore a scarlet kaftan lined and trimmed in sable and baggy scarlet breeches and yellow boots, and his snow-white turban was garnished with a spray of diamonds that flashed when he moved. At his waist was a curved sword whose hilt and scabbard were alive with precious stones. In his hand smoked a long-barrelled pistol, its fittings chased with silver. His eyes were brown and fixed on Mattias's own, and in them was something that looked like admiration, and something more – though it could not be so – that felt to Mattias like love.

The brown gaze did not waver and Mattias did not blink. And in this moment the soul of the man and the soul of the boy reached out and were entwined, for no good reason that either might explain and with a power that neither dared question, for it came from God.

In time Mattias would learn that this warrior was a captain of the Sari Bayrak, most ancient and valorous guardians of the Sultan's arms, and that his name was Abbas bin Murad. For now he was simply a man. A man whose heart contained no trace of malice.

Behind the captain sat two more scarlet riders. In the street beyond, villagers fought fires and rushed back and forth in dismay, dragging furniture from hovels and ferrying children and old folk from the flames. Riding through this tumult like paladins among sheep, a dozen more scarlet horsemen wielded lances and whips as they harried the chastened foot soldiers from their pillage.

17

Abbas sheathed his pistol in a saddle-mounted sleeve. He looked at the woman draped violate and nude across the horse. He looked again at Mattias and he spoke. His tongue was not the same as that of the devils and though Mattias didn't know the words, he knew what he asked.

'*This is your mother?*'

Mattias swallowed and nodded.

Abbas saw the dagger in his hand, and his shirt plastered to his body with spilled blood. Abbas pursed his lips and shook his head. He glanced beyond Mattias and Mattias turned: the first man he'd stabbed lay unmoving. The second crawled half-naked in the dirt, blind and faceless and mewling in self-pity though rended lips. Abbas made a motion with his hand. One of his lieutenants rode forward and drew his sword and Mattias stared in wonder at the flawless damascene blade. The lieutenant stopped by the mewling wretch and leaned forward. The etched sword rose and fell with hardly a sound and a head rolled into the gutter in a spate of gore.

Abbas rode over to Mattias and held out his hand.

Mattias let go of his mother and wiped the blade on his sleeve and stripped the tang of its rags and wiped that too. He held the blade by the tip and gave it to Abbas. He felt no fear. The moment Abbas touched the dagger his brow rose in surprise. He held the flat against the back of his hand and surprise was confirmed. Mattias realised the steel was still warm. Abbas gestured with the dagger.

'*You made this?*'

Again Mattias understood the question if not the words. He nodded. And again Abbas pursed his lips. He nudged his horse towards the house and leaned across and slid three inches of the dagger into a crack between doorframe and wall. He threw his weight against the tang and Mattias flinched as the blade canted over, folding far further than he would dare bend it, the tang almost flat to the wall, and panic lanced through his gut as the steel snapped – but the steel did not snap. And when Abbas let go, the blade sprang back to the true. Abbas withdrew the dagger and examined it again and looked at Mattias. And both knew he'd forged a piece of appalling beauty. Then the dagger vanished into the captain's *dolama* and Mattias knew he'd never see it again.

Abbas gave orders and Mattias watched as the second lieutenant wheeled and rode away. The first, who hadn't sheathed his damask blade, trotted to the two kneeling rapists, they whose lust would never be slaked. They blubbered and pleaded and befouled themselves, and he prodded them into a stumbling run and chivvied them back down the street.

Abbas turned and reached behind the cantle and unhitched a milk-white blanket there rolled. He tossed it to Mattias and Mattias caught it. It was woven of the finest lamb's wool. Mattias had never handled an object of such high quality before and so gentle was its touch to his roughened hands that he feared that he'd damage it. He stared at Abbas blankly, baffled by this gift. Abbas gestured to his mother, spreadeagled and outraged in the shambles.

Mattias felt his throat go tight and tears stung his eyes, for the gift was not of a blanket, but of a woman's dignity, and this kindness pierced him to the core. But a warning flashed on the captain's face and on instinct Mattias understood. He pulled the tears back inside. He didn't let them fall. And Abbas saw this and again his estimation rose and he nodded. Mattias turned and unfurled the blanket and it fell like a caress across his mother. His tears rose again as she vanished forever beneath it and again he quelled them. She was dead, and yet not dead, for she filled his heart with a love that burst its buckles and he wondered if she was even now in Heaven and if God would ever let him see her again. Then he heard Abbas's voice and turned. Abbas repeated the phrase. And though he didn't understand, Mattias felt the comfort of their intention. He remembered their sound.

In the months to come he would hear them again many times and would learn their meaning.

'*All flesh is dust*,' said Abbas.

From his saddlebag Abbas produced a book. Its green leather binding was worked in a golden script of fabulous design and as if letting God direct his hand he opened it at random. His eyes scanned the chosen page and stopped, as if arrested by something noble and sacred and apt, and he looked up from the book and pointed at the boy.

He said, '*Ibrahim*.'

Mattias stared back without comprehension.

Abbas pointed again with an insistent gesture: '*Ibrahim*.'

Mattias realised that this was the name by which the captain intended to call him. The name, in fact, that Allah had decreed he be called, for the book randomly opened was the Holy Koran. Mattias blinked. His mother was gone. Britta and Gerta were gone. His home was gone. And his father would return to a howling pit where he'd left prosperity and kin. The scarlet captain waited on his tall Arabian grey. Mattias stabbed a finger at his own chest.

He said, '*Ibrahim*.'

With this gone too was the name that his father had given him.

Abbas nodded and closed the holy book and stowed it. The lieutenant returned with a saddled horse and he handed the reins to Mattias and Mattias realised he was to leave with these scarlet riders, and the wide world gaped before him like a chasm. Abbas was not offering him a choice. Rather, Mattias had been chosen. He did not falter. He mounted the horse and felt its living strength between his thighs and from this high prospect the world was already changed and more than he knew. He bent to the horse's ear and, as his father had taught him to say before the shoeing, he whispered, 'Don't be afraid, my friend.'

Abbas wheeled away and the lieutenant followed. Mattias

looked down at the blanket-shrouded body and thought of his father. He'd never know the magic his father would have taught him, nor the love that was the greatest of his spells. Had the black blade snapped – had Mattias let those tears fall down his cheeks – perhaps the riders would have left him to bury the slain. But this he could not know, for he was a boy. Mattias stifled his anguish and urged his new mount onward. He did not once look back. Though he could not know this either, War was now his master and his trade, and War was jealous, and demanded love only of itself.

As they trotted up the street, past burning hovels and villagers with gazes cast down, Mattias saw the remains of the last two devils. Their decapitated bodies soaked in enormous puddles of blood and the whited eyes of their heads stared into the mud. Their chastened comrades stood in sullen ranks under the guns of their Turkish betters. These men, Mattias would learn, were the irregulars who flocked to the Sultan's banner in search of plunder – landless failures and criminals, Wallachians and Bulgars, the floating scum without discipline or skill who crave the wages of war. The execution was to demonstrate that this was now the fiefdom of the Sultan and that all that lay upon it belonged to him. Every grain of wheat, every cup of wine, every sheep, every mule, every village. Every man, woman and child. Every drop of rain that fell. All this belonged to his August Majesty, as, now, did belong young Ibrahim.

Thus, in the year of 1540, Mattias the blacksmith's son became a *devshirme:* a Christian boy gathered in the Gathering and drafted for the Slaves of the Gate. Across many strange lands he would travel, and many strange Things he would see, before the fabled minarets of Old Stambouli rose gleaming in the sun by the Golden Horn. Because he was a killer before he was a man, he would train in the Enderun of Topkapi Saray. He would join the violent brotherhood of the janissaries. He would learn strange tongues and customs and the many arts of war. He would learn that God is but One and that Mohammed is his Prophet and would yearn to fight and die in Allah's name. For the unknown fate towards which he rode was to dedicate his life to God's Shadow On This Earth. To the Padishah of the White Sea and the Black. To the Refuge of All the People in the World. To the Sultan of Sultans and King of Kings. To the Lawgiver, the Magnificent. To the Emperor of the Ottomans, Suleiman Shah.

PART I

A WORLD OF DREAMS

SUNDAY 13 MAY 1565

Castel Sant' Angelo, the Borgo, Malta

The situation, as Starkey saw it, was thus.

The largest armada since antiquity, bearing the finest army in the modern world, had been dispatched by Suleiman Shah to conquer Malta. Turkish success would expose southern Europe to a wave of Islamic terror. Sicily would be ripe for the picking. A Moslem reconquest of Granada would not be unthinkable. Rome itself would tremble. Yet these strategic rewards be as they might, Suleiman's most passionate ambition was to exterminate the Knights of Saint John – that singular band of healers and warrior monks known to some as the Sea Knights and to others as the Hospitallers, and who in an age of Inquisition yet dared call themselves '*The Religion*'.

The Grande Turke's army was commanded by Mustafa Pasha, who had broken the knights once before – and in a citadel immeasurably stronger than this one – at the celebrated siege of Rhodes, in 1522. Since then, Suleiman – who, despite his many achievements, placed his sacred duty to conquer the world for Islam at the forefront of his Policy – had overthrown Belgrade, Buda, Baghdad and Tabriz. He'd crushed Hungary, Syria, Egypt, Iran, Iraq, Transylvania and the Balkans. Twenty-five Venetian islands and every port in North Africa had fallen to his corsairs. His warships had smashed the Holy League at Preveza. Only winter had turned him back from the gates of Vienna. No one doubted the outcome of Suleiman's latest *jihad* on Malta.

Except, perhaps, a handful of the knights themselves.

Fra Oliver Starkey, Lieutenant Turcopolier of the English Langue, was standing at the window of the Grand Master's office. From this prospect, high in the south wall of Castel Sant' Angelo, he could see the complex geography of the battlefield to come. Encircled by surrounding heights, three triangular spits of land formed the boundaries of Grand Harbour, the Sea Knights' home. Sant' Angelo stood at the apex of the first peninsula and dominated the main town of the Borgo. Here were crammed the Auberges of the Knights, the Sacred Infirmary, the conventual church of San Lorenzo, the homes of the townsfolk, the main docks and warehouses, and all the bristling paraphernalia of a tiny metropolis. The Borgo was barricaded from the mainland by a huge, curving enceinte – a curtain wall studded with defensive bastions and teeming with knights and militia at their drill.

Starkey looked across Galley Creek towards the second spit of land, L'Isola, where the sails of a dozen windmills turned with a strange and incongruous tranquillity. Squares of militia wheeled in formation, the sunlight winking from their helms, and, beyond them, naked Moslem slaves chained in pairs strained to the overseer's whistle as they hauled blocks of sandstone up the counterwall of Saint Michel, the fortress that sealed L'Isola from the mainland. Once the siege commenced, the only communication between L'Isola and the Borgo would be the fragile bridge of boats across Galley Creek. To the north, half a mile across Grand Harbour at the seaward tip of the third peninsula, stood Fort Saint Elmo. This was the most isolated outpost of all, and once under siege it could only be accessed by water.

The entire vista seethed with preparations. Fortification and drill; excavation and entrenchment; harvesting and salting and storage; burnishing and honing and prayer. Master serjeants roared at the pikemen and the hammers of the armourers rang. In the churches bells pealed and novenas were held and women prayed to Our Lady by day and by night. Eight out of ten of the defenders were unblooded peasants with homemade leather armour and spears. Yet in the choice between slavery or death, the proud and valiant Maltese had shown no hesitation. A mood of grim defiance hung over the town.

A movement caught Starkey's eye and he looked up. A pair of black-winged falcons plunged earthward through the turquoise sky, as if they would fall forever. Then they broke and soared in unison and sailed without visible motion for the western horizon, and in the indefinable moment that they melted into the haze, Starkey imagined them the last birds in the world. A voice from across the spacious room behind him broke the spell of his reverie.

'He who has not known War has not known God.'

Starkey had heard this unholy motto before. It never failed to disturb his conscience. Today it filled him with dread, for he feared he might soon discover that it was true. Starkey turned from the window to rejoin the conference.

Jean Parisot de La Valette, the Order's Grand Master, stood at his table of maps with the great Colonel Le Mas. Tall and austere, in a long black habit emblazoned with the Cross of Saint John, La Valette was seventy-one. Fifty years of killing on the high seas had forged his sinew and so, perhaps, he knew whereof he spoke. At twenty he'd survived the blood-soaked tragedy of Rhodes, when the tattered remnant of the Order had been exiled to the waves in the last of their ships. At forty-six he'd survived a year as a slave in the galley of Abd-ur Rahman. When others would have taken high office within the Order – and on the safety of land – La Valette had chosen decades of ceaseless piracy, his nostrils stuffed with tobacco against the stench. His brow was high and his hair and beard were now silver. His eyes had been bleached by the sun to the colour of stone. His face seemed cast from bronze. To him news of the invasion was like some rejuvenating elixir in an Attic myth. He'd embraced the prospect of doom with the ardour of a lover. He was tireless. He was exuberant. He was inspired. Inspired as one whose hatred may at last be unleashed without pity or restraint. What La Valette hated was Islam and all its evil works. What he loved was God and the Religion. And in these the last of his days, God had sent the Religion the blessing of War. War at its apotheosis. War as manifestation of Divine Will. War unfettered and pure, to be fought to its smoking conclusion through every conceivable extreme of cruelty and horror.

He who has not known War has not known God? Christ had never blessed the pursuit of arms in any fashion. But, then, there were times when Starkey was certain that La Valette was mad. Mad with the premonition of outrageous violence. Mad with the knowledge that the power of God flowed through him. Mad because who else but a madman could hold the destiny of a people in the palm of his hand and foresee the slaughter of thousands with such equanimity? Starkey crossed the room to join the two old comrades talking over the map table.

'How much longer must we wait?' said Colonel Le Mas.

'Ten days? A week? Perhaps less,' replied La Valette.

'I thought we had another month.'

'We were wrong.'

La Valette's office reflected his austere temperament. The tapestries, portraits and fine furnishings of his predecessors were gone. In their place, stone, wood, paper, ink, candles. A simple wooden crucifix was nailed to the wall. Colonel Pierre Le Mas had arrived that morning from Messina with the unexpected reinforcement of four hundred Spanish soldiers and thirty-two knights of the Order. He was a burly, battle-scarred salt in his late fifties. He nodded to Starkey and indicated the chart on the table.

'Only a philosopher could decipher these hieroglyphics.'

The map – somewhat to Starkey's chagrin, for he'd overseen

the delicate cartography himself – was densely annotated with cryptic notes and symbols of La Valette's devising. The Order of Saint John was divided into eight Langues – or Tongues – each according to the nationality of its members: those of France, Provence, Auvergne, Italy, Castile, Aragon, Germany and England. La Valette traced the defensive enceinte that sealed the Borgo in a great stone curve from west to east, pointing out the bastion he'd assigned each Langue.

'France,' he said, and marked the far right, hard against Galley Creek. Like Le Mas, La Valette was of that most belligerent of breeds, a Gascon. 'Our noble Langue of Provence is next, here on the foremost bastion.'

Le Mas said, 'How many are we of Provence?'

'Seventy-six knights and serjeants at arms.' La Valette's finger moved westward along the chart. 'On our left is the Langue of Auvergne. Then the Italians – a hundred and sixty-nine lances – then Aragon. Castile. Germany. In total five hundred and twenty-two brethren have answered the call to arms.'

Le Mas furrowed his brow. The number was pitifully small.

La Valette added, 'With the men you brought we have eight hundred Spanish *tercios* and two score gentleman adventurers. The Maltese militia number a little over five thousand.'

'I hear Suleiman sends sixty thousand *gazi* to drive us into the sea.'

'Including seamen, labour battalions and supports, many more than that,' replied La Valette. 'The Dogs of the Prophet have pushed us back for five hundred years – from Jerusalem to Krak des Chevaliers, from Krak to Acre, from Acre to Cyprus and Rhodes – and every mile of our retreat is marked with blood and ashes and bones. At Rhodes we chose life over death, and while to all the world it is an episode bathed in glory, to me it is a stain. This time, there will be no "surrender with honour". We will retreat no more. Malta is the last ditch.'

Le Mas rubbed his hands. 'Let me claim the Post of Honour.'

By this Le Mas meant the locus of greatest danger. The post of death. He was not the first to request it, and must have known this, for he added, 'You owe it to me.'

To what this referred Starkey did not know, but something passed between the two men.

'We'll talk of that later,' said La Valette, 'when Mustafa's intentions are better known.' He pointed to the edge of the fortifications. 'Here, at the Kalkara Gate, is the Post of England.'

Le Mas laughed. 'An entire post for one man?'

The Ancient and Noble Tongue of England, once among the Order's greatest, had been destroyed by the bloated philanderer and heresiarch, Henry VIII. Starkey was the only remaining Englishman in the Order of Saint John.

La Valette said, 'Fra Oliver *is* the English Langue. He is also my right hand. Without him, we'd be lost.'

Starkey, embarrassed, changed the subject. 'The men you brought with you, how do you rate their quality?'

'Well-trained, well-equipped and all devoted to Christ,' said Le Mas. 'I squeezed two hundred volunteers out of Governor Toledo by threatening to burn his galleys. The rest were recruited on our behalf by the German.'

La Valette raised one brow.

'Mattias Tannhauser,' said Le Mas.

Starkey added, 'He who first forewarned us of Suleiman's plans.'

La Valette glanced up into space, as if to conjure a face. He nodded.

'Tannhauser brought the intelligence?' said Le Mas.

'It wasn't an act of charity,' said Starkey. 'Tannhauser has sold us a colossal quantity of arms and munitions with which to prosecute the war.'

'The man is a fox,' said Le Mas, with no small admiration. 'Little takes place in Messina that escapes his notice. He has a way with men, too, and would surely make a stiff companion in a fight, for he was a *devshirme*, and spent thirteen years in the Sultan's corps of janissaries.'

La Valette blinked. 'The Lions of Islam,' he said.

The janissaries were the most ferocious infantry in the world, the elite of Ottoman arms, the spearhead of their father the Sultan. Their sect was composed entirely of Christian boys, raised and trained – through a fanatical and unforgiving strain of Bektasi dervish Islam – to crave death in the name of the Prophet. La Valette looked at Starkey for confirmation.

Starkey rifled his memory for the details of Tannhauser's career. 'The Persian conquest, Lake Van, the crushing of the Safavid rebellions, the sack of Nahjivan.' He saw La Valette blink a second time. A precedent had been set. 'Tannhauser gained the rank of janitor, or captain, and became a member of the bodyguard of Suleiman's first-born son.'

La Valette said, 'Why did he leave the janissaries?'

'I don't know.'

'You didn't ask him?'

'He wouldn't give me an answer.'

La Valette's expression changed and Starkey sensed that a plot had been born.

La Valette embraced Le Mas by the shoulders. 'Fra Pierre, we will talk again soon – of the Post of Honour.'

Le Mas understood he was dismissed and walked to the door.

'Tell me one more thing,' said La Valette. 'You said Tannhauser had a way with men. How is his way with women?'

'Well, he has an admirable bevy of nubiles working for him.' Le Mas coloured at his own enthusiasm, for his occasional lapses into debauchery were well known. 'Though I hasten to add that they're not for hire. Tannhauser hasn't taken Holy Orders and in his shoes, well – if the man has a taste for women – and good taste, mind – it's not something I'd hold against him.'

'Thank you,' said La Valette. 'I won't.'

Le Mas closed the door behind him and La Valette took to

his chair and tented his fingers. 'Tannhauser. It's not a noble name.'

To be considered for entry as a Knight of the Order of Saint John, a man had to prove sixteen quarterings of nobility in his bloodline. It was a concept in which the Grand Master placed great faith.

Starkey said, 'Tannhauser is a *nom de guerre* – borrowed from a German legend, I believe – which he took while serving Alva in the Franco-Spanish wars.'

'If Tannhauser spent thirteen years in the Lions of Islam he knows more about our enemy – his tactics, his formations, his moods, his morale – than anyone in our camp. I want him here in Malta – for the siege.'

Starkey was taken aback. 'Fra Jean, why would he care to join us?'

'Giovanni Castrucco sails for Messina at noon, on the *Couronne*.'

'Tannhauser will not be persuaded by Castrucco.'

'Quite,' said La Valette. 'You will go with him. When Castrucco returns, you'll bring this German janissary back to Malta.'

'But I'd be gone for five days – I have innumerable duties here –'

'We will survive your absence.'

'Tannhauser wouldn't join us if we dragged him here in chains.'

'Then devise another way.'

'Why is he so important?'

'Perhaps he is not. But even so.'

La Valette stood up. He walked back to the map and scanned the terrain that thousands would soon contest with their lives. 'This battle for our Holy Religion will not be won or lost by some great stroke,' he said. 'There will be no brilliant and decisive manoeuvre, no Achilleus or Hektor, no Samson with the jawbone of an ass. Such tales are constructions of hindsight. There will only be a multitude of smaller strokes, by a multitude of lesser heroes – our men, our women, our children – none of whom will know the final outcome, and few of whom will even live to see it.'

For the first time Starkey saw something like dread in La Valette's eyes.

'The flux in God's crucible is infinite in possibility, and in that final outcome only God will know who it was that tipped the balance: be it the knight who died in the breach, or the waterboy who slaked his thirst, or the baker who made his bread, or the bee that stung the foeman in the eye. That is how finely the scales of war are weighted. That's why I want Tannhauser. For his knowledge, for his sword, for his love of the Turk or his hatred, either one.'

'Forgive me, Fra Jean, but I assure you Tannhauser will not come.'

'Does the Lady Carla still plague us with her letters?'

Starkey blinked at this *non sequitur* and at the triviality of its subject. 'The Countess of Penautier? Yes, she still writes – the woman doesn't know the meaning of refusal – but why?'

'Use her as your lever.'

'Against Tannhauser?'

'The man likes women,' said La Valette. 'Let him like this one.'

'I've never met the countess,' protested Starkey.

'In her youth she possessed a great beauty, which I'm sure the years have done little or nothing to dim.'

'That may well be, but at the very least she's a woman of noble birth and Tannhauser is – well – a near barbarian –'

La Valette's expression forestalled all further discussion.

'You will sail on the *Couronne*. You will bring Tannhauser back to Malta.'

La Valette took Starkey's arm and walked him to the door.

'Send in the inquisitor as you leave.'

Starkey blinked. 'I'm not to be privy to your conference?'

'Ludovico will be faring with you on the *Couronne*.' La Valette observed his confusion and essayed a rare smile. 'Fra Oliver, know that you are dearly beloved.'

In the antechamber outside, Ludovico Ludovici, judge and jurist of the Sacred Congregation of the Inquisition, fingered his rosary with the blameless impassivity of an icon. He returned Starkey's look without expression and for a moment Starkey found himself unable to speak.

Ludovico was in his forties, Starkey's own age, yet the bristles of his Pauline tonsure were crow-dark and had not retreated a fraction from its widow's peak. His forehead was smooth, his face was beardless, and the overall impression of his skull was of a huge stone sculpted by primordial forces. He was long in the torso and broad in the shoulders and he wore the white scapular and black cape of the Order of the Dominicans. His eyes shone like spheres of obsidian and lacked any trace of either menace or warmth. They regarded the fallen world about him, as if they'd regarded it since Adam, with a frankness of perception that excluded the possibility of joy and horror both, and with an extraordinary order of intelligence that sought to breach the inmost core of whomsoever he subjected to their gaze. And behind this dwelt the shadow of a fabulous melancholy – of a regret that evoked some notion of perpetual mourning – as if he'd seen a better world than this one and knew he'd not see it again.

Make me the guardian of the secrets of your soul, said the fathomless black eyes. *Lay your burdens upon my back and life eternal shall be yours.*

Starkey felt both an urge to confide and an ill-defined anxiety. Ludovico was Pope Pius IV's special legate to the Maltese Inquisition. He travelled a thousand miles a year in search of heresy. Among other noted exploits he'd sent Sebastiano Mollio, renowned Professor of Bologna, to the flames of the Campo del Flor. He'd guided Duke Albert of Bavaria in his brutal restoration of the One True Faith. During his cleansing of the Piedmont he'd dispatched an entire train of prisoners bearing burning tapers of penitence to the *autos da fé* in Rome. Yet Ludovico's humility was profound; too profound to be an act. Starkey had never seen so much power worn so lightly. Ludovico's function on Malta was to seek out the Lutheran heresy among the brethren of the Order of Saint John; yet he'd made no arrests. If anything this inaction had made him all the more feared. Did La Valette want Ludovico safe in Sicily? Or were there other intrigues in play? Starkey realised he'd been staring for an unseemly time.

He bowed and said, 'His Excellency, the Grand Master, awaits you.'

Ludovico rose to his feet. With a swift movement and a rattle of beads he tied the rosary around his waist. Without a word, he walked past Starkey into the office. The door closed. Starkey's relief was tempered by the thought of two days' voyage in the Dominican's company. He headed for his quarters to prepare for the trip. He did not excel at subterfuge and dishonesty; but in these modern times only a fool confused devotion to God with morality. He loved La Valette. He loved the Religion. In the service of either one – and no matter the cost to his soul – Starkey was prepared to do anything at all.

TUESDAY 15 MAY 1565

The Villa Saliba, Messina, Sicily

. . . In short, military considerations continue to prevent me from authorising your passage to the island of Malta. However, I am able to suggest other means by which your most earnest ambition might be realised.

In the port of Messina is a man called Mattias Tannhauser, whose origins are far too ravelled to illuminate here. Suffice to say that he marches to the beat of his own drum. While he is a denizen of the lower orders, has little respect for the law and is rumoured to be an Atheist or worse, I can warrant he is a man of his word and have no reason to believe he would do you any harm. Neither do I have any reason to believe he will help you. At the same time, I cannot predict the power with which a gentlewoman of your grace and beauty might appeal to such nobler instincts as he may possess.

I will not deceive you, My Lady. Captain Tannhauser's presence on Malta would be to our advantage in the fight against the Grande Turke. To date, owing us no loyalty and being cognisant of the dangers, he has shown no inclination to join us. If you were to persuade him to make the voyage on your behalf, I would be in a position to grant your passage as his escort. The

Couronne *leaves Messina at midnight, tonight. If the most recent intelligence proves accurate, it will be the last Christian ship to beat the Turkish blockade.*

You will find Tannhauser at a tavern at the southern end of the waterfront, called the Oracle. I can hardly bring myself to recommend that you visit such a sordid establishment in person, but you will likely find him unresponsive to the usual couriers. How you approach him, then, depends upon the urgency with which you wish to press your suit.

Conscience obliges me to repeat my previous warnings: that a state of war exists upon the island and the danger of death or enslavement for all those there resident during the coming days is grave in the extreme. If I can offer you any further help or counsel, you will find me in Messina, until the Couronne *sails, at the Priory of the Knights of Saint John of Jerusalem.*

Starkey's handwriting was the most beautiful Carla had ever seen. She wondered how many hours he had spent as a boy perfecting the graceful curves, the elegant transitions between the broad down strokes and fine up strokes, the unvaryingly accurate spacing between each letter, word and line. It was writing as emblem of power. Writing to make a king mark exactly what was said – as indeed kings did, for Starkey drafted the Order's diplomatic correspondence. Carla had never met him. She wondered if he were as polished as his calligraphy, or if he were a dusty, withered monk bent over a desk. She thought of her own boy and wondered if he could read or write at all. And at yet another such reminder of her failure in her duties as his mother, her stomach clenched with pain, and her desire to return to Malta – and her fear that she'd never do so – climbed a new pitch of urgent intensity.

Carla folded the letter and squeezed it in her hand. She'd been corresponding with Starkey for six weeks. His previous prohibitions of her return had been the replies of a busy man dealing with trivia and making the effort only out of respect for her noble origins and family name. Over the same period, she'd asked many of the sea captains and knights passing through Messina if they'd take her to Malta. She'd been heard with the utmost chivalry, and the occasional promise of action, yet here she remained, watching the rise of the sun from the Villa Saliba.

Grand Master La Valette had decreed that anyone unable to contribute to the island's defence was a 'useless mouth'. Hundreds of pregnant women, the elderly and infirm, plus an unspoken number of the dwindling Maltese aristocracy whether infirm or not, had been shipped across the Malta Channel to Sicily. Any native Maltese who could hold a pike or a shovel remained on the island, regardless of age or sex. Carla – in their eyes a feeble noblewoman they would feel obliged to protect – was dead wood. Furthermore, all space on the galleys returning to Grand Harbour was reserved for fighting men, materiel and food, not for idle ladies with an inexplicable wish to die. Carla despised idleness and certainly did not consider herself feeble. She managed her own, modest, estate in the Aquitaine alone. She was under no man's authority or sway. She and her good companion, Amparo, had ridden across the Langue D'Oc under the protection of nothing more than God's Grace and Carla's wits. The recent Huguenot war had left scars and a modicum of peril in its wake, but they'd reached Marseilles unscathed and shipped for Naples and Sicily without disaster. The fact they'd come so far unaided and unaccompanied had shocked many they had met, and, in retrospect, Carla admitted an impetuous, perhaps even foolhardy, aspect to their journey, but once she'd made the decision the thought that they might not get at least this far had never crossed her mind. For a woman long resolved to dictate her own existence, then, the weeks spent sweltering in Messina had been infuriating. Starkey's letter was her first intimation of hope. She now had potential military value. If she could get this man Tannhauser on the *Couronne*, by midnight, she'd be allowed to travel with him.

In all her negotiations with Starkey, sea captains and knights, she'd never revealed her reason for wanting to go home. To have done so would have confirmed her in their eyes as the unbalanced female they already believed her to be. Only Amparo knew. Yet Carla guarded her motives out of more than mere diplomacy. She kept her secret out of shame. She had a son. A bastard son, stolen from her arms twelve years before. And her son, she believed, was in Malta.

She opened the glass-paned doors that overlooked the gardens. The Saliba, distant relatives of her own family, the Manduca, had retreated to Capri to escape the Sicilian summer and had given Carla use of their guesthouse. It was elegant and comfortable, and came with a cook, a maid and an openly contemptuous steward named Bertholdo. She'd already asked Bertholdo to arrange delivery of a message to Captain Tannhauser, at the Oracle, but the elaborately counterfeited shock which had greeted her request had convinced her it would take days to get him to obey. In any case, Bertholdo's inveterate hauteur would likely ensure the failure of his mission, if not life-threatening injury to his person by the Oracle's proprietor.

Carla looked out into the garden. Amparo knelt in the flowerbeds, rapt in communion with a tall white rose. Such eccentricities were normal for the girl and the freedom of spirit to indulge them made Carla feel jaded. An idea crossed her mind as she watched. Carla had no fear of going to the Oracle in person. To do so had been her first impulse. She'd negotiated often enough with the merchants of Bordeaux. She knew, rather, that to beard the notorious Tannhauser in his lair would be to assume the weaker position. If he could be lured to come to her, here amidst the trappings of power, the advantage would be hers. Amparo, she now sensed, would bring Tannhauser to the Villa Saliba far more surely than she could herself. If the usual couriers would not do, Amparo would be the strangest messenger the man had ever received.

Carla walked out under the palm trees, upon whose shade the flowers depended for survival. Amparo kissed the white rose and stood up to brush the dirt from her skirts. Her eyes stayed on the flowers as Carla stopped beside her. Amparo seemed calm. On rising she'd remained overwrought by what she'd seen in her vision glass the night before. The images she reported from her glass were so diverse, so extraordinary, that when one of them achieved some overlap with reality Carla was inclined to believe it mere coincidence. Laying coincidence aside, symbols could bear any meaning according to their interpreter's desires. Yet Amparo never interpreted. She only saw.

She'd seen a black ship with red sails crewed by tiny monkeys blowing trumpets. She'd seen a huge white mastiff with a collar of iron spikes and bearing a burning torch in its jaws. She'd seen a naked man, his body covered in hieroglyphs, riding a horse the colour of molten gold. And as the man had ridden by, an angel's voice had told her, '*The gate is wide but the path thereto is like a razor's edge.*'

'Amparo?' said Carla.

Amparo turned her head. There was always an instant when Carla expected her to keep on turning and gaze into the distance, as if eye contact caused her pain and she'd rather seek something of beauty invisible to all but she. This had been Amparo's habit during their first months together and it remained her habit still with everyone but Carla. But Amparo looked at her directly. Her eyes were of different colours, the left as brown as autumn, the right as grey as Atlantic wind. Both seemed alive with questions that would never be voiced, as if no words yet existed with which to frame them. She was nineteen years old, or thereabouts; her exact age was unknown. Her face was as fresh as an apple and as delicate as blossom, but a marked depression in the bones beneath her left eye gave her features a disturbing asymmetry. Her mouth never curved into a smile. God, it seemed, had withheld that possibility, as surely as from a blind man the power of sight. He had withheld much else. Amparo was touched – by genius, by madness, by the Devil, or a conspiracy of all these and more. She took no sacraments and appeared incapable of prayer. She had a horror of clocks and mirrors. By her own account she spoke with angels and could hear the thoughts of animals and trees. She was passionately kind to all living things. She was a beam of starlight trapped in flesh and awaiting only the moment when it would continue on its journey into forever.

'Is it time to play?' asked Amparo.

'No, not yet.'

'But we will.'

'Of course we will.'

'You're afraid.'

'Only for your safety.'

Amparo glanced at the roses. 'I don't understand.'

Carla hesitated. So ingrained was her habit of caring for Amparo that to ask her to enter a den of thieves seemed a crime. Yet Amparo had survived the streets of Barcelona, childhood years of violence and privation that Carla dared not imagine. Cowardice was not Amparo's flaw, even if, in her heart of hearts, Carla believed it her own.

Carla smiled. 'What need starlight fear of the dark?'

'Why, nothing.' Amparo frowned. 'This is a riddle?'

'No. There's something I want you to do for me. Something of the greatest importance.'

'You want me to find the man on the golden horse.'

Amparo's voice was as soft as rain. She saw the world through the eyes of a mystic. Carla was so familiar with the lens of Amparo's imagination that she no longer found it so unnatural. Carla said, 'His name is Mattias Tannhauser.'

'Tannhauser,' repeated Amparo, as if testing the integrity of a newly cast bell. 'Tannhauser. Tannhauser.' She seemed satisfied.

'I must talk with him today. As soon as possible. I want you to go into the port and bring him back here with you.'

Amparo nodded.

'If he refuses to come –' continued Carla.

'He will come,' said Amparo, as if any other outcome were unthinkable.

'If he will not come, ask him if he would receive me at his earliest convenience – but today, you understand. Today.'

'He will come.' Amparo's face shone with the mysterious joy that was as close as she came to a smile and which, in its way, was more than compensation.

'I'll tell Bertholdo to prepare the carriage.'

'I hate the carriage,' said Amparo. 'It has no air and it's slow and cruel to the horse. Carriages are a nonsense. I'll ride. And if Tannhauser won't come with me, he's not the man who will walk the razor's edge – and so why would you want him to receive you later on?'

Carla knew better than to argue. She nodded. Amparo started to walk away, then stopped and looked back. 'Can we play when I return? As soon as I return?'

There were two unvarying elements in Amparo's days, without which she became distressed: the hour they spent each afternoon playing music, and the session she spent at her vision stone after dark. She also went to Mass every morning, but in order to accompany Carla rather than from any sense of piety.

'Not if Tannhauser is with you,' said Carla. 'What I have to say to him is urgent. For once our music must wait.'

Amparo seemed astonished at her foolishness. 'But you must play for him. You must play for Tannhauser. It's for him that we've practised for so long.'

They'd played for years and so this was absurd and, in any case, Carla found the idea quite unthinkable. Amparo saw her doubt. She took hold of Carla's hands and pumped them up and down as if dancing with a child.

'For Tannhauser! For Tannhauser!' Again she made his name peal like a bell. Her face shone. 'Imagine it, my love. We'll play for him as we've never played before.'

* * *

THE BEGINNING WITH Amparo had been hard. Carla had found her while taking her early morning ride, on a crystalline February day when the mist still smoked around her horse's knees and the first cherry trees were in bloom. The mist concealed Amparo from view and their paths might never have crossed if Carla hadn't heard a high, sweet voice piping like the sorrow of angels across the landscape. The voice sang in some dialect of Castilian and to a melody of its own devising which carried the wing beat of death. Whatever its meaning, the song's otherworldly beauty made Carla draw in her mount.

She discovered Amparo in a break of willows. Had she not already known from the voice, she'd have been hard pressed to say whether what lay curled around a trunk, half-buried under a mass of rotting leaves against the frost, was female or male, or whether it was human at all but a woodland creature of fantastic origin. Apart from a filthy pelt drawn about her throat, and the remains of a pair of woollen hose, she was naked. Her feet were large for her build, and blue, as were the hands clasped together between her breasts. Both of her arms, from shoulders to wrists, were blemished by livid bruises, as was the pale, translucent skin stretched across her ribcage. Her hair was raven-black and coarsely chopped and pasted to her skull by clots of mud. Her lips were purple with cold. Her eyes of different hues showed no sign of anguish or self-pity, and in not so doing seemed to Carla more piteous than any she'd ever seen before. Amparo would never say how she came to be in the forest, starved and filthy and frozen near to death. She would rarely speak of any past at all, and only then to answer yes or no to Carla's guesses. But later that day, when she submitted to Carla bathing her with hot water, there was blood and slime clotted around her pudenda, and some of the marks on her body were from human teeth.

On this first encounter, Amparo would not look her in the eye. It would take weeks before she would do so and it remained an honour seldom granted anyone else. When Carla dismounted and took her by the arm, Amparo screamed so piercingly that Carla's horse almost broke free of its tether. The animal's distress brought Amparo springing to her feet. She comforted the horse and murmured softly in its ear, quite unconcerned for her own pathetic estate. When Carla wrapped her cloak around Amparo's shoulders, Amparo didn't demur, and though she declined the saddle she was content to walk alongside holding the bridle. Thus, seven years before, had Amparo arrived at Carla's household, accompanying her mistress home with the long green cloak trailing behind her, like some barefoot and ragamuffin page in a tale untold.

The members of Carla's household, her priest, her very few acquaintances in the village, and those local gossips whose numbers were far greater, were unanimous in thinking Carla ill-advised – indeed, as mad as the girl herself – in taking the waif to her bosom. Amparo, then hardly in her teens, was prone to violent outbursts at obscure provocations, and to spending hours in conversation with the horses and dogs, whom she serenaded with a passion in her silvery voice. She refused to eat meat or fowl of any kind, sometimes disdained fresh bread, and on her preferred diet of nuts, wild berries and raw vegetables never added an ounce to the emaciated condition in which she'd been found. Her refusal to look the priest in the eye, and the fact that her own were of different colours, were sure signs, it was commonly agreed, of diabolic leanings.

Carla stood by the girl through tantrum and trance, through the sudden disappearances that could last for days, through the social humiliations and offers of exorcism, and through Amparo's apparent inability to reciprocate her affection. She seemed insensible to the feelings of others; or if not insensible, entirely indifferent. Yet in the loyalty Amparo developed towards her, in her sharing of the discovery of her vision glass and the revelations it provoked, in her struggle to learn basic etiquette and the tenets of proper bearing, and most of all in the naïve genius she brought to their study of music, Amparo revealed a love deeper and more enduring than most mortals know. They were curious friends, then, yet no two friends were ever closer.

Did Carla love the girl, she sometimes wondered, because of some spell cast in the mirror of recognition? That mirror in which all those who've been cast out may see themselves? Or because, in her isolation, she needed someone to love and the girl just happened to be there? Or was love not always some conspiracy of isolation, recognition and chance all intermingled? It didn't matter. The girl won her heart. It was Amparo, who had no past, who'd inspired and propelled Carla on this quest to redeem her own.

'I WON'T GO to Messina until you tell me,' said Amparo. 'Shall we play for him or not?'

Carla's heart quickened at the thought. Such things weren't done. To invite a man – a man of dubious reputation – to a strange villa and without so much as an introduction subject him to their Art? It was unheard of. Tannhauser would consider them mad. Her mind told her that to play for him would be folly. Her heart said it would be magnificent. Amparo waited for her answer.

'Yes,' said Carla, 'we'll play for him. We'll play as we've never played before.'

Amparo said, 'You will take me with you, won't you? If you left me behind, I couldn't bear it.'

She'd asked this question innumerable times since they'd started on this journey but from now on things might change. Would Starkey permit it? Would Tannhauser? For the first time, Carla answered without knowing if she could keep her promise. 'I'll never leave you behind.'

Again, the unsmiling glow of joy illuminated Amparo's face, and another inspiration sprang forth. 'Wear the red dress,' she said.

She saw Carla's face.

'Oh yes, the red dress,' insisted Amparo. 'You must.'

Carla had commissioned the dress, during their sojourn in Naples, for reasons she couldn't fathom even at the time. The bolt of silk had captured her: a fantasy of colour that had travelled across desert and sea from Samarkand. The tailor had seen its reflection in her eyes and had clasped his hands in communion with some vision of her own that she couldn't yet see, and he'd promised her a union between the silk and her heart's desire whose harmony would delight a pillar of stone.

When she'd first donned the dress a week later, her skin had sighed and her heart had hammered and something close to panic had choked her throat, as if she'd been reminded of something in herself that she feared above all things, and which she'd long since determined to forget. When she'd left the dressing room, Amparo's eyes had widened and swum with tears. When she'd stood before the looking glass, she'd seen a woman she didn't know, and who could not be. And though at once she prized it more than anything she owned, she knew she'd never wear the exquisite garment, for the moment in which she might become the woman in the glass – would dare to be that woman – would never come. The dress was made for a woman in bloom, and she was a woman whose spring and summer had gone. The dress lay in her trunk, swaddled by the tissue in which its maker had wrapped it.

'The occasion has never been apt,' said Carla. 'And surely is not so now.'

'If not now, then when?' asked Amparo.

Carla blinked and looked away. Amparo persisted.

'If Tannhauser is to walk the razor's edge, then you must match him.'

There was logic to this; but it was Amparo's logic. 'No matter how remarkable he may be, he'll not be wearing red silk.'

Amparo took this in and shook her head with sadness.

'Now, enough of these foolish fancies,' said Carla. 'Please, be on your way.'

She watched Amparo run towards the house and wondered what it must be like to live without fear. Without guilt or shame. As Amparo lived. Carla had felt an intimation of such a life on that morning in the springtime recently passed, when they'd started out for Sicily from the Aquitaine. Two madwomen on a journey that she knew they'd never complete. That morning she'd felt as free as the wind in her hair. Carla walked back to the guest-house. She'd go to the villa's chapel and say her rosary and pray that the girl succeeded. If Amparo returned from the Oracle alone, their quest would be over.

TUESDAY 15 MAY 1565

The Oracle Tavern, Messina, Sicily

HARSH WHITE LIGHT and the sewage-tainted stench of the harbour spilled through the warehouse doors across a mongrel horde of nations and men, its members drawn from the criminal and military classes, and among them a sense of excitement was general. Pickers, sailors, smugglers, soldiers, *bravi*, painters and thieves crowded the rough-hewn trestles and poured their wages down their gullets with the gusto of the long and justly damned. Their talk, as always, was of the imminent invasion of Malta and of the cruel and degenerate Turks and the perversions of Islam. Their ignorance of all these topics may well have bordered on perfection, but as long as they kept drinking, Tannhauser had no reason to complain. He intended to profit from the war no matter who was victorious, so he kept his own peace, as is a wise man's practice, and invested his attention in his customary late breakfast: today an exceedingly tasty blood sausage from the Benedictines of Maniacio, washed down with a raw red wine brewed by the same.

His shoulders filled a massive walnut chair, upholstered in shabby green leather and embellished in gold leaf with the legend '*Usque Ad Finem*'. It was known as 'Tannhauser's Throne' and a brisk thrashing, followed by violent ejection into the reeking gutter without, awaited any sot drunk enough to imagine he might rest there. He had only lately come to be a man of business and property, and that against all previous expectations, but he felt that his new vocation fitted him well and, as in every endeavour in which he engaged, he gave himself up to it body and soul.

The tavern had evolved, as if of its own accord, from the anteroom of the warehouse from which Tannhauser plied his trade as a dealer in arms. The table at which he ate stood in an alcove among the gantried casks to the rear and from whence he could observe the whole room. This alcove was draped in carpets of exotic origin and fabulous design, which lent his office the air of a caravanserai. On the table was a broken clock from Prague, whose innards he intended to repair with components of his own manufacture; and beside it a brass astrolabe, by which one could calculate the position of celestial bodies, and which Professor Maurolico in person had taught him how to use; and heaped around these instruments were tomes of curious provenance, written in a variety of languages – not all of which, admittedly, Tannhauser could understand – and from certain of which, when in his cups, he would declaim *gazels* in Turkish and laments by Fuzuli and Baki. His library also included Brucioli's banned translation of the New Testament – a feat for which the man had died in the Inquisition's gaols – and tractates by Ramon Lull and Trithemius of Sponheim, and books of Natural Magick, wherein were expounded the opinions of ancient philosophers and the causes of Wondrous Effects. Amid these quaint paraphernalia, with his densely thewed forearms and their heathen tattoos, and his scarred countenance and bronze hair and lapis lazuli eyes, Tannhauser seemed to his fellows like a Mogul from some remote and outlandish demesne, and this was to his liking, for in mystery lay the notion of power, and in power lay his own notion of freedom.

As Tannhauser finished the sausage and drained his wine, Dana sashayed over to take his plate. She was supple and full and all abloom with youth. Along with the three other women who served the tables, Dana was from Belgrade. The four had been saved from a corsairs' brothel in Algiers when their ship was captured by the galleys of the Religion. Tannhauser, in his turn, had saved the girls from the brothels of Messina, though not without some violence on the docks, all of it to the cost – it hardly need be said – of a gaggle of thwarted pimps. For this deed the ladies considered him gallant, not least because they were surprised to discover that whoremongering, along with vomiting and pissing, were forbidden within the Oracle. Even so, the girls made a handsome contribution to his business, for men came to slake their eyes as much as their thirsts, the latter intensified greatly by frustrated lust. Since the girls knew that unwelcome attention was punished with even greater severity than the use of their master's chair, they paraded their charms without shame and with a singular lack of pity, both of which attitudes Tannhauser wholeheartedly admired.

Dana raised a glazed earth jug and gave him a smile that was demure by design alone. He resisted more wine by placing one hand over his beaker but failed to prevent the other from caressing the calf beneath her skirt. Her skin was cool and smooth and luscious to his touch, and she brushed her breast again his cheek and murmured some Serbian endearment beneath her breath. He shifted in his seat, admirably aroused, and slid his hand up higher beneath the cotton. She'd shared his bed, and a number of spontaneous assignations in the bowels of the warehouse, for the last few weeks, and with the frequency of these trysts now climbing to several times a day, he knew he should know better; but the idea of a visit to his chamber, with the wine and sausage settling on his stomach, presented itself as one whose attractions were vast. Love was good for the digestion and while he had a number of chores to perform he could think of none, at that moment, that could claim great urgency. He inhaled her body's perfume and sighed. A short nap afterwards and what further joy could the Cosmos possibly offer?

His palm cupped her buttock and his fingertips settled in the muscular cleft of her arse, and he was inspired to wonder at the boundless perfection of Creation when it took such form. Dana tugged at his hair and he pushed back his chair. Yet in his erotic reverie he'd lingered too long. Before he could take her arm and steal away, Sabato Svi emerged from the Oracle's depths and sat himself down at the table.

Beyond a courteous nod, Sabato paid Dana, and the glare with which she fixed him, no mind at all. He spread a place among the books for his elbows and shook the oily curls that dangled from under his yarmulke and smiled with the deep-set eyes in which there always burned a flame of Divine Madness. Sabato plucked a letter from his sleeve and Tannhauser flinched. He could not quite bring himself to withdraw his hand, but out of a vague sense of etiquette he kneaded Dana's flesh with lesser vigour and mustered a greeting.

'Sabato,' said Tannhauser. 'What news?'

'Pepper,' said Sabato Svi.

Sabato was a Jew of fearless temper from the Ghetto of Venice. At twenty-seven he was ten years Tannhauser's junior and his senior in matters vital to their prosperity. They'd been partners for half a decade yet in all that time had never quarrelled, even when some oversight had left them facing slavery or worse. He delighted in provoking outrage by slyly calculated slurs, by walking out in mimed fury as an arduous negotiation reached its climax, by asking impertinent questions of ruffians thrice his size. Yet with few, if memorable, exceptions, Sabato contrived to emerge in a position of advantage. Tannhauser was chary in his affections, for those he'd favoured had proved themselves too prone to calamity, but if anyone was destined to bury him it was Sabato Svi. Tannhauser loved no man more.

'I've told you before,' said Tannhauser, 'I know little or nothing of pepper and have no great itch to learn more.'

'And I have told you – before – everything you need to know,' Sabato replied, 'which is that its price better than quadruples between a warehouse floor in Alexandria and the market stalls of Venice.'

'If – that is – I can avoid the tonnage tax and the bastinado –'

'Which, as always, you will.'

'– and if I'm not taken and chained to the oar of a galley by El Louck Ali –'

'Who is on his way to join the Sultan's armada, along with Torghoud Rais, Ali Fartax and every other corsair in the Mediterranean.'

'And from where will Suleiman's Mamelukes sail to Malta? Alexandria!' countered Tannhauser, with satisfaction.

Sabato waved the letter towards the dockyards beyond the doors. 'Look at the Genoese. They cower in the bay like cockle pickers – but for a man like you the sea has never been safer.'

Tannhauser, always a fool for any challenge to his prowess, paused in his fondling. Dana flexed her buttocks to signal disappointment and he continued, but more pensively than before. If he could avoid the Moslem fleets converging on Malta – which with timing and luck was likely – the rest of the sea, for these few weeks, would indeed be uncommonly quiet. With the uncanny timing he'd come to expect of women, Dana ran her fingers through his hair.

'I have no love of the sea,' Tannhauser said. 'It's a stony field I've ploughed for far too long and I have many essential duties to occupy me here.'

Sabato glanced at Dana's breasts and she pouted obscenely in riposte.

'Mattias, my friend,' said Sabato, 'eighty-five quintals of Javanese pepper lie waiting for us in Egypt.' He fluttered the letter below his nostrils as if it were perfumed with myrrh. 'And in a warehouse exclusively favourable to our suit.'

Tannhauser caught a glimpse of the Hebrew script. 'Moshe Mosseri?'

Sabato nodded. 'Eighty-five quintals – and in a month it will be gone forever.' He leaned forward. 'Every city in Europe screams for pepper. The French won't even eat soup without it. Imagine Zeno, D'Este and Gritti trying to outbid each other. Have you any idea how much they'll pay?'

Tannhauser scowled.

'You'll be in Alexandria in three weeks – make up the lading with mace, beeswax, silks – and in eight we'll be counting our gold in San Marco's Square.' Sabato had a wife and two sons in Venice, for whom he pined, but Tannhauser knew him, and sentiment alone wasn't reason enough to go home. 'Would you like to hear my estimate? A conservative estimate?'

'If I must.'

'Fifteen thousand florins. More likely, twenty.'

The sum was so enormous that Tannhauser was moved to withdraw his hand from Dana's skirt and massage his jaw. Stubble rasped on his fingers, and Dana clucked with outrage, but the sum remained just as fabulous as before.

Almost as an afterthought, Sabato added: 'For the outbound leg I've secured a load of sugar cane.'

Sabato sprang these enterprises at such an advanced stage of planning that Tannhauser was left with little option but to carry them through. The success of the Oracle had been conspicuous enough that they were able to open up new lines of credit, and quarry their old ones, more or less as they pleased. Tannhauser probed, without conviction, for another impediment.

'A sailing master? A ship? A well-found ship, mind, not one of the worm-raddled sieves you've sent me out in before.'

'Dimitrianos. The *Centaur*.'

The thought of the evil stench, the weeks of boredom and blistering sun, and the Greek's interminable puling over his losses at cards and backgammon provoked an unwelcome squall through

Tannhauser's digestive organs. Out of consideration for Dana, he suppressed the urge to break wind. 'Put too many irons in the fire and some will cool,' he said. 'Besides, I've no love of the Greek, either.'

As expected, this demurrer was ignored. 'The Greek is waiting and his pockets are empty. We can load within three days. The best time to embark –' Sabato shrugged and smiled as he passed the burden to Tannhauser, '– depends as always upon your information.'

Tannhauser had one foot in each of two hostile worlds. To the Venetians, the Spanish rulers of Sicily and the Knights of Malta, he was a condottiere captain of infantry, late of Alva's Italian campaign and the slaughter of the French at Saint Quentin, and now an estimable merchant in opium, arms and munitions. To the Moslems he was Ibrahim Kirmizi – Ibrahim the Red, veteran of the bloodbaths of eastern Anatolia and Iran. He knew the Ottoman way, its manners and languages and rituals. He moved among them as the native he once had been and, in some regions of his heart, would always remain. He had associates in Bursa, Smyrna, Tripoli and Beirut; he'd shipped silks and opium out of Mazandaran; and no man in Christendom knew the Stambouli Shore – and Eminonu and Uskudar and the Buyuk Carsi, and their baths and hostelries and bazaars – as well as he. In Messina he was thick with those of the pilots, overseers and sailing masters who might supply valuable intelligence – of goods and vessels in transit, of competitors on the rise or fall, of confiscated cargoes up for auction, of raiders and intrigues abroad, of changes of political fortune overseas. He also canvassed the slaves in their dockside gaols, and the Moslems most of all, for they were mute to everyone else. These men brought tidings from the Barbary Coast that no one else could provide. When news travelled so slowly, a few days' foreknowledge could be precious, and that of a few weeks without price.

It was thus that his dealings with the Knights of Malta had

begun, when he'd seen with his own eyes from the Unkapani quay of the Stambouli Shore the raw timber keels of Suleiman's new fleet, and had realised that such intelligence might make him and Sabato Svi wealthy men.

They'd embarked from Old Stambouli that very night, Sabato for Venice to broker a supply of powder and arms, and Tannhauser for Messina, to lease the warehouse, and thence on to Malta to treat with the Religion. The priceless advance news of Suleiman's fleet he gave them for free, to establish his bona fides and to secure a lucrative contract to supply them with arms. 'War is a river of gold,' he'd promised Sabato, 'and we will stand with buckets on its bank.' And so it was, for the Religion's appetite for gunpowder, cannon and ball had proved insatiable, and with rich lands all over Catholic Europe their pockets were deep.

'My information,' Tannhauser said to Sabato Svi, 'is that we're rich and getting richer whether the French put pepper in their soup or sprinkle it over their privities for the pox.'

Sabato laughed, with the infuriating cackle he inflicted on those he had bested. Dana bumped her haunch into Tannhauser's shoulder, but the pleasures of her skirt had been soured. With a gesture he sent her away and she acquiesced with another rancorous glare at Sabato Svi. Tannhauser watched her hips swing out of sight then turned and planted a forefinger on the tabletop.

'You ask me to spend two months at sea when the bloodiest contest of arms in the memory of the living is about to take place on our doorstep.'

'So now we come to the nub. Rather than advance our station, you'd sit prattling with the wine-swillers and sifting gossip from the docks.' Sabato tossed his head at the scurvy entourage crowding the trestles. 'You've spent so much time with these swinish guzzlers you're taking on their virtues.'

'Peace!' said Tannhauser, without effect.

'The arms trade has been good but the cannon won't roar forever. We own little property. We own no land. We own no ships.' Sabato waved a contemptuous hand at the rafters. 'This is not rich. This is merely the chance to become so – a chance to dream.'

'I have no great faith in dreaming,' said Tannhauser. His last dream had been to forge a blade that his father might be proud of, and his father had never seen it. That dream had left him with an emptiness he'd never been able to replenish. He said, 'We will talk no more of pepper, at least for today.'

Sabato caught his change of mood and placed a hand on Tannhauser's thickened forearm and squeezed. 'Melancholy doesn't suit you. And it's bad for the liver – like the air in this filthy hole. Let's take a ride to Palermo and see what profitable mischief we might raise.'

Tannhauser clapped his own hand on top of Sabato's and grinned. 'You damnable Jew,' he said. 'You'll have me sweating on the Greek's ship within a week. And you know it.'

Tannhauser looked up as the open double doorway fell dark and a hulking silhouette extinguished the light. It was Bors of Carlisle, *de facto* manager of the tavern and the last of the unlikely trinity that kept the Oracle afloat. Earlier that morning, during their daily training session, Tannhauser had caught him on the cheekbone with the pommel of his sword. Bors had made no complaint, but his blunder hadn't left him in the gentlest of moods and the indigo lump beneath his eye was plain to see. On the weighing scale at the customs house, Bors had tipped the balance at twenty stone, much of it packed into his thighs, arms and chest. Since his face appeared to have seen use as a smith's anvil, the bruise didn't seem out of place, yet as he barged into the tavern he heard some slighting reference to the fresh blemish. Worse still, it was followed by a reckless round of drunken laughter. Without breaking his stride, Bors swung by the offender and punched him in the neck with a colossal fist. His victim tumbled, choking, among his fellows and Bors continued across the room to take his habitual place at

Tannhauser's left hand. As he did so, Dana set down a jug and his personal drinking cup.

The cup had been artfully fashioned from a human skull. Bors filled the skull with wine and drained it and filled it again, then in a belated fit of manners filled Tannhauser's beaker with what little remained. He tossed the jug back to Dana and she went to recharge it. Bors had iron-grey hair and the advance of baldness was offset by enormous eyebrows, a fine beard and the wiry tufts that curled down from his nostrils. He nodded to Sabato Svi and turned to Tannhauser.

'A red ship has docked,' said Bors, 'at the Wharf of the Hospitallers.'

'You see?' said Tannhauser to Sabato. 'The Religion's iron is yet hot. The gold rolls in.'

Bors continued, 'I've had Gasparo load the wagons and saddle our mounts.' He looked at Sabato Svi. 'Would you have him saddle yours?'

Sabato shook his head. 'The Religion's money is welcome but they regard me as one of the murderers of their Christ.'

'They are holy men of the Baptist,' countered Bors and crossed himself.

'The slave pens of the Religion groan with Levantine Jews whose prayers are for the Turks – as are my prayers too,' said Sabato Svi. 'The rumour's already afoot that the Jews of Istanbul have financed the invasion, and while it's false – as such libels always are – I wish it were so. When Malta falls every Jew alive will praise God.'

'Since they're all bound for Hell, let them praise whoever they wish.'

Sabato looked at Tannhauser. 'I've ransomed two Alexandrian captives myself – hence Moshe Mosseri's good favour.'

'You've been content to trade weapons for the knights' gold,' observed Bors.

'I'm more than happy to profit before they're wiped out,'

Sabato replied. 'What kind of fanatics would die for a scorched rock?'

'They've gathered there to determine the Will of God, by a noble contest of arms,' corrected Bors. 'And if we don't fight the Moslems in Malta we'll one day have to fight them in Paris, for the conquest of the world is their grand plan.'

'We?' said Sabato Svi.

'Your time will come too, believe me,' said Bors. 'Furthermore, the knights have assembled the most doughty bevy of manslayers anyone's ever seen in one place.' He looked at Tannhauser. 'They will harrow Hell on that island – and you and I are not among them to test our mettle.' He clenched a barrel-shaped fist in anguish. 'It's a violation of the natural order.'

'Mattias has made an end with killing and war. I thought you had too.'

Bors ignored Sabato and scowled like a gigantic infant. 'This broil will make Saint Quentin seem like May Day capers.'

'No,' said Tannhauser. 'Like two old ladies lighting votive candles in church.'

'Then you agree!' said Bors, hope rising in his breast. 'And this red ship will be our last chance to play our part. Let's pack our war chests and load them on the wagons now. Destiny calls. Don't tell me you can't hear it.'

Tannhauser shifted, for the blood was up in his spine too, and the reproach in Bors's eyes was hard to meet. In Sabato's face, by contrast, he saw the horror of seeing their plans collapse wholesale. Tannhauser toyed with his ring, a cube of Russian gold with a hole bored through its centre. Its weight lent him wisdom.

'Bors,' he said, 'you're my oldest and most steadfast companion. But we three contracted to become rich men together and such we are becoming and so we have done. Whether we rise or fall, it's battle of a different sort we're engaged in now. Remember the motto you coined for us, *Usque Ad Finem*. Until the End. Until the very end.'

Bors concealed his thoughts behind the upraised skull cup of wine.

'However,' continued Tannhauser, 'the English Langue would welcome you with a huzzah. If you want to seize this last occasion to go, then go. No one here will think you false.'

Tannhauser looked into Bors's eyes: grey with a nimbus of yellow around the iris and set in puckered nests of scarred and wrinkled skin. If Bors did choose to join the war of the Cross against the Crescent, Tannhauser would sail with him. Bors did not know this, for he wasn't the kind of man to expect any sacrifice on his behalf, but Sabato knew all too keenly and he waited with bated breath. Dana brought a fresh jug, well aware that her charms were rendered impotent by this conference. Bors gave a blunt growl and refilled his cup.

'Perhaps it is no coincidence,' said Bors, 'that I'm the only uncircumcised man sitting at this table.'

'That disharmony, at least, could be corrected,' said Tannhauser.

'You'd have to cut my head off first.'

'Both of which procedures could only improve your humour,' said Tannhauser. 'Come now, give us a decision, man. Are you with us or with the fanatics?'

'As you say, we are contracted together, in the rise or in the fall either one,' grumbled Bors. He raised his wine. 'Until the bitter end.'

Sabato Svi blew his cheeks with relief.

Tannhauser stood up. 'Let's go and peddle our wares.'

In his chamber Tannhauser changed into a burgundy-red silk doublet banded in diagonals of gold. He buckled on his sword, a Julian del Rey with a leopard's head pommel in silver, and scraped a hand across his stubble in lieu of a shave. He had no mirror but was confident that he'd cut the grandest figure on the waterfront. Bors called his name, and an obscene jibe, from the street below and Tannhauser went to join him.

Eight two-wheeled ox carts waited outside, the great beasts stoic in the sun. The carts were loaded with gunpowder, brass cannonballs, willow charcoal and pigs of lead. Bors sat his bay with impatience while Gasparo held Buraq by his reins.

Tannhauser said, 'Gasparo, how goes the day?'

Gasparo was a sturdy youth of sixteen, shy but loyal to a fault. He grinned for answer, abashed at the honour of being asked. Tannhauser clapped him on the back and turned to Buraq, whose affection filled him at once with an infinite joy. Buraq was a Teke Turkmen from the oasis of Akhal, a breed that the ancients considered sacred and called Nisaean. Genghis Khan had ridden such a horse. The swiftest, the strongest, the most graceful. He held his head high and with inborn majesty. His coat was the colour of a newly minted gold coin. His tail and short, tufted mane were the colour of wheat. Tannhauser fed him on mutton fat and barley and would have housed him in the Oracle had his partners let him. Buraq dipped his Roman nose and Tannhauser caressed him.

'Call him the most beautiful,' he said and Buraq snorted and tossed his long neck.

Tannhauser mounted and as always felt at once like a Caesar. Buraq needed no bit, so lightly did he respond. The devotion of horse and rider was complete. Buraq moved off as if the whole expedition was his idea and the drivers cracked their whips and the oxen strained in the traces and with the riders in the lead the wagon train began its procession through the harbour.

If Sicily as a whole was uncongenial to those of nonconformist temper, Messina, which through millennia had known conquerors by the dozen, was open to foreigners, rogues and entrepreneurs of every stripe. It was an independent republic, as populous as Rome, and paid the latest – Spanish – invaders presently stripping the island to the bone as little mind as it had paid the Romans, the Arabs, the Normans and all the rest. It was turbulent and rich, and with the sanctuary of Calabria only two miles across the straits, it harboured the lawless high and low in enormous numbers. The Governor looted more for the Spanish Crown in a single year than the rest of the island yielded up in five. On the Church's part, the Holy Inquisition formed a veritable legion of kidnappers, killers and thieves, and numbered in its ranks knights, barons, merchants, artisans, criminals of every kind and, it went without saying, the bulk of the civil police force. As a place for a man such as Tannhauser to make his fortune, it had no equal.

The Bay of Messina formed a perfect sickle-shaped harbour, protected by fortified jetties and the cannon of the monumental Arsenal that commanded the sea. Behind it stood the old walled city itself, the outlines of its towers and campaniles warping in the noontide heat. The vast docks were forested with masts and spars and reefed sails, and through the sparkling light that bounced up from the water, barges stacked with baskets and bales plied the strand. Apart from a sprinkle of fishing boats and coasters, and a Spanish galleass patrolling out in the offing, the sea beyond was still, for most mariners were waiting out these dangerous days until the Grande Turke's intentions were better known.

The Wharf of the Knights Hospitaller was a half-league distant from the Oracle and on their way Tannhauser and his entourage clattered over the cobbles past chandlers and ropewalks, spice magazines and granaries, bordellos and money changers and drinking dens similar to their own. They rode past towering cargo cranes powered by slaves inside the rims of giant treadle wheels, and past careened galleys stretched out amidst the smell of oakum and pitch; past food vendors roasting tripes and gambrels festooned with the carcasses of fresh-skinned lambs; past street cleaners shovelling excrement into reeking, fly-blown carts; past limbless beggars and barefoot urchins and mendicants pleading for alms; past women arguing prices with stallholders; past bands of swaggering *bravi* with their sneers and hidden knives; past a thousand cursing voices and a thousand breaking backs. The colossal scale of the enterprise, which abounded for as far as his eye could see, reminded Tannhauser that Sabato Svi was right: they were not yet rich enough. He resolved to pay his respects to Dimitrianos on the way home and secure some decent rations for the voyage.

The *Couronne* was long and sleek, a hundred and eighty feet from stem to stern and only twenty feet in the beam. It was designed, like all the knights' ships, for speed and attack. The hull was painted black and the huge lateen sails were blood-red. The gold eight-pointed cross woven thereon dazzled the eye. On the wharf to welcome the ship in their long black mantles stood a score or so knights of the Religion. All wore swords over their robes and looked ready for any hazard. Tannhauser assumed they'd arrived in recent days from the most distant priories of the Order and indeed the features of some were distinctly German or Scandinavian, and of others likely Spanish or Portuguese. They were taking it in turns to embrace a slender brother who stood among them. When the man turned this way to greet the next, Tannhauser recognised Oliver Starkey. Their eyes met and Tannhauser saluted and smiled. Unease flickered over Starkey's fine-boned face; but then he too smiled and nodded, and turned back to his brethren. Tannhauser motioned to Bors.

'Let's conclude our affairs with the captain and seek out Brother Starkey later.'

As Tannhauser stepped up the main gangplank, Bors put a hand of warning on his arm. Three men came down the walkway, the sun at their backs. Two wore Dominican robes, and odd companions they made because one, in size, would have made two of the other. Behind them came a Spaniard in his twenties, lean as a whip and dressed in a fine black doublet. His eyes and mouth were depraved and he had the look of a murderer. At his waist hung both dagger and sword. The larger of the monks walked with the bearing of a prince and the humility of a pauper.

His path was arrayed against Tannhauser's and as he passed from the glare of the light, Tannhauser saw his face and felt his gut clench.

Tannhauser said, 'Ludovico Ludovici.'

'The inquisitor?' said Bors.

The world in which Tannhauser lived might well have seemed wide to the mass of common men; but because of that very selectivity it was smaller than the map on which he moved. The map of villainy was smaller still. He felt his skin stretch taut around his skull.

He said, 'Ludovico sent Petrus Grubenius to the stake.'

Bors took his shoulders and tried to manoeuvre him out of Ludovico's path. 'The past is past. Let's look to our business.'

'I was a brute and Petrus made me a man. He was my teacher. He was my friend.'

'And it's a fool who cherishes an enemy he can't fight.'

Tannhauser yielded to Bors's strength and took a step back; but he didn't take his eyes from Ludovico's face and he saw that the inquisitor now studied him as he approached. The shorter monk, a sallow cove with disdainful features and sweating under two heavy satchels, made to walk past them as if skirting a noxious midden, but at the last moment Ludovico stopped and turned and regarded Tannhauser with courtesy. He indicated his waxy confrère.

'May I present Father Gonzaga, the legate of our Holy Office in Messina.'

Gonzaga, perplexed by Ludovico's tarriance, managed a nod.

'This is – Anacleto.'

The soulless young Spaniard stared at Tannhauser without warmth.

'I am Fra Ludovico. But in that respect you seem to have the advantage.'

Ludovico's voice rolled over him, calm and deep as a windless sea. Yet beneath its surface lurked monsters. Tannhauser gestured to Bors. 'Bors of Carlisle.' Then he gave a short bow. 'Captain Mattias Tannhauser.'

Ludovico's attention was engaged. 'Your reputation goes before you.'

'Every cock is king on his own dunghill,' Tannhauser replied.

The bluntness of the remark took Ludovico by surprise and his sensual mouth broke into a smile, as if discovering how to do so for the first time. An affronted gasp escaped Gonzaga's throat. Anacleto watched Tannhauser as a cat watches a bird in a barnyard. Bors watched Anacleto, and fidgeted with fingers that would rather have held a knife.

'You're a philosopher,' said Ludovico. 'And a keen one.'

Despite the old hatred rekindled within, Tannhauser found himself warming to the monk. A sign that Ludovico was more dangerous than he could imagine. Tannhauser shook his head. 'Your Grace flatters me. I'm a fortunate man but a simple one.'

This time Ludovico laughed out loud. 'And I am a humble priest.'

'Then we meet upon the square,' Tannhauser replied.

By now Gonzaga's astonishment was aimed at his master.

Ludovico said, 'Tell me from whence you know me, Captain Tannhauser. If we'd met before today I would surely remember.'

'I saw you only once, and at a distance, and many years ago. In Mondovi.'

Ludovico looked up into the distance, as if conjuring a scene from a memory detailed and vast, and he nodded. 'Apart from myself, you were the tallest man in the piazza.' His gaze came back around and the shadow of an obscure sorrow crossed his face, and Tannhauser knew that they both could recall the same pillar of flame and the feral acclamation of the same bestial mob.

Ludovico said, 'The world is awash with evil, now as then, and the evidence of Satan's handiwork is everywhere apparent.'

'I'll not gainsay you,' said Tannhauser.

'There was wickedness afoot among the Piedmontese,' said

Ludovico. 'Purity of faith had been impaired by war and malignant doctrines flourished. Discipline had to be restored. I'm happy that you were not numbered among the guilty.'

Tannhauser spat on the dockside and covered the phlegm with his boot. 'My wickedness is too common to invite the attention of such as thee,' he replied. 'In Mondovi, you murdered uncommon men. Men of uncommon learning. Like Petrus Grubenius.'

A change in the light in Ludovico's eyes showed cognition of his victim's name; but he said nothing. Tannhauser pointed due south, towards Syracuse.

'It wasn't far from here that the great Archimedes was murdered too, by an illiterate Roman soldier, for writing mathematical ciphers in the dust.' He turned back to Ludovico. 'It's a comfort to know that in the centuries stacked high since, Rome's admiration for learned men has not diminished.'

No man there had ever heard an inquisitor accused of murder. To hear it twice left both Bors and Gonzaga pale with stupefaction.

Ludovico took it all with equanimity. 'My comfort is the triumph of order over anarchy. And heresy – which is the enemy of good order – is rooted in the vainglory of learned men. He who hears the Eternal Word has no need of learning, for learning in itself is no virtue at all and is often the road that leads to infinite darkness.'

'I'll agree that learning confers no guarantee of virtue, for the evidence stands before me.' Tannhauser could feel Bors's eyes drilling into his skull, but the mood was upon him. 'As to darkness, broader roads lead thereto than that of knowledge.'

'What good is knowledge without fear of God?'

'If God needs human agents to make us fear Him, then you must tell me what paltry manner of god He must be.'

'I am no agent of God,' said Ludovico, 'but rather of the One True Church.' He pointed to the knights on the jetty. 'These noble Knights of the Baptist, whose valour I imagine you honour, are come to defend the Cross against the Red Beast of Islam. The war that Mother Church struggles to survive is more desperate by far. The enemies ranged against Her from every quarter are more terrible and more ubiquitous, and the very worst are spawned from within Her own bosom. The duration of the Church's war will be measured not in weeks, or even in years, but in millennia. And at stake is not an army, or an island, or a mere people, but the destiny of all mankind for all eternity. My purpose, then, is not to spread fear, but to defend the Rock upon which Peter founded Christ's congregation.'

'I do indeed honour these knights,' said Tannhauser, 'but they come to cross swords with the bravest fighting men in the world; not to torture the powerless and execute the meek.'

'And the Paradise of the Saints will be their reward. But you, too, wear a sword. If you believe in your inmost heart – in that place where even you hear the Voice of God – that you would rid His world of evil in ridding it of me, then I urge you, now, to draw your sword with gladness and strike me dead.'

The more the man talked, the more Tannhauser liked him, and the more he was convinced that he would rid the world of a very great menace indeed by striking him dead. He smiled. 'I'll match words with you no longer,' he said, 'for I concede I cannot best you.'

'The challenge was issued in earnest,' said Ludovico. 'And your comrade, at least, believes you might take it up.'

Tannhauser looked at Bors, who was indeed poised as if to spring on him. At Tannhauser's expression, and somewhat sheepishly, he relaxed.

'It is not my purpose to rid the world of evil,' said Tannhauser. 'But rather to accumulate wealth – and even a little learning – and to die of all the vices my allotted span will allow me to indulge. I turned my face from God a long time ago.'

'Believe me, man, He lives within you as surely as He lives

within me,' said Ludovico. 'And, just as surely, He will judge me for each of my deeds as He will judge you for yours.'

'Then perhaps – on Judgement Day – we'll stand in the dock together, side by side.'

Ludovico nodded. 'Of that, too, we may have no doubt at all.'

Ludovico glanced at Gonzaga, who was not only visibly shocked by what had passed but was also straining not to drop the satchels in his fists. Ludovico turned back to Tannhauser.

'Let us pray that by then the Grace of God will have freed us both from sin.'

'I thought you priests reserved that power to yourselves.'

'Opinions differ, scholastically speaking,' Ludovico replied. 'The priest may absolve you from the punishment due to sin – which is Damnation – but if, as some of the higher authorities hold, the malice of sin is defined as obduracy of heart, then that can only be broken down by Sorrow.'

'You've dispensed a deal of sorrow too,' said Tannhauser.

'Who among us has not?' He waited and Tannhauser nodded. Ludovico said, 'And if Sorrow opens the gate to the Grace of God, then what right man would shun it?'

Tannhauser didn't answer. Ludovico smiled, with a hint of melancholy.

'But I'm keeping you from your business. Despite your shameless blasphemies, perhaps you'd accept a humble priest's absolution before we part? It would ease my conscience, even if it won't ease yours.'

Tannhauser glanced at Anacleto and caught the ghost of a smile on the cupid lips. He hesitated. But churlishness was not his habit and he lowered his head. Ludovico raised his hand and made the sign of the cross.

'Ego te absolvo a peccatis tuis in nomine Patris et Filii et Spiritus Sancti, Amen.'

Tannhauser looked up. He realised that Ludovico had the coldest eyes he'd ever seen.

'*Asalaamu alaykum wa rahmatullahi wa barakatuh*,' said Tannhauser.

'Until we meet again,' said Ludovico.

'I'll bring my own firewood.'

Tannhauser watched the Dominican stride away with Gonzaga panting in tow. Anacleto's lupine figure brought up the rear. At ten paces distant he made a point of looking over his shoulder. Tannhauser held his eyes and Anacleto turned away and the trio were lost in the tumult of the port.

'Would you have us all on the rack?' seethed Bors. 'I've never seen such folly.'

'The eagle doesn't hunt worms,' Tannhauser replied. 'Ludovico's prey is the Religion.'

'I saw his face when he absolved you,' insisted Bors. 'As if he were sending you to the gallows. Or the stake. Mark my words, that blessing will prove a malediction.'

Tannhauser slapped him between the shoulders. 'Blessing or curse, I've no more faith in one than in the other, so let's to work.'

The captain of the galley was the Cavaliere Giovanni Castrucco, whom Tannhauser knew, and so the civilities were brisk and he and Bors were invited on board to have the bill of lading stamped and endorsed by the purser, and to arrange the loading of the cargo, which would occupy the rest of the day. The payment would be credited to their bank account in Venice; the Order never reneged on its debts. The *Couronne* would leave on the midnight tide: the Turkish vanguard might turn up any hour and Castrucco was eager not to run a blockade. When the business was done, Tannhauser and Bors headed back down the gangway and found Oliver Starkey on the quay. Tannhauser stretched out his hand and Starkey took it.

'Brother Starkey. This is a pleasure I didn't expect.'

'Tannhauser.' Starkey turned to shake Bors's hand too. 'And Bors of Carlisle.'

He pronounced his countryman's name with ironic amusement.

It was true that Bors's sobriquet was somewhat extravagant, smacking as it did of noble birth; but then so too was 'Tannhauser'. They'd chosen their *noms de guerre* over a bottle of brandy in Milan, while looking to hire their lances out to Alva. The unmapped mud hole from which Bors hailed was at least located near Carlisle; 'Tannhauser' was stolen from some ballad of chivalric fancy, an old troubadour's tale concerning a knight who was plagued by women and exiled from the City of God as a result. But a name had a power all its own, illegitimate or not, and theirs had done them proud, then and since.

'What brings you to Messina at this late date?' Tannhauser asked.

'You do,' said Starkey.

'If you want more men, I dare say I could round a few up – though most will be drunk and all of them scum of the earth –' He stopped at the patent want of interest in Starkey's face. 'But I forget my manners. Come and dine with us at our table –'

'Forgive me, Tannhauser, but I have not the heart to dissemble.' Starkey's unease was manifest. 'I do not come to trade, but to ask a boon.'

'You're amongst friends. Ask and be damned.'

'I came at the Grand Master's urgent command to entreat you to make common cause with the Religion, in the war against the Grande Turke.'

Tannhauser blinked. He stole a glance at Bors.

Bors smoothed his moustaches and licked his lips.

'In short,' said Starkey, 'the Grand Master wants you to join us.'

'In Malta?'

'In Malta.'

Tannhauser stared at Starkey with such incredulity and apprehension that Bors dropped his hands to his knees and roared with laughter. So raucously, indeed, and with such jubilation, that the sailors reefing the lateens and the stevedores sweating at the wagons stopped in the midst of their chores and turned to gape.

TUESDAY 15 MAY 1565

The Oracle – Messina Gate – the Hills of Neptune

Tannhauser returned from the *Couronne* in a sour humour. Starkey had mounted every type of persuasion – moral, political, financial, spiritual and tribal – in an attempt to recruit his allegiance. He'd promised him glory, riches, honour and the gratitude of Rome. He had begged, cajoled and browbeaten. He'd invoked the *Summae* of Thomas Aquinas, the authority of Saint Bernard of Clairvaux, and stirring examples of heroes ancient and modern. He'd done all but accuse Tannhauser of lacking courage. Yet Tannhauser had answered these bribes and propositions with an absolute refusal to take up arms for the Religion. The Maltese Iliad, as Starkey styled it, would have to go ahead without him. He hadn't killed a man in years and while his conscience was generally untroubled by such deeds it wasn't a practice he missed. As a reward for the morning's travails, he promised himself a bath back at the warehouse. Bors rode alongside him in a vexed silence of his own. As they approached the Oracle, Bors nodded towards a horse tied up in the shade outside the doors and said, 'Trouble.'

Tannhauser saw that the horse was a splendid bay mare, expensively saddled and caparisoned. With a handful of exceptions, the tavern's customers had no more chance of owning such a beast than they had of gaining election to the College of Cardinals. As they passed the Oracle's doors on their way to the stables, Tannhauser ducked his head to glance inside and found a peculiar commotion within. The uproar spilled from a mass of scurvy drunkards, crowded shoulder to shoulder in the manner of spectators to a brawl. He dismounted at once, handed Buraq's reins to Bors, and stepped to the threshold to peer over the heads of the unwashed.

In the middle of the saloon a long, bony whip of a girl in a forest green riding dress whirled like a dervish, arms outstretched like wings, amid a horseshoe of rowdy patrons, seated and afoot, who shouted lewd suggestions in Sicilian slang and threw pieces of cheese rind, candle wax and bread at her head. The girl was plainly demented, though bombarded as she was with obscenities and debris she could hardly be blamed for that. To make matters worse, and in ripe provocation of her tormentors' primitive fantasies, she chanted his own name in a piping voice as she revolved.

'Tannhauser! Tannhauser! Tannhauser!'

Tannhauser sighed. He rearranged his sword so as to hang in a more imposing fashion and strode into the tavern with every appearance of knowing exactly what to do.

The louts were making such rare sport that few noticed his entrance, which galled him even more. As a squat, ox-necked individual leaned back from his bench, his arm cocked to hurl some piece of trash at the girl, Tannhauser grabbed him by the nape and bounced his face on the tabletop with such an excess of force that the other end of the trestle leapt in the air and spilled a shower of beer across the seated.

'Back to your ale, you pigs,' he roared.

To his gratification, the din collapsed into silence. The girl stopped in mid-spin and looked at him without a trace of giddiness. As far as he could tell in the murky light she had one brown eye and one grey, a sure sign of an unbalanced temperament. Since the eyes were perfectly matched in the spirit with which each shone, and this in spite of the cruelty to which she'd been subjected, he was intrigued. If her face was somewhat lopsided and she was far too thin and her hair looked as if she'd cut it herself, without the aid of a mirror, he couldn't help wondering what it would be like to make love to her. The dress didn't give much away, but an educated guess suggested magnificent breasts. To his surprise, he discovered a pleasant and rapid stiffening within his leather breeches.

'Tannhauser,' said the girl, in a voice that, to his ear, rang with music. Her eyes were fixed on his chest rather than his face, but she was entitled to be nervy.

'At your service, signorina,' he replied with a flourish and a bow.

Her eyes flickered past him and he turned as Ox Neck regained sufficient of his wits to rise unsteadily from his bench and clench raised fists. Before his dazed gaze could locate his foe, Bors fell upon him from behind with grim delight. The girl seemed unperturbed by the brutal events that ensued, as if violent spectacles in tawdry settings were not beyond her experience.

'Do you speak French?' she asked in that language.

Tannhauser coughed and spread his shoulders. 'But of course,' he replied in the same. With what he considered admirable fluency, he asked the girl her name.

'Amparo,' she replied.

Lovely, thought Tannhauser. He indicated the sanctuary of his alcove, with no little pride in its exotic furnishings and decor, and said, 'Mademoiselle Amparo, come, please. Let us sit.'

Amparo shook her head, her eyes still on his chest, and replied with a torrent of words that Tannhauser realised he could not understand. Or rather, he recognised one word in five while the rest hurtled by and left him befuddled. He'd grown up speaking German among his family and as a boy of twelve, in the janissary school, draconian discipline had forced him to master languages and scripts of absolute foreignness. He'd subsequently learned Italian with relative ease. During his sojourn with Petrus Grubenius, whose every sentence would wander through rhetorical byways before reaching its point, he'd acquired a love of that extravagance which the Roman tongue invites from certain temperaments. Messina had also made him a passable Spaniard. But French was a cursed tongue, encrusted with irrationalities of pronunciation, and what vocabulary he had, he'd learned from soldiers.

He raised his hand to stop her.

'Please,' he said. The furtive eyes of the rabble were upon him and the sound of their grumbling and farting made conversation hard. He indicated the doors. 'Let's talk outside.'

Amparo nodded and he held out a protective arm. She ignored it and skipped past him to the waterfront, where he joined her with the horses in the shade. He found her staring at Buraq, whom Bors had tethered up alongside her mare. Clearly, she had an eye for fine horseflesh.

'This is Buraq,' said Tannhauser. He retreated into Italian and hoped that if he spoke slowly he'd be understood. 'He is named for the winged horse of the Prophet Mohammed.'

She turned and met his gaze directly for the first time. If she wasn't exactly pretty, she cast a powerful allure. Her face, misshapen he now saw by a violent depression of the bone beneath her left eye, glowed with an ecstasy that disturbed him. She had about her an elemental innocence at odds with the manner in which she'd handled the tavern. She said nothing.

Tannhauser tried again in his stunted French. 'Please, tell me how I can help you.'

He listened as Amparo spoke to him as if to a simple-minded child, and though this enabled him to gain some idea of what she said, he couldn't shake the feeling that this was exactly how she viewed him. She talked a good deal of nonsense about a naked man – it was possible he misunderstood this detail – on some kind of horse, at which she gesticulated towards Buraq, and about a dog with a fire in his mouth and other fragments of what sounded like mystic fancy. But beyond these riddles he managed to glean that she wanted him call upon her mistress, one Madame de la Penautier – a contessa, no less – at the Villa Saliba in the hills beyond the city.

'You want me to visit the Contessa de la Penautier, at the Villa Saliba,' he said, to confirm at least that much. The girl bobbed her head. As far as he could tell, she hadn't explained the purpose of such a conference. 'Excuse me,' he said, 'but why?'

Amparo looked perplexed. 'It is her wish. Isn't that enough?'

Tannhauser blinked. His experience of French countesses, or for that matter their maids, if such Amparo was, was nonexistent. Perhaps they always summoned a gentleman in this manner, and perhaps all their maids were as strange as this elfin girl; but probably not. Nevertheless, it was a novelty and he was flattered. And after all, where was the harm? Tannhauser took a moment to compose his reply.

'You may tell the Contessa that it will be my pleasure to visit the Villa Saliba tomorrow, at her convenience.' He smiled, pleased with his increasing mastery of the loathsome tongue.

'No,' said the girl. 'Today. Now.'

Tannhauser cast a glance from the slender shade into the shimmering furnace of a Sicilian summer afternoon. The prospect of his perfumed bath retreated. 'Now?' he said

'I will take you to her at once,' said Amparo.

There was a sudden dangerous aspect to the girl's expression, as if she might start whirling and shouting at any refusal. Due to what he now viewed as the dark years of his celibacy – for such was the rule among the janissaries – Tannhauser had only come to know the gentler sex at an advanced age. It was a fact known only to himself that he'd been twenty-six before he'd abandoned virginity. As a result, he invested women with a power and wisdom he suspected they didn't deserve. Yet he balked at the thought of appearing less than gallant before a contessa, or even her maid.

'Very well,' he said. 'The air, for my health, will be good.'

He gave her what he hoped was a charming smile, but received none such in return. Amparo turned and skipped to her mare and sprang into the saddle with admirable litheness. She revealed a flash of muscular calf and, beneath the bodice of her dress, enough movement to confirm his hopes about the size of her breasts. She looked down on him with exaggerated patience. Tannhauser hesitated, unused to being marshalled in this way. Bors appeared, wiping blood from his knuckles, in the doorway. He looked at the girl in green, then cast a questioning glance at Tannhauser.

'I'm invited to call on a lady,' Tannhauser announced. 'A contessa, no less.'

Bors snorted with salacious laughter.

'Enough,' said Tannhauser. He strode to Buraq.

'He is your father?' asked Amparo matter-of-factly.

Bors, whose French was in fact superior to Tannhauser's, stopped laughing.

Tannhauser took his turn. 'No. But for certain he is old and fat enough to be so.'

Amparo said, 'Then why are you asking his permission?'

Tannhauser too stopped laughing, appalled that she had made this interpretation.

'You'd better go to your contessa,' said Bors, 'before this creature bests us both.'

Tannhauser mounted. Before he could lead the way, as was his intention, the girl clattered away across the cobbles at a brisk trot.

THEY RODE THROUGH streets rendered empty by the vicious heat and which hummed with the faeces and flies that infested the gutters. At the city's northern gate they passed cartwheels fixed to poles, upon which were lashed the disembowelled corpses of blasphemers, sodomites and thieves, their hides so sunburned, their flesh so desiccated, that even crows and maggots now shunned them. On the spikes to either side of the gate was a collection of beak-flayed heads. Leaving such eyesores behind they ascended the Hills of Neptune, where the air was surpassing sweet and falcons in great variety patrolled the Monti Peloritani.

Via discreet enquiries of the girl, Tannhauser gained an impression of the Lady Penautier as a tough and resourceful young widow who ran an estate in the Aquitaine all on her own. Of the deceased husband Amparo had no knowledge, for his death had pre-dated her arrival, but the contessa had never shown signs of missing his companionship. While no accurate figure could be elicited, it seemed that the Lady was not yet thirty years old, and was possessed of considerable beauty.

For the moment he was content to note that Amparo had long fingers with almond-shaped nails and a neck as graceful as a swan's. Beneath the green silk, stained black by sweat beneath her arms, her breasts were even larger than he'd appreciated, a fact emphasised by her build, which he now preferred to see as slender rather than thin. If she barely looked at him at all, it was no doubt due to shyness. Tannhauser learned, with relief, that Amparo was a Spaniard and had spent much of her later girlhood in Barcelona. Castilian gave him the chance to correct the impression that he was an idiot. He spoke of the port and the fine old cathedral to be found in that great city, though he'd never been there himself and had acquired this knowledge second-hand. Amparo met his enthusiasm with silence and he returned to asking questions, which she was, at least, always polite enough to answer.

She and Madame had travelled from a village near Bordeaux, but beyond that her grasp of geography was weak. To Amparo, Marseilles, Naples and Sicily were no more than stepping stones scattered on the waters of a vast unknown. For two women travelling alone such a journey was reckless in the extreme; not least because they had scorned an armed escort. Yet Amparo declared herself content to follow her mistress 'to the edge of the world'. Such loyalty was uncharacteristic of hired labour – or of relationships between females in general, in Tannhauser's experience. By the time they reached the bougainvilleas that announced the end of their ride, Tannhauser was more intrigued than ever.

The Villa Saliba was a pile of marble in the modern – ostentatious – fashion. Tannhauser felt that a residence such as this would suit him well. The villa itself, however, was not their destination. They left their horses to be watered at the stables, then Amparo led him to a fabulous garden devoted to white and red roses. It was shaded by palm trees and myrtles and its location and design were superbly conceived. Tannhauser noted with satisfaction that there were none of the ubiquitous magnolias that would have smothered the delicate scents. Beyond the garden stood a much smaller yet still splendid house of cool white stone.

Amparo stopped before the rose beds and crouched down by a particular white bloom, as if to reassure herself of its health. Tannhauser watched her for a moment as she murmured to it in a language that was neither French nor Castilian. She was indeed a singular creature. As if she had read his mind she turned from the bloom and looked up as if daring his scorn.

'In Araby,' he said, 'they say that, once upon a time, all roses were white.'

With a passionate curiosity, Amparo straightened up. She took in the red blooms thickly clustered, and then looked at him again.

'One evening, beneath a waning moon,' Tannhauser continued, 'a nightingale alighted by such a rose – a tall, white rose – and when he saw her he fell at once in love. Now, until that time, no nightingale had ever been heard to sing –'

'The nightingales couldn't sing?' asked Amparo, eager to confirm this detail.

Tannhauser nodded. 'They passed their lives in silence, from one end to the other, but so brave was this nightingale's love – for this exquisite white rose – that a song of wondrous beauty burst from his throat, and he threw his wings about her in a passionate embrace and –'

He stopped, for the girl seemed entranced, and there was a look of such poignant rapture in her face that he feared to tell her the climax of the tale.

'Please,' she pressed him, 'go on.'

'The nightingale clasped the rose to his breast, but with such wild passion that the thorns pierced his heart, and he died with his wings wrapped around her.'

The girl's hands flew to her mouth and she took a step back, as if her own heart had been pierced. Tannhauser pointed to the red flowers.

'The nightingale's blood stained the rose's white petals. And that is why, ever since, certain roses bloom red.'

Amparo considered this for some time. With grave sincerity she asked, 'This is true?'

'It is a tale,' said Tannhauser. 'The Arabs have other tales of roses, for they hold them in special regard. But the truth of a tale is in the gift of the one who hears it.'

Amparo looked at the blood-red blooms around her.

'I believe it is true,' she said, 'though it is very sad.'

'Surely the nightingale was happy,' said Tannhauser, not wishing to dampen her spirits. 'He won the power to sing for his brothers and sisters, and now they sing for us.'

'And the nightingale knew love,' said Amparo.

Tannhauser nodded, this vital observation having escaped him heretofore.

'It's a better bargain than most of us make in death,' he said.

For the first time since they'd met, her eyes rose to meet his own directly. They were larger than he'd realised and she turned them on him as if stripping herself naked.

'I will never know love,' she said.

Tannhauser almost blinked but held fast.

'Many people believe that,' he said. Indeed it was a conviction he shared himself, but did not say so. 'Some fear the madness and chaos love brings in its wake. Some fear themselves unworthy of its glories. Most are proved wrong in the end.'

'No, I cannot love, like the bird who could not sing.'

'The bird found his song.'

'And I would be a bird if I could, but I am not.'

Tannhauser could not deny a strange affinity for the girl. He didn't know why.

'You're the man on the golden horse,' she said.

Now that they'd left the quagmire of French behind, he understood this phrase, which she'd used earlier on at the tavern with such great excitement. A golden horse. Buraq.

He shrugged. 'Yes.'

Amparo turned and walked towards the guesthouse. Tannhauser followed, feeling somewhat like a large, ugly dog in train to a wayward child. In passing he noted the feline sway of her hips and the splendid drape of the linen adorning her hams. The building's lengthening shadow fell across a wooden bench, equipped with floral-patterned cushions, which overlooked the garden and the sea. With a gesture, Amparo invited him to sit.

'Wait here,' she said.

Amparo walked through a pair of glass-paned doors and left them open as she disappeared inside. Tannhauser could see only a few feet within. The ceiling appeared to be decorated with the vulgar interpretations of classical myth so popular with the Franks. The rear of the salon was shrouded in gloom and between gloom and doors – as if some elvish aura had been left by Amparo's passage – a shower of golden motes tumbled through the air.

Tannhauser settled on the bench, whose comfort delighted him. In the distance the sea was a mirror of white and gold held up to the sun, and across the straits of Scylla and Charybdis the hills of Calabria quavered in the afternoon heat. The air was the most fragrant he'd tasted in months and the roses and the hills and the water took him back to a private courtyard in Trebizond, in the palace where Suleiman Shah had been born, and where Tannhauser had sworn an oath to protect the emperor's first-born son.

The only flaw was an awareness of his own smell, formerly undetectable, of tavern, docks, sweat and the erotic antics he'd indulged in the night before. It was probably of no consequence, as the Christians were a filthy lot with a morbid fear of water, yet the missed bath was missed indeed. His fondness for immersing himself in water was a habit learned in Turkey, where the Prophet demanded that the faithful be pure for at least the Friday noon prayer, and most especially after the defilement of sex. Here it was considered an eccentricity. He inhaled deeply. There was no doubt about it, he stank. Perhaps that was why Amparo had left him in the garden.

His concerns were truncated by a gust of divine sound. A sound so divine, and of a beauty so pure, that it took him a moment to realise that it was music. And so lovely was this music that he couldn't bring himself to turn and seek its source, for it seized control of his nerves and so penetrated his heart that he was robbed of the power to do aught but fall for its spell. Two instruments, both stringed. One plucked, one bowed. One light and nimble, the notes falling soft as summer rain, the other dark and surging as the tides of a storm-racked night, the two dancing, one with the other, in a fierce and elemental embrace.

He closed his eyes in the shade, with the scent of the roses in his throat, and let the music roll through his soul, a sarabande which caressed the face of death as lovers caress the face of their beloved. The darker instrument overwhelmed his senses with waves of ecstatic melancholy, in one moment brutal with exaltation, as delicate as candlelight in the next. Nothing he had known, not merely heard but known, had prepared him for such transcendence. What possessed him to allow his soul to yield to its force? What sorcery could conjure such spectres and send them roaring through his heart and on and away into an eternity nameless and unknown? And when each note ended where did it go? And how could each be and then not be? Or did each one echo until the end of all things and from one far rim of Creation to the other? On and on the music rose and fell, and segued and flowed, with an exuberant hope and a demoniac despair, as if invoked from skin and wood and the gut strings of beasts by gods no priest or prophet had ever worshipped. And each time he knew that the music must die, depleted by its own extravagant longing, it resurrected itself again, and yet again, falling and climbing from one peak to the next, howling for more of itself, for more of his soul, that soul now borne along by the torrent unleashed from the locked places inside him of all that he'd done and all that he'd known and all that he'd seen of horror and glory and sorrow.

Then with the same shocking stealth with which the sound had arrived, silence stole its place, and the universe seemed empty, and in that emptiness he sat.

Time re-established its dominion and once more the scent of the roses and the cool of the breeze and the weight of his limbs crept back into his awareness. He found that he was sitting with his face in his hands and when he took his hands away they were wet with tears. He looked at the wetness with amazement for he hadn't wept in decades and had thought it no longer in him. Not since he'd learned that all flesh is dust, and that only God is great, and that, in this world, tears are for the comfort of the defeated. He wiped his face on the burgundy sleeve of his doublet. And just in time.

'Chevalier Tannhauser, thank you for coming.' The voice was almost as lovely as the music. 'I am Carla de la Penautier.'

He stood up and composed himself and turned and found a woman watching from some yards distant on the path. She was petite of build, somewhat narrow in the hips but long in the thigh, and perhaps shapely in the calf with finely turned ankles, though these latter attributes were based in speculation, for her legs were concealed by a dress that was something to behold. It was the colour of pomegranate juice and of such sensuous cut and fabrication that it was all he could do to keep his mouth from falling open. The dress clung to her body like oil, like lust, and shimmered with slashes of light with every movement she made. He felt his fingers twitch and stilled them. He seized control of his senses and dragged his attention to her face.

Her features were strong and clear, her irises green and rimed, as if with ink, by thin black circlets. Despite her name, she didn't look French but had the bones and hauteur of a Sicilian. Her hair was the colour of honey and shot through with yellow, as if one of the Norman conquerors had left his seed in her blood. The hair was forced into a knot but would spring into golden waves if given its freedom. His eyes returned, despite his better judgement, to her bust. The dress was fastened at the front by an ingenious arrangement of hooks and eyes, and thereby buttressed her breasts – which were of modest dimension and a quite stunning whiteness – into two exquisite hemispheres. The hemispheres were separated by a cleft into which he would happily have fallen forever. The outlines of her nipples were just visible and, if he were not mistaken, appeared to grow more prominent under his gaze. But perhaps he flattered himself. In any event, she was a beauty, true enough.

He returned his eyes to her face, upon which two high spots of colour had appeared. If Amparo embodied a hardiness that had failed to extinguish her innocence, Carla possessed an air of sadness contained by courage. That and more. Much more, for he knew, on instinct, that the demoniac instrumentalist was she. He liked her at once and bowed.

'My pleasure, Madame,' he said. 'But I must confess at once that I'm no chevalier.'

He smiled and Carla returned the favour, as if involuntarily and with a warmth he sensed she rarely felt or revealed.

'If you wish, you may call me Captain, as I've held that rank or its equivalent in a variety of armies. I should add, however, that I am now a man of peace.'

'I hope you'll forgive me for not greeting you more promptly, Captain.' Her Italian was refined, with an accent he couldn't place. 'Amparo insisted that we play music, as is our habit. Without habit, she becomes distraught.'

'Then I'm in her debt,' he said, 'for I've never heard the like. Indeed, delight has never transported me nearly so far.'

She inclined her head at the compliment and he seized the opportunity to revisit the dress, which was quite the most fabulous he'd seen and which clung to her body in much the way he might have done himself, given half the chance. To meet two desirable women in a single day was a welcome novelty. It was a shame they were such close associates; but that conundrum could wait on another day. He met her eyes again. Could she read his thoughts? He laughed. How could she not?

'Do I amuse you?' she said, smiling again.

'I amuse myself,' he replied. 'And I'm filled with the joy of this unforeseen encounter.'

He inclined his head in what he hoped was a gracious gesture, and she accepted with the same, and made a better job of it. He brushed the back of his fingers against his jaw, and was reminded that he was unshaven and that his mien was in general uncouth. Unsure of how to proceed, he took refuge in simplicity.

'Please, My Lady,' he said. 'Tell me how I may serve you.'

TUESDAY 15 MAY 1565

The Abbey of Santa Maria della Valle

Even a man's inmost thoughts are known to God. As too are that man's fantasies and fears, his shame, his dreams both waking and asleep, and most of all those unborn desires whose existence he dares not acknowledge, even to himself. From such occult desire springs spiritual error. And spiritual error was the source of all human evil. Hence, desire had to be scrutinised – and policed – with unceasing vigilance. Ludovico Ludovici stood nude and sweating in the abbot's gold and marble lavatorium. There he cleansed his flesh of the penetrating stench of the galley. As he did so he scrutinised himself. The quality of his mind, and the elemental forces of his body, made him more vulnerable than most to the abuse of power. And his power was immense. He was not only the plenipotentiary of His Holiness, Pope Pius IV, but the secret agent of Michele Ghisleri, inquisitor General of All Christendom.

In Ludovico's hand was a piece of coarse sacking with which he wiped his face and the vault of his skull. He dipped the sack in a barrel of fountain water, sweetened with flowers of orange and leaves of wild betony. He could have used Red Sea sponges and soft white linens and any number of rare aromatics and balms, for these rooms had been placed at his disposal and the abbot lived in splendour, but luxury was a snare for the weak and unwary. He'd slept on stone for thirty years. He fasted, dawn till dusk, from September to Easter. He wore a goat's hair shirt on Fridays. He ate meat only twice a week, to preserve his intellect. And for all that he loved conversation, he practised silence unless his work demanded otherwise. Mortification of the flesh was the armour of the soul.

He wiped his neck and his shoulders. The water cooled him. He was obliged to determine the fate of two human beings. He always gave such matters the gravest analysis, and these two cases in particular weighed on his soul. Ludovico rinsed the sackcloth and wiped his arms.

Ludovico had grown up in Naples, the richest and most vicious city in the world. Born into a family of courtier diplomats and intellectuals, he was the second son of his father and his father's first wife. He'd entered the University of Padua at the age of thirteen and joined the Dominican Order a year later. He was sent to study at Milan where his mind won him a chair in theology and ecclesiastic law. Encouraged by his father *to seize all opportunity with shrewdness and daring*, he went to Rome in his early twenties and won his doctorate in the same subjects. There he caught the eye, in turn, of both Pope Paul IV, Giovanni Carafa, and the inquisitor General, Michele Ghisleri. It was to restore the moral purity of Italy that Carafa, in '42, had established the Holy Office of the Roman Inquisition and had thereby unleashed the purges that had kept the prisons full ever since. A young man of Ludovico's brilliance and piety was rare, and Carafa had recruited him with a brief to strike at men in high places, *for upon their punishment, the salvation of the lower orders will depend.*

In a time of dire conformism, in which the tongue up the arse was the most efficient way to prosper, original minds found few spheres in which to flourish. To Ludovico, the Inquisition was just such a realm. He was honoured to be an inquisitor. Terror and Faith were its tools, but in his view the Black Legend was false. A tiny handful of executions, inflicted with due diligence on the deviant, and with every juridical right of the condemned rigorously observed, had prevented the deaths of many hundreds of thousands. These figures were not in dispute. Luther had played midwife to a Devil's Era, in which Christian slaughtered Christian in monstrous numbers not for land or power but simply because each was Christian. It was a paradox – an absurdity – that Lucifer alone could have designed. The obscene and constipated monk had drenched the whole of Germany in blood, and that more horror was to come was scorched across the map in letters of fire. In France the carnage had only just begun, at Vassy and Dreux. The Low Countries were a dank pool of Anabaptism. Heresiarchs sat on the thrones of England and Navarre.

Only in Spain and Italy were people free from being slaughtered by their own countrymen. In Spain and Italy the Holy Office had strangled the Lutheran viper at its birth. The campaign in northern Italy to wipe out the Protestants had been the greatest political achievement of modern times. That it was not widely celebrated was testament to the skill of its execution. If Turin and Bologna and Milan had fallen, as a hundred Catholic cities only a few days north of the Alps had fallen before them, Lutheranism would be lapping at the gates of Rome. Italy would be engulfed in catastrophic violence. And Spain, which controlled the Italian south, would have been drawn into the holocaust. The whole of Christendom would have torn itself apart. And might do so yet. Ludovico never doubted that the Inquisition was a very great force for good. The Inquisition protected Mother Church. The Inquisition prevented War. The Inquisition was a boon to depraved and fallen mankind. Those who opposed the Inquisition dishonoured God.

He rinsed the sacking and squeezed it and wiped the smell of excrement from the pores and hairs of his marble-pale calf and thigh. As he did so he averted his head so as not to see his privities. The vanities of intellect and power he'd held in check. Inspired by Tomas de Torquemada, he'd refused all high preferments, including a red hat offered by two successive popes. He'd remained a simple friar. At very much greater sacrifice, he'd rejected chairs of theology and law in a dozen superb universities. Having grown up in opulence to find it enfeebling and empty, the attraction of riches escaped him. He lived on the road, calloused to need, unshackled by human community, bound only to Christ and his vows, an ambassador of ecclesiastic terror, the wayfaring sword of the Sacred Congregation. In all this his conscience was clear. Yet once he'd been consumed by desire. Once he'd submitted to a power more profound than his Faith. He'd been dragged to the verge of apostasy by Love.

He rinsed the sacking again and scrubbed his other leg. Lust was the oldest of his enemies and, though it no longer plagued him with the tenacity of youth, it was not wholly vanquished even now. Yet lust was of the flesh, and its masks transparent, and could be transformed into an offering of pain. Love had come cloaked in the guise of spiritual ecstasy and had spoken with the Voice of God. Nothing before or since had seemed more sacred and even now he sometimes wondered if all that he had learned were not flawed, and if the accumulated wisdom of centuries were not false, and if that Voice was not indeed the text of the Almighty's best instruction. And there – again – was the danger. The buried seed awaiting its moment to bloom. The spectre of the woman he had loved and, as these meditations now revealed, loved still, had returned from the gloom of the past to challenge his Fidelity. And not merely her spectre, but her person. Her living flesh. She was here, not an hour from where he stood aroused and naked.

His yard throbbed monstrously between his legs. He felt it pant and strain like a hell dog on a gossamer leash. He rinsed and squeezed the sacking and wiped the sweat and grease from his groins and his pubes. He wiped his balls. He wiped his member and held on as a spasm of carnality overwhelmed him.

In his mind, with perfect clarity, he saw her on her back on the grassy bank, splayed amid burgeoning wildflowers whose fragrance besotted them both. Slender and nude and white as milk she was, her face tipped back, lips parted in ardour, her nipples purpled and clenched, her spread thighs open, her vulva swollen, her flawless arms flung wide. She wanted him. She trembled and cried out and her green eyes rolled and fluttered with the extremity of her wanting. It was her wanting – of him – which pushed him to the brink of derangement. Of her wanting of him he'd never have his fill.

A wave of yearning rose and crested, foaming from the floor of his bowels, and he groaned as demons screamed to let the wave explode. A few seconds stolen from the ocean of time and the agony would pass. But only for a while. He felt his Guardian Angel at his shoulder, felt his cold spectral hand touch his head to remind him: this was how the Devil had lured him before, with the lie that in committing the lesser sin he could somehow forestall the commission of the greater, as if evil was something one could sip from a crystal cup and not a foetid swamp into which one plunged headlong and vanished.

'God spare me,' he cried. 'God forgive me.'

For an instant he thought he'd succumbed. But the sackcloth was unsoiled, as were the tiles at his feet, and the wave and its demons receded. He dashed his face with fountain water. He gave thanks to Saint Dominic. He rinsed the cloth and wiped his belly and his loins, and rinsed again. He wiped the plates of his chest. He reflected on the circumstances of his fall.

HE WAS THEN twenty-six years old, and in Malta on behalf of his patron, Michele Ghisleri, who'd required the resignation of the Bishop of Mdina to make way for a favourite nephew. To be entrusted at such an age with an errand of such delicacy was a tribute to Carafa's faith in him. But Ludovico met a girl, on the coast road high above the surf, and he fell under her enchantment. Her name was Carla de Manduca. The image of her beauty settled in his heart and kindled a flame that tormented him without cease. Flagellation only exacerbated his salacity and, though he prayed for the obsession to leave him, its grip became stronger. He sought her out in the hope of discovering she meant nothing, and his folly was compounded. They walked and he agreed to hear her confession. Among sundry trivial sins she admitted to impure thoughts. Of him. She took him to see the idol of the giant pagan goddess that had stood on the island since the race of men was young. And there they made love, he no less virginal than she.

There followed weeks in which their Fascination grew, and while Ludovico sinned he stripped the Bishop of Mdina of all the dignity he had. He broke his aged spirit with the zeal of the young and reduced him to a worm crawling for forgiveness. Then he banished him to a cell in the Calabrian wastelands. His cruelty was fanned by transgression, and guilt had curdled his bowels and distempered his mind. Madness and apostasy loomed and with it not only perdition but public shame for the Ludovici in Naples and the betrayal of His Holiness in Rome. At the very moment he'd decided to abandon his calling in favour of the girl, Ludovico was betrayed himself. He was summoned by the prelate of Malta to hear that the girl's parents had made a charge of infamous conduct against him. In panic and despair he fled to Rome and confessed his dire iniquities to Ghisleri.

The wily Ghisleri, as penance and reward, sent Ludovico to Castile, to learn the art of inquisition from the foremost Spanish master, Fernando Valdes. In homage to Saint Dominic, Ludovico walked barefoot from Rome to Valladolid. It was a journey of revelation and spiritual rebirth, and he was received on his arrival as a holy fool, possessed by the living spirit of Jesus Christ. And perhaps by then it was so, for by this supreme act of will and mortification he'd forgotten Carla. Now, these many years later, it seemed that he had not. And neither had God, nor the Devil, for one or other had placed her here, again, within his reach, to tempt him into error and menace his soul.

Ludovico never knew at the time what intrigues informed his sudden disgrace in Malta. More recent enquiries had revealed that the ruined bishop counted La Valette, then Admiral of the Navy, among his allies, and that La Valette had been behind the charge of misconduct. Ludovico held no grudge against the man. Grudges were for the weak. He would orchestrate the fall of La Valette for other reasons. As to Carla, he meant her no ill. If she had indeed turned against him – a fact which could not be verified – she'd been young and his heart could do no other than forgive her. Yet even if he allowed her to jeopardise his soul, he couldn't let her jeopardise his work. He was sure she was unaware of his presence in Messina. But if she returned to Malta, his plans would be imperilled. He would be imperilled. His reputation, his authority, and with them the ambitions of his patrons in Rome. Who knew what the woman wanted? Who knew what deformities time had wrought upon her mind? And if the past could recapture him with such violent energy, it could capture Carla – with wayward passions, be they of love or hatred, that no one could foretell or control. His own fate was immaterial. But he was the instrument of the Church. He could not allow her to blunt its edge.

He rinsed the sackcloth, his ablutions almost complete, and wiped his armholes and his arse. A period of retreat in the company of the Holy Sisters would hardly do her harm. If Carla was safely secluded with the Minims, was there any need, then, to dispose of Mattias Tannhauser as well? Ludovico had been ignorant of the man's existence – and of Carla's presence – until the voyage from Grand Harbour on the *Couronne*, when Starkey had taken Ludovico into his confidence. Starkey was convinced that Tannhauser would not be won over to the Religion's cause.

La Valette, however, had suggested a stratagem in which Carla would recruit the German on their behalf.

Ludovico hadn't discouraged Starkey's plan. When the stratagem failed, he didn't want Starkey to suspect that he was the cause. 'You mustn't appear to beg for Her Ladyship's help,' Ludovico had counselled. 'Rather, let her feel she's the beneficiary of your kindness. Exaggerate the unlikelihood of success. Paint Tannhauser in dark colours, so that the ray of her hope is faint.'

'Why so?' Starkey's tone had revealed that he'd plotted the opposite course.

'Because it will excite her ingenuity to the utmost. In the manipulation of men's hearts, women love to attempt the impossible. It flatters the only power they're given to wield, which is the power of desire. As to Tannhauser, use the contrary technique. Exhaust every argument. Push him hard. Push him to the point of giving insult, so that his dignity insists on refusal. Then, when the Lady Carla makes her play, it will flatter his vanity that the decision to go to Malta is his alone.'

Even as Ludovico had supported and refined Starkey's plan, he'd resolved to thwart it, for it threatened the success of his own schemes. Schemes so fantastic in complexity they made poor Starkey's ruse seem a prank. Ludovico's purpose was to bring the Knights of Saint John under papal control. Many had tried and failed. Two centuries before, the Papacy had conspired in the brutal extermination of the Templars, but the Hospitallers were too strong, and too remote and too well loved, for so crude a solution to work. The Turkish invasion created a unique possibility, the study of which had occupied Ludovico on Malta. If the Religion's stronghold were destroyed, their vast holdings across Europe would be sequestered by local princes and monarchs, most particularly in France. If the knights survived, in glory, they'd be even less vulnerable to the Vatican than before. Unless, that is, the Grand Master's throne were occupied by a man whose allegiance was strictly to the Holy Father. Ludovico had such a man in mind. His present mission to Rome was to acquire the means to install that man in power. Nothing could be allowed to compromise Ludovico's dignity and thereby his work.

He would never let Carla set foot on the island of Malta.

LUDOVICO LEFT THE lavatorium and donned a clean habit.

The German, Tannhauser, was formidable, yet the man was willing to indulge in dangerous passions. A vain man. A foolish man. His insolence on the dock had confirmed it. He might well take pity on Carla. He might well be flattered to accept the role of her champion, no common honour for a scoundrel such as he. And no doubt she had the means to pay him. Ludovico had also sensed the man's sexual potency, as men of similar stripe, like beasts, often do. He felt a stir of jealousy and cautioned himself, yet equivocation was hardly necessary. The man was a blasphemer and a heretic. As Michele Ghisleri had counselled, in regard to prominent noblemen, *Remove the man, and you remove the problem.*

Ludovico made his way to the abbot's parlour, where Gonzaga awaited instructions.

Gonzaga was a *commissarius*, a local priest who acted for the Inquisition and supplied information. He had a vicious streak, which Ludovico mistrusted, but was well liked, perhaps for that very reason, by the familiars in Messina. These latter, of whom there were many, Gonzaga had flattered by founding a brotherhood, the Congregation of Saint Peter Martyr. Familiars were lay servants of the Holy Office, ready at all times to perform the duties of the tribunal and permitted to bear arms to protect inquisitors. It was an honour eagerly sought, not least because it conferred immunity from secular justice. High-born or low, *limpieza de sangre* – purity of the blood – was required, for no convert of Jewish lineage could serve the Holy Office.

In the parlour, Anacleto, as always as much apparition as human being, stood inside the door. Ludovico had found him in Salamanca, in '58, where he'd been asked to examine him for signs of diabolic possession. The young nobleman, then eighteen, stood guilty of incest with his sister, Filomena, and of the murder of both his parents when they'd caught the two siblings *in flagrante delicto*. Anacleto didn't deny these horrifying crimes, nor did he repent of them. Filomena had been hanged, and her corpse consumed by swine, while Anacleto watched. His execution, too, was a formality. But something in the youth's black soul had touched Ludovico. Moreover, he'd seen in him a tool of great value: a man without conscience, capable of any heinous deed. A man who would give undying loyalty to the person who redeemed him. Ludovico spent four days with the youth and forged an unbreakable bond. He extracted Anacleto's penitence and absolved him. More than that, he gave him a higher purpose and a reason to live. Thus immunised by the Inquisition, Anacleto had accompanied Ludovico and Fernando Valdes on their relentless sweep through Castile, which climaxed in extravagant *autos-da-fé* in Valladolid, where the Emperor Philip himself attended the burnings. Anacleto had been his master's shadow ever since, always ready to protect him and to keep Ludovico's hands unstained by blood.

Gonzaga stood up and bowed. Ludovico gestured that he sit.

'This being the territory of Spain,' said Ludovico, 'and under the jurisdiction of the Congregation's Spanish arm, I have no formal powers here.' He held up a hand to forestall Gonzaga's offer of all necessary authority. 'Nor do I seek such powers. However, it is in the most urgent interests of His Holiness that by eight o'clock this evening two tasks be accomplished without fail.'

'Our familiars include the best of the city constabulary,' blurted Gonzaga. 'My cousin, Captain Spano, will give us every assistance.'

'By what means these tasks are accomplished, and by whom,

I don't want to know. Neither action should be seen as the work of the Holy Office, but rather of the civil authorities. Both tasks require subtlety and speed in different measure.'

'Yes, Your Excellency. Subtlety and speed.'

'In residence at the guesthouse of the Villa Saliba is a noblewoman named Carla de la Penautier. She's to be taken to join the Minims at the convent of the Holy Sepulchre at Santa Croce, for a period of prayer and contemplation lasting no less than one year.'

The Holy Sepulchre was perched on a waterless crag as fissured as the face of woe, some three days' journey into Sicily's scorched interior. The Minims were so called because their enclosed order of nuns practised a rule of unusual severity. They lived in absolute silence and abjured meat, fish, eggs and all dairy stuffs. Ludovico thought of Queen Juana of Spain, confined to a darkened room for thirty years, and considered Carla lightly treated.

'She will not go willingly, but such a retreat can only be of benefit to her soul.'

Gonzaga assumed a pious expression and bobbed his head.

'She must not be charged with any crime, civil, moral or heretical,' said Ludovico. 'Commit nothing to paper. Only a fool puts something into writing that he may accomplish by speech alone, and speech, at that, which lays claim to no third witness. Do you understand?'

Gonzaga crossed himself. 'Your Excellency, all will be as you ask.'

'The second task will require the use of arms – sufficient to subdue a man both skilled in combat and loath to yield. He may have confederates. We met this man this morning, on the dock.'

'The German,' piped Gonzaga. 'I should have acted sooner, for the man is half-Moslem and partnered with a Jew, but he's not without powerful friends in the Religion.'

'Tannhauser is a criminal. Evasion of customs, bribery of state officials, doubtless more. This must not be seen as an ecclesiastical matter. Have the civil constabulary handle it, but see they move swiftly and with force.'

'Must the German be taken alive?' enquired Gonzaga.

'Tannhauser's life is immaterial.'

'I shall have them arrest the Jew, too,' said Gonzaga.

Ludovico considered the ubiquitous hatred of Jews to be vulgar and without logic. Unlike the Lutheran scum, they presented no threat to the Church. He said, 'That's their affair.'

'Their goods shall, of course, be confiscate to the Congregation,' said Gonzaga. 'We're entitled to our share.'

'Have I not made myself clear?'

Gonzaga paled. His mouth writhed with an apology he dared not utter.

'It is my wish,' said Ludovico, 'that the Holy Office leave no trace of their hand in this affair. It must be – and must be seen to be – an entirely civil matter. If the Holy Office should be implicated in these proceedings, in any way, you will be found most direly wanting.'

Gonzaga glanced at Anacleto and found himself the object of the gaze that a cobra bestows upon a toad. 'All will be as Your Excellency commands,' said Gonzaga. 'No papers, no third witness, no trace. A civil matter only. I shall not take a penny for my Congregation.'

Gonzaga waited, as if for some kind of praise or reassurance. Ludovico stared at him until the man's squirms disgusted him.

'You've much to do, Father Gonzaga. See that it's done.'

As Gonzaga scurried out, Ludovico felt a whisper of anxiety. He'd never entrusted such matters to Gonzaga before. Desperate as the man was to please, he reeked of that excess of zeal and petty ambition so common among provincial functionaries. Yet Gonzaga was the local eminence. It was a shame Tannhauser should fall to so base a creature. As to Carla, he'd reconsider her fate in due course.

Ludovico went to the window and looked down into the

courtyard below. Saddled horses waited to carry them to Palermo. There he'd take the measure of the Spanish Viceroy, Garcia de Toledo, before embarking on the journey to Rome. After the Viceroy of Naples and the Pope, Toledo was the most powerful man in Italy, and in the matter of the invasion of Malta more important than either. La Valette had asked Ludovico to pressure Toledo into sending a relief force; but that part of his plan would await his return from Rome. In Rome he would muster the means that he needed to secure Toledo's obedience.

That and more. In Rome he would also prepare for his return to Malta and his infiltration of the Religion. In the right hands, the Religion could live up to their name and become true champions of the Church. The Order was sworn not to fight against fellow Christians; but like all matters of policy, that could be made to change. The European war against Lutheranism would prove more bloody than anyone could imagine. The Religion's arms and prestige would be invaluable – if they survived the Turkish invasion. But that was in God's hands.

In God, Ludovico's trust was absolute.

They took their leave of the abbey. The sun was high and hot. The Palermo road was clear. They rode north with the wind of History at their backs.

TUESDAY 15 MAY 1565

Guesthouse of the Villa Saliba

Tannhauser rose from the bench like a wolf aroused from some primal dream, lithe and at once alert, yet still caught in the toils of another world. As he towered above her, whatever expectations she'd had were swept away in the moment that turned his lucent blue gaze upon her own. His face was battered yet still youthful. A black powder burn disfigured his neck by the left hinge of his jaw. A thin white scar bisected his brow on the same side. His hair swung over his face as he stood up and the eye gleaming through it evoked an untamed creature regarding a world too civilised and cramped to call home. When he swept the hair aside the impression faded, and she was sorry. His lips parted when he smiled to reveal chipped and uneven teeth and a hint of cruelty. His burgundy-red doublet was striped with diagonals of gold and was of fine quality. His high boots shone. The ensemble was completed, yet compromised, by leather breeches of somewhat tawdry complexion.

Carla was alarmed by her reaction. Simply by standing up he'd pierced the sexual twilight to which she'd long condemned herself. He stirred her blood in a way she hadn't thought possible. She invited him into the parlour to take some refreshment and he paused to study her viola da gamba on its stand.

'The gambo violl, yes? This is your instrument.'

He said this as if he knew it could be no one else's, and this pleased her.

'It was the passion of my childhood and youth.'

'I commend you on your choice,' he said. 'I've admired the music of gambo in the salons of Venice, where fine practitioners abound, but I never before heard such sinew and fire in the playing.' He smiled. 'I might even say such fury.'

Carla's stomach fluttered.

'And the composition?' he asked.

'An improvisation of our own.'

'Improvisation?'

'An invention – an embellishment – on a dance suite in the French style.'

'Ah, the dance,' he said. 'If all dance were so spirited I might have studied the art myself, but I am ignorant of it.'

'It can be learned.'

'Not on the Messina waterfront. Or at least not in any style that you would recognise.' He held his hand to the neck of the violl, but stopped short of touching it. 'May I?' he asked. 'I've never studied such a marvel before.'

She nodded and he whisked it from the stand and examined it with a close eye for the carvings and inlays and for the grains of the maplewood back.

'Astounding geometry,' he murmured. He looked at her. 'I understand that the shape is conceived around an arrangement of concentric circles, of overlapping diameters. The harmony of the geometry produces the harmony of sound. But of course you know this better than I.'

In fact she did not and was stunned by his recondite learning, but while she couldn't bring herself to nod, she didn't deny it. He peered through the F-holes for a signature.

'Who made this masterpiece?'

'Andreas Amati of Cremona.'

'Superb.' He plucked a string and watched its vibration. 'The transmutation of movement into sound – now there's a mystery for you. But the transmutation of sound into music is more mysterious still, wouldn't you say?'

Carla blinked, too taken by his observations to venture an answer. Tannhauser appeared not to expect one. He held the violl at arm's length and spun it back and about, looking it up and down with genuine enchantment.

'My old friend Petrus Grubenius said that when beauty and purpose are married in perfection, there one may find magic in its truest form.' With the violl still suspended he looked at her and smiled again. 'If I were bold enough, I'd venture that such a notion would encompass that dress, too.'

Carla felt her cheeks burn. She felt inadequate to the compliment and to acknowledge it seemed improper. A sense of sin clenched inside her. Such fears and doubts had hedged her life for as long as she could remember. Yet in these few moments he'd blown through all that dust like a wind through a long unopened room.

She said, 'Do you believe in magic?'

He took no offence at her shunning his tribute and replaced the violl on its stand. He did so with the precision of a man whose intimacy with the physical was natural and deep.

'I have no truck with incantations, sorcery and the like, if that's your meaning,' he said. 'Such false arts stand on fancy and superstition – and, as Plato said, to Dionysus, *Philosophy should never be prostitute to profane and illiterate men*. No. Magick takes her name from Ancient Persia, where a "magician" was a wise man who expounded the divine mechanics inherent in Nature. Men such as Zarathustra – or Hermes Trismegistus. The Egyptians considered Nature herself a magician. In that sense – the sense of wonder at the mystery in all Things – there's nothing I believe in more heartily.'

Carla's hopes of bending this man to her will began to fade.

He pointed to the second instrument. 'And this one?'

'A theorbo.'

He picked up the double-stringed lute and examined its construction with equal curiosity.

'The girl also plays like one possessed,' he said. 'But by angels rather than demons.'

He looked at her and again she felt lost for an answer.

'I'm confounded by her mastery – there are more strings here than I can count.'

'Amparo has a gift. I have merely the benefit of long practice.'

'You give your powers short weight.'

She was relieved when Bertholdo, the steward, entered with a silver tray filled with two crystal beakers and a pitcher of mint cordial. Bertholdo wrinkled his nose and cast a disapproving look at the brawny intruder. Tannhauser appeared unperturbed by this discourtesy. Bertholdo set the tray down, filled the beakers and turned to Carla.

'That will be all,' she said.

With a barely perceptible flick of his head, Bertholdo turned to leave. He stopped as if stabbed between the shoulders by Tannhauser's voice.

'Hold there, boy.'

Bertholdo turned, his lips white.

'Is it not the custom for a servant to bow before his mistress when taking her leave?'

She saw Bertholdo consider a riposte, which was not beyond his impudence, but he saw in Tannhauser's expression that the risk of a sound thrashing was far too high. He bowed to Carla with exaggerated subservience. 'Forgive me, My Lady.'

Carla suppressed an unkind smile. Bertholdo beat a swift retreat and they sat by the table. Tannhauser glanced at the pitcher and his thirst was evident. She took up her beaker so that he might take his. The coldness of the glass provoked another of his wolfish grins.

'Snow from Mount Etna?' he said. 'You're well provided for.' He raised the beaker. 'To your health.'

She sipped and watched as he drained the cordial in one and set it down with a sigh.

'An exceptional beverage. You must let me acquire the recipe from your boy.'

'He would probably add some hemlock.'

Tannhauser laughed, the sound easy and rich, and she realised how little of men's laughter she'd heard in her life, and what an impoverishment that was.

'He regards me as his inferior, yet is obliged to serve me. It's a lash he applies to his own back, but I hope you'll forgive me for rubbing some brine into his wounds.'

Carla refilled his glass, disarmed by his directness. As she did so she was aware of his eyes taking in the way she moved, and she wondered if she did so with adequate grace. As she set the pitcher down it clinked against the beaker and the beaker toppled and panic flooded her belly. But his hand swooped – that was the word – and took the falling glass and raised it to his lips without a drop spilled.

'You're too kind,' he said, and drank again. 'And so, My Lady, I ask again, how may I serve you?'

Carla hesitated. His frank blue gaze robbed her of her tongue.

'In my experience,' he said, 'there's much to be said for boldness in such matters.'

She swallowed. 'I arrived here some six weeks ago. Since then I've found that all doors are closed against me. I'm given to believe that you represent my last and only hope.'

'I'm honoured,' he said. 'But you must tell me which door you'd have me open.'

'I seek a passage to the island of Malta.'

She might have said more but the shock he conveyed by the sudden stillness of his features struck her silent. Once again she was reminded of a wolf. This time one who'd heard the footfall of the hunter.

He said, 'You're aware of the recklessness – the folly – of such a venture.'

'I've been schooled in the many hazards in more detail than I cared to hear a hundred times. I'm now expert in the cruelties of the Turk and the grisly prospects that face the Maltese people. Despite the many flocking to the battlements to die, I'm deemed unfit to decide on such a course for myself.'

'Surely it's not the battlements, or death, that you seek.'

'No. I seek only to increase the burdens upon the Religion with the danger to my welfare, to waste their food and water, and to generally conduct myself as they see me – a conceited and useless woman of less than sound mind.'

The buried anger that escaped in her voice startled her. Tannhauser said nothing and she flushed. She stood and clasped her hands and turned away from him.

'Forgive me, sir, but as you see, I am desperate.'

'They've been evacuating useless mouths for weeks, thousands of them,' he said, 'and their reasoning can't be faulted. At the siege of Saint Quentin the defenders shoved them outside the gates at spear point, where they perished in the most unhappy manner.'

'I won't dispute your assessment. I am a useless mouth.'

'Why do you want to go to Malta?'

Carla didn't turn. 'I am a Maltese.' She'd never claimed such an identity before, for her family was Sicilian by blood. But the instinct seemed true. She said, 'It's my home.'

'One doesn't run into a burning house because it's home,' he said. 'Unless there's something precious left inside. Something one is willing to die for.'

'My father lives on the island, in Mdina.' She was long dead to her father. He would have been as dead to her if not for the pain in her heart that kept his memory alive. Tannhauser didn't reply. She knew her explanation was weak and she wondered what was in his face, but didn't turn. She added, 'What daughter wouldn't wish to be at her father's side in such dark times?'

Tannhauser said, 'You ask me to risk my life. If you intend to do so on the basis of a lie, you could at least speak that lie to my face.'

She looked down at her hands. The fingers had turned white. Still she didn't turn. She managed to say, 'Sir, you've been generous with your time. Thank you. Perhaps you should now leave.'

She took a step towards the door and it was all she could do not to run. She didn't hear him move, yet he appeared before her in a trice, blocking her way with his eyes as much as his bulk. His face was once again half-veiled by his hair.

'I heard you play on your gambo violl,' he said. 'After hearing truth in its purest form, any falsehood is painful on the ear.'

She dropped her eyes and tried not to compound her humiliation by breaking into tears. She was not accustomed to tears. Nor to making such a fool of herself.

She said, 'You must find me contemptible.'

He took her arm without answering. His touch steadied her. When she dared look at him she found a strange compassion, a need to comfort her, which sprang from some private anguish of his own. He flicked his head at the ceiling and its splendid decor.

'Rooms like this were built for telling lies in,' he said. 'Let's return to the garden. It's hard to play false among roses. And if what you have to say is bitter, their fragrance will sweeten its taste.'

Her heart suddenly felt that it would burst if she didn't open it now.

'I have a child.' She stopped. She took a breath. 'I have a son, a son I haven't seen since the hour in which he was born.'

The sympathy in his eyes turned a deeper colour.

She said, 'This is my secret and my prison. This is the door I hoped you'd be able to open.'

'Come,' Tannhauser said. 'Tell me everything.'

* * *

THEY SAT IN the shade of the palms and a breeze from the sea excited the scent of the myrtles and the flowers. She found herself looking into his eyes. He was right. Lies had no place here. And secrets seemed senseless. Yet at the last, she balked.

'I am a coward,' she said. This, she felt, was no lie. 'This you are entitled to know.'

'A coward could not have come so far.'

'If I tell you everything, you'll despise me.'

'Is this a game you play to win my pity?'

She stumbled on. 'I mean only that your sufferings, whatever they may be, are surely greater than mine, which are of my own making.'

'My sufferings are not the subject of this meeting,' said Tannhauser. 'But to assuage your conscience, which seems to me oversensitive, suffice to say that I'm enjoying life to the full and am in fine fettle. As to wickedness, shame or disgrace – for some such phantom seems to stand between you and speaking your mind – be assured that I've committed crimes beyond your reckoning. I'm not here to sit in judgement, but to decide if I'll do as you ask, and take you to Malta.'

'Then it's possible? Despite the Turkish blockade?'

'The Turkish fleet has not yet arrived. And not even Suleiman Shah has the ships to encircle forty miles of coast. A small boat, a good pilot, a moonless night. Reaching the island is the least of the challenges we'd face.'

She realised he'd already mapped the entire endeavour in his mind and her stomach lurched with curiosity tinged with fear. For the first time the reality of what she'd set herself to do rose up before her. Her emotions suddenly calmed, for in practical matters she was proud of her noted hardheadedness. 'What other hazards lie ahead?' she asked.

'Steady now,' said Tannhauser. 'I would know more about this boy. How old is he?'

'Twelve years old.'

Tannhauser pursed his lips, as if this detail was significant. 'And his name?'

'I don't know. The privilege of naming him wasn't mine.'

'Can you tell me anything else? His family? His trade? His appearance?'

Carla shook her head.

'This world is hard on babes,' he said. 'How do you know he's still alive?'

'He's alive,' she said with vehemence. 'Amparo saw him in her vision stone.' She regretted this outburst, guaranteed as it was to confirm her evident foolishness.

Rather, he was intrigued. 'The girl is a scryer?'

The word was unknown to her. 'A scryer?'

'A medium to the supernal world, one who may commune with spirits, or receive occult intelligence or foreknowledge of things yet to come.'

'Yes, Amparo claims such powers. Angels speak to her in tongues. She has visions. She saw you – a man on a golden horse.'

'I would not mount so firm a conclusion on the back of a horse,' he said. 'I'm not willing to be bound by prophecy. At least not yet.'

She nodded. 'You're right, of course. The man she saw in her stone was covered in hieroglyphs.'

Tannhauser recoiled as if punched in the chest. 'I would see this remarkable shew stone.'

'I'm perplexed, sir,' she said. 'I was given to understand that you had little faith in God.'

'In these benighted times such libels can cost a man his life.'

'I meant only that I'm amazed by the credence you're prepared to give Amparo's visions.'

'Charlatans abound, but Amparo is quite without guile. Even so, purity of heart is no defence when it comes to the Inquisition. Indeed, such purity is all the more damning. I knew another with such insight and he paid the price.' He dropped his eyes for a moment, as if the memory were a grim one. 'But then we're all lost in a universe infinitely larger than we can know. Or even imagine.'

He looked at her.

'My friend Petrus Grubenius believed that even the sun is at the centre of nothing more than its own small handful of cosmic dust. What is visible, what is known, is little compared to what is not, and most notions of God thrive on our ignorance. Yet the existence of the stars and constellations – and their influence upon us – of angels good and bad, of realms and hidden forces that lie beyond our grasp and beyond our dreams, does not require the existence of a governing deity. Nor does the fact of being demand a theory of Creation, paradox though that may seem, for if Eternity has no end, then perhaps it had no beginning. That there is flux is evident, for here we are, tossed like wreckage on a turbulent sea. That there are countless subtle patterns worked into that flux is evident too. Even blind Chaos has its purpose. And Fate is a web whose threads we acknowledge only when once entangled. But pattern or purpose or no, religion brings forth mighty legions of fools, that they may call each other devils and deny the inner nature of Things. There is no God but Allah and Mohammed is his messenger, yes. And God sent His only begotten Son to die on the Cross, yes. I've worshipped at mosque and altar both, because I was told to, and I obeyed. But I heard God's voice in neither, nor felt His Grace. In the end, I heard only the braying of the book burners and the whimper of an inextinguishable fear.'

Carla stared at him. She felt more disconcerted than ever. Yet she realised that she knew Things that he did not. 'I don't have the learning to contradict you,' she said, 'but I know that the cruelty of men cannot be laid at God's door.'

'That's a comfort I'll remember at my execution.'

'The Grace of God is a gift.'

She said this with enough conviction to give him pause. He nodded in respect.

'Then I've not done enough to earn it,' he said. 'The approved means, so I've been told, is through a surfeit of sorrow, a commodity which the Roman Church prizes highly.'

'The Grace of God can't be earned. It can only be accepted – by you no less than any if you'd open your heart. If you'd open your heart to the love of Our Lord Jesus Christ.'

'No doubt.' He smiled in a way that left her feeling patronised. 'But let's leave that to another day and settle the matter in hand. Who was the boy's father?'

She hesitated. 'A monk.'

'Well, well. Tell me more.'

'I was fifteen years old, my father's only child. My pregnancy brought extreme shame upon my family and, I was told, hastened the death of my dear mother.'

Tannhauser snorted, as if he reckoned this latter an odious fable.

'Be that as it may, my father had the infant taken away as soon as he was born. I never saw my babe again and know nothing more of his fate.'

'A common enough tale,' Tannhauser said.

Carla flinched.

He shrugged. 'Anyone may fall into the trap of passion. Sicilian fathers are jealous of their daughters' virtue. And when it comes to shirking the consequences of lust, priests have a firm advantage over most. The Messina docks swarm with such foundlings and their lot is grim.' He bunched one fist to reassure her. 'But if your boy is alive, he'll be strong. Have you any idea where he was placed?'

'The foundlings are usually taken to the Sacred Infirmary, in the Borgo, then placed with a wet nurse. Once they're weaned, boys are raised in the *camerata* – the orphanage – until the age of three, then, if a family is available, they're fostered.'

'Twelve years,' he mused. 'That's a long time to wait before attempting to reclaim your child.'

'As I told you, I'm a coward.'

His mouth twisted with impatience. 'This face you put forward, of one who lacks courage, is a false face. Your actions contradict it at every turn. Be assured, it does not become you and it will not win my pity. On the other hand, the truth might.'

'I was considered unfit for the better kind of marriage that my father had planned,' Carla began.

'There are remedies for such problems,' Tannhauser said. 'The dried blood of a pigeon or a hare, for instance, which when moistened by –'

'Sir, faking my virginity was not an option to which I gave great thought. Mdina is not Paris and fornication is not in fashion. The oppression under which I laboured was very considerable. My parents were united against me and my only solace was the God you so elegantly deny. I repeat I was fifteen years old. My marriage contract – with a man whose very name was unknown to me – was agreed by the time my son was born. After my child was taken, I fell into a profound melancholia, and in that state was shipped to the Aquitaine. I do not want your pity. At most I seek to charter your expertise.'

She paused to control the anger in her breast. He didn't speak.

'The Spanish Crown,' she continued, 'allows inheritance of a noble title through the female line and in this inhered my only apparent worth. I was fortunate. The husband that the marriage agent secured was a rich and elderly widower who wanted to strengthen his petition for a title, and who was too sorely ailed by dropsy to want me at all. Indeed, he died within two years of our union. However, the letter patent was purchased from the King of France before he died, and my stepson – who is older than me – now comports himself the Comte de la Penautier. I, as per the successful outcome of the contract, inherited property and income enough to see me through my days. So as you see, sir, I am the product of a class far too civilised to resort to the blood of pigeons.'

Her bitterness was not lost on Tannhauser. He inclined his head.

'I consider myself chastised and beg your pardon,' he said.

At this moment, Carla didn't feel disposed to grant his wish.

'In mitigation,' he said, 'let me tell you that as a youth I entered a world from which women were entirely excluded. A society of men within which women were barely acknowledged to exist. A man who knew women – who desired them, who dreamed of them, who might love them – was weak. The janissaries were strong. It was not until I left their hearth, and abandoned every belief and broke every vow, and found myself in Venice, that I rediscovered the company of women at all. Because of this hiatus, women remain for me a very great mystery and even now I sometime give offence where none is intended.'

No man had ever spoken to her with such frankness. His intention was surely not to captivate her, yet he did. For form's sake she said, 'No offence is taken and my pardon is granted.' Yet she sensed that he had not related this merely to excuse himself. She said, 'Why do you tell me this?'

'I will never know women in the way that other men do. By that same token, I hear your story in a way no other man can.'

She stared at him, lost for a reply.

'You never held your babe in your arms,' he said. 'You never gave him suck. You never held his hand to guide him through his follies and his fears.'

She took a sudden breath, as if stabbed, and turned away.

'The babe was denied the things that any babe needs, as you were denied the things that any mother needs. You had no power to prevent this heinous crime, yet the guilt lies not where it belongs – with those that committed it – but with you, always, like a tombstone crushing your chest. Sometimes you wake in the night and you cannot breathe. You see the babe's face in your dreams and your heart breaks into pieces. His cries echo through an emptiness that nothing on this earth can fill. And, with time, the knowledge of your innocence scourges your conscience more cruelly than any evil you could ever do.'

She turned to look at him. His eyes were fierce but held no malice.

'Yes, I hear your story,' he said. 'I understand. And better than you may imagine.'

Carla felt tears burn in her throat. She swallowed.

'How can you speak of these things with such poignant feeling?'

'Never mind,' he said. 'Let me ask you again, for you haven't answered: why do you seek the boy only now?'

She gathered her wits, and mastered her sentiment and cleared her throat.

'Some three months ago the Chevalier Adrien de la Riviere rested at my house for the night on his way to Marseilles, where he hoped to take ship to Malta. He knew of my origins and was sure of a civil welcome. When I learned that the island would likely fall to the Turk, I knew that I had to find my lost son, no matter what the cost, and for no matter how short a time God might allow us to be reunited.'

Tannhauser showed no sign of finding this irrational. He nodded for her to go on.

'I told myself this was absurd. But that same night I had a visitation. I saw Her by my bedside as vividly as I can see you now, Our Lady with the Holy Child Jesus in Her arms. I received in that moment a profound consolation. I realised that finding my boy was not a foolish whim. It was the Will of God. If I could not lay at least that claim to the truth of my own existence, then my life would continue as a sham. For I will tell you, Captain Tannhauser, my life has been a sham since the day I let them take my boy away from me – and did not raise my hand to stop them.'

Tears blurred her vision. She feared he'd think them tears of self-pity, when in truth they were tears of rage. She brushed them away. Tannhauser pondered her in silence.

'There,' she said. 'I've told you everything. Now tell me if you'll accept my commission and at what price. Whatever the latter may be, I will pay it.'

'The monk who fathered the child,' said Tannhauser. 'Who was he?'

'Have I provided inadequate of scandal for you to take back to your tavern?'

Tannhauser laughed, the rich easy laugh of before, and she was possessed by the sudden urge to strike him.

'It would take a riper tale than yours to amuse that rabble,' he said. 'No, my question is pertinent. Fornication may not be in fashion but there are more than a few knights' bastards running round Malta. If your lover – I use the word with all respect – was a Hospitaller, and if he's among those there gathered, it would be as well to know it.'

'He was not a knight but a friar, of a different monastic order. He fled from Malta, without warning, before I myself was aware I was expecting a child.' She paused to contain another welling of anger. 'I've heard nothing of the fellow since.'

'He broke your heart,' said Tannhauser.

Carla waited until she knew her voice would be steady. 'It took me many years to forget his face. And I would forget his name if I could. But tell me to speak it and I will do so.'

He conceded the point with a wave of his hand. 'You speak with the anger of unhealed wounds,' he said. 'But as long as he's not the Bailiff of Lango, or some other such eminent knight, the fellow is of no consequence to me. Forget him by all means.'

He rose from the bench and prowled a dozen paces round the rose beds. Then he stopped and walked back towards her.

'So the task in hand, if I have it right, is to sail to Malta, evading the Turkish blockade, find a twelve-year-old boy of whose name and appearance we are ignorant, and then, with his acquiescence – which, by the way, cannot be taken for granted – retrace our path to Sicily without being hanged, either as deserters by the knights or as spies by the Grande Turke.'

She looked at him, hardly able to speak. Her consternation puzzled him.

'Do I misrepresent the endeavour?' he asked.

'No. You broaden it beyond my expectations.'

'How so?'

'You'd bring my boy back to Sicily?'

He spread his palms. 'Is there any other point in going?'

'I'd never seen beyond the dream of finding him and avowing myself his mother.' Carla felt her throat contract. She swallowed. 'A passage to Malta and a moment of reunion – perhaps, with God's blessing, a moment of forgiveness – are all I dared imagine.'

'Such moments may well expiate your sins and soothe your conscience. They may even bring you consolation and joy. But they won't spare you or your boy from Turkish steel. At that age he'll be in the battle line, make no mistake. The Maltese make up the bulk of La Valette's garrison. They'll bear the brunt of the fight. And the brunt of the dying.'

Carla felt sick. 'Do you believe the fight is without hope?'

'I wouldn't say that, but it's a brave roll of the die for any sporting man. Five faces favour the Turk, I should say, and but one the knights of the Religion. But whoever wins or loses my point stands. Victor and vanquished both will pay dearly in blood. Unless you want to make the journey only to watch the boy die, we must spirit him away.'

'Spirit him away?' The phrase thrilled her. 'Can that be done?'

He sat back down on the bench beside her.

'I've smuggled bulkier cargoes out of tighter havens. But first we must find him.'

'I will know him when I see him, believe me,' she said.

'Of course,' he said, without a trace of confidence. 'But we can hardly ask La Valette to pull every youth in the Borgo out of the line so you can take your pick.'

As quickly as it had soared, her heart plummeted. She'd travelled all this way on the basis of a fairy tale, so absorbed by her adventure in the wider world that she'd failed to consider the simplest practicalities. She was a fool. But Tannhauser, it was ever more clear, was nothing of the sort.

'The Maltese have the Roman Church bred into the bone,' he said. 'The boy must have been baptised, bastard or not, and his name duly entered in a parish register. If your information on the orphanage is sound, there should also be some record at the Sacred Infirmary.'

'But as you've pointed out, we don't know his name.'

The effort he expended in concealing his expression made her feel her stupidity more keenly. 'Indeed. But you do at least remember the date of his birth.'

'The last day of October, fifteen fifty-two.'

As with the boy's age, his birth date seemed to strike him with some significance.

'All Hallows Eve,' he said. 'The Sun in Scorpio.' He shook his head. 'Strange roads, Madame Contessa. Strange roads indeed have brought us to this garden above the sea.'

He didn't elaborate and before she could ask his meaning he clenched his fist.

'But why did you not come to me much sooner? Six weeks you've been here? Why, we could've been in and out, with no more danger than that of drowning in the channel.'

Bile rose in her throat. 'Until this morning I was unaware of your existence.'

Suspicion furrowed his brow. 'And who made you thus aware?'

'Fra Oliver Starkey, of the English Langue.'

She saw anger flare in his eyes, like the blue at the heart of a flame, and she feared he would abandon her. Why Starkey's name so provoked him, she didn't know.

'Brother Starkey was most complimentary of your talents.'

'I am sure he was.'

'His letter –'

'His letter?'

'His letter said you were a man of remarkable ability, who feared nothing and held all authority – moral, legal and religious – in outright contempt.' Why this should flatter him she wasn't sure, but she believed it would. 'He said that, above all, you were a man of your word.'

'The Englishman is more crafty than I gave him credit for.'

At last she felt she had some useful intelligence to offer. 'Fra Starkey said he could offer us a passage, on the *Couronne*.'

His mood showed no sign of getting brighter. 'I don't doubt it.'

'The *Couronne* leaves on the midnight tide.'

'It will leave without us.'

He snuffed out the anger and smiled.

'War has a long arm, and its fingers are around my throat, but I will yet give it the slip.'

'Would the *Couronne* not be the surest way of getting there?'

'Perhaps. But a bargain made with the Devil is best reserved for an hour more desperate than this one.'

He paused, as if at the brink of a steep drop. Then he nodded.

'Entrust the arrangements to me and forget Brother Starkey. You'll hear from me within two days at the most.'

It took her a moment to realise that with these words he'd agreed to her request. She wanted to speak but couldn't find the words. Tannhauser rose from the bench and bowed with conspicuous gallantry. He indicated the house.

'Now, if I may, I'm curious to see the girl's shew stone. Her vision glass.'

Carla stood up. 'We haven't discussed your payment.'

He hesitated, as if he'd already set his price but thought it exorbitant.

He said, 'If I return you and your son, safe, from Malta, I would have you marry me.'

Carla was stunned. She thought she'd misheard him. 'Marry you?'

He seemed abashed and coughed. 'Wedlock, Holy Matrimony, the reading of the banns. So forth.'

For a moment her instincts thrilled. Dormant impulses stirred deep in her pelvis. She swayed with a sudden headiness. She felt his hand take her arm. She looked at him. His eyes were so clear she could read nothing in them. She didn't know what it was he saw in her face, but he read it as some form of horror.

'The request is a gross impertinence,' he said. 'Yet my motives are not ungentlemanly, merely avaricious. Even the faint flavour of nobility that such a union would give me would be invaluable to my enterprises. The price I ask is high, yes. Given our relative stations, perhaps outrageous. But so is the risk inherent in your quest. We may contract, of course, that I have no rights to your property or your income, which I do not covet. Furthermore, you have my word of honour that I won't take unwelcome advantage of our arrangement.'

The joy of her naïve fantasy vanished. This was business; nothing more. They were as distant from each other in temperament, as well as in station, as any two individuals could be. She had no right to think ill of him. Indeed, she'd never held any man in higher esteem. And in return for what he offered, the price was trifling. Even so, something inside her, which had in this last hour bloomed back into life, withered away. She tried to keep her voice even, and felt she sounded cold.

'You misunderstand the complexities of nobility,' she said. 'Marriage alone would allow you the appearance of a title, but no more.'

'May I legitimately comport myself a count – and insist on being addressed as "My Lord" or "Your Excellency" or some other such obsequious courtesy?'

'I believe you may.'

'Then the appearance is worth a fortune, no matter how fraudulent, and I shall be more than satisfied.'

Very well,' she said. 'My title has been bartered away before. At least this time it is a matter of my own choosing.'

'Then we have a bargain?'

'Shall I have an attorney draw up a contract?'

'A handshake will do for now.'

He held out his hand. It was large and rough, with the calluses of a sword hilt on the palm. She reached out her own hand to take it and he pulled back.

'May I add a rider to our pact?' There was a sly amusement in his eyes.

The charm he was able to exercise was infuriating. 'You may try,' she said.

'On our return, you will play for me again on your gambo violl.'

A confusion of sentiments rose within her. 'Why are you doing this for me?'

His brow flexed. 'Because I consider the bargain fair and a boon to my business.'

'Your faith in my intuition may be frail,' she said, 'but I sense you enter this venture with deeper motives than simple business might entail.'

Tannhauser considered her – for what seemed like minutes but could only have been seconds. He seemed to calculate how much he should reveal of himself, and she sensed that at the core of that self was a sorrow as deep and enduring as her own. Perhaps even deeper. If he'd taken her into his arms, she wouldn't have resisted.

Tannhauser said, 'I once knew another mother who fought for her boy.'

'That's all?'

'The mother lost,' he said.

Carla waited. But on this matter, Tannhauser said no more.

He smiled with his broken teeth. He stretched out his hand.

Carla took it and he squeezed and a sudden shiver rippled across her skin.

She wished they'd sealed their bargain with a kiss.

TUESDAY 15 MAY 1565

The Messina Road – the Oracle

Tannhauser rode through hills painted violet and gold by the set of the sun. The women of the Villa Saliba had laid him like greyhounds fetching down a deer, yet he was gratified.

Amparo, for one, was a find. Her sexual allure, of which she seemed ignorant, itched at his mind and privities. Her shew stone had proved a marvel. Most such stones were spheres of pure crystal. Grubenius had owned a speculum of polished obsidian. Amparo's device was an optical contraption – constructed merely as a novelty – but with the mantic genius that paves the way to knowledge she'd recognised a higher function within it. It was a brass tube with an eyepiece at the fore end, while at the nether end two slim, triple-spoked wheels, also of brass, rotated about a spindle, one flat against, but independent of, the other. Between the spokes of each wheel was laced an intricate fabrication of stained glass fragments. Down the bore of the tube were fixed two slender strips of mirrored glass, their reflecting surfaces opposed at thirty degrees.

On first glance the wheels appeared dark, but when pointed at sunlight, or a candle flame, a multiplicity of colours was revealed, and when the wheels were spun with a flick of the fingers, the colours and the sum of their parts whirled through amazing combinations that stunned the eye. Any movement of either wheel changed what could be seen, and Tannhauser understood that by altering the speed of their rotation, and of their speed relative to each other, Time itself was broken up into particles infinitely small. Furthermore, the temper of the field of vision depended on the source of illumination – the closer to the flame, the more incandescent the colours. The smokiness of the candle, the intensity of the sunlight, the texture of the intervening ether, all these elements changed what was changing even as they themselves were changing too. And when the wheels rolled into stillness, and a particular combination of colour and light was chosen by Chance, there for an instant was a shard of eternity captured. In short, within the girl's vision glass was a model of the Cosmos – of the mighty flux, of Fate itself.

Sometimes Amparo would see nothing but the beauty of the colours; at others, images of startling clarity would fill her mind. Sometimes she would hear the voice of angels. No one could know the future; Amparo did not claim to do so. But among the infinity of Things that one day might be lie all the Things that will be. It was possibility she saw within the vortex. What could be lay waiting in the crucible of what was yet not. This, it seemed to him, was what Amparo, albeit by instinct, understood.

Night fell as he approached the northern gate. In the last of the twilight a two-wheeled carriage clattered up the road towards him. The driver wore a helmet and a breastplate and the matchcord of a musket glowed down by his seat. As the vehicle trundled by, a young, rat-like face peered out from under the hat of a priest. Tannhauser thought on them no more. He passed the watchman at the gate and crossed the city. That final frenzy that marks the end of the day had all but passed and the streets were soon quiet. He rode along the waterfront to the Oracle.

Tonight he would drink too much and slake his lust upon Dana. Perhaps, he thought, this impulse was somewhat ungallant, for it was Amparo and the Lady Carla who'd inflamed his fancy. But such was life. He wondered what sound each would make in the throes of love. The ferocity of Carla's attack upon the gambo echoed still through his mind. Furthermore, she was clearly of high intelligence, an erotic force he hadn't encountered before. He imagined peeling off that red silk dress, though he doubted she would ever consent with such as him. Her one experience of romance had brought her punishment and shame, and exile from all she loved. She was entitled to be cagey. Even so, he shifted in the saddle to give his member room.

Along the waterfront darkness was general, broken by yellow pools from the lanterns of the ships. The new-risen moon above the sea was a day past full. A hundred yards hence stood the Oracle and a curious crowd stood clustered about its doors. Tannhauser stopped. Beyond the crowd he caught the glimmer of torchlight on a pair of steel helms. The helms belonged to men at arms. City constables. And crowds were prone to gather about misfortune. A murder at the tavern? There'd been none to date, thanks to Bors, but it was far from impossible.

Then Tannhauser heard the threnody of a scream.

It was muffled by walls and distance but clear enough. A surge of fear swept his bowels. In an extremity of pain such as the fading scream announced, most men sounded strangely alike.

Yet Tannhauser knew that the cry came from Sabato Svi.

He dismounted and led Buraq through the passage between the chandler's and the ropewalk. To the rear of the buildings that fronted the docks lay a maze of workshops, wagon pens, storage yards and stables, all threaded without design by crooked alleys barely wider than his shoulders. He picked his way through the dark by the shreds of moonlight. Buraq followed quietly behind. As he approached the rear of the warehouse he heard another scream, much more piercing here, and saturate with terror and desolation.

Sabato Svi was being tortured.

Buraq felt his master's distress and blew his nostrils in sympathy. Tannhauser hawked the gall from out his throat. He tethered Buraq to an iron hoop in the wall and reassured him. He unrolled the cuffs of his high leather boots to protect his thighs and crotch and drew his sword. He stole towards the warehouse, its roof a stark black parapet against the stars. He stopped on a feral instinct. He'd heard no sound. But above the stink of the alley, a smell of sweat and leather not his own. Then a hoarse breath. He shaded his brow against the starlight above and relaxed his eyes into the darkness. A hulking shape lurked – there – against the paler dark of the wall. Tannhauser took a step closer. The smell was distinct. He whispered.

'Bors.'

The shape moved sideways, crablike, and ducked towards him. A crossbow emerged at two paces, aimed at his chest. Tannhauser poised ready to strike, should his judgement prove him false. Bors's face appeared. He canted the crossbow skyward against his hip. His grizzled features were drawn. He kept his voice low but couldn't quite still its tremor.

'City police. Two outside, four within. Cuirasses and helms. Two hackbutts and a pistol stand inside.'

'Do we know them?'

Bors shook his head. 'Not from our patch. They're led by the scrawny inquisitor from the *Couronne*.'

Tannhauser fancied he could hear the clank of the wheels that cause the Universe to turn. One of those moments when the architecture of your ambition was revealed to be a brothel built on sand; when the needle of the compass broke and all the clocks stood still; when the future you'd imagined and the future which gaped at your feet parted company forever.

Tannhauser said, 'What do they want?'

'I came up from the cellars towards the end of it. They were looking for you.'

'And Sabato?'

'He had to make a dispute of it – mocked them something fierce – and they struck him down. Young Gasparo took that hard.' Bors's mouth twisted. 'And they shot him dead.'

Tannhauser felt a grinding inside his skull. It was his own teeth.

'I kept my head down,' said Bors. 'When the police cleared the tavern, I shuffled out with the rest. No one played me false.'

'Dana? The girls?'

'I left them safe and sound with Vito Cuorvo, then came back.'

Another agonised scream rang out. Bors grimaced.

'Where are the villains now?' asked Tannhauser.

'They scoured the building and regrouped in the tavern. From the rear, our way is open.'

'The inquisitor is one of the four?'

Bors nodded. 'We've three police inside, one of them a captain. We must beware of alarming the other pair outside.'

'A cry or two they'll credit to poor Sabato, but we can't allow gunfire.' Tannhauser indicated the crossbow. 'Are you steady?'

'Steady as a rock.'

Bors cradled the crossbow in one elbow and dug a three-inch stub of candle from his jerkin. He unhooked a small iron pot from his belt and flipped the ventilated lid. Inside glowed a burning lump of charcoal.

'An inquisitor and five constables,' Tannhauser mused. 'That'll put us as far beyond the law as men can be.'

Bors's face was already grey with that knowledge.

'If we two run now,' said Tannhauser, 'I doubt that they'll pursue us across the straits.'

'If anyone had foretold that I would risk my dirty neck for the sake of a Jew, I'd have laughed in their face.' Bors mustered a grin. 'In any case, I don't believe you.'

Tannhauser clapped him on the back. Bors lit the stub of tallow from the coal in the pot. They slipped inside the Oracle by its light.

* * *

THE DARKNESS INSIDE the warehouse was complete and without the candle they'd have blundered. Tannhauser picked his way through what remained of their stock until he found a bundle of javelins racked with the pike shafts. He cut the binding cord and sheathed his sword and chose three of the slender spears, five-foot staves of ash tipped with needle poignards. He tested each for balance. At short range they were lethal as a musket and far more nimble.

As they crept towards the tavern at the front of the building, lamplight spilled across the floor from the doorless portal. With it came a shrill tirade that was almost ecstatic with bigotry. Tannhauser heard the word 'Jew' shrieked as if alone it were an insult without rival. Sabato vented a curse that was swollen with agony. Then his voice was choked off and replaced by a guttural gagging. Tannhauser's bowels churned and his legs felt so weak he feared they'd fail him. He quelled the urge to vomit. It had been a long time. He reminded himself that this was normal and he breathed deep and even and the jitters passed. Bors snuffed the candle and hefted his crossbow. Tannhauser edged to the portal and peered beyond.

He saw two constables and their captain, armed as described. The captain, who was plump as a partridge, stood with arms akimbo and watched the alcove. From the alcove came Sabato's groans. Tannhauser could see neither Sabato nor the priest. Of the two constables, one stood amid the deserted trestles, midway to the front door. His arquebus was shouldered and the match hung smouldering from his fingers. The second constable lounged on a bench, his long gun propped between his knees, and drank from a jug. Tannhauser reckoned the first to be nine paces distant, the second at no more than five. He pulled back and mimed drinking with his thumb then stabbed a finger at Bors. Bors dipped one eye around the architrave and withdrew. He gave Tannhauser a nod.

The shrill voice rose from the alcove. 'Blood and circumcision!

How many good men have you reduced to beggary with your poisonous schemes and lies? Where is your gold, Jew? The gold you've stolen from us – from we who've shown you so much Christian kindness! We who let you live among us, as if you were a man and not a rabid, thieving dog! What devil brought you to our country? God did not invite your fiendish brood! The gold, Jew! The gold!'

Tannhauser hefted a javelin in his right hand, the two spares balanced in his left. He gave Bors the nod, then propelled himself two paces into the tavern. As his front foot landed and his arm blurred past his ear, he heard the snap of the crossbow behind him and the hiss and crunch of the quarrel. The constable grunted as the javelin struck him below his breastplate and bored through his pubis. The poignard hurtled two feet further through his lower gut and tumbled him beneath the trestles, where he twitched and blinked and gasped as animals pierced and dying often will. Tannhauser filled his hand with a second shaft and turned on the captain, who gawped at him with a shock too early for terror. Tannhauser advanced. The captain's podgy hand flapped towards the snaphaunce in his belt, but the pistol was no more a threat than the panic-soured fart that squealed from his arse.

'Think of your wife,' instructed Tannhauser. 'Think of your children.'

The captain did so; and what little remained of his resistance was undermined. Tannhauser put the javelin to his throat, then turned and tossed the spare across to Bors. He pulled the pistol from the captain's belt. It was a splendid piece, equipped with the latest Spanish stone lock; the kind of weapon a banty little turd would reckon his vanity demanded. Tannhauser blew the powder from the pan and returned it to the captain's belt. He looked yonder and saw young Gasparo. Gasparo lay on his back by the stairs with a bloody hole stoved though his chest. The boy had been loyal and had died for it. Tannhauser quelled a terrible urge before turning back on the captain. The captain's jowls trembled against the spear point as he tried to resurrect some shadow of his former authority.

'My name is –'

Tannhauser lashed a backhand across his cheek. The heavy gold ring laid him open to the bone. 'You can keep your name,' said Tannhauser. 'I'll have no use for it.'

The captain whimpered and clenched his eyes. Tannhauser glanced backwards over his shoulder. One constable slumped over the trestle, his face and beard as bright as enamel with gore. The quarrel of the crossbow had caught him behind one eye and was lodged so deep in his skull that the bone had half-stripped the fletching. Tannhauser's victim lay clenched and panting on the flagstones, awaiting the arrival of a tide of pain so monstrous that he dared neither move nor scream, and hardly dared to breathe. Tannhauser turned towards the alcove. The priest stood staring at the floor, as if he hoped that this tactic might render him invisible.

Tannhauser looked at Sabato Svi.

Sabato sat on Tannhauser's celebrated chair. His jaws were wedged apart by an iron pear crammed into his mouth. A screw and a key protruded from the end of the pear, for cranking its diameter to ever more painful dimensions. Tannhauser glanced down. Sabato's hands had been nailed to the chair's armrests. Tannhauser met his dark eyes and saw that something had been torn from his soul. Something he would spend a lifetime trying to recover without success, for such is the harvest of torture.

Tannhauser turned to Gonzaga.

'You. Priest,' said Tannhauser. 'Take that atrocity from his mouth.'

Gonzaga didn't dare raise his head.

'If I hear him so much as sigh,' continued Tannhauser, 'you will foot the bill.'

Gonzaga scrabbled for the crucifix of the rosary beads belted around his waist and mumbled some hogwash in Latin. The gesture made Tannhauser's mind flare white with rage. He strode across the room. The javelin whirled though a half-circle in his fingers. As he bore down on Gonzaga the wretched inquisitor finally jerked up his face.

'Mercy, Your Eminence!' he cawed. 'Mercy in the name of Christ!'

Tannhauser drove the javelin through the instep of the priest's left foot. Gonzaga shrieked and clung on to the shaft. Tannhauser tore the crucifix away and a shower of black beads spilled across the floor. He looked down into the two revolving tunnels of abject terror bored into the priest's paling face. He held the crucifix before them. He spat on the cross and phlegm bespattered Gonzaga's contorted features.

'You're proud of your cruelty, aren't you, priest?' He threw the crucifix to the flagstones. 'I was thirteen years a Turk. And this is nothing.'

He shifted his weight and levered the poignard deeper through the splintering foot bones. Gonzaga had not a breath left to scream with, nor could he find the strength to take one. His mouth gaped wide without sound. His quivering lips turned purple.

Tannhauser seized him by the throat.

'You haven't even begun to understand cruelty. But you will understand it now.'

He twisted the javelin free and drove it through Gonzaga's other foot. Gonzaga started to crumple at the knees. Tannhauser held him upright. There was a venerable school of thought that held that acts of this vicious character reduced a man to the level of his enemy. Tannhauser did not subscribe to this philosophy. Again he gouged the spear deeper and felt the pain bubble though the windpipe clenched in his fist. The squalid priest's eyes rolled white and he gargled for his life. Tannhauser was distracted by an anguished grunt from the chair. He turned.

He looked at Sabato Svi and in his eyes he saw fear. He realised that a pall of mortal dread lay about the room, and that he alone was now its source. He withdrew the spear and shoved the screeching priest across the room. Gonzaga slithered in his own bloody footprints and hit the floor at the captain's feet. Tannhauser laid the javelin on the table. He looked at Bors.

Bors laughed and said, 'When is it my turn?'

Tannhauser went to Sabato. With care he unwound the key of the iron pear until it shrank to a size whereby he could pull it from his mouth without further injury.

'Forgive me,' said Tannhauser.

Sabato rolled his jaws and spat blood. He was white with shock, but though he had no violence in him, he was as tough as the nails that pinned him to the chair. Tannhauser examined them. Their flat heads protruded two inches above the backs of Sabato's hands.

'Can you endure a little longer, my friend? We're not yet safe.'

Sabato produced a grim smile. 'I'll be here.'

Tannhauser grabbed the javelin and walked towards the prisoners. He stooped over Gonzaga and crammed the iron pear between his lips. He hammered it home with the heel of his hand and felt the snapping of teeth.

'Stand up,' he said.

The priest could do no more than grovel and moan.

'Stand up! Stand, I say!'

The priest struggled to his perforated feet and stood there shuddering, his nostrils snorting for air above the iron gag. Tannhauser shoved him across the room towards Bors.

'Strip him.'

With as much violence as possible, Bors began to rip Gonzaga's habit apart. Tannhauser turned and grabbed the chubby captain by the neck. He manhandled him towards the constable still panting over the javelin in his belly. He pushed the captain's head down.

'Look at him.'

The spear point had gored the man's innards and sought the

easiest exit, which was his anus. His breeches were clotted with excrement and leaking blood. The captain gagged. With the broad side of his boot, Tannhauser kicked the butt of the spear and drove it four more inches through the man's entrails. The man doubled up with a terrible groan. The captain unleashed a stream of vomit all over his writhing subordinate. Bors laughed.

Tannhauser cast his eyes about the desecration of his tavern: over the empty trestles and benches, the guttering pools of yellow light, the lurching swathes of darkness and shadow, the blood pooled black as petroleum on the flags. He turned back to the captain, his fat little face slack with fear in the tenebrous light. He grabbed him and spoke into his ear.

'Look about and feast your eyes upon what you've wrought.'

The captain did so with a grimace of dismay.

'See the dead, the dying, the horror. See the barbarian laughing. The priest naked. The crucified Jew. Witness the vengeance of your enemies.'

The captain hunched his shoulders round his vomit-clogged beard. With the bloodied point of the javelin Tannhauser lifted up the captain's chin so he could look into his eyes.

'Know that you are in Hell. And that we are its demons.'

Puke foamed from the captain's nostrils as he tried not to sob. He wrapped his arms over his head like a bewildered child. Tannhauser stepped back to the dying constable and spun the javelin and punched the needle tip through the man's temple and into his brain. The crunch ran up his arm and the man fell still. He'd murdered a constable sworn to the Spanish Crown. His life had become one thing, and not another. He was once more a killer. So be it. He felt the drag of the bone as he plucked the spear free. He looked at the captain.

'Torment or mercy,' he said. 'You have a choice.'

So desperate was the captain's relief at clinging on to life that he broke his silence. 'Great lord, Excellency, I am your servant.' He stifled a sob. 'I am at your command.'

Tannhauser pointed to the corpse. 'Drag him to the wall, over there.'

As the captain bent to his work, Tannhauser glanced at Bors and indicated the dead man bleeding on the trestle. Bors lumbered over and laid down his weapons and scooped up the corpse in both arms. He lugged him to the warehouse doorway and flung him into the dark. Gonzaga stood trembling and nude among the black and white tatters of his robes. Bors went back to the bench and took up the arquebus. He stabbed the muzzle hard in Gonzaga's ribs.

'Kneel,' he said. 'Kneel like a dog.'

Gonzaga fell on to his hands, choking on the pear, and Bors laughed again.

Tannhauser picked up the second arquebus from the floor. He blew on the match and went to the window and cracked a shutter and peered outside. Two more constables and a score or so of idlers milled about in the street. He snapped his fingers at the captain, who dropped the body by the wall and trotted over.

'Clean your beard,' said Tannhauser.

The captain scrubbed nostrils and chin with his sleeves.

'You have two men outside,' said Tannhauser. 'You must be angry with them.'

Confusion filled the captain's face. 'Angry?'

'I am angry with them. They've done nothing to disperse the rabble. It's an outrage.'

'An outrage, yes, yes,' agreed the captain.

'If you would spare their lives, as well as your own, you will order them to fire their guns and clear the street. Then you will dismiss them for the rest of the night. Tell them to go home. If you find them loitering, they will be flogged.'

'Flogged raw!' babbled the captain.

'When you've given them their orders, you will slam the door on them. Because you are angry.'

'I am furious!' yelled the captain.

Tannhauser glanced at Bors, who'd positioned himself out of sight of the door, arquebus to his shoulder, the javelin close to hand. Tannhauser prodded the captain forward.

'If you step outside,' said Tannhauser, 'we'll kill you all.'

Before the captain could think too hard, Tannhauser opened the left-hand wing of the doors. The captain, free at last to vent himself and in a manner in which he believed himself expert, poured all the emotion of his ordeal into the tongue-lashing he laid on his two inferiors. When the threat of a flogging was expanded into a variety of mutilations and a double hanging, Tannhauser poked the javelin into his arse. In mid-sentence, the captain slammed the door shut on his minions. He looked to Tannhauser for approval. Tannhauser took the pistol from the captain's belt. Without being asked, the captain handed over a powder flask worked in brass and a pouch of ball and patches.

'Join Father Gonzaga,' said Tannhauser. 'On your knees.'

As the captain hurried to obey, convinced that he'd secured his tormentor's goodwill, two gunshots thundered outside. Tannhauser reprimed the pistol and took another look through the shutters. The crowd were in flight, leaving a pair of groaning bodies on the cobbles. The two constables laid into a third prostrate figure with their gun butts. Such was the price of gawking. Tannhauser belted the pistol and added the arquebus to Bors's collection.

Bors nodded towards Sabato. 'I'll go and fetch a claw hammer.'

Sabato twitched with alarm and Tannhauser shook his head. 'Let's do it without breaking his hands.' He took a lamp from one of the trestles and hurried into the warehouse and located his tool chest. He retrieved a fine-toothed hacksaw and hastened back. He re-examined the nails through Sabato's hands.

He said, 'I paid fifteen gold scudi for this chair,'

'You were robbed,' said Sabato Svi.

Tannhauser went to work with the saw in short, rapid strokes.

'So our Sicilian adventure is over,' said Sabato Svi.

'There'll be other adventures, grander and more lucrative.' The first nail head dropped off. 'Don't move.' He started on the second.

'At least you won't have to sail to Egypt, with the Greek.'

'There'll be more pepper too. It grows on trees.' The saw topped the second nail and Tannhauser laid it down. 'Let the hand go loose,' he said. He took hold of Sabato's left wrist. With his other hand he interlaced his fingers through Sabato's and hooked them under the palm side of his knuckles. 'Loose, I said.' Tannhauser whipped the hand up from the nail.

'There. Now, the other. Loose.'

In another moment Sabato was free. He rose from the chair and worked his fingers gingerly, then clenched his fists, surprised.

'Flesh wounds,' said Tannhauser.

Bors called from the window. 'The street is clear.'

The three friends congregated around the prisoners, who grovelled on elbows and knees in the flickering gloom. Between the priest's splayed hands was a puddle of drool. Both men stank of their own soil. Tannhauser looked at Sabato.

'They're yours if you want them.'

The captain's voice quavered from below. 'But Your Excellency –'

Bors booted him in the teeth.

Sabato shook his head. 'It would give me no joy.'

Tannhauser indicated the captain to Bors.

'Kill him.'

Bors dropped the muzzle of the arquebus to the base of the captain's skull and let fall the match. There was a brief pause, which the captain filled with the wail of one who knew he was about to die with neither absolution nor unction. Then the contents of his skull exploded from his brow in a sooty blast of flame and befouled the flagstones. Gonzaga recoiled as his face was splattered with brains and fragments of lead. Bors laid down the gun and hauled the gagging and naked priest to his mutilated feet. He grabbed the iron pear by its key and tore it from Gonzaga's mouth, leaving a mass of broken stumps in its wake.

'See how the priest has shat himself,' said Bors with disgust. He brandished the iron pear. 'We should've shoved this up his arse.'

'Father Gonzaga,' Tannhauser said.

Gonzaga shuffled in a circle, his naked thighs dripping brown filth, and stared at Tannhauser's boots. He was no longer a human being, but a sack filled with terror and despair.

'It's time you made a clean breast,' said Tannhauser, 'and now that you're alone, you need have no more fear of your comrades.'

Gonzaga blinked with incomprehension. Bors stomped on the remains of the captain's head. Gonzaga swayed with nausea and Bors gave him a slap on his shaven pate.

'You hear that, priest? Friendless and alone.'

Tannhauser said, 'You've worked this atrocity on orders of Brother Ludovico?'

Gonzaga nodded. 'Fra Ludovico. Yes, oh yes.' He hesitated, then blurted, 'And to crucify the Jew was the captain's order, not mine. Of that deed I am innocent.'

'He speaks like a lawyer,' said Sabato.

Bors said, 'I hate lawyers.'

He grabbed Gonzaga's head with both hands and rammed his thumbs into the nostrils with such great violence that they popped asunder. Gonzaga screamed, his tongue waggling forth through broken teeth. Bors let go. From the nearest trestle, Tannhauser took a half-beaker of wine and gave it to the priest. The priest took it with both hands. He waited.

'Drink,' said Tannhauser. Gonzaga drank. 'Tell me, why does Ludovico turn against us?'

Gonzaga lowered the beaker. Rivulets of gore trickled from his ruptured nose and over his chin. 'Why?' He groped for the courage to answer. 'Why, because – because –' He quailed and gave up and hid behind the beaker. Bors struck the beaker from his hands. Gonzaga loudly befouled himself again. He clasped his hands to Tannhauser. His face was a haggard portrait of one for whom God no longer had meaning and who wanted only to live at any price. Tannhauser wondered how often Gonzaga had seen such a portrait himself, and he felt no pity.

'Speak freely,' said Tannhauser. 'And have no fear of offending us.'

Bors sniggered. Yet Gonzaga clung on to Tannhauser's every word.

'You are a Moslem,' he said. 'A heretic, an Anabaptist, a criminal. You consort with Jews. You disdain the Holy Father.' He pointed to the curious tomes heaped on Tannhauser's table. 'The forbidden texts are there for all to see.'

'That wouldn't be enough for Ludovico to show his hand. Tell me the real reason.'

'Your Excellency, Ludovico told me nothing more.' His eyes flicked at Bors. 'Nothing at all. Your impertinence on the docks seemed more than reason to me.'

Bors lurched forward. 'Let me tear his scrawny cock off.'

Tannhauser stopped him with his arm. Gonzaga clutched at his privities and shivered. 'I was ordered to leave the matter in the hands of the police.'

Bors strained to escape. 'But you thought you'd nail my friend to a chair instead?'

Gonzaga closed his eyes.

'There must be more,' said Tannhauser. 'Tell me everything. Everything that passed between you.'

Gonzaga struggled to form his thoughts. 'There was a second task. Ludovico ordered the seclusion of a noblewoman, in the convent of the Holy Sepulchre at Santa Croce.'

Though he already knew the answer, Tannhauser said, 'What was the woman's name?'

'Carla de la Penautier, of the Villa Saliba.'

Sabato and Bors both turned to stare at Tannhauser.

'When was this task to be accomplished?'

'It's accomplished already. Tonight.'

Tannhauser recalled the priest in the carriage at the gate. 'By whom?'

'The qualificator of our Sacred Congregation, Father Ambrosio.'

'Does this creature have the face of a rat?'

Gonzaga simpered. 'Oh, yes, exactly so, Your Excellency.'

Tannhauser glanced at Bors and Bors struck the priest in the kidneys with his fist. Gonzaga fell. Tannhauser pulled him to his knees by one ear.

'Will the noble lady be harmed?'

Gonzaga struggled for breath. 'No. Ludovico gave strict orders to the contrary.'

So, the mysterious monk who had deflowered the young contessa, and unknowingly left her with child, was Ludovico Ludovici, and Ludovico wanted the slate to be wiped clean. It was as tangled a web as Tannhauser had been caught up in. But how had Ludovico known that Carla had beseeched his aid in getting to Malta? Through Starkey? Inadvertently, perhaps. But Gonzaga wouldn't know the answer and Tannhauser didn't ask.

'Where are the charges written against us?' asked Tannhauser.

'None were prepared. We were forbidden to commit anything to paper.'

This much, at least, was good news. 'And where is Ludovico now?'

'He left to see Viceroy Toledo this afternoon. From Palermo he goes on to Rome.'

'On what business?'

'I don't know. Grand Master La Valette's, perhaps. And his own. Always his own. He'd never confide such matters in me.'

Tannhauser considered him. He nodded to Bors. 'He's nothing left to tell us.'

Sabato Svi walked away.

Bors drew his dagger. He hesitated. 'I've never killed a priest before.'

Gonzaga started babbling in Latin. '*Deus meus, ex toto corde poenitet me omnium meorum peccatorum eaque detesto . . .*'

Tannhauser took the dagger from Bors. 'Neither have I.'

He silenced Gonzaga's last prayer by stabbing him behind the collarbones and cutting the pipes from his heart. During the rebellion of the False Mustafa, when the janissaries massacred thousands in the streets of Adrianople, Tannhauser had found this method to be more certain than cutting the throat. And the blood was neatly contained inside the chest. Gonzaga died without a sigh. Tannhauser let him fall and returned the dagger.

He said, 'It's much the same as killing anyone else.'

Bors wiped the dagger on his thigh and sheathed it. 'And now?'

Tannhauser pondered. Santa Croce lay inland, in the mountains south-west of Etna. The route thence from the Villa Saliba – the Syracuse road – wound due west of the Oracle, past Messina's southern gate. Ambrosio and his escort would not yet have reached the Villa Saliba. Carla, he hoped, would have the sense not to offer resistance. And Amparo? But speculation was idle. He had more than time enough to cut them off on the Syracuse road. He suddenly felt a little nauseous and realised why.

'I haven't eaten since breakfast,' he said. He indicated the corpses. 'Let's stack this filth in the warehouse. Then, while I fill my belly, we can talk.'

Tannhauser watered Buraq, rubbed him down with a sack and left him out back with a bag of crushed oats and clover. When he returned, Bors had sluiced the floor with vinegar to clear the stench. Poor Gasparo was laid out on a trestle. While Bors went to pillage the kitchen, Tannhauser hastened to his chamber and retrieved his medicine chest.

When he returned, Bors had laid the table with bread and cheese and wine and a quarter of cold roast swan. He added a bottle of brandy and three dainty glasses. Sabato Svi sat with his head in his bloody hands. His shoulders were shaking. Tannhauser set his medicine chest on the table and opened its lid. He wrapped his arm round Sabato and felt the muted sobs in his chest. He waited while they stilled, then he said, 'Show me your hands.'

Sabato scrubbed his face on his sleeve, then took a deep breath and let it out. He avoided Tannhauser's eyes. His beard was all mucked about with mucus and blood. Tannhauser took a cloth from the chest and started to wipe his face. Sabato took the cloth and did it himself.

'You must think me less than a man,' he said.

'I heard you spit in their faces. No man could have been braver.'

Still Sabato kept his face turned. Tannhauser glanced at Bors.

'I've shat myself for much less, believe me,' Bors declared.

Sabato looked at Tannhauser. His eyes were haunted. 'I've never lost everything before.'

'The Oracle?' said Tannhauser. 'They've but broken a chain around our ankle.'

Sabato said, 'That isn't what I mean.'

Tannhauser nodded. 'I know. Yet, in losing everything, you win the chance to discover all that is precious.'

Sabato saw that he spoke from the heart. He nodded.

'Now, let me see those hands.'

Tannhauser took a stoppered bottle from the chest. He'd learned some battlefield medicine out of necessity and had picked up a number of vulnerary remedies from Petrus Grubenius. Apart from the method of their infliction, Sabato's wounds were unremarkable, being already closed into small puckered holes that hardly bled at all. Tannhauser cleaned them with witch hazel and sealed them with oil of Hispanus. He decided against a bandage.

'Let the sun and air heal them,' he said. 'Keep them dry, for dampness will make them purulent. If you must conceal them, I've some kidskin gloves in my armoire to which you're welcome.

They'll hurt more in the days to come than now, but even so, you must keep moving the fingers or you'll lose the use of them.'

Sabato flexed his hands. He was pale and his natural ebullience seemed dimmed, though far from extinguished. Since bravado was the order of the hour, Tannhauser sat down in his chair and nodded to Bors, who filled the crystal tulips with brandy. Tannhauser handed one to Sabato.

'These things knock the wind from your chest,' he said. 'Yet here, in fire such as this, is our mettle retempered.'

Sabato looked him in the eye. He raised the glass. '*Usque Ad Finem*.'

Bors and Tannhauser raised their glasses too. 'Until the End.'

They tossed the brandy down and Bors recharged the glasses.

Sabato Svi said, 'Burn her.'

They looked at him.

Sabato said, 'You speak of fire. Let's burn the Oracle to the ground.'

Tannhauser looked at Bors and saw that he too, in his mind's eye, was watching a blazing inferno of all they'd wrought, and with nothing short of awe.

'Magnificent,' said Bors.

'Sabato Svi,' said Tannhauser, 'you've revealed yourself to be a poet at the last.' He raised his glass. 'To the fire and be damned.'

'The fire.'

They drank. The glow of boldness arising from Tannhauser's belly was most welcome. He turned to the food and started on the roast fowl. Sabato, as if reluctant to let poetry stand alone as justification for arson, added sound reason to his suit. 'Most of our coin and credit is lodged in Venice. When we join it, we'll be well beyond the reach of the Spanish Crown.'

'True,' Tannhauser agreed.

'And a fire in the harbour will keep the city occupied at least until noon, by which time we'll be gone.'

'With a dozen quintals of powder still in store, so will half the waterfront,' said Bors. He'd stripped the captain of three fine rings and was testing them on his little finger. Not one of them would fit. He put them in his pocket and drank more brandy.

Tannhauser said, 'I'm to Malta.'

Sabato looked at him. Bors chuckled and recharged his brandy yet again.

Sabato said, 'So I go to Venice alone.'

'Your wife and children await you,' Tannhauser said.

'Only death awaits you in Malta.'

'Not for me,' Tannhauser replied. 'Like you, I have no squabble with the Turk.'

'So it's the contessa, La Penautier – she who stands behind this disaster,' said Sabato.

'She's innocent of everything but love,' Tannhauser replied. He ignored the looks which greeted this. 'The inquisitor, Ludovico, is behind our ruin, no one else. He wanted to deny the contessa any chance to disgrace him.'

'Everything but love?' said Sabato Svi.

'The kind you will appreciate. Love of her only child. Her son.'

'And her chance to disgrace the inquisitor?'

'I realised this only tonight, but Ludovico is the boy's father.'

Both Sabato and Bors looked to him for more. He shook his head.

'A fatal power beyond all telling has entwined the Lady Carla's path with mine. Don't press me further. Suffice to say that we all will stand to profit from the relationship.'

'How so?' asked Bors.

'When our bargain is successfully concluded, she and I will be married, and you will find yourselves in partnership with an aristocrat. A count, no less.'

'Count Tannhauser?' said Sabato.

'I've settled on "Count von Tannhauser". And I have it on good authority that thereafter you must call me "My Lord".'

'I'll drink to that,' said Bors, and proceeded to do so.

Tannhauser saw the doubt in Sabato's face. 'Sabato, tell me that such a title isn't worth a fortune. To all of us.'

'If you're dead it won't matter if you're a king,' Sabato replied.

'Fate has laboured hard to sever the knot which bound we three to this endeavour. Yet here we are and severed it is. Each must do as he must.'

Sabato said, 'I'll come to Malta with you.'

'That's the only foolish thing you've ever said to me.'

Sabato frowned. Tannhauser leaned forward.

'Sabato. These many years you've called me brother, and no name was ever sweeter to my ear. But you must go home, to Venice, and hold our future ready for our return. I've no desire to fight in the Maltese war. You may dismiss Bors's smirking. We'll be a month behind you at most. Dimitrianos can get you to Calabria by dawn.'

Tannhauser stood up. He looked at Bors.

'Under the floor of my chamber you'll find sixty odd pounds of Iranian opium.'

Bors was aggrieved. 'Why wasn't I told before?'

'If you had been there'd be much less.' Tannhauser tapped the chest of remedies on the table. 'Ship this too, and all the liquor and sweetmeats you can find. Give Dana and the girls forty gold scudi apiece –'

'Forty?' Bors gasped rarely, but he gasped at this.

'Tell them not to tarry in Messina. If Vito Cuorvo ships them to Naples, he can take our ox carts as payment.'

'I'll take the girls with me to Venice,' volunteered Sabato.

'No,' said Tannhauser. Dana's heart would be sore at his disappearance, but circumstance left him no choice; and anyway, perhaps he flattered himself. 'Travelling alone you'll attract little attention. With four luscious girls you'll attract a mob. The girls must do for themselves, as must we all.'

Sabato nodded and Tannhauser turned back to Bors. 'Wait for

me on the *Couronne*. Don't let Starkey leave without us.' Tannhauser opened his arms to Sabato Svi. 'Wish me good fortune, for Adventure calls and I'll need it.'

Sabato Svi stood up. 'Let no one rank common friendship alongside ours.'

They embraced. Tannhauser suppressed the ache of love in his chest. He stepped back.

'Now,' he said, 'I must go, for I've two more men to kill before the midnight tide.'

TUESDAY 15 MAY 1565

The Syracuse Road

The interior of the carriage was pitch dark and the creak of springs and clatter of wheels were the only sounds she could hear. The only indication of the priest on the opposite bench was a smell – of sweat and onions and stale urine – which turned Carla's stomach when it wafted her way. She kept her face to the edge of the blind over the window, grateful for the thin stream of air and the occasional glimpse of starlight. When she'd opened the blind earlier on, the priest had drawn it back down without a word.

She'd not been told the priest's name nor upon whose authority he acted. He'd told her only that she was to embrace a life of contemplation, at the convent of the Holy Sepulchre at Santa Croce. Apart from a cloak to cover her red silk dress, she'd been forbidden to bring possessions. She hadn't argued for she knew she wouldn't need them. Sicily was the edge of the world. Beyond its cosmopolitan ports – in mountains more uncivilised than any in the vastness of Spain – little had changed in a millennium. A season, a year, a decade, a lifetime, an era. A world in which such notions possessed scant meaning. A world that had watched the passing of civilisations one after another, the empires of the mighty falling like leaves. A world ruled by mortification and blind obedience. She could vanish into this wilderness, as inconvenient women had vanished before: her hair shorn, her indecent dress torn off, bound to permanent silence and indentured to implacable icons masquerading as God. She realised, furthermore, that to all practical intents she was already gone.

HER ABDUCTION HAD been accomplished with a curious lack of drama. An armed man and a priest appear, unannounced. No sign of Bertholdo; thankfully, nor of Amparo. Just two strangers, one wielding – absurdly, for did they expect to shoot her? – a smoking musket. No, she had broken no law. No, she was not placed under arrest. No, she could not know the purpose of this treatment, nor upon whose authority it was ordered. The priest knew nothing about her. He knew only what he was ordered to oblige her to do. All her questions would be answered in time, no doubt, but for now she would serve her best interests by joining the priest in his carriage and keeping her peace. The priest, she felt, saw in her dress alone good reason for arrest and confinement. In the constable's eyes she'd seen a plea that she not force him to manhandle her too roughly.

To be dragged to the carriage screaming would have done no good. It would only have added loss of dignity to loss of liberty; and it would have implicated Amparo in the catastrophe. The sense of helplessness evoked Carla's oldest nightmares. As she mounted the effort required to keep her head high, she was once again fifteen years old and walking to the carriage that took her from her father's house for the very last time. This time a voice inside her had rebelled and urged her to fight. But fight how? And with what? And to what end? And what of Amparo? At the moment of Carla's arrest, Amparo was spinning her vision glass. The priest's costume gave no indication of his order or whom he served, but the fact that he'd been chosen to carry out this sinister task suggested the Inquisition. Tannhauser had warned her that

Amparo's gifts were dangerous. The thought of her being tortured or burned filled Carla with the greatest horror. Amparo was better protected by remaining unknown, even if it meant abandonment. Amparo would survive. She'd make her way to Tannhauser. He'd admired the girl in a way no one else ever had. Not even Carla. He'd protect her. She couldn't entangle Amparo's fate with her own.

These calculations had propelled her into the carriage without resistance. Yet unlike the last time, when her father's agent had taken her away from Malta, she now saw her role within a larger machinery of oppression. In every moment, and throughout the human world, each was exercising power over another. It was a perfect simulacrum of a painting of Hell she had seen in Naples, in which grotesques trod each other down into the flames, thinking only of themselves. Hadn't she been rowed to Sicily by hundreds of human slaves? To whom she'd given not a thought beyond protesting their foul smell? She'd known nothing about them or what they had done to deserve such degradation, and she hadn't asked. Just as this priest, conducting her to oblivion, knew and cared nothing about her and did not ask. In the end she was no better than he. She was just another grotesque, lost – damned – in the self-serving riot of human existence.

Even so, she wondered what she'd done to provoke her abduction. All that had changed since yesterday, or the day before, was the arrival of Starkey's letter and Tannhauser's visit. Her imprisonment in a convent could not possibly profit either. Perhaps she'd been spied on. By Bertholdo? But on whose behalf and for what reason? The only candidate was her father, Don Ignacio, in Mdina. She'd made her desire to return sufficiently public that he might have got wind of it, not least because she'd brandished him as her motive. She could believe that he despised her enough, even now, to prevent her going home. Her confinement among self-flagellating nuns would strike a man of his religiosity as apt.

But she still couldn't find the heart to hate him. There was hatred enough without her donating her portion.

The carriage rocked on through the night. The priest's breath befouled the tiny space. They slowed to grind their way up a steep hill. She hoped the coachman would invite them to spare the horse and to get out and walk. She wished, if he should do so, that she might find the means to run away. In her ridiculous boots and her ridiculous dress. She wished she were a man, like Tannhauser, who'd never endured the feebleness of being a woman. No wonder he found them a mystery. They accepted a slavery that didn't even flatter them with chains.

The carriage stopped altogether, a speed scarcely slower than they'd been making up the grade, and she felt the clunk of the brake against the wheel. Then she heard a rough, threatening challenge, its words muffled by the blinds. Vague sounds and cumbersome thuds emanated from above, and the challenge was repeated. There was a gunshot, inches away it seemed, shocking in its unexpected violence. The little priest jumped in the dark. The shot was followed by a cry and the crash of someone falling – it could only be the coachman – and the horse started forward and the carriage lurched and then stopped as the brake creaked and juddered against the wheel rim. The invisible priest made no attempt to investigate. Instead he fell quite still and odours more repellent than before seeped forth. Carla opened the blind and the priest didn't stop her.

After so much suffocating blackness, the light from the moon and the carriage lamps seemed huge. The landscape revealed – the glittering silver swathe of the distant sea, the yellow clusters scattered across the port far below, the pale grey hillside falling from the edge of the road – filled Carla with exhilaration. She looked at the priest huddled opposite. She couldn't see his eyes but his body was rigid and his lips appeared to tremble in silent prayer. She realised, with some surprise, that she felt no fear, despite the fact that bandits swarmed these hills. Tannhauser was right. She wasn't without courage of a sort. If the priest feared what lay outside, she did not. She swung open the carriage door and climbed out.

There was a flash in the moonlight as Tannhauser lowered his sword. The blade dripped a viscous black liquid. He was on foot and in his left hand he held a pistol from whose muzzle curled a last grey tendril of smoke. His eyes were like blue coals afire in the sockets of his face and his hair blew wild and his lip was curled and once again she was reminded of a wolf, this time one who'd been disturbed at the site of a kill. This was no less than fitting, for tangled head down in the traces, and with his cuirass streaked and gleaming with same black liquid, was the body of the coachman.

'Are you hurt, My Lady?' asked Tannhauser, as if, perhaps, she'd turned her ankle.

Carla shook her head. She looked at the coachman. She'd never seen a man recently killed. 'Is that man dead?'

'Dead as a stone, My Lady.'

He paused, as if waiting for her to swoon or otherwise embarrass him. She felt no inclination towards the former and was determined to avoid the latter, yet could think of nothing useful she might say. She looked up at the star-spangled heavens.

'It's a beautiful evening,' she ventured.

Tannhauser favoured the sky with an educated glance. He slotted the pistol in his belt.

'Indeed,' he agreed, as if she'd said something wholly pertinent. 'Orion the Hunter is down and Scorpius has risen. The stars have judged in our favour.' He looked at her. 'But men, I'm afraid, will not.' He nodded at the carriage. 'Is the priest within?'

She nodded. 'I'm afraid I know neither his name nor whom he serves.'

'His name is Father Ambrosio and he serves the Inquisition.'

It seemed perfectly fair that he should know all this while she did not. 'Is he armed?'

'Only with his faith.'

'Then from eternity, at least, he has nothing to fear.' He pointed to the far side of the carriage. 'Yonder stands my horse – and my good companion – Buraq. He's mistrustful of strangers but let him take your measure and show no timidity – a warm word if you have one – and he'll let you mount him. Wait for me at the foot of the hill.'

She realised that he intended to murder the priest, and in blood so cold she wondered it wasn't frozen in his veins. She looked at him and he forced a smile to reassure her, and she saw that he was a killer of the darkest stripe, and that for all his broad intelligence and largeness of heart, there was a defect – a hole – in his conscience that was almost as wide. She wondered what had made the hole and how long it had been there. It saddened her, because the cause must have brought him great anguish, and the cost must have been so high that he had forgotten how much he had paid. She thought to object to the murder, but he was taking this stain on his soul for her advantage and she held her tongue. She'd offer no more false faces. She'd not insult the man with pious hypocrisy. She'd embrace the world in which she found herself so bloodily embroiled. She'd learn at last to be true to her inmost self.

'I wish to stay here with you,' she said.

'I will join you shortly,' he said. 'There's no need to be afraid.'

'I am not afraid. Though I know not how, this disaster is of my making. I will not hide from its consequences.'

'Perhaps you don't understand,' he said, 'but I'm going to slay the priest.'

A thud rocked the inside of the carriage and she turned to look. Ambrosio had fallen to his knees, his fingers knotted. His thin face beseeched her with a doleful supplication.

'He grovels for his life, as most do,' Tannhauser said. 'But if I spare him he will do us further harm, you may take my word.'

She looked Tannhauser in the eye. 'Do not delay on my part.'

Tannhauser, both shocked and relieved by her phlegm, rubbed the back of his hand across his mouth. 'You're sure.'

She nodded. He stepped past her to the carriage doorway and studied the priest.

'These creatures are like rats. They come out only at night.'

The priest cringed and Tannhauser struck his hat off with his palm.

'Who sent you on this base and unmanly errand?'

Ambrosio's mouth opened and closed. Tannhauser leaned in and clamped one hand to the tonsured crown of his skull. With a short stroke of the sword he docked the priest's ear. Carla flinched as Ambrosio uttered his first, pitiful response and rivulets black as brimstone poured down his neck. His eyes flicked towards hers with bewilderment and terror. No, she told herself, you will not look away. Tannhauser turned the priest's face towards his own.

'Answer me, dog.'

Ambrosio heaved for breath. 'Father Gonzaga, of the Congregation of Saint Peter Martyr.'

'Good. What were your orders?'

'To convey the signora to the convent of the Holy Sepulchre at Santa Croce, to be retained there indefinitely for the good of her immortal soul.'

'And what of Gonzaga's master, Ludovico?'

The name shocked Carla more than any of the singular events she'd so far endured. She'd not heard it uttered in thirteen years. She waited for Ambrosio's answer.

'I've not heard tell of His Eminence in months – since he went to Malta.'

Tannhauser bent to the hole in Ambrosio's skull. 'Now you must die. And know that if your God has indeed made a Heaven and a Hell, Lucifer will rub his hands as he watches you burn.'

'Jesu!'

Tannhauser canted the sword steeply and drove it through the notch of his throat. Ambrosio emitted a bubbling gasp and his hand clawed at Tannhauser's back in a final embrace. Tannhauser shoved him to the carriage floor and cleaned his blade on the dead man's robes. The blood was tenacious and it was a moment before he was satisfied. While Carla stood and watched, as if from the window of a dark and stirring dream, Tannhauser reshaped the world like a bloodstained mason, tearing down one wall even as he threw up another. He sheathed his sword and drew a dagger.

'Where is your good companion?' he asked. 'Amparo.'

'At the villa. My abductors were unaware of her existence, I didn't enlighten them.'

'Then you did right well.'

She watched him cut the dead coachman from the traces and she stepped back as he hefted the corpse like a bale. He crammed it into the carriage on top of the priest and closed the door. He examined his gold striped doublet as if for stains. His satisfaction in finding none was that of a man so practised in butchery that the result was no more than he expected. He wiped his hands on his hams and stripped the breeching, crupper and hip strap from the coach horse.

He said, 'I've concluded from the conspiracy mounted against us that Ludovico is the father of your boy.'

'I regret not telling you sooner. Perhaps you'd have avoided this calamity.'

Tannhauser shook his head. 'The die was already cast. When I got back from your villa, a pack of city constables sought to ensnare me.'

He led the coach horse free and soothed it with words and caresses. He nodded towards his own mount by the roadside. As if to forestall the impression that his offer was mere gallantry, and thus a source of contention, he said, 'Please, Buraq has carried me far today and will appreciate the lesser weight.'

In the moonlight the animal appeared as white as milk.

'He looks as pure as an allegory of Virtue,' she said.

Tannhauser said, 'I'm sure he'd say the same of you if he could.'

Leading the coach horse by its harness, Tannhauser steadied Buraq as Carla hiked up her skirts and mounted with ease. She saw Tannhauser take in her short leather boots, and his delectation aroused her. Buraq accepted her calmly and she felt at once his wonderful strength and poise. She thrilled to his beauty, his nobility, his smell. She thrilled to the stars and the night. She thrilled to the man who stood by her and studied her legs with such unabashed appreciation. Tannhauser handed her the coach horse's reins.

She collected her wits and said, 'You say the constabulary waited?'

The smile that had lurked behind his eyes that afternoon reappeared. 'The Messina police force will be understrength for a while.' The ghost smile vanished and something cold fled through his spirit. 'They killed young Gasparo, for standing tall in defence of Sabato Svi. They put Sabato Svi to the torture, because he is a Jew. Both men honoured me with their friendship.'

'I'm sorry,' she said.

'When the powerful turn against us, we must act as the powerful act, which is in one's own interest, and without morality or mercy. We killed them like dogs and my conscience rests easy. So be assured: no one is left alive to speak your name in any of this – no one except Ludovico. But he will keep his peace, for his part in this debacle would shame him before those even mightier than he.'

He took her arm at the wrist and squeezed. His fingers bit her bones, as if his intention was to rouse her from her dream.

'Ludovico has gone to Palermo, and thence to Rome. Go back to Amparo. The priest here never took you and of this butchery you saw naught. Say nothing and no one will ask. Take Buraq, and care for him, and return to France, tomorrow, as if none of this took place.'

Tannhauser's grip was painful. But he'd roused her from her dream in the moment she'd first seen him, with his face still damp with tears in the garden of roses. God had willed that she take this path and by this path He graced her. This was what she knew, here and now, with the great horse breathing between her thighs, and the stars on fire above, and the bite of a man's fingers on her flesh.

'I'm to Malta,' said Tannhauser. 'The stronghold of the Hounds of Hell. Starkey will have his way, after all. But I will find your boy, come what may. And I will bring him home safe to your arms.'

Carla did not doubt him. Yet she said, 'I'm coming with you. That was our bargain.'

He considered her in silence, his eyes unreadable. He released his grip and turned and walked away. She watched him manoeuvre the carriage to the rim of the road. He pushed it over the edge and the carriage and its morbid cargo rolled away into the dark. He returned and mounted bareback on the coach horse.

'The red ship sails at midnight.' Tannhauser glanced at the moon with an educated eye. 'If we're to collect the girl, we must hurry.'

'Amparo?' She'd been sure he wouldn't welcome the added burden.

'In an imbroglio such as this,' he said, 'a scryer and her vision are not to be scorned.'

He wheeled and set off down the hill at reckless speed. Buraq followed of his own accord, as sure as he was fleet. Carla rose from the saddle and threw back her shoulders. The wind blew through her hair. She felt as if she'd grown wings.

WEDNESDAY 16 MAY 1565

Messina Harbour, the COURONNE

THE *Couronne* WAS half a mile offshore when the Oracle exploded. The ensuing fire was immense and the whole bay glimmered yellow with its light. Of the human chaos unleashed along the docks, all Bors could see were tiny, desperate figures etched against the flames.

As they ploughed on into the darkness, the uproar of the waterfront was drowned by the creak of timber and cordage, by the dip and sweep of fifty-two huge oars, by the boom of the gong and the crack of whips and the jangle of shackles and chains. On the open rowing deck below, slaves chained five to a bench bent over the looms. They shat and pissed where they sat, on sheepskins still sodden with the filth of the day before. Bors crammed tobacco up his nostrils and leaned against the rail. The Oracle was dead, but life was good. The distant, desperate figures were in their world, and he was content to be in his.

Mattias had arrived at the wharf just as Giovanni Castrucco and Oliver Starkey seemed about to come to blows over how much longer they could wait. Bors, reluctant to waste more powder than was needed when it could be used to kill the heathen, had freighted eight of the dozen quintals left in the warehouse to the *Couronne*, along with their war chests, harness and supplies and the muskets of the vanquished constabulary. Mattias, by contrast, hove up on a bareback horse, encumbered by two women and a collection of musical instruments, like a covey of troubadours who'd lost their way and found themselves bound for perdition. For a man who'd slain two priests and three officers of the Crown, Mattias conducted himself with admirable poise, and in herding his brace of *femmes* and his golden stallion past the eyes of the astonished knights had even exhibited a charming congeniality. But Mattias was nothing if not a firm hand in a pinch.

Mattias stood now up on the quarterdeck, conversing with the famous Italian captain and the Lieutenant Turcopolier as if for all the world he were their equal and not, as was now the case, the most wanted man in Sicily, if not the Empire. Bors grinned. The man was a marvel. And look at the expression on his face, as if he were as perplexed by the waterfront inferno as were they. It was no surprise to Bors that the Grand Master wanted him for the fight. But the old pirate would get double value, for when it came to slaughter Bors could show these fighting monks a trick or two himself.

The women that Mattias had taken under his wing? Only God knew what further trouble they would bring. They stood beside Bors at the gunwale of the *rambades* watching the shore, the contessa and wild-eyed girl. He'd given each a half a lemon with which to combat the stench of the slaves and they wafted the fruit beneath their noses with a dainty air. The contessa kept looking at Mattias on the bridge. Bors could see that all her hopes – and who knew what dreams? – were now firmly invested in his friend, and a woman's hopes and dreams were as heavy as any burden known to man, especially when going to war. The girl beside her took no interest in the ship and its malodorous hurly-burly, but stared at the flames, the only thing still visible on the dark and distant shore, as if they exerted an enchanting force, as if she could see something in them that others could not. The women would make life more hazardous. Decisions would be blurred. Love would poison the well and whoever drank from it. But Bors's sacred vocation was to watch Mattias's back, and watch it he would.

At an overrespectful distance from the women, and looking at the vanishing shore of Europe, were a score or so of knights in black doublets. Their breasts bore white eight-pointed crosses cut from silk, and these crosses shone with an eerie glow in the moonlight. They spanned forty years in age, but most looked under thirty. All sported strong, warlike beards. All murmured Paternosters. The knights were obliged to recite one hundred and fifty Paternosters every day, but since accuracy in the count was hard to keep they rarely stopped, and at sea they prayed for hours in a mystic trance. Each man gradually fell into the rhythm of another, until they chanted the prayer in unison, and Bors felt a chill down his spine, for the sound of so many killers in perfect harmony was a sound to set a block of stone atremble. He saw that the contessa had joined the knights in their incantation, and that the girl had not.

Bors looked back to Sicily. They were sailing to a bloodbath, yet he craved it. Craved it more than gold, more than honour. Only in battle were the shackles of morality broken. Only on the field of blood, where all prior investitures were rendered null and void, was a man stripped to the nub of his being. Only there could transcendence be found. The greater part of human kind toiled and died without ever knowing such ecstasy. Once known, all else lost its savour. Horror – in which the world abounded anyway – was a small price to pay to know it again. With a rattle of blocks and the snap of canvas and rigging, the huge red lateens dropped from the yards and swelled in the breeze. An enormous cross of gold shone on the mainsail. Mattias appeared at his side and slipped an arm through the crook of Bors's elbow.

'So,' said Mattias, 'your wish is granted. The natural order is fulfilled.'

'I wouldn't have wished it at quite so hefty a price,' Bors replied.

'At the least you'll fetch back some tales to tell by the fireside.'

Bors tipped his head towards the women. 'And you've brought minstrels in skirts to accompany our revels.'

'Where we're going, music will be more precious than rubies,' said Mattias. 'But mark me now and remember. I've no mind to see this fight through to its end. We're going to spirit a boy from the jaws of war.'

At the age of nine, or thereabouts, Bors had struck his father to the ground with a hoe and stowed away on a curragh out of Carlisle to join the army of the King of Connaught. Thinking of this, he frowned. 'What boy would want to be thus spirited?'

'Perhaps he will not. But I don't intend to offer him the choice.'

'Whoever he is,' said Bors, 'I'm in his debt.'

Mattias shook his head and grinned. And Bors thanked God Almighty that somehow on the long and crooked road he'd earned such love. Bors would have ridden with Mattias if he'd planned to kidnap Satan from his deep and fiery throne. With a squeeze of Bors's arm, Mattias disengaged and joined the women.

Bors turned back to the spume churned up from the deep by the blades of the oars. On some other quarter of this ancient sea, tens of thousands of *gazi* approached their own moment of truth. Fifty gruelling days crammed cheek by jowl in the Sultan's ships. After such confinement, landfall would see them howling for Christian blood. Bors had never fought the Lions of Islam, but if Mattias were any guide they'd be a handful. The prospect made his thighs and bowels shake. The reasons that had brought them here, Mattias and his women too, no longer mattered. The God of War had spoken and they'd rallied to his call. The rhythmic litany of the knights seeped into his chest.

'*Pater noster, qui es in caelis, sanctificetur nomen tuum. Adveniat regnum tuum. Fiat voluntas tua sicut in caelo et in terra. Panem nostrum quotidianum da nobis hodie, et dimitte nobis debita nostra, sicut et nos dimittimus debitoribus nostris. Et ne nos inducas in tentationem, sed libera nos a malo. Amen.'*

On a red and black ship, across a black and silver sea, they sailed by the light of the moon towards Hell's Gate. When the knights began their litany afresh, Bors joined them.

FRIDAY 18 MAY 1565

Kalkara Bay, the Borgo, Malta

ORLANDU HAD HUNTED the greyhound since first light, when a cannon shot had woken him from his roofless billet by the creek and he'd seen the animal's lean silhouette against the sky. Crimson corrugations of cloud broke from the east, like an army of the night in flight from the scourge of day, and the breeze, never cooler or sweeter than at dawn, carried on its wings the voices of men singing psalms.

At the second cannon shot the greyhound turned towards him. They weren't more than a dozen feet apart, the dog looking down from a stack of canvas-bound crates on the Kalkara dock. A beam of early light escaped the clouds and he saw that the dog was pure white. Its ears snapped erect and they studied each other, the dog and the barefoot boy, the one as clean of limb as God could have made him, the other scabbed with bites and tarnished with gore. Orlandu grabbed his butcher knife from the capstones by his head and slowly stood up. The hound's eyes were mournful and bright. His soul was unconcealed. His nobility pierced Orlandu's heart.

As far as Orlandu knew, this white greyhound was the last living dog on the island. Whether it was so or not, not a bark or a howl was to be heard throughout the town. Whether it was so or not, Orlandu intended to kill this beautiful white hound before the morning was done.

At the third cannon shot, the greyhound leapt from his station and vanished into the streets with the stealth of a phantom. Orlandu plunged into the Borgo in pursuit, and so intent he was on tracking down his prey that the sun had cleared the horizon before he remembered. He stopped. Three shots from Castel Sant' Angelo was the signal all had awaited with measureless dread. The Turkish armada had been spotted out in the offing. The Hordes of Islam had arrived at Malta's shores.

The slaughter of the dogs had taken three days. This was the fourth. Their extermination had been decreed by Grand Master La Valette. In the siege of Rhodes, it was said, La Valette had seen the people eat rats and dogs. Furthermore, the dogs had eaten the corpses of the slain. He had determined that, on Malta, death would come to all before any such degradation would be tolerated. Orlandu had heard it said also that of all living things La Valette's most tender love was reserved for his hunting dogs. Before making his decree public, La Valette had taken his sword and killed his six beloved hounds by his own hand. Afterwards, it was said, La Valette had wept with pity.

If the decree was simple enough, its execution proved more taxing than anyone expected. Many whose dogs were to hand followed La Valette's example and killed them themselves. But the policy couldn't be concealed from the animals so condemned. By nightfall of the first day, alerted by the yowls of their fellows and with their masters turning against them on every side, dogs domestic and feral alike had banded together in wild-eyed packs in which they roamed the streets and alleys of the city. Since the city was walled and surrounded by the sea, escape was not possible; and sanctuary was denied.

Since dogs are strangely like men in this respect, the packs were led by the most savage and cunning among them. In such large numbers, and fuelled by terror and the stench of the pyres on which their carcasses were daily burned, these packs proved highly dangerous and ever more bold. Since the hunting and killing of dogs was a lowly task, beneath the dignity of the fighting men and knights, and since everyone who could walk was engaged in preparations for the war, and since it was not fit work for women, a serjeant at arms lit on the idea of using the waterboys recruited to serve the battlements during the siege. Orlandu, who'd been assigned to the Bastion of Castile, had been among the first to volunteer.

For the Religion he would have volunteered for anything. Like all the lads, he looked upon the knights as gods on earth. He'd been given a boning knife – honed to a crescent by long use and razor-sharp – and told that since they'd soon be killing Moslems, they might as well start on dogs, who before God were but beasts of a similar order, the principal difference being that the latter smelt less vile and would not go to Hell. This observation set Orlandu to wondering whether or not dogs had souls. He was assured by the chaplain, Father Guillaume, who blessed the juvenile butchers before they set off on their crusade, that they did not, any more than a sheep or a hare, but so particular was the way in which each canine met its death, and so poignant was its love of life, that by the first sundown Orlandu was convinced to the contrary.

When each dog was killed the boy took the carcass to a wagon by the Provençal Gate, where the dead dog was gutted so that its entrails could be used to poison the wells of the Marsa once the Turks arrived. What remained was taken to the bonfire of hair and bone outside the walls. By the end of the second day, by which time most of the boys had begged to be excused these hideous duties, Orlandu's tattered clothes were stiff with the excrement and gore of the animals he'd killed and gutted and hauled off to the pyre. His inflamed flesh ached with more bites than he could count. He was nauseated. He was drained. He was glutted and revolted by slaughter. And he decided that Father Guillaume was right about their souls after all, for to believe otherwise made the work too harrowing to bear.

He slept on the docks alone, on a pallet of sacked grain. When he rose and scouted the alleyways for prey, people stepped aside, as if he were a bedlamite lately escaped from a refuge for the deranged. At first he imagined that this was because he stank, but the look in the eyes of the baker from whom he bought a breakfast loaf told him that it was because he inspired a repellent awe. The baker feared him. After this he walked taller and wore a stern and impassive countenance in the manner of the knights. From the tanner he procured a piece of sheepskin, and he rubbed the hide in chicken fat, and tied it nap-to-skin around one forearm. Thus armoured, he was able to tempt a dog's jaws before cutting its throat.

Even so, the teeth bruised his arm to the bone, for it was the fiercest and canniest of the outlaw curs that had survived the cull to date, and by the second nightfall his left hand was blue to the knuckles. The watchmen on the docks shared sweetbreads and kidneys, roasted on the coals of their brazier; they pressed him for news of the hunt, and he joined in their vulgar laughter at things he'd not found funny at the time. They asked him how many he'd killed. He couldn't remember. Twenty, thirty, more? They glanced at his bruises and wounds when they thought him distracted and exchanged mysterious looks and thought him strange. He left them to their fire, and by the time he lay down again upon his sacks and looked up at the stars, he was not the boy who'd risen the day before. Not yet a man, perhaps, but a killer of sorts, which was almost as good. How much harder could it be to kill a Moslem?

He was a bastard and, because an outcast whether he liked it or no, he'd chosen a life on the waterfront over slavery on the pig farm where he'd been raised. He laboured in the docks, careening the galleys, boiling pitch and graving the filth-sodden hulls. Repulsive work; but he was free. And free to dream: of being a pilot in the Religion's navy. Tonight he stared at the sky and watched the polestar in the Little Bear's tail. He fell asleep and his slumbers were troubled, by malevolent spirits and menacing dreams, which were dark and bloody and bereft of consolation.

Daybreak brought the beautiful pure white greyhound, watching Orlandu as if it knew his dreams and had stood a sentinel's vigil over his sleep. At first he thought it a spirit, and with that his belief in canine souls was restored, not to be shaken again even when the vision proved corporeal. When the white greyhound fled into the purple shadowed streets, Orlandu followed.

Like a ghost in a fable that expounded the nature of futility, the white hound led him through the hovels of Kalkara Creek, and on into the city, and towards the voices raised in praise of the reborn day. The conventual church of San Lorenzo stood shrouded in a spectral violet light. Its open doors pulsed yellow against the monumental façade and Orlandu's soul was drawn through the sacred portal. He left his knife by a buttress and tiptoed through the arch. The flagstones were cold against his feet. The plainsong made him shiver. He dipped his fingers in holy water, genuflected and crossed himself, and crept towards the yellow shimmer within. San Lorenzo was the church of the Knights of Saint John the Baptist. Orlandu had never been inside its doors before. His heart pounded and he hardly dared breathe as he pushed on through the vestibule. Beyond the two broad pillars that flanked the nave, the interior opened before him and his senses were stunned.

The whole convent of the Religion stood assembled as one and the stones shook as half a thousand soldiers of the Cross raised their voices to God. The monks of war stood rank upon rank in their plain black robes, meeker than lambs and fiercer than tigers, bound by love of Christ and Saint John the Baptist, proud of bearing and fearless, and singing, singing with a roaring exaltation. Smoking incense drifted about the aisle and made him dizzy. The vast space glowed and flickered with countless burning candles. Yet it seemed that every ray of light emanated from the tortured figure of Christ raised high above the altar. That was where Orlandu's gaze, along with that of every other in that mighty congregation, was drawn: to the gaunt and noble visage of He who'd suffered and died for all mankind, to the bloody crown of thorns and the hands clawed in pain, to the pierced and emaciated body that twisted on the Cross, as if His final throes were not yet over.

Orlandu was filled with sorrow. He knew that Jesus loved him. A sob escaped from his chest and he clasped his bruised and bloody hands and fell to his knees.

'I confess to almighty God, to blessed Mary ever Virgin, to blessed Michael the Archangel, to blessed John the Baptist, to the holy apostles Peter and Paul, and to all the Saints that I have sinned exceedingly in thought, word, and deed, through my fault, through my fault, through my own most grievous fault.'

He was not alone in his plea for forgiveness, nor in his weeping. Tears shone without shame on the faces of many monks. Sorrow and joy filled the church to its vaulted rafters. Not since the tragedy of Rhodes had so many brothers of the Religion assembled in one place. If no man among them believed that such a number would ever gather again, it was because every man there had come to Malta to die for his Faith. God had called their monastery to war. Fire and sword were the holy tools of their creed. Caught up the vortex of worship around him, Orlandu embraced this fate as willingly as any. He too yearned to die for Christ the Redeemer. Yet his instincts didn't desert him. He turned in time to see the chaplain, Father Guillaume, bear down from the corner, his face a mask of fury at the ragged intruder. Orlandu scrambled to his feet and fled through the vestibule into the lilac light of day. He snatched his knife from where it lay by the buttress and sprinted round the corner of the church.

There, as if engaged in a game whose rules and finale he could not be expected to grasp, the pure white greyhound stood waiting.

In the improved light Orlandu saw that the hound's sleek flanks – the ribs jutting out, though he wasn't poorly fed – were disfigured by recent knife wounds. Others had tried to kill him, then, and had failed. With his eyes still wet and his chest still close to bursting from his communion with the knights, Orlandu's stomach cringed at the prospect of butchery. But La Valette had killed his hounds, the hounds he'd loved above all living things. He'd killed them for the people and for the Religion and for God. To tempt the animal closer, Orlandu considered extending the fat-soaked hide still bound about his arm; but to trick this dog, as he'd tricked the feral curs of yesterday, seemed ignoble, and perhaps unholy. He displayed the knife to the greyhound.

The greyhound turned and skipped away.

Orlandu ran after him.

THROUGHOUT THE MORNING, as the cool was broken and the heat rose fierce and high, Orlandu pursued and lost and tracked and found, and lost and tracked again, the fugitive hound. Back and forth across the Borgo, from the Provençal Gate in the huge landward walls to the dockyards of Galley Creek, from Kalkara to Sant' Angelo, through markets and middens, through sunlight and through shadow. And as boy and dog charted every alley and street, the town itself was transformed into a hive of terror.

Drums pounded and trumpets echoed and bells tolled. Bewilderment and turmoil rippled through the population. The common folk had not expected the Turks for another month. Every hard-worn face was pallid with dismay. Many ran into their houses and locked their doors. Others ran hither and thither with a frantic want of purpose. And all across the island those not yet inside the walls rushed towards the Borgo to claim sanctuary. The peasants brought with them every living beast that could be worked or eaten. On the backs of donkeys and carts, and across their own stubborn shoulders, they loaded the last of the crops they'd harvested early and the fruits of which every orchard had been stripped. They brought their children and their wives, and their vegetables and goats, and those small precious things that remind a person of their life and what they have been. They brought their icons and prayers, their courage and their fear. And in every direction smoke spiralled into the sky. Every blade and morsel of crops not fit to reap and of provisions that couldn't be carried were put to the torch and burned. They scorched the land. Their own land. They poisoned every well with the entrails of dogs and lethal herbs and faeces. Nothing was left behind them for the Turk, for the Turk was here.

It seemed as if the whole of Malta were on fire.

Only once did Orlandu pause in his pursuit, at the harbour where he'd begun and which now seethed with tumultuous commotion. He'd taken neither food nor drink since the brazier of the watchmen the night before, and out of nowhere he felt sick, and the faces of the horses and the people began to spin before his eyes. He found himself retching on elbows and knees, the earthy tang of mule droppings in his nostrils and the acid scalding his throat. He pressed his forehead to the cobblestones and retched a mouthful of gall. Then a pair of bony hands seized his shoulders and hauled him to his feet.

He closed his eyes to stop the whirling and was guided to an upturned bucket for a seat. Something wet and sourly sweet was pushed into his mouth and he chewed and swallowed. His stomach clenched on the wine-soaked bread. He held it down as bony fingers filled his mouth with more. As quickly as it had come the nausea and giddiness retreated. He blinked and discovered his rescuer.

The old man's eyes were as bright as those of a child, and his nose was so hooked that it seemed to meet the bristles on his pointy chin. Orlandu knew him at once. It was Omar, the old *karagozi*. Behind him stood the tiny, ramshackle theatre at which he plied his singular trade. The *karagoz* man had been a feature of the docks for longer than any could remember. Some said he'd been here since before the knights had arrived. He was the oldest person Orlandu had ever seen, older even than La Valette or Luigi Broglia, and along with every other child, and many a weary seaman and stevedore too, he'd often delighted at the antics of the shadow puppets the old man brought to life on the muslin screen. Apart from the slaves who trudged by in chains, Omar was the only Turk on Malta. No one knew how he'd got there or why he'd stayed, and perhaps by now old Omar knew not himself. He was harmless and brought laughter and so no one seemed to care that he was a Moslem. He was also thought to be crazy, for he lived alone in a barrel, and he accompanied the mime of his paper marionettes with gargles and grunts and squeals such as no sane person would ever know how to make.

'Aha! Aha!' cackled Omar, pointing at Orlandu's bites. 'The dogs it is! The dogs!'

He followed the garbled Maltese with a diverse series of barks of remarkable accuracy and finished with a mournful howl and a toothless grin. Orlandu nodded and Omar offered him more bread and wine and Orlandu ate.

'The Grand Master knows. He knows all!' Omar pointed to the tower of Castel Sant' Angelo. 'They dance for his tune! Turks! Romans! Demons! All! They serve his will. Yes!'

Orlandu, bewildered, nodded encouragement, as one does with a madman.

'Dogs, men, children, women, poof!' Omar mimed an eruption with his hands then dusted them clean with an extravagant gesture and presented his empty palms. 'The dogs show the way!' He mimed the sharpening of a knife. 'The Master spits upon the whetstone. Yes!'

Orlandu understood not a word the old man had said. Out of

gratitude he replied, 'Yes!' and was rewarded by another display of Omar's gums. Orlandu's strength had returned. This talk of the Grand Master stoked his will to complete his task. He stood up from the bucket, towering over the *karagozi*, and found his limbs to be sound. For the first time he noticed that a galley had berthed at the dockside. Its mariners swarmed the rigging to reef the red sails. A new contingent of knights was disembarking.

The Navy of the Religion consisted of seven galleys. He'd scraped barnacle and weed from the excrement-saturated timbers of every one. This was the *Couronne*. Among the lads of the town, especially those honoured to serve as waterboys, it was a matter of pride to recognise and name as many of their noble heroes as they could. Each sighting was noted and recounted with much argument as to who were the deadliest fighters, the most intrepid mariners, the closest to God. But all the knights on the *Couronne*, supervising the unloading of their horses and gear, were unknown to him. These late arrivals must have travelled from the most distant of the Order's commanderies, perhaps in Poland or Scandinavia, or even Muscovy, fabled lands at the far end of the earth, where magic flourished and pagan tribes still roasted captured knights in their armour.

He saw a well-known figure descend the gangway, though not one rated high for his ferocity. It was Oliver Starkey. Behind him came two strangers of fearsome stature and mettlesome bearing, who by their dress were clearly not knights at all. He guessed they were *soldados particular* – gentlemen adventurers – drawn to Malta by chivalry and faith and the prospect of action and glory. They drew no pay and answered to no one and fought with whom they chose. These two suggested little that was chivalrous or gentlemanly, though for action they surely were born. The first was as broad as an ox cart, with rough-cropped hair, an iron-grey beard and many scars. He wore a brass-studded Brigantine war vest and had festooned himself with weapons, including a two-handed German breach sword slung over his back and, cradled in one arm, a wall gun whose bore would accommodate the handle of a broom.

The taller of the men was more striking still. He had a lion's mane of hair that flamed like burnished bronze in the high sun. Among the plainer garb of the knights, his doublet striped with gold struck a note of bravado, and he wore high, cuffed boots that came halfway up his brawny thighs. At his hip he wore a sword and in his belt was a long-barrelled pistol of intricate design. A martial kind of men, whether noble or not. Orlandu conceived a new fantasy. He'd never be a knight, for his blood was lowborn and impure, but he might aspire one day to be such a man as these.

Behind them came two women. He hadn't seen a woman disembark in months, but felt little curiosity. In the presence of such giants as now bestrode the gangway, women were tiny birds of the dullest plumage. He was far more taken by the magnificent golden stallion that the younger of the women led behind her. He'd never seen its like and he'd seen many, for the horseflesh of the knights was of the finest. The steed could not be the girl's, or even – at least so he hoped – her mistress's. It had to belong to the man with the lion's hair. Splendid as it was, his interest switched abruptly as the Grand Master, La Valette, came to greet the newcomers.

Orlandu straightened his shoulders and stiffened his spine. Perhaps La Valette would glance his way and see his wounds and realise that, like him, Orlandu too was a killer of dogs and thus be proud of him. See him stride along the quay, like a panther despite his years and taller by a head than most, the bustle of the dock parting as he approached, his black habit swishing about his feet, a simple dagger belted at his waist, his hawk's eyes fixed forward yet seeing everything. Yes, surely seeing Orlandu too, though he didn't look his way.

La Valette had fought in eighty-seven sea battles, some said eighty-nine. La Valette had slain a thousand Turks by his own hand. La Valette had survived the galley bench of the evil Abd-ur Rahman. La Valette had survived the terrible siege of Rhodes and had been dragged to the ships by his comrades because, despite that all was lost, he'd wanted to fight on. Not even the Emperor Philip in far off Castile, or the Holy Father in Rome, could sway La Valette. His harangue of the militia, the week before, was quoted by the boys as if it were scripture.

'Today our faith is at stake. The battle to be fought on Malta will determine if the Gospels – the words and deeds of Christ – must yield to the Koran. God has asked us to sacrifice the lives that we have pledged Him. Happy are those who die in His sacred cause.'

Happiness filled Orlandu's chest. When he prayed to God, God, in his mind's eye, looked like La Valette.

La Valette now welcomed the two intrepid adventurers and, with brief but impeccable graciousness, the women, then he fell at once into conversation with the lion-haired stranger and they walked back along the dock towards Castel Sant' Angelo. They passed not ten paces from where Orlandu stood and he held his breath. As La Valette spoke, and pointed out various landmarks, the stranger shot a glance across the quay, through the toiling figures of the stevedores, and Orlandu found himself pierced by flame-blue eyes. He almost reeled, as if a physical force had shoved him; but he held his ground and the blue gaze turned away.

As the women passed by, Orlandu paid little attention to the older and more regal of the two. Her face was turned in conversation with Oliver Starkey. But the girl who led the golden stallion stared at him directly, with an expression he couldn't read. Her face was unbalanced and strange, and he wondered if she had the power to curse him, for she looked at him over her shoulder as she passed out of sight. Orlandu attributed her interest to his grotesque appearance. He hoped that his bloody demeanour had impressed the blue-eyed stranger. The ox-like bruiser brought up the rear, nodding congenially to the labourers about as if they'd turned out to welcome his arrival. When he saw Orlandu, he laughed and tipped the long barrel of his musket in salute. Orlandu tingled with pride. What a day! What men! He thanked God that he was here and now, among such remarkable fellows and in such remarkable times.

'A world of dreams! Aha! Aha! Yes!'

Orlandu turned back to Omar. The *karagozi* was exposing his gums and rocking from one foot to the other, as if he himself had choreographed these events like the shadows in his plays.

'Yes,' agreed Orlandu, without understanding the old man's meaning. 'A world of dreams.' He searched the cobbles and found his butcher knife and picked it up. 'Thank you.' He dipped his head. 'I must go.'

Omar made a spider-like running motion with his fingers. 'The white djinn! Yes!' He barked twice and howled.

Orlandu nodded. 'Yes. Now I must go.' He started away.

'The garden of the –' Omar's Maltese failed him. But like many denizens of Grand Harbour, like Orlandu too, his head contained fragments of a dozen tongues. The Borgo was a Tower of Babel. Omar's hands undulated upwards to illustrate the growth of plants, then he mimed throwing a drink down his throat and pulled a face as if the taste were bitter. '*Le jardin du physique*,' he said, in French.

Orlandu nodded, for his French was fair.

Omar lapsed back into Maltese. 'The house of the Italians. Yes!'

At the rear of one of the Italian auberges was a walled physic garden, where Father Lazaro, Master of the Sacred Infirmary, cultivated shrubs and herbs with medicinal powers. As well as being the greatest warriors in the world, the Hospitallers were also the greatest physicians. But what did the old man mean? Omar pointed down the alley; but there was no sign of the greyhound.

'*Dans le jardin!* The white djinn! Yes!'

Omar threw back his head and howled at the sky.

* * *

ORLANDU HAD NOTHING to lose, and madmen often know things that right men do not. He headed through the panic-stricken town towards the physic garden. The North African sun was as pitiless as despair and he was grateful for the shade of the narrow streets. In those that were neither cobbled nor flagged, where the common folk lived, dust raised by the tumult flew up in clouds and clung to his hair, coated his tongue and powdered his rags. Every yard teemed with refugees seeking shelter for their families and their goats. Orlandu considered their fright with scorn, but they were peasants, naturally timid and unused to war, and it was to be expected. The knights would protect them, the knights and the other fighting men – the *soldados particular*, the Spanish *tercios*, the Maltese militia, the dog killers like himself. He set an example by walking tall and without fear. He pressed on towards the auberge.

Each langue of the Religion had its own auberges. The younger knights and all the serjeants at arms slept in austere dormitories. The commanders and senior knights had their own homes bought with the *spoglia*, the prize money yielded by their pirate caravans. The Italians, the largest and richest langue, had several buildings, including their own hospital, on the foreshore of Galley Creek. The wall of the garden of Father Lazaro's auberge was six feet high. At the rear was a wrought-iron gate.

Orlandu peered through the gate. Sure enough, the white greyhound stood in the lee of the far wall, nibbling the slender leaves of a dark green shrub as if to salve its wounds. Orlandu's compulsion to his duty lay in his belly like a heavy rock. He could not shirk it. In entering the garden he knew he risked a flogging, or even a spell in the dungeons of Saint Anthony, yet if he asked permission he would surely be denied. It was as if the dog had sought this sanctuary for that very reason. He raised the latch and opened the gate and the hound turned and looked at him, ears cocked forward, its graceful figure perfectly still.

Orlandu closed the gate behind him.

He walked along the path between the plants. As he approached closer he saw the hound's eyes for the first time. They were large and moist and black as Oil of Peter. They were filled with inexpressible sadness. They pierced him to the core. At the last moment the hound fell on to its side and splayed its legs in the air towards him, as if hoping its belly would be tickled and that this invitation to play would spare its life. With a shock Orlandu saw that the dog, as he'd assumed it to be, was in fact a bitch.

Orlandu squatted on his haunches and the bitch sprang up and pressed her tapered skull and long white neck into his chest, her pink tongue extended as she panted in the heat. Orlandu put an arm around her shoulders. She was all bone and lungs and muscle, but her fur was as sleek as velvet and he felt her beating heart throb against his hand. The knife in his fist trembled. It would be no great sin to steal back out the gate and leave her here in the shade.

'God will forgive you.'

Orlandu went down on one knee and turned and in so doing he clasped the greyhound closer still. At a door in the rear of the auberge stood a monk. His hair had receded to a grey fringe around his scalp. His voice was kind and his eyes were as sad as the hound's. Orlandu recognised Father Lazaro, for Lazaro had nursed him through a childhood fever of the chest many years before. Few of the knights deigned to learn Maltese at all, for it was the language of 'the little people', but because the peasants and townsfolk were his most frequent charges, Father Lazaro was fluent. He was not a knight of the Order, but a chaplain. He walked towards Orlandu.

'You would also earn my gratitude,' he said. 'To my shame, this chore proved more painful than my courage allowed.'

'She's yours, Father?' blurted Orlandu.

'I inherited her, because she showed no great love for the kill. Last night I sent her away so that someone else – someone like you – would bear the burden of her fate. For that I must beg your forgiveness.'

Orlandu bowed his head. His heart now beat as rapidly as the hound's. He became aware of his filth-caked feet, his tattered shirt and breeches, the shredded and stinking sheepskin bound to his arm, and all the evidence that he, unlike this gentle and holy monk, was a seasoned murderer.

He said, 'Father, if you please –' His throat was dry and he swallowed. 'Please would you hear my confession, afterwards?'

Lazaro stopped beside him and put a hand on his head. The touch caused a healing comfort to seep through his body. 'You must not do this against the voice of your conscience,' said Lazaro, 'for that would be to disobey God, and it's better you disobey our Grand Master.'

'What's her name, Father?'

Lazaro removed his hand and in so doing he seemed, to Orlandu, to seal the greyhound's doom. Lazaro said, 'It's best you don't know.'

'Why?'

'Because, man or animal, it's easier to destroy a victim that has no name.'

'Please, Father, but whether I know her name or nor, it will not be easy. I'd like to be able to remember her in my prayers.'

'I call her Persephone.'

Orlandu didn't understand, but he spoke the name. 'Persephone.'

Lazaro watched the hound lick Orlandu's throat.

He said, 'It seems that she will forgive you too.'

Orlandu gritted his teeth and put the point of his knife to Persephone's chest.

In emulation of the knights, he whispered, 'For Christ and the Baptist.'

He drove the knife home until his fist hit the prominent breastbone. Persephone let out a scream that was almost human and squirmed with alarming power beneath his arm. Orlandu squeezed tighter and half-withdrew the blade and canted the angle and drove it home again. He felt something clench and then burst around its point and in an instant all her strength melted into nothingness and the long white neck fell across his lap.

Orlandu pulled the blade free and beads of crimson spilled down the snow-white fur. He wanted to drop the knife, but couldn't litter the garden with such trash. Without wiping it, he slid it through the back of his rope belt. He began to take the carcass in both arms, to carry it away to the gut cart and thence to be burned, but Lazaro put a hand on his shoulder.

'I'll do the rest. Leave her here.'

Orlandu laid the carcass on the earth beneath the shrub. He made the sign of the Cross.

'Father, do dogs have souls?'

Lazaro smiled. 'It's no sin to hope that they do. And since you and I must take good care of our own souls, we will go to Father Guillaume to confess together.'

Although Lazaro was not a Knight of Justice, and had never, therefore, reckoned at all in the ranks of his military heroes, Orlandu was overwhelmed by this honour. He bowed, once again ashamed of his lowborn appearance.

'But first,' said Lazaro, 'you must let me dress those wounds before they putrefy.'

Lazaro walked back towards the auberge. Orlandu hesitated to follow, unable to believe he was meant to go inside. Lazaro turned and beckoned him and Orlandu followed. The room beyond the threshold was cool and dark and smelled of pungent scents intermingled together. Lazaro scrubbed Orlandu's bites with brine and painted them with unguents and Orlandu bit his cheeks and made not a sound.

When he'd finished, Lazaro said, 'You have seen the ships?'

'The ships?'

'The fleet of the Grande Turke.'

Orlandu remembered the cannon shots at dawn, the consternation in the streets, but so bedevilled had he been by catching the hound that he'd forgotten the cause of the alarm. He shook his head. 'No, Father, but I would like to.'

Lazaro led Orlandu up a stair to the auberge roof. From here Orlandu could see across the sandstone houses and Kalkara Bay to the gibbets on Gallows Point and the open sea beyond. The bright blue waters of the offing were obscured by a strange, multi-coloured carpet, which quavered like an apparition in the heat. It was enormous, its farthermost edge fringing the horizon and its eastern margin obscured by Monte San Salvatore.

As Orlandu squinted, he realised that the immense carpet was composed of warships. The sun sparkled from gilded prows and silver plaques, and the colours were of brilliant silk awnings and extravagant banners and billowed sail, and in a silence ominous and huge massive banks of oars rose and fell like the beating of wings. The ships were moving south. And there were hundreds of them. Hundreds? Orlandu rubbed his eyes and looked again. The Navy of the Religion boasted seven galleys, and Orlandu had believed it the mightiest in the world.

He sensed Lazaro watching him and on an impulse encouraged by the old monk's patience, he said, 'Father, is this a world of dreams?'

Lazaro considered him, and his rheumy eyes assumed a melancholy sheen.

He said, 'When we enter the Kingdom of Heaven, perhaps it will seem so.'

MONDAY 21 MAY 1565

The Auberge of England

Majistral Street was empty.

The whole of the tiny city seemed to hold its breath.

Every fighting man was on the great enceinte. The womenfolk sheltered indoors from the deadening heat and whispered prayers to their icons and saints. The foreboding crept like mist into the Auberge of England and heightened Carla's frustration. Idleness galled her yet there was no pressing work to keep her occupied. Oliver Starkey's assumptions had been proved correct: she was a useless mouth. She joined Amparo in the parched and scrubby garden. Mattias arrived at noon. He wore a fluted cuirass, a pistol and a sword and carried in his left hand a wheel-lock rifle. Wedged beneath the same arm was a morion helmet.

'The Turk stands at the gate,' he said. 'The Maltese Iliad begins. I thought you might wish me luck before I join them.'

Since Carla's return, the Borgo had boiled with excitation. Despair competed with jubilation. Emotions were tossed on the tides of rumour that flowed at every street corner. The Turks were heading south, then heading north. The Turks, having seen their defences, would flee back to the Golden Horn. The Turks had already landed at Marsamxett. The Turks would conquer the island within a week. Spies were reputedly abroad. And saboteurs. And assassins sent to murder the Grand Master in his bed. Guards were mounted on the sandstone plugs that sealed the underground granaries and cisterns of water. The giant two-hundred-yard chain that barred the mouth of Galley Creek was cranked up from the sea floor by its capstan. Turkish galleys prowled the open sea. The Borgo, L'Isola and Saint Elmo's were now cut off from the rest of the Christian world.

Amid such turmoil, Carla's own concerns were small indeed, yet this was the land of her birth – and in which she'd given birth – and she was elated to return. Of all the townsfolk it was the boys, whose numbers seemed unlimited, who exhibited the greatest exhilaration. They never walked while they could run. They fell silent only when a knight passed by. They mimed combat in the streets, stoked by dreams of heroic sacrifice in which their own deaths featured as the most heroic of all. Half of them were barefoot and many carried small weapons – knives, carpenter's axes, hammers, staves – that seemed quite futile to the task. Their faces were bronzed and bright with lean, hard life. Yet while all of them moved her, none of them provoked any instinct to suggest he might be her son.

The knights were solemn and undaunted for they were God's martyrs. Armoured monks strode past Carla on the street as though she had no more significance than a butterfly, each occupied by thoughts of duty and his place among the Saints. The Maltese menfolk had a grimmer view. Compared to the knights they were poorly armed and armoured. Being ten times more numerous they had no doubt that they would die in much greater numbers. Those with wives and children reassured them, then headed for their posts. These men fought for much more than God. Their women bore the greatest weight of all. They eased the fears of their men and kept their own to themselves. They stored food and exchanged remedies for wounds. They readied their hearts for the death and mutilation of their loved ones. Love was the fragile and hidden counterweight to overwhelming fear.

Carla found herself stranded. Her request to work in the hospital had been denied; so had her application to work in the commissary. The latter service in particular she felt well equipped to improve, but the fact that in the Aquitaine she managed a farm, a vineyard, a wine press and two score tenants counted for nothing. She feared she'd be given no role beyond that which the knights had imagined: that of a vain and feeble woman to be fed and protected. Oliver Starkey had donated his own small house in Majistral Street for her use. The house was austere and masculine, with an overabundance of books. Her chamber contained a single hard bed and a writing desk. Amparo was provided with a cot in the adjoining room. The house communicated with the Auberge of England next door. Since the latter had been vacant for years, Mattias and Bors had seized possession.

She'd seen little of Mattias since their arrival. On the voyage from Messina he'd spent hours in conversation with Starkey and Giovanni Castrucco, and by the time they'd disembarked he'd known more about the military situation, the Order's disposition of its forces, its supplies and morale, its communications with Mdina and Garcia de Toledo, than all but a handful of knights themselves. On arrival La Valette had engaged him in a tour of the enceinte and the likely Turkish positions, and Mattias had returned that evening with two stout youths who carried between them a crate of beeswax candles, a firkin of wine and four roasted chickens.

THEY ATE IN the auberge refectory. Mattias brought news that the Turks had anchored to the north, in Ghain Tuffieha Bay, which Carla knew well. There was alarm that the Turks would attack Mdina, but he believed it a feint and had advised La Valette not to be drawn out. His knowledge of the Turk was encyclopaedic, and she sensed his pride in their valour and sophistication and a wistful affection for their ways. Despite his reluctance to become embroiled in war, the titanic drama now unfolding had clearly captured his fancy.

'I've been roped into certain obligations,' he said. 'I'll be busy until the Turks have disembarked and their intentions are better known, but once I've proved my loyalty I'll be free to do as I please, for on such freedom my worth to La Valette will depend.'

This was too opaque for Carla, but Bors knew him better.

'You'll go out among the heathen?' said Bors.

'With the right gear, which is easily acquired, I can pass as one of them more easily than I pass among you Franks.'

'And if you're caught?' said Carla.

'In the meanwhile,' said Mattias, ignoring this query, 'I leave it to you to investigate the records of the church of the Annunciation, the Sacred Hospital and the *camerata*.'

'What should I tell them?'

Mattias said, 'You tell them that you seek the boy's identity because he is to assume an unexpected legacy.' He glanced at her mouth, a habit he'd begun to indulge with increasing frequency. 'A legacy of some value. You are acting on behalf of the boy's benefactor, whose trust you enjoy, and whose privacy you're obliged to protect.' He spread his hands, as if nothing could be simpler. 'Thus you tell not a single lie while giving no hostages to fortune. No one would be so churlish as to question a woman of your noble piety and poise.'

His lucent blue eyes flickered, as if against his will, to her throat and her cleavage. She knew that he desired her carnally and in his mind had his hands on her body. With liquid intensity, Carla desired him too. The fact that she'd seen him cast lascivious glances at Amparo only served to increase her longing. Mattias rose from the table and beckoned Bors.

'We're to the bastions, to take the measure of the mercenaries and militia. Men reveal certain thoughts in darkness that they keep to themselves in the light.'

With that he left her to wonder what his hands might have felt like.

ON SATURDAY HE stopped by on his return from a reconnaissance with the news that an advance guard of three thousand Turks, including a division of janissaries, had landed at Marsaxlokk Bay, five miles to the south. They'd sacked the village of Zeitun and outflanked the Christian patrol, which had only escaped with the bitter loss of several knights dead and captured. One of those taken by the Turk was Adrien de la Riviere, for whom Carla had provided shelter some months before. When she asked as to his fate, Mattias told her he'd be tortured by experts in the craft, and then put to the bowstring. That night Carla slept poorly. La Riviere had seemed indestructible in youth and gallantry. She wondered what she'd done in bringing her companions to a world so perilous and cruel.

ON SUNDAY SHE saw Mattias not at all.

By that evening the Turkish Commander in Chief, Mustafa Pasha, and the bulk of his vast army, had disembarked at Marsaxlokk Bay. They were setting up camp in the flatlands of the Marsa, to the west of Grand Harbour. Carla learned from Bors that there'd been fierce debate as to the wisdom of letting the Turks land unopposed, but La Valette's view, supported by Mattias, had won the day. The Christians lacked the numbers to chance open battle on the beach. Better to let the Turks splash against the walls. As darkness fell, the watchfires of the vanguard of janissaries could be seen in the hamlet of Zabbar, only one mile distant across the undulating ochre hills beyond the walls.

THROUGH THESE DAYS Amparo said little, taking in the maelstrom of activity through watchful eyes and making of it things that only she knew. She'd set herself to revive the small garden at the rear of the house, squandering water on the struggling blooms with the justification that if all the humans were to die, as she'd heard with tedious frequency that they would, then the least they could do was leave something of beauty as their monument. Her vision stone showed nothing in these first three evenings of their residence, as if a curtain had been drawn across its window into other worlds, and Carla was not sorry, as such prognostications could only have been cheerless. They'd played no music together, as it seemed ill-fitted to the general mood of gloom. Their instruments lay in Carla's room, untouched.

On Monday, when Mattias came to visit on his way to the opening of hostilities, Carla and Amparo were pulling weeds on their knees in the neglected garden. Carla turned to find him smiling, as if a sight so preposterous were a tonic.

'I'm glad to see you approach our dire estate with such aplomb,' he said.

Carla dusted fine dry dirt from her hands and walked towards him. Her heart raced at the sight of his face and the sound of his voice and she wondered how evident this was.

'We'd like to make ourselves more useful,' she said, 'but there's little we're allowed to do. Father Lazaro told us that the infirmary is yet another male domain. We are, of course, barred from approaching the walls.'

'When the infirmary overflows into the streets, Lazaro will change his tune.'

That he seemed so cheerily certain such horror would come undermined her gladness.

'Have you turned up any sign of our boy?' he asked.

His use of 'our' boy touched her. She shook her head. 'There's no one with his birth date, or close to it, known to the *camerata*. In the Church of the Annunciation, the closest recorded births are a week to either side. Both were girls. The monks at the infirmary were too busy to answer to my enquiry.'

'There'll be time, though the sooner we fly this coop the better.'

They were standing close and for a moment neither spoke. His brawny bulk stirred her and she felt herself stiffen with anxiety. The impulse to retreat was at odds with the urge of her heart, but it was the stronger of the two. From the distance came a concert of martial harmonies: drums and horns and pipes of a foreign character that wavered with a poignant heroism, and for the first time something human attached itself to Carla's idea of the Turk. Mattias heard the music too and cocked his head. She felt again the stab of remorse at having lured him into a conflict he'd sought to avoid.

'Forgive me,' she said.

'For what?' he replied.

'I've brought Death into your sphere.'

'He's one of my oldest acquaintances. Dwell on it no further.'

He bent his face towards hers and she realised he intended to kiss her on the mouth. Before she could conquer it, instinct made her pull her head back. She regretted it at once, but it was done. She hadn't kissed a man in half a lifetime, but she could hardly explain that now and ask that he try again. Mattias blinked and turned away, untroubled it seemed, and it was as if the moment had existed only in her mind. He called to Amparo in Spanish.

'Amparo, what news from your vision glass?'

Amparo watched from a distance. At being included against her expectations, she brightened and skipped over. She seemed more at ease with Mattias than with any other person Carla had known, including, she felt with a pang, herself.

'The glass is dark,' she said, 'ever since we boarded the ship.'

'So the angels have abandoned us,' he said, with a carefree smile. 'With all these thousands calling on their aid, it's no surprise.'

Amparo appeared crestfallen by her failure. Mattias rallied her.

'I've a favour to ask, if I may,' he said. 'There'll be a deal of noise and shooting throughout this day. Buraq is not trained to war, and he has a sensitive soul. If you could pass an hour or two in his company, I'd be in your debt.'

Amparo swelled with the honour. Her eyes shone with adoration. Carla's fondness for Mattias increased in equal measure and she regretted again avoiding the swoop of his mouth.

'Oh, gladly,' said Amparo. 'Buraq has the noblest of souls.'

'All horses are nobler than just about every man, but Buraq is a prince without equal,' Mattias agreed. 'You'll find him at the stables of the Grand Master, by Castel Sant' Angelo.'

Amparo threw her arms round him and kissed him full on the lips. Carla felt her cheeks turn hot as Mattias slid his arm around her waist and held her close, and then closer still, and Carla had to turn away. Then he let her go and Amparo stepped back, her own colour rising.

'I've never gone into battle with a kiss on my lips,' he said. 'It sets a most admirable precedent.'

Carla suppressed her chagrin. She didn't know where to look.

'Two might serve even better,' said Mattias.

Carla looked at him and he grinned. Her cheeks burned more fiercely still, and some perverse fit of temper almost made her refuse. Her mind was tangled with emotions she couldn't fathom. She willed herself to lift her face and Mattias bent and kissed her on the mouth, not with the violence she expected and which she more than a little desired, but with a tenderness that stole her senses. The moment of contact stretched into forever and she clenched her eyes as tears welled up from nowhere, for his kiss seemed to plumb the abyss into which her womanhood had been cast so long ago. And no sooner had his mouth covered hers than he pulled away. She was left having sipped at a pleasure too intense to be compassed. She turned away to master her emotions.

'I shall now be safe from all harm,' he said.

Carla spun back towards him. 'Please,' she said, 'promise me you'll take every care.'

'Audacity is a virtue of youth,' he said, 'and I've left both far behind.'

They accompanied him through the auberge and paused on the threshold to Majistral Street. Two dour serjeants of the Order were passing by, and between them they dragged a strange and ancient man with eyes of uncommon brightness and a toothless crescent-moon face. His hands were tied fast behind him and, as Carla wondered at his crime, she saw a dark expression cross Mattias's face.

'The earth calls that old man,' he said. The expression was unfamiliar to Carla, but Mattias didn't elaborate. He said, 'I'd best be to the walls.'

'I'll pray for you,' said Carla. 'Even though you do not fear God.'

'I welcome all prayers on my behalf, no matter which god hears them.'

He gave them both a final glance, saluted and set off down the street. Beyond him she glimpsed the old man, his gait hopping and frantic between the relentless stride of his guards. The ancient threw back his head and emitted a mournful, yapping howl and Carla suddenly realised that in all she'd witnessed since arriving there'd been neither sight nor sound of a dog. How strange, she thought. A serjeant cuffed the ancient with a fist and the three of them disappeared around the corner.

Mattias followed them, and though she willed him to do so, he didn't look back.

She turned on the step and found Amparo as doleful as she. Carla took her in her arms and they held each other tight. She felt Amparo's heart beat and its quickness matched her own. Fear for Mattias clenched her stomach; that and perhaps something more. Perhaps she was falling in love. She looked at Amparo and wondered if the girl felt the same. Her instinct said that she did.

More than instinct: it was written on Amparo's damaged face. If so it was, Carla told herself, then it must be God's Will and God had His reasons. She set herself to embrace whatever He ordained. Some wisdom so profound that it could only have come from Christ rose up within her. In the days that were to come, there could be no surfeit of Love, whatever its nature. Without Love they would be nothing. Worse than that, they would be damned.

MONDAY 21 MAY 1565

Bastion of Castile – Bastion of Italy – Bastion of Provence

Orlandu gazed from the high stone battlements – for hours – as a vortex of red dust bloomed above the horizon to the south and the legions of the Sultan Suleiman emerged from its coils. The Moslem horde drew up in immaculate order until they covered the ochre hills beyond the Grande Terre Plein and so glorious and brave was the spectacle that some of the knights there watching wept without shame.

Orlandu, in recognition of wounds sustained in the slaughter of the dogs, had won a coveted place on the Bastion of Castile, which jutted forth from the left of the enceinte at the base of Kalkara Bay. The outer bulwark was lined with *arquebuceros* and the acrid smoke of their match cords stung his eyes. Most of them were Castilians from the *tercios* of Sicily and Naples. Their corselets and gear varied, for each man managed for himself. Their uniform, such as it was, was a small red Burgundy cross patched on to their jerkins. They were grouped in bands of six, and called themselves *las camaradas*. Behind them stood the Maltese infantry with their half-pikes. They were dressed in homemade leather armour and simple casques. Interspersed among the foremost ranks, the Spanish and Portuguese knights sounded the only note of grandeur, their shining armour covered by their crimson war coats, each breast emblazoned with the plain white cross of Crusaders. Orlandu squatted on the lid of a water butt, at the rear of these lines, and from this vantage took stock of the enemy deployment. The contrast in brilliance between the opposing armies stunned his senses.

The Grande Terre Plein was an apron of flat land, a thousand feet across, which unrolled from the ditch outside the city walls to the heights of Santa Margharita. Upon these heights the horde was now assembled. The Turks were caparisoned in more splendour than Orlandu knew existed, a dazzling array of vivid greens and blues, of radiant yellows and fierce reds, of gleaming musketry and pole arms and damascened blades, of massed white turbans and high bonnets, of fluttering pennants and gigantic standards garnished with scorpions and elephants and herons and hawks, and with crescent moons and the Star of David, and with twin-bladed swords and exotic calligraphs wondrous to behold. Even the mounts of the cavalry, drawn up in two huge squares on either flank of the summit, were chanfroned in gold and armoured with polished bronze. And all this pageant was iridescent with shimmering silks and sparkled like the surface of the sea as the sun winked from a fortune in gilded ornament and jewels, as if this mighty host had journeyed to this distant field not to fight a battle, but to mount a festival of wild and exorbitant splendour.

Orlandu suddenly wondered why indeed they were all here, and what had brought them so far, and why God had blessed him by placing him here to see it, and his chest filled with an excitement so intense he could hardly breathe. If the Sultan's extravagant multitude appeared inexorable, then the immense city walls toothed by the Religion appeared impregnable, and so absolute was this contradiction that Orlandu thought that these two foes must reach some cordial agreement and go their ways. For a moment he felt fear: that all this might indeed melt away, like an unforgettable dream that ended unfinished. He didn't want the horde to turn back. A cataclysm such as this now poised before him was given to few to witness from one end of Time to the other. The faces of the knights told him so. The stones beneath his bare feet told him so. Something rooted in his gut and bone told him so. And because everyone there present beneath that burning azure sky knew that this was so too, Orlandu realised that the cataclysm was already here, and that it stood unhindered by all jurisdictions and controls, and that nothing in Heaven or on Earth could stop it now.

He turned at a sudden disturbance. Two serjeants at arms manhandled a manacled figure along the allure. The prisoner had a strange, bobbing gait and as Orlandu gained a clearer view through the staves of the pikes, he saw that it was Omar, the old *karagozi*. His mouth was jammed with a knot from a ship's rope. As Omar was dragged along the wall walk to the Bastion of Italy, Orlandu lost sight of him. Then he looked beyond and saw that canted over the ditch, on the wall's foremost prominence above the Provençal Gate, a gallows had been erected. From the gallows swung a noose, etched as black as ink against the turquoise sky.

When Omar reappeared it was beneath the gallows. They stripped him naked of his rags and his bones poked like deformities through the shrivelled mantle of his skin. Orlandu watched as they pushed the *karagozi* to the wall's sheer edge and looped the noose around his neck. Omar was too old and crazy to be a spy. And he never strayed far from his barrel. Orlandu looked out at the heathen massed on the hills. Their every eye seemed fixed on the bow-legged ancient, who stooped and jiggled and drooled beneath the longarm. And Orlandu understood.

The Religion were hanging Omar because he was Moslem.

And it was true, thought Orlandu.

The old *karagozi* was a Moslem.

And his world of dreams was over.

Somehow Orlandu knew that so too was his own.

* * *

TANNHAUSER HAD BEEN honoured with a station on the Bastion of Provence. La Valette himself was but a few yards distant on the allure and with him stood his young page, Andreas, and the great Colonel Le Mas, and a clutch of other stern grandees. Tannhauser had never encountered a society so concerned with rank and purity of blood. In the empire of the Ottomans a slave could become a general or a vizier, if such was his quality. Admiral Piyale, whose ships even now surrounded Malta, was a Serbian foundling from Belgrade. Yet if it had to be said that for the mass of Frankish nobles knighthood had become a charade, the elite of the Religion were as busty a fraternity of killers as ever Tannhauser had seen. They were twelfth-century barbarians with modern arms. And without doubt they were spoiling for a fight.

As the army to which he'd devoted a third of his life spread across the heights, turbulent waves of memory rolled through his heart. The soldiers of God's Shadow On This Earth had never looked more beautiful. No other word would do. They were also terrifying, in a way he'd never been privy to before. The flawless precision with which forty thousand troops arrayed themselves across the hills was alone enough to loosen a man's entrails. The quality of their weapons was outstanding, as was, too, the quality of the men. To have transplanted all this wholesale – to a scorched rock halfway round the world – was a marvel of raw power.

He saw the Topchu artillery crews drag colossal serpent-mouthed culverins into place. He saw the Sipahis and Iayalars, and the yellow banners of the Sari Bayrak and the crimson of the Kirmizi Bayrak, and between these latter cavalry corps he saw the silk pavilion of Mustafa Pasha as it suddenly arose, shining like an orb of gold on the rugged skyline. Above Mustafa's pavilion the *Sanjak i-sherif* was unfurled, the black war banner of the Prophet, inscribed with the *Shahada. There is no God but Allah and Mohammed is His Messenger*. Mustafa's blood ancestor had carried that same banner into battle for the Prophet himself. This fact too filled Tannhauser with awe, for the ghost of the Prophet hovered atop that hill; and Mustafa and his legions knew it, for they felt his sacred hand on every shoulder.

Tannhauser saw pennants identifying regiments he'd once known for their deeds and temper, and alongside whom he'd fought in the wastelands around Lake Van. But among the *orta* of janissaries he didn't see the standard of his own – the Sacred Wheel of the Fourth Agha Boluks. The janissaries were as close to a notion of country as Tannhauser had ever known. His feelings for their hearthstone, his loyalty, his love, had been as profound as La Valette's for his Holy Religion. In abandoning their ranks so many years ago, he'd abandoned part of his soul; yet had he not done so, he'd have lost his soul entire, for such would have been the price of the dark deed required of him. Despite that their pipes and tambours still stirred his blood, and his heart, he now faced his former brothers on the field of battle. He waited with a pounding in his chest and a tightness in his throat for a sound he'd never heard but had only voiced.

The mighty Lions of Islam were about to roar.

When each of the great squares of troops, mounted and afoot, had finally taken its position in the order of battle, the haunting ululations of the marshalling horns and the rousing melodies of the *mehterhane* band abruptly ceased, and the great wheeling movements stilled, and a vast and unearthly silence fell across the field. A silence and a stillness such as that which must have reigned over the first dawn of Creation. Amid that stunned tranquillity tens of thousands of souls, Christian and Moslem, considered each other across the gulf for which they would sacrifice their lives, and the merged beat of their hearts was all that sent a ripple through the silence or the stillness, either one. A strip of dirt and a pile of stones lay between them. This dirt and these stones they would contest as a proxy for eternity.

It was a moment in which Tannhauser understood, and he was not alone, that whatever any man might accomplish on this field, this battle was just another marker on a grave-strewn road. A road stretching back seven centuries before any man here was born and which would carve its bloody furrow for centuries uncounted yet to come.

Tannhauser might have wished himself elsewhere, but he was here, and could be nowhere else, for this was his fate. The straight and the winding road at last were one. And he realised – for the first time since a cold spring morning in the glow of a mountain forge – that the Moslems were the enemies of his blood. He was a Saxon. A man of the north. Now, as he confronted the implacable men of the east, he felt his origins flow through his deepest marrow.

Bors, whose presence on the Post of Honour had also been contrived, turned from the Grande Turke's display and inhaled, as if of a toothsome aroma, and looked at Tannhauser.

'Can you smell it?' whispered Bors.

Tannhauser watched his grey English eyes as they creased up in a smile.

'Glory,' said Bors.

Tannhauser didn't reply. Glory was more potent than opium. He feared its grip.

Bors looked along the fortress walls, then at the vast and shining panoply on the heights. 'Can it be possible?' he said, with awe. 'That most of these men are to die?'

Tannhauser looked at them too. Again, he gave no answer, for there was no need.

With their jewel-encrusted display the Grande Turke had struck the first blow against the morale of the defenders. The Religion now struck back. La Valette gestured to Andreas and the page bowed and strode to the bulwark, where he delivered the Grand Master's order to a brother knight. The knight raised and lowered a sword that winked in the sun.

Tannhauser turned.

Beneath the gallows above the Provençal Gate stood the naked and trembling figure of the old puppeteer, whom Tannhauser had found himself following, step for step, from Majistral Street. A serjeant at arms stepped up and with the butt of a spear he struck the puppeteer between the shoulders. What dignity the ancient had clung on to was robbed and his legs buckled under him like weeds, and he befouled himself, and with his dying cry muffled by the knot crammed hard betwixt his gums, the old man toppled into space. The drop seemed long. Then the rope cracked like a gunshot over the plain and both armies watched the *karagozi* as he jerked and danced like a puppet in his own theatre, sixty feet above the floor of the ditch below.

La Valette had decreed that a Moslem be hanged for every single day the siege continued. Tannhauser thought this a brilliant ploy, not just because its ugliness was the perfect rebuff to the splendour of the Turk, but because it declared to both armies that this conflict's end would only be marked by the extinction of one or the other. As regards the defenders, the choice of the old *karagozi* as inaugural victim was also inspired. The old puppeteer was known to every islander and, indeed, was held in a certain communal affection. For most, he was the only human face that Islam had. Now he squirmed beneath the gallows' arm with the contents of bowels and bladder dripping from his gnarled toes. With this single stroke La Valette had made the whole population accomplice to a cruel and iniquitous murder. He'd rendered every heart there stony. He'd bound them together as monsters in the eyes of their foe. If this fight was to be fought at a savage and amoral extreme, every man on the Christian walls now knew it.

At the end of the rope, the old man's spasms ceased, and he rotated lifeless and obscene above the Grande Terre Plein.

Colonel Le Mas raised his sword and threw his voice across the flatlands in a roar.

'For Christ and the Baptist!'

As Le Mas's voice faded, the Christians crowding the ramparts took up the cry. It rolled outwards to left and right and from one crowded bastion to the next in a crescendo of fury, and it spilled across Galley Creek and along the walls of Fortress Saint Michel, and on its way the pledge was garnished by the taunts and obscenities of the soldiery. The battle cry found its echo across the waters of Grand Harbour on the ramparts of distant Saint Elmo's. Then it was gone.

The Turkish horns wailed again and the culverins on the heights bucked like dragons in chains and flame spouted from their mouths and *guerre à outrance* was commenced.

A score of stone cannonballs arced visibly towards the Borgo. As the missiles punched great divots in the walls of Castile and set the masonry atremble beneath their feet, a regiment of Tüfekchi janissaries charged down the hills and across the plain. Tannhauser watched as they fanned into triple firing ranks – the perfection of their geometry astounding – and their long-barrelled pieces rippled with light as the muzzles swung down to the aim. The muskets issued a volley and the marksmen vanished behind a bank of smoke. They seemed to many to be out of range, but Tannhauser knew better. He ducked behind a bulwark and the hum of the balls was lost in the loud, bright bangs of those that struck the armour of the knights. La Valette's young page was shot in the throat and Tannhauser watched him fall at his master's feet. La Valette flinched not at all and motioned for the bearers to remove him.

Tannhauser straightened up and laid his rifle across the wall.

His armour and helmet were stifling and there was no shade. He mopped his brow with the scarf he kept tucked in his sleeve. The smoke unrolling on the plain thinned out and he watched the front-rank janissaries reload their guns. Beneath their tall white bonnets their faces were blurs. He braced the Spanish butt against his shoulder and took aim at a man in the centre of the line. He made a reckoning for the drop and squeezed the trigger. The wheel sang against the pyrites and the rifle thundered. He'd neglected to bring wax for his ears. He peered above the plume of the discharge. His victim lay without moving in the dust. A comrade stepped on his corpse to take his place. And that was that. Tannhauser, once again, was at war. He felt a hand clap him on the shoulder.

'God's bread!' said Bors. 'I'd say you could lay claim to the first kill.'

'No,' said Tannhauser. 'That prize belongs to the hangman.'

Christian arquebuses exploded down the length of the enceinte but they couldn't match the Turkish nine-palm muskets. On the plain a sheet of red dust was kicked up as every shot fell short. The provost marshals screamed at their men to hold their fire and before the dirt could settle a fresh wave of *gazi* came howling through the haze and unleashed a second volley of their own. From the Bastions of Italy and Castile the Religion's cannon belched flame into the thickening fog and the gun teams fell on the recoiling beasts to drag them back into place and swab the bores. The big brass cannonballs bounced from the clay as if Satan himself had cast them and clove screaming tunnels of gore through the Ottoman ranks. A cheer went up from the battlements and musket fire sang from the stones and a battalion of enraged knights invested the Provençal Gate and hollered that it be opened that their blood lust might be appeased.

Tannhauser turned from this theatre of the crazed and found Bors grinning.

'That brass is likely our munitions,' said Bors.

Tannhauser grounded his rifle butt and measured a charge of powder down the barrel. Glory? No. Not yet. Not at this distance. And he hoped not to get any closer. At least the better part of him so hoped. Like killing priests, killing former comrades was much like killing anyone else. If he felt anything at all it was a dark shade of joy and the thrill of that power which was once the jealous preserve of vicious gods: to strike a man's life from existence by a single bolt of thunder. Through the taste of the gunsmoke the kisses of Amparo and Carla yet lingered on his lips. What a splendid pair they were. And what a splendid life this was.

Tannhauser resolved to be cheerful.

He turned to Bors as Bors squinted down the length of his wall gun.

'Did you bring any wax?' said Tannhauser.

Bors jabbed a finger at his ear to indicate that it was plugged. 'Did I bring any what?'

MONDAY 21 MAY 1565

The Heights of Santa Margharita – the Grande Terre Plein

According to Allah's Will, they'd been fighting hand-to-hand for six hours. In the rays of the westering sun the exhausted belligerents cast elongate shadows that danced on the blood-slaked plain, as if not merely men but their ghosts were possessed by a delirium. And yet this was only an overture to a drama yet unconceived.

Abbas bin Murad, *aga* of the Sari Bayrak, sat on his coal-black Arab at the head of his brigade and could not but note that among the hundreds of corpses strewn like laundry across the field, the ratio of the Faithful to the Infidel looked not less than ten to one. This in itself could be accepted. There was no greater joy than to die for Allah and in the service of Suleiman Shah, the Refuge of All the People in the World. But the spies who'd assured Mustafa that Malta could be taken in two weeks would forfeit their lives. Abbas hadn't fought the Franks since the wars in Hungary decades before. At the Drava they'd slaughtered Ferdinand's Austrians wholesale and sent their commanders' heads to Constantinople in clay jars. And when, in '38, Ferdinand had been rash enough to retake possession of Buda, the Sultan's campaign along the Danube had been a promenade. But these Knights of John the Baptist – these Children of Satan – were of a different mettle altogether.

The two knights, French and Portuguese, taken prisoner outside Zeitun, on Saturday, had been tortured for thirty hours by Mustafa's most experienced interrogators, and neither had uttered a word beyond prayers to their god. When, finally, they'd broken, each knight – independently and in absolute ignorance of the other – had sworn that the weakest spot in the Christian defence was the Bastion of Castile. In fact, as this afternoon's assault had made brutally clear, Castile was the strongest point on the whole enceinte.

Abbas glanced at the ancient slave, still scorching on the gibbet above the plain like a manikin in some demoniac invocation. The execution was a barbarous insult, which Abbas had taken for bravado at the time. But when the gates of the fortress swung open and a throng of knights clanked forth to wade with sword and mace among the janissaries, this illusion had been banished. The Hounds of Hell had attacked with such rabid savagery that it seemed the janissaries would have no choice but to retreat. They did not do so, despite the cost, for the Tüfekchi would have rather died to the last man. Honour had been satisfied and a murderous standoff obtained. The knights were confined to a square of steel around their drawbridge. The long day waned and Abbas sat and watched the anarchic morass of dust and gunsmoke and arms, the flash of muskets and blades, the lamentations of the maimed and disembowelled. The hard, baked clay of the plain had become a moist red mud of blood and urine and soil, and slithering in the filth of this opening sally, each side had taken some measure of its foe.

Abbas, still waiting for his orders to join the fray, turned to look at his men. As expected he found them undaunted and eager for action. But the sun had clipped the edge of the mountain to the west – Monte Sciberras, he believed – and if they didn't go in soon, they wouldn't be blooded at all, at least today. His aide-de-camp pointed and Abbas wheeled his mount. From Mustafa Pasha's golden pavilion on the hill, a messenger hurtled down the slope.

Mustafa was an Isfendiyaroglu. His ancestor had carried the Prophet's war banner during the conquest of Arabia. At seventy, his personal valour was legend, as was his violent temper and his profligacy with his men. Mustafa had personally humbled the Knights of Saint John at Rhodes, in '22, when only the august mercy of the youthful Suleiman had spared the Order from annihilation. The dogs had rewarded this beneficence with forty years of terror, inflicted for the most part on Moslem pilgrims and merchants. This error would now be corrected. The stronghold of the Hounds of Hell would be razed to the dirt and only their Grand Master spared to kneel before the Padishah in chains. But this would not be accomplished in two weeks. The grim thought entered Abbas's mind that it might take as long as two months.

He cast about the battlefield once more. The Christian ditch was deep and the walls formidable. The fortifications were crude but shrewdly conceived. The gallows on the bastion again caught his eye. It was said that after death human souls could meet, in the dreams of the men and women of this world. Would anyone, Abbas wondered, welcome the hanged slave into his sleep? Or the janissaries bloating in the scarlet heat of the twilight? The messenger's dust drew closer. Abbas knew that he brought orders for the *silahadar* to attack. He beckoned the regimental trumpeter to his side. He drew his sword. He murmured:

'*All praises and thanks be to Allah, Lord of all worlds,*
The Compassionate, the Merciful, Ruler of Judgement Day.
You Alone we worship, And of You Alone we ask help.
Show us the straight way,
The way of those upon whom You have bestowed Your Grace,
Not the way of those upon whom lies Your wrath,
Nor of those who wander astray.'

PART II

MALTESE ILIAD

MONDAY 4 JUNE 1565

The Monastery of Santa Sabina, Rome

LUDOVICO COMPLETED THE ride from Naples to Rome in a shade over three days. The way was dusty and gruelling. Anacleto rode at his side. They prayed as they rode and folk of every estate bowed down as they passed, as if they believed them vengeful revenants committed to some fell purpose whose nature was best unknown. They passed numberless pagan catacombs and tombs, markers of a mighty power now consigned to oblivion. They ate in the saddle and lost count of the number of horses they exhausted on their way; Ludovico's endurance too was tested to its bounds. Yet this he welcomed, for he needed to steel his sinews for the ordeals to come.

Through this state of extreme fatigue the streets of Rome, seething under the starlight of a torpid summer night, seemed more than usually dreamlike and depraved. He entered the Porta San Paolo with cowled head, for spies were always abroad and he shunned recognition. Along the streets of the Ripa, pimps and prostitutes brazenly sought his custom, undeterred by his monastic garb and offering tender boys if such were his fancy. Exotic birds and animals – parrots squawking obscenities, spider monkeys, lemurs, tiny green dragons on red silk leashes – were brandished in his face. Toothsome aromas from the vendors' cooking fires assailed his palate, but he resisted their call. In this squalid latter-day Sodom there was much to resist.

Rome was a theocratic dictatorship yet its ruling influence was not Jesus Christ but Lust. Lust for gold and property and beauty, for sex, food and wine; for titles, grandeur and ostentation, for intrigue and betrayal; above all, for power. Raw power in more myriad incarnations than existed anywhere else in the world. Even piety was craved and was for sale alongside all other commodities. In contrast to the industriousness of the north and the Spanish domains of the south, idleness abounded in Rome, both among the teeming masses of the destitute, who prowled the wretched slums like toothless dogs, and the rapacious legions of the rich in their opulent palazzos. Vast quantities of cash – milked from the faithful in every corner of Christendom, borrowed from the rising clans of international bankers, and extorted from the rural economy in papal taxes – poured down Rome's throat in a ceaseless bacchanal of carnal indulgence. The churches and cathedrals were theatres of bathhouse art where the genitals and arses of leering pederasts were plastered over every wall, and boylike martyrs writhed in erotic torment, and paedophiliac fantasies posed as aids to devotion. Teenaged cardinals who could barely recite a blessing swaggered down the Via della Pallacorda – from tennis court to gambling den to brothel and back – protected by insolent bands of hired *bravi*. In a city that could not boast a single great guild or profession – in which it was no easy task to get a horse shoed – the only industry that flourished was prostitution, and with it the French disease and anal warts, and every doe-eyed girl, every smooth-skinned boy, seemed destined for a semen-soaked mattress. Outside the city, whole armies of bandits – jobless soldiers, the dispossessed, a vast criminal detritus from the Franco-Spanish wars – ravaged the countryside. And through the high passes of the Alps the poison sea of Protestantism – Calvinists, Lutherans, Waldensians, Anabaptists, heretics of every breed and persuasion – swelled towards the shores of the Holy See.

Ludovico walked across this cesspool as Christ had walked on the water. The prelates who gorged themselves in marbled halls – beneath pornographic tableaux of rutting dryads and at tables that groaned with fat meats, pastries and liqueurs – regarded his raw-boned austerity with fear. And so they should, for he despised them. During his last sojourn Ludovico had destroyed the Bishop of Toulon, one Marcel D'Estaing, who was a notorious homosexualist with a weakness for diamonds and women's clothes. While the Bible, Saint Paul, Aquinas and numerous other authorities condemned both fornication and sodomy, a close reading revealed that nowhere was sex with boys listed as a sin, either venial or mortal. This oversight explained the great ubiquity of cherubic males – the *bardassos* – in the city's many bordellos. In neglecting to exploit this loophole and indulging in sex with adult men instead – it was said he was more familiar with the sight of his toes than with the inside of his church – the Bishop of Toulon had sealed his fate. Ludovico had the blubbering prelate sewn up in a sack and thrown in the Tiber.

Yet laced through this sordid estate of sodomites, voluptuaries and thieves was that network of remarkable men to whom Rome owed its survival as the fulcrum of the Christian world. Men of devotion, ruthlessness and ability who, without soldiers, without ships, and with coffers filled with little more than promises, attempted to steer the policy of nations and secure the moral destiny of Mankind. Men possessed by the most potent lust of all: the compulsion to shape the clay of History as it spun on the wheel around them. Ludovico and Cardinal Ghisleri were two such men. Their army was the Holy Office of the Roman Inquisition.

At last the two travellers dismounted in the Dominican fortress-monastery of Santa Sabina. Ludovico sent Anacleto to take his supper with the monks. Officially, Ludovico served Pope

Pius IV, Giovanni Medici. In truth he served Medici's sworn enemy – and, with luck, the pontiff-to-be – Michele Ghisleri. Ghisleri greeted Ludovico with joy and they retired to the cardinal's rooms for a simple meal.

LUDOVICO LISTENED TO the latest news as he ate. A rash of murderous plots in the College of Cardinals between the French and Hapsburgian parties had culminated in a knife fight in the half-built transept of Santa Maria degli Angeli. Next winter's famine – a certainty since torrential rains had caused the second catastrophic crop failure in a row – had triggered a frenzy of profiteering in grain futures, from which the Pope expected to bloat yet further his fortune. Four thousand beggars had been driven outside the walls at spear point, in order that they might starve to death elsewhere. The miasmas from their corpses had caused a plague scare and the riots that resulted had only been suppressed by burning down a section of labourers' boarding houses, with the loss of some several dozen lives.

In the Eternal City, it seemed, all was much as usual.

As it was, also, throughout Europe. The Spanish Hapsburgs and the French Valois remained at daggers drawn over a variety of squabbles, including various disputed fragments of Italy. The two royal families had used Italy as a battleground for a century, carving it up between them this way and that, and according its natives little more respect than they did the aborigines of Mexico. Charles Quintus had even sacked Rome itself and imprisoned the Pope. His son, Philip, now systematically looted the country's richest regions – Milan and the north, Naples and the south. Every Italian patriot, including Ludovico and Ghisleri, loathed both dynasties with passion. An Italy independent of Spanish and French invaders alike was their long-held dream; but its realisation had been thwarted, most of all, by a succession of corrupt popes who lacked the vision or leadership to bind the various Italian states together. That and a lack of diplomatic and military resources. These political crises, long unresolved, were what drove Ghisleri's desire to claim the papal throne.

Ludovico finished his cheese and broached with Ghisleri the subject that had brought him so far: the fate of the Religion, its place in the larger scheme, and the part Ludovico might play.

'Malta?' said Ghisleri. He was white-haired and bony and at sixty-one his mind was keener than ever. 'Most of these fools can't mark it on a map, yet this summer the city talks of little else. Every Royal House in Europe wants to wrap itself in the cloak of borrowed glory.' He snorted. 'Even Elizabeth, the English heresiarch, has had the gall to order masses for the knights' deliverance. As for Medici, you'd think he was standing on the battlements waving a sword – instead of lying in bed while his boys take it in turns to suck his cock.'

'Medici is a pimp,' agreed Ludovico. 'If he knew I were here in your rooms he'd have my life. But I enjoy his trust.'

'Good.' Ghisleri gave Ludovico's arm a squeeze. 'Good.'

Giovanni Medici was Pope Pius IV. He'd reigned for almost five years and on merit – intellectual and otherwise – should never have ascended the Chair of Saint Peter at all. His only qualification for the office had been three decades of toadying in the Vatican's shadowy precincts. After three months' bitter stalemate in the Conclave of '59, his election had been a sordid compromise – paid for by the Farnese clan – to prevent Ghisleri's accession to the papal throne. Medici was no friend to the Inquisition. He was soft on heresy and had opened the gates of the gaols and set free many dissidents. Corrupt to the bone, he'd created forty-six new cardinals – more than in the entire previous century – with each paying his price in one coin or another. And in an attempt to buy immortality, he'd lavished the millions of scudi screwed from the pockets of the peasantry on further architectural embellishment of his gaudy capital.

Now Medici was old and weak. His neglect of the twofold threat from Lutheranism and Islam had earned him many new enemies. Among his more fanatical detractors there were rumours of assassins. It was widely known that the most he'd done for the Order of the Knights of Saint John in their present troubles was to send a paltry ten thousand scudi from his gold-plated lavatory. In this feverish political season, the valour of Malta was a reproach to papal indolence. Medici was now desperate to be seen as Malta's champion. It was this need that Ludovico intended to exploit.

'What is the mood of the knights?' asked Ghisleri.

'Defiant,' replied Ludovico.

'Can they win?'

'With God's favour, La Valette believes they can.'

'And you?'

'If the knights prove as fanatic as their word, yes, they might well prevail.'

'The Religion and the Inquisition should be natural allies. The sword and the book.' Ghisleri tugged on his beard. 'And under the aegis of a cleansed and revitalised Vatican –'

Ludovico punctured his fantasy. 'La Valette trusts no one outside the Order.'

'Including Medici?'

'Especially Medici. Medici ignored La Valette's ambassador for months.'

'Trust me, Giovanni Medici won't survive the year,' said Ghisleri.

Ludovico wondered how so. To wear the Shoes of the Fisherman, Ghisleri would have liquidated every red hat in the conclave. But Ghisleri's expression suggested he ask no more.

'If His Holiness's successor' – by this Ghisleri meant himself – 'could count on the political allegiance of the Order – a victorious Order, the heroes of all Europe – he'd wield a power that no pope has enjoyed in generations.'

Ludovico nodded. All popes wanted to control the Knights of Saint John: for their military power and their great prestige, for their vast lands and wealth. If the Vatican seized the reins of the

Religion, its power would once again rival that of a major nation-state. But no pope had ever succeeded in winning this prize.

'Princes respect victory even more than purity of blood, and certainly more than piety,' rasped Ghisleri. 'The Religion, if it survives, would embody all three. Such ambassadors – already woven through the bloodlines of the European aristocracy? – they'd be priceless.' His rheumy eyes shone in the candlelight. 'If I – if the Vatican – could forge an alliance with the Religion and use it to unite the Italian princes – and win the favour of the French – then might we begin to counter Spanish power. Then might Italy forge its own destiny, as in times gone by.'

'The knights scorn European bickering,' said Ludovico. 'They live to fight Islam. They still dream of Jerusalem.'

'Do you?'

'I dream of an Italy freed from foreign armies, and ruled and united by the Church, as do you. But you will never win the allegiance of the knights while La Valette reigns. He's too entirely French, and a Gascon to boot.'

'You've given some thought to a solution,' Ghisleri said.

'We must engineer the election of an Italian as the knights' Grand Master.'

Ghisleri's brow furrowed. Ludovico knew why. The Religion's electoral college was the most complex ever invented, superbly devised to prevent any outside interference, especially from Rome. On the death of a Grand Master his successor had to be elected within three days. This alone sealed the process among those knights present on the island at the time. Even so, seventy-two hours of feverish intrigue invariably followed – bribery, arm-twisting, blackmail and extravagant oaths – among the brethren of the eight competing langues. Many went about wearing masks to disguise their allegiances, so Ludovico had been told. The knights, after all, were a heady distillation of noble blood and carried in their veins the most ancient of aristocratic vices: an obsession with power. Their intricate electoral system, developed over centuries, had only made the contest the more furious.

'Is it possible?' said Ghisleri.

'The mechanism of the election is Byzantine,' said Ludovico. 'Each langue meets in its own chapel and elects one knight to represent it. These eight then choose a President of the Election. They also choose a Triumvirate consisting of one knight, one chaplain and one brother serjeant at arms, each from a different langue. From this point the President, plus the original conclave of eight, take no further part in the proceedings. The newly convened Triumvirate now choose a fourth member, then these four choose a fifth, then the five choose a sixth, the six a seventh, and so on – each new member from a different langue than the one preceding – until their number totals sixteen electors. At least eleven of these electors must be Knights of Justice, but none may be a Grand Cross. These sixteen – at last – cast their votes for the new Grand Master, with the President using a casting vote in the event of a tie.'

Ghisleri took all this in. He said, 'An Italian Grand Master would be marvellous. And I've fixed as many elections as any man in Rome. But given these fantastic safeguards? How?'

'With your blessing,' said Ludovico, 'I intend to become a Knight of the Holy Religion.'

Ghisleri stared at him.

'Once inside the convent,' continued Ludovico, 'I can canvass for the appropriate candidate.'

'And who is that?' said Ghisleri.

'A brilliant soldier – admired by every langue for his leadership in war – and a man you yourself know well.'

'Pietro Del Monte,' said Ghisleri.

Ludovico nodded. Del Monte was Prior of the Langue of Italy and Admiral of the Religion's navy. At sixty-five, his reputation was unsurpassed.

Ludovico went on. 'His only weakness – a lack of political

sophistication – is to our advantage. He'll be susceptible to your – or I should say, the pontiff's – needs. And the other langues will find him the least disagreeable nominee against their own aspirants.'

'How so?' asked Ghisleri.

'In the face of the Turk, any of the brethren would lay down his life for the others. Yet they do not lack for internal rivalries. The French have dominated the order for most of the century. The Spaniards, Catalans and Portuguese resent this bitterly. A Frenchman, De L'Isle Adam, lost Rhodes, and even La Valette is not unsullied by intrigue and disaster – eighteen thousand Spaniards slaughtered at Jerba; the failure to liberate Tripoli; Zoara was their worst defeat since Rhodes. It was French treachery that lost Tripoli in the first place and La Valette not only freed the culprit, Gaspard Vallier, from gaol but also promoted him Bailiff of Largo. Even in peace the French and Spanish squabble and politics is never more vicious than in time of war. Each camp would oppose the other's candidate. It won't take more than the application of reason – and the distribution of the necessary favours – to make Del Monte the wartime heir assumptive.'

'You know this for certain?'

'The knights are practical men. Battle is unpredictable and La Valette's love of war exceeds all other passions. Hell's legions could not keep him from the walls. If La Valette were to die in battle' – at this Ghisleri's brow rose – 'then the usual electoral machinations would be impossible, or, rather, suicidal. Morale would demand that a new Grand Master be ordained at once. And in such dire circumstances the serious contenders can be counted on one hand. Del Monte is one of them. With my help, he would win.'

'And if Del Monte is dead too?'

'Mathurin Romegas, General of the Galleys and a great hero, is to be counted on that same hand. Less pliable, perhaps, than Del Monte but a good son of Italy.'

Ghisleri tented his fingers and looked down at the table. He was troubled.

Ludovico said, 'The Cross is not given to those with weak backs.'

Ghisleri raised his eyes. 'If La Valette were to die in battle. And if not in battle?'

Ludovico said, 'Your conscience should not trouble itself. Nor should you be apprised of any more. All I need is your blessing to join the Religion.'

'My blessing, should I give it, is the least of your needs. Entry to their Order is a prize not easily won. More to the point, they'll hardly welcome an inquisitor into their ranks.'

'I've done nothing to incur their enmity – to their surprise – and I enjoy the respect of La Valette, for I've promised to argue his case before the Holy Father. Two further steps will win me their affection. The first is to make a significant military contribution to their defences.'

'At this late date that's beyond the powers of Rome.'

'But not beyond the Spanish Viceroy of Sicily, Garcia de Toledo.'

'Toledo will intervene or not based on the interests of himself and Madrid.'

'Quite. At present, the risks of providing the large reinforcement that La Valette has begged for are too great. But consider this, for we can be sure that Toledo has done so. If the Religion defeat the Turk unaided, all glory is theirs. If, rather, the Religion are annihilated, then a Turkish army ground down to the bone by a bitter siege and stranded on a barren island a thousand miles from home would be tempting prey for the kind of army Toledo will have mustered in Sicily by early autumn. The Religion's tragic demise followed by a brilliant *reconquista* would carve Toledo's name on the Stone of Ages.'

'Is he capable of such perfidy?'

'He's Castilian.'

'And the Emperor Philip too would let Malta fall?'

'If he could thereby regain it as a purely Spanish stronghold, why not? Charles Quintus leased Malta to the knights just to get them out of his hair after their expulsion from Rhodes. At the time the island was impoverished and of little strategic importance. But that was forty years ago – before Suleiman's maturity, before the disasters in North Africa, before Quintus split the Empire between his sons, before Luther split Christendom down the middle. Since the knights arrived in Malta, the world has turned upside down.'

Ghisleri shook his head. He was not yet convinced.

Ludovico said, 'Toledo hesitates because the loss of both Malta and of Spain's Mediterranean fleet would be a disaster too great to bear. And where the Turks are concerned, disaster has far too many precedents. Toledo will bide his time and see which way the wind blows. But if I can persuade him to send a small relief – say a thousand men? – then Toledo can claim he did his best, and La Valette's knights will cheer me to the echo, inquisitor or no.'

Ghisleri weighed the possibilities. 'But can our Congregation muster the required inducements? Bribing the rich is expensive, which is why I'm not pontiff already. Toledo is no pauper, nor is Spanish cupidity mere legend.'

'The advancements, wealth and sacred relics within the gift of the Holy Father far exceed those of our Congregation. The Vatican could provide more than enough to bribe not only Toledo but key elements within the Religion too.' Ludovico leaned forward. 'Let Medici pay the piper. While we call the tune.'

Again Ghisleri tugged on his long white beard. 'Your stratagem would appeal to Medici as much as his successor. And you'd carry the full authority of the papal will.'

'Tomorrow,' said Ludovico, 'I'll feign my arrival in Rome and report to Medici as if to him alone. The Pope will provide the instruments and promises I need.'

'Then you'll return to Malta?'

'To Sicily and Garcia de Toledo, and thence to Malta.'

'And if Malta has already fallen to the Turk?'

Ludovico didn't answer. He stood up. 'Once I show my face at the Vatican, I'll be watched for the remainder of my stay. We two shall not meet again before I leave.'

Ghisleri frowned. 'You said two steps were needed before the Religion would take you to their bosom. What is the second?'

'I will join the knights on the ramparts and blood myself in battle with the Infidel.'

A different set of emotions coloured Ghisleri's eyes. He reached out a hand and placed it on Ludovico's arm. 'I beg you, go no further than Sicily.'

Ludovico looked at him without reply.

'You're closer to me than any son could be,' Ghisleri said. 'And every bit as dear.'

Ludovico, unaccustomed to affection, found himself moved. Still, he did not reply.

'You are yet a young man,' said Ghisleri. 'One day you could wear the Fisherman's Ring yourself. Indeed, that is my hope and my prayer.'

Ludovico knew this. He'd envisaged every step that it would take, like a path of boulders strewn across a torrent. Yet he craved to achieve the impossible. He craved La Valette's downfall. He craved the judgement of battle. These petty cravings, he believed, were the expression of a power both fundamental and profound: the Will of God.

'Do you forbid me to go?' he asked.

Ghisleri sighed. He shook his head. 'And if you die?'

Ludovico said, 'I'm committed to God's keeping. Do I have your blessing?'

'As member of our Holy Congregation? Or as a Knight of Saint John?'

'As whatever I need to be to serve the Will of God.'

TUESDAY 5 JUNE 1565

The Waterfront – the Borgo – the Night

NIGHT. WIND. STARS. Sea. Stones.

The days were hot and had no pity, but the nights were cool, as this one was cool, and Amparo's green linen dress wasn't enough to keep her warm. She wrapped thin arms about her knees and shivered in the breeze. The shallow undulations of the sea were ribboned with silver and a gibbous moon lay low amid Heaven's dust. Direction meant nothing to Amparo, any more than did Time. From where she sat, tucked among the stacks of lumber on Kalkara Bay, these gentle friends – wind, sea, stars, moon, night – were all she could know and they brought her comfort. In her lap lay her shew stone in its cylinder of leather. She'd tried to read the secrets in its glass by the light of the moon but the Angels hadn't spoken. All she had seen were whorls of colour. Pretty patterns but no more. Had the Angels fled from the hatred that flourished all about her? Or because Amparo was in love and no longer needed their guidance?

Tannhauser was out among the heathen, somewhere beyond the monstrous walls that closed them all inside and made her feel trapped. With neither him nor Buraq to fill the hours, the day had passed slowly. The quartermaster had scolded her for wasting water on her flowers and she'd had little else to do but watch them die. By sunset, Tannhauser had not returned. Exhausted by the waiting and the worry, she'd wandered to the waterfront to take the silence. Silence had been all but driven out of this place. Cannon shook the earth from sunrise to dusk. From the infirmary random screams pierced her spine. Men shouted or muttered prayers. Whips and whistles and curses drove the work gangs, poor wretches in chains, who in this city of endless high walls were forced to build yet more. In the auberge, Carla brooded, for she could not find her boy. Perhaps, though she had not said so, Carla was also downcast because Tannhauser had taken Amparo as his lover.

As far as the unknown boy was concerned, Amparo had few feelings at all. It was a quest that required events long dead be linked to those of a future that didn't exist, and this riddle perplexed her. A few hours either side of the present moment were as far as her imagination ever extended. Tomorrow was far away and yesterday was gone. Ambition was a mystery and her memories few. She hoped the boy would be found, for it would make Carla happy. Until Carla had appeared from the willows, like an Angel from her glass, Amparo's life had been one of enduring all things. Since then her life had been sowed with wonder and beauty. Amparo loved Carla. But the search for the boy was an enterprise in which she felt she had no part.

As to Tannhauser, she loved him with a wild and terrible passion that shook her to her blood, to her core, to her inmost heart and soul. She'd loved him since he'd told her the tale of the nightingale and the rose. The blood-red rose who'd killed the one who adored her. Tannhauser had brought her the yellow leather slippers she was wearing now from the Turkish bazaar. He'd brought her the ivory comb, chased with silver and floral arabesques, which she wore in her tangled hair. He made her howl in the night when she lay beneath him. He made her weep as he slept while she lay on his chest and feared he would die. Amparo knew herself to be unlike all other women. How or why she could not explain, but always had it been so. She thought she'd known sex. It had always been around her: in the rutting of the bulls that her father had raised; in the squalid hovels she'd shared in the course of her wanderings; in the cramped and violent streets of Barcelona; in the figure of the sweetmeats vendor who'd kicked her face in; in the farmhands who'd laughed while they held her down and who'd pissed on her when they were done. In the world she'd shared with Carla, of music and horses and peace, such things had been unseen, never spoken of, so utterly excluded that Amparo at first had found it strange. Then years had passed, and she'd forgotten them, and for her, as for Carla, sex had become a mystery left neglected and unknown. And then she'd seen Tannhauser naked. Her heart had almost stopped to witness the calligraphs and wheels and crescent moons and the red forked dagger with a dragonhead hilt, with which his arms and thighs and calves were bravely tattooed. Truly he was the man she'd seen in her vision stone. She'd shown him her own nakedness, with a wild and shameless joy, and she'd given herself to him, and he'd taken her.

Tannhauser and Carla would be married, perhaps. This fact left her unmoved and she did not dwell on it, for it was a matter for a future far away. It did not seem to her that they were in love. It did not seem to her that Carla wanted him, for she hadn't said so. Amparo had seen her flinch from his kiss in the garden of the auberge. And if Carla never spoke of such things, then what could she know of them? Her dejection must be for the boy alone, Amparo reasoned, and with a lighter heart she gave the matter no more thought.

'*Hola*.'

She turned to the voice without alarm, even though its owner had appeared without a sound. It was the youth, rather, who seemed startled to have come across her. His face was lean and smooth and unbearded, his features not yet fully grown; yet he was as tall, if not as broad, as many of the Maltese men. His hair was stiff with dirt and he wore a leather jerkin crudely studded with brass-headed nails. His breeches were ragged and tied up with a rope and his feet were calloused and bare. A butcher knife was shoved through his rope belt. A man-boy. She recognised him from the dock when they'd first arrived. He'd been caked in crusted blood and the old puppeteer had danced him a crazy jig. She looked at him without speaking. He shuffled and regained his wits.

'You speak the French?' he said, in that tongue, and then in Spanish, 'Spanish?'

She nodded and perhaps he took this to mean both for he went on to speak in a patois composed of each. 'Are you hurt?' he asked, seeing the way she hugged herself.

She shook her head. He looked back and forth along the waterfront.

'This is not a good place for you,' he said. 'It's not safe, for a girl.'

Amparo pointed up to the sky and he looked up. For a moment she thought he'd find this nonsensical, but when he looked back at her he nodded, as if her meaning couldn't be clearer.

'The stars, yes.' He swelled his chest and pointed about the firmament with his finger. 'The Virgin. The Great Bear. The Little Bear.' He glanced at her to see if this impressed her. 'But here is not safe. The soldiers. The *tercios*.' He paused as if he'd suggested something indelicate. He studied her, fists on his hips as if this were his domain. He said, 'You're cold.'

Without waiting for an answer he turned and ran out of sight, his feet slapping on the capstones until silence fell. She wondered if Tannhauser had returned. She was about to leave for the auberge to find out when the footsteps returned and the boy reappeared with a threadbare length of fabric whose original function was obscure but which now, it seemed, served him as a blanket for he draped it over her shoulders and pulled it around her. It smelled of brine. She took up the slack and wrapped it tight.

'You're kind,' she said.

He shrugged. 'I saw you. With the German.'

'The German?'

'The big man.' He spread his chest and put a hand on the hilt of his knife and mimed a manly swagger. 'The great captain, Tannhauser. He spies on the Turk for La Valette. He moves among them like a wind. He cuts their throats while they sleep.'

This account of Tannhauser's activities disturbed her. She didn't believe it.

'And the other, the English, like a bull,' continued the boy. 'And the *belle dame*. You came with them on the *Couronne*, when the warships of the infidels were first seen. Yes?'

Amparo remembered the way he'd looked at Tannhauser and how the boy's eyes had met her own and how in them she'd seen the ghost of the life she'd left so far behind. She saw it again now, in his unvarnished honesty, in his poignant and desperate pride. She nodded.

'I saw you too, with the old puppeteer.'

'The *karagozi*,' corrected the boy. He looked sad.

Amparo had returned to the dock later that day and the old man, unprompted, had laid on a performance in his theatre of dancing shadows, squawking in a fantastic mixture of tongues. It seemed to portray a rich man asking a poor man to die on his behalf, with the promise of great rewards in the blessed hereafter, but if the meaning had been less than clear the choreographed paper figures of his puppets had brought her delight. When she'd indicated that she carried no coin and couldn't pay him, the *karagozi* had fallen to his knees and kissed her feet. She hadn't seen him again since the soldiers had dragged him down the street on the day of the battle.

'Where is he now?' she asked.

'In Hell,' said the boy.

'No,' she said. The thought wounded her. 'Hell wasn't made for such a soul.'

He thought about this; and perhaps he agreed. 'But for sure

the *karagozi* is dead.' He mimed a noose snapping about his neck and dropped his head, and she flinched. The boy grinned, as if this were what made him a man and her a mere girl. Then his eyes snapped towards something in the dark and he put a finger to his lips and pointed to the ground.

'Look,' he whispered.

A long, slender lizard scuttled across the dock in the pale light and stopped a yard away to observe them with protuberant eyes. The boy dived and his hand flashed out and Amparo cried 'No!' and he grabbed it by the tail. The lizard squirmed and its tail snapped off in his hand. The shorn creature scampered away into the dark. The boy squatted on his haunches beside her and showed her the scaly object.

'Gremxola,' he said. 'Very clever. They break so they can live. They survive.'

He threw the tail away and looked at her, their faces now level.

'So,' he said, 'they have cast you out.'

Amparo blinked at this absurdity. He gave her a rueful smile, his teeth white and uneven in his sunburned face.

'Me too. In, out. In, out. That is the game. But I am not sad. When the Turks have killed very many, the chevaliers will let me fight with them in the line and if I don't die, I'll become a big man too. That's the way forward in this life, to kill many. Tannhauser, La Valette, all of them. For killers the world is open – it is free – and I want to see it. This island is all I know. It is small. It is mean. Each day the same as the next.'

'No day is the same as the next.'

The boy was undeterred. 'You have seen the world. Is it as wide as they say?'

'Wider than anyone can know,' said Amparo. 'It is beautiful and it is cruel.'

'There are many green trees,' he said, to prove his learning. 'More than you can ride through in a week. And there are mountains too high to be climbed. And snow.'

'Trees and snow and flowers and rivers so wide you can't see one bank from the other,' agreed Amparo. The boy nodded, as if this confirmed what he'd heard. There was in his eyes the passion of a fabulous dream, and the thought that their light might be extinguished made her sad. 'But what if you die here, in the war?' she said.

'I will be welcomed into Heaven by Jesus and all His Apostles.' He crossed himself. 'But I'm too clever to die, like the gremxola. You are the one in danger. You don't believe me, but don't worry, I know Guzman, an *abanderado* with the *tercio* of Naples, and he knows the English bull – Barras?'

Amparo nodded. 'Bors.'

'Bors. Yes. I will ask Guzman to speak with Bors, and they will take you back in. Tannhauser would not put you to live on the docks, of this I am sure, but perhaps he is out there' – he threw an arm towards the darkness beyond the bay, – 'killing Turkish generals, or setting fire to their ships.'

As his fantasies became more extravagant, Amparo was disturbed. 'How do you know what Tannhauser does?'

'The men on the Post of Castile talk of him,' he said, as if to imply that he was to be counted among their number. '*Los soldados particular*. Even the knights regard him. The door of La Valette is open to Tannhauser as to no other. Only Tannhauser dares to go out among the fiends.' As if noting her distress he added, 'Don't be afraid for Captain Tannhauser. They say he will never die. Tannhauser knows the Turk. Tannhauser knows the Sultan Suleiman himself. And perhaps the Devil too. But tell me, was it the *belle dame* who cast you out? What did you do?'

'I'm not cast out,' she said. 'I live at the Auberge of England.'

He studied her afresh, and with a shadow of awe. 'Then why are you here?'

'I came here for the peace.'

'The peace?' The idea seemed to baffle him. He stood up. 'I

will guard you back to the auberge. It is the home of Starkey, the last of the English. I know it well, very well, yes.'

He rose to his feet. He seemed so set on gallantry that Amparo couldn't refuse. She stood up too. She slipped the blanket from her shoulders and handed it back. He took it, as if he now considered it a shabby and offensive thing to have offered a woman so obviously grand. He balled it and tossed it in the lumber stacks. He noticed the leather cylinder around her neck.

'What is this?' he said.

Amparo slid the case beneath her arm. 'It is a curiosity,' she said. He pursed his lips as he realised that this was all she'd let him know. She said, 'Tell me your name.'

'Orlandu,' he said. He added, 'When I leave to see the wide, wide world, and become a fine person and a man of honour, I shall be Orlandu di Borgo.'

'Why do you live here, on the waterfront?' she asked.

'Here I am free.'

'Where's your family?'

'My family?' Orlandu's lip curled. He made a short, axe-like gesture with the edge of his hand. 'I have cut them,' he said. 'They are not fine people.'

She would have asked more, but his face suggested he would not give it, and that it was a subject that caused him pain.

'And your name?' he said.

'Amparo.'

He smiled. 'Very fine. Spanish, then. Are you a noble, like the *belle dame*?'

She shook her head and his smile broadened, as if this bound them even closer. She wondered if he wanted her, and having wondered knew that he didn't. He wanted to be a man, with so palpable a desperation it made her ache too, but he was still too much a boy to know real desire. In a flash she wondered, also, if this was Carla's boy.

She said, 'You will meet Tannhauser when he returns. I will

tell him you are a gallant, who protected me from the *tercios*, and that it would please you to shake his hand.'

Orlandu's eyes boggled.

'Would that please you?' she asked.

'Oh verily,' said Orlandu. 'Verily indeed.' He scrubbed at his hair, as if already grooming himself for the occasion. 'When?'

'I will speak with him tomorrow,' she said.

Orlandu grabbed her hand and kissed it. No one had ever done so before.

'Come now,' he said. 'Let me take you home, before the moon goes down.'

Amparo hoped he was the boy Carla sought. She liked his heart. If he was not the boy, she wondered if they couldn't make believe that it was so.

FRIDAY 8 JUNE 1565

Auberge of England – the Outlands – Castel Sant' Angelo

'*Allahu Akabar! God is most great! Allahu Akabar!*
I bear witness that there is no God but Allah.
I bear witness that Mohammed is the Apostle of Allah.
Come to prayer!
Come to prayer!
Come to prayer!
Come to success!
Allahu Akabar!
There is no God but Allah.'

Tannhauser woke at the break of day to the poetry of the muezzin's call. For seventeen dawns the *adhan* had drifted from the Corradino Heights and through the windows of the auberge. After so many years among the Franks, the music haunted him – depending on his dreams – with awe, with dread, with pride, with a readiness for battle; with an obscure anguish whose nature he could not define. It didn't matter that the words were indistinct. The *Al-Fatihah* was engraved on what passed for his soul and would never be erased.

'*Guide us to the straight way,*

The way of those upon whom You have bestowed Your Grace,
Not the way of those upon whom lies Your wrath,
Nor of those who wander astray.'

There was a void in his heart as large as the universe around him, and within it he found no Grace, no way that seemed straight, nor any guide thereto. And even by his own lights, he'd wandered as far astray as a man might get without running into the gallows. Amparo's arm stirred across his chest and her fingers, propelled by some tender dream, caressed his neck and she sighed. Tannhauser breathed in her scent and with it the hope inherent in the bright new day.

A pale citrus light breached the deep-silled, glassless windows and awakened the glow of her skin where she lay coiled beside him. The sheet had been thrown back and was twisted about her thigh. Her head lay in the bight of his shoulder, her hair lay black across her cheek and her shadowed lips were half-parted and the colour of precious garnet. Her flanks revealed the outlines of her ribs as she breathed and he craned his head an inch or two to study the curve of her arse. She appeared to him quite a beauty, despite that her face and her mind were imperfect and strange. His privities were engorged and became more so as he ran his palm down the muscles of her back. His fingertips palpated the burls of her spine and slid down them one by one, until they abandoned the hardness of bone to nestle between the curves that so delighted him. To such sensual abundance a man could abandon himself forever, if the world would but permit it. But of all worlds this one would not, for its very heart was stone. He considered arousing her slowly, with kisses and dextrous wiles, for he knew by now that her body was as greedy for his hands as his hands were for her. Thereafter he'd engulf her with his bulk and slide inside her and pound her into the mattress, a practice for which, he also knew by now, her appetite was admirably large.

His desire lurched towards the overpowering and he shifted his weight and reached down to unlimber his balls. As he did so

Amparo murmured and rolled on to her back. Her breasts sloped to either side of her chest, the skin faintly marbled with blue where they hung fullest, and he watched her nipples, no longer softened by the warmth of his body, grow dark in the cooling air. No void within troubled him now. The turbulent ache that filled it, the thoughts of her that increasingly filled his mind, the consuming abandon that filled as much of his days as he could spare, would all stand condemned as sinful and abhorrent by the Believers of the various camps among whom he was stranded. Yet, willing as he was to admit vices and crimes without number, he could find no wrong in the transport Amparo brought him. Half a mile from where they lay entwined, other interwoven bodies were crammed by the thousand in a reeking ditch for the nourishment of seagulls and crows. Both those whose corpses filled it, and those whose hands had made it so, were destined for the fields of Paradise shrived of all sin; but of the guilt of the fornicators dozing the sunrise away, there was no doubt.

He scooped Amparo's hair back from her face and looked at her, and so peaceful were her features, so innocent of care and of any knowledge of the madness into which she had thrust herself – so like a child's – that he couldn't bring himself to expel her from such an Eden. And so uncharacteristic was this impulse to restraint that he wondered if this feeling in his heart were not Love. He studied her further: the faint creases encircling her throat, the various textures of her unflawed complexion, the smooth contours of her belly, the sheen on the swell of her thigh, her pubic hair. He brushed his lips over hers, so softly that she didn't stir. He blinked and sat back against the wall.

This was absurd. What manner of man was he becoming? They'd barely left the room for two days, a commendable indulgence even by his standards, and it had addled his brain. With as much stealth as possible, he rose to his feet. He turned and looked down on her. He kissed her again. Addled indeed. He heard the clank of armour and muffled protests of despair in the street outside, and though he knew what he would find he went to the window.

Two serjeants at arms of the Religion, Aragonese by the look of them, marched a naked, manacled Turk up Majistral Street. The scars that corrugated the latter's back, like a subcutaneous infection of bloated worms, marked him as a galley slave. In his mouth was a knot of old rope to stifle the prayers he tried to utter on his way to the gibbet. In accord with La Valette's decree, this slave was the eighteenth Moslem to be hanged since the puppeteer had been launched from the Bastion of Provence. It was a drawback of this billet that the condemned trudged by the window every morning, and Tannhauser made a note to ask Starkey if some other route might not be used. The eighteenth slave reminded him that he'd already tarried on Malta for far too long.

He'd hunted high and low to find the name – and less than a name, a memory, a trace, a rumour – of a boy born on All Hallows Eve in the year of '52, and he'd found nothing. If Carla's boy was still alive, Tannhauser was having doubts that he was on the island. He'd considered persuading Carla to leave right now, before war devoured them, but his pride balked at admitting to defeat. Anyway, Carla would not give in. He collected his boots and clothes from the bare oak floor and made his way naked down the stairs.

In the garden at the rear of the auberge he'd had two slaves install a double hogshead filled with seawater. In the ground beneath this tub, Tannhauser and Bors had buried a chest containing fifty pounds of their opium. As the war progressed, its value would soar, and they aimed to make a killing on their departure. Tannhauser relieved his bladder in the dust and vaulted into the barrel, cursing as the cold water shocked him. He slid down on to his haunches, the brine rising to his throat, and he settled back to watch the sky as it turned from a seashell-pink tinged with grey to a pale and gentle blue. He'd pass the rest of the day in sweltering heat and in these frigid moments he found a comforting nostalgia for mountains and snow. It was thanks to the tub, at least in part, that his affair with Amparo had started.

ONE MORNING AS he lay soaking, she'd skipped over the garden wall, as if, to her mind, walls were constructed for that precise purpose alone, and had come over to the tub without any discernible bashfulness or shame to admire his tattoos.

He'd explained the tattoos' significance, and told her something of the sacred cult of the janissaries, who lived in barracks with their *babas*, their dervish fathers, and who shunned the company of women and recited poetry at their fires, and who craved death in the service of Allah above all things. But while in the content of this lecture she feigned not a scrap of interest, he found her more than fascinated by his flesh, which she poked and stroked with her long, almond-nailed fingers, and this proved a provocation far beyond his endurance. He'd not intended to make sport with either of his female charges, for in the thicket of love disaster was always lurking, but, he had reasoned, life was short and could get shorter at any time. He'd clambered from the tub in a state of unconcealable arousal and by some mutual and spontaneous combination of leaping and sweeping she'd wound up cradled across his arms, whence he'd carried her to the room where she now lay sleeping.

He was a fool but there it was and here he sat. As the water's cool cleared his mind of sleep and lust, and of morbid memories of Islam, and of the conundrum of loving one woman – if love it was – while planning to marry another, he reviewed his situation in what was surely the strangest of all the places on the Earth.

SINCE THE FIRST, inconclusive, battle on the 21st, Tannhauser hadn't taken part in any fighting, a fact entirely to his satisfaction. The Turks had not yet sealed the Borgo from the country surrounding, for their attentions were elsewhere – upon Saint Elmo's – and it was no great feat to sneak out of the Kalkara Gate before the sun was up. He'd thus made numerous sallies into the outlands beyond the enceinte in the guise of an opium trader from the *ordu bazaar*, the Turkish army's mobile commissariat, which was pitched beyond the hills on the Marsa plain.

As was the Ottoman way on major campaigns, this market constituted a town – transplanted from across the sea – of some one hundred and fifty tents and silk pavilions. From these premises, a multitude of merchants plied their crafts and trades. Barbers, butchers and surgeons; confectioners, grocers, metalsmiths; tailors and bootmakers; apothecaries; armourers, gunsmiths, harness makers, farriers; chandlers, wheelwrights and masons; there were even jewellers and goldsmiths to tend the many riches with which the officers and *beys* festooned their garb and their weapons. These merchants serviced the army but were independent. Since the Ottoman gentry nursed a mistrust of banks, they carried their wealth in their baggage wherever they went, and the money that swilled through the bazaar made Tannhauser glad.

From beyond the bazaar came the sweet smell of thousands of bread kilns, the bricks freighted in the ships from Old Stambouli. A stream of camels and ox carts toiled back and forth between the Turkish camp and Marsaxlokk, the natural harbour on the island's southern shore where the Sultan's armada was anchored. Here Tannhauser saw displayed the administrative genius that lay behind Ottoman supremacy. Hundreds of supply ships and galleys discharged hundreds of thousands of quintals of barley, flour and rice; iron, copper, lead and tin; honey, butter, hardtack, oil, lemons and salted fish; flocks of sheep and herds of cattle; firewood and timber and fascines; pavilion furniture and tents; gunpowder in vast quantity; the enormous four- and five-ton screw guns of the siege train; silver and gold coin for the soldiers' wages; ice for the generals' sherbet; and every ounce weighed and calculated in a *tour de force* of logistical insight and finesse.

Tannhauser wished Sabato Svi could see it too. A thousand Oracles in a thousand years could not have accomplished anything near such a feat. Tannhauser considered himself a fellow of uncommon resourcefulness, and even daring, but before this vast and teeming portrait of Suleiman's audacity, he felt dwarfed. To place at hazard, in the ultimate game of chance, so many lives, and so much pride and prestige, and the ransoms of so many kings, and with the whole world watching on, was an act of near madness that made Tannhauser's wagers on Fortune seem timid indeed. Suleiman Shah was indeed the King of Kings. Yet, large or small, it was the gamble that gave life its savour and which made war, above all other endeavours, so eternally irresistible to the species.

Thus emboldened by Suleiman's example, Tannhauser rode through this ceaseless torrent dressed in fine green robes, a white turban and a scimitar of elegant splendour. Buraq, whose golden coat and Asian blood aroused a deal of admiration, completed his disguise.

The smells, the colours and sounds, the refined precision of the Ottoman machine despite the chaos of conquest, rekindled in Tannhauser something more than memory. Beyond the walls of the Borgo, Malta was already part of the Sultan's realm and it evoked for him a way of being – of feeling and perception, of walking, talking and laughing – that was forged through his mettle to its core. Like any man returning to a world he'd once inhabited but had abandoned, he felt a sweet pain in his heart, most poignant when an *orta* of janissaries marched by, with their tall white *borks* and nine-palm muskets and warlike bearing. But if ambiguities of the heart sometimes troubled him, the clarity of his mind remained unmuddled. In the janissaries he'd been a *kullar*, the Sultan's slave, chanting prayers to a faceless and monstrous idol and killing with blind obedience on behalf of a rapacious race not even his own. Now he was a free man. The follies in which he might entangle himself were at least of his own choosing and design.

Since the Ottoman civil service and merchant classes were largely composed of Islamicised Christians, his fair skin and blue eyes provoked no suspicion. Since he could discuss with erudition the problems of damp powder, the price of nutmeg, the quality of steel and the perpetual lack of patience displayed by military officials high and low – and since he joined their daily prayers with absolute fluency – no one questioned his legitimacy. He made discreet gifts of opium and gold, as if to ensure future favours but in fact to loosen tongues. On occasion, to establish his pre-eminence over quartermasters and merchants, he'd reveal by an inadvertent gesture the janissary wheel or the Zulfikar sword tattooed on his either arm and at this they would blanch with respect and change their tune. He avoided contact with the encamped divisions of officers and fighting men against the slim chance of being recognised. In any case, all gossip flowed through the bazaar and the merchants and victuallers had, in sum, a far better knowledge of Mustafa's troop disbursements and morale than did most of his army's captains.

By such means Tannhauser learned that the island was presently occupied by something over thirty thousand *gazi* of the Sultan and more than as many again in labour battalions, engineers, oarsmen and auxiliary supports. He learned also that at least a further ten thousand reinforcements were expected from a variety of pirate and North African allies. Hassem, Viceroy of Algiers, had embarked from the Barbary Coast with six thousand elite Algerians. El Louck Ali, Governor of Alexandria, was to bring a corps of Egyptian engineers and Mameluke troops. The great Torghoud Rais, 'The Drawn Sword of Islam', was en route with a dozen galleys and two thousand seasoned corsairs. Killers from two score nations and two great creeds and dozens of tribes swarmed this Tower of Babel, in which all carried swords in their hands and hate in their hearts. Only War could invite so many to such a carnival.

The intelligence Tannhauser gathered was of such value to La Valette that he earned the kind of access to Oliver Starkey that only the seven priors of the langues routinely enjoyed. On returning from each reconnaissance, he made sure to bring some small gift for the guards on the Kalkara Gate – honey, choice cuts of lamb, pepper and mace, sweet cakes of almonds and raisins – and to ask their views on the campaign and to share some piece of news from the Turkish lines. This stoked their sense of importance and with it the trust in which they held him and which he knew he would one day exploit. His reputation was thereby established at either end of the Religion's hierarchy and, since fighting men like little more than to discuss each other's deeds, therefrom it spread through all those in between. This process was done no harm when he produced a dramatic coup from his first solitary foray, on the night of the 21st, in the aftermath of the initial clash of arms.

THAT EVENING – WITH the war's first corpses cooling on the Grande Terre Plein – Mustafa Pasha had convened a war council with Kapudan Pasha Piyale, High Admiral of the Fleet, and all his generals. Present throughout this meeting was a member of Mustafa's bodyguard, a Macedonian youth of remarkable beauty who was a Christian by birth. After the council ended, by a stroke of luck Tannhauser fell into a parley with this same young Greek.

Campfires guttered in the dark of the Marsa plain and in the distance he and the youth heard tambours and pipes, and the drone of the janissary poets chanting their tales. They roasted wild garlic on the points of their knives and they talked of their origins and their travels and of the kin they'd left behind. They discussed the fighting to come and the fearsome reputation of the Religion. And after an hour, with a pantomime of reluctance overcome by good fellowship, Tannhauser gave him a Stone of

Immortality, of which he carried a supply in a mother-of-pearl box.

Tannhauser had learned of the stones from Petrus Grubenius, who had learned, in his turn, in Salzburg, from the great Paracelsus himself. In truth, Tannhauser had a poor conception of the true alchemical recipe, but his own worked admirably well. In the kitchen of the Auberge of England, he rolled out pills of raw opium and marinated them overnight in a brew of citrus oils, brandy and honey. Next day he sprinkled them with fine-flaked gold, pared from a Venetian ducat, and glazed them hard in the sun. What contribution the gold made to their potency he didn't know, but it gave the stones a compelling allure, by firelight or by day, and contributed no end to his promotion of their powers. He showed the youth the pill flecked with yellow in his palm.

'In Eternity,' he told him, 'there is no sorrow.'

The Macedonian's eyes suggested that he'd known his share and more.

'Neither is there fear, nor anger, nor desire, nor even will,' continued Tannhauser, 'for in Eternity, all men partake in the Divine Intelligence as a drop of water partakes in the wide blue sea. Thus are we freed, and thus are we made whole, and thus do we return to the fundament and source of all Things.'

He placed the gold and black pill in the Macedonian's hand as it were a Host.

'These stones – the Stones of Immortality – open a window to that metaphysical realm. They give a glimpse of what it might be to exist as pure spirit – of the infinite peace that awaits us – unyoked from the many shackles of our mortality.'

Tempted though he was to indulge, Tannhauser feigned popping a stone in his mouth, and the Macedonian swallowed his. His name was Nicodemus and he was eighteen years old. Tannhauser instructed him to look at the fire around which they sat cross-legged and Nicodemus did so, and they passed another hour in silence, and while Tannhauser tended the blaze

Nicodemus fell under the mystic spell of the stone. When he saw the youth rocking back and forth to some internal rhythm all his own, Tannhauser pointed at the fire.

'In the dance of wind and flame,' he explained, 'and in the transmutation of the wood into heat and light, and at the last into ashes and dust, we see a portrait – or as the Ancients would say, a *microcosmos* – not only of our lives, but of the Chaos into which all Creation will one day subside.'

Nicodemus stared at him, as if he were a very great sage indeed.

'You understand,' said Tannhauser, knowing that it mattered little whether he did so or no. Nicodemus nodded. His eyes sparkled in the firelight, pupils small as the heads of pins, and quavered in their sockets like oiled marbles. 'Good,' said Tannhauser. 'Now let us watch the fire as it dies, and take courage therefrom for the hazards yet to befall us.'

They watched. And the fire at last collapsed into ruby embers and lay throbbing in the night like the excised heart of an infernal beast, and by then Nicodemus was in that place where all disconsolation had been banished and was no more. And in this mute and ecstatic state, Tannhauser loaded him on to Buraq, and stole him away to the Borgo.

Bors had mounted a long watch for Tannhauser's return and he ensured that the two were not shot down as they approached the mantlet and wicket of the Kalkara Gate. For Nicodemus, as Tannhauser led him through the narrow city streets and across the broad wooden bridge to Castel Sant' Angelo, it was a strange reconversion and rebirth, but no less real for that. The city was proliferate with crucifixes, icons and shrines, many smoking with incense and votive lights, and Nicodemus began to cross himself at each. The stern faces and pious aura of the knights who flanked the way, and who escorted them through a labyrinth aflicker with torches to the Grand Master's office, filled him with trembling and awe, as did the symbol of the Christ, everywhere to be seen on surcoats and robes. Though midnight was past, La Valette was in conference with his piliers, and on meeting him the Macedonian fell to his knees, as if at the feet of a living saint, and professed his love for Christ Our Lord, and begged to be rebaptised and to be accepted back into the fold of the Lamb of God.

When La Valette learned that the youth was called Nicodemus, he raised one brow, and there were murmurings from the brother knights, because it seemed there was a character of some significance in the Gospel of Saint John – who had, indeed, spoken with John the Baptist himself – who bore that very same name. If Tannhauser found this unremarkable, for after all every man there present, including himself, bore some name from the Bible, the brethren took it as a sign of God's favour and told Nicodemus that gladly would the chaplains be called and gladly would his soul be born anew. Nicodemus then told them all that had passed at the latest Turkish war council. And it was this.

Following the rebuff before the Bastion of Castile, there were fierce divisions in Mustafa Pasha's camp, which was no surprise to Tannhauser at all. If the Turks had a weakness it was that the army on campaign, unless led by the Sultan in person, was plagued by latent jealousies and by the rivalries and intrigues of the commanders. Mustafa had been in favour of capturing the northern city of Mdina – where La Valette had stationed his cavalry under Copier – before pressing home the siege of L'Isola and the Borgo. But Admiral Piyale had insisted that his armada was not safe in its present anchorage of Marsaxlokk, exposed, as he mistakenly believed it to be, to the Gregale winds.

Piyale was the conqueror of Oran, Minorca and Jerba. He was husband to Suleiman's granddaughter. He was the Sultan's favourite. And Piyale had argued for the capture of Fort Saint Elmo as the first step of the campaign. This would open the safe, adjacent anchorage of Marsamxett to the Turkish fleet. Not only that, but the capture of the fort would allow them to enfilade Sant' Angelo and the Borgo with naval cannon fire from Grand Harbour. Since the Turk's chief engineer had attested that the tiny fort was weak and would fall in less than a week, the council had concluded that their next assault should be focused against Saint Elmo's.

NICODEMUS'S ACCOUNT CAUSED consternation. There were some eight hundred men stationed at Saint Elmo's, premium troops that comprised a third of all the trained soldiers and knights at La Valette's disposal. Arguments were advanced for the fort's evacuation and destruction. For a token resistance by a skeleton crew for the sake of honour. For its immediate reinforcement. But that the fort would indeed fall was not in question.

La Valette turned to Tannhauser. 'Captain Tannhauser, what say you?'

Tannhauser sniffed. 'Is a week's resistance the best your men can do?'

Some among the grandees bristled with offence, but La Valette stilled them.

Tannhauser went on, 'If so, evacuate them now. It will only give Mustafa a victory with which to stir the blood of his *gazi* – something you'd be wise to avoid.'

La Valette nodded, as if this reflected his own view. 'Tell me then, how many days' resistance would turn their victory to humiliation?'

'Humiliation they'll never stoop to. Would dismay suffice?'

'Dismay will do.'

Tannhauser thought about it. Among its many other prodigalities, War demanded that the arts of mathematics, augury and the reading of men's minds be raised to their highest degree. Time, materiel, men, morale, corpses. It was an algebra that could only be attempted by groping in one's gut and a gut, at that, which had itself roiled through eternities of violence and fear.

Tannhauser picked a target he considered impossible. 'Three weeks.'

La Valette pursed his lips and raised his eyes. Watching him, Tannhauser recalled that the trials upon which La Valette's gut could draw included the siege of Rhodes. Even among the janissaries of four decades thereafter, the primeval ferocity of Rhodes remained legend. At Rhodes, they said, the starving remnants of the Religion had risen from holes in the snow like fiends whose only nutriment was human blood. La Valette considered a pandemoniac vision known only to himself and lowered his eyes.

He said, 'Twenty-one days it shall be.'

Before objections could be raised to this boast, Le Mas seized his moment. 'Excellency, my men and I stand ready to hold you to your promise. The Post of Honour.'

The Post of Honour was the post of certain death and Tannhauser felt a constriction in his throat. He was fond of Le Mas, with whom he'd passed some riotous and less than monastic nights at the Oracle. As the leaders of the various langues competed to volunteer, Tannhauser quelled a sudden urge to join them. This was dangerous company to keep.

Tannhauser said, 'I've seen the Turkish siege train. It's enormous.'

The chorus of self-sacrifice was curtailed.

'A dozen eighty-pound culverins, basilisks that fire three-hundred-pound stones, forty-pounders by the score. And Torghoud will bring a siege battery of his own.'

'Torghoud is expected?' asked Le Mas.

'Any day,' Tannhauser replied.

Le Mas turned to La Valette. 'Then I restate and redouble my claim. The Post of Honour.'

'They'll pound Saint Elmo's to rubble,' said Tannhauser.

'By God's Grace,' La Valette said, 'Saint Elmo's will be defended to its rubble.'

'Then I won't seek to dissuade you,' said Tannhauser. 'But the

Ottomans fight with the spade as much as the sword. You must do the same. The Borgo is weaker than you think.'

La Valette concealed a flicker of annoyance. 'How so?'

Tannhauser indicated the chart spread out on the map table. 'With your permission?'

La Valette nodded and the grandees gathered round as Tannhauser ran a finger along the line of the main enceinte. 'Sandstone blocks, yes? Ashlar cladding filled with rubble.'

La Valette nodded.

'The Ottomans use a scientific system,' continued Tannhauser. 'Iron shot to smash through the cladding, marble and stone in rotation to loosen the rubble. These walls are immense, but they will fall. When the Mamelukes arrive, these bastions' – he pointed them out, – 'will be mined, despite the ditch. Mustafa's engineers would dig him a tunnel back to Egypt if he so ordered.'

'This is no more than we expected,' said La Valette.

'If Saint Elmo's can indeed buy you so much time, you must use it to build. You've a thousand slaves rotting underground. Here – at the Post of Castile, a second wall –'

Heads craned forward to watch his finger sketch a line on the map.

'A second wall, invisible from the heights – with gun casements here, and here – to break their hearts when they come howling through the first.'

'Why Castile?' asked La Valette.

'Pride,' said Tannhauser. 'Mustafa is galled by yesterday's reverse. He is enraged. And Turkish rage is of a quality I've never seen in the Frankish soul. Moreover, if he attacks Castile, he can protect his right flank with batteries on San Salvatore. Further still, the plain is most narrow at that point, for his miners and engineers.' He indicated the fortress of Saint Michel. 'If he then assaults L'Isola in concert – as I would in his shoes – your garrison will be stretched to either extremity of the enceinte. And if one or the other breaks, it will be all over, bar the shouting.'

La Valette glanced at Oliver Starkey, as if to convey that the benefits of Tannhauser's recruitment had exceeded all expectations. Then he turned his sea-grey eyes on Tannhauser. They were the coldest he'd ever seen, and he'd seen them all. Even Ludovico Ludovici's were more recognisably human; they at least had known love. Tannhauser formed the discomfiting impression that La Valette entertained an identical opinion of him. He blinked and turned back to the chart. He stabbed at the plan of Borgo town.

'These streets – here, here, here – more walls. A funnel. Demolish these buildings for a field of fire and when they come through, break them again.'

'The battle's hardly begun,' said Le Mas, 'and you already have the infidels in our midst.'

Tannhauser said, 'In Mustafa's mind it's a certainty.'

'Captain Tannhauser is right,' said La Valette. 'The work will help the people understand what lies in store, and what is demanded.'

The gaunt Castilian Zanoguerra spoke up. 'Captain, our common soldiers speak of the janissaries as if they were demons. What can you tell us to allay their superstitions?'

'Superstitions?' said Tannhauser, miffed. 'The janissaries are men of God, much like yourselves, and man for man the equal of any one of you.' He ignored the snorts, for they would learn soon enough. 'But they're lightly armoured and Mustafa will waste their lives. This is his weakness. He is an Isfendiyaroglu, a blood descendant of Ben Welid, the Prophet Mohammed's standard-bearer. He is fearless. He is feared. He is master of all war's arts and siege above all. But he is intemperate. He is vain. He is proud. Break his pride. Husband your men.' He glanced at La Valette. It wasn't done to criticise the Grand Master but if he couldn't speak his mind he was of no use to them. 'Yesterday's sally outside the Provençal Gate was wasteful, rash –'

'We slaughtered them ten for one,' said Zanoguerra.

'You can't afford to spend the one for the ten,' countered Tannhauser. 'Mustafa can. Mustafa will. Bravado will seal your doom. Let the janissaries make the bold gestures. For although they are men among men, they are only men. They will tire of being squandered. They will tire of bad food and filthy water and brutal heat. Sap their faith in Allah's favour, drop by drop. Undermine Mustafa's pride.' He looked at La Valette. 'But if you would break the Turkish heart – and I can name none who've ever done so – you must harden your own beyond measure.'

La Valette said, 'You won't be offended if I say you think like a Turk.'

'On the contrary,' Tannhauser replied. 'They regard you as base barbarians.'

To the surprise of all gathered, La Valette laughed as if he couldn't have been more flattered. It was at this moment that Nicodemus chose to fall headlong in a swoon, right before the crucifix hung on the wall and at which he had been gazing for some time.

Tannhauser strode to kneel beside him and rolled him on his back. It was not unknown for the Stones of Immortality to prove as good as their name; some never woke again from Infinity's dream. But Nicodemus's breathing was regular and on his lips was a smile. When next he made a batch of stones, Tannhauser resolved to be less generous with the opium. The knights, who had also gathered round and who had no knowledge of the youth's intoxication, read in his collapse a sign of religious rapture. Tannhauser didn't disabuse them. With Le Mas's help he hoisted the youth from the floor and over his shoulder.

'We will talk again,' said La Valette.

Tannhauser staggered forth, for the Macedonian was no midget, and carried him to the auberge. A few slaps roused him next morning and, still in a state of rapture, Nicodemus was baptised in San Lorenzo and the stain of Islam washed forever from his soul.

* * *

TANNHAUSER, STILL STEEPED in his barrel of brine, now detected woodsmoke and the smell of coffee drifting from the open door. In the bazaar he'd secured a copper ewer and coffee set, some delicate cups from Izmit – in turquoise trimmed with gold – and two sacks of roasted beans. In Nicodemus he'd secured someone who knew how to prepare them in the necessary fashion. The Macedonian, who treated Tannhauser with the reverence accorded to a magus, was now resident at the Auberge of England, and since – disappointingly, to Tannhauser's mind – neither of the two women evidenced any great interest in culinary skill, he'd taken on the honour of cooking Tannhauser his breakfasts.

Tannhauser climbed from his tub of brine, cooled and refreshed, and let the air dry his skin before he dressed. While eating sheep's kidneys, goat cheese and fried bread, he pondered the conundrum of the contessa's boy. They'd been on the island for almost three weeks and if the boy were here, they hadn't found him. They still didn't know his name. The baptismal registers of the churches in the Borgo had proved barren ground, and this despite the fact that the priests of twelve of the island's outlying churches had brought the registers with them when they'd fled from the Turk. During his forays into the outlands Tannhauser had searched a further seven of the churches and chapels in which Malta abounded. He found a further five parish registers buried beneath the altar stones, but these too had produced nothing.

His design for finding the boy by this method – which had seemed so inspired while drunk on music, roses and cleavage – had proved no less ridiculous than the endeavour as a whole. The urge to impress a woman had led innumerable men of good sense into disasters otherwise avoided. It was small comfort to think he was the latest in a line of fools that stretched all the way back to Eden.

There were hundreds of boys in the city. It was no easy matter to identify among them a bastard born twelve years before on All Hallows Eve. It occurred to him now that such a foundling might not even know his own birth date. Illegitimacy was a touchy subject in this community, where a surly pride was ubiquitous among the Maltese and high reputations, especially regarding piety, were jealously protected among the knights. And in burying the sexual crimes of its celibate servants, the Roman Church enjoyed an expertise honed throughout a millennium of frequent practice.

'I will know him when I see him,' Carla had claimed. But if so, she hadn't seen him yet. Tannhauser had searched every unwashed face for echoes of Carla and Ludovico. On one day he would spot half a dozen youths who appeared the very image of one or the other; on the next those very same physiognomies would mock his gullibility. He even saw boys who might pass for the fruit of his own seed. And all this was to assume that the boy was here at all, rather than long dead or at that moment being buggered in a Libyan brothel or a cardinal's bed. Tannhauser had considered telling Carla that he'd found the boy's tombstone in one of the remote country graveyards beyond the walls. How much grief could she feel for so abstract a figure? But it was not so much grief as defeat that would cloud her eyes and he didn't want to dull their lustre, especially with a lie. Carla seemed to view her life as a tale of surrender without resistance; the strong were ever reluctant to forgive or excuse their failures. Her search for the boy was Carla's last battle; if she lost it he feared that she'd never have the heart to fight another, and that he would hate to see.

He washed down a mouthful of kidney with his wine. He contemplated an alternative deception, inspired by Amparo while he'd grappled with the buttons on her dress on his return from the midnight conference. This was to substitute an impostor from among the numerous orphans in the city. She'd befriended some such ragamuffin on the docks and had asked if she might introduce him. It would be easy enough to gain such a boy's trust, educate him in the advantage of such a stratagem, and get him to claim the appropriate birth date, which could be validated by a simple piece of forgery in one of the parish registers he'd taken. All would be content, and they could make a prompt escape from this island of madness and death.

He found himself staring at the last morsel on his plate with a sudden nausea. Honour was a monstrous curse. It led more surely to destruction than any vice. Love and respect for women was even worse, being capable of spoiling an excellent breakfast among much else. He signalled Nicodemus for the coffee. He sipped the healthful brew and waited for his spirits to rally. He hadn't yet been to Mdina, the island's formal capital. La Valette was in contact with its garrison via his famous Maltese scouts, but the journey was hazardous. Nevertheless, the boy had been born in Mdina and it had to be done. If the trip proved as fruitless as the others, he'd persuade Carla that their quest was over.

He rubbed his face with both hands. His only present desire was to return to bed and Amparo's arms, but it was some form or other of such desires that had brought him to this hardship in the first place. Carla had asked him to bring her to Malta and he'd done as much and more. He'd put some colour in her cheeks. He'd given her a taste of adventure. They'd failed, but with honour. Surely she could lay her demons to rest on that basis. He'd brought lambs into a den of wolves and this weighed heavily on his mind. Surely his obligation now was to take them out again. Would she deny him his noble title by marriage? He'd neglected to specify this circumstance in the details of their bargain; more evidence of his witlessness when braced by a fine pair of breasts. He was uncommonly fond of Carla, more than he'd so far been willing to admit. A man could do much worse in the matter of a wife. Yet he'd muddied those waters too by giving in to Amparo's charms. This had wounded Carla, there was no denying it, and a clawed fist squeezed at his entrails. If only the contessa had been a little more receptive. If he hadn't bungled the kiss he'd tried to steal in the garden. In all truth he'd taken that as revulsion and hadn't been surprised. And what of the powerful emotion he'd felt on watching Amparo sleeping not an hour before?

Damnation. He was shackled by invisible chains. Tortured by psychic instruments of fiendish manufacture. A shrewd man would arrange his own departure without further ado. But he was not a shrewd man, or so it seemed, and he concluded these futile ruminations with a weighty sigh.

'You are troubled, My Lord,' said Nicodemus.

Tannhauser grunted and lowered his hands. The Macedonian's looks were striking, with dark, intense features of perfect symmetry and proportion. His black, long-lashed eyes looked out on the world with the violated innocence of icons on the walls of the Aya Sofy. It was probably these qualities that had promoted him to Mustafa's personal guard, for old men find reassurance in the mirror of youth. They spoke in Turkish.

'I'm too easily given to introspection,' said Tannhauser. 'It's not a habit you should cultivate.'

'You showed me the way back to Christ,' said Nicodemus. His eyes shone with the idealism of one too young to know better. 'My life is yours.'

Tannhauser smiled. 'I am not a religious man.'

'You see to the heart of things as only a religious man could.'

Tannhauser saw no reason to contradict him. Loyalty, whatever its basis, was a precious commodity. Nicodemus pulled up the sleeve of his shirt to reveal a bronzed and sinewy forearm, and around it a bangle of stippled yellow gold. He stripped the bangle off and held it out.

'Please,' he said. 'Accept this from me. It will ease your troubles.'

Tannhauser examined it. It was an incomplete circlet and heavy, perhaps seven or eight ounces, and masculine in character. There were random variations in the metal's hue and the finish was not of the finest: the marks of the smith's hammer could be seen in the repoussage work and the symmetry was imperfect. Yet all the same it proclaimed itself superb. The gold was an inch and a half wide at its centre and tapered to an inch at either end. The terminations were fashioned into the heads of roaring lions. He turned the bangle in the light and saw that it was inscribed in Arabic along its inner face. He read it out loud:

'*I come to Malta not for riches or honour but to save my soul.*'

He looked at Nicodemus. He wondered who'd given it to the youth, and why; but he wasn't sure he wanted to know the answer. Tannhauser wrapped the bangle round his wrist. He felt an inexplicable warmth flow through his chest. The inscription, perhaps, imbued it with some supernal potency.

'I will treasure it above all other possessions,' said Tannhauser. He held his arm up and the bangle shone with a dull, almost ochre, glow. 'It contains a power that the eye cannot see.'

Nicodemus nodded, solemnly.

Tannhauser said, 'Before he was crowned Sultan, Suleiman Khan trained in the goldsmith's art.'

'Yes,' replied Nicodemus. 'So did I.' Tannhauser looked at him. 'At least, I was apprenticed for five years. I was never admitted to the Guild.'

The bangle's minor flaws now made sense. 'So this is of your creation.'

Nicodemus nodded. 'From forty-nine pieces of gold.' He said this as if the coins had been in payment for something that should never have been sold.

'Then you transformed something base into something of beauty,' said Tannhauser. 'There is no higher magic.'

A shadow of melancholy persisted in the Macedonian's face.

Tannhauser smiled. 'Let me embrace you.'

Nicodemus stepped forward and Tannhauser clasped him to his chest. 'Now, go and rouse Bors from his pit.' He let go. 'And cook something tasty for the women while I'm gone. They eat like sparrows.' Nicodemus turned to leave and Tannhauser stopped him. 'Nicodemus. You have eased my troubles.'

Nicodemus's face brightened with a smile. He bowed and left. Tannhauser went to the door and the sunlight struck bursts of radiance from the bangle. Only gold looked and felt like gold. All else was prone to deceive, which was why men loved it. He felt a faint tremor through the soles of his boots as the sound of dozens of explosions reached the auberge. The siege guns had opened up from the slopes of Monte Sciberras. Another day had begun at Fort Saint Elmo.

FRIDAY 8 JUNE 1565

Hospital Piazza, Castel Sant' Angelo

Bors swallowed his disgruntlement at missing a cooked breakfast and wolfed bread and cheese and swigged wine as they walked across the town.

'The women are driving me mad,' Mattias said.

Bors feigned surprise. 'What have the fair and tender maidens done now?'

Mattias blew his cheeks. 'Do they need do anything, other than breathe?' He spread his palms, as if the victim of forces mightier and more cunning than he. 'I have the one but I want the other too.'

'The contessa?' said Bors. 'I'd have thought her too haughty for you.'

'She casts a fascination without even knowing it.'

'Well, I dare say you'd find a torrid welcome in her arms – if you stopped swiving her dearest friend and abased yourself. By the look of her she hasn't been molested since her boy was born. Though, of course, they're much craftier in concealing these matters than we.'

'If it were only a question of lust there'd be no great riddle. But I have affection for each.'

'Hold now,' said Bors. 'Love at the best of times is a faithless pimp.'

'I did not say love.'

'Then let us argue the number of angels that may dance on the head of a pin.'

Mattias said, 'Go on.'

'In war love becomes a contagion,' expounded Bors. 'Much-loathed rivals become brothers, malice becomes firm fellowship and strangers clasp each other to their breast. Look at La Valette. I'd wager that six months ago any number of the Spanish or Italian knights would've danced a jig of joy to see a knife between his shoulders. So at least I've heard. But the man now walks on water. But why?' He paused for drama. 'Because Love is the horse that pulls the gut cart of War. Why else would we come back for more? As for women and war, never is their flesh softer or their virtues more bright or their gentleness more welcome to the soul.' He looked Mattias in the eye. 'And never is the hole between their thighs a deeper pit in which to fall.'

Mattias was silent for a while as he took this in and Bors was gratified. In the normal run, Mattias had an answer for everything. 'So what is your advice?' he asked.

'Advice?' A short laugh escaped Bors's throat. 'There's a whore in the lee of Galley Creek that I can warmly recommend, though she tips the scales at not much less than I do. The sight of her naked is alone a marvel never to be forgotten.'

'My question was in earnest.'

'Then so is this answer. The only game here is to stay alive. And to be in love – or in lust – is to play with a dangerous handicap.' He shrugged. 'But I waste my breath, for the game unfettered is no game at all, as least for the likes of you. My advice, then, is to swive them both and let the Devil take his due. It won't be until all this is over that you'll know what any of it means. And even then.'

Mattias brooded on this as they entered the piazza outside the

Sacred Infirmary. His attitude changed as he saw Father Lazaro come out and walk down the steps.

'Hold,' said Mattias, 'for I've a bone to pick.'

He bowed to Lazaro, who gave a cautious nod in return.

'Father Lazaro, Mattias Tannhauser, late of Messina. I hope you won't find me insolent, but I've a boon to ask. The Lady Carla is eager to bring some comfort to the wounded, a fact of which you are aware, yet she is denied any opportunity to serve. I was hoping you and I might reach some bargain in this matter.'

'The care of the sick is the most sacred work of the Order, and is not a fit subject for bargaining,' said Lazaro. 'In any case, only we have the necessary skill.'

'What skill does it take to hold a man's hand and whisper some words of hope?'

'She is a woman.'

'The sound of a woman's voice will give a man better reason to live than all your elixirs and potions mingled together.'

'Our men will survive through prayer and the Grace of God,' said Lazaro.

'Then the contessa is sent by God. She's spent half her life on her knees.'

'No lay women are allowed in the Sacred Infirmary.'

'The only thing that excludes them is your pride – or should I say vanity?'

The monk gaped at his effrontery. 'Should we open the doors to every woman in the Borgo?'

'No doubt you could do worse,' said Mattias. 'Nevertheless, it can be no great feat to make exception for an aristocrat like her.'

Lazaro seemed unwilling to yield. Mattias placed a hand on the monk's shoulder. Lazaro flinched, as if no one had taken such a liberty in his life. 'Father, you are man of God and, if you will forgive me, advanced in years. You cannot imagine what the sight – the presence, the perfume, the aura – of a beautiful woman can do for a fighting man's spirit.'

Lazaro looked up into the battered and barbarian face looming over his own. 'I'd hoped to avoid raising this objection, but I have heard that the Lady Carla is not as pious as you claim.'

Mattias raised one brow in warning. 'You have me at a disadvantage, Father.'

'Is she not living with you in a state of mortal sin?'

'You disappoint me, Father,' said Mattias. 'Bitterly so, if I may be so bold.'

Lazaro's mouth puckered into something resembling the anus of a sheep. Mattias glanced at Bors. Bors turned away to stifle a snigger.

'Such gossip is both idle and pernicious,' Mattias continued. 'Did not Moses himself list the bearing of false witness as a crime?' His eyes darkened. 'I myself have no good name worth defending, but as the Lady's protector I would advise you against such slurs upon her honour.'

'Then it's untrue,' said Lazaro, nervously.

'I'm shocked that the brethren should entertain such salacious tittle-tattle.'

Lazaro, somewhat embarrassed, offered a feeble defence. 'Perhaps you do not know this, but the Lady left this island under a cloud.'

'She told me so herself, for she's quite without guile. The shame you refer to – and there was plenty to go around – belonged to others more powerful than she and to her not at all. Besides, it was long ago. Is your piety so exorbitant that you've abandoned Christ's message of forgiveness? Would you banish the Magdalene from the foot of the Cross? Shame on you, Father Lazaro.' As Lazaro reeled under this tirade, Mattias took a step back and softened his tone. 'If you chose to be more Christian, a pound of Iranian opium might find a way of reaching your apothecary. Perhaps even two.'

Lazaro blinked, by now quite confused. 'You're hoarding opium? While the hospital is filled with direly wounded?'

Bors recalled the weighty stash beneath the water tub. Mattias feigned a sad smile.

'Perhaps I've earned the low esteem in which you hold me, Father Lazaro, even though we were strangers before today. But hoarding opium?'

Lazaro retreated. 'Perhaps the plight of my patients provoked too hasty a conclusion –'

'However,' went on Tannhauser, hand palm-raised, 'at great personal risk, and considerable expense, I might acquire said drugs on your behalf from the Turkish bazaar.'

In a seizure of repentance, Lazaro grabbed his hand. 'Forgive me, Captain, I beg you.'

Mattias inclined his head in a gracious gesture. 'The Lady Carla will be honoured to accept your invitation.'

Lazaro's face corrugated with worry. 'But will the Lady Carla have the strength for such grim work?' Lazaro looked up the steps to the cloistered hospital. 'There are sights in there that would turn the strongest stomach – and break the stoutest heart.'

'The contessa's heart is of gold. But if her stomach proves too weak, then your pride will be vindicated, and hers justly chastised. You will find her and her companion at the Auberge of England.'

'Her companion?'

'Amparo. If it's vulgar gossip you seek, she's the woman with whom I'm living in sin.' Lazaro blinked. Mattias made the sign of the Cross. '*Dominus vobiscum*,' he said.

And off they went.

Dominus vobiscum, thought Bors. To a priest. Only an ignorance of manners could produce such cheek; but ignorance played little part in anything Mattias did.

Castel Sant' Angelo rose above Grand Harbour like a huge floating ziggurat, its sheer walls descending in stepped sandstone tiers to the water's edge. From Sant' Angelo's roof, the view across

Grand Harbour to Fort Saint Elmo was unequalled and as they ascended the last stone stairway Bors's heart hammered hard with more than just exertion. He'd been invited to the emperor's box and not even Nero had ever staged a circus as spectacular as this.

They emerged into the blinding sun in time to be deafened by a salvo from Sant' Angelo's cavalier. The great gun platform, whose timbers shook and creaked with the force of the blast, had been constructed to provide a better field of fire on the Turkish positions. Spouts of smoke barrelled above the crystal waters far below and Bors shaded his gaze to watch the gunners. They fell upon the sixteen-pounders as if upon dangerous animals in want of restraint. They were stripped to the waist for all that the day was yet cool, their red mouths heaving in the sulphurous air and every inch of them painted black as tar with powder waste and grease. Their filthy hides were runnelled with sweat and patched with weeping ulcers caused by the burns that went with the job. And all of them, nine to a crew, cursing God and the Devil and the dear old mothers that had borne them as they wrestled the great bronze beasts back into position, the whites of their eyes rolling bloodshot and their faces all covered in soot, as if this were a satanic *commedia* and they its minstrels infernal and deranged.

'I was a gunner's mate at the age of nine,' said Bors, 'in the army of the King of Connaught. I still bear the marks.'

'Concussion to the brain can last a lifetime,' agreed Mattias.

Bors laughed. 'As will my oath never to work with artillery again.'

In the high, clear morning sky dozens of vultures on broad black wings wheeled above Fort Saint Elmo in placid anticlockwise gyres, their orbits perfectly stacked one above the other by that mysterious science known only to their breed. A tall, slender monk stood on the allure of the north-west wall, studying the monstrous birds as if he would fathom their secret. Starkey cut as scholastic and unwarlike a figure as one could imagine, yet he'd done his time on the Religion's caravans, ravaging the Levantine coast and Aegean Isles and mauling Ottoman ships in the Ionian Sea.

Mattias said, 'There's our man.'

As they circled the vast, flat roof towards Starkey, Bors said, 'What news of the contessa's boy?'

'I've one last place to look. If I find no sign of him there, it'll be time to take our leave.' He looked at Bors. 'Sabato waits in Venice. And you can boast that you stood with the Religion.'

'Desertion's not something to boast about. And if they catch us, they'll hang us.'

'I'm deserting no one,' said Mattias. 'I gave no bond and signed no contract. Despite which I've given priceless service for not a penny piece in pay. That debt I intend to collect.'

Bors knew Mattias of old. 'You have a boat?'

'Not yet. La Valette has concealed a score or more of feluccas all about the coast, for use by his messengers to Sicily. It can't be more than a day's work to find one.' Mattias read his expression and stopped at the foot of the stone stairs to the allure. 'We've both better things to do than die in this manure pile. At present the country to the south is but sparsely patrolled, but when Saint Elmo falls, Mustafa will invest this city and the risks of escape will be multiplied. My notion is to sell off our opium in the bazaar – where we'll get a better price and may trade for pearls and precious stones rather than gold – and make sail for Calabria within the week.'

'What if the Lady Carla decides to stay?'

'I can't create her son out of clay. And love is no more worth dying for than God.'

'Praises be.'

'Will you leave or stay?' asked Mattias.

Bors shrugged. 'I suppose the smell of glory will have to do.'

'Good.'

'But how will all four of us get through the Kalkara Gate?'

Mattias didn't answer.

They mounted the stair and as Bors cleared the parapet he gasped. Less than half a mile distant across the harbour the entire Turkish army surrounded the small, beleaguered outpost of Fort Saint Elmo. Monte Sciberras bulged from the water like the back of a half-submerged ox, its spine tapering down towards the fort, which was perched on the seaward tip of the rocky peninsula. The hill gave a fine advantage to the Turkish artillery but its flanks claimed not a stalk of vegetation, nor even a handful of dirt in which such might have thrived. Virgin nature offered nothing in which to entrench either guns or troops, but like a virgin the mountain had been raped by the engineers. From as far away as the Bingemma Basin thousands of African blackamoors and Christian slaves had scraped hundreds of tons of earth from the island's meagre topsoil and hauled it in sacks to the mountain's barren slopes. They'd woven gabions – huge wickerwork baskets – from willow branches brought in by their ships. Then they'd filled the baskets with boulders and rubble and with the corpses of those fellow labourers shot down in droves by the marksmen of the fort. These gabions were formed into a series of redoubts from which the muzzles of the Turkish siege guns pointed and roared, vomiting iron and marble at Saint Elmo's walls.

At further prodigious cost in Turkish lives, trenches had been hacked into the rock and now extended, web-like, down the slopes to wind all the way around the fort's southern aspect. From these slits in the stony ground, janissary marksmen picked at the men on the ramparts and at anything that sailed across the water, which in daylight was nothing at all. From the shore of Marsamxett Bay beyond the fort, where timber and brushwood screens provided concealment, more snipers fired at any Christian who showed his head on the western walls. Below the massive gun batteries, the whole steep hillside swirled with the regimental pennants of the Moslem warriors thereon massed in their thousands. Canary yellows vied with vivid scarlets and parrot greens, the silk all shiny and the sun winking silver from the hieroglyphs adorning the flags. At the centre of all this pageantry and gunfire, Saint Elmo's smoked like the throat of an awakened volcano.

'How they love bright colours, these Moslem swine,' said Bors. 'What do those banners say?' he asked.

'Verses from the Koran,' said Mattias. 'The *surah* of Conquest. They exhort the Faithful to slaughter and vengeance and death.'

'And there you have the difference between us,' said Bors, 'for when did Jesus Christ ever call for such horrors?'

'Evidently, Jesus Christ knew he did not need to.'

The embattled fort itself was shaped like a star with four main salients. Its landward curtain and bastions were presently obscured by smoke and dust. Its rear and eastern flanks fell sheer into the sea. After fifteen days' bombardment its original shape and design could only be guessed at. The walls that faced batteries on the hill were rent by breaches and the masonry gaped like teeth in a crone's mouth. Masses of rubble had cascaded into the ditch beneath the wall and these hillocks were brightly carpeted with the bodies of Turkish fanatics already slaughtered. Ferocious wave attacks, lasting hours at a stretch, had alternated with bombardments, and more were expected that day.

Despite all this, the bullet-tattered standard of Saint John – a white Crusader cross on a blood-red field – still flew above the ruins, and from the crumbling battlements and improvised counterwalls came a steady crackle of muskets and the blast of cannon. So far, against every calculation of attackers and besieged alike, the massed Turkish assaults had been repulsed. As the defenders died by day, La Valette replaced them by night, with men rowed out across the harbour from Sant' Angelo's dock. There was never any shortage of volunteers and Bors did not wonder. He clenched his fist on the hilt of his sword and wished that he were with them. A hand squeezed his arm.

'You've tears in your eyes,' said Mattias. 'I thought you English knew better.'

Bors scowled and swatted the offending orbs with either hand. 'No, all we are fit for is boasting in alehouses – of the feats of valour we saw but did not take part in.'

Mattias glanced over at Starkey. 'Your countryman seems a good deal more phlegmatic.'

It was true: Starkey was observing the holocaust with no more emotion than a spectator at a game of bowls. 'Starkey doesn't plan to steal away like a thief in the night.'

Mattias ignored this and walked along the allure and Bors followed.

Starkey turned in greeting. 'I hear you've turned my house into a sink of iniquity.'

'As Jesus told us,' Mattias replied, 'man cannot live by bread alone.'

'Christ spoke of spiritual matters, as even you well know.' Starkey turned to Bors and spoke in English. 'You're a son of the Church, I've seen you at Mass.'

Bors heard his native tongue so rarely that its sound seemed peculiarly foreign; yet its music always moved him. 'Yes, Your Excellency. A good son.'

'How did you come to fall in with so godless a man?'

'On a cold night, in a damp ditch, when Mattias wasn't long for this world. With God's help, I nursed him back to life.' There was no point flattering a man of Starkey's influence, but a stab at piety could do no harm. 'Now, God willing, I hope to guide him towards eternal life too. That is, back into the arms of Mother Church from whence he came.'

Starkey seemed to enjoy hearing the language as much as he did. 'You have a mighty task on your hands.'

'Mattias was taken by the Mussulmans when only a boy, and saw his family butchered in the bargain, so I beg you to forgive his blasphemies, which are indeed many. Christ still speaks to his heart, if he would but listen.'

Starkey studied him and said, 'I do believe you're sincere.'

Bors blinked. What kind of scoundrel did Starkey take him for? 'In matters of religion I am always sincere.'

'No doubt you discuss things of great importance,' said Mattias in Italian, 'but I've matters of my own to broach.'

'The subject was eternal salvation,' said Starkey. 'Your salvation.'

'Then you can help me,' said Mattias, 'I've a mind to visit Mdina, but in the bazaar I learned that Marshal Copier's cavalry regard any foragers, scouts or watering parties much as wolves regard rabbits. I'd rather not be hacked to pieces and need more protection than that afforded by my wits.'

'They've served you well enough to date,' replied Starkey.

'The Turks aren't so quick to indulge their bloodlust,' said Mattias. 'They're a civilised race. They enjoy talking. Armoured knights on horseback are poor of hearing, especially when they see a man in a turban.'

'Would you take the Lady Carla with you?' asked Starkey.

This took Bors by surprise, and he would have stumbled, but Mattias reacted as if no question could have been more natural. 'Not today, though it is her wish, as she'd like to be with her father through these dark days. But without a *passe porte* – for her and her guardians – I wouldn't be allowed to take them beyond the walls. May I take this as an offer to provide us with such a safe conduct?'

Guardians, by God, thought Bors. Just like that. With a passport through Kalkara Gate – and a boat – they'd all be gone.

'Then My Lady hasn't found this boy of hers,' said Starkey.

Mattias had intended the high command to remain ignorant of this matter, lest they interpret it for what it was, a motive for treachery. But again Mattias replied without a blink.

'Do you know the boy and where he might be?'

It was Starkey, rather, who blinked. He shook his head. 'In the years before our Grand Master was elected, the moral conduct of the Order became degenerate. Men are only men. Young knights join the Order full of pride and chivalric dreams, and find a life of fasting and privation at the edge of the world. Holy Vows were made but not always kept. There was dicing, whoring, drunkenness, even duelling. Only the severest discipline can stop young men from doing what young men do. La Valette imposed it. As he says, *Our vows are inhumanly hard by design. They are the hammer and the anvil by which our strength is forged.*'

'You've avoided my question,' said Mattias. 'Do you know the boy?'

'I've no idea who the Lady Carla's son might be – nor with whom she transgressed.' He looked discomfited. 'Was it a member of the Order?'

'The contessa's boy was born on All Hallows Eve,' said Mattias.

He'd avoided revealing the boy's pedigree. That the inquisitor, Ludovico, was his father was sufficient reason. The matter was scandalous enough as it was.

'I wouldn't count on the boy knowing that,' said Starkey. 'The Maltese are a primitive, insular breed and very pious. What will you do if you find him?'

'I shall reunite him with his mother.'

'She may be unpleasantly surprised. The life of a swineherd can eradicate every vestige of noble blood.'

'The contessa has a tender heart.'

'And after that? Can we continue to rely on your allegiance?'

'I've proved my fidelity to the Religion.'

'A careful answer,' said Starkey.

'To a question some would take as a mortal insult,' Mattias replied.

Starkey retreated with good grace. 'No man stands higher in the Grand Master's esteem.'

'Then I'll give you reason to raise it even further – and to send me to Mdina as well.'

Mattias pointed over Starkey's shoulder. Starkey turned. They all looked towards Gallows Point, the spit of land that, with Fort

Saint Elmo, formed the jaws of the entrance to Grand Harbour from the open sea. True to Mattias's predictions, Torghoud Rais had arrived with his fleet on 30 May. He'd installed his siege guns on Gallows Point and these now battered Saint Elmo's from the east. Even as they watched, these batteries fired a cannonade at the smoking fort.

'The Turks are pouring three hundred rounds an hour into the fort,' said Tannhauser. He indicated the channel across Grand Harbour. 'And Torghoud's guns menace your resupply boats. Instead of killing waterboys and camel drovers, let Copier's cavalry do some man's work. Send me to Mdina and I'll guide a company of his horse to Gallows Point.'

'As always,' said Starkey, 'your boldness shames me.'

'And the *passe portes*?' said Mattias.

A sixteen-pounder roared from the cavalier and Bors watched the ball in its flight across the bay. It landed amid a covey of blackamoors extending a Turkish trench and left a tangle of yowling human wreckage as it bounced on down the slit.

'Come with me,' said Starkey, 'and I'll draw up the necessary papers. I can also tell you where to find the Lady Carla's father, Don Ignacio. He's in ill health, and may not be sympathetic, but if anyone knows something of the boy, it will be him.'

Starkey made for the steps. Mattias followed. Bors felt a pang at losing this Olympian vista. 'Your Excellency,' he said. Starkey stopped. 'With your permission, I'll stay and spot for the gunners. I see a good number of their shots going to waste.'

Starkey nodded. 'I'll instruct the crews.'

Mattias said, 'Today is the Moslem Sabbath, so their attack will be unusually fierce.' He took Bors by the shoulder and pointed to the Turkish redoubts on Monte Sciberras. 'You see the big white turban?'

Bors scanned the tiny figures through the powder haze. 'I see a thousand white turbans.'

'One is larger than the rest, to indicate high rank. The green robe. There above the six-gun emplacement, the dragon-mouthed culverins.'

Bors, still scouring the battlefield, stopped as he found a huge white turban balanced on a green-robed figure the size of pin. 'I have him.'

'That's Torghoud Rais.'

Bors felt his lip curl.

'He sleeps in the trenches with his men,' said Mattias. 'He shares their food. They adore him. His death would be worth a division. Lob some shot his way and chance may do the rest.'

Mattias turned and Bors grabbed his arm. 'Good fortune, my friend.'

'Tell the women I'll be back tomorrow night.'

Bors watched Starkey and Mattias descend the wall stair and cross the roof. A sixteen-pounder boomed from the cavalier and Bors turned to watch the ball's trajectory and judge any necessary correction. He inhaled with joy. This was the life God had given him. He crossed himself and gave thanks to Jesus Christ.

FRIDAY 8 JUNE 1565

Mdina

In the heat-stunned wane of the day the winding streets of Mdina put Tannhauser in mind of Palermo. The houses were grand in the Norman style but gloomy, as if built by men too much in awe of their own importance. At the end of a blind alley off King Ferdinand Street he found, as directed, the Casa Manduca. He knocked and a sallow, grey-haired steward, perhaps sixty years in age, opened the door. He wore a dark blue velvet coat from which stains had recently been sponged. He looked and smelled as if he rarely left the building. He bowed as if to do so pained his back. He stared at Tannhauser's chest without meeting his eyes. Strange servants served strange masters and Tannhauser wondered what he'd find inside.

'Captain Tannhauser,' he said, 'for Don Ignacio.'

The steward led him down a hall in which the lamplight flickered on lugubrious family portraits and depictions of martyrdom, none of them, in Tannhauser's view, of high artistic merit. They passed an unlit staircase and a number of closed doors. The rugs underfoot were moth-eaten, the furniture dour and as heavy as the building itself. It felt like a mausoleum, built to inter a fantasy of grandeur lost. This was where Carla had grown up. In a dark and suffocating tomb of provincial piety. He imagined her youthful spirit struggling to soar in such a prison. His own already gasped after twenty paces. He felt pity for the girl that she'd once been and understood better the restraint that marked her as a woman. Tannhauser felt no surprise that she'd never returned and his tenderness towards her deepened. He couldn't avoid the thought that by sending the girl into exile, no matter how cruelly, Don Ignacio had done his daughter a favour.

The steward opened a pair of lacquered doors and stood aside without making an announcement. The air that gusted forth was musty and stifling, a foetor saturate with urine, flatus and decay. It filled Tannhauser with the urge to flee – from loneliness, from despair, from life sustained at a price not worth the paying. He looked at the steward. Familiar though he must have been, the steward bore the expression of a man trying to quell an intolerable nausea. He bowed from the waist and indicated that Tannhauser enter alone. Tannhauser, regretting that he didn't have to hand a sprig of rosemary with which to cram his nostrils, walked inside as if stepping in a bath of vomit, and the steward closed the lacquered doors behind him.

A DEEP ARMCHAIR with a footstool was set within the light of a blazing fireplace. In it sat an old man, his skull as hairless and pale as a maggot. He was wrapped in a fur-lined robe, its colour dark brown in the firelight. Down one breast the robe gleamed with mucus, though whether from the bloodless slit that passed for his mouth or from the enormous lesion distorting his lips and invading his right cheek, Tannhauser couldn't tell. The man's white beard was clotted and sticky too. The body within the robe appeared as shrivelled as a waterless plant and the etiolate hands protruding from the sleeves were blotched with large brown spots. The eyes that peered out at him were black, with yellow rims about the irises. Tannhauser couldn't tell how much the old man could see, but sensed that it wasn't much more than the blur of the fire. This was Don Ignacio Manduca. Tannhauser decided it would be premature to introduce himself as Don Ignacio's son-in-law-to-be.

'Do not be alarmed by my affliction,' said Don Ignacio. He spoke Italian with the local accent. His voice was without a quaver, the last manifestation of a strength that barely clung to existence. 'It was sent by God as punishment for my sins. If I were to rail against His judgement, I would forfeit the mercies of Purgatory, and so I ask you to accept it, as do I.'

Tannhauser took a step closer and looked at the lesion again. It was a purple-edged crater with a raw, weeping floor and extended from the rim of his ear to the edge of one nostril, and from his temple to the angle of his jaw. Beneath the jaw, his neck bulged with tumours, as if a cluster of quail's eggs had been buried beneath the skin.

Tannhauser said, 'Only the vain fear ugliness of the flesh, Don Ignacio. And of all the vices, vanity is the one which least befits a man.'

'Well said, Captain Tannhauser, well said.' He squinted. 'That has the ring of a *nom de guerre*, if I may so note.'

'You have the instinct of an adventurer,' Tannhauser replied.

'An adventurer?' Don Ignacio nodded and grimaced with what Tannhauser took to be pleasure. 'Yes, yes, though you might not think so seeing me now. Do I take it you're wanted for a crime in some far-flung corner of this sick and benighted world?'

'For many crimes, in many corners.'

Don Ignacio laughed like a crow at his carrion. 'Then you may count on sanctuary here. I fought for Charles Quintus at Tunis, thirty years ago. Under Andrea Doria. I knew many a *Landsknecht* back then. Didn't they torch Rome for Quintus too?'

'And imprisoned the Pope in his own gaol.'

Another dry cackle. 'Bold fighters, the Germans, but only as good as their pay. Does La Valette pay you well?'

'The Grand Master pays me not at all.'

'Then he's a fool, though that's no news to me. If you wish to speak of vanity speak of the knights. The Religion. Bah.' Scorn further contorted his deformed lips. 'You'd think Christ was nailed to the Cross for them alone. And Frenchmen to boot, or controlled by them, more or less. More vanity in a Frenchman than lies howling in the bilges of Hell. You'll forgive my blasphemies, I know, for all Germans are godless at heart. Too much of forest and wilderness in their souls. But the knights vex me, strutting about our island, reshaping our polity to their convenience. And with not so much as a by your leave. Nor am I alone in these sentiments. Without their crusade the Turks would've left us alone. Corsairs, yes, we've been seeing off those dogs for five hundred years. But an army fit for the reconquest of Granada?' He snorted and slavered and drew a trembling hand across his mouth. 'But I take up your time. How may a dying man help the mighty Religion?'

'I'm not here on behalf of the Religion,' said Tannhauser, 'but to ask a personal boon.'

'I enjoy a rogue's company and it's been a good while. Ask what you wish.'

'I represent the Lady Carla, your daughter.'

The grotesque face turned towards him, as if trying to make out Tannhauser's features in the gloom. 'I have no daughter.' His voice was like a trap snapping shut. 'I will die childless and without heirs. By God's will my line is over, and I am the last of the Manduca.' He indicated the house above them. 'All this will go to Mother Church if, God willing, She survives this invasion to claim it.'

'The Lady Carla doesn't seek your property, or even your acknowledgement.'

'The Lady Carla is a whore.' Don Ignacio's liver-hued lips contorted and gouts of malodorous phlegm sizzled into the grate. 'As was her mother before her. Truly it is said that marriage is a bargain in which only the entrance is free.'

Veins seemed to writhe on his flaking scalp and the tumours

bulged in his neck and the malignant crater shone like evil in the firelight, as if he were already chained and screaming in some lower circle of perdition. Tannhauser waited while the old man lanced his own boils.

'Not a drop of my blood flows in Carla's veins. A chevalier of Auvergne was her father, one of the pure and holy knights – oh yes – who cavorted in my bed while I defended the Empire. And no sooner was Carla herself of an age to spread her legs, than another of the glorious brethren stepped into the breach. They deposit their sacred seed between trips to the confessional.' His spidery fists clenched, the thumbs and forefingers rendered immobile and twisted by gouty deformities. 'My forefathers built this house as conquerors. In my custody it was turned into a brothel.'

The news that Carla shared no kinship with this creature could hardly have been more welcome. Tannhauser kept the contempt from his voice. 'Does Carla know she's not your daughter?'

Don Ignacio stabbed a knobbly finger at the ulcer eating his face, and no doubt eating his mind away too. 'What do you think is the cause of this obscenity? Decades of deception and pretence. Lies. Lies. Lechery and lies. And shame and sham and fornication and whispers of mockery and laughter behind my back. No. Carla knows nothing.'

Don Ignacio leaned forward with a doleful expression. He exchanged his morbid self-loathing for a more poignant torment. 'I raised her as my own,' he said, his voice not far short of a wail. 'And not merely to protect my honour but because I loved her more dearly than any other living soul. Ask her to swear – by the Virgin of Sorrows – and she will tell you as much herself.'

The man seemed to think he deserved some sympathy; perhaps even admiration.

Tannhauser could not have been more revolted by this display.

'And yet for all that – for all that I loved her – she betrayed me and the name I'd bequeathed her with a whoreson of the Baptist.'

'Her lover was no knight of the convent but a Dominican priest.'

'Knight, priest, Dominican, a pox on them all.'

The old man's histrionics confirmed Tannhauser in his view that when misfortune befell the privileged they bore it with far less dignity, and a great deal more self-pity, than did the rest of the human race. He said, 'Tell me, Your Excellency, what was the fate of Carla's child? Her son. What was his name? Who raised him and where?'

Ignacio's eyes gleamed with malice. 'So at last her conscience pricks her. Believe me when I say that it's better that my daughter never knows.'

Tannhauser sighed and wiped his brow. The heat and the foetor were appalling. 'I'm as keen to find this boy as she is,' he said. 'I ask this favour as a personal courtesy to me.'

Don Ignacio summoned a degenerate leer, made the more grotesque by his deformity. 'So she's opened her thighs for you too.'

Tannhauser grabbed him by the rabbit-fur lapels of his robe and hoisted him from the chair. Beneath the heavy velvet he was even more wasted than Tannhauser expected and he flew into the air with a wail of outrage. Tannhauser crammed him to the hearthstone and grabbed his neck, his own stomach turning as the tumerous eggs undulated under his fingers. Don Ignacio's outrage vanished and turned to terror as Tannhauser pushed his diseased face to within inches of the searing flames crackling in the grate. The raw pink floor of the crater glazed over and its leaking suppurations popped and sputtered in the heat. Don Ignacio screamed.

'You disgusting old cuckold. Tell me how to find the boy, you turd, or this night will prove a long one, even for you.'

The old man cried out into the flames that charred his brows.

'The boy is dead!'

Tannhauser dragged him from the hearth and hurled him back into the chair. His hand was sticky with the slime from the robe.

He wiped it across the unravaged half of Don Ignacio's face. The skin was so fragile he felt it almost tear. As the old man heaved for breath, Tannhauser leaned over him, one hand on either of the armrests.

'How do you know this?'

The slit mouth gaped and closed. 'He was rowed out to sea and tied in a sack and –' He stopped as he sensed how close he was to further torture. 'He was not the first. The sea floor is littered with bastards!'

'You let Carla believe the boy was abandoned as a foundling. Why?'

'Would I tell her the truth and have her scream infanticide?'

Tannhauser restrained himself to prodding the old man in the belly. 'You're too soft in the gut to have done such a deed yourself. Who did you send to perform this dreadful crime?'

'The first time I was betrayed, when Carla was born, I swallowed my pride. I bore the whispers and the downcast eyes in the street. The second time –' The memory of intolerable rage silenced him with its enormity.

Tannhauser cared nothing for the old man's soul. He reached for his throat, then remembered the slithering eggs, and settled for another jab at the scrawny belly.

'Tell me. Who did you send?'

'My steward, Ruggiero.'

The double doors opened and the steward appeared beyond the threshold. He observed Tannhauser, and his master's terror, without discernible emotion.

'Did His Excellency call?'

Tannhauser straightened and turned his back on the wretched old count and walked towards the steward. The steward took two steps backwards. Tannhauser closed the door on the hellhole behind him.

'Ruggiero.'

Ruggiero ducked his head. Decades of crippling servitude had made the man unreadable and, perhaps, had purged him of his capacity for human feeling.

Tannhauser said, 'You serve a monster.'

Ruggiero said, 'Sir, you are a brave and hardy soldier. Therefore, do you not serve monsters too?'

Tannhauser slammed him into the wall. 'Don't bandy words with me, slave. I represent the Lady Carla – whom in night's darkest hours you must remember all too well.'

Ruggiero blinked, otherwise the habitual blandness of his expression did not change. 'It was ever my pleasure to serve the young contessa.'

'By murdering her newborn child?'

The flicker of shock was brief and confined to Ruggiero's eyes. He attempted to extricate himself from the wall. 'With your permission, sir?'

Tannhauser considered him. Then he stepped back.

Ruggiero took a lamp from a nearby stand. 'Come with me, sir, if you please.'

TANNHAUSER FOLLOWED RUGGIERO down a corridor and up a narrow stair, then along a series of passages and up more stairs, until he was sure it would take him an hour to find his way back out. The thought of the sack in the sea filled his throat with gall and his heart with grim echoes of his own vile crimes – his motives in resigning from the Agha Boluks – for the steward's observation had been right enough. He had served monsters too. A third stair and a door, which Ruggiero unlocked, brought them to a large room with leaded windows. He took these to be Ruggiero's private quarters. A bed, an armoire, an armchair, and, under the windows, a writing desk. A carving of the Madonna in creamy white stone. The rewards of a lifetime's service. Ruggiero set the lamp down and used a key to open a drawer in the desk. Tannhauser glanced inside. It was empty but for a piece of paper, folded several times and sealed with red wax. Ruggiero took out the document and turned.

'Can you read?' he asked.

Tannhauser snatched the document and studied the seal by the lamplight. Its mark meant nothing to him but it was unbroken. Imprisoned beneath the wax were two lines of writing. He cracked the seal with care and prised off the wax with a thumbnail. The first line of the writing read: *Madonna della Luce*. The second recorded a date: *XXXI Octobris MDLII*.

All Hallows Eve. 1552.

Tannhauser's mouth turned dry and he swallowed.

'Madonna della Luce,' he said. 'The name of a church?'

Ruggiero nodded. 'Here, in Mdina.'

Tannhauser unfolded the paper. It was covered with a screed of Latin in a fine hand. He stopped at the first word, heart racing. He read on. He recognised Father, Son and Holy Spirit. *Domine*. A name: *Orlando*. Another: *Ruggiero Pucci*. At the bottom was a signature.

His gaze was drawn back to the first word: *Baptizo*.

He looked at Ruggiero's eyes. Guilt stalked them. So did fear. Tannhauser handed the document back. 'My Latin is patchy.'

Ruggiero didn't take the document. Instead, he recited from memory. '*Baptised this day, 31st October 1552, a boy, Orlando, as witnessed by Signor Ruggiero Pucci, his guardian.*' His voice caught with emotion and he coughed to conceal it. '*Hear our prayer, Lord God, and guard this thy chosen servant, Orlando. May strength never fail him now for we have traced upon his brow the Sign of Christ's Cross.*' Ruggiero cleared his throat again. 'It is signed by Father Giovanni Benadotti.'

Tannhauser waited for the rest of the tale.

'I have served Don Ignacio since I was a child. Everything I am I owe to him. As a young man he was of stainless character, charitable and just, with the gentlest of hearts.'

'I'm not here to mourn your master's fall from grace.'

'May I sit down?'

Tannhauser indicated the chair and rested a haunch on the desk. Ruggiero took a breath.

'Don Ignacio was possessed by devils that night – the night the child was born. Perhaps they possess him still. When I left by the rear gate with the babe in my arms – and with the sack that would be his shroud in my coat pocket – I intended to carry out my master's orders. As I'd carried out every order he'd ever given me.' He hesitated.

Tannhauser said, 'I've obeyed my own share of evil commands. Go on.'

'The boy made not a sound, as if he knew what his birth entailed, and this tore at my heart more piteously than if he'd screamed without cease. I couldn't bring myself to consign him to Limbo, which even though it lacks for flames is a circle of Hell. I took him to Father Benadotti at the church of Our Lady of Light, to be welcomed into Christ's temple. Baptism would ensure eternal life. I stood godfather to the child, as there was no one else to answer for him, and when he was anointed with the holy chrism my tears fell on the boy's face. That was when Benadotti understood my purpose. He made no accusation, but he looked at me as if . . .'

Ruggiero wrung his hands. He pressed on.

'I couldn't look into the good priest's eyes. When the rite was over he took me into the sacristy and entered the boy's name in the parish register, then prepared the document you hold. He let me read it, then sealed it, and locked it away. He told me that once he had assurances that the child was in good hands, I might collect this certificate of his birth. If not, the certificate would stand as proof of a monstrous crime.'

Tannhauser glanced down again at the signature. 'The boy was baptised, the priest showed decency and wisdom. What then?'

'I fell to my knees and begged forgiveness for the murder in my heart, but Benadotti refused to confess me. He gave me the name of a woman in the Borgo. She would find a wet nurse, if I was so minded. If I was not, then I was never to enter his church again, for, just as surely, and no matter what penance I paid, I would never be allowed to enter the Kingdom of Heaven.'

Tannhauser almost grabbed him by his lapels. 'You spared the boy?'

'I took him to the Borgo that very night.'

So close had Tannhauser been to giving up hope that this news almost rendered him voiceless. But he needed more. 'What is the name of the family that took him in?'

'Boccanera.'

'And they raised him?'

Ruggiero bobbed his head. 'The father worked in the shipyards, until he was crushed while careening a galley.'

'Do you know the boy still?'

'I last saw him when he was seven years old, when the agreement to pay for his upkeep came to an end – a stipend I provided from my own pocket.'

'Orlando Boccanera,' said Tannhauser. 'So as best you know he's still alive and in the Borgo?'

Ruggiero nodded. Tannhauser took the statue of the Madonna from the desk and thrust it in Ruggiero's hands. 'All this you swear by the Holy Virgin, and upon your life, which shall be forfeit, and upon the damnation which is certain if you lie.'

'All of it,' said Ruggiero. 'I swear by the Blood of Christ.'

'Orlando Boccanera.' Tannhauser muttered the name again as if it were a charm. 'You never told the contessa what you'd done. Why?'

'By the time I had placed the infant with Boccanera and returned from the Borgo, My Lady Carla was gone, on a galley bound for Naples. The marriage contract was already sealed. I never saw her again. My master Don Ignacio prefers things neatly done.'

'He does, does he?'

Tannhauser thought of Carla and his heart was pierced. Packed into a stinking boat while yet torn and exhausted by childbirth. Still stunned by grief and ignominy and banished to the unknown terrors of a foreign and far-flung land. And at only fifteen years old. It was not the first time Tannhauser had observed the ruthlessness and cruelty with which the Mediterranean Franks were capable of treating their own kin; especially when it came to shame and family honour. Sexual misdemeanours drove them to madness. To murder. Tannhauser was not overdelicate when it came to acts of wickedness, but this one made his blood boil. A stratagem sprang to mind.

'Well,' he said. 'I like things done neatly myself.'

Ruggiero shrank back in his chair.

'As steward of the estate, are you familiar with all of Don Ignacio's affairs? Or merely the keeping of accounts and the collection of rents and so forth?'

'All of them, sir. His Grace depends on me entirely.'

'And you have the craft and learning to draw up a simple legal document, let's say in the manner of a deathbed testament – a will – in which the Don might make clear his wishes for the disposition of his worldly goods?'

Ruggiero stared at him.

'Have you lost your tongue?' said Tannhauser.

'Yes, I could draw up such an instrument.'

'And it would carry the force of law? That is, would it withstand challenge by the lawyers of the Church?'

'That I cannot say. At the very least the will would require witness, by a gentleman of good reputation.'

'Here he stands.'

Ruggiero shifted in his chair. 'Then I would say that such an instrument would have at least a fair chance of legal recognition, depending on the skill of its advocates.'

'That bridge can be crossed later.' Tannhauser wagged the certificate in his hand. 'Once you'd retrieved this, the priest's threat was void. Why did you preserve it with such care?'

'I hoped that My Lady Carla might one day return.'

'You never thought to write to her?'

'Often.' Ruggiero withered under Tannhauser's stare. 'I was too afraid. Of reawakening the scandal. And Don Ignacio's anguish. His rage.'

Tannhauser recalled the creature rotting by the fireside down below. 'I won't blame you for that,' he said. 'In any case, Carla is here. In the Borgo.'

Ruggiero rose to his feet, as if she'd entered the room in the flesh.

'She is in your debt,' said Tannhauser. 'As am I. Now.'

He pocketed the certificate and produced his mother-of-pearl box. He flipped it open and shook two of Grubenius's pills into his palm. They gleamed, oily and flecked with yellow in the light of the lamp. Ruggiero looked at them.

'These stones are the most potent physic yet known. Opium, quintessence of gold, minerals and decoctions known only to the sages. They banish pain, and soothe even the most tormented of minds, which they imbue with the gentlest character. Yet in excess they are fatal to the strongest constitution. If a man were sick and frail, and suffering intolerable pangs, these would bring him succour. And who would question the dying wish of such a man – especially if that wish were to bequeath his property entire to his beloved daughter?'

Ruggiero saw the justice of this ploy; yet old loyalties cling. He didn't answer.

'Would you question such a wish?' said Tannhauser.

Ruggiero said, 'No.'

'Good,' said Tannhauser. 'Then fetch pen and paper.' He put the certificate in his pocket. He wanted to see Carla's face when she read it. 'Later,' he said, 'you can fetch Don Ignacio a priest. A soul as black as his will need all the final sacraments the Church can offer.'

SATURDAY 9 JUNE 1565

Gallows Point

THE MOON WAS down and they travelled by starlight in the footsteps of their canny Maltese guide. They rode with muffled harness and led their mounts on foot along sheep trails and treacherous defiles. In the sky above the rimrock, the tail of the sea goat pointed their way south. They left the high country and swung east and followed the Gorgon's Eye towards the coast. They encountered no Turkish patrols. No man spoke. It was a rum business, Tannhauser reflected, to travel in the company of killers whose names one did not know, especially at night. The weight of the gold round his wrist reassured him: *Not for riches or honour but to save my soul.* The priest's certificate in his pocket brought him cheer. In the cool before dawn he led thirty-five knights under Chevalier De Lugny to the crest of Monte San Salvatore and they stopped and took in the prospect there unfolded.

A shallow mist lay across the lowland. Within it, less than half a mile distant, glowed the dull red embers of the campfires on Gallows Point. A single brighter fire marked the perimeter, and Tannhauser imagined the watchmen warming their hands and talking of home. The knights wore half-armour and did not carry bucklers. Their mounts wore no armour at all. The monks of war dismounted and lengthened their stirrups for the charge. To keep the animals quiet they cowled their heads with silken scarves and walked them down the hill to Bighi Bay. A thousand feet short of the watchfire they stopped knee-deep in the mist, like a company of ghouls from some netherworld recently arrived, and with many an impatient glance at the eastern horizon they unlimbered their arms. The water was too black to be seen and in the circle of their silence the gentle rhythm of its lapping seemed loud. While there was yet time to kill, the knights knelt down by their steeds, reins looped round their elbows, and they crossed themselves and they bent their heads to their sword hilts and their lips moved in soundless prayer above the fog.

They remained thus genuflected until the first intimation of dawn was signalled by birdsong. The indigo sky hauled a wide swathe of violet from beneath the far horizon and as the violet brightened swiftly into lilac and mauve the knights crossed themselves again and rose to their feet. The silk scarves were stripped and the horses blew their nostrils and pawed the sand, and stirrups and harness creaked as the knights remounted and knotted short their reins. They rolled their shoulders and they flexed and pronated their elbows to free the greased joints of their gear. In the uncertain light their faces were as short of pity as any Tannhauser had seen. The ground before them was as flat as a ballroom floor, patched with parched marram grass and with no rock or shrub in sight to impede their promenade. They drew up in a shallow echelon with De Lugny and Escobar de Corro at their centre and from somewhere on distant Corradino there drifted the ghostly and keening echo of a song:

'*Allahu Akabar.*
Allahu Akabar.
Allahu Akabar.'

De Lugny raised his lance and the knights moved out and picked up speed. Unlike the enemy who rode light, short-backed

Arabians and Barbs, the knights rode huge beasts of mixed northern European and Andalucian blood, bred for the strength to carry two hundred pounds at a charge and trained to be as eager for blood as were their masters. Tannhauser stood on the beach and stroked Buraq's head and watched them go. He'd played his part and had no appetite for the fray, let alone a wound. Even so, it was a spectacle not to be missed. He mounted and drew his scimitar and watched from the saddle.

At five hundred feet the wedged and rampant horsemen were running flat-out and nothing on earth or above could have called them back. He saw the rind of the rising sun emerge above the armature of the point and in the oblique light streaming across the flatlands the helms and burnished back plates of the riders shone an iridescent pink. Thus gaudily adorned by the newborn day they thundered down on the encampment and set about the sleep-dazed defenders with a gusto fuelled by righteousness and hate.

Human figures leapt to their feet in panic and were just as swiftly dashed back to the ground. Maces whirled and bludgeoned and lances ran through naked flesh and axes rose and fell amid sudden sprays. Sword blades fluttered red above the roseate armour. A rising clamour of terrified mules and belated alarums and death shouts and wasted commands fractured the crystalline morning, and amid the hue and cry could be heard the names of Jesus Christ and John the Baptist, of Allah and the Prophet, and, as always when men meet their maker in a circumstance of horror, the word 'mother' in various tongues from the mouths of sons who would never see her again.

Tannhauser nudged Buraq and started in at the trot.

As he reached the perimeter watchfire, in which the entrails of an unseamed corpse lay purple and steaming, a pair of fleet-foot refugees stumbled forth from the carnage. Seeing Tannhauser's white turban, his dark green kaftan and his golden Mongol horse, they ran towards him in blind hope of salvation.

They had the look of Bulgars or Thracians, and were helmless, and their eyes rolled in their faces like portraits of the deranged. They weren't much more than boys. But even had he been inclined to mercy, he couldn't let them know him at some later time and place. He slew the first with a single stroke as he grabbed for Buraq's bridle and hot blood sprayed the animal's chest and he sidestepped away. The second man he clove unto the brain from behind as he abandoned his comrade and fled like doomed game. Up ahead, De Lugny's riders had swept the camp as far as the seven bronze siege guns commanding the bay and they wheeled about for a second pass in spumes of hoof-tossed sand. Tannhauser reined in Buraq and flicked the gore from his blade while it was still wet and he watched the knights' bloody venture wend to its close.

Of the seventy-odd artillerymen and levies, most lay dead or squirming with dire wounds. The rest either tried to flee or howled to Allah or rallied to the call of their commander, who stood with a red-crescent standard by his saffron-coloured tent. All such choices met with a similar outcome. De Lugny's knights, their steeds half-blown by the charge, retrawled the camp at a canter and slaughtered the Moslems to a man. Their weapons and harness were slathered with brains and gore. Their snorting war mounts stoved in ribs with their shoulders and crushed skulls with their iron-shod hooves and snapped at fingers and hands with their great square teeth. The encampment's commander and his guard were lanced like a bevy of swine and as the Turkish standard was brandished aloft in triumph, some knights dismounted to ransack the ruin for trophies and to finish the groaning wounded where they lay.

Tannhauser urged Buraq into the shambles. He bent across his neck to murmur a *gazel*, for the animal was gentle and a stranger to the reek of battle's consequence. As they headed for the saffron tent, the prayers of the wounded were silenced one by one, until only the sounds of victory remained. The knights, by habit so dour, were exhilarated by the totality of their success and smiles flashed abroad and jubilant praises were offered to the Saints and coarse jokes cracked about this dismembered body or that severed limb. Yet this didn't curb the efficiency they brought to their chores. They slaughtered the captured mules in squealing droves and smashed the butts of drinking water apart. By the edge of the bay those detailed to demolish the artillery mounts and to hammer spikes into the touchholes of the guns went about their work with a will. Others rolled kegs of gunpowder, stacked thereabouts in abundance, into the shallows, where they stove them open with their axes and vented their contents in the brine. Sacks of flour, and provender by the barrel and the bale, followed too, until the shoreline resembled the wake of a disaster at sea. And all of this without the use of fire, though it would have been swifter, for they'd yet to make the long ride back to Mdina and their numbers were small.

The ground in places was boggy with entrails and gore; Buraq tossed his head in distaste, and Tannhauser steered around such spots as he sought out the Chevalier De Lugny. In skirting the splayed and tangled slain who'd made their final stand by the tent, Tannhauser spotted a nine-palm musket on the ground. Its match still smouldered. Its stock was pinned beneath its owner's corpse. The blue-black hue of the damascened barrel, which seemed to glow from deep within its substance, and the arabesques of silver wire with which the ebony woodwork was inlaid, announced the hand of a master gunsmith. He marked its location in the wrack and rode up to De Lugny, who was mounted and was issuing orders to Escobar de Corro. De Corro asked some question that Tannhauser didn't catch.

'Leave for the Borgo now,' said De Lugny, 'and take this.' He handed de Corro the captured crescent-moon standard, 'It will stir their spirits.'

De Lugny turned to Tannhauser and nodded.

'A fine morning's work, Captain Tannhauser,' said De Lugny.

'The Angelus bell not yet rung and not a single man lost or wounded. Accept my compliments on behalf of Marshal Copier.'

'Don't tarry too long,' said Tannhauser. 'When the battery fails to open fire, Torghoud will read this state of affairs and send Sipahis in the hope of an ambuscade.'

'Let him do so,' scoffed Escobar de Corro.

Tannhauser gave him a glance, but expressed no opinion. 'With your permission, I'm away.'

De Lugny raised a crimson-glistered sword in salute. 'With God's blessings.'

Tannhauser rode back a few yards and stopped and dismounted and retrieved the Damascus musket, which on closer encounter was finer than he'd supposed. He stripped a pouch of balls and a powder flask from the corpse. The man dead was young and exquisitely featured. He'd been lanced through the base of the skull. In his turban was a spray of rubies set in white gold. Tannhauser stripped that too. As he remounted and canted the musket against his thigh, he caught Escobar de Corro's eyes on the long blue barrel, as if it were a prize he'd marked out for himself. He looked into Tannhauser's eyes and Tannhauser paused to give him his chance; but Escobar said nothing and Tannhauser wheeled away, as eager as was Buraq to leave the stench of that reeking field behind them. The sun had cleared the horizon and they rode towards it. By nightfall he hoped to secure the boat that would take him away from this island of fanatics and fools. He stroked Buraq's neck with a sudden pang of anguish.

In Turkish he said, 'I can't take you with me, old friend, but to whom shall I bequeath you? Christian or Turk?'

SATURDAY 9 JUNE 1565

The Sacred Infirmary – Auberge of England

Carla dipped a silver spoon into a silver bowl and raised a mouthful of broth to the poor man's lips. He opened them and took the broth and swallowed, not with hunger or enjoyment for he was beyond such sensations, but out of some sense of duty and, she realised, to please her. His name was Angelu, a fisherman by trade who would go to sea no more, for he was now blind and his hands resembled lumps of discoloured wax in which broken twigs had been embedded.

Along with scores of other seriously wounded, he'd been evacuated from Fort Saint Elmo after the eight-hour Turkish assault had been halted by nightfall. Angelu's head had been drenched in a gobbet of wildfire, hurled by his own comrades at the Turks. In scraping the incendiary jelly from his burning scalp he'd charred both hands to the bone. He sat huddled on a chair, the least agonising posture he could find. The roasted vault of his skull was like an obscene tufted cap pulled over his ears, and it gave off a corrupt odour which overpowered that of the applied salves and lotions. Angelu had already received extreme unction and Father Lazaro didn't expect him to survive another night. Carla did not believe that Angelu wanted to.

Lazaro had brought her to the Sacred Infirmary that morning. Carla had asked to serve yet she'd been fearful. Fearful of her lack of skill and knowledge, of the stern-faced brethren, of the fortress-like hospital itself. Part of her wished she hadn't complained about her uselessness. She despised it, yet days passed in emptiness passed quickly. Easy to gaze at the world until sunset threw a veil on it. Easy to dream without remembering of what. Lazaro marched her to the infirmary as if to a gallows; or so it felt to her. In fact it was to something more daunting by far.

The main ward of the hospital was two hundred feet long with a series of shuttered windows along its southern aspect. The arched entrance was framed by Maltese stone. Above the arch was carved *Tuitio Fidei et Obsequium Pauperum*, the Order's motto, which she read to mean, *Defenders of the Faith and Servants of the Poor*. Two rows of fifty beds faced each other across the centre aisle. Each bed had a red curtained canopy over its head, with a good mattress and fine linen. Armour, clothing and weapons were bundled beneath. The patients were served their food on silver plate, for the monks placed great store in purity. The floor was tiled in marble and swabbed thrice a day. Thyrus wood burned in censers to cleanse the air and mask putrefaction and drive forth the flies. At the far end was an altar for the twice-daily celebration of the Mass and behind was mounted the crucified Christ. On the wall facing the windows hung the treasured banner under which the knights had abandoned their stronghold of Rhodes. It displayed the Virgin and the Infant Christ above the legend: *Afflictis Tu Spes Unica Rebus.*

In all that afflicts us You are our only Hope.

Father Lazaro proclaimed it the finest hospital in the world, with surgeons and physicians to match. 'Our Lords the sick,' said Lazaro, 'want for nothing that we can give them. It is here in the Sacred Infirmary that the true heart of the Religion is to be found.'

The drifting incense, the murmur of prayer, the reverential concentration of the monks as they moved from bed to bed to wash and feed and dress the wounds of their Lords gave the hospital the atmosphere of a chapel and this induced a sense of tranquillity otherwise unimaginable among so much suffering. It also enabled Carla to master the horror of her first encounter.

After the flood of wounded in recent days the ward was almost full. Though fresh corpses were carried from the ward each dawn and the wounded were discharged as soon as their lives were out of danger, space would soon run out. Like Angelu, most of the patients were young men of the Maltese militia or Spanish *tercios*. Few of them would be whole again. Lazaro and his colleagues had performed numerous amputations and trepannings and, as best they could, had repaired the grotesque facial injuries that abounded. Those pierced or shot through the gut lay stiff as planks, panting lightly and slowly turning grey with the agony of death. Those afflicted with monstrous burns suffered most of all. From the distance beyond the protecting walls came the constant rumble of cannon fire.

On arrival she was to wash her hands and feet in the lavatorium, and change into slippers to keep out the dust of the streets, for cleanliness was pleasing to God. She was forbidden to touch any wounds or dressings. She could serve food, wine and water but could not wash the patients. If they needed to pass water or defecate she was to inform one of the brothers. If she noticed fresh bleeding, fever or pox, she was to inform one of the brothers. If a man requested Confession or Holy Communion, or appeared close to death, she was to inform one of the brothers. She was to speak in a soft, gentle voice. As much as possible she was to encourage Our Lords to pray, not only for their own souls but for peace, victory, the Pope, the liberation of Jerusalem and the Holy Land, the Grand Master, the brothers of the Order, the prisoners in the hands of Islam, and for their own parents, whether alive or dead. Because the sick were the closest to Christ, their prayers were the most powerful of all, more so, even, than those of the cardinals in Rome.

Lazaro took her down the ward, where she was conscious of the eyes turned at once upon her. Those of the serving brothers were shocked. Those of the wounded flickered, as if glimpsing a divine apparition from within a nightmare. Some of the seasoned troopers licked their lips and exhaled sighs. She felt herself blushing and her grand intentions teetered. What good could she do here? She was in the middle of more raw pain than should ever be assembled underneath one roof. However, she'd be damned, at least to herself, if she retreated. She wasn't without tools, she told herself. She had Faith, and it was strong; she had much of Love to give; she even had a modicum of Hope. She steeled herself and walked tall. Then Lazaro stopped and introduced her to poor Angelu. Silent, blinded, helpless. Deformed beyond the wildest dreams of cruelty.

Angelu, she realised, was to be the test of her devotion.

CARLA SAT WITH him all day long and the man uttered not a word. To some of her questions he replied with a single nod; to others he shook his head. The questions were simple, for her Maltese was poor. Although she'd grown up here it had been a language used only for speaking to servants and grooms and this fact now shamed her, for this man and thousands like him were dying in her defence. Yet her voice provoked some animation in his twisted posture. Within the dark torture chamber that his body had become, he was aware. She took out her rosary and prayed and in his silent and sightless vigil Angelu prayed with her. At least so she believed.

At times pity overcame her and tears rolled down her face and her voice faltered, but she offered her pity to God and begged His forgiveness for her selfish concerns. She fed Angelu and lifted cups of wine and water to his lips. She wondered why he didn't speak and if, perhaps, he couldn't – if perhaps the fire had scorched his throat raw too – but it wasn't her place to ask, only to serve. She prayed with him and for him and for them all and as the hours passed and Aves flowed through her like an endless and sacred song, her horror vanished, for horror was merely the complaint of her own fragile senses and was itself another wound to the man so afflicted before her. Then her pity vanished too, for pity was to see him as less human than she. And even her sorrow subsided to its embers and an incandescent Love filled her being, and she realised that Christ had entered her, body and soul, with a power beyond her experience or vision. Christ's love surged through her with the force of revelation and she understood, and she knew, that through such love all sins were forgiven, even those atrocities that surrounded her in such profusion. She wanted to tell Angelu and opened her eyes to look at him: at his half-skull and half-face, at the opaque, blistered orbs that bulged beneath shrivelled eyelids and sloughing brows, at the withered claws that quivered at the ends of his arms. Angelu was walking his own road to Golgotha. It was he who had invited Christ into her heart.

She said, 'Jesus loves you.'

Angelu's head jerked back and his mouth twisted open, and she didn't know what this meant, or if she'd hurt him, or if he hadn't heard what she'd said. For a moment she was afraid.

She said again, 'Jesus loves you.' Then she said, 'I love you.'

Angelu's lips trembled. His breath shuddered. She reached out and put a hand on his shoulder. It was the first time she'd dared touch him. Quietly, for even in this darkness his strength had not deserted him entire, Angelu lowered his head and started to cry.

LATER, THEY HEARD Mass and she helped him to kneel while they took Communion, and if he said 'Amen' neither she nor the chaplain heard him. Afterwards, she served him beef broth from the silver bowl, and, seeing that he had no appetite, she put the food aside, and since the ward was busy with the meal time, and suddenly thinking that it might disturb him not to know who his strange companion was, she told him, as best she could, something of herself, and her purpose in returning here, which was to find her lost son, whose name she did not know. Angelu said nothing and by now she was sure that he was quite unable to do so. Then Carla too fell silent and she wondered if she should not tell him too about Mattias Tannhauser.

That day she'd prayed for Mattias, with his image in her heart, more often than for any other. He was German – a Saxon – a race of which she'd neither knowledge nor experience, but which by reputation was marked by brilliance and barbarity in equal measure. He'd not a drop of noble blood in his body, yet carried himself among the Knights of Saint John, a sect obsessed with such notions, as if born into the purple. His admiration of the Turks seemed to exceed his opinions of those he called the Franks, yet he'd turned his hand against them. He'd murdered a priest without a tremor of conscience, yet gentleness and courtesy were rooted in his nature to a depth she'd seen in no other man she'd known. He believed in no God that he could name yet was filled with spirit. His carnal appetites, like his passions for beauty and knowledge, were uninhibited and vast, yet he'd watched everything he owned burned to ashes without a word of regret or reproach. For all his brutal pragmatism, he'd taken her part on a whim and was even now chasing a phantom across this deadliest of terrains. He perplexed her utterly.

Was this man really to become her husband? Was she to become his wife?

His affair with Amparo, the vehement erotism of its conduct and of the feelings it had stirred within her own nocturnal thoughts, had challenged her emotions to a struggle she'd fought hard to master. The man was entitled to his fancies; he was a soldier of fortune and a man of the widest world; she could expect no less; and he'd given her no promise in respect of romance. The marriage was a contract as dry as those he struck for timber and lead. But could that really be so? Had she not felt in him something more? Or had he only sensed her fear of carnal relations?

That fear was deep and unexamined, for to examine it was impossible without the resurrection of her memories of Ludovico.

Her physical passion for Ludovico had been every bit as ecstatic and uninhibited as Amparo's was for Mattias; perhaps more so, for the latter pair had crossed no forbidden boundaries, while she and Ludovico had shattered every rule both sacred and profane. That transgression had lent their ardour a compulsive, delirious intensity that had lured her so far into madness that she was terrified of going near it ever again. And not merely into madness but into a tragedy that laid waste to her life and to her family, that had cost her her nameless child, and whose consequences even now threatened the lives of those she loved. Memory still made her nauseous with fear and guilt and shame. Memory still aroused her most painful sexual longings – when she let it do so; which she did not. Dry as timber and lead was the way her marriage to Mattias ought to be. She would be a spinster wife and cause no more chaos. And if, despite her waning hopes, she found her son, that would be an outcome for which she'd always thank God.

Even so, jealousy tormented her.

She wanted Amparo to be happy; to see her so filled Carla with joy. And yet, at one and the same time, it also dripped acid on her heart. The crudeness of her fantasies revolted her: but yes, Carla wished that it was she who moaned in the night beneath Tannhauser's brawn. She craved tenderness and kisses and the look of love. She wished that he'd brought her a silvered comb from the Turkish bazaar. Such pettiness filled her with self-loathing; and to spare herself she'd started avoiding Amparo. Yet Amparo was not to be blamed for giving herself to such a man. Amparo tolerated moderation as a wild horse the bridle. Amparo had known tragedy that made her own seem trite. If either deserved such happiness, it was the girl. And in this God was just and all-wise. He'd given Carla this trial to strengthen her soul. She would see it through. The thread that bound the three of them together was fragile, and around them violent forces were daily unleashed. Carla prayed that she wouldn't be the one to break it. No matter what she felt, she would do nothing to come between them. This, she realised, was the reason she found herself in the infirmary. In the infirmary, problems such as jealousy were trifles.

Dusk fell and the monks lit three lamps, which would burn all night to protect the sick from illusions, dubiousness and error. The two serving brethren assigned to the night watch moved from bed to bed with a candle in one hand and a jug in the other. 'Water and wine from God,' they said to each patient. La Valette paid a visit before the darkness outside was complete. He said little, and possessed little natural warmth that Carla could feel, yet his presence was an inspiration to the wounded men, who all but climbed from their sickbeds to salute him. He noted Carla sitting by Angelu and one brow briefly rose on his high forehead. He said nothing to her and left soon thereafter to a valiant chorus of cheers.

As La Valette disappeared, Father Lazaro came up to Carla and indicated it was time for her to leave. He offered no words of praise, yet his manner seemed warmer than before and she sensed she'd acquitted herself with honour. As Lazaro walked away, she turned to Angelu.

'I must go now, Angelu,' she said. 'Thank you for all you've given me.'

She stood up.

'Will you come back again, My Lady?' said Angelu.

She looked at him. It was the first time he'd spoken all day. And by the way he asked the question she felt as if he'd placed his life in her hands. For a moment she was choked.

'Yes, of course,' she said. 'First thing tomorrow.'

Angelu held out his two congealed fists, as if he'd clasp them together if he could. 'God bless you, My Lady. May He guide you safe and sound to your boy.'

Carla's eyes filled. Her voice deserted her. She turned and hurried away for the arch.

CARLA LEFT THE ward with her chest constricted by turbulent emotions. She'd given something of herself, something pleasing to God. The feeling was unfamiliar. And marvellous. Her life had been one of taking and being taken from. She'd bobbed like a cork on its waters. Her acts of charity had been abstract, investments in an eternity she didn't deserve. She'd adopted Amparo to assuage her own isolation. To have someone to mother. Even her quest to find her boy was, in part, to allay the guilt that gnawed at her heart. But today Christ had filled her with Divine Love, a love of all Creation, a love even of her own wretchedness, for it was true, all, that it was here among the wretched that Christ was most readily found. She passed back between the rows of the wounded, their pain transmuted into murmured prayer, their moans stifled by the stoical pride that bound them. Later, when the night boats from Saint Elmo's brought fresh mayhem, there would be screams from the surgical slabs, where Lazaro would spend the hours of darkness steeped to the elbows in gore.

The evening air at the threshold was so sweet that her senses swooned and her head whirled about and she stopped and closed her eyes for fear of falling. Cannon still crashed to the north, louder out here. As her throat cleared of incense she detected on the breeze the smell of cooking fires and meat and she felt hungry. Hunger as she'd never known it. Hunger earned. How strange to feel so alive at the centre of so much death. How terrible. In all the world there was no more tragic place than this, yet she wouldn't have wished herself anywhere else. The life she'd known, the woman she'd been, seemed infinitely far away. What would she become when this was over?

She felt a hand on her arm. 'Carla?'

She opened her eyes and found Amparo looking at her. There was a brightness in her eyes, a love that filled her. In her hair was the ivory comb, beautifully worked. Carla found that this gift no longer galled her, and she was relieved. Amparo appeared radiant. Or was it that Carla now saw the world anew and could see the radiance in things she'd been blind to before? Emotion rose again in Carla's throat, joy and sadness intermingled. Without speaking, Amparo embraced her and Carla clung to the girl and felt strangely like a child, the more so for the strength in Amparo's arms, a strength she hadn't known was there for she'd never leant on it. Carla's world was turned upside down. Yet, suddenly, she felt free. Amparo stroked her hair.

'Are you sad?' Amparo asked.

'Yes.' Carla raised her head. 'No. Sad but in a good way.'

'Sadness is never bad,' said Amparo. 'Sadness is the mirror of being happy.'

Carla smiled. 'I'm happy too. Especially to see you. I've missed you.'

Amparo said, 'I want you to meet my friends.'

Amparo had never claimed friends before, but she'd changed too in these days. No longer confined to the round of Carla's life, she came and went like a bird uncaged. She was closer in spirit to these people than Carla could ever be, and she wandered their streets and wharves with an anonymous liberty that Carla could never know. Carla looked down the hospital steps, where two young Maltese stood waiting. The older of the two, perhaps twenty, had a freshly bandaged stump where his right forearm had been. She recognised him from the ward. He'd arrived last night and had been discharged this evening. His face was still grey with pain, his eyes still hollowed and stunned by the shock of battle.

The younger, not much more than a boy, perhaps fourteen, was barefoot and unwashed. The smooth, adolescent flesh that might have softened his features had been burned away by the life he'd led to leave razor cheekbones and an aquiline nose. His eyes were dark and wild, as if he could scarce contain the energies locked within him. He carried a cuirass and helmet slung across the blade of a sheathed sword, which she assumed belonged to the other. Unlike his companion, who'd dropped his eyes when she looked at him, he looked at her with a brazen curiosity. She wondered, in her heightened state of mind, what it was that he saw.

Amparo introduced the armless man as Tomaso. He backed away, dipping his head in respect. The younger, taller youth made a poor job of stifling a grin of delight.

'This is Orlandu,' said Amparo.

Orlandu gave an elaborate bow and she wondered if he were not mocking her. 'Orlandu di Borgo,' he said. With glee he added, 'At your service, Madame.'

His teeth were bright in his dirty, sunburned face. Carla stifled a smile of her own. 'You speak French,' she said.

He shrugged. 'French, Italian, Spanish. All. Spanish, very good. Very good. From the harbour, the knights, the voyagers.' He pointed a finger at his ear, then his eye. 'I listen, I watch. Some Arabic too, from the slaves. *Asalaamu alaykum*. This means, *Peace be upon you*.'

His showing off suddenly reminded Carla of Mattias. 'And your friend?' she asked. 'Does he speak many tongues?'

'Tomaso speaks only Maltese, but he is brave, very brave. We work with the ships. Now he fights with the heroes, at Saint Elmo.' His French had degenerated into a mixture of languages but remained fluent enough. Carla nodded. Tomaso, unhappy to be the centre of attention, ducked his head in silence. Orlandu said, 'You are the contessa who searches for the lost boy. The bastard.'

Carla blinked. She looked at Amparo, whose eyes contained the vital question. At the same time they overbrimmed with hope. *Please tell me it's him.*

'Have you found him yet?' asked Orlandu, bold as brass.

Carla felt suddenly beleaguered. 'You know about this matter?' she said.

'Of course. Everyone knows. The great captain asks. Tannhauser.' He spoke the name as if exceedingly proud to know it. 'The big English too. They ask, the people hear, they talk. You are surprised?'

Orlandu's surprise that she might be so made her feel stupid, yet she found his bravado too charming to care. Could it really be him? She searched in her belly and her heart, and felt no yearning. She felt a flutter of panic. She shook her head.

Orlandu said, 'I don't think you will find him.'

'Why not?' said Carla.

'Twelve years old, yes? Born on the Eve of All the Saints, yes?'

'Yes.'

He flashed his teeth. 'I know the news. I hear. I watch.' He pointed into the night with the sword. 'This morning, Captain Tannhauser razed the cannon of the Turk on Gallows Point.'

Carla's anxiety took a new turn. 'Where is he now?'

'Tannhauser?' Orlandu shrugged with exaggerated mystery. 'He comes. He goes. They say his horse, Buraq, has wings.' He glanced at Amparo, as if she were the source of this legend and he wished to confirm its authenticity. 'Amparo says I may meet him. With your permission.'

'Surely. But tell me, why won't I find the boy?'

'Because you have not found him yet,' he said, as if nothing could be more obvious. 'No one knows such a boy.'

'How old are you, Orlandu?'

He groped for the word, his fingers coiling and uncoiling in his palm. He said, 'Seventeen.' He saw her total disbelief and backed down. 'Fifteen! Yes, I think. Soon. At least.' He shook the sword. 'Old enough to fight the Turk, when they will let me. I've killed dogs, many dogs, and the Moslems are no different.'

'When is your birthday?' asked Carla.

Orlandu's confidence was momentarily blunted. He shrugged. 'Birthdays are for children. Rich children.'

'I also have no birthday,' said Amparo.

'It's true?' said Orlandu.

Amparo nodded and Orlandu's sense of worthiness was restored.

'I was born in spring,' said Amparo.

'And I in autumn,' said Orlandu. 'This much I know.'

He looked at Carla and must have seen the turmoil within her for he recoiled a little and smiled and shook his head. 'Me? Your boy?' he said. He shook his head again. 'I would like, oh yes, but I don't think so.'

'Why not?'

He shrugged and confirmed the prejudice that she'd dared not admit to herself. 'You are too fine,' he said. 'Look at me.' She did so. The flurry of hope died within her. Orlandu smiled in vindication. He said, 'Do you think I'm the boy you seek?'

Tomaso shifted his weight and Carla felt ashamed for keeping him standing in the street. She didn't give Orlandu an answer. She looked at Amparo.

'Why don't you invite your friends to come and eat with us?'

Orlandu's eyes bulged. Amparo nodded to him.

'Yes,' said Amparo. 'Come and eat with us at the auberge.'

Orlandu spoke rapidly to Tomaso, who shuffled with reluctance and shyness. Orlandu, without discernible sympathy for his friend's injured state, grabbed him by his good arm and smiled at Carla. 'Thank you, Your Lady, very much. We come.'

At the Auberge of England, Nicodemus cooked flatbread and lamb and Orlandu's excitement was uncontained when he learned that at some point in the proceedings the great Captain Tannhauser was expected to arrive. In the meanwhile, he did not want for thrills, for Bors returned from the batteries of Sant' Angelo's cavalier, his face black with powder and hauling a two-gallon demijohn of wine, and found himself more than fit substitute for the youth's blind adoration. Orlandu sat at the refectory table with the barbarous Englishman and Tomaso, hero of Saint

Elmo's, and he translated between the three, and who could deny him his pride at being accepted as a man by two such men as these?

As they ate and drank they talked of the grim and murderous siege across the water, of the prodigious valour of the defenders and the suicidal courage of the janissaries, and of the miracle it was that the fort had already held for seventeen days. Even the hardiest of Saint Elmo's knights, related Tomaso – Le Mas, Luigi Broglia, Juan de Guaras – did not believe they could survive another three or four sunsets, despite the nightly reinforcements. No man there expected to live, except, perhaps, the Maltese swimmers who'd been ordered, when the fall came, to take to the water and fight another day. At times Orlandu's eyes shone with tears, and Carla wondered why gallantry moved men's hearts with a power nothing else could match.

As dessert Nicodemus served bread fried in butter topped with marzipan and sugar, and was roundly declared a cook of genius, and the talk turned to the future of the campaign. Maps were traced by candlelight on the tabletop, with fingers and the tips of knives in spilled wine. Strategies were argued, for and against, and the cunning of Torghoud, whom Bors had sworn to kill from the cavalier, and the rage of Mustafa Pasha, were pitched against the brilliance of La Valette. Bors told tales of his late adventures in the wars of Charles Quintus, and of Tannhauser's exploits under Suleiman's horsetail banners. And at each account Orlandu's eyes became wider and more brimful with martial yearning. And though she did not speak, Carla was saddened, for thus were the myths of war nourished and replanted, even by those who must have known that they were warrants for cruelty and madness.

Yet perhaps they did not know, or could not so allow it, for their fascination was inexhaustible and the subject turned to weapons and the supremacy of Turkish musketry and the weakness of Turkish armour and the merits at close quarters, respectively assessed, of axe and mace and halberd and dagger and pike, of the various widths and cross-sections of swords and of their hilts and lengths, and of the war hammer, which Bors thought much underrated and a tool without compare.

Throughout this the women were as shadows on the wall, and while Amparo seemed content to enjoy the warmth and convivial company, Carla was overcome by fatigue. In any case, she couldn't square this celebration of fighting with the sorrow crammed into the ward of the Sacred Infirmary. Mattias did not return and none knew when he might. She excused herself, to a chorus of blessings and thanks, and retired to a deep and instant sleep.

She awoke to a hand on her shoulder and found Amparo standing by the bed with a candle in her hand. The girl was wrapped in a towel and could hardly contain her excitement.

'Carla,' said Amparo, 'it is Orlandu! It is Orlandu after all!'

Carla swung her legs from the mattress and stood up. Her heart was ahead of her mind for it had leapt into her throat. She grabbed Amparo's hand. She managed to say, 'Orlandu?'

'Tannhauser says Orlandu is your son.'

Carla's head spun and she almost sat back down. She felt a trembling desperation constrict her chest. She took a deep breath. Orlandu was her son. Orlandu was her son.

Tears blurred her vision. She said, 'Orlandu is my son.'

'Isn't it wonderful?' said Amparo.

Carla hurried past her and grabbed her cloak. Then she hung it up again. She couldn't go to greet him in her nightgown. She turned to her plain black dress spread over the table. Her hair, she thought. It was tangled from sleep. The boy would hardly care, of course. But even so.

She took another deep breath. 'Tell Orlandu I will be down in a few moments.'

Carla stripped her nightgown over her head and threw it on the bed.

Amparo said, 'Orlandu isn't here any more.'

Carla swayed with a terrible premonition. She closed her eyes and opened them and looked at Amparo. The girl's joy, still real, was now overshadowed. Carla steeled herself.

'Where is he?' she asked, with all the calm she could summon.

'I don't know. Tannhauser and Bors have gone to find him, on the wharf.'

Carla retrieved her nightgown and pulled it back on. The cloak would have to suffice after all and her hair be damned. 'The Kalkara wharf?' she said. She took the cloak from its hook and looked about the floor for her boots.

'No,' Amparo replied. 'Sant' Angelo's.'

Carla stopped with the cloak half-unfurled about her shoulders.

Her day in the infirmary had made her all too keenly aware that Sant' Angelo's wharf was the point of embarkation for the slaughterhouse of Fort Saint Elmo.

A cry escaped her throat.

Carla ran barefoot down the stairs and out into Majistral Street.

SATURDAY 9 JUNE 1565

Zonra – Marsaxlokk – Auberge of England – the Wharf

A LONG DAY but a good one, reflected Tannhauser, as he trudged bone-tired through the Borgo for the Auberge of England. Good for him, at least. He'd just reported to Starkey, where his various deeds had received all due admiration, and where he'd found the Christian high command in a state of shock following twenty-four hours of crisis at Fort Saint Elmo.

After seventeen solid days of desperate hand-to-hand violence, the Turks held Saint Elmo's ditch, had captured the defensive ravelin outside the main gates and had built steps and bridgeworks to a colossal breach that gaped in the south-west perimeter. This extremity had provoked a mutiny among the younger knights, who had determined to sally forth to die like men, rather than wait like penned sheep in an indefensible ruin. La Valette, with characteristic genius, had sent word to the rebels 'to flee to the safety of the Borgo'. Accused of something very close to cowardice, despite the inhuman courage they had proven time and again, the sorry mutineers – doomed to return to the contempt of the entire Order – had begged the Grand Master not to relieve them of their duties and swore absolute obedience to his every command.

As Tannhauser left Sant' Angelo, a reinforcement of fifteen knights and ninety Maltese militiamen was mustering on the wharf to cross the water. And welcome to it, Tannhauser thought. For, with a modicum of luck, he would by this time tomorrow be making his own shameless retreat – across the wine-blue sea to the coast of Calabria.

After leaving De Lugny's cavalry that morning on Gallows Point, Tannhauser had traced the coast for two miles south in search of the Order's hidden sailing boats. He reached the sea hamlet of Zonra without finding one. The hamlet – a dozen fishermen's cottages – had been sacked by the Turks and the houses stripped of everything that would serve as firewood – furniture, doors, architraves, window frames, roof joists. All that remained of what had been a tiny jetty were timber pilings sawn off below the waterline. He followed the shore for another hour, skirting every foot of a Y-shaped bay without success, and began to wonder if La Valette hadn't stationed all his boats to the north. Most boats would be hidden to the north, for that placed them closer to Mdina and Sicily too; but all? He pressed on until the water's edge threw up a rocky outcrop. It was sheer enough to defy all but determined mountaineering and extended some twenty yards out into the waves. His smuggler's instinct was aroused.

Like most men, Tannhauser never learned to swim. He stripped and waded out along the rock face. By its seaward tip he was throat-deep and forced to fend off flares of panic as the brine washed into his mouth and the shale shifted beneath his feet. He held his nerve and rounded the apex. There was a shallow cove beyond – less a cove than a wrinkle in the shoreline – and with the salt stinging his eyes and setting him to cough, he saw nothing to remark. He was about to curse his own cleverness and grope his way back to dry land when a movement on the surface caught his eye. It was no more than a false note in the bounce of the light on sea and rock, but he wiped his face and looked again, and there it was: the hull of a twelve-footer in the bight of the rock face. A cunning length of canvas had been nailed along the landward gunwale and draped across the boat so that the free edge hung in the water. Thus sodden, it gave the boat the appearance, at more than a few feet distance, of just another shelf of grey coastal stone. From a passing galley a hundred yards out or more – the only viewpoint any Turkish eyes would enjoy – the vessel would be quite invisible.

Such was Tannhauser's joy that he lost his footing and vanished below the brine. His mind reeled until he clapped both hands to the rock, found his feet and thrust himself back up to gasp at the air. He was humiliated that a medium he'd otherwise mastered could render him so helpless, but he crabbed along the outcrop's far face and at last reached the craft without drowning. With the sea here waist-deep and with his toes once again clenching rock, he peeled back the canvas and hauled himself aboard.

In the bottom lay two pairs of oars, a rudder, a mast and a furled lateen. There was a barrel of water, a pitch-sealed chest – he presumed of biscuit – and stowed in a trap bolted on to the gunwale were a knife, fishhooks and line, and a compass wrapped in oilcloth. Sicily was fifty miles due north; the Calabrian coast, where no one wanted his head impaled on a spike, only fifty miles more.

He untied the boat from two iron hoops nailed into the rock and rowed her back round the shoreline. She cut the shallow waves like a blade and with the lateen up and a breath of wind would outrun any galley on the sea. At the shore he collected his gear and left Buraq with a bag of rolled barley. He rowed the boat north across the bay and pulled in at Zonra. He dragged the boat up the beach and careened her in the seaward lee of a roofless stone outhouse. He covered it with the canvas and an hour's worth of hand-shovelled shale. From the sea it couldn't be distinguished from the outhouse wall. From land, only a determined search would unearth it, and since the hamlet was waterless and lately gutted, the Turks were unlikely to return. From here, on foot – and even with two women in tow – they could be under sail within three hours of leaving the Kalkara Gate.

Tannhauser dressed, marched back to Buraq, wrapped his new Damascus musket in a blanket, and continued south to Marsaxlokk Bay, where the bulk of the Sultan's fleet yet lay at anchor. Supply ships plied to the North African ports and back, and the beaches teemed. He watered Buraq and joined their afternoon prayers, and took tea and honeyed almonds with an Egyptian navigator. They talked of Alexandria and Tannhauser gleaned that Admiral Piyale remained too chary of the Gregale winds to commit more than a dozen galleys to the blockade. Some patrolled the Gozo channel and the rest prowled the mouth of Grand Harbour, both of which sectors Tannhauser could readily avoid. It was to secure the northern anchorage of Marsamxett that the battle for Saint Elmo still raged.

With this welcome news boosting his confidence in a happy passage home, Tannhauser fell in with a mule train taking firewood and flour to the army's bread kilns on the Marsa. He told the captain of their Sipahi escort of the attack on Torghoud's battery, of which the fellow was unaware. As often before, he was treated to a vision of the Religion from the Turkish point of view. A cult of satanic fanatics. Less soldiers than criminals. Slavers, pirates, human devils, perhaps even sorcerers. A plague to be extinguished for the sake of peace and the good of the rest of the world. It took no great shamming on Tannhauser's part to agree.

At the main Turkish camp on the Marsa he took to the bazaar and renewed his acquaintance with certain of its denizens. They drank yoghurt with salt and coriander, and he learned how savage the Turkish losses had been at Saint Elmo's. Several janissary *orta* had been virtually wiped out by their refusal to retreat. Though the campaign was proving more arduous than expected, no one doubted that their Sultan would prevail, according to God's Will.

When merchants ran the world, they all agreed, there would be harmony among nations; but until that distant date they would profit as they could.

The virtues of Malta's harbours were much discussed, as were the uses to which they would be put when absorbed into the Sultan's dominions. Under the evil hegemony of the Hounds of Hell, the island was little more than a barracks and a market for slaves. Under the Ottomans it would prosper. Here, at the crossroads of half a dozen major trade routes, and with Christian piracy eliminated, fortunes would be made. These traders were poised to stake their claim; that was why they'd come so far and at such risk. Tannhauser found himself envious. Then he realised that when Malta became a wellspring of Turkish cash, he and Sabato Svi could dip their bucket from as far as Venice. Despite periodic bickering, the Serene Republic had always held first place in Ottoman trade. He put this thought, in broad terms, to the gathered merchants, who received it with enthusiasm. One knew Sabato Svi by reputation and Moshe Mosseri in person. Jews were trusted and respected. Tannhauser imagined Sabato's eyes at the thought of twice the business at half the distance.

It occurred to him that this required the Turks to triumph at the Religion's expense. But the fact was that if the Religion was wiped out, no one would mourn for long. Masses would be said and the dead honoured. Monarchs, princes and popes would squabble over their lands. Those who hated La Valette would pay wordy tribute to his reputation, as a means to inflating their own. The knights would vanish from memory along with the cause for which they'd died. And Time would consign their name to the shelves of history, alongside dynasties, tribes and empires too sundry to number.

'Who are the Greeks now, despite a thousand years of Byzantium?'

He muttered this thought out loud and the others looked at him strangely, perhaps because the answer was evident to all.

Those Greeks with any talent were the slaves of Suleiman Shah, and grateful to be so. The rest were peasants scraping a living from the rocks. He gathered his wits and gave them the benefit of his expertise in the market for pepper. From Malta they could ship direct to Genoa, Barcelona, Marseilles, and cut out the Venetians altogether. Prices were bandied and unspoken calculations furrowed their brows. The remains of the day slipped by in such altogether civilised speculations. The coffee was strong, the cakes were sweet and no man spoke of murdering another. The sun fell behind the high country to the west. The muezzin called. Tannhauser joined his friends at prayer and impostor and blasphemer though he was, he found it a comfort. Afterwards, the Galata grain dealer most intrigued by his forecasts in pepper, and who had friends in the Mendes family, let slip the rumour that Mustafa planned to surprise Saint Elmo's with a night assault next day, on the infidel Sabbath.

With this titbit to feed to Starkey, Tannhauser left the encampment and rode Buraq through the dark to the Kalkara Gate. With Mustafa obsessed with Saint Elmo's, the Borgo's eastern flank was thinly patrolled and he met no trouble on his way. A day to find Orlando Boccanera. Surely no more than two or three. The boy had been raised in the Borgo and that was most likely where he'd be. Then he'd take the ones he cared for from this hellworld and leave the rest to God's Will.

When he reached the Auberge of England on his return from Sant' Angelo, Majistral Street was deserted and the sky above was clear and indigo blue. The moon was waxing and would be bright for a week to come; but it set between one and two and wouldn't endanger their nocturnal flight to Zonra. Five was a large number to get past the watch on the Kalkara Gate, even with the *passe portes* to Mdina. But where else could the guard imagine they were going? He smiled. The women would be absolute proof against any suspicion of defection to the Turks.

He entered the refectory and found Bors and Nicodemus playing backgammon. Bors wore that expression of ecstatic anguish which is unique to compulsive gamblers on the verge of a heavy loss. Asleep with his head on the table was a third man he didn't know. A bandaged stump swung from his shoulder. Amparo slid from nowhere and threw her arms about him and he gave her a squeeze and a kiss on her luscious lips. She was more oddly beautiful than ever. Her lean, asymmetrical face was split by the candlelight, the fractured cheekbone lost in shadow, and he found that he missed it and wouldn't have wished her unblemished even if it could have been so. In her hair she wore the ivory comb and he was touched. He let go of her and she, with reluctance, of him. He rested the Damascus musket in its blanket against the wall.

'So,' said Bors, 'the Great Khan returns.' Runnels of dried sweat striped the gunblack on his face and gave him the appearance of a giant and unruly child. 'What news from Mecca?'

Tannhauser saw the demijohn. 'Is there any wine left?'

'No.'

'Supper?'

'The cook is occupied.'

Nicodemus rolled the dice and Bors cursed vilely and banged the table with his fist. The night was yet warm and Tannhauser considered the cool water in his tub. Why not? He unbuckled his scimitar and unbuttoned his kaftan. He watched Nicodemus clack white bones around the backgammon board with fluent expertise.

In Turkish Tannhauser said, 'Nicodemus, let him win. Imagine he's but a small boy, whom you love tenderly.'

'That's how he plays,' said Nicodemus. 'But why should I throw the game?'

'It would bring tranquillity for all and tonight I would value it. And it will be a shrewd investment for future contests.'

Bors rolled the dice and cursed again. 'These dice are bewitched. What did the Greek dog just say?'

'He told me he'd like to bugger you, but is waiting until you bathe.'

'He's already buggered me, a dozen times. I may need to borrow some gold.'

'You're playing for gold?'

Bors scowled, his huge, filthy hand hovering over the board. 'What news, I say? What news?'

Tannhauser said, 'They're warming our dinner in Calabria.'

Bors momentarily forgot the game. He looked at him sourly. 'And a pilot?'

'We have a compass. I'm our pilot.'

'Magnificent.'

'I've also identified the contessa's boy.'

Bors returned to scanning the board with thinly veiled rage, then plunged his hand as if into a nest of scorpions. The black bones slammed home. 'I'm not interested,' he growled.

'Where's Carla?'

Amparo answered. 'She's asleep.'

'Then I'm for a bath,' said Tannhauser.

Bors ignored him and scooped the dice into the leather cup. Glowering with menace he banged it down in front of Nicodemus. 'Roll and be damned, you Moslem fiend.'

Tannhauser saw the alarm on Amparo's face and smiled. 'Pity him,' he said. 'Bors was the finest backgammon player in Messina, or so he thought.'

'Once again I find myself trapped among the circumcised,' said Bors. 'Here, in the bastion of the Catholic faith. It's against the natural order.' He watched the roll of the dice then froze like a cat spying a wounded mouse as Nicodemus made a flagrantly incompetent move. 'Go take your bath,' said Bors, 'and leave the men to their business.'

TANNHAUSER WENT TO his cell and stripped and took a towel and went to the garden. When he got there he saw a flash of ivory and silver. Amparo was already immersed in the tub beneath the stars. He stopped. This was a novel concept and a rum one. His bath wasn't something he was in the habit of sharing. He was more than content to be soaped, scrubbed, oiled, embrocated, and so forth, at least by a woman, but to swill about in the same water? Amparo's face loomed above the ironbound rim, angelic and pale and lovely in the moonlight. It was clear she had no idea that this act was radical, but in such artlessness lay much of her matchless charm. It would be unkind to ask her to leave and even worse to refuse to get in. He walked over and tested the contents with his hand. The water still held the day's heat. His body would be soothed, not shocked, and with this prospect his dilemma became more acute. Then the same silver light that lit her face gleamed from two majestic white hemispheres. They broke the water's surface like the hero's reward in some ancient and erotic myth, and the dilemma was wiped from his mind like a shadow from a screen. The frankness of the gaze that she directed at his fast-engorging privities further mocked his squeamishness, and without further ado he vaulted over the edge and splashed in beside her.

He'd intended the tub to relax his limbs and to empty his mind of excitements for a spell. The immaculate slither of milky flesh that wrapped itself about him sabotaged both these possibilities at once. He restrained himself from instantaneous congress and let his hands roam about her thighs beneath the brine.

'You razed the Turkish guns today,' said Amparo.

It wasn't a memory he wished to revisit. With his lips on her neck, he merely grunted.

'Was it terrible?' she said.

'Terrible?' he mumbled, perplexed. Perhaps she was trying to soothe him. 'We killed many men,' he said. 'But with such worldly matters you needn't be concerned.' He kissed her throat. He ran his fingers into her hair. One breast filled his hand, as if of its own volition, and he sighed from deep in his chest as bliss overpowered him. Yet he remained obscurely pestered by her query. Such topical questions were not what he'd come to expect from her.

'Amparo, how do you know about the guns?' he said.

She said, 'Orlandu told me.'

Tannhauser's arousal receded with a disconcerting abruptness. He stood up and she slid from her perch across his thighs. 'Orlandu?' he said. 'Who is Orlandu?'

'My friend from the harbour. I told you, he thinks you a great hero and wanted to meet you.' He vaguely recalled this matter but had paid it no mind. Amparo continued. 'He was here in the refectory. He shared our supper not an hour since.'

'How old is this friend of yours?'

'He says he's fifteen, though he isn't sure.' She understood his agitation. 'He doesn't believe he's Carla's son, and neither does Carla.'

Tannhauser wasn't reassured. 'What's his family name?'

'Orlandu di Borgo.'

He laughed, but without humour. His vision of escaping the island shimmered before him and with it a nameless dread that he had to resolve with all speed.

'Who's the man at the table, with the missing arm?'

'Orlandu's friend, Tomaso.'

'Wait here,' said Tannhauser. He levered himself over the rim.

'Are you angry with me?'

'On the contrary. Just be patient.'

He hurried to the door of the auberge and realised he'd left the towel behind. He didn't turn back. The slap of his feet on the tiles seemed abnormally loud. He reached the refectory to a peal of exuberant laughter from Bors, who looked up as he entered.

'The tide has turned!' roared Bors. The sweat marks on his cheeks looked like tears of joy. 'Justice has forged her masterpiece!'

'Wake the Maltese,' said Tannhauser.

Bors reacted to his tone by leaning over and prodding a finger as thick as a broomstick into the sleeping man's ribs. Tomaso jerked up, confused by his surroundings, still the worse for several pints of wine, and alarmed by the nude and dripping figure that hulked from the candlelit shadows.

'Orlandu Boccanera,' said Tannhauser.

Tomaso looked about the table as if to point him out, his blurred eyes roving about the dark when he didn't find him. It was answer enough.

Tannhauser said, in Italian, 'Where does he live? The house of Orlandu?'

Tomaso looked around as if for help.

'I know where Orlandu sleeps,' said Amparo. Her head peeped around the doorframe. She was wrapped in the towel.

'Good,' said Tannhauser. 'We'll get dressed at once.'

As he turned away, Tomaso said something that none of them understood. He pointed to a spot on the floor by the wall. Tannhauser rapped the table with his fist. 'Bors?'

Bors turned and looked and said, 'That's where Tomaso's sword and armour were stacked.' He blew his cheeks. 'I'd say young Orlandu must have taken them with him.'

Tomaso spoke again and the words included '*Sant' Elmu*'.

Tannhauser looked at Bors. 'Tell me I just misheard him.'

Bors wiped a finger across his moustache. 'Well, the lad was all afire to join the broil. And I dare say we stoked it.'

'He's twelve years old,' said Tannhauser.

'In cuirass and helm he'd look man enough and more. He wouldn't be the first to lie about his age, to go for a soldier. And, I must say, the lad has a quick and ready tongue when he wants to wag it.'

Tannhauser felt the floor falling out of his bowels.

He said, 'You're coming with me, to Sant' Angelo's wharf.'

'But the game,' said Bors. 'I have him on his knees!'

Tannhauser ran to his cell to grab his boots and a pair of breeches.

Tannhauser and Bors double-timed it through the narrow streets. Between the crenellated rim of the curtain wall and the silhouette of Castel Sant' Angelo the town was a pool of darkness. As they got closer to the fortress, voices and groans rang out, and they passed stretcher-bearers hauling the day's injured to the infirmary by torchlight. The evacuees were distinguished not merely by their wounds but by an absence in their eyes, as if horror had robbed each one of something precious. They ran on.

Castel Sant' Angelo stood on its own rock, separated from the Borgo by a canal. The bridge across the canal led to the foot of the castle and to the curving wharf from which the boats set sail to Saint Elmo's. The bridge was jammed with a desperate and bloody human traffic. Tannhauser browbeat his way past the provost marshal and they shoved their way through the press with all necessary callousness. On the bare stones of the wharf lay bodies that had expired during the crossing. Beside them lay a dozen more who looked unlikely to make it across the bridge. Spilled gore abounded, in puddles and gelid lumps, and it clung to his boots as he hurdled the dying and the dead. Two chaplains moved among the moribund, smearing chrism on their foreheads and nostrils and lips.

'Through this holy unction may the Lord pardon thee whatever sins or faults thou hast committed.'

The evacuees brought with them the tang of the siege across the harbour: gaping wounds, raw fear, the whiff of violent chaos. La Valette always made a point of seeing off the fresh volunteers; that Tannhauser couldn't see him boded ill. They pushed on. A captive Turkish officer – bloody, half-naked and festooned with chains – was driven past them, and Tannhauser heard a fragment of his murmurings.

'Hold fast to the rope of Allah . . .'

'That fellow's in for a nasty shock,' observed Bors.

Tannhauser pressed forward, hardly listening. Bors was undeterred.

'In the dungeons of Saint Anthony, the torturers keep a giant blackamoor on hand – treat him like a king, food, wine by the bucket. When they want to loosen a fresh Turk's tongue they strip him down and bend him over a hogshead and have the blackamoor sodomise him, while they stand about cheering and laughing, and reminding him that that's how old Mohammed took his pleasure.' Bors laughed himself. 'The results, they say, are a wonder to behold.'

Tannhauser made no comment and looked about. The waters of Grand Harbour shone like quicksilver, its surface shimmering in the wake of two departing longboats and their dipping oars. Each contained twenty-odd men and sundry supplies. At a lamplit table sat a brother serjeant with a ledger and a quartermaster whose manifests were swimming in a spilt pot of ink. Unbrotherly words flew back and forth. Tannhauser recognised the serjeant, a Lombard called Grimaldi, and he rapped his knuckles on the table to draw his attention.

'Brother Grimaldi, I must know if a certain man left with the volunteers.'

'Tonight?' asked Grimaldi

'Tonight. By the name of Orlandu Boccanera.'

The quartermaster didn't appreciate the interruption. 'You've no authority here. We have work to do.'

'Work?' Tannhauser leaned his hands on the table and looked down on him. 'This morning I directed the raid on Gallows Point. So tell me, book-keeper, how many Turks have you slain today?'

The quartermaster rose to his feet, his hand crossing his waist to the hilt of his sword. Despite that Tannhauser remained bent forward, the man was still obliged to look up at him.

'Who are you, sir?'

'I advise you to keep to spilling ink, my friend,' said Bors,'and leave the spilling of blood to such as we.'

'Sit down,' said Grimaldi. 'This is Starkey's man.'

The quartermaster walked away, muttering a Paternoster to calm his ire. Grimaldi leafed through the muster roll. His finger stopped near the end of a column of names.

'No Boccanera here. But we have one *Orlandu di Borgo*,' said Grimaldi. 'The fellow was as impudent as his name.' He tipped his beard towards the harbour. 'He's in the last boat yonder.'

Tannhauser straightened and turned and gazed across the water. Far out in the night, and beyond all hope of recall, the oars of the rearmost longboat feathered the quicksilver. For the sake of a fantasia on pepper, one cup of coffee too many, or a quick dip in his tub, the cornerstone of his policy lay in pieces. Orlandu was on his way to the post of certain death. For all the ups and downs of recent weeks, Tannhauser had never succumbed to a feeling of dismay. But he did so now. He turned from the water and his spirits sunk yet lower.

Running barefoot through the blood, her hair flying wild about her shoulders, was Carla. She saw his face and stopped. And Tannhauser felt as if he'd stabbed her through the heart.

SUNDAY 10 JUNE 1565 – PENTECOST

Shrine of Our Lady of Philermo – Auberge of England – Castel Sant' Angelo

The icon of Our Lady of Philermo hung in a chapel in the church of San Lorenzo. After the Right Hand of John the Baptist, the knights considered the icon their most sacred relic. Saint Luke had painted it, so some said, and a miracle had carried it to Rhodes on the waves of the sea. When Suleiman conquered Rhodes, the surviving knights had taken the icon with them. The Madonna's face was primitive, almost without expression, yet her eyes contained all the sorrow of the world. She'd been known to weep real tears and numerous miracles had been credited to her powers. Carla knelt before the icon and prayed; and if not for a miracle, then for guidance. On this day, when the Holy Ghost had descended upon the Apostles, surely she could hope for that. Outside it was dead of night and the church was empty.

'Fate is against us,' Mattias had told her, as she stood stunned and ankle deep in the blood of the wharf. 'Let me take you back to Italy. To France. To stay here is to die, and for what? Put this business behind you and start life anew.'

She'd promised him an answer by morning. She'd come to the shrine of Philermo to find one. She was yet in shock from the knowledge that Orlandu was her son. At a distance of inches and despite an exposure lasting hours she'd failed to recognise her own flesh. She'd allowed him to slip through her hands into certain death.

She didn't doubt his identity. As soon as Amparo had told her she'd known it was so. Ruggiero's story of the baptism, the letter of Father Benadotti: of these confirmations she'd had no need. She'd felt a bond with the boy, had warmed to him at once, yet she'd put it down to his urchin charm, his friendship with Amparo, the power of Christ's love that had filled her soul in the Sacred Infirmary. Amid all that she'd felt no explicit sense of maternal recognition. Vanity. Vanity. What had she expected? To feel pangs and spasms in her womb? To see a halo glow about his head? She was no mother. She'd never given suck. How could she expect to know him? Her fantasy of herself had condemned him. That and also, she realised with shame, her social bigotry. Charming as he'd been, he was filthy and uncouth, a barefoot lout who'd boasted of killing dogs. Some inbuilt sense of station had blinded her eyes and stifled her heart, the curse of her supposed nobility. She thought of her father, Don Ignacio. Mattias had seen him.

'Your father begged your forgiveness for stealing your child,' said Mattias. 'And for condemning the boy to a life of such lowly character. The most bitter of his regrets were for the heinous cruelty he inflicted upon you. If I may quote his very words: *I loved her more dearly than any living soul.*'

At this she'd wept, for the thought of her father's hatred had been a wound.

'Don Ignacio was dying,' said Mattias. 'When I left he could count his time in this world in hours. The priest was with him. Your father took great consolation in the thought that you'd returned. I presumed to tell him that he still enjoyed your affection and respect, and that your forgiveness was already certain, and for this he blessed me. Perhaps I misrepresented you, but a dying man deserves charity, despite that his sins were vile.'

Carla wept again before the icon. With love for the kindness of Mattias. With grief at her father's passing. With desperate gratitude for Don Ignacio's love, for in some small corner of her heart she'd never lost her belief in it. With sorrow for Orlandu and the pain of her own folly. She sensed a figure enter the side chapel behind her and she stopped her tears.

It was La Valette.

He knelt at the rail beside her and fell at once into deep devotions. He did not acknowledge her. He seemed almost in a trance. She thought of the burdens upon his conscience. His fears for the Maltese people. The men he dispatched daily across the harbour to their deaths. The mistakes – his own most of all – that must have dispatched even more. Carla looked up at the figure of Our Lady and asked Her what she should do. And Our Lady told her.

After his labours of recent days Mattias was entitled to his rest and Carla waited until he awoke before seeking him out. He stayed in bed into the afternoon and she wondered if he'd taken a soporific. Or perhaps he was preoccupied with Amparo. The thought of them still caused waves of nausea; but for this she chastised herself and not them. When Mattias at last emerged he seemed low in spirits. They met alone in the refectory, where he ate his food without appetite. They talked of this and that, then he asked after her intentions concerning the future.

'My right place in the world is here,' she said.

He took this with a grim glance across his coffee cup. The cup was tiny and beautiful and looked absurdly dainty in his walnut-knuckled fist. 'Orlandu won't be coming back,' he said. 'At least not whole.'

'My place is here whether I ever see Orlandu again or not.' She watched him attempt to contain a bleak frustration. He was not a man much given to dejection – indeed his resilience in the face of misfortune astounded her – and it hurt her to see him so dispirited. Especially on her part. She reached out her hand and touched the back of his. 'You want me to leave the island and I understand why –'

'That I doubt very much.' His voice was curt and she felt rebuffed. He added a rider. 'You've never seen the Turks sack a town. You'd be raped for hours, perhaps days. Then, with luck, you would be butchered. Without luck, you'd be sold and shipped to a brothel in North Africa.'

She flinched at the brutality of his language. 'But it's impossible to leave Malta.'

'Have I lost your confidence?' he said.

'Certainly that is impossible.' She smiled but he didn't reciprocate. 'No. God has granted me the vocation – the calling – that's eluded me all my life. That's why I must stay.'

'We're surrounded by the Called,' said Mattias. 'They're hacking each other to pieces as we speak.'

'I will be doing no hacking,' she said. 'I wish only to serve the people – those who suffer in the footsteps of Christ. I'll accept whatever Providence ordains.'

He turned away and flicked the grounds from his cup and refilled it from the copper ewer. Then he stared into his brew and avoided her eyes. She knew he thought her a fool, but for once she knew that she was not.

'Mattias, please, hear me.' He looked at her. She continued. 'You've done everything that any man could and much more. You've brought me on a great journey, you've been my guardian and guide. I was searching for my son and I lost him, yet again, but I've been given something else – something infinitely precious – that I didn't expect to find.' She remembered their first conversation in the rose garden. She said, 'Let us call it the Grace of God.'

Mattias nodded. He said nothing.

'If my quest to find Orlandu has led me to this knowledge – of my own soul, my own place in God's heart and creation – then I will not count it a failure. And neither should you.'

'And Amparo?' he said. 'Must she stay and die with the fanatics?'

'I am no fanatic.'

'I speak of those who between them will reduce this city to dust.'

'Amparo has always been free. I do not command her. She loves you, Mattias.' She hesitated. 'I love you. I love you both.'

Mattias flinched, as if this information only added to his burdens. He retreated once again into his coffee.

'As to our bargain,' she continued, 'I will gladly keep it if you wish. We could marry before you leave and draw up the papers. You would have your title.'

He waved his hand. 'We're beyond such trifles now. And you deserve a better mate than me. Your commitment is to something noble. More than noble. Do you want my blessing?'

'There's nothing I would cherish more deeply.'

He smiled his smile of old. 'Then it's yours, free and full,' he said. He stood up. 'But there are matters I must ponder for myself.' He bowed, with the primitive gallantry that had touched her before. 'Will you excuse me?'

Carla stood up too. 'Of course. In any case I must go to the infirmary.'

He offered her his arm. 'Then I'll claim the honour of escorting you.'

Carla put her hand on his arm and it felt good. She feared she'd never see him again. She still yearned for his love. And yet, she'd made her peace with herself. She could ask for no more.

When she got to the infirmary, Lazaro told her that Angelu was dead.

TANNHAUSER AND BORS sat between the merlons on Sant' Angelo's battlements like two idling boys, their feet dangling over the clear blue water a hundred feet and more far below. They shared a goatskin of wine and a crock of olives and watched the set of the sun behind Monte Sciberras. The ochre smoke of the siege guns lent the sundown an infernal glow. From the cavalier behind their grandstand the cannon spouted a salvo of iron and woe. Across the bay, Fort Saint Elmo seemed not much more than a heap of disintegrating boundary stones, yet in breach of every statute of probability its blasted precincts teemed with unhinged defiance.

'It's a paradox,' said Tannhauser, 'that men committed to dying should cling with such tenacity to life.'

'Glory,' said Bors.

He looked at Tannhauser and Tannhauser's heart lurched with an unexpected sadness at the wild grey eyes and the gnarled northern face.

'All mortal chains broken, all moral debts waived,' continued Bors. 'Not praise or honours or grand renown – but rapture, and a foreshadowing of the Divine. That is Glory.' He filled his throat with wine and swallowed and wiped his lips. 'But you know that joy as well as I. Deny it if you will and I'll call you a liar.'

'Glory is a moment that can only be known in Hell.'

'That's as may be, yet what else in this world compares? Money? Fame? Power? The love of women?' He snorted. 'A moment, yes, but having once seen its light, all else is gloom.'

Tannhauser's gloom was rooted in other causes. 'Getting my hands on this boy is like trying to catch lice in someone else's crotch. Unpleasant, frustrating, hazardous and with no happy end in sight.'

'The lice usually find you, though the boy came close.' Bors emptied another prodigious draught down his gullet and offered the skin to Tannhauser, who shook his head. 'Are we for Calabria, then?' asked Bors. 'And will the fair and tender ladies come with us?'

'After praying to Our Lady of Philermo, Carla has decided that her place is here, in the Borgo. Divine Providence, the Grace of God, will guide her way henceforward. She will martyr herself to the sick, or some such nonsense.' He waved his hand. 'Such was the gist.'

'Well there's no gainsaying Providence,' said Bors. 'Do I recall it was a pound of opium that oiled her way through Lazaro's door?'

Tannhauser did not need this reminder. His motives for arranging that favour now seemed wholly unfathomable. 'I asked her if Amparo was obliged to stay in this splendid theocracy.'

'And?'

'Amparo is free to do as she pleases.'

'Surely these are glad tidings,' said Bors. 'All are content, so it seems, and you can leave with conscience clear and a gaudy girl on your arm.'

Tannhauser scowled. 'If ever I were to hear the Voice of God, this would be a welcome moment.'

'So you're not content.'

Tannhauser gazed across the bay. Saint Elmo's had been scourged by marksmen and bludgeoned by cannonades since first light. Here and there, the rosy glint of the sunset reflected from helmets and pauldrons in the overclouding dust. Somewhere among the rubble, Orlandu di Borgo was getting his first taste of warfare; if he'd survived this long.

'It doesn't sit right with me to leave a thing unfinished,' Tannhauser said. 'And most especially to be thwarted at the last.'

'You've taken beatings before. The bruises will fade.'

'The boy's brain was stuffed with evil myths.'

'We talked of weapons and such. Is that a crime?' Bors sniffed and raised the wineskin and lowered it again without drinking. 'What else could we have discussed? The price of pepper?'

'He's a child. If he doesn't die they'll ship him back crippled. In either event he'll never be the things he might have been. He'll never do the things he might have done. He'll never know the things he might have known.'

'Such is life.' Bors raised the wineskin again and poured at length.

'He'll be robbed of his birthright before he's had the chance to collect it. As were you and I both.'

'Us?' said Bors, almost choking. He wiped his lips. 'Do we not walk tall?'

'Only among apes.'

'Surely this war is righteous, even if I might allow that others are not. We can't have a crowd of greasy heathen forcing us to rub our faces in the dirt, while we spout their gibberish and bend our heads to Mecca. Look what they did to you.'

Tannhauser said, 'When you know that men can be trained like dogs to believe and do anything – anything at all – it makes you value your own counsel and be suspect of every other.'

'Cheer up, man, and quit this dreary philosophising. It will change nothing. Besides, you love killing. So do I. And a good thing too, for without killers there'd be no war and without war –' He stopped as his thought ran into the ground. 'Well, there you are – without war we'd have nothing to talk about at all.'

Tannhauser took the skin and rifled a drink. He stared at the sea between his feet. The thought of the drop made him dizzy. There were other falls just as sheer. Perhaps more sheer still. He looked up across the bay at Fort Saint Elmo.

'So,' said Bors, who knew him all too well, 'you've decided to go over to the cauldron and bring back the boy.'

Tannhauser didn't answer.

Bors said, 'If you want my opinion, that is the Voice of God.'

'After dark, Mustafa plans to storm the breaches,' Tannhauser said. 'A night attack by the Turk is something to behold.'

'Then let me bring him back for you,' said Bors.

Tannhauser laughed. 'I'd never see either one of you again.'

'You doubt my good faith?'

'Never. But a madness rages out there which even at this close range cannot be imagined, and you're too prone to catch it and rave. Even I fear its glamour.'

'Then take me with you. Let me sip from the chalice and I'll row you back to Venice by myself.'

Tannhauser shuffled back between the crenels of the embrasure and managed to stand up without plunging to his death. He looked east across Bighi Bay. In the thickening twilight Gallows Point was a hive of Turkish industry as Torghoud's men drilled out the spiked cannon and rebuilt the batteries and constructed a defensive palisade against further attack. Yesterday's dawn seemed a long time ago; and tomorrow's seemed far away. Perhaps Carla was right. Perhaps they were all right. Embrace Providence. And let God's Will be done.

'It's hard for thee to kick against the pricks,' he murmured.

'What?' said Bors.

The guns of the raised cavalier bellowed again and balls sucked the air above their heads as they passed by. Some seconds away, in the dusk beyond, another handful of lives were about to be blighted and didn't yet know it.

'Come,' said Tannhauser. 'Let's see if the Grand Master has granted my wish.'

SUNDAY 10 JUNE 1565 – PENTECOST

Auberge of England – the Crossing – the Post of Honour

Tannhauser bent over his war chest and stacked various items into a knapsack. Ten slabs of opium wrapped in oilcloth, various medicaments and decoctions, two bottles of brandy, half a dozen crocks of sweet preserves – quince, apricot and strawberry. The knapsack's contents comprised such gifts, bribes and wheel-grease as might be needed. He didn't dwell on any eventuality that might leave him prone to consuming these goodies himself. Carla hadn't yet returned from the infirmary, and he was content to avoid the explanations and farewells.

'What are you doing?'

He turned towards the soft, musical voice with a clenching in his gut. Amparo lingered in the yellow light and shadows at the door of his monastic cell. He smiled. 'Where I am going two things become priceless above all others, while gold and precious stone become worthless as dirt. Can you guess what those things might be?'

She replied without hesitation. 'Music and love.'

He laughed. 'You've outriddled me, and I dare say you're right. My answer is less poetic.' He hefted the knapsack on the bed where his armour was baled. 'Things that ease pain and things that taste sweet. But at least I can put them in a bag.'

'Are music and love not welcome in Hell?'

He walked over to her. Her eyes were black and fearless and he fought the inclination to lose his soul within them. 'On the contrary, the Devil himself craves them.'

'You go to bring Orlandu back from the war,' she said.

He nodded. On impulse, he said, 'Can you keep a secret?'

'Better than anyone.'

To his surprise, he found he didn't doubt it. 'After that, I plan to escape the war itself, and return to Italy. Will you come with me?'

'I'll go anywhere you want me to.'

Her mouth half-opened and her body swayed, as if to counter the desire to press herself against him. He pulled her into the room by her arm and took her by the waist and pushed her against the wall. She raised her face and he kissed her. She didn't close her eyes and neither did he. Hers were full of questions. Perhaps they mirrored his own. They'd already slaked certain needs not an hour before yet his nether parts swelled with lubricity. He let go of her, before retreat became unfeasible, and stepped away.

'When will you be back?' she said.

'Tomorrow night.'

He shouldered the knapsack and grabbed the baled armour and his wheel-lock rifle, freshly oiled and primed. The pistol he'd left in the chest. He pointed to the Damascus musket, still wrapped in a blanket and stacked by the wall. The elaborate Ottoman powder flask and the pouch of balls hung from it.

'Would you bring those for me?' he asked.

IN THE REFECTORY, Bors brooded over his wine. As Tannhauser dumped his gear on the table, Bors made a point of not looking up.

'Well, this is a sour farewell for an old friend,' Tannhauser remarked.

Bors scowled and fended him off with a hand.

Tannhauser took the blanketed gun from Amparo. 'Since you never fail to have one, give me an opinion.' He tossed the musket broadside across the table.

Bors stood up and caught it with both hands and by reflex tested its weight. His eyes gleamed. He laid it down and unfastened the ties. He unwrapped the blanket, and as the silver, ebony and steel were unveiled he let out a connoisseur's sigh. The weapon leapt into his hands as if it was alive, and he threw it to his shoulder and sighted and swept it in an arc across the room, the silver chasing and the nine-palm damascened barrel winking in the light above the table lamps.

'Perfection,' he muttered. 'Perfection without price.' He lowered it and with the effort of one extracting his own teeth laid it back on the blanket in a pointed display of the triumph of good manners over covetousness. 'Unique. Exquisite. With that I could shoot the bollocks off a Mussulman at five hundred feet.' He added, teeth gritted, 'If I ever get that close to one.'

'It's yours,' said Tannhauser.

Bors stared at him and Tannhauser thought he saw his lip tremble. Bors's hands moved to seize the musket, then stopped and hovered above it. 'You're sure, now? If I pick it up again you'll have to take it from my corpse.'

Tannhauser nodded. 'It will come in handy at Saint Elmo's.'

Bors seized the gun and caressed it, marvelling, his face shining. As his eyes pored over the scrollwork he froze and his head snapped back towards Tannhauser. 'At Saint Elmo's?'

Tannhauser said, 'Get your gear.'

CARLA MADE HER way back from the hospital in darkness. Today was Pentecost, *Pascha Rosatum*, when the Holy Ghost had descended on Christ's Apostles in tongues of fire, and at Mass in the ward they'd strewn the altar with rose leaves and the nature of what God required of her became clearer. Angelu had died the previous night and his body had been removed before she arrived. With Angelu's death, certain of her vain fantasies had been laid to rest. Jacobus, with whom she'd spent the morning, had died at noon. A man no one could identify, and whose face was too dismantled by sabre cuts to identify himself, had died with his hand in hers in the minutes before she left. They would have ejected her at sundown, but she'd fought with the monks and won. At last her habit of getting her own way had been put to good use. She'd grieved with each man, and had found that each time she thought her heart was about to break, it had become stronger, and the living presence of Christ more powerful yet. If she held hands of men, then Jesus held hers.

When she reached the auberge she thought no one was there, until she searched the monks' cells and found Amparo crying quietly. She lay on the palliasse clutching her ivory comb. Lying on the sheet was the brass cylinder of her vision glass. Carla had never seen her cry before. Without speaking, Carla knelt down and stroked her hair.

'They've gone across the water,' said Amparo. 'To Hell.'

'To Saint Elmo's?'

'I've heard many people talk of it. They all call it Hell.'

'And who has gone there?'

'Tannhauser. Bors. They say they're going to bring Orlandu home.'

A pang of anxiety and guilt pierced Carla's stomach. But she was learning to master those old enemies too. 'They act out of Charity, and God protects them. They'll be back.'

'I looked in the shew stone, and I couldn't see him. I couldn't see Tannhauser.' Wetness bubbled from her nose. She wiped it with the back of her hand and took a deep breath. 'Oh, how I love him so.'

Carla saw how overwhelming and bewildering this notion was

to her. She took hold of Amparo's hands and squeezed. 'Mattias is a good man,' she said. 'With a large heart.'

'Do you love him too?'

'Yes, in my way.' She smiled. Almost to her own surprise, it was not a false smile. She said, 'I've seen how he looks at you. I saw it from the earliest moment, when you showed him the roses in the garden.'

'He told me the nightingale was happy in death, for he knew love. But perhaps Tannhauser does not.'

Carla didn't understand the meaning of the nightingale. But it wasn't time to ask. She said, 'I'm sure he does. And I'm just as certain that he will not die.'

'I'm afraid,' said Amparo. 'I've never been afraid before.'

'Love always brings fear,' said Carla. 'They travel hand in hand, for to know love is to know that you may lose it. To love takes courage and strength. But you have both.'

'Will you stay with me tonight?'

Carla lay beside her on the palliasse.

Amparo said, 'Can we play our music again? Together?'

'Yes,' said Carla. 'Soon.'

With a flick of her finger she snuffed the wick of candle in the molten wax and darkness fell. They lay in each other's arms and neither spoke, neither did they sleep, and each eased the terrible aching inside the other. After a while, the guns that had been silent since sundown exploded with renewed thunder, and they pulled each other closer in the dark.

THE WATER WAS as still as the night and the only sound they heard as they left Sant' Angelo was the dip and sweep of the oars that drove them onwards. The moon was three days short of full and apart from the charcoal crescent pared from its leftmost face it was as radiant as joy. It had just passed through the meridian and, a few degrees shy of its shaded rim, the Scorpion's head shone as bright. In this Tannhauser read a benevolent augury.

At the worst it could do no harm.

The men in the boats were silent, each huddled in his own round of darkness. Each knew that the only way to be carried back home was in the cradle of his own mutilation. They took comfort in the knowledge that death, when it came, would be a martyr's and that their sacrifice might purchase life and freedom from the yoke of Islam for those they loved.

Tannhauser and Bors sat in the rearmost of three boats, among which were disbursed fifty Maltese and Spanish soldiers, twelve professed knights and serjeants at arms of the Order, sundry supplies, ten shackled slaves and a number of sheep which were hooded to stay their bleating. The great black shadow of Monte Sciberras loomed to their left and such a multitude of torches and fires glowed thereon that they rivalled the teeming firmament laid out above. At the seaward edge of the slope, beyond the sharp angulation that bent the shoreline south of Fort Saint Elmo, a Turkish labour battalion was throwing up what looked like a palisade, though as a defence against what Tannhauser could not tell. Then a keening song threaded through the stillness. The graceful rise and fall of the imam's voice, its rhythmic repetition, stirred his heart. The Koran was Allah's instruction to Man and Arabic the language in which He'd spoken. It couldn't be translated into any other. Though the words at this distance were indistinct, the reaction it evoked within him – the reflexive tightening in his belly, the sudden thinness of the air in his lungs, the throbbing in his ears and temples – left him in no doubt, for he had heard them too many times before, on too many bloody fields.

The words and rhythm were those of *Al-Fath*, the *surah* of Conquest.

To the beat of the imam's song, Tannhauser murmured in Arabic, '*If any believe not in Allah and his Messenger, We have prepared for those who reject Him a Blazing Fire.*'

Bors gave him a look.

'Hark,' said Tannhauser, 'the Lions of Islam roar.'

A holocaust of frenzied explosions rent the darkness of the mountainside asunder, as not far short of five score siege guns unleashed an opening salvo that sucked the breath from their chests. Flames roared orange and yellow and blue from the dragon-mouthed bores of the culverins and showers of sparks wafted upwards on the balmy night air. In the brief but dazzling light thrown by the muzzle blasts, they saw soldiers massed on the slopes in enormous squares. Soldiers massed by the thousand and the tens of thousands.

And all of them eager and willing to see the Face of God.

'Christ's wounds,' said Bors, with awe.

In the stunned silence that followed the monstrous barrage an imam shrieked an exhortation to the thronged Believers. The *gazi* horde responded as one with a roar of exaltation that was louder and more terrifying by far than the anger of the cannon.

'Allahu Akabar!'

The cry swept across the water like the wind from Hell's gate. None in that Christian company had ever heard its like and the blood of every man ran as cold as the waters of the Styx.

'Allahu Akabar!'

'For Christ and the Baptist!' shouted Bors, for he did not like to be outdone, and the men in the boats took up the riposte. Yet they were few, and they went unheard, and the horde's throat opened yet again.

'Allahu Akabar!'

And Tannhauser knew in that moment, as did other men there, and not among the Moslem ranks alone, that this was the primordial howl of his inmost heart. The howl that had echoed down millennia. It was the voice of a god whose power had been ancient when all other deities were unborn, whose dominion subsumed all lesser faiths and creeds, whose reign would see all other idols crumble into dust. It was a behest to kneel at the Altar of War. An invitation to relieve that thirst which would afflict men always, and which would never be wholly quenched. Tannhauser's breath caught in his chest and tears sprang to his eyes. He brushed them away and breathed in the Quintessence of the meaning of mortality. This was what it was to be a man. This, and not some thing other than this; be that high or be that base.

'Oh my God,' said Bors. And his eyes too were all ashine. 'Oh my God.'

The Moslem battle cry subsided into a formless din of rage and the martial janissary bands struck up and volleys of musket fire blazed. Then horns trilled and the banners flaunted high and the horde invincible rolled down the slope towards Saint Elmo's.

The fort replied with cannon blasts, and arquebuses crackled along the bastions. Turkish flares exploded high above and as the first wave hit the ditch and strove across the improvised bridgeworks, dazzling jets of wildfire erupted from the trumps on the Christian ramparts and burning hoops spun down through the banished dark to ensnare the foe. Within minutes the entire southwest salient was ablaze with burning men and erupting fireworks and pools of flame. Enough light was thrown for Sant' Angelo's sixteen-pounders to open up, and balls screamed high above the convoy and ploughed furrows of bloody outrage through the Moslem charge. Acrid smoke crept out across the water towards them and roiling spirals climbed across the face of the moon. The oarsmen bent to their looms and pulled and the boats slid on through the heat and the fog as if ferrying their lading of Argonauts to the far side shore of Damnation. Then a volley of gunfire barked, not three hundred feet alee, and a cry in Spanish went up.

'The infidels are on us!'

Tannhauser peered ahead through the silvered gloom. A Turkish flatboat had slipped beneath the smoke and had raked the leading transport with a broadside of musket fire. The transport was a turmoil of screaming sheep and desperate men, oars tangled and askew, drifting without direction as the Turks laid off at thirty feet and recharged their pieces. A number of Turkish archers harried the stunned Christian survivors with vicious flights of arrows from their goat-horn bows. There were few guns on the Christian boats, the shoulder arms of Saint Elmo's being passed on from the dead to the living. The second transport swung clear of the first and pulled hard for Saint Elmo's dock. A wise choice in the circumstance. There was every chance that Tannhauser's lot would receive the second volley. Then the Turks would be at leisure to extinguish them all. Bors threw the Damascus musket to his shoulder.

Tannhauser stopped him. 'Save it, man.'

'I haven't come this far to drown like a blasted sailor.'

'Nor I.'

They were seated in the front third of the boat, near five brethren of the Aragonese Langue dressed in full battle harness. Caballero Geronimus Aiguabella, of the Priory of Gerona, was in command. Tannhauser grabbed him and Aiguabella, a razor-faced fanatic with cyes as black as glass beads, turned to listen.

'Move your brethren to the stern, so that their weight will raise the prow.' Tannhauser pointed, then illustrated with his hands. 'Then order the helmsman to ram the Turk amidships, on the oblique. Do you understand?'

Aiguabella blinked and looked across the water to envisage Tannhauser's ploy.

'At the last moment, on your order, our rowers must ship their oars,' Tannhauser said. 'The Turkish sweeps will form a ramp to carry us over, and the infidel's craft will be left capsized in our wake.'

Aiguabella took this in and looked at him. He seemed dubious.

Tannhauser said, 'It's that or take their fire. If we slow down enough to take them on hand-to-hand, they'll rake us stem to stern.'

Aiguabella said, '*Bueno*.'

He rapped out orders to his knights and led the unsteady,

clanking procession to the stern. The Maltese helmsman, singing out the rhythm in a calm and salty voice, had the rowers already heaving at a full pelt. The whoosh of their breathing matched the rattle of the oarlocks and sea spume topped the gunwales with every stroke. If one had to attempt so reckless a manoeuvre at sea, Tannhauser thought, one could not wish for better than a Maltese hand on the helm. As he unlimbered his rifle the longboat changed course to bear down on the Turkish vessel, now just two hundred feet distant. He and Bors were now the foremost of their crew and they could see the Moslem musketeers as they struggled, cramped and pitching, to reload and prime. They were dressed in a motley of costumes and numbered two score. Shouts of alarm were exchanged as they saw the Christian prow foaming through the quicksilver, and their frenzy increased and their rowers hoisted their oar blades out of the water to pull away.

'Corsairs!' said Bors. He blew his gun match to a fierce yellow glow. 'It's sweet to pull a corsair's trick upon them.'

'Their helmsman,' said Tannhauser. 'Do you see him?'

'Oh yes,' said Bors.

Bors wedged his foot against a bench and braced his elbow against his knee and shouldered his piece. For two strokes of the oars he let the rise and fall of the bow flow through his body. As it rose a third time he squeezed the trigger and held steady as the match sprang into the pan. The nine-palm barrel bucked and boomed and Tannhauser ducked below the gunsmoke to watch. The Moslem helmsman was plucked from his seat and vanished in the foggy blackness beyond the stern.

'Straight through the chest,' chortled Bors. He kissed the water-dappled steel of the musket barrel. 'What a baptism for my beauty. Her very first shot. I'll call her *Salome*, in honour of John the Baptist. Salome was a filthy Moslem, was she not?'

'There were no Moslems in those days,' Tannhauser informed him. 'There were only a dozen Christians or thereabouts.'

Bors took this as a jest. 'But bitches aplenty, of that much we can be sure.'

Tannhauser aimed his rifle and watched as the corsair rowers found their stroke and shunted their flatboat forward. The Algerians were stranded broadside. In order to swing stern-on they'd have to backwater and pull, starboard versus port, but without the helmsman to guide them confusion was king. Another man leapt to the tiller and Tannhauser, waiting for such a ploy, fired on the rise of the oarstroke and draped him among his compatriots coughing blood. The collision was now inevitable. He slipped the rifle across the bench beneath his thighs and hoped to keep the lock dry. He grabbed either gunwale, both feet braced, and hung on for grim life. Bors stuffed the wick of his gun, still burning, down his boot top and followed suit. Arrows flew towards them and slammed quivering into the hull. They closed the last hundred feet with alarming speed, their momentum irresistible. The bank of Moslem oars dipped the water before them. The longboat took leave of the sea. There was a roar from Aiguabella and Tannhauser heard the jangle of looms in the rowlocks as the oarsmen hauled in their shafts.

The teeth of the corsairs shone in their snarling faces, Algerians by the look, and a dozen belated musket blasts flashed wild. Then wood splintered and groaned and Tannhauser clung for his life as the prow rose before him and his bowels dropped inside him and all he could see was a flash of the star-speckled sky. There were screams and curses and the rush of the sea below as it swamped the corsairs. His guts welled up again as the prow plunged steeply back down. Then he was drenched as water cascaded the bows. They were level again, rocking and pitching but afloat, and he heard the looms run out again to steady them. He turned.

In their wake floated the overturned hull of the corsairs' flatboat. Around it splashed a shoal of desperate men with gasping mouths and arms aflail. From the remnants of the first Christian transport came a chorus of huzzahs. Aiguabella had the helmsman bring them round, and the crew rose from their benches like grim harpooners, and as the Algerian flotsam blubbered their last orisons, the Maltese finished them off with the blades of their oars.

THEY PULLED into Saint Elmo's dock and Tannhauser's relief at feeling solid ground beneath him could not be described. Beyond the looming and ragged silhouette of the crumbling fort the sky flared a fiery yellow shot through with smoke. Great chunks of masonry had been blasted from the ramparts and lay half-submerged at the foot of the sheer rock bluff upon which the eastern wall was built. Their welcome was warm but brisk and they climbed the steps in the stone behind Aiguabella and his brethren. On dry land the knights were as nimble as goats in their armour. Tannhauser hefted his baled helmet and cuirass, which he hadn't worn in the boat for fear of the water.

'If we're going into the broil I want more steel than this against my hide.'

Bors said, 'Then let's go and find ourselves some dead men.'

As they reached the gate Tannhauser asked the guard where he could find the field hospital, and was directed towards the chapel at the fort's northern end. They cleared the postern gate and there they stopped and gaped, for any such spectacle as that which lay before them was seen by few. Of those, far fewer still would live to recount it.

The inner ward of the fort was a crater-pocked wasteland across which no man dared to stray. Its cracked and pulverised flagstones were littered with iron and granite balls, some big enough to sit on, and blotched with sinister stains so numerous that in parts they merged together to paint whole sections of the yard a gelatinous black. Here and there stood the outlines of smaller buildings, demolished either by cannon fire or design. Their materials had been used to throw up the rude breastworks that zigzagged all about the open ground, for there was scarcely a square foot of the interior that wasn't exposed by now to Turkish musketry.

The north-western wall to their right gaped with holes and a second bulwark had been built behind it from cannibalised stones, earth, splintered timbers and bedding. This defence work was presently unmanned and had the air of a folly erected by a madman and abandoned in a fit of pique.

On the southern side, facing the captured ravelin and the main Turkish positions on Monte Sciberras, the curtain wall could no longer rightly be described as any kind of wall at all, but was rather a vast heap of rubble – more befitting cave dwellers than a modern army – scraped into a crude defensive embankment. Even as they watched, chains of slaves toiled in the moonlight to the whistle and the whip, naked and ghostlike in their caked raiment of dust and sweat and blood, heaving chunks of masonry from one pair of bleeding hands to another until the stones regained the rampart from whence they'd fallen. The rim of the V-shaped ravelin on the Turkish-held ground beyond now loomed higher than the Christian defences. From behind its protecting veil came the intermittent bark of hostile musket fire.

But the ravelin was a distraction. The brunt of Mustafa's night attack was directed against a huge breach in the western apex of the fort's southern salient. It was there that the light of the flames, the brilliance of the fireworks and the desperation of combat were most intense.

The garrison at this point comprised perhaps five hundred Maltese militia, whose courage and tenacity had stunned everyone, and the Turks most of all, plus two hundred and fifty of the legendary Spanish *tercios*, and eighty or so knights of the Order. Half of the whole were engaged in repelling the wave of assaults. Lookouts were posted at various points around the perimeter to give notice of a secondary attack. A few Christian cannon bellowed from their ravaged and precarious emplacements. The bulk of the reserves were drawn up in the lee of the west wall and protected from the ravelin's marksmen by the improvised inner bulwarks and breastworks. Freed Christian slaves – criminals, homosexuals, heretics – were employed to collect shot from the yard to feed the guns. Freed Jews were employed as stretcher-bearers, and these crept back and forth from the front in an intermittent stream, carrying stricken men on wattles towards a stout building prominent among those clustered under the northern – seaward – wall.

Tannhauser's eyes roved the fiery and tempestuous melee. Where in all this havoc was Orlandu? He had no skill in arms and no great strength. Where danger was so ubiquitous, he could easily have met the same fate as the slain strewn in abundance about the bailey.

'You know Orlandu,' he said. 'To what use would you put him?'

Bors frowned. 'Powder monkey? Waterboy?'

Tannhauser had spotted four batteries within the fort. There was a fifth, he understood, on a cavalier raised outside the fort and connected to the northern seaward wall by a bridge. Orlandu had been here only a day. 'Powder monkey I don't believe. It takes too much schooling and drill in the hazards of fire.'

Bors was all too eager to agree. 'Waterboy would put him in the thick of the fray.'

THE CHAPEL'S INTERIOR flickered with candles and was perfumed with incense and thyrus smoke. The benches had been removed for use in the breastworks and the wounded lay supine on the flags or sat slumped in anguish against the walls. A chaplain wearing the rich red vestments of *Pascha Rosatum* said Mass at an altar stone scattered with rose leaves, and that someone had troubled to convey the leaves to this locus of ugliness and horror seemed at once both marvellous and crazed. Cries of pain rang out from those under treatment by the surgeons, of which latter there were only two. They stood across a table in the quag of congealed blood that befouled the chancel floor. They were as incarnadined as butchers and their faces were grey with that peculiar fatigue that comes from the infliction of torment in the quest to heal. A man writhed on the altar table between them and beneath his screams the rhythmic burr of a bone saw could be heard. Despite their inhuman tribulations, and the fact that they'd slept hardly two hours in twelve for the last fifteen days, the surgeons radiated a steadfast composure – perhaps even a careworn serenity – that was more affecting and majestic than anything Tannhauser had seen. The knights were the Hospitallers, after all, and these grave heroes were the guardians of the holy flame.

Inspired by such placid nobility, or perhaps by the discovery that screaming usually hurts, the rest of the patients lay quiet and waited their turn. Arrayed inside the vestibule and wrapped in clean white shrouds were the bodies of five dead knights awaiting transport to the vault of San Lorenzo. As Tannhauser had hoped, their armour and swords were stacked beside them. The knights treated their own dead with particular delicacy and, contrary though it was to reason, would never think of passing their harness on to the common soldiers whose longevity it would have extended – and whose corpses were consigned to the sea with lesser ceremony. Tannhauser pointed to the equipment.

'Choose quickly and well. Greaves, cuisses, shoes. Gauntlets if they'll fit.'

'Where are you going?' asked Bors.

'To give wool today so that we might take sheep tomorrow.' He unlimbered his knapsack. 'Remember my motto: *a man with opium is never without a friend.*'

While Bors rifled through the gear of the bulkiest shrouds, Tannhauser approached the altar. He watched the surgeons complete the amputation of a leg below the knee. They sealed the stump with a most ingenious arrangement of skin flaps, and with only the most subtle use of the cauterising iron, and this gave him the chance to gain their attention.

'Is that the new technique recommended by Paré?' he asked.

The surgeon who had the air of being in command looked at him with surprise. 'You're most well informed, good sir.'

'I was at Saint Quentin, where Monsieur Paré was surgeon general and took his stand against excessive use of the fire iron.' He recalled that Paré was a Huguenot, and thus a heretic, and hoped that he hadn't made the wrong impression. 'I assume you approve.'

'The results speak for themselves.'

Tannhauser held out his hand. 'Mattias von Tannhauser, of the German Langue.'

'Jurien de Lyon, of Provence.'

Jurien hesitated to shake, for his hand was bloody, but Tannhauser clenched it undeterred. He told the noble surgeon that he was La Valette's commissioner for the inspection of defences, and showed him the Grand Master's seal on the parchment he'd acquired from Starkey. He then engaged Jurien in a discussion of the state of the wounded, and commended his policy of only sending to the boats those with some hope of survival and return to duty. He swiftly impressed Brother Jurien with his knowledge of Natural Magick and vulnerary potions, secrets learned from Petrus Grubenius, and he proceeded to take from his knapsack a number of hemp bags whose contents he described.

'In this we have comfrey, pirole and aristolochy, leavened with featherfew and agrimony. Boil the poultice in a ratio of one ounce to two measures of wine, and having mixed a pinch of salt with them, bind the herbs to the wound. The wine which remains may be taken as a decoction – a spoonful morning and evening is enough.'

Jurien de Lyon, familiar with this regime, nodded and expressed his thanks.

Tannhauser produced a stoppered glass flask full of garnet-red oil. 'Oil of Hispanus – linseed and camomile extracts rectified with bay berries, betony, cinnamon and Saint John's wort. A few drops taken in black wine, thrice daily, helps heal wounds by contracting the nerves that inflame them. Keep the stopper tight, or the virtue will fly out and vanish.'

There was so loud a clatter from the vestibule that it cut through the groans of woe, and unease provoked him to be more generous with his last donation than might otherwise have been necessary. He rose from the knapsack with two oilcloth slabs of opium.

'This will need no introduction. Opium from the poppy fields of Iran.'

Jurien almost took a step backwards. 'Fra Mattias, you are Heaven sent.'

'Like all such marvels, the poppy is God's bounty, albeit that it flourishes best in a land of Shiite devils. Accept these small contributions, then, from your German brother.'

Jurien, despite a canny glance into the knapsack, was moved by this benevolence and assured him that no favour he could ask would go unsatisfied. As he judged the fellow honourable to a fault, Tannhauser buckled up the knapsack and entrusted it to Jurien's safekeeping.

On his way through the vestibule he did the unthinkable and stole a dead knight's sword. He chose on instinct and therefore chose well. Even inside the scabbard the sword felt like an extension of his arm. His own rapier, by Julian del Rey, could not be bettered in a street fight but was too delicate for the work that lay ahead. For battle one needed a tool with the resilience of a ploughshare. He left the del Rey by the corpse and slipped outside.

He found Bors in an alley by the chapel, standing among a heap of steel and trying to lever his barge-like feet into a pair of bear-pawed sabatons. Tannhauser marked them as big enough to fit over his own boots and examined the rest of the collection. There were no complete leg fitments of a length to suit him, so he levered out some rivets to dismantle what was there, rolled his boots down to the knees, and crammed a pair of shynbalds down the front. He found poleyns that with some stomping could be reshaped to accommodate his knees. He unrolled his boots back up the groins and stuffed their tops with thigh plates. The ensemble chafed here and there but was preferable to a scimitar across the shins. He dismantled his own bale and donned the fluted cuirass, which had been forged in Nuremberg by Kunz Grunwalt. Bors helped him buckle on the pauldrons and vambraces. Bors surrendered the sabatons but disputed the single pair of full-finger gauntlets to fit either one of them. On account of the Damascus musket, Tannhauser won and stuck them in his belt. Bors found a pair of armoured mittens and made do. Their helms were morions, high-crested and open-faced with cheek and jaw guards tied beneath the chin with red silk ribbons. With each man fifty pounds heavier, they cradled their long guns and started round the western perimeter towards the flames.

As they passed among the reserves they enquired about Orlandu. No one knew him. He was fresh meat and no one cared. The age-old mathematics was at work: the longer you survived, the longer you were likely to survive. Under conditions of this severity, where eight-hour assault followed hard on twelve-hour bombardment, veterans were forged in two days and saw more bloodshed than most other troops during ten years' service. Those who'd been here since the start of the siege – eighteen days ago, now – and among whom many of the *tercios* were numbered, were made of a different clay altogether. They squatted in the dust, their halberds and partisans on the ground beside them, dead men every one, saying little and possessed of an unnatural, hollow-eyed tranquillity. Their clothes were tattered and their boots cut to pieces by the rubble. Their hair and beards were clotted with filth, their faces with scabs and sores. Most sported wounds, crudely dressed, and missing fingers and arms in slings, and burns and painful limps, which they bore with the fatalistic fortitude of injured dogs.

The knights stood grouped by langue at the head of each company: French, Auvergnoise and Provençals. The Italians and

Aragonese, they learned, were presently in the thick. The hiss of steel on whetstones mingled with the sound of Paternosters. Discipline was tight. Morale seemed higher than should have been possible. Whatever weariness the soldiers felt, and it was etched on their spectral faces, the air crackled with some invisible communal force. They would have invoked the Holy Ghost to explain the phenomenon, but Tannhauser had felt it before, on the far side of the wall where Allah was claimed as its arbiter and source. Was this the difference over which these warriors were hacking each other apart? Over the name – the word – for the same essential concept of Divine Oneness? Or was there no Divine, and was this binding force the creation of men alone, men who found themselves thrown together for reasons which none could explain, men bound by merest accident: by birth, by geography, by Fate?

Tannhauser had stood on that far side and known the same tingling in the blood that he felt right now. To fight and die in any shared cause, whether for good or evil, or for any god, ancient or new, would evoke the selfsame compulsion in them all. Bors had hit the nail. The same Love. The spell was overmastering. Despite himself he found his heart yearning for the fray. His mentor, Petrus Grubenius, would have despaired.

You came here for the boy alone, he reminded himself. Amparo awaited him, and her eyes, which when they looked into his saw only him. A look such as he'd never seen, except in memories so long lost they stood more in the way of a dream. Only here, amid the stench of powder smoke and bear grease and blood did he realise that he loved her. Yet did he love this stench of war even more? Was he too far fallen from whatever grace he'd been born with? And was the boy no more than a phantom of his own creation, summoned to lure him back to the gutters of blood where he belonged? And what of the contessa, whose hand he had won? Carla's heart, too, called out to his across the abyss. Two fine women and one fine war competed for his attention.

'I must be as mad as the rest,' he muttered to himself.

'Mattias,' growled Bors.

Tannhauser came to and looked at him.

'What's wrong, man? You're staring at the moon as if you expect to find some answer there. You won't.'

'Do you think this will cost us our souls?'

'Pah. If so, we got a good price. I know you well – you consider things too deeply. Out here you should let me do the thinking. My brain's not confounded by idle musings and womanly conceits.'

'Womanly?' Tannhauser took a step towards him.

'That's better. Look now, Le Mas is here. He calls us.'

Tannhauser turned as Colonel Pierre Vercoyran Le Mas lumbered towards them. He limped and had a ladder of fresh stitches running across his jaw and down his neck behind his gorget. He smiled and held out both arms to clasp Tannhauser. His breastplate was thickly encased in an apron of stiffening gore.

'Didn't expect to see you here,' said Le Mas. 'There's surely no profit in it and I never reckoned you a suitor for martyrdom.'

Bors said, 'We were told the air here was conducive to good health.'

Le Mas inhaled through his nose. 'Truly, it is sweet. But in earnest, now.'

'We've come to take a boy back to the Borgo,' said Tannhauser. 'On the Grand Master's orders. Orlandu Boccanera. A runaway. He may style himself Orlandu di Borgo.'

'A boy of such importance must deserve a high style. I know him not, but I'll pass the word. I'll say this, if he was a boy when he arrived, he's a boy no longer. But come and look for yourselves. My Provençals and a crowd of your Spaniards are going into the line.'

Le Mas hoisted a halberd, its several vicious edges freshly honed. Bors unslung his enormous German two-hander.

'Give Mattias a half-pike,' said Bors, 'or one of those lovely Turk-whittlers.'

'There'll be arms aplenty up front,' said Le Mas.

When men are gathered for a ruction it takes more than mere will to stand aside. Tannhauser submitted to events and they accompanied Le Mas to where he roused his section from their rest. Some seized the chance to empty their bowels and bladders, and they shook themselves down and shouldered their pole arms and checked each other's gear. Tannhauser stood in line at the water butt and emptied two quart-full dippers down this throat. Then he fell in beside the colonel at the head of the column. Le Mas, despite the general din, conversed as if strolling down a country lane.

'Who's at the helm of your tavern, the Oracle? The Jew?'

'The Oracle is in worse repair than this fort. Ashes are all that's left.'

'How so?'

'Thc Inquisition.'

'Then my conscience is even heavier. I'm glad to have the chance to beg your pardon.'

'For what?'

'When I blew in from Messina, I told Fra Jean – La Valette – what a bold species you were, how you'd recruited the ex-*tercios* as a favour to me, so forth, and he took an uncommon interest. And, it must be said, that for all his piety he's a dextrous and unscrupulous mind. Next I knew you were in his chamber, when you conjured Mustafa's Greek out of thin air. So, I'm to blame for you being here, if there's blame to be placed.'

'It took a greater parcel of rogues than you and La Valette.'

'Did the parcel include women?'

Tannhauser looked at him and Le Mas laughed. 'He asked me, you see, Fra Jean, *Is he a ladies' man?* he said. And I said, well –' He looked at him. 'Well, I ask you, Mattias, what would you have wanted me to say?'

He laughed again, and so did Tannhauser and if there was anything to forgive it was forgiven, and they marched on until the fractured limit of the curtain wall loomed to their right. There the din in Tannhauser's ears became a Devil's Requiem, and the entreaties to God in a dozen different tongues, the oaths and maledictions, the clang and whicker of thousands of brandished blades, the crackle of wildfire and the blast of guns, mingled and whirled skyward like the clamour of fiends intoxicate. Flames brighter than day and hot enough to work brass flared up and down the line. Along the southern salient of the star-fort's western horn, a mined section of curtain wall fifty paces wide had collapsed into a craggy embankment. Across the jagged crest of this yawning breach, an immense crowd of men fought like maddened animals for possession of a heap of stones. And despite his most earnest efforts to walk a peaceful mile and ignore the call of the Beast, Tannhauser found himself, once more, on the floor of its pit.

MONDAY 11 JUNE 1565

The Gantlet – the Bailey – the Causeway

LIKE A SPECK of migrant life in a forest primeval, Orlandu wriggled and crawled through the thicket of half-pikes and halberd shafts that filled the cramped gap between the front and second ranks of the defenders. As he picked his course along the boulder-cobbled gantlet, which was coated, as was he, in a reeking compost of piss, vomit, entrails, shit and spilled blood, his mind was occupied wholly by the task of finding the next squalid patch of ground upon which to advance. He had no surplus faculty with which to observe the progress of the fight, much less to care about its outcome. His head felt like the clapper of an alarum bell. His own vomit clung to his leather breastplate and chin and had already been trodden into the foetid paste underfoot. His anus strained painfully to open itself, even though he'd shat himself void of all but a watery mucus before he'd joined the fray. His body was a mass of bruises from the tattoo of boot heels, spear butts and elbows that punished his passage. When he scrambled over the fallen or the dead, he minded them only as obstacles and not as men. If he felt terror, it was as the fish feels the sea, as an immersion so absolute he was unaware of it. This was his third foray down the tunnel of wood and steel; and the work was getting no easier.

A finger jabbed him repeatedly in the ribs but so insensible was he by now to any such insults that the hand had to grab him by the neck and heave him up to his feet from his elbows. He found a wide, bearded face yelling down at him from beneath a dented morion, the eyes demonic in the light of the flames, and he gaped at it in stunned incomprehension. The *tercio* jabbed his finger downwards and Orlandu, open-mouthed and panting in the hot and ammoniac air, turned and looked. The tub he was dragging behind him by its rope handle was empty. The *tercio* spat into it to register his disgust and yelled again. Orlandu rose to his feet and changed direction, too bedazed to feel either offence at the invective or gratitude for the respite. The *tercio* kicked him up the arse and he lurched back through the ranks and down the embankment to the rear.

All the warnings against snipers were forgotten. Like a creature only lately taught to walk on his hind legs he tottered across the bailey's shot-strewn wasteland. The empty tub bounced willy-nilly behind him. At the door of what had been the stables, in the seaward lee of the eastern wall, he stopped and let go of the tub and slumped into a wall. His helmet, stuffed with sacking to make it fit, slid from his head and he let it lie where it fell and grabbed at the soaking sackcloth which still clung about his skull. He wrung out half a pint of sweat and scrubbed his face. His eyes stung and something infantile surged within him and his chest shuddered and he realised he was about to cry, not in sadness or fear or even relief, but as a child sobs, out of a boundless bewilderment and helplessness. Before he could give vent, some counterinstinct rose equally unbidden, and hammered the child back down, and Orlandu gritted his teeth and caught his breath.

For Christ and the Baptist. For the Religion and his countrymen. For Malta. His spirit recovered. He wrapped the damp sacking around his head and replaced his helmet. He dragged the empty tub into the stables, which now served as the field commissary. The cook, Stromboli, looked up from among his bottles, barrels and baskets and waved the knife with which he chopped the loaves.

'Where have you been?' he snapped in Italian. 'The soldiers thirst.'

Orlandu spat on the floor, set the empty tub down and gave it a kick. In Maltese he said, 'I've been crawling in the shit, you old turd, what have you been doing?'

Stromboli, Orlandu now learned, had spent enough time in the markets dealing with the locals to understand. He lunged over and fetched Orlandu a stiff clout round the side of the head.

'Bread and wine from God. That is what I do. And without me the battle would be over.'

He stabbed his knife at three other tubs which waited in a row, each filled near to the brim with hunks of bread dipped in olive oil and soaking in a marinade of red wine, salt and revitalising herbs. Earlier, a chaplain had blessed these supplies and sprinkled them with holy water. While it was true that these refreshments kept the fighting men on their feet, Stromboli gave no credit to Orlandu for delivering them to their mouths.

'Quickly now. And do not spill. And keep to the walls, or the food will be spoiled with your brains.'

Orlandu held his tongue. He picked up the nearest tub by both handles, caught his balance, the tub bouncing into his bruise-blackened thighs, and staggered out of the door. There he set it down and shovelled up a dripping handful of the damp red mush, as the soldiers did when he dragged it along the battle line, and crammed it into his mouth. He gulped it down, hardly chewing at all on the soft, succulent crusts, and found it more delicious than anything he'd ever tasted. It was the first time he'd had the wit to eat himself and at once he felt new strength suffuse his belly and limbs. Stromboli was a bastard, but his tubs were filled with an elixir. Bread and wine from God. He reached down for another handful and the blunt edge of Stromboli's knife cracked down across his wrist.

'The food is for the soldiers, not the pigs!'

Orlandu hefted the tub and lurched off into the darkness that shrouded the bailey. The ropes cut into his fingers and his forearms burned, as then did his arms and shoulders and chest, his back, his belly, his hams and calves. The cheap leather cuirass he'd stolen from the barrel-chested Tomaso had chafed his hips and elbows to the bone. His breath scorched his throat. He thought of John the Baptist in the Desert, surviving on only locusts and wild honey. He thought of Christ at the Pillar. He thought of the knights in the forefront of the broil, already hours and hours in the breach and with God only knew how many hours more to go. He was weak; but he would become strong. He'd already carried this tub further than the others. His body screamed. The ropes slipped in his blistered fingers. He would have to set it down. No. Another ten paces. At eight the rope slid from his left hand, taking his skin with it, and the tub canted over and a great wave slopped from the lip and on to the ground.

He glanced back, mortified, but Stromboli was gone. He thanked Saint Catherine that here in the lee of the wall the flagstones were sound and not pulverised to dust. With both hands he scooped the spillage back into the tub. Fat green flies from the mass of decomposing bodies heaped outside the walls buzzed down in swarms to claim their share and he waved them away without effect. The wine stung his skinless palms but he left not a crust behind. He rolled up his sleeve and buried what he'd scraped up within the unspilled portion and gave it all a good stir and then swallowed another handful. It tasted just as marvellous as the first. The burning in his muscles had gone. He took off his helm and dropped it by the wall. Let the Turks split his skull, he didn't care. He cut the damp sackcloth with his knife and wrapped the pieces round his hands. The sweat stung too. He'd give himself two more rest stops before reaching the front, and next time only two all told. He looked across the yard to the seething nocturnal encounter.

Flares and incendiary rockets exploded above the toiling mankillers. At a distance from the foot of the slope a fresh section of men had drawn up. At their head Orlandu recognised – in part because he was laughing – the celebrated French adventurer Colonel Le Mas, bravest of the brave and even in this company reckoned a man among men. Who else could find something to laugh about in such a dire place? With a thrill Orlandu wondered if Le Mas might take God's bread and wine from this very tub. Imagine. He swore to keep his head up this time. In any case he should wait until he knew he wouldn't obstruct their manoeuvre. Le Mas gesticulated to two large companions, larger even than he, and they laughed, too, and one, a bull of a man, threw to his shoulder the longest musket Orlandu had ever seen, its barrel feathered with silver under the flares, and a plume of white smoke flew towards something high on the unbreached parapet. A body fell, and as the bull lowered the gun with a proud cock of his head towards the others, the second man removed his helmet and handed it to him, and Orlandu saw that this was Captain Tannhauser, and that the other must then be Bors, who'd called Orlandu 'my friend' and promised to teach him backgammon. Tannhauser too snapped a long gun to his shoulder and fired, with great speed it seemed. A second bundle of colourful robes plunged from the wall. A pair of Turkish snipers picked off like hares. What marksmen. Tannhauser spoke as he retrieved and replaced his morion and the three of them laughed again. Imagine. Laughing!

Orlandu lifted the tub by the ropes and started forward. His hands sang with pain. No spilling, he swore. He hoped they wouldn't notice him until after his next rest stop, when perhaps he could convey greater strength than he possessed. He began running in short, reeling steps, the mush swilling round, and the burning returned to his muscles almost at once. His face contorted and his lungs roared. He kept his eyes peeled for any sign that the three men might see him, but he was in shadow and they were not. He had to move out from the wall. He felt the ropes slip again and he stopped and grounded the tub and cursed it. He planned the next leg to take him closer than necessary to Bors, who would surely call him over, and introduce him to Tannhauser and Le Mas, as any friend would. Or he could offer them the food. And Bors would tell Le Mas that his good friend Orlandu deserved more fitting duty than hauling a tub of wine through the shit and –

Strange horns ululated and an exhausted cheer intermixed with obscene jeers suggested that the Turkish assault had been driven back. Orlandu thanked the Virgin, for perhaps now the troops could go and get their own bread and wine. The three men looked up the slope, where the mass of defenders were moving aside in good order to open a gap in their centre. Tannhauser and Bors handed their long guns to an orderly and donned their gauntlets. Then each drew a sword and rolled his shoulders. Another horn, this time a Christian trumpet. Whistles. Banners with various insignia waved to instruct their respective companies. Le Mas's section formed up in a wedge. The wedge pointed its apex at the gap still opening at the top of the bloody slope, and the reserve started up the embankment through the curtain of hot ochre smoke.

Did this mean the battle wasn't over? Would the Turks be crazy enough to come back? Orlandu grabbed his tub and tottered along the wall to find out.

Le Mas's section spread themselves across the breach and the men who'd held it until midnight withdrew. They were steeped as if in mud by the liquid products of combat, and relief precipitated in them a sudden exhaustion. Le Mas's Spaniards piked the Turkish wounded where they lay and what corpses remained they kicked down into the ditch. Under cover of the fight, the Turkish sappers had filled in several sections of the ditch to form short causeways. They'd also thrown across bridges fashioned from masts. Out among the foul eddies of smoke there must have been four hundred fresh bodies in ragged piles, some still moving and muttering from the Koran. Many were charred and still smouldered in pools of wildfire. Beyond the fallen, Tannhauser saw bands of *yerikulu* limping from the field, dragging maimed comrades between them as they trudged back to the scorn of their *aga*.

Bors said, 'Your janissaries have decided on an early supper.'

Tannhauser shook his head and pointed to the green robes and white turbans tangled in the ditch. 'Regular infantry, Azebs of the *yerikulu*. The janissaries will come next.'

Bors pointed, 'What are those in aid of?'

At twenty-pace intervals at the foot of the breach, orderlies had rolled huge butts into place and nailed plank footbridges to their rims. They were filling them with seawater from barrels on a cart.

'If you get a taste of wildfire,' said Le Mas, 'you jump in the butts to cool down.'

He indicated the parapets to either side of the breach, where the wildfire crews assembled their batteries. Brimstone, saltpetre, linseed oil, salt ammoniac, turpentine, pitch and naphtha. The Turks added frankincense and tow to make the wildfire stick, the Venetians hammered glass and aqua vitae. Against the parapet walls, mouth-upwards, the crews stacked rows of trumps – brass pipes fixed to pike shafts that were filled with the incendiary brew. When lit and pointed, the boil within the pipe belched forth streams of fireballs. The crews stacked crates of fire-pipkins by the crenels. The Turks called them *humbaras*: fist-sized clay pots sealed with paper, pierced by a fuse and filled with jellied wildfire. The most ingenious of the fireworks were credited to La Valette's invention: hoops of pithy cane were soaked in brandy and Oil of Peter, then wrapped in wool and steeped in the same inflammable liquors used in the trumps. When ignited they were hurled with tongs into the advancing Moslem ranks to horrible effect. The crews had a hellish job. Tannhauser grabbed Bors and shifted position in the line to be further out of range of an accidental spill.

A pot of camphorated balsam was passed about and they rubbed it into their beards against the stench. A smatter of sniper fire buzzed overhead. One of the *tercios* was hit in the face and his comrades dragged him to his feet and sent him stumbling rearward.

'Give me some room,' said Bors.

He needed it to wield the twelve-inch grip and scalloped sixty-inch blade of his German two-hander. He whirled the sword round his head to warm his sinews and the blade whistled in a huge figure of eight about and before him. With the dexterity of a lady folding a fan, Bors fetched the huge sword in and planted it between his feet.

Tannhauser donned his gauntlets and examined the sword he'd taken from the chapel. The blade was three feet long with a flattened diamond cross-section. He judged it something over two pounds in weight. Italian. Hopefully Milanese. He put his tongue to the edge and tasted blood but felt no pain. He strode to the stack of fallen arms collected by the orderlies from the breach. He chose a five-pound mace with a steel haft and seven flanged blades welded to the core. A spiked finial four inches long was screwed into the top. He headed back to the line and turned to the man on his right, a short but powerful veteran with flinty eyes.

Tannhauser raised his sword in salute. 'Mattias Tannhauser.'

The knight returned the gesture. 'Guillaume de Quercy.'

The man to Guillaume's right, a beak-nosed Provençal wielding paired short swords, bent forward and did the same. 'Agoustin Vigneron,' he said.

The exchange was enough to cement their fraternity and they

said no more. With a Gascon to one side and an Englishman to the other, he couldn't ask for more. The *mehterhane* band struck up. Pipes, kettledrums and bells. Even now there was no sound more stirring to his ears. Trumpets blew. The banner of Saint John was flaunted, the white cross luminous in the moonlight. A chaplain raised an icon of Christ Pantocrator in one hand and rang a bell with other and began to recite the Angelus:

'Angelus Domini nuntiavit Mariae.' The Angel of the Lord declared unto Mary.

Aves were chanted en masse and the power of the Virgin invoked.

'*Pray for us, O Holy Mother of God.*'

'*That we may be made worthy of the promises of Christ.*'

'*Pour forth, we beseech Thee, O Lord, Thy grace into our hearts . . .*'

The front line of knights clambered up the scree to the blood-steeped ridge and Tannhauser climbed up with them. He was the only man on that field without a prayer on his lips, for it seemed to him that any deity worth addressing would condemn the elation rising in his chest and that all the gods of mercy would sleep this long night through.

The knights and serjeants occupied the forefront of the line, and the Spanish and Maltese, perhaps three hundred, moved up behind, the points of their half-pikes and glaives filling in the gaps in the armoured wall. Tannhauser studied the ground at his feet, kicked some loose debris aside, noted the irregularities and planted his left foot forward, the sword in his right hand pointed down and the mace haft canted against his hip. Awareness now was all. Awareness of his own small sphere whose boundaries were defined by the man to his either side and by whatever appeared from the night at the tip of his blade. He reminded himself to breathe regularly and deep. It was easy to forget in the fray, and to lose one's wind was fatal. Breathing. Posture. Footwork. Underneath his armour sweat streamed forth from every pore, for the heat of the night was fierce and unforgiving. His mouth was dry. He was stationed at the throat of a Turkish causeway. Three men wide in a pinch, it formed an uneven apron against the gantlet and he stood on its leftmost edge. The Gascon, Guillaume, stood athwart its centre and Agoustin Vigneron braced its far right. To his left Bors commanded the lip of the ditch. Bors rooted in his pocket and brought out a pair of smooth white pebbles. He popped one in his mouth.

'Didn't I tell you this would be grand?' he said.

He offered the second pebble. Tannhauser took it and sucked and his dryness was eased.

Bors said, 'Mind you watch my back.'

The martial rhythms of the *mehterhane*, the stomp of thousands of feet, the clank of metal, the shrill descant of the imam's pleas to Allah, fashioned themselves into a mighty wheel of sound which rolled from the flame-lambent shadows beyond the ditch. In its wake five janissary *orta*, horsehair standards aloft and banners writ with the *Shahada* aflutter, roared from the throat of night and flung themselves at the causeways and across the corpse-swollen ditch.

The Christians goaded them on with a howling invitation to the dance. Mixed within it Tannhauser heard a Babel of prayers in Latin and a clutch of vulgar tongues. To Santa Caterina and Sant' Agata. To Sant' Iago and San Pablo. To Christ and the Baptist. Pray for us sinners. Thy kingdom come. Thy will be done. Now and at the hour of our death. Amen. The most popular invocation, as if the man were beatified already, was La Valette and the Holy Religion.

At twenty yards the oncoming ranks unleashed a shower of *humbaras*, the burning fuses tailing showers of sparks. Tannhauser watched them arc over, poised to leap away, but luck was with him. They sailed overhead and he felt flares of heat behind him and heard squalls of horror and panic but didn't turn. At the same time the Devil's bondsmen in the Order's firework crews unleashed squealing torrents of liquid death from the trumps, and huge burning hoops traced yellow spirals in the air as they sailed forth. The tightly packed janissaries were ensnared by twos and threes in these circles of flame. Their blue cotton robes flared up as if made of paper and like the damned chained together in perdition they tore at each other as they writhed and burned and died.

So fierce was the coruscation on either wing that the field incandesced as bright as noontide. Through this holocaust the vanguard's human tide roared on undaunted. They brandished a gallery of melee arms and with their wild eyes and long moustaches and tall, white bonnets embellished with wooden spoons, they suggested a race of deranged cooks who'd been banished from the kitchen of a madhouse. They spilled into the ditch. They charged the burning bridges. They surged across the fire-drenched causeways.

Tannhauser picked his first opponent from the horde now pouring down the funnel. The man's boots were black – the *orta*'s janitor. He carried a *mizrak* spear overarm and a rectangular Balkan shield. Tannhauser advanced a step out on to the apron to give himself room and dropped the mace along his thigh. He opened his chest just enough to invite the spear and as the down thrust came he pulled his right leg back in an oblique turn and deflected the shaft with his sword and drove the spike of the mace into the thus exposed armpit, sliding his hand up the haft for a shorter grip. The man bellowed, as any man would, and his lung popped and his feet left the ground, and as Tannhauser took him backwards and down, he swiped the sword across his throat and half-severed his head.

He turned his face from the spray and snapped the sword back up to block a scimitar blow from above and he brought his head up with it and straightened his legs, hammering the crest of his morion into a face. Blood and sweat flew and he lunged up with mace, still held short, and drove the spike through the belly of the man's jaw and heard the crunch of bones, the man squirming like a gaffed tunny, blood streaming down from his nostrils and eyes, and Tannhauser shielded himself with this new prey, and shuffled head on into the melee, breathing and blowing as Turkish blades hacked the man's arms off, thrusting with the Milanese sword, chain mail scraping on the steel as it pierced a gut and encountered spine. He twisted it back out, and sucked and blew, teeth gritted, and flung the gaffed and armless wretch at the charging feet of the next, who stumbled and fell to his elbows. Tannhauser lengthened his grip on the mace and coshed him and killed him with a blow, the flanges biting through the rear of the skull and dyeing the white bonnet red.

Straighten up, breathe and blow, shake the sweat. He wheezed. His chest was tight, his gorge scorched. He felt nauseous and weak. He was too far forward. Get back.

The horde shouldered each other in their frenzy to get through the choke point, their weapons constricted, one shield obstructing another. Spot the openings. Swallow the scalding bile. Kill him, kill them, kill them all. A blow glanced off his helm and hammered into his pauldron. Spike him in the privities, stab him in the neck. The fellow fought on from his knees, blinded by the fountain from his arteries, still scrabbling with his blade for the joints in Tannhauser's plate. Tannhauser drove the finial through his temple and stepped back. Now backstep again. Keep them at bay. He threw an upward swordcut to the thighs and a backstroke to the guts and a thrust to the chest, in deep and twist. Don't look in his eyes. He's done. And breathe, you fool, keep the knees loose, ignore the battle cries. Get back. Movement to the left – below – a face in the ditch, slash him in the eyes, forget him, face front, step back, here he comes, X-block, no room to swing, struggling face to chest, breath hot and sour, he's strong – oh yes? – pommel strike, open him up, cosh him on the shoulders, collapse his chest, die, die, stab him in the belly, and out, and again, and out, and some steel in the throat for the Sultan, and step back – but over there – no, step back now, patience, breathe, shake the sweat, blow it off. Still too far down the causeway. Exposed. Ten seconds' rest. Or five. He had no choice.

He leaned on his sword and panted.

The first ten minutes were over and he felt sick to the gut and drained. His body already begged for light refreshment and eight hours' sleep. Where was the strength and wind he'd once possessed in abundance? He was shaken. He'd never fought men so difficult to kill, so reluctant to die even when they were dead. These janissaries were maniacs and he was not; not any longer. The night stretched before him and he couldn't see its end. He was afraid, not of death, but of the effort. Yet his second wind would come. That or a shared grave in the bloody ditch. To the clank and hiss of hammer and sword, Guillaume de Quercy and Agoustin Vigneron drew level on the causeway, each soused from helm to greaves in sweat-speckled gore, and their beards all matted and agleam, as if they'd supped from a barrel of molasses.

Tannhauser roused his pride. He couldn't let himself be shamed by a pair of Frenchmen.

The three of them stood abreast at the mounting redoubt of corpses piled at their knees, and proceeded to impale the Turkish foemen as they scrambled over their dead. Swift and cruel it was, with bludgeon and spike and blade, and the Maltese ventured up behind them with their pole arms and gave them some respite from the sheer weight of flesh. The blue-robed assault began to founder on the wall of spears, and a fresh shower of *humbaras* arced across the charnel. Tannhauser crouched beneath them and the pikemen stumbled back in disarray, ash staves aclatter as flames bloomed yellow among them. Those drenched in burning jelly fled for the water butts, and each man for himself it was, for the butts couldn't hold them all. And in that instant the tables were turned, for on to the vacant ground the pikemen had abandoned behind them the Sultan's *gazi* sprang up from the ditch, and the assault across the charnel pile renewed, and out on the causeway the three armoured brothers found themselves surrounded and outflanked.

'Back to back!' roared de Quercy.

De Quercy's war hammer flashed and the pick sank up to the haft in a face and tore it half away. Tannhauser swivelled and the pauldrons of the three clashed together. Shoulder to shoulder in a circle of woe they stood, and woe was all their assailants found to greet them. Like a band of cornered wolves they ravaged and butchered all that stirred in reach, hostile blows ringing from their harness as they gave up the ground they'd won and shuffled back through the flames towards the line, their footing unsteady on the smouldering mattress of the mutilated and slain.

The dense smell of roasting human meat was repulsively appetising, and Tannhauser's mouth filled with juices. A fair-skinned youth ran himself through on the point of Tannhauser's sword, and with such frenzy did he come that his chest hammered hard into the quillions. He spiked the squalling youth in the head with the finial and like a farmer pitching a wheat bale he hefted him aside, and a slash came at his head and Tannhauser parried with the mace haft and he chopped the Italian blade into a leg as hard as cedar. The fellow dropped to his knees and Tannhauser worked the sword down into his chest, and an uncontrollable nausea exploded up his gullet and his mace dangled by its wrist loop, and he doubled up over the sword, with both hands gripping the crossguard, and he vomited a torrent of gall and phlegm in the dying man's screaming face. Tannhauser clenched his watering eyes, the gastric spasm shunting the blade in deeper. He leaned on the hilt until the fit had passed, then he spat and hauled his blade free, and kicked the corpse aside, and blinked and shook his head, and sweat and mucus flew, and through the blur he saw two tall-hatted heads bearing down the causeway towards him. He braced himself to take their blows, then a scalloped blade whistled by and both heads vanished as one, the skulls splintering apart in a welter of eyeballs and brain and liquid ropes. A gaping gorge and a half set of teeth topped the second pair of shoulders, and as it toppled out of view he saw Bors wrangle in the huge two-hander and plant its point down into a third head as it bobbed up from the ditch.

Bors paused, his mouth heaving wide in his blood-boltered face. 'I asked you to watch my back.'

Tannhauser also battled to catch his breath. 'Fighting fit I'm not,' he admitted.

There was a lull in the assault and the four men fell abreast and they bludgeoned and stabbed those wounded within reach, and then they rested, and for a moment the causeway boasted no life standing but their own.

'The queer thing is,' said Bors, 'they look – well – much like us.'

'Slavs, Greeks, Magyars, Serbs,' said Tannhauser. 'Even some Austrians.'

'Never did warm to Austrians,' said Bors.

They regained the line and assumed their stations. Tannhauser felt improved. The purge of his stomach had done him good. As he spat out the sour residue his eyes caught a tub of bread and wine shunting by. He cradled his sword in his elbow and stooped and shovelled up a gauntlet of mush and slaked it down his throat in one. It was marvellous. Sweet and salty at once. With a hint of rosemary? He called Bors and pointed to the slowly disappearing vat. Bors bent to help himself. Tannhauser turned back to the shambles and recruited his spirit.

Thus the second ten minutes had passed, or so he guessed. His body felt limber, his chest as sound as a drum. His mind was crystal clear. He had his second wind. He rolled his shoulders and loosened his hips and settled down to meet what was yet to come. It could only get worse, but he was up for it. A fresh wave of fanatics foamed from the dark towards the causeway. They wore yellow *dolamas* and bronze helms: janissaries of the elite Peyk division, toting sneaky lassoes and halberd-like *gaddaras* and *zemberek* crossbows with bolts as thick as your thumb. He blew out his breath and took a deep one. As the champions of the Religion braced themselves, Bors fetched up alongside him smacking his lips. He caught Tannhauser's look.

'Well?' said Bors.

Tannhauser clapped him on the back and smiled and said, 'Glory.'

MONDAY 11 JUNE 1565

No-man's-land

When dawn broke above the eastern battlements its uncertain light lent the oily banks of smoke a yellow hue, and somewhere beyond that ochre gloom the Turkish horns sounded recall, and the vanquished remnants of a dozen janissary *orta* drifted into the fog like scourged wraiths and then they were gone. Along the blood-slaked crest the tatterdemalion soldiers of the Cross watched with stunned indifference as the foemen disappeared, too exhausted to comprehend that the night was theirs and that their banner would greet another day.

Tannhauser sank to one knee and leaned on the crossguard of his sword and rested his forehead on his gauntlets and closed his eyes. For a few precious moments he was alone in a measureless silence, into which he voiced no questions and from which no answers came. Then he heard the ululating murmur of the wounded, and a succession of hoarse sobs, and prayers raised not to praise God but to beg Him for forgiveness.

Tannhauser lifted his head. His neck was stiff and painful from the weight of his helm and the numerous blows it had borne. His gauntlets were caked in a burgundy mud, which crumbled away in flakes as he eased them off. His hands were blue with bruises and his knuckles ached as he flexed them. The bangle on his wrist bore the imprint of two scimitar cuts in the gold. *Not for riches or honour but to save my soul.* He stowed the gauntlets and planted the mace into the ground and rose to his feet. He sheathed his sword. The air was unwholesome and turning putrid as he breathed. The brightening day unveiled a hellscape so baneful and repugnant that no artist would dare portray it for fear of placing a curse upon his gift.

Beyond the shattered ramparts on which he stood – and steeped in a foetid marinade of blood, human offal, entrails, brains and the evacuated contents of thousands of bladders and bowels – lay the bodies of some fifteen hundred Moslems. They overflowed the groaning ditch and spilled across the befouled and pestilent no-man's-land like the stain of some unnatural catastrophe. And Tannhauser felt ashamed. Then he felt ashamed of his shame, for it was a lie, and killing, at least, was honest. Here and there pools of wildfire flickered still, and an arm rose and fell, and a contorted shape struggled vainly from the reeking broth before yielding to the pull of the fresh-slain dead and falling back into the mire to struggle no more.

'All these men were born Christian?'

Tannhauser turned to Agoustin Vigneron. The Frenchman's eyes were swollen and bloodshot and his voice was scorched to a rasp.

'Most of them,' Tannhauser said.

Agoustin shook his head. 'How terrible that their souls are now damned forever.'

Tannhauser denied his own despair the luxury of expression. He left the mace standing upright in the rubble, like a pagan shrine to his own evil, and went to find Bors.

He found him out in no-man's-land, slumped face down and helmless against a yellow-costumed mound of janissary dead. His right hand still clutched a dagger in a corpse's chest. Tannhauser lumbered towards him in his tattered boots, stumbling through the debris as wounds to his ankle and knees made themselves apparent. Bors was insensible, and to judge by the rattling stridor in his throat he was choking on his own blood. It took two attempts to roll his steel-clad bulk on to his back. Tannhauser recoiled, momentarily repelled by what he saw. Bors's face appeared half cut away. A broad, deep slash gaped from above his right brow to the left angle of his jaw, the nose and cheek so split that bones and cartilage and gums and teeth gleamed along its course. The right side of his face was so severed from its moorings that it was sliding down over his chin. His contorted lips were blue. The bleeding was spectacular but could not, on rapid reflection, be called torrential.

Tannhauser mastered his horror and with his left hand pushed the drooping flesh up into place and pulled open the mouth and reached inside with his fingers. He scraped out a thick, gelatinous plug and a broken tooth and flung the mess aside. Bors wheezed. Tannhauser shoved his hand back in, deeper still, and evacuated another viscid mass. Bors retched and threw his head and shoulders forward, and he heaved up a dark red swill into his lap, and his hands flailed to grab on to his knees, and his chest exploded in a violent spasm of coughs.

The fist of dread in Tannhauser's gut unclenched. He grabbed the dagger from the corpse and cut through the straps down one side of Bors's cuirass. With the convulsions racking Bors's frame, it was a job but he got it done and he stripped the heavy plates on to the ground. With his chest freed from this constriction, Bors coughed his lungs clear and his mind quickly followed, or at least to the extent that he tried to take Tannhauser by the throat. The bloody flap masked one eye and the other was swollen shut and for the moment Bors was blind. Tannhauser seized the groping wrists to avoid being throttled.

'Bors, it's Mattias. The fight is done. It's Mattias.'

'Mattias?' The bloody and sightless face swung up.

'Yes. The fight is done,' he repeated. 'We bested them, for now.'

'Am I undone?' His voice was slurred by the deformities.

'No, you've just acquired a badge to justify your boasting for the next twenty years.' Tannhauser pulled off Bors's bloody steel mittens. 'Can you stand? Take my hands.'

Bors spat and hauled himself upright and caught his balance. 'Hold still,' said Tannhauser. He pushed the drooping flap of brow back into place against the exposed skull bone and an eye blinked in the early light. 'Here.' Tannhauser took Bors's right hand and guided it so that he could keep the flap pinned in place with his own fingers. Tannhauser slung the stripped cuirass over his shoulder by its surviving straps.

'Hang on to my arm,' he said.

'Do you take me for a woman?'

Bors located his two-hander and stubbornly retrieved it and used it as a stick. They crested the dire embankment and Bors stopped and turned to take in the vista with his one good eye. 'Christ's wounds!' he said.

It was as good an inventory of the night's work as any and Tannhauser, with nothing to add, just nodded in accord. But Bors's exclamation was in response to something other than the carnage. He pointed with his free hand and Tannhauser looked.

Twenty-odd paces distant a slender, bareheaded figure squatted on his heels atop the tangled monstrosity of corpses choking the ditch. His filth-rimed leather cuirass was too big for his chest and with his long, thin arms poking out it gave him the look of a scarab on a hill of dung. In his fingers he examined something that glittered when it caught the light, perhaps a brooch or a jewel-encrusted dagger. Some lupine intuition made him raise his head and he stared right at them, his face as soiled as his harness. Teeth gleamed in the dirt and he raised one hand in salute.

'Yes indeed,' said Bors. 'By my oath, that's Orlandu di Borgo.'

THE BOY RAN over at their beckoning, pausing to grab Tannhauser's abandoned mace. The boy had been watching him, then. The feeling was curious. Orlandu stopped before them, proud as a gamecock to have been summoned by two such giants of the field, and he saluted. Beneath the grime, and lean as he was, his features were flushed with the sap of youth. His eyes were a strong yellowy brown. A fine nose and delicate lips. A quick-witted lad by the look of him and, at a guess, capable of low cunning. All of which met with Tannhauser's approval. He fancied he could see the ghost of Carla – an innate sensitivity perhaps – and, more surely, the long limbs and capacity to brood in the brow of his father, Ludovico.

'So you are Orlandu Boccanera,' said Tannhauser.

'Orlandu di Borgo, My Lord,' corrected the youth, sassy as you please. He dipped his head. 'And you are the bold Captain Tannhauser.'

Tannhauser said, 'You've led me a merry old dance.'

The boy assumed a guarded expression, as if accused of mischief but puzzled as to what. The glittering object was nowhere in sight.

'What did you steal from the dead?' said Tannhauser.

He watched Orlandu contemplate deceit. Tannhauser held out his hand. The boy's arm fluttered and a dagger appeared in his palm. Artfully sleeved. He gave it to Tannhauser with the rueful air of one seeing something precious vanish forever. The sheath was of moss-green leather, tipped and chased with silver. He slid the dagger free. Its hilt was set with an emerald.

'This is a *hancher*,' he said. 'The accoutrement of a *corbacy* at least. A Turkish knight carried this. You could shave with it if you could but lay claim to a beard.' Orlandu shrugged, determine to mount a brave face to his loss. Tannhauser slid the blade back home. '*To the lion belongs whatever his hand may seize*,' quoted Tannhauser. He handed the dagger back and the boy licked his lips. 'Don't let the Spaniards see it, or you'll have to stick it through their ribs.'

The dagger vanished as quickly as it had appeared and Tannhauser smiled.

'Come,' he said. 'Bors is in need of some needlework, and I don't want him to stand in line, for it's going to be a long one.'

'Am I to serve you, My Lord?' asked Orlandu. The prospect seemed to delight him.

Tannhauser laughed. The weariness begat by the tragic nocturne eased. It was an auspicious place to have caught up with the boy. They were all alive, after all, and across the bay, and beyond the Kalkara Gate, his famous boat was waiting at Zonra. Amparo's arms waited too and a smile on Carla's face. The tide had turned at last. More. It was already sweeping him home to the coast of Italy.

'Are you to serve me?' said Tannhauser. He unslung Bors's armour and dumped it in Orlandu's reedy arms. 'Why not? At this date it will make a welcome change.'

FRIDAY 15 JUNE 1565

Saint Elmo's – the Barbican – the Solar – the Wharf

By the time Tannhauser got Bors to the chapel a pyre of amputated limbs already filled the bailey with the smell of burning meat. The sheeted dead were stacked outside in the dust and they had to fight their way inside though a morass of mutilated bodies, to whose groans for mercy Tannhauser closed his ears. Inside the chapel, a Mass in thanks for their victory was in progress at the altar. Mere inches from the chaplain, the scarlet-aproned surgeons plied their bone saws. Hoping to spare Bors as much agony as possible, Tannhauser located his knapsack and produced a bottle of brandy, which Bors rifled down his throat while employing the flat of his sword to defend his greed.

Tannhauser picked his way through the afflicted, slithering here and there on the ubiquitous clots, and braced the surgeons. Beleaguered by his entreaties, Jurien de Lyon forsook a Spanish soldier whose congealing entrails dangled about his crotch, and inserted twenty-seven sheepgut sutures into Bors's face. By the finish – and the improvement was quite remarkable – Bors's reassembled features were the colour of a rotting aubergine and so swollen that he was sightless altogether. Tannhauser shouldered the knapsack, drained the surviving inch of brandy, and guided Bors's blind and staggering frame back out across the carpet of the hapless.

They found some shade and Orlandu raised his standing by providing a fine breakfast of ox liver, red onions and a skin of wine. Shortly thereafter, Orlandu was assaulted by an enraged and withered monk wielding a copper ladle and only Tannhauser saved this Stromboli from being knifed with the *hancher* blade. Yet so odious and ungrateful did the old man prove to be that Tannhauser, a mite testy after six hours in the breach, dispossessed him of the ladle and bent it so tightly round his throat it turned him blue.

'Go and peel your onions and whatnot,' Tannhauser told him, 'while the fighting men replenish their energies.'

As he settled to his nap, Tannhauser noted that this exchange had further endeared him to the boy. He awoke as stiff as a board and in more agony by far than he'd felt at the battle's close. As evening came and the day cooled it became clear that Bors was unwilling to 'flee to the Borgo' on account of 'this scratch'.

'I will never live it down!' he bleated.

Bors's passage across the harbour had already been secured, in exchange for a crock of apricot jam, ahead of a large number of far worthier cases. The boats would be so crammed with the sorely afflicted that Tannhauser was unable to acquire berths for himself and Orlandu. Anything was possible, but pride, or shame, or exhaustion, or some regrettable combination of the three, persuaded him to delay their return until the following night. After so brutal a reverse, Mustafa would need days to prepare another assault and the danger was acceptable. To mollify Bors's drunken truculence, Tannhauser fed him a lump of raw opium that would have killed two lesser men, shoved a pound of the stuff inside his shirt, and three hours later herded him like a steer to the waiting transports. Bors, who'd been further gentled by the return of his Damascus musket, was by this time under the illusion that he was being dispatched to Saint Elmo's rather than sent away from it, and it was with relief that Tannhauser finally watched him slide across the water.

On Tuesday and Wednesday the boats were again filled to the gunwales with the limbless, the dying and the blind. Standing side by side on the wharf with both Le Mas and the noble Jurien, Tannhauser quailed at presenting so cowardly a spectacle. He spent these days sleeping as much as the continued bombardment allowed. He helped Le Mas in deciding where best to lay the batteries and was careful to take no part in repelling the minor but vicious night raids by which the Turks continued to harass them. While taking care not to make a nuisance of himself, Orlandu stuck to him like a shadow, thus evading many arduous chores, and was solicitous to as many of Tannhauser's needs as he could satisfy.

Tannhauser saw no logic in bewildering the boy by revealing the true nature of his interest in him. Who knew what effect such shocking revelations might have on his callow brain? The instinctive liking he'd felt for the boy on first meeting deepened and grew. Orlandu laughed easily, the most admirable of virtues in Tannhauser's book, and his stoicism was commendable. Given the right education, he would make a fine rogue and adventurer. Carla would have him studying the Quadrivium, no doubt, but that was surely the superior road to travel. It occurred to him that – as the boy's stepfather to be – he would have some say in these matters, and he resolved not to encourage him in sin and to set an upstanding example wherever possible. In the meantime, man and boy took pleasure from the latter's education in the use of firearms.

At sundown on Thursday, with the fiery orb's departure tinting the gunsmoke pink, an emissary of the Pasha, nervous as a fledgling thespian, climbed atop the ravelin before the barbican and requested a parley. At Governor Luigi Broglia's request Tannhauser attended the battlements to translate for the commanders.

Tannhauser and the Turkish ambassador shouted across the twenty yards that parted them. Mustafa, it turned out, was offering terms for the fort's peaceable surrender. This gave the morale of the grandees a considerable fillip. Broglia was a gnarled Piedmontese in his seventies who bore several fresh wounds with insouciance. He produced an unkindly smile, his lips puckered by the prominent gaps in his teeth.

'Mustafa's arsehole must be raw,' he said. 'What terms does he offer?'

'Mustafa swears by his beard,' rendered Tannhauser, 'and by the tombs of his holy ancestors, and by the beard of the Prophet, blessed be his name, that he will grant safe passage to any member of the garrison who wishes to leave tonight.'

Le Mas pointed to the noxious mire of decomposing corpses that more or less begirded the fort. 'Tell him – by the beards of his women – that we've tombs aplenty for him and his offspring too.'

'Safe passage to where?' said Broglia.

Tannhauser asked the emissary. He would have accepted the offer in a trice.

'To Mdina,' he reported. 'No man who retires will be molested.'

'Is he to be trusted?' asked Broglia.

Tannhauser's heart fluttered with hope. 'These are grave oaths, comic as they may seem to you, and publicly made. He wouldn't blaspheme in front of his own troops. And Mustafa kept his word to you at Rhodes, did he not?'

Broglia, along with La Valette, was one of the tiny and dwindling elite who'd survived that legendary epic. He grimaced, as if the memory of that surrender still soured his tongue.

'Tell Mustafa we're resolved to die where we stand.'

Tannhauser turned to convey this unwelcome riposte.

Broglia stopped him with a hand. 'Better yet, let his ambassador die where he stands.' He indicated the German wheel-lock cradled in Tannhauser's elbow. 'Shoot him.'

Tannhauser blinked. It was all the time he needed to decide that moral delicacy would earn him no distinction with those present. He threw the rifle to his shoulder and the emissary, alert to the likelihood of such perfidy, caught the movement and turned to retreat from his perch. With a matchlock gun against him, he might have succeeded, but the wheel-lock ignited its charge on the instant the trigger was pulled. The sixteen-bore lead ball punctured the unfortunate ambassador mid-spine and pitched his broken body down the ravelin's far side. Le Mas chortled and, as a furious but inconclusive musket duel brought the peace conference to a close, Tannhauser retreated to the gatehouse. Before he could take his leave, collect Orlandu and head smartly for the wharf, he was invited to a war council in the solar, and his excuses were not accepted.

The solar – the grand chamber of the fort's inner stronghold – itself bore signs of battery. The groins in the vault sported cracks, a pair of trusses clung on by dint of wedged splinters alone, piles of fallen plaster scattered the floor and dust motes danced in the light of the candles and lamps. But Stromboli provided well and Tannhauser found himself tucking into one of the sheep that had accompanied him across Grand Harbour. He dined with Broglia, Le Mas, De Medran, Miranda, Aiguabella, Lanfreducci and Juan de Guaras. They ate and talked at a splendid oak table, still wearing their gore-scabbed harness in case the alarums sounded. The topic was of how best to extend their defiance at the most exorbitant cost to the Turk. Maimed and enfeebled though most at that table were, the talk of combat vitalised their spirit. Their conviction that God's design and their own were one and the same was irrefragable. A singular jocundity reigned, from which Tannhauser felt excluded. He was feasting with madmen. Then Captain Miranda, not a professed knight but a Spanish adventurer, asked Tannhauser for his opinion.

'As the Arab proverb has it,' he said, 'an army of sheep commanded by a lion would defeat an army of lions led by a sheep.'

De Guaras almost rose from the table and Tannhauser hastened to assure the fierce Castilian that he was not the sheep commander in question.

Tannhauser said, 'If Mustafa had more patience and cunning – which are virtues just as leonine as courage – he would leave some few batteries, solidly defended, on the hill along with those on Gallows Point, and move the bulk of his army to besiege the Borgo. He could batter this fort from three directions, at his leisure, you'd receive no further reinforcements, your morale would wither quickly, and the apple would fall from the tree. It's the fact that Saint Elmo's is cast as the prize of this epic that keeps you fighting so hard. If you were relegated to a sideshow . . .' he shrugged.

'Well?' said Le Mas. 'Is the dog that cunning?'

'No,' said Tannhauser. 'Mustafa's methods were forged in other wars, in times now past, and the leopard won't change his spots. Mustafa's counsel is his rage and the thrill of sending men to die in battle. He'll continue this offensive to the bitter end. Since you murdered his ambassador – an insult hard to surpass – Mustafa will determine to overwhelm the fort at his next attempt. Which I guess will be in no more than three days.'

A certain gloom hovered about and Tannhauser thought this the moment to make his exit. But Le Mas clapped him on the shoulder, which since it was still black and blue almost made him gasp with pain. 'An admirable shot, by the way,' said the brawny Frenchman. 'Plucked him like a quail from the covey.'

'At that range I could've hit him with this table,' Tannhauser said.

Le Mas smiled, 'I wasn't commending your marksmanship, but rather your élan.'

There was a ripple of mirth and their spirits were restored. A toast was raised to the hardness of Tannhauser's heart. His attempts to escape their company and sneak away to the boats were roundly thwarted, and a fine brandy from Auch was produced, and they cajoled him to tell tall tales of distant campaigning in Nahjivan and the Shiite marches, and to describe the Temple in Jerusalem, which no other there had ever seen, and to expound on the bloodstained career of Suleiman Shah. Their prejudices were affirmed to hear that Suleiman had ordered the strangling of his own two sons, and of their sons too, by the notorious mute eunuchs of the seraglio. They were amazed to discover how like their own were the sacred rules and customs by which the janissaries lived, and they were moved to learn that Tannhauser had once worn their colours, and the grandees looked at him through altered eyes, and Tannhauser didn't feel so alien in their company any more. De Guaras asked him why he'd left the janissaries, and Tannhauser gave a false answer, which was that he'd rediscovered Jesus Christ, and this pleased them. But not even Bors knew the true reason, for of the many dark deeds that might have caused Tannhauser shame, the deed that lay behind his disaffection was the most despicable of all.

By the time he finally left, and somewhat unsteadily, the transports had long vanished into the night. As Tannhauser made his bed in the shelter of the chapel, with Orlandu curled at his feet like a watchful dog, he felt sad for the old men of the Religion, for all of them were old in spirit, shackled as they were to a world and a dream long dead. And he thought of Amparo, and his heart knew a different ache. And he thought of Carla and her green eyes rimed with black and her red silk dress and her martyr's heart. And of Sabato Svi in Venice and the money they'd make. And he reminded himself, as he fell asleep, that the rare and noble brotherhood of the knights was not a thing to be seduced by, for in the end it was a cult of death, and of such fellowships as those he'd had his fill.

* * *

On the day following, Friday the 15th, the Turks renewed their bombardment. The bakery was destroyed. Sixty- and eighty-pound balls bounced around the bailey, dismembering anyone in their way. Hunched behind the breastworks and crumbling curtains, the dust-powdered defenders scuttled about like ants under assault by barbarous children. No one doubted the end was near. Tannhauser resolved to leave that night no matter what the cost.

As darkness fell, he concluded his bargain with the serjeant who marshalled the departures from the wharf, and a random pair of would-be evacuees were abandoned on their wattles by the postern. Orlandu staggered gamely down the steps, brutally overburdened with Tannhauser's knapsack and tackle. They shouldered their way to the edge of the quay through a press of stretcher-bearing slaves and crippled fugitives, cleared out a spot on which to stack their gear, and waited for the longboats to glide in.

'Why do we retreat?' asked Orlandu.

'Retreat?' scoffed Tannhauser. 'You begin to sound like Bors. If we stay, we will die, and popular though that ambition is hereabouts, it forms no part of our plan.'

'Everyone here will die? De Guaras? Miranda? Medran?' He paused as if stunned by his own imagination. 'Colonel Le Mas?'

Perhaps battle had so befogged his wits that he thought his heroes immortal.

'All of them,' Tannhauser replied. 'It is their choice and their calling, but not mine. Nor should it be yours.' He inclined his beard across the water. 'Somewhere beyond this lunacy a wider world awaits, in which men such as we may prosper and make a mark more seemly than a florid inscription on a tomb. Indeed, no one at Saint Elmo's will leave so much as that.'

'They will leave their names.'

'Those few who will are more than welcome to. I've already outlived Alexander and that's a mightier comfort to me than his name is to him. For what that name was worth, the poet Dante consigned him to the bowels of Hell.'

'Alexander?' said Orlandu.

'You see? Your ignorance shames you. You're equipped for little more than lugging a tub of swill through the mire. Is that craft or achievement to be proud of?'

The light in Orlandu's eyes dimmed and he lowered his face to hide his hurt at amounting to so little in his hero's reckoning. Tannhauser quelled a pang. It would do the boy good. To aim high required some knowledge of where one stood.

'Couple your vitality to my counsel,' he said, 'and you'll learn that there are joys beyond the worship of martyrs.'

Orlandu rallied. 'What is your plan?'

'Our plan, boy.'

Orlandu brightened. Not a sulker then. Good.

'Yes,' repeated Tannhauser. 'Our plan. But if we don't get off this wharf we fall at the first rub, so more of the plan later, for here come our transports.'

The first of three longboats had appeared to the south-east, the oars sparkling silver as they rose and fell. The Milky Way teemed about the Archer, and the moon, only two days on the wane, was an hour up. The bay, then, could not have been brighter. The longboat was loaded with men and supplies and, as became lamentably apparent at thirty yards' distance, a chest-high barrel of fresh Greek fire was roped into place amidships. It was at this range that the Turkish guns opened up.

Tannhauser realised at once that this was the purpose of the new Turkish palisade whose location had baffled the onlookers from the fort. It was a screen of wooden piles, earth and gabions that ran down the eastern slope of Monte Sciberras right to the water's edge. Here, it was now clear, a battery of light cannon and a unit of Tüfekchi musketeers had been stationed, thus craftily shielded from the guns of both Saint Elmo and Sant' Angelo. The flash of their muzzle blasts on the surface of Grand Harbour and the unspooling tendrils of gunsmoke were all that could be seen. That and the calamitous results of their marksmanship.

A spray of splinters, water and airborne body parts exploded from the foremost transport, which foundered, oars wheeling, as Tannhauser's gut roiled inside him. An instant later, the butt of wildfire, smashed open by a ball and ignited by the gun match of a seaborne *arquebucero*, erupted in a yellow volcano which lit up the bay for a quarter of a mile around and sent flaming balls of the sticky incendiary liquor spouting aloft.

A number of fiery projectiles arced towards the crowd of lame and wounded on the wharf, and panic swept the throng and a frenzied scuffle for safety broke out around him. Agonised screams vied with shouts of desperation as loaded wattles tumbled in the scrimmage. Tannhauser, his prime site at the quay's edge now precarious, started to claw his way further landward. Then a pair of fist-sized fireballs splattered square among the press and the whole mass recoiled in two separate and expanding circles from their respective points of impact. One circle collided with the other and chaos was compounded as those scourged with flame barged to find relief in the water. The pressure of the mob was irresistible. For all his strength, Tannhauser was shoved backwards. The Milky Way flashed overhead and his back crashed into the water and his ears fell abruptly deaf to the dockside uproar.

For an instant the coolness was a delight, then he realised he was sinking with a flailing, human millstone atop his chest. He shoved and caught a kick in the gut and sank further down. The coolness reached his feet as his high boots filled to their tops. He kicked out with no more effect than if he'd been buried alive in sand. He ripped off his helmet and waved his arms, his bearings lost in the void. Nothingness gaped beneath him. His lungs refused his commands not to burst and convulsed of their own accord. Panic shot through him, as swift and brief as lightning. When the water rushed through his nostrils and throat, the sensation was a marked improvement. The blackness in which he was immersed spread like warmth through his mind and with it came a relief he hadn't thought possible. An image of Amparo came and went. And then he heard, as clear as a bell, his mother's voice call out his name. '*Mattie*.'

So that was it, he thought. That was my life. Did I do so badly?

He thought: you could have done worse. But it would have taken a mighty effort.

He came to with his face pressed into a slab of wet capstone. It was dark and he had the sensation that someone was jumping on his back. Saltwater gushed from his mouth and stung his sinuses. He couldn't move and the pounding continued. He realised he was alive and that the place he was returning from had been one of a peace so profound it could only have been his death. The pounding on his shoulder blades was more than he could bear and he mustered the strength to throw an elbow behind him. He hit something solid and the assault stopped. Hands rolled him over on to his back and he flopped there and wheezed. Orlandu, his hair dripping water, looked down at him and grinned.

'Lugging a tub of swill through the mire?' he said, with glee. 'Oh yes, and lugging a tub of lard out of the water.'

FRIDAY 15 JUNE 1565

Amparo's Rock

AMPARO SAT ON a craggy outcrop of the island of Sant' Angelo and watched two bullet-splintered longboats return across the black and silver bay. She shivered in the cool of the night and her heart ached inside her breast and she felt inconsolably alone, and this she found strange, because alone was her most familiar home and hearthstone.

She knew that Tannhauser wasn't with the boats, as he'd not been with the boats of previous nights. She'd watched them all since Bors had returned. She'd watched every oar stroke, every ripple that they'd made on the water. Why Bors and not Tannhauser? From the bloody cargoes of the boats now pulling past her, from the explosion that she'd seen light up the harbour, she knew that from now on the desolated fort across the bay was beyond all help and reinforcement. But she knew Tannhauser was alive. She'd seen his face just moments ago. He'd found a great peace and had wanted her to know it. Then he'd gone, and she'd been afraid, for she couldn't find him in her heart and she thought him dead. And then she'd felt him again. No longer at peace, it was true; but alive. In that moment she conceived the notion that as long as he knew she loved him, he wouldn't die. Yet of her love she'd never spoken. How could she? There were no words sufficient to convey it. How then could he know? And how could she make it so?

From the leather cylinder around her neck she took out her weirdstone and put her eye to its bore and pointed the brass tube at the moon. She spun the wheels of stained glass. She saw nothing but a vortex of colours. Since coming to the island she'd lost her power to see. Perhaps her loss was due to the malign aura of war. Or perhaps because she had fallen so far in love.

She sat on the rock until the moon completed its journey through the night and hung as if sad and haunted over the western rim of Creation. The eastern horizon purpled at her back and in the pale violet light she saw that two score Turkish warships had entered the bay, and were drawn up stem to stern in an unbroken chain that curved out of sight beyond the headland where Tannhauser was trapped. At the seaward tip of the peninsula flares bloomed in a garland of fire around Saint Elmo's throat. A vast arc of gunfire rippled across the mountain's slopes as four thousand musketmen, in a single immense rank, discharged their pieces. The galleys rolled at anchor as their deck guns boomed. The face of Monte Sciberras seemed to vomit forth the contents of the molten earth beneath it as a hundred diabolic siege guns roared in unison. Somewhere at the centre of that inferno stood her love.

A stain spilled down the mountainside and she watched without blinking and her heart shrank within her and her blood ran cold as ten thousand voices raised in hatred raped her soul. From the fractured rim of the fort a meagre salvo crackled in reply and a tattered banner was brandished against the retreat of the night.

She realised that she had seen this in her shew stone after all. Endless chaos. The rule of misrule. The abyss into which all harmony and structure had been cast forever. She raised the vision glass one more time and aimed it at the not yet risen sun. She spun the wheels. The colours turned and slowed, and redness flooded into her, and drenched her mind, and she thought it was blood, then for an instant, an instant terrible and infinite and true, the red became a dress, and a woman wore it, and the woman in red swung from the end of a rope tied about her neck.

The glass fell from her hands into her lap. For a moment she was deaf to the roar of the guns and blind to their fire, and to the birth of the day and the smell of the sea she was numb, and to the cool of the morning breeze her skin was calloused. On her tongue was a taste as flat and lifeless and bitter and cold as brass. She sealed the vision glass in its leather case. She stood up on the rock. And she threw the glass into the sea.

It disappeared without a splash. And if with the weirdstone's vanishment something precious inside her died, something new was born. She would face the future without prognostication, and the present as she'd never dared face it before: with Hope. The Angels had abandoned her. And she didn't know how to petition Almighty God, for she'd never thought to call on Him before. She turned her back on mortal chaos and closed her eyes and laced her hands.

'Please God,' she said. 'Protect my love from harm.'

She opened her eyes. From beyond the farmost curvature of the world, a vermilion sun ascended the cloud-bruised sky. And in answer to her prayer she heard nothing but the rage of Moslem guns.

SATURDAY 16 JUNE 1565

Saint Elmo – the Ramparts – the Forge

THE MOST SURPRISING discovery Orlandu made about battle was that it was work. The fear, the stench, the horror, the rage, the random gusts of panic and exhilaration, the hatred and loyalty and valour, all these had formed some part of his fantasy, erected upon the tales he'd heard all his life. Because the tales were brief, the battles in his imagination were settled with a few rousing moments of crisis and high drama. But six, eight, ten hours of massed combat was mostly composed of grinding and exhausting tedium, like quarrying stone in blistering heat while somebody tried to stab you in the back. It was the most arduous and back-breaking labour ever devised and Orlandu, who'd spent his days scraping galleys, was no stranger to toil. At times a pair of depleted warriors from either camp would stop in the middle of a duel by mutual agreement, and lean upon their spears as if upon shovels while they caught their breath. Then they'd nod and start again and fight until one or the other was slain.

The first assault that day had been by maniacs: fiends dressed in the skins of leopards and wolves and wild dogs, the sun flashing from gold-plated helms, and utterly careless of their lives. Iayalars, Tannhauser called them, who chewed hashish and smoked hemp and chanted through the night to stoke their frenzy. Some even charged stark naked, their privates all adangle between their thighs. They waded across the swill of faeces and maggots, and trampled through the black and bursting corpses that enswathed the enceinte, and kicked a path through the flap and squawk of vultures too glutted to fly. They came at the walls with scaling irons and ladders and were slaughtered by the *arquebuceros* and the enfilading cannon of the salients, as if their only purpose was to fill the groaning ditches with their meat.

As the remnants crawled back up the mountain, a host of dervishes howled their way to Paradise. After them came the Azeb infantries. And from the blinding glare of the meridian sun, to the jangle of their bands and the pounding of their drums, the janissaries joined the fray. Time and again they rolled down the hill and up the pestilent counterscarps to scale the walls, there only to tumble from the ramparts like bloody surf.

It made no sense.

Tannhauser had elected to avoid the rigours of the line by employing his marksmanship. Along with his wheel-lock rifle, he picked a Turkish seven-palm musket from the stockpile of captured weapons and with Orlandu to load the latter he crawled about the ramparts behind the pikemen, sniping from the embrasures and wreaking a horrible toll on Mustafa Pasha's officers. Half a dozen times he took a shot at the Pasha himself, who directed the theatre of madness from the ravelin, with Torghoud Rais at his side. But Allah must have protected the wizened commander, for though Tannhauser dropped three guardsmen at Mustafa's very feet, that was one mark he couldn't make, and nor could anyone else.

For Orlandu, carrying twelve pounds of musket, a ten-pound sack of balls and a heavy flask of powder was hardly less brutal than dragging the tub of mush, and more terrifyingly onerous by far. It took twenty-two steps to load and fire a musket, and twenty-one of them were left to him. Under fire, the game became a nightmare. The misfires shamed him. The overloads and double loads, whose recoil almost blew his hero off the allure, earned him a curse and a clout. The pike butts and elbows were as heedless as before. And the overheated barrel scorched his hands. Sparks fell in streams down the neck of his breastplate, which was itself an oven. Black powder stung his eyes and smoke peeled his throat. At times he found himself weeping as his fingers dropped the flask. He wasn't allowed to shoot because he'd waste a precious shot. Yet despite his bouts of anger, Tannhauser carried him through. With a word of praise or a piece of advice. With a slap on the back or a grimy smile. With a jest and a peal of laughter. With unguarded looks of affection that Orlandu had never seen in his life before.

The maelstrom roiled about the teetering walls from one end of the day to the other. When the blood-red round at last went down on another festering harvest of bloating dead, the Moslems bent before Allah's will and retired, and the defenders knelt by their weapons and praised Christ. Orlandu had no breath left for his Saviour. He slumped against a merlon, musket in his lap, and fell at once into a slumber. Before he could dream a hand hauled him upright and held him firm while he found his wits. Tannhauser cradled both long guns in his arm. His eyes were shadowy hollows in his skull.

'Come, boy,' he said. 'Keep me company while I eat.'

THAT EVENING TANNHAUSER fell into melancholy and said little. As soon as he'd finished his meal, Orlandu fell asleep on the ground where he sat. He woke on an instinct, in the silence of the early hours, and saw Tannhauser's long silhouette cross the moonlit bailey. Sleep called Orlandu back and his aching body begged him to pay heed, but something stronger pushed him to his feet and he followed, picking his way through the gun stones that littered his path.

Orlandu caught up with him at the door to the armourer's

workshop. Tannhauser carried a helmet and a lamp and seemed amused yet glad to see him. Neither spoke as they went inside and there Tannhauser paused to inhale the smells, which were of sacking and bear grease and cinders and coal, and notably wholesome after the pestilential miasma that reigned outside. Orlandu watched as he strode to the forge and set down the lamp and helm and raked the ashes for a coral pink residue of embers. From these he coaxed flames and he called Orlandu to work the bellows – gently now – and showed him how to feed in the coke and build the coal bed, and once again Orlandu was in awe of his expertise and felt the crush of shame that he was such a know-nothing. Tannhauser stripped the helm of its padding and laid it on the coals and they watched the seep of colour into the steel.

'When I was your age,' said Tannhauser, 'this was my intended trade. A blacksmith was all I wanted to be, and I thought it the greatest art in the world.' He shrugged. 'No doubt I was right. But it wasn't to be. I've lost what little knack I had, but it soothes me to shoe a horse from time to time, or work a piece of metal in the fire.' Orlandu was about to ask him why it wasn't to be, but Tannhauser said, 'See how the colour turns.' He pointed. 'Fetch me that peen hammer.'

Tannhauser grabbed the helmet with tongs and put the heated portion over the anvil's horn and set to working it four inches from the crown.

'After I lost my own in the harbour last night I couldn't find another helm to fit me.' He looked up from the anvil. 'You're a fine swimmer. A strong one too.'

Orlandu glowed. 'I could teach you,' he said.

Tannhauser smiled and went on hammering. 'I dare say so, but not in the time we have left. Could you swim the bay to Sant' Angelo, as the messengers do?'

'Oh yes, easily.' Easily was a boast, but he could do it.

Tannhauser returned the helmet to the coals and pumped the bellows.

'Then that is what you must do. Tonight.'

Orlandu stared at him. The fierce blue eyes were in earnest. Orlandu felt sick without knowing why. He shook his head.

'I order it,' said Tannhauser.

Orlandu felt a pressure in his chest he couldn't resist. He said, 'No.'

'Have you not had enough of battle? Of weariness and filth?'

'I serve you.' said Orlandu. He took a step backwards.

'That is a start. The first rule of serving is to obey.'

'I'm not a coward.' Such was the strange panic in his gut, the heat inside his head, that this statement seemed false on his tongue. He was full of fear.

'Nothing could be clearer. Nevertheless, you must go.'

'Nevertheless, I will not.'

'You have the makings of a very poor soldier.'

The words seemed an insult yet Tannhauser spoke them with approval. He transferred the glowing steel to the anvil and for some time said nothing, lost in his smithing as he extended the newly fashioned bulge around the helm's circumference and expanded the heat-dulled steel towards the rim. Orlandu prayed that the argument was won and that he wouldn't be banished from Tannhauser's side. The prospect of such exile filled him with a horror so intense he wanted to vomit. Nothing he'd felt while crawling along the gantlet came close to the terror that filled him now. He watched Tannhauser's hands, drawn in by the hypnotic rhythm of the hammer and the gradual submission of that which wasn't meant to yield.

'It takes earth and water and fire and wind to make steel,' said Tannhauser. 'Therein lies its strength. My father told me that God forged men from the same materials, but simply in different proportions. It is the proportions allocated of each that determines the qualities of a piece of steel. This helm must be hard but not flexible, therefore the heat we use is gentle and we will quench it only once. But a sword must bend without breaking or losing its fettle, and a gun barrel must contain the explosions unleashed within it, so these steels require diverse techniques and proportions proper to their purpose. And so it goes. Do you understand?'

Tannhauser looked at him and Orlandu nodded, again lamenting his ignorance but thrilled by the thought of such mysteries. His terror was fading away.

Tannhauser continued. 'The solving of these riddles – of matching the most apt of an infinitude of possible proportions to a particular purpose – has been the work of millennia, passed down from fathers to sons, and from master to pupil, each, with luck, learning more than the last. And so it should be in the blending of those elements that make up the temper of a man. The knowledge is there, if we would but listen. But in the matter of forging their own mettle, men are stubborn and vain, and place more faith in the voice of their own inclinations than in the counsel of the wise.'

Tannhauser treated him to a smile, but one which disturbed him.

'Yet stubborn though men are, and hard to believe as it may be, boys are more stubborn still.'

Orlandu shuffled and the panic returned as he realised that the argument was far from over. He tried to change the subject. 'Where is your father?' he said, with exaggerated curiosity.

Tannhauser chortled at the crudity of this stratagem. He returned the fire-blackened helm to the coals and exchanged the hammer for a lighter one.

'My father is far away, and my prayer is that his peace is rarely disturbed by any thought of me. But you will not escape the issue. I came to this cesspool for one reason only, and that was not to die – for Jesus Christ, the Baptist, the Religion or anyone else. I came here to take you back to the Borgo.'

'You came for me?' said Orlandu.

Tannhauser nodded.

'Why?'

'I've asked myself that question many times over, and found many different answers, none of them satisfactory. At a certain point "Why?" is no longer important. De Medran died today and so did Pepe de Ruvo. Miranda has a bullet in his chest. Le Mas is burned by wildfire. Again, there are many reasons why, and at this point none of them matter. You'll swim back to the Borgo, if not because I order it then because I ask it. Go to the Auberge of England. You may serve Bors and the Lady Carla until I return.'

'But how will you return? The boats were shot to pieces again tonight and, well – I'm sorry to say this – but you can't swim.'

Tannhauser pulled the helmet from the fire, frowned, buried it in the ash to cool. 'I have my own way out of here, but it's not for you. Now do as I say. Go.'

Orlandu felt his eyes film with tears, and a sadness clenched his throat with a pain more intense than any he could remember. He felt grief and the fear that verged once more on blind terror. He would lose Tannhauser forever. He'd never had anything to lose before. Without Tannhauser there was – what? These days in his company, despite the exhaustion and madness, were the most precious of his life. The fullest. The dearest. Before Tannhauser there had been nothing. All he could recall of it was emptiness. To be cast out, to return to that emptiness, seemed worse than death. Tannhauser took him by the shoulders and stooped so their faces were level. The eyes that had looked at him – smiled at him – with such comradeship now stared at him from the shadows with no more warmth than a pair of blue stones.

'The Borgo is where I need you. You have no place here. I don't want you around.'

Tannhauser pushed him away and turned back to the forge.

'Now go.'

Orlandu stifled his tears and a violent rage swept through him. Words and thoughts were lost in the thicket of emotions choking his chest. He turned and ran from the armoury and out into the bailey. He ran on, sobs breaking from his throat. He ran across the courtyard and through the postern and down the stone stairs to the quay. A pair of guards dozed on the steps. They watched him with that absolute lack of curiosity that attends bone-tiredness. Orlandu caught his breath and stood staring into the water at his feet.

A single idea sprang from the turmoil inside him. He stripped off his boots and breeches and shirt. He dived into the harbour. He knew the spot. On the fourth dive to the harbour bottom, twelve feet below, his fingers brushed against it at the limit of his breath and he came up empty-handed to gasp for air. On the next plunge he found it at once and kicked his way back to the surface and climbed up on to the quay holding Tannhauser's helmet.

He sat with it in his lap and used his shirt to wipe it clean of mud and weed. If he must leave, at least he could do something to make Tannhauser smile, to make him proud. Something to wipe out the memory of those stone-cold eyes. And of the child's tears that had stung his own. As he polished the steel until it shone bright in the moonlight, he stopped with a sudden understanding and his gut turned over inside him.

He – Orlandu – was the boy the contessa had been seeking.

And Tannhauser was in her pay. He cared nothing for the Religion. Or Christ. Or for him either. Orlandu was no more than merchandise, something to be sold and passed on, forever in pawn to the will of others, as he'd always been before. As he'd been since the day he was born. In himself, he was nothing. The rage inside returned and consumed him.

He pulled on his breeches and his too-big boots. When the sound of the hammer reached his ears he realised he was back in the armoury, with no memory of the distance in between. He could hardly breathe, not from the exertion of running but from the band of anger and heartache crushing his chest. Tannhauser looked up from the anvil and saw his face and blinked.

Orlandu threw the helmet. It clattered across the flags to Tannhauser's feet.

Orlandu fought the stinging in his eyes. He said, 'I do not serve you any longer. And I stay here – because I am free – and I will die like a man for the Religion.'

He didn't wait for a reply. His anger was already waning and in its place rose a terrible yearning to be taken into Tannhauser's arms. He ran to escape the confusion bursting his skull. Outside he sat down against the wall and hugged his knees and tried to return to that state which had existed before all this had happened. Before Tannhauser had beckoned him to come across the field of dead. Before he'd known the scourge of love. The Lady Carla his mother? He didn't believe it. His mother was a whore, as Boccanera had told him a thousand times as accompaniment to a kick. Across the bailey, knights were making their way to the chapel as dawn broke. Orlandu heard Tannhauser's hammer strike up again and he felt abandoned.

Agoustin Vigneron stopped as he passed by. He looked down at him.

'Come to chapel, boy, and ease your woes,' said Vigneron. 'It's Trinity Sunday.'

THURSDAY 21 JUNE 1565 – CORPUS CHRISTI

The Borgo – Saint Elmo's

THE PRE-DAWN DARK seemed more impenetrable today, its gloom thicker, its resonant promise broken, and the sun when it rose was pale, sickly and wan. Or perhaps, thought Carla, it was only a spell cast by thousands of sombre hearts as they tried to excite their spirits for a feast overclouded by doom. She woke Amparo with difficulty and dressed her like a child, for she'd fallen to a black melancholia and rarely left her bed. Bors too took some rousing from his stupor of opium and drink, a state sought more to dull his anguish than the pain of his healing wounds. Carla's own anguish, her guilt at the disaster she'd wrought for Tannhauser, was keen enough. But someone had to spread Christ's love and she felt blessed that it was she. She extracted Bors's oath to see that Amparo attended the procession, for it might inspire her. Then she left to take her own place, dressed and veiled in black.

Carla had been invited by Father Lazaro to join the brethren of the hospital and those of the wounded who could walk. Without intending it, she'd become a revered figure in the infirmary. Her prayers and companionship were craved by the maimed. Her name was called out in the darker watches of the night. If someone survived against expectations, her powers were given credit. When someone died holding her hand, none doubted that he was accepted at once through Heaven's Gate. She attributed none of this to herself. She knew she was no more than a channel for God's love. Yet in this she found a kind of ecstasy.

The general sense of grief that pervaded the city was induced by the ordeal of brave Saint Elmo's, whose survival for so long was perceived as a miracle and whose fall was expected any hour. The relief that Garcia de Toledo, Viceroy of Sicily, had promised by the 20th had not arrived, and no one any longer expected it. Every prayer was offered for the souls of Saint Elmo's dead and the souls of those soon to join them. With a breaking heart, Carla prayed for Mattias and his deliverance, and for Orlandu, her son, whom she'd known so briefly and failed to claim, but whom she loved no less for that.

The Corpus Christi pageant was as grand as the hard-pressed townsfolk could make it. Apart from the soldiers on watch, every Christian who could walk or be carried turned out to take part. The streets teemed wall-to-wall as the procession wound its way to San Lorenzo. The Grand Master led his knights in escorting the Blessed Sacrament – Corpus Christi, the Body of Christ – in a magnificent gold monstrance wreathed with lilies, and some folk wept that such flowers still existed in the wasteland their world had become. The icon of Our Lady of Philermo, dressed in red damask and pearls, and the icon of Our Lady of Damascus were carried aloft. Men mocked up as demons mimed their terror of the Divine Presence. At the head of the pageant, preceding the Holy Eucharist, children dressed as angels sang the Panis Angelicum in a portrayal of the Nine Heavenly Choirs.

At points the procession stopped for the casting of Holy Water and for Benediction, and the Tantum Ergo Sacramentum of Aquinas was sung. Candles burned and incense smoked and a child led a lamb by a harness of red ribbons. Banners waved to

Santa Catarina and Santa Juliana, and to John the Baptist and the Virgin of Sorrows. And the brethren of the Sacred Infirmary carried the precious Madonna and Infant standard of Rhodes: *Afflictis Tu Spes Unica Rebus.*

In all that afflicts us You are our only Hope.

Bands played and church bells pealed while the Turkish siege guns thundered across the bay. By the time the procession reached the square of San Lorenzo, the power of God flowed through them like a sacred river and their hearts were lifted in spite of all that they endured and in all that twenty thousand there was not a soul present who wished to be anywhere else in all Creation, for they knew that here, above all places in this mortal and fallen world, the Lamb of God loved each and every one.

On her return from the Mass, Carla glimpsed Amparo in the crowd. The dullness in her eyes had gone and the lustre of her skin had returned and her body was once again as lithe as a cat as she wove through the press. Then Amparo was gone and Carla's heart felt lighter. She made her way to the infirmary to pray for the wounded, and for Mattias and for her son.

The solemnity of the Corpus Christi celebration did not forestall the daily ritual at the slave pens. Though few but his executioners bore witness, the thirty-second Moslem prisoner of the siege was picked from his fellows. They gagged him with rope to stifle his heathen gibbering and they dragged him through the backstreets where the procession for Christ did not go, and they prodded him up the wall stair to the gallows of Provence and there they noosed his neck and watched him die.

IN THE SMOKING shell of Saint Elmo's across the water, Tannhauser searched the grounds and found Orlandu at work with a gang of Maltese soldiers. They were hauling rocks up the scarp to the western breach, where the heat was intense and the sky was dark with flies. The boy was naked to the waist and sweating and caked with dust. As Orlandu stooped down in the rubble, Tannhauser placed a crock of quince jam on the rock he intended to lift. Orlandu blinked, as if dispelling a mirage, then straightened and looked at his former master.

'That,' said Tannhauser, of the jam, 'is the most coveted prize left to this entire company.' He brandished a hand. 'Your companions here would fight for it as fiercely as they fought for this breach – if they knew it were here. What say you help me finish it?'

Orlandu wiped the back of a hand across his mouth. He glanced at the jam without replying. Tannhauser picked up the crock and tossed it in the air and Orlandu's hands flashed out to catch it before it smashed. Tannhauser laughed and wrung a grin from the boy.

'Come,' said Tannhauser. 'We've pouted like women long enough. And comfort yourself with the fact that no man ever sold his pride for a higher fee.'

While the Turks from four points of the compass had sniped and bombarded without cease, Orlandu had avoided Tannhauser day and night. It was clear that he nursed wounded feelings and that his Latin blood seethed over insults of his own concoction. Tannhauser had left it to hard labour to cool him down. He'd kept an eye out for his safety and employed certain others to do the same. Tannhauser took him now to the forge, which he'd seized as his own domain following the death of the armourer. Three days' solitude at the anvil, refurbishing damaged harness and drinking nostalgia's wine, had restored his inner contentment. The big news from the front – the Drawn Sword of Islam, Torghoud Rais, mortally wounded in the head by a cannon shot from Castel Sant' Angelo – had reached him as if from far away. The end was nigh for Saint Elmo's ragtag garrison. By his calculation this weekend would see Mustafa conclude the siege. Time, then, to mollify the boy for his departure.

Tannhauser brewed the last of his coffee on the firepot and while gun stones battered the donjon above and shook showers of plaster from the vaulting, they ate the jam with a wooden spoon and both of them found it hard not to weep with pleasure. Tannhauser didn't press the boy as to his intentions, for the cult of death had swallowed him and his intentions were plain. Instead, Orlandu pressed him.

'I am the boy you were looking for, born on All Hallows Eve, yes?' asked Orlandu.

'You are he,' said Tannhauser.

'How do you know this?'

'It was writ down by the priest who baptised you and sworn to by a man of devout character. Orlandu Boccanera.'

'I disown the name Boccanera, for he was a pig, and the father of pigs, and never claimed me for his own. He sold me like a mule to the ship scrapers. I will die as Orlandu di Borgo.' He looked at Tannhauser as if expecting disputation.

'Orlandu di Borgo it is,' Tannhauser replied. 'Though you might claim another name – and a truer one – if you had the wit.'

'Then it's so? I am the bastard of the Lady Carla?'

'You are her son.'

'Boccanera told me my mother was a whore.'

'Perhaps he considered her such, if indeed he knew who she was, which I greatly doubt. In that he wasn't alone. Men, and pigs, are hard on women who sacrifice their virtue, especially for love.'

'True love?' said Orlandu.

'I know the Lady Carla,' said Tannhauser. 'She wouldn't have given her virtue for anything less.'

Orlandu's eyes shifted, excited, absorbed. 'And my father? Who was my father?'

Tannhauser expected this query and masked his answer with a smile. 'That's a secret the Lady Carla keeps to herself, as is a woman's right.'

Orlandu, clearly, had already explored this conundrum. 'One

of the knights of the Religion, yes? Such a lady would never – sacrifice her virtue – to anyone less.'

'I'm sure her taste was as refined as one would expect.'

'Perhaps one of the great knights here at Saint Elmo – or in the Borgo, yes?'

At the sight of the boy's joy an unexpected sadness squeezed at Tannhauser's heart. 'There's no doubt in my mind,' he said, 'that your father was a most extraordinary man.'

'Then I have noble blood?' asked Orlandu.

'If you wish,' said Tannhauser. 'Those who boast of it value it higher than virtue, but in my view blood counts for little – or nothing – in itself. Jesus and his disciples were humble men, as were Paracelsus and Leonardo, and the great majority of men of proven genius in every age. And more than a few of the vilest scoundrels alive may call themselves noble. Superiority of mind and character – if such is our ideal of nobility – does not flow in our veins, but stems from the manner in which we conduct our lives. To answer your question, I'd say that by either measure you have a just claim.'

Orlandu hesitated, as if battling with a notion he knew to be foolish but which had plagued him with more tenacity than any other. Finally, he blurted, 'You are not my father.'

Tannhauser smiled, and again he was moved. 'No, I'm not, though I'd be more than proud to be so. However, if luck is with us, it's possible that a variant on such a relation may come to pass.'

This was too oblique for the boy and Tannhauser didn't elaborate.

'Why, then, is he not proud to be so?'

'Who?'

'My father.'

'He doesn't know you exist, at least in my understanding. Your mother never told him, to protect his honour.' Tannhauser saw other unasked questions in his eyes and added, 'Do not think ill of the Lady Carla for abandoning you. It was not her wish to do so. Powerful men robbed her of any choice in the matter, and treated her most cruelly, when she wasn't much older than you.'

Orlandu took this in gravely, and nodded.

'Your mother has travelled very far and risked many perils to find you again. I know you're always present in her heart.'

Orlandu blinked twice and Tannhauser wondered if this was the moment to persuade him to leave. He'd been a fool, looking back, not to educate the boy sooner. If he had, they might not be sitting here now but, rather, running up the sail on his boat. But that milk was spilt and here was indeed where they sat. Let the boy come to the notion of leaving by himself.

He said, 'Noble or blacksmith, each must work out his own destiny as best he can.' He stood up. 'Speaking of which, I've a deal of work to do here. If you're willing, I could use a good hand.'

THEY SPENT THE day planishing divots and freeing seized joints and for each it was as happy a day as he could remember. At sundown Orlandu went to the chapel to hear Mass and take Communion and to give thanks for the knowledge of his origins. Tannhauser finished his repairs to a twisted couter and vambrace. He drank some brandy and fell into a doze on a palliasse on the floor. He awoke from oblivion by the fading light of the forge and he thought himself quite lost in an erotic dream: for Amparo stood in the shadows looking down on him.

He climbed to his feet, making, he hoped, a good fist of hiding the aches and pains that racked his joints. When he turned he expected the apparition to have vanished in the air. But he looked at her again and it had not.

Amparo was wrapped in a ragged crimson war coat emblazoned with a cross. Her hair was plastered to her skull and dripped with water. It was the water that made him realise this was no dream and that she stood there in the flesh. Her slender arms and muscular calves were bare; her feet were coated in wet dust. The baggy linen surcoat adhered to the peaks of her breasts and he knew that beneath it she was nude. He was at once aroused. The slit between the coat's shoulders revealed pale white collarbones and a long, tanned neck. Her eyes shone in the glow of the embers and her face was as enraptured as a mystic's. He wondered how long she'd stood there watching him sleep.

He glanced about the forge. They were alone. He looked down into her face and questions either pointless or to which he knew the answer slipped through his mind unvoiced. You swam the bay? Who brought you here to the forge? Why did you come? She was here. He searched for the anger to scold her, for two dependants in Hell he did not need, but found only gladness. He slipped his right hand through the surcoat's open flank and took her by the waist.

Her skin was cool and smooth, barely dry. The muscles against his thumb below her ribs were taut. His left hand brushed damp locks from her cheek and stroked her scalp and cradled the back of her skull in his palm. Emotion so intense that it caused him pain welled up in his chest. She was no dependant but an Angel come to give him the strength to endure. The touch of her – the existence of her – was so gentle, so lovely, so utterly other than all else that stood around him, that his senses were overwhelmed and his limbs trembled beneath him and he thought for a moment he might fall. Amparo threw her arms around him.

'Lean on me,' she said.

He rallied and smiled and pulled her closer. He said, 'Amparo.'

Her lips parted and he bent his face to hers and kissed her and pulled her against him closer still, as if he'd squeeze her body inside his own, if he could. He felt her fingers digging through his shirt as if she felt the same, and he felt the bristling of his beard against her skin, and his palm against the small of her back, and his member pressing hard against her belly. She lifted one knee and wrapped her leg about his thigh and pushed herself against him with a passion both artless and exuberant.

He took his lips from hers and looked at her again. She was immaculate. She was, in all things, true. He slid his hands on to her breasts, moisture lingering in the creases beneath them, and his memory of their magnificence was shamed by the beauty they embodied now. Love and desire became one, each as overmastering as the other, and he pulled the red surcoat over her head and sucked her nipples and stroked her swollen vulva until she trembled and clung on to him and mewled with pleasure in his ear. He turned her about, her eyes bedazed and rolling with transport, and he bent her across the cold steel face of the anvil. He unfastened his flies and unlimbered himself and she rose up on tiptoe to receive him. He bent his knees to get beneath her and entered her from behind and her feet left the floor and she called out to God and convulsed with each slow stroke, her head thrown back and her eyelids aflutter, and her cries filled the forge until she squeezed him from inside and he exploded to a prayer of his own within her body. They fell to the surcoat on the ground and Tannhauser held her in his arms and he stroked her hair while her body was racked by sobs.

He didn't ask her why she wept for he doubted she had an answer. When she quieted, he rose and stoked the firepot bright and stripped off his clothes and made love to her again on the crimson war coat spread across the ground. She gave herself to him like some creature wild and untamed and so did he give of himself and neither one spoke, for this cradle of insanity and horror had been made by men and words, words perverted from the very lips of gods, and so here were all words lies and they did not need them.

He amused her with small acts of tomfoolery and they laughed, and they slathered in his sweat and pawed at each other's skin with the wonder of simpletons. He toasted heels of bread and sugar on the coals and they ate, and he brewed tea in an old helmet and they drank. She explored the tattoos on his arms and legs with her lips. The eight-spoked wheel, the Zulfikar sword, the crescent moons and sacred verses. She sang him a song in some dialect he didn't understand but whose sentiment he did. He recited erotic *gazels* in Turkish while he aroused her. They made love again and when they were done they lay sated on the palliasse and watched the red light from the coals grow dim.

At last he sensed people moving in the yard and went naked to the door to peer outside. Armoured monks were clanking across the bailey towards the chapel and their pre-dawn prayers. There were few who did not limp and many leaned on pike shafts or comrades for support. The night was almost over and its spell would soon be broken, and for all that it had seemed an eternity, it was now revealed as an instant, and like a conjuror in a carnival show Time had worked its paradox once again.

He went back into the forge and dressed and wrapped Amparo in the surcoat. He picked her up and she cupped her hands around his face and he carried her out beneath the stars and across the wasteland. As he walked he felt as if he held in his arms a being from another world, where violence had no purchase and all living things were kind, and it seemed to him that she weighed no more than the breeze. He took her through the postern and down the steep stair hacked in the rock to the quay. He kissed her and he looked at her and he didn't want to let her go. But go she must, and before the dawn and the Turkish guns made the journey too hazardous. He set her down on the capstones and she made no fuss.

'I'm watching over you,' she said. 'Did you know?'

He said, 'I've felt your breath on my cheek a time or two.'

She stroked his face, his beard, his lips, her eyes liquid and dark.

She said, 'I love you.'

His throat tightened. He didn't reply and didn't know why. He didn't know how to. Amparo pulled the war coat from her shoulders and she dropped it to the quay. For a moment she stood before him, nude and pale as ivory. He kissed her again and released her. Then she turned and dived into the water and foamed away and Tannhauser wished he'd said more.

From the chapel came the sound of singing and from the mountain came the muezzin's call and in the east the indigo paled over San Salvatore. Thus the world turned, though Tannhauser did not. He stood and gazed across the bay until Amparo's fragile figure had long been swallowed up by the last of night.

FRIDAY 22 JUNE 1565

Saint Elmo – Sant' Angelo – the Bailey

The violent circus of murder and prayer recommenced at first light and raged throughout another broiling day. The Turks wallowed through a moat of corrupting bodies and spilled viscera, their feet puncturing distended bellies that sometimes exploded into flame from the vapours therein. As the sun crawled past its meridian, griddle-hot armour sizzled and smoked with sprayed gore and men collapsed for want of air in the foetor and their brains boiled inside their skulls and they spasmed and died, and if the Devil was looking on he must have rubbed his hands, for even in his own demesne there could be no spectacle more demoniac than this.

Tannhauser wished for the fort's final hour to come, for with it – according to his plan – would come his only chance of survival. Yet each time the line of defenders wavered or was breached, and the crazed escalade of the Turks seemed about to overwhelm them, some madman would rally – Lanfreducci, de Guaras, or, time and again, Le Mas – and in a delirium of butchery that would spread like a contagion, the Christians would drive the slithering invaders backward into the ditch.

Tannhauser plied his rifle from the allure, cursing God, cursing them all, cursing the recalcitrant boy at his heels. He kept Orlandu alive. He fought vertiginous waves of lunacy of his own, when the urge to plunge in would importune him and reason itself seemed insane and death the only logic to be embraced. The hallowed music of self-sacrifice rang in his ears, with its promise of eternal renown and a swift release from sorrow; but he'd heard it before and the tune was false and its notes were the screams of the dying.

'Keep your head down, boy,' he roared.

He grabbed Orlandu by the throat and hauled him to cover. In the storm of unhinged courage, the fear in the boy's rolling eyes was a beacon to steer by. He let go and squeezed the bewildered youth by the arm. 'We will see this day through, do you hear me?'

Orlandu nodded. At that moment Tannhauser was down on one knee, his rifle canted on his thigh. A vicious blow took him in the side and spun him round and almost pitched him over the allure. He teetered over a drop of forty feet on to jagged rubble. Orlandu grabbed the arm that squeezed him and held his master fast. Tannhauser righted himself and shuffled behind the protection of the merlon and explored himself with his fingers.

He'd taken numerous hits on his fluted cuirass, and a couple more to his helmet, without sustaining anything worse than bruises. This ball had caught his left hipbone below the plating's edge and had ploughed on into the muscle of his lower back. He could feel the hard lump of lead beneath the skin. It hadn't gone deep into his organs and wouldn't kill him soon. Putrefaction, however, though slower, was as sure a way to go. From his pouch he took a damp rag in which he'd wrapped pellets of comfrey and featherfew. He chewed one briefly and inserted the cud into the hole. The bleeding stopped and on reflection, he didn't feel too poorly. Orlandu stared at him with anguish. Tannhauser mustered a grin.

'That's twice you've saved me, boy. Now fetch me some water, for I'm parched.'

* * *

On the roof of Castel Sant' Angelo, Oliver Starkey and La Valette watched the sun go down behind a veil of vermilion fog. Many of the senior knights stood with them, murmuring Paternosters and the Little Office. Over on the headland, Saint Elmo's sat in a blazing round of fire. From time to time the smoke lifted to reveal the scaling ladders raked against the walls, and the colourful teeming of the Moslem horde, and incendiary liquids cascading down the blackened sandstone, and the bright flash of armour along the battlements and breach. At times the fight appeared to rage in silence. At others, bedlamite gusts of noise would carry across the bay. Despite the inferno of violence the banner of Saint John still fluttered, tattered but unvanquished above the flames.

The Turks had been sure that it would take no more than a week to conquer the star-shaped fort. Even La Valette had not expected his boast of three weeks to be fulfilled. Yet, for the valiant of Saint Elmo, this grim Friday was the thirtieth day of defiance.

Starkey looked at La Valette. The old man remained tireless, even when Starkey stood swaying on his feet, and he nightly sacrificed an hour of sleep to pray to Our Lady of Philermo. His labours were prodigious. He'd supervised the design and construction of the new inner walls almost brick by brick. He'd completed yet another audit of the stockpiles of food and wine in the caverns beneath the town. He'd then repeated his calculations and repeated them again, and on that basis had doubled the rations of the slave battalions, from whose limbs he would now squeeze an extra two hours' labour every day. He'd ordered mass graves to be dug over on L'Isola and covered them with wicker wattles to prevent alarm. He made daily tours, randomly timed, of the hospital, the bastions of the various langues, the gun batteries, the markets and armouries. His dour, masculine charisma gave people wherever he went the strength to endure. His religious demeanour bolstered and nourished their fidelity, for he was the

Defender of the Faith made flesh. In his weather-beaten face, which evermore looked cast from bronze, they saw an absolute absence of self-doubt and a perfect absence of pity. The daily hangings of the Moslem prisoners of war reminded them that, much as they feared the Turk, they should fear the Grand Master more.

As he watched his brethren dying across the water, La Valette appeared as serene as a portrait of Jerome. He knew that even the epic of Saint Elmo was but a prelude to the greater fight to come – for L'Isola and the Borgo. Yet this was one moment when Starkey found La Valette's composure unsettling. Almost inhuman.

Starkey said, 'The Greek poets used the word "ekpyrosis" to describe their heroes. Achilleus, Diomedes, Ajax. It means to be consumed by fire.'

'Our heroes are not consumed yet,' said La Valette. 'Listen.'

Turkish horns wailed forth from Monte Sciberras, heavy as the breast of anguish in the crimson gloaming. The watchers held their breath. Then, from the embattled walls across the water, came a ragged cheer. Starkey could hardly believe it.

'Was that a huzzah?' he said.

The cheer was raised again from the smoking ramparts. The voices of the doomed brethren pierced the heart of every man there standing on Sant' Angelo's lofty allure. Some burst into tears and felt no shame. As the Turks withdrew up the hill, La Valette turned to Starkey, and Starkey saw that he had been unkind, for the eyes of the old man too were filmed with tears.

La Valette said, 'Even the Ancients knew not such men as these.'

To ADVANCE HIS climactic stratagem, Tannhauser buried his last five pounds of opium, along with his Russian gold ring, under a stone in the floor of the forge. He extinguished all signs of the disturbance with ashes and straw. In the less secure hiding place of the splintered timber vaulting of the solar, he'd earlier concealed his wheel-lock rifle and its key, along with powder and ball. He took the last bottle of brandy from his knapsack and walked out into the bailey, favouring the wound in his hip. The Turkish lead was still in him, but as hundreds of horribly wounded carpeted the stones outside the chapel, he felt in no position to beard the surgeons. In any case, the untreated wound might yet prove useful to his escape.

In the middle of the open ground a bonfire blazed, wherein the knights burned everything that might be valued by the Turks. Food, lumber, furniture, tapestries, wildfire hoops, pike staves, arquebuses; even those sacred icons and paraphernalia that might be desecrated by the fiends. There was no surer sign that Saint Elmo was facing its end. The chapel bell tolled and the flames were sucked up into the darkness. A strange sense of peace reigned over the night.

Orlandu sought Tannhauser out by the bonfire's light. He was naked but for his breeches and his scrawny body and dirty face and wide, dark eyes made him look even younger than his years. Around his neck by a cord hung a cylinder sealed with oilcloth and wax. This latter Tannhauser was gratified to see. It contained a letter to Oliver Starkey, in his own hand, detailing certain observations on the state of Mustafa's forces and the number and size of his siege guns and, in anticipation of Orlandu's desire to return to Saint Elmo's, a request that under no circumstance was the boy to be allowed to do so. He also asked that Starkey do what he could to ensure the comfort and safety of the women.

'I have a commission from Colonel Le Mas,' announced Orlandu.

'A great honour,' said Tannhauser. 'Tell me more.'

'I'm to deliver these dispatches to La Valette and tell him what has taken place here.'

'I hope you'll include the saga of my own brave doings.'

'Oh yes. You'll be mourned as much as any other hero. Probably more.'

Tannhauser laughed. 'Do not bury me yet, my friend. Tell La Valette that the fox plans to run with the hounds.'

'What does this mean?'

'He will know.' He held out his hand and Orlandu shook it. 'Mind the Turkish marksmen on the shore. Swim underwater until –'

'I know how to swim.'

'So you do. Bear north a quarter of a mile before you turn.'

'I know the way too.'

'Tell Bors and the Lady Carla to endure until I see them again – and don't let them think I mean in the hereafter. Tell Amparo she is in my heart.'

Orlandu blinked as his eyes filmed. He threw his arms round Tannhauser in a sudden, emotive embrace. Tannhauser suppressed a flinch as his wound was mauled. He returned the embrace with one arm.

'We'll meet again, too,' he said. 'Mark my words. Now, be off.'

Orlandu turned and loped away across the yard and was lost to the blackness beyond the flames. Tannhauser was hugely relieved. He tracked down Le Mas. The Frenchman was monstrously afflicted by sword cuts and burns, but despite all that was still on his feet, dispensing words of encouragement to the brethren and relaying the cannon at the breach in time for the morrow. Having already confessed his sins to chaplain Zambrana, and taken Communion, he was able and willing to share in Tannhauser's brandy.

They sat in two splendid chairs that Tannhauser had rescued from the bonfire and he thanked Le Mas for the favour of dispatching Orlandu. He told him something of the boy's story, which Le Mas acknowledged a tale, though by no means the most unlikely that one might cull from their fellow adventurers.

'Many an account of folly's wildest escapades will die here

untold,' said Le Mas. 'In the end, every man's life is but a tale told to him that's lived it, and to him alone. Hence are we all alone, except for God's Grace.'

They drank and dwelled on what had passed. Fewer than four hundred defenders were still able to stand at the breach, and of those only a handful lacked serious wounds. That day alone, the bloodiest yet, two thousand Moslems had been slain, and by Le Mas's reckoning seven thousand or more lay rotting outside the walls. The Religion's total loss, when it came, would amount to fifteen hundred.

'Five for one isn't bad,' he said, 'considering how badly we're outgunned. We gave your heathen pause. If they had any sense they'd pack for home tomorrow.'

Neither said, though both knew, that Mustafa could afford to lose seven thousand far more readily than the Religion their fifteen hundred.

'Sense is generally in short supply on this island,' said Tannhauser. 'I should tell you that if I can work the masquerade, I intend to join the foe in the guise of one of your Turkish prisoners of war.'

Le Mas looked at him, rifled brandy down his throat, then looked at him again.

'Taking account of the fact that you are a German,' he said, 'you are the wiliest man I ever knew. If you were French, you'd be the equal of La Valette himself.'

'Then I have your blessing.'

'Godspeed,' said Le Mas and handed him the bottle.

'Tell me,' said Tannhauser. 'How many Turkish slaves do we have left?'

Le Mas said, 'I should say no more than a dozen. Why?'

Tannhauser took a swallow. 'If they're liberated, they'll be mining the walls of the Borgo within the month. Perhaps even fighting in the Turkish line.'

'Very true,' concurred Le Mas. 'An observation that had

escaped me. And it would be a pity, would it not, if one of those filthy swine were to betray your stratagem?' He looked at Tannhauser. 'Perhaps more than a pity.'

'A catastrophe,' said Tannhauser.

'Marvellous,' said Le Mas. He threw his head back and laughed. 'Marvellous. God forgive me, but I do love men who have no scruples about war. After all, without them, how ever could we fight one?' He seized the bottle again, wincing at the pain the movement caused him. 'Rest easy. I'll have them all put to death, after breakfast.'

Tannhauser soothed his conscience with the thought that at least the condemned prisoners would have time to say their morning prayers. He soothed it further by digging out a pair of the Stones of Immortality. He showed Le Mas their marbling of gold and explained their properties, both healing and mystic, and they each washed one down with the brandy and then they sat and watched the mighty constellations wheel about the sky above. The Great Bear straddled the north. To the south, Scorpius was bright. A perfect half-moon had risen in Aquarius. Tannhauser – as was his habit whenever the bounds of augury could be stretched – read into this sequence a favourable omen. Speaking for himself, he would need it.

All about the bailey the remnant of the garrison bedded down, each man pondering the knowledge that this would be his last night on Earth. The crackle of the bonfire died away and a balmy silence enfolded the two good friends, a silence in which they could believe themselves the last living men in the world. They linked their arms in the darkness and this was a boundless comfort to both, and Le Mas sang a Psalm of David into his beard and tears rolled down the scars on his face as he made his peace with God. After a while, the brandy and opium wrought their spell. Le Mas fell asleep. Now alone, or so it felt, and swaddled in darkness, Tannhauser gazed at the firmament and slipped into a blissful trance wrought by stars and eternity.

And in that trance he wondered just how it might be, that in a Universe as beautiful as this one some room had been put aside for the likes of him.

SATURDAY 23 JUNE 1565

Saint Elmo's Fall

TANNHAUSER COUNTED HIMSELF fortunate to have indulged the comfort of opium the night before. Its soothing effect lingered on and made the task of keeping his nerve seem almost plausible. This advantage was welcome, for the Turks today forwent their usual bombardment. The dragon-mouthed muzzles of the siege guns gaped from heights in silence. Saint Elmo's last battle would be settled toe-to-toe with cold steel.

Forty-odd professed knights of the Italian and three French Langues, a hundred or so Spanish *tercios* and two hundred stalwart Maltese squared up on the gore-blackened stones of the southern breach. Juan de Guaras and Captain Miranda, both too badly injured to stand, commandeered the chairs from which Tannhauser and Le Mas had been roused and they'd had themselves strapped into the seats. The chairs and their mutilated occupants were ferried to the top of the embankment and there they both sat, swords across their laps, and watched the Turkish army on the slopes above. There, janissaries, dervishes, Iayalars, Sipahis and Azebs waited for the cries of their imams and the blast of the horns.

Since honour had long been banished from the field, some

savage and primeval pride must have directed the final Turkish assault, for they ignored the unmanned walls, which they might have escaladed with ease, and the abandoned gatehouse, and the numerous lesser breaches through which they might now have swarmed unimpeded. Instead, the entire army, with a deafening assertion of Allah's greatness, foamed roaring down the mountainside like some river provoked to boil by the End of Days. Its only mark was the bloody gantlet where so many of their comrades had died – and where the Christian devils even now sang hymns and jeered them on. The disparity in their numbers was almost comic. Yet the defenders would not go down without shoving the thorn a final inch through Mustafa Pasha's side. To Tannhauser's astonishment, as he watched the unhinged bloodfest from a squint in the fore of the keep, the Religion held their ground for over an hour.

Sword and dagger, half-pike and mace. Bellows of rage and agony. Heartfelt prayers. Luigi Broglia, Lanfreducci, Guillaume de Quercy, Juan de Guaras, Aiguabella, Vigneron, all of them bathed in blood in the ferocity that bloomed around the chairs. Tannhauser saw Le Mas's halberd carving bright arcs in the early light, and his heart went out to him. If not for the heady tranquillity bequeathed by the poppy in his gut, Tannhauser would have been hard pressed not to join him. He ached to do so. But the die was cast once more. There would be no Glory for him today; just survival or an ignominious death. If the latter, he was at least dressed for the part.

He was naked but for his boots, already long tattered, which he'd cut down to six inches below the knee and rubbed down with ashes and charcoal. They now looked looted from a corpse. Nicodemus's golden bangle, with the inscription that now mocked him, but which he was loath to abandon, he'd clasped around his ankle and bound up with rags. In the other boot he stowed the last of his Stones of Immortality. He'd caked his torso with the filth in which the fort abounded. Although he'd not the benefit of a mirror, he was confident of looking every inch a heathen slave. Le Mas, closer to the Divine than he'd ever been and with much expression of mirth, had assured him so when they bade each other farewell. Le Mas, engaging with the spirit of Tannhauser's deception, had had the Turkish prisoners penned in the stables and shot dead, rather than knifed as might have been expected. Now Tannhauser's bullet wound would further validate his pretence to be the only survivor.

Tannhauser needed just one more prop for his performance and as he studied the last-ditch stand – there it was. A half-armoured figure reeled down the embankment and crashed among the rubble in a rise of dust. He rolled prone and dragged off his helm, as if he were drowning, then rose to his hands and knees and vomited blood. He crawled a few feet, back towards the battle, then slumped to his elbows. He raised his right hand to his forehead, then to his breast and his left shoulder, then collapsed on his face without moving with his sign of the Cross incomplete.

Tannhauser turned to go, then heard the shrill calls of the marshalling horns and looked back. To the blood-elated cheers of the Christian remnant, the Turks were withdrawing. It was only to re-form for the last push, to be sure; but even so. Le Mas had held the breach one last time. No more than ninety men yet stood alive on the gantlet. Most of the Spanish and Maltese were dead, the core of knights preserved by their superior armour. As they gathered in a phalanx around the chairs of de Guaras and Miranda to await the end, Tannhauser ran down the stairs and into the bailey.

He'd awoken with a dappling of fever on his brow and his legs felt unsteady and the wound in his back burned like hot charcoal. He stumbled to the dead knight, still propped up by his knees, and he joined him in the dust and hauled him up by his arms. The head flopped back. It was Agoustin Vigneron. Stabbed in the throat. In conception this had seemed simple. The execution was more taxing. He grabbed the corpse under the crotch and shunted him over his shoulder, the cuirass stripping the skin from his sunburned neck. He clenched the dead thighs tight and planted one foot solid and pushed himself upright. He heard the roar of combat and a mighty clash of colliding steel nearby. The river would soon swamp the rampart and flood down into the fort. He staggered across the bailey towards the stables.

The burden of corpse and metal almost broke him. His skull pounded fit to burst and his legs were tubes of jelly and his chest wheezed and bile scalded his throat. Only fear gave him the strength to reach his goal. He let the corpse fall from his back in the stable doorway and fell to the cobbles. When he caught his wind he looked up.

Inside the stable a swathe of tangled and naked dead lay heaped upon the straw. A mere dozen among thousands. But these unarmed and wretched few had been murdered for his sake alone. He stilled the prick of conscience, for conscience was the truest madness here. He turned away and looked across the yard and saw the end. The tall white hats of the janissaries closed with the men in steel. In a frenzied terminal ecstasy of gore and blades, the chairs of the brave went over and Fort Saint Elmo's fell.

Broglia. De Guaras. Miranda. Guillaume. Aiguabella. Men with whom he'd fought and drunk fine brandy. Lives committed to war at last swept into eternity by its tide. Le Mas was torn to pieces, his severed limbs brandished aloft. Moments later his great head appeared, bobbing on the point of a spear.

Tannhauser needed see no more. He looked down at his chest. He too was slaked in blood. He felt more of the same dribbling down his back. He looked at Vigneron sprawled at his knees. Tannhauser drew the dead man's sword and dropped it nearby. He drew a dagger from the dead man's belt and with its tip dug the poultice from the wound in his hip and freshened the edges until it bled. He drove the dagger into Vigneron's neck. Then he draped himself across the corpse in a sculpture of struggle.

He closed his eyes, his hand on the hilt, and unconsciousness drifted towards him. And with it came pictures. Of Amparo and the boy, and of Carla and Bors and Buraq, and of Sabato Svi. His mind began to slip away and he hauled it back. He opened his eyes and saw the tanned complexion of Agoustin Vigneron's face, the bristles in his nostrils, the boils on his chin, the lifeless sheen of his eyeballs. He inhaled the yeasty stench of weeks of privation, of urine evacuated by death and so rectified by thirst it was almost black. He felt the obscene resistance of the dense dead flesh that pillowed his cheek. Tannhauser had crawled through the bowels of human darkness and here now he lay in its excrement, fighting druggy sleep on a comrade's corpse with spilled blood cooling on his skin, surrounded by the foetor of the still rotting dead in a charnel house of murdered slaves, and pretending to be that which he was not. And yet what was he not? Everything a man might hope to be except alive. He told himself to think Turk. To dream of Old Stambouli. To pray in the language of the Prophet. He heaved for breath and sang, and his parched and cracking voice was as hollow as the breast of desolation.

'*By the winds that winnow with a winnowing, And those that bear the burden of the rain, And those that glide with ease upon the sea, And those Angels who scatter blessings by Allah's command, Verily that which you are promised is surely true. And verily Judgement and Justice will come to pass –*'

Footsteps bored through his raving and a rough hand seized his shoulder. He rolled free, taking the dagger with him, and with his last strength rose up on one knee, one foot coiled to spring, letting madness whisper in his ear, his teeth bared, the blade outflung.

A pair of janissaries, lean and young, stood over him, scimitars raised, the heat of victory upon them. Yet at the sight of him they stepped back and the younger reached out a hand and pushed the sword of his companion down. They took in Vigneron's corpse and the littered Moslem dead. They saw the Sacred Wheel of the Fourth Agha Boluks tattooed on Tannhauser's arm in dark blue ink. They saw the twin-bladed sword of Dhu'l Fiqar in red. They saw his circumcised organ. On his thigh they saw the *surah* of *Al-Ikhlas: He is Allah, the One. Allah-us-Samad, the Eternal, Absolute. He begetteth not, nor is He begotten. And there is none like unto Him*. Comradeship filled the janissaries' eyes.

'Peace be upon you, brother,' said the younger man.

The elder said, 'By Allah's will, you're among friends at last.'

Their swords came up at a sudden sound behind him and Tannhauser turned. Old Stromboli emerged from the stable's shadows. He had an axe in his hands. He saw Tannhauser and gaped. Tannhauser sprang as if crazed and covered the ground between them in two lupine strides and he stabbed Stromboli in the heart and watched him die. He let the old man fall. He turned to the young lions. They looked at him with renewed respect.

Tannhauser said, '*Allahu Akabar*.' Then he fell back to the ground.

THEY WRAPPED HIM in a blue silk cloak and fed him honeyed tea and dried beef, and he sat on a giant gun stone in the shade and watched as the Turks slaked their anger on those few of the Christian defenders still breathing.

Nine knights had been taken alive, de Quercy and Lanfreducci among them. They were stripped stark naked and forced to kneel in the yard. They sang Psalms of David until horns and drums announced Mustafa Pasha's arrival. He crossed the ditch on a pearl-grey horse and looked at them only once before ordering them all beheaded. One by one their raised voices died until Lanfreducci sang alone, and the executioner's sword hummed, and his body splashed forward into the crimson lake that stained the yard. The wounded splayed in the open outside the hospital were speared where they lay. The chaplains were dragged from the chapel and butchered like hogs on the blood-soiled steps. The uncounted wounded within, by the clamour of their screams and orisons, were slaughtered where they lay on the chancel floor.

So ubiquitous were the dead on this scorched acre, so monotonous had the sight of atrocity become, that Tannhauser felt little beyond a dulled sense of shame. Even when they brought out Jurien de Lyon, and hacked off his limbs and privates and cleaved his skull, his horror was merely abstract. Jurien, who had sewn Bors's face back complete, whose vast and sacred knowledge of Healing could not be redeemed from fifty thousand minds thereabouts, whose fingers held skills that entire nations could not muster: all that extinguished in a spasm of triumphant malice. When all such extinctions were multiplied, even by the few that Tannhauser had seen of the many in which the world overbrimmed, one could see the clock of civilisation running backwards. Aye, and old Stromboli too had been a wonderful cook.

The heads of the knights were gathered and spiked on top of palings on the seaward walls, where observers from Sant' Angelo might see them. The banner of Saint John was hauled down, and stomped into the dirt and drenched in urine, and the standard of the Sultan fluttered up the halyard in its place. It was over and it was done.

Despite the heat of the day Tannhauser shivered and he pulled his cloak about his shoulders. His ague was now beyond doubt and rising within him. The wound in his back was a red-hot lobster crawling beneath his skin. His blood was poisoned. A throbbing circlet of fever tightened round his skull. The possibility crossed his mind that he'd escaped a glorious exit only to rot on a filth-soaked palliasse and die of plague. He winkled his last opium pill from his boot and washed it down with tepid water. He threw himself upon fate. Then fate rode through Saint Elmo's gates to greet him.

'*Ibrahim*?'

Tannhauser looked up from the gun stone and the movement

caused the sky to spin above him. The sun had crested the wall and blinded his vision and sweat poured stinging into his eyes. He pushed back the sudden blackness that loomed in his skull and wiped his face. He raised his hand for shade and blinked and saw a knot of men on horseback and the yellow banner of the Sari Bayrak, oldest of the Sultan's cavalry. He rose to his feet and swayed and sat back down. A silhouette dismounted and a face loomed over his own. A face polished and austere and engraved by the decades that had passed since last he'd seen it. But the eyes were unchanged in their refinement and compassion afflicted them still. A hand reached out and scraped the hair back from Tannhauser's face.

'It is you,' said Abbas bin Murad.

'Father,' Tannhauser mumbled.

He stood again and spiralled towards the ground and was captured by Abbas's arms. He heard Abbas give commands. He tried to speak but failed and strong hands lifted him into a saddle. He held on with his thighs. He craned his head, searching for Abbas. Instead of Abbas he saw something else, indistinctly, as if in a dream. He saw a gang of Algerians emerge from the postern to the wharf. One of them held a rope. The end of the rope was tied round Orlandu's neck. Tannhauser stared, then pointed, wheeling his head to find his saviour.

Abbas appeared, mounted, beside him, a steadying hand extended to his shoulder. 'You're sick,' said Abbas. His expression was grave. 'You will come with me.'

'The boy,' said Tannhauser. 'There.'

Abbas ignored these ravings and ordered two of his men to take him to his tent. Tannhauser twisted in the saddle and looked about. Contrary to his hopes, Orlandu was no product of the opium or the fever either one. There the boy stood, blood in his eye, and leashed like a dog by corsairs. Tannhauser pointed again and almost fell from the saddle. Abbas grabbed his arm. Tannhauser groped the mist of his pyrexia for a stratagem that might work. He didn't find one. The mist thickened and his vision turned red. He grabbed at the horse's mane.

He said, 'I was thirsty and the boy gave me water.'

Then the sun went out and all turned black and empty.

SUNDAY 24 JUNE 1565
THE FEAST OF SAINT JOHN THE BAPTIST

Castel Sant' Angelo – Auberge of England

Oliver Starkey prayed for La Valette and for his own contaminate soul. The reason lay in the clotted and hairy heap piled up by Sant' Angelo's cavalier. Even as he prayed yet more severed heads – human heads – were tipped from bulging sacks on to the roof like the crop of an obscene harvest. The lips of the slain were blue and drawn back from the teeth in rictal agony. The whites of sightless eyes bulged dry and lustreless in the sun. With dire jests and a debate over the most suitable charge of powder, the gunners grabbed the sundered heads by their beards and proceeded to cram them four and five at a time down the muzzles of the cannon. There were dozens of them, dozens of heads, more than Starkey could bring himself to count, and he wondered what penitent impulse it was that forced him to bear witness to this crime. Surely one, at least, who considered it so should be here; for just as surely, Jesus wept in witness too.

Dawn had seen four wooden boards washed up on L'Isola's shores. No one knew how many more had been washed out to sea. Crucified to each board was the nude and headless corpse of a Knight of the Order. A cross had been hacked into the flesh of each pallid breast. Lamentation flourished and, too, a poisonous hatred for the Turk. La Valette received this news as he emerged from daybreak mass. On seeing the mutilated corpses, tears of rage and grief had filmed his eyes. Deaf to Starkey's counsel, he'd ordered every Turkish prisoner captured since the siege began to be hauled out from the dungeons and decapitated.

'All of them?' said Starkey.

La Valette said, 'Let judgement be administered by the people.'

This decree was made public and the Maltese rose to the call. The prisoners were dragged to the beach and there, with the zeal of the Devil's Own, the executioners swung their swords through hair and bone. Shackled Turks calling out to Allah were cursed to Hell's hottest reach as they were slain. Some fled, clanking, for the sea and were butchered in the surf like ravined game. Those who refused to kneel were hacked through the ankles and trodden down and beheaded with their faces in the sand. Stoical courage and pleas for mercy alike were met with scorn, for these were not men but Moslems, and this was the work of the Lord, and none among the killers doubted that God would smile on his work.

By the time all the cries were silenced, and the most tenacious sinews severed, and the corpses cast on the tide and the heads gathered up by their dripping locks and bagged, an immense burgundy stain befouled the strand and Starkey could not shake the sense that his soul was no less tainted.

The battery on Sant' Angelo's cavalier now belched behind him. A shower of smoking skulls, some flaming from the scalp and beard, exploded from the muzzles and arced across the bay towards the Turkish lines. Jeers of malice went with them. If Mustafa would dabble in atrocity, then let him take a lesson from masters of the trade. La Valette showed no further emotion. As Starkey watched the gunners swab the barrels, and the loaders grabbed more heads from the ghastly pile, he said, in Latin, '*And many shall rejoice in his birthday*.'

La Valette looked at him.

Starkey faltered under the gaze. He added, 'So said the Archangel Gabriel of John the Baptist.'

La Valette said, 'Many shall rejoice in the death of every Moslem on this island.'

From there, La Valette went down to the main piazza with his entourage and issued a proclamation to the throng, which declared that every Turkish captive from now on – once the torturers had done their work – would be surrendered to the people, without quarter, to be torn apart as they saw fit. Starkey watched as the populace cheered him to the echo and chanted his name and praised God. Then Starkey walked away. By an appeal to shocking savagery, a defeat had been transformed into some kind of victory. Though a victory over what, Starkey did not dare wonder. La Valette alone knew how to give them a chance to survive, Starkey didn't doubt it. But he thanked his Lord Jesus Christ that his own duty was to follow and not to lead.

Carla saw the barrage and thought the projectiles were incendiaries. On learning that the flying objects were burning human heads, a spectacle that in the normal course of her life she would have found impossible to believe, she discovered that she was disgusted but not surprised.

Cruelty and the grotesque were the normal course of life, now. If she was troubled by this realisation, it was because she'd never felt more fulfilled. War had condensed her universe to caring for other people and life had never had more meaning. It was not a meaning she could put into words. She was freed from absorption in her own small miseries and concerns. She knew, at last, that living was precious, rather than something to be endured. Anger and horror were futile; so too were victory or defeat. In a world of hatred and woe, she resolved to feel neither. Thy will be done. Jesus was in her heart and He loved her. This was all she needed to know.

She saw the monstrous barrage as she made her way from the infirmary to the auberge. Father Lazaro had lent her tweezers and a scalpel to remove the sutures from Bors's face. She met the latter in the street, into which he had blundered on hearing the news of the display. He was gratified to see a second volley – indeed, he let loose a halloo of joy – and for fear of missing a third insisted on fetching a chair so that she could perform her task outside. Since the light there was much better and the task fine, Carla didn't object.

The sutures were buried in a thick scab that bisected Bors's face in a crusty brown diagonal. The symmetry that the surgeon had restored to his features was remarkable, and by his own account Bors would not swap the scar for a ruby ring. By paring the scab back she was able to cut the sheepgut threads, but to pull them out required more strength than she was happy to use. After a number of ineffectual tugs, Bors said, 'Heave away.' She did so and the first stitch slipped free. Bors barely flinched.

'Five Maltese swimmers escaped from Saint Elmo's yesterday,' he said. 'They witnessed the final moments.'

Carla tackled the second stitch. Her hopes for Mattias and Orlandu, like her guilt that they'd met their end through her dereliction, were stored in a deep place in her heart that she'd chosen, for the present, not to visit.

'I have spoken with three of them,' continued Bors, a little aggrieved that she hadn't shown more curiosity. 'No one has any news of Mattias or your boy. Yet none saw either of them die.'

'Then there is hope,' she allowed. 'And we must pray that they have endured.'

'If any man alive could intrigue his way out of that bloodbath, it's Mattias. The man is a fox. But the girl has taken it hard,' said Bors.

Carla nodded. Amparo's moods were storm-tossed. In some

ways she'd reverted to the wild and violated creature Carla had found in the forest – withdrawn, mercurial, lost to God. Carla had persuaded Lazaro to let Amparo work in his physic garden. She hoped she could persuade Amparo to do so.

'Did you know she went to visit him?' said Bors. 'Ouch.'

A trickle of blood ran down his cheek as Carla let slip the knife. She said, 'Amparo went to Saint Elmo's?'

'Swam across the bay in the night – without a stitch on,' said Bors. 'And I'll admit, that of all the wondrous events I've seen since I got here, that was the most agreeable.'

Carla imagined Mattias and Amparo making love. Her stomach lurched, despite her higher intentions. As if to further feed the snake of jealousy, her pelvis contracted with desire and she felt her cheeks burn red. She wasn't as full of God's Grace as she liked to think, then. She tried to bite her tongue, but failed.

'You didn't stop her?' she said.

Bors looked at her. He was a man who wasn't ashamed to enjoy the sight of burning heads flying through the sky. To ask such a man a question was to ask for truth in its bluntest form. She wondered if the redness she felt on her cheeks were visible.

Bors said, 'Such news is hard for you to bear. I understand. But the chances remain excellent, and improve by the day, that we're all going to die on this rock. Who, then, would be so mean of spirit as to stand in the way of so fine and unlikely a romance?'

'I haven't stood in its way,' said Carla.

Bors smiled, with great warmth. 'And it does you credit. For what it's worth, Mattias is mightily torn between the two of you lovelies. So, between you and me, the game is not over.'

The anxieties, the anguish – the hopes – that she thought she'd banished returned in an instant. She didn't want to compete with Amparo. She wouldn't. Yet. She wanted Mattias.

'Do you truly believe he's still alive?' she said.

'Though I'd be making the wager alone,' said Bors, 'I'd lay money on it.'

The guns on the castle boomed and Bors leapt to his feet to watch the skulls smoke by. He shook his head in admiration, then settled back into the chair and picked up his thread.

'Mind you,' he said, 'there is a darker side to that coin. If Mattias and your boy are still alive, they're in the hands of Moslem fiends.'

THURSDAY 5 JULY 1565

The Waterfront – the Kalkara Gate – the Venerable Council

AMPARO SLEPT ON the waterfront beneath the stars. The sound of the sea soothed her. It lulled her into dreams of Tannhauser's forge and of his hands and lips on her body and of his breath on her cheek and his moans in her ear, as did too the balmy heat of the night and the cold of stone on which she lay.

During the days she tended Lazaro's physic garden and found a patch where the wild roses grew. Their buds were mashed with sage flowers, myrtle and horehound in one of his many ingenious salves. She otherwise avoided human society as much as she could. She spent many hours grooming Buraq and she rode him bareback round the paddock and soothed his fears when the cannon crashed. These days most of her conversation was with Tannhauser's golden horse, and she could not have wished for a gentler or lovelier companion.

The movement of the Turkish guns to the Corradino Heights, the impending attack on the Borgo and L'Isola, the litany of death and suffering, the tales of valour endlessly repeated, the intrigues of the knights, the faithlessness of the Viceroy, the fathomless evil of the Turks – none of these things concerned her.

People imagined they mattered and, more astounding to her yet, that their talking about them mattered, too, and might even change them. She found their chatter dreary, their recitation of woes without purpose, and their ponderous attempts to involve her in their lives a drain on her energy and spirit. The price of their company was high. It made no sense to pay for what she didn't want. People sucked her dry. She was happy to stand outside their realm. Her own interior, her communion with wild rose buds, Buraq's affection and beauty, all these were far more compelling and gave her strength. Yet others viewed her solitude as a malady, as if they had not troubles enough of their own to attend. So Amparo remained aloof and without regrets. It had always been thus. Let them think her a dolt, as long as they left her alone.

She awoke to the sound of oars and sat up. A mist the colour of milk lay over the water, lit as if from within by the waxing moon. She watched longboats glide through the vapour one by one and head into Kalkara Creek. A dozen at least and all of them empty but for skeleton crews of rowers. They slid through the nebulous dark with a quiet urgency, the disembodied oarsmen faceless and mute, like traffickers in emptiness ferrying no one into nowhere. Then the last boat rounded the point and melted into the mist and all trace of their passing was gone.

Gone, leaving no more of an imprint than she would leave on this world, she thought, and the thought brought her comfort. Only in worlds other than this one did things last forever. Her night with Tannhauser belonged to such a world. It was and then it was not and yet would always be. Only moments of beauty enjoyed immortality. Everything else combined – all the grand vanities for which so many laboured and died – could claim not even the magic of a daydream. She lay back down on the rock, the boats forgotten. She stared at the teeming firmament. Would the stars in their courses also one day disappear? She'd ask Tannhauser, when next they met, for despite bleak prospects, she knew that they would. Somehow. Somewhere.

Bors had volunteered for the night watch at Kalkara Gate. Since the contessa's pitiless scolding for his – admittedly excess – indulgence, he'd forgone the succour of opium and sleep had since deserted him entire. Even brandy by the bottle proved poor surrogate. And it went to show that if virtue was rarely its own reward, it was sometimes the source of others, for if he'd been lying besotted in his bed, he'd have missed the latest turn in this remarkable tale.

A hot, wet wind had blown a mist in from Tunisia and the first he knew of the excitement was a convoy of sparsely manned longboats which threaded their way down the creek and suddenly swung for the opposite shore, which was only six hundred feet distant across Kalkara Bay, but shrouded in fog.

Next, a party carrying torches marched through the streets and at their head walked La Valette. Bors checked the match on his musket and blew the coal bright. The sally gate below creaked open and he watched the party exit and head to the shore. Starkey, Romegas, Del Monte and bailiffs galore. As if the Pope himself were expected any moment.

Then the longboats loomed through the mist and, as if returning from some kindred netherworld beyond the veil of this one, they proved full to the gunnels with armed and armoured men. Hundreds of them. As each phantom band disembarked, their boat turned back across the creek and returned with yet more men and their baggage. The fresh troops poured into the Borgo through the Kalkara Gate.

Bors slipped down the steps and bearded one of the new men passing by. An Extrameño called Gomez. Four galleys sent by Garcia de Toledo had sailed down from Messina and some days before had disembarked this precious relief, under Melchior De Robles, on the north-west coast of Malta. They'd laid up in Mdina and sent a messenger to La Valette, and on the happy chance of the summer fog had marched beneath its cover for the Borgo, skirting south of the Turkish camp and crossing the slopes of Monte San Salvatore to the farside bank of Kalkara Bay. Daring fellows all, they were forty-two Knights of the Order, twenty Italian 'gentleman adventurers', plus three Germans and two English of similar ilk, fifty seasoned artillerymen and six hundred Spanish Imperial Infantry. It was hardly the twenty thousand they'd been hoping for, but La Valette embraced them for the heroes that they were.

A new figure emerged through the gate, a big man who stood for a moment in the torchlight as if to savour his return. Bors's eyes were drawn by the exquisite quality of his armour – a fluted cuirass in black enamel. He wore it over white monastic robes. A sword rather than a rosary was belted round his waist. Something in his posture and the set of the shoulders, in the carriage of his giant head, made Bors's blood run cold. He wore a magnificent black salet, with nose and cheek guards in the old Venetian style, and its vault was crested with a relief of Christ on the Cross. This helm he now removed and held beneath his arm and he genuflected to the cobbles and crossed himself and gave thanks. Lethal as this company was, he looked like a leopard running with the wolves, and as he rose back to his feet his eyes gleamed black as marbles in the flames. He took a deep breath and cast his gaze about, like a man inspecting a soon-to-be-conquered kingdom.

'God's wounds,' muttered Bors to himself.

A new figure emerged from the gate behind the first, leaner, more delicate, yet as deadly as a serpent in his poise. He too removed his helm to reveal the depraved mouth – the sensual yet empty eyes – which Bors remembered well from the Messina dock. Anacleto scanned the walls and Bors turned away and climbed up the steps to the parapet.

Ludovico Ludovici was back. It was time for the mice to tread softly.

* * *

THAT NIGHT LUDOVICO met with La Valette and all the Bailiffs of the Venerable Council. Also present was Melchior De Robles, the commander of the relief, who was not a member of the Religion but a Knight of the Spanish Order of Santiago. Ludovico had won the latter's confidence on the voyage from Messina. It was Robles who made it clear to the Venerable Council that Ludovico had persuaded Toledo to send the reinforcement.

The mood of the Council reflected the state of the town, which was grim. Overcrowding was extreme and exacerbated by the knights' demolition of a swathe of houses for defensive purposes. A colony of tents had been established for the refugees, on L'Isola, wherein the newly located Turkish siege guns were wreaking havoc. Food was not a problem. Each inhabitant received three one-pound loaves per day, and the reserves of grain, oil, salted meat and fish remained vast. However, despite filling the cisterns beneath Sant' Angelo and storing forty thousand barrels, the water supply was approaching a critical level, all wells and springs being located outside the walls. Shaving, washing and laundry had been prohibited and those who'd broken this rule, most of them women, had been flogged in the piazza. Among the bleating and the gossip of the multitude, violent disorder had flared at the water distribution points, and these riots had only been stalled by providing a supply of prisoners on whom the mob could vent their discontent. Certain of the louder mouthed grumblers had been birched to the gallows and hanged.

Despite these efforts they would shortly face the gravest extremity of want. What water there was had to be preserved for the garrison. A diviner had been deployed and was digging holes all over both peninsulas. If he failed, La Valette explained, it would be necessary to expel a large section of the little people outside the walls, to fling themselves upon the mercies of the Turk. Since in this circumstance the risk of rebellion would be great, it was a decision he would take when left with no other choice. But he wanted the Council, and them alone, to know that they might have to turn their weapons on the populace.

No one protested. Admiral Pietro Del Monte, a sturdy, powerful man with a beaky nose and velvet eyes, sat through these exchanges in silence, casting the occasional glance at Ludovico. Like La Valette, Del Monte was a study in old age held at bay by a life of action. La Valette caught one of Del Monte's glances and turned to Ludovico.

'Fra Ludovico,' he said, 'what is your reading of Garcia de Toledo's intentions?'

Ludovico paused, as if to gather his thoughts, then answered in the calm bass tones that he knew would elicit rapt attention. 'At present no reinforcement of the size you dream of exists.' He spread his hands in an appeal to reason. 'Bear in mind that the recruitment, transport and disposition of such an army, in which tasks Toledo is vigorously engaged, will represent the largest Mediterranean adventure by a Christian power since his predecessor attempted the capture of Jerba.'

He said this innocently as if, unlike every other at the table, he was unaware that La Valette had been one of the advocates of that luckless expedition. La Valette made no comment.

Ludovico continued, 'A fleet is gathering in Seville to bring four thousand troops, and men from every garrison in Italy are being dispatched with the greatest urgency. I understand that it will take some time to muster them. Weeks at least.'

A murmur of dismay rippled about the table. La Valette stilled it with a hand.

'You would be mistaken to read into this delay any sign of conspiracy,' said Ludovico. 'As pledge of his good intentions, Toledo has sent his own son, Federico, to fight alongside us.'

Federico had accompanied the relief; Ludovico had persuaded him in person to join the cause. The pressure on Toledo was now private as well as political. Nods of approval, vigorous from the Spaniards, grudging from the French, went around the table.

'I can also assure you,' Ludovico went on, 'that His Holiness Pope Pius is making every effort on our behalf.' He noted that his use of 'us' and 'our' passed without any demurrers. 'The Holy Father has urged all right Italian gentlemen to join the Order's colours, in particular, the Knights of Santo Stefano.'

A number of contemptuous snorts were unsuccessfully stifled. The Order of Santo Stefano, crudely modelled on the Religion, had been established only four years before by the Pope and his distant relative, Cosimo de Medici. In this company they were regarded, not altogether fairly, as a gang of bloated plutocrats barely able to climb aboard their horses.

'Perhaps they can send us some paintings,' growled Del Monte.

There was a round of welcome laughter and Ludovico smiled along with them. The moment was ripe to play the first of the several instruments with which he'd been equipped, before leaving Rome, by Pope Pius and Michele Ghisleri. From his lap he produced a leather satchel bearing the papal arms and handed it to La Valette, who recognised at once the round lead seal that signified an Apostolic letter of the highest significance.

'When the right moment comes,' said Ludovico, 'His Holiness hopes that this will prove more formidable than cannon.'

La Valette broke the lead seal to a breathless silence and removed the vellum within. The letter's red wax bore the imprint of the Fisherman's Ring. He broke this seal too and unfolded the letter. The Council waited while he read it. La Valette, visibly moved, indeed too moved to comment, passed the document to Oliver Starkey, who sat at his right hand. Starkey scanned the Latin text and cleared his throat.

'It is a Bull, promulgated June eighth, which grants plenary indulgence of all sins to all Christians who fall in our war against the Moslems – brethren of the Order, soldiers, slaves, civilians, women. All.'

Murmurs circulated the table. The Bull meant that every man, woman and child who died in the battle for Malta was granted absolute remission of all temporal punishment for their sins, whatever the latter might be. For a people more than familiar with hardship, torture and suffering of every kind, the knowledge that in the hereafter they'd spend not an hour enduring the rigorous toils of Purgatory – as opposed to the centuries that each expected as his lot – would have an effect on morale beyond all reckoning.

'His Holiness in his wisdom spoke truer than we can know,' said La Valette. 'This is worth five thousand men, though I trespass to put a price on it.'

He turned his iron-grey eyes on Ludovico and Ludovico knew that whatever expectations the Grand Master had harboured of his mission to Rome, he had exceeded them.

'At the right moment, as you say, this will restore faith and courage to the faintest heart.' La Valette stood up. 'Let us each acknowledge that in helping to effect the relief, and in delivering at such hazard this precious Blessing from Our Holy Father in Rome, we owe Fra Ludovico a debt we'll be hard pressed to repay.'

The other Bailiffs rose and dipped their heads towards Ludovico. Ludovico stood and humbly returned their bows. He bowed to La Valette last. 'Your Excellency,' he said, 'I have not returned to Malta to conduct the affairs of the Vatican or of the Holy Office, but rather to fight. I have Our Holy Father's special dispensation to do so.'

Someone hammered the table in approval.

La Valette said, 'We're honoured that you should make such a spiritual sacrifice.'

If irony was intended by this comment, no one but Ludovico seemed to hear it. He turned to the Admiral of the Fleet and head of the Italian Langue, Pietro Del Monte. 'I therefore beg your permission, Admiral, to be quartered with your soldiers and to serve in their ranks.'

'With the soldiers?' Del Monte shook his head. 'As a son of Naples, you are invited to berth with the knights at the Auberge of Italy, and most welcome.'

After the Council was adjourned Ludovico accompanied Del Monte to the Auberge of Italy. He declined the offer of a private cell, insisting instead on a strip of flagstone in one of the dormitories, where some hundred and forty Italian knights were berthed. He learned that over thirty of their fellows had died at Saint Elmo. He was indifferent to luxury, and in the dormitories information would be plentiful. As Del Monte took his leave, Ludovico detained him for a moment and played his second card.

He showed Del Monte a silver chain from which hung a silver cylinder, the size of a finger, and showed him the ingenious screw which secured the cap. The silver was engraved with the Cross and the Lamb of God, the Baptist's symbols. The interior was padded with kidskin, which protected a slender crystal phial nestling within. The phial, on removal, was seen to contain a quantity of dark umber residue at the bottom.

'I'm instructed to deliver this personal gift to you and the Langue of Italy from Cardinal Michele Ghisleri, who prays hourly for your safe deliverance and trusts that this Sacred Relic – duly attested by the most eminent and exalted authorities – may afford you protection and deliverance in the days to come.'

Del Monte took the phial in his sea-weathered hand as if afraid his mildest touch would shatter the glass.

Ludovico said, 'It is a drop of the Blood of Saint John the Baptist.'

Del Monte's eyes filled and he fell to his knees and his hands shook as he pressed the phial of Holy Blood to his lips and prayed. Never was true Devotion more sincerely embodied. The sight gave Ludovico satisfaction. Del Monte's favour was certain and though the man didn't know it – and never would – he already formed the foundation stone of Ludovico's plan. These first steps in the intrigue had been neatly taken. Yet much else remained. Foremost was the task of establishing his fitness to join the Order.

And that required battle.

* * *

On the day following the arrival of the small relief force, Mustafa Pasha sent an envoy to sue for peace. The terms were identical to those that the Religion had accepted at the siege of Rhodes and were as generous as possible short of a Turkish withdrawal. If La Valette would surrender possession of the island at once, then he and all his knights were guaranteed a safe passage to Sicily, with their arms, relics, standards and honour intact. The lives of the population would be spared and they would become the subjects of Suleiman Shah and as such enjoy his protection, including the freedom to worship any deity in any manner they chose. For any number of good reasons, any intelligent and peace-loving man would have grabbed this offer with both hands. La Valette listened with the appropriate courtesy. Then he ordered that the envoy be taken to the gallows at the Provençal Gate and hanged.

PART III

THE WINNOWING WINDS

SUNDAY 15 JULY 1565

Fortress of Saint Michel – L'Isola

LUDOVICO STOOD ON the bastion of the Fortress of Saint Michel and listened to the unhallowed wail of the call to prayer. Devils in thrall to the rantings of a desert lunatic. By the standards of his own erudition he knew little of Islam, but more than enough to recognise a creed that was antithetical to higher reason and designed to excite and beguile the most primitive minds. As such it would no doubt continue to find a large constituency among the lower races. Yet as long as it could be contained to the barren lands in which it thrived, history would consign it to irrelevance – or at worst to the role of a shackle on the stride of mankind.

Ludovico's informers had told him everything that had taken place here in his absence. Mattias Tannhauser had died at Fort Saint Elmo. Tannhauser's oafish confederate, Bors, was a dog to be left sleeping. The story of the boy Tannhauser had tracked down, and who had also perished, had caused Ludovico anguish. More than he could have imagined. He'd fathered a son. Where he might have expected shame, he felt pride. Where indifference, a penetrating sadness. The boy was an abstraction; yet he stalked Ludovico's mind. So did Carla. Ludovico had made no attempt to seek her out. He feared the power she wielded over his heart and thereby his will; and larger priorities loomed, not least this day. From a quarter-mile distant, in the pitch-dark shadows of Santa Margharita, came the clatter of gear and the rumble of footfalls by the thousand. The Red Beast of Islam was awake and eager for blood.

Anacleto was beside him on the allure. Matchcords glowed along the ramparts, as if in clandestine observance of forbidden rites. Interspersed between the musketmen, the Knights of Saint John stood tenebrous and silent and grim, like the sentinels of some outpost in a land where entry was forbidden to all but the damned. Ludovico turned to watch the sunrise. Against the backdrop of the eastern sky, slashed with crimson cirri as if by knives, he saw a clutch of human silhouettes in the middle distance. There was a struggle. Then an emaciated figure was launched from the gallows on the foremost Bastion of Provence.

As if with that macabre spectacle something in the unseen enemy snapped, the darkness of the overlooking heights exploded with muzzle blasts and a hail of metal and stone lashed Saint Michel. A wedge of masonry and a cloud of rocky spicules swept a cluster of defenders into the yard. Fierce sounds buzzed in Ludovico's ears, which, never having been shot at before, he belatedly understood to be Turkish bullets skirring by. In the rising light he watched a lone and terrified jackhare flee its violated den in the Ruins of Bormula. It scampered for the fortress as if its gates might swing open to offer sanctuary. Then hard on the jackhare's dust and scarcely less swift, a bedlamite horde roared out from the purpled badlands, weapons and banners aloft, and baying like dogs in praise of their false god and his degenerate prophet.

Chain-shot, grape and ball erupted from the bores of the Christian guns. Yet the swathes of execution that scourged the Moslem ranks failed to slow their progress by an inch. They charged for Saint Michel as if for the door to Paradise, great scaling ladders strung out between them, grapple ropes draped about their shoulders and festooned with arms of every length and variety. To greet their arrival, cauldrons of simmering pig fat were manhandled to the machicolations. The Maltese porters spewed curses in their alien tongue, not only at the noxious fumes that scathed their eyes, but at those bleeding and dismembered comrades who squirmed underfoot, and on to whose caterwauling flesh scalding gobbets of the sizzling brew now spilled. The clamorous babel and the brimstone vapours and the anguished throes of the afflicted soon swamped whole sections of the allure, as if Hell had overflowed through some warp in the fabric of Creation and here had its escapees at last found refuge. Ludovico was a scholar of power and fear. In this his first battle, he witnessed the apotheosis of their union.

Mustafa Pasha's war engine had laboured towards this moment since the fall of Fort Saint Elmo. The vast architecture of siege guns and gabions had been dismantled piece by piece and hauled from the slopes of Monte Sciberras to those of Santa Margharita, Corradino and San Salvatore. Trenches hacked in the sandstone by his pioneers wound through the Bormula towards the walls of L'Isola; and beneath the ground mines advanced towards the citadel's foundations.

Because the entrance to Grand Harbour was denied to his fleet by the batteries of Castel Sant' Angelo, Mustafa had built a highway of greased timbers across the back of Monte Sciberras itself. Then his blackamoor slaves spent three days under the lash and – in a feat which filled the watching knights with wonderment and dismay – they dragged scores of Piyale's war galleys, one at a time, directly over the mountain from Marsamxett Bay. As they loomed above the rimrock the ships squealed down the tortured planking like beasts goaded into a shambles. The ropes and chains that retarded their descent hummed from the monstrous strain, some snapping with lethal force to scythe the labourers. And as the massive boats teetered down the scarp towards the waters flanking L'Isola, their keels smoked black in the tallow and flickered with gouts of flame as the grease ignited, as if this were a convoy from Hades, and its captains so impatient for cargo they'd come to take the living rather than the dead. Now eighty such vessels all told, and their deck cannon too, menaced the fortifications that lined the shore.

From every point of the compass, from the high ground and the harbour and Gallows Point, the two Christian peninsulas, the Borgo and L'Isola both, were thus entirely enfiladed by Turkish artillery and for the last ten days had been bombarded from dawn till dusk. Scores of women and children in the overcrowded town had been battered to death. Dozens of homes had been destroyed. Now every Turkish gun pounded Saint Michel.

Ludovico ignored the Turkish missiles and watched the carnage wreaked on the Moslem horde. He took his lead from Admiral Del Monte and Zanoguerra and Melchior De Robles, who observed the bouncing cannonballs, and the suffering strewn in their wake, with the grim sang-froid of pallbearers. Their bastion overlooked the harbour and Bormula both, and provided a panorama of the onslaught as it surged from land and sea. In the spearhead of the assault were the Algerians.

Hassem, Viceroy of Algiers and victor of the sieges of Oran and Mers-el-Kebir, had arrived the week before with five thousand *gazi* and the corsairs of El Louck Ali. Hassem led the attack from the heights of Margharita on Saint Michel's landward walls. His lieutenant, Kandelissa, led seaborne troops from the shores of the Marsa to the west. The latter came in scores of foaming longboats, oars and weapons flashing in the rise of the sun and imams chanting *surahs* from the prows.

The shore of L'Isola was defended by a palisade of stakes, lodged in the sea floor and linked by lengths of chain. The longboats rammed this barrier at maximum speed but the chains shrieked as the stakes keeled over and snarled the desperate vessels in a lethal web. The Christian *arquebuceros* on the overlooking walls raked the disembarking troops with volley after volley, yet the fanatics breasted the blood-swollen tide and ploughed through abandoned oars and corpses with a calm Ludovico found astounding. They dragged their ladders with them from the bullet-whipped spume and regrouped on the shore, and they interlocked their shields against the rain of shot and fire pipkins from above, and there on the beach the Star and Crescent was unfurled. Kandelissa rallied the faithful and a black flight of arrows arced through the dawn. On his word, and declaring God's greatness, the Algerians began their escalade of L'Isola's walls.

Ludovico was dressed in half-armour down to the cuisses, his diamond-black carapace – a gift worth a baron's ransom from Michele Ghisleri – was made by Filippo Negroli of Milan. It was so perfectly articulated that movement was hardly more difficult than in his robes. By his profession as a priest he was not allowed to shed blood, but Pope Pius had granted him a dispensation *in foro interno* to fight in this crusade. Like a plague of gargantuan vermin the Algerians mastered the ditch and infested the walls. Boiling oil sluiced smoking down the murder holes and scalded the clamouring infidels seething below. Pipkins of wildfire bloomed and the smell of burning flesh rose to choke the besieged. As the sun climbed towards its zenith and draped the furnace plain in a shimmering veil, Algerian battle standards fluttered atop the walls and God ushered Ludovico to his moment of Truth.

Ludovico was assigned to Knight Commander Zanoguerra, who led a flying section of a score of Spaniards and Italians held in reserve for the greatest crisis. Among them were three brethren who had special orders from Del Monte to watch for Ludovico's safety. Two were Italians: Bruno Marra of Umbria and a young Sienese novice called Pandolfo. The third, a fierce Castilian, was Escobar de Corro, seconded from the cavalry in Mdina. They all of them turned.

Beyond the grinding windmills just to the north a vast explosion and a fountain of limbs and flame consumed the seaward extremity of L'Isola's wall. Even here, at the opposite end of the peninsula, where the fortifications angled inland from the water to face the heights, fragments of airborne debris clattered against their harness. Only the explosion of a powder magazine could explain such vast destruction. They watched as a bastion and its curtain wall slid down through the dust cloud and into the water. Kandelissa's Algerian banners bobbed up the slope for the smoking ruins. Zanoguerra turned to his section.

'The time has come to perish for our Holy Faith.'

Zanoguerra led them along the seaward allure at a run. Their route lay through chaos and was as slippery as the floor of an abattoir. The angle and weight of the enemy's scaling ladders made them difficult to dislodge from the wall – when burdened by dozens of men, quite impossible – and all along the battlements Moslem and Christian panted in sweating embrace for possession of the walls.

Some paces ahead a Maltese militiaman paused while spearing a Moslem on the rampart's edge – held him piked through the chest and coughing blood, his Mohammedan comrades screeching from their perches on the scaling ladder behind him. The Maltese pulled down his breeches with one hand, and squatted, and with the speed and aplomb of a man clearing his throat he squirted forth a large and steaming turd. Then he whipped his breeches back up and returned to the task of shunting the steel spike deeper through his victim's lungs. As Ludovico got closer, another Algerian scrambled over the shoulders of his impaled comrade, who stubbornly clutched the pike shaft with both hands to prevent its withdrawal from his breast. The Maltese relinquished the pike but too late, for, as he drew his dagger, the Algerian gained the crenel and hacked him with a scimitar in the neck. The Maltese charged the Algerian about the knees, stabbing him with his dagger in the thighs, the crotch, the loins, bringing him down, crawling on top of him between the merlons, their heads bobbing above the sheer drop to the beach, each man grunting, wheezing, each man drenched in the blood of the other and both in that of the first – still speared, still perched on a slippery rung, still coughing scarlet spray, still fighting as he ripped off the Maltese's helm and pulled his hair and gouged at his eyes and jammed his thumbs into the gaping wound in his neck to tear it further open.

Ludovico lunged across the dying Maltese and ran his sword into the speared man's gaping mouth. He felt the snap of breaking teeth and the crunch of the sword as it penetrated skull or spine. His own spine shivered at the sensation. He withdrew the blade in a spout of bloody vomit and guided the gore-tarnished point beneath the body of the Maltese and rammed it deep into the Moslem flesh there pinned beneath. Anacleto joined him and thrust his sword through the melee. The tangle of squirming men convulsed in a grotesque and frantic spasm, and Ludovico stepped back, his foot detecting the moist surrender of the turd, then all three men, Algerians and Maltese alike, teetered over the edge and cartwheeled into space and plummeted down to swell the mass of bodies heaving below.

Ludovico caught his breath. In his chest – in his limbs, in his throat – a nameless ecstasy arose like the force of Revelation. He looked at Anacleto, who nodded once and turned away. Ludovico was a killer of men. The knowledge elated him.

He raised his face into the blinding light and thanked God.

They charged onwards.

Zanoguerra's elite closed with the Algerians at the breach and left the debris reeking with brains and limbs and bowels. The sails of the windmills cast intermittent bands of shade across the disputants and Ludovico threw himself into the fight. Ignoring the clatter of blades on his pauldrons and salet, he hacked and thrust two-handed, and smashed his steel-clad elbows into narrow brown faces, and stabbed with all his might into the fallen who crawled at his feet. He heaved on the dust-choked air and called on Saint Dominic for strength. Anacleto seemed to flank him on every side at once, darting between the scimitars and striking underhand blows at the otherwise engaged, and saving his master's life more times than he knew.

Zanoguerra exhorted the cowed militia from the ruins, stoking their spirits with invocations of Christ and urging them to lay down their lives for the Holy Religion. Then a musket ball bored him through the chest and he fell among the dead. As the jackals of the Prophet mobbed his corpse, panic swept again through the militia and they fled the bloody couloir to shelter among the mills. An exuberant hurrah swept the Moslem throng and they rallied and turned to surge once more up the rubble. Ludovico and Anacleto and the few Castilians left formed a cordon round their stricken commander, and a steadfast handful of Maltese joined their band athwart the rupture, and they chanted the Paternoster in readiness for the end:

'*Pater noster, qui es in caelis . . .*

'*. . . sanctificetur nomen tuum.*'

'*Thy kingdom come.*'

'*Thy will be done, on earth as it is in heaven.*'

'*Give us this day our daily bread . . .*'

'*. . . and forgive us our trespasses . . .*'

'*. . . as we forgive those who trespass against us . . .*'

'*Et ne nos inducas in tentationem:*'

'*. . . but deliver us from evil*'

'*Amen*'

'*Pater noster, qui es in caelis . . .*'

The Algerians stormed up the rock-strewn grade and Ludovico glanced down. For the first time he noticed that an arrow jutted out from his thigh. He had no memory of its impact. Anacleto cut a niche in the shaft with his sword and snapped it short. Ludovico thanked him.

'My God,' said Anacleto. 'Look.'

Ludovico turned. The refugee women of the tent town were climbing up the scree in a crowd. Their skirts were hitched round their waists and they scavenged weapons from the slain, and as they took to the ramparts and closed hand-to-hand with the fiends, Ludovico felt his eyes blur with tears. Beyond these Maltese Amazons, the Langue of Auvergne under Sieur de Quinay and a company of Spanish infantry crossed the bridge of boats spanning Galley Creek. Ludovico plunged back into the fray and tremendous slaughter was joined all along the shore.

It took two hours to drive Kandelissa and his *gazi* back to their boats. Those among the Moslems who surrendered were butchered in the sand. Those found half-drowned were knifed in the shallows by the Maltese women. With the news that their shorefront assault had failed the heart drained from the landward assault. Del Monte's Italians drove Hassem and his Algerians from the walls, then sallied out from the gates and massacred the laggards in the Ruins of Bormula. The sun sank behind Monte Sciberras in a multihued fantasy of saffron and pink, and as Ludovico watched the last of the Moslem boats pull out of range, flocks of vultures circled the corpse-glutted beach. In the waters surrounding the peninsula countless lifeless bundles bobbed in the surf and swimmers splashed out from the beach to harvest the floaters of their jewels and silver and gold. Thousands of Algerians would never see home. But the cost to the Religion had been high. In the dolorous exhaustion of the aftermath Del Monte appeared by Ludovico.

'Battle is a monstrous business,' Del Monte shrugged. 'But it gets beneath your skin.'

Ludovico looked at him. He felt light-headed, his vision slashed with instants of absolute blackness. He raised his scorched voice to an audible rasp. 'With your blessing, I wish to make my profession as a Knight of Saint John.'

His legs buckled and Del Monte held him upright. Ludovico rallied. He followed Del Monte's gaze and saw that his boots were filled to their tops with murky fluid and curdled blood. Del Monte called a younger knight and told him and Anacleto to take Ludovico to the hospital.

'As to your induction into the Convent,' said Del Monte, 'leave it to me.'

Of the walk to the hospital, across the bridge of boats, which heaved and rocked with the exodus of halt and maimed, he remembered little. To make better progress through the rabble his escorts laid about them with the flats of their swords. An unknown peasant woman gave him wine from a skin; he didn't know why. When they reached the Sacred Infirmary they found such chaos and confusion that his escorts refused to abandon him. They made to carry him the extra few hundred yards to the Auberge of Italy, or so, in his dazed condition, he vaguely grasped. As they turned, Ludovico stopped and fought against their hands.

There, across the gore-caked anteroom, he saw a woman bent over a convulsing mass of wounds, which he realised was a naked man that she pinned to a table. Her arms were crimson to the shoulders. Her hair had fallen loose and was plastered to the gouts that smeared her face. But neither this nor the carvings of exhaustion on her brow could mar her beauty, still less the tenderness of her countenance. He tried to call out but his throat failed him. He envied the man on the table. Jealousy pierced his bowels. And more than his bone-deep fatigue, more than his wounds, more than the ecstasy and horror that had taxed his soul, it was the sight of her that brought him to his knees.

It was Carla.

As the last of his senses slid from his grasp and the young knights let him fall, he realised that he loved her still, and an abyss as deep as eternity opened inside him. He loved her despite the years of virtue and discipline. He loved her despite the jeopardy to his duty. He loved her with as dark a desperation as that which had bewitched him once before.

WEDNESDAY 1 AUGUST 1565

The Borgo – the Hospital – the Auberge of England

Beneath the light of the Milky Way the streets of the Borgo lay silent and derelict and pale, like a ghost's faded memory of a civilisation ruined long ago. Midnight was near when Carla left the Sacred Infirmary and crossed the piazza. The flagstones stank from the vinegar used to cleanse them of blood and waste, and the smell increased the dizziness of her exhaustion. For the last two weeks the night had been rent by random Turkish bombardments, and she picked her way through the streets with an eye for cover. Everything – including those sleeping outdoors – was powdered with sandstone dust. Gun stones would crash without warning through the roofs of overcrowded hovels. The Sacred Infirmary had been hit several times. Cannonballs bounced down the narrow cobbled alleys like playthings in an awful game. Even at rolling speed they were capable of shattering a limb and it had taken several gruesome incidents to teach the town's children not to try to catch them.

Without religion to comfort them, bind them and, most of all, keep them occupied, the spirit of the people and the soldiery would have broken long ago. At La Valette's command a more or less constant flow of holy rites had been maintained. Funerals and mass burials were conducted with great ceremony. Requiem masses, Benedictions, novenas, vigils and public processions were a daily occurrence. Rare icons and relics were displayed for public veneration and then removed. The feast days of saints scarcely recognised, even by the pious, were announced and commemorated. A handful of baptisms and three unlikely marriages had been conducted with special joy. In these ways, in their fortitude and courage and in their kindness to each other, the people proved themselves worthy of God's protection.

But the other tie that bound them was a fervid hatred of Moslems, whom they considered inherently murderous, treacherous and cruel. Much conversation concerned their inhuman character. The Order's two thousand galley slaves, most of them repairing walls under Turkish gunfire, bore the brunt of this spite. The random acts of violence that they suffered went unpunished. When a line of women at the food depot had been chopped into raw meat by a Turkish cannonball, dozens of slaves had been murdered with shocking cruelty. Nicodemus when he ventured out – and he did so more and more rarely – was treated like a man with a pestilent disease, even in church. Carla walked past the slave gangs, past their skeletal frames and suppurating sores and haunted faces, with a burning sense of shame.

'You can do nothing,' Fra Lazaro told her. 'War makes villains of us all.'

Seventy-two days had passed since the old puppeteer had been hanged. Everyone had lost something of their sanity and their soul. Terrified and insomniac and sheltering in cellars and tunnels by night, and cowering in the debris from musket fire and arrows by day, the population lurched ever closer to despair. Some even hoped for the next Turkish attack: it would at least break the grinding, fear-soaked monotony; and maybe it would bring their trials to an end. Carla was not among these latter. She had not forgotten – she could never forget – the aftermath of the assault on Saint Michel.

THE WOUNDED HAD started to arrive when the battle was done, when the bridge of boats had been opened – at last – to the injured. Until then the casualties, who'd swollen since early morning into a parched and wretched horde, had been detained by armed guards on the far side of the creek. Fra Lazaro had sent across three of the town's Jewish doctors to do what they could and with the din of the slaughter a mere three hundred feet distant the Jews had toiled like angels in the scorching and bloodstained chaos. Carla hadn't been alone in her desire to volunteer, but Lazaro had some notion of what was to come and refused to risk the lives of his staff.

Even Lazaro was stunned by the scale of what followed. The exodus of the wounded across the slippery, lurching planks was too harrowing to describe. The knights were favoured first, an injustice accepted by all as the way of the world. Then came a torrent of panic which the provost marshals tried and failed to control. People slipped through ropes into the creek where they drowned. Others fell into the boats and expired in tangled, suffocating piles. Others yet were trampled to death. From the Borgo end of the boat bridge the townsfolk bore the fallen on blankets and wattles to the hospital; those with strength to do so hobbled or crawled; members of either group expired in droves along the way. By the time the evacuation was complete the streets along the route displayed a wall-to-wall mantling of russet sludge.

The Sacred Infirmary was the best equipped and staffed in the known world – the Knights of Saint John of Jerusalem had made it so – and with two hundred beds it was also one of the biggest. Large-scale slaughter was itself no innovation, but the human detritus was usually left on the battlefield to die. No institution had ever attempted to handle such numbers of casualties before.

To try to save them at all was an act of madness harnessed to faith. But try they did; and they were overwhelmed.

The walls and floors of the operating room were awash with gall and gore. Crews of Maltese women sloshed back and forth, swabbing up the crimson slime with mops soaked in vinegar. Then the mops became inadequate, and they were driven to using shovels to clear the fat, blackening clots, which multiplied under the slabs like obscene forms of life. Sweating surgeons wielded mallets to induce unconsciousness in their charges. They exhausted sheepgut twine by the spool and called for their instruments to be resharpened time and again. Rotten teeth snapped on wooden gags, for the precious narcotic sponges quickly ran out. Arrowheads and musket balls and shards of bloody masonry – plucked and quarried from the depths of groaning flesh – skittered about the tiles underfoot. The smells of cauterisation hung in a pall. Among competing yells of agony and command, chaplains knelt in habits saturate with blood and dispensed Extreme Unction with unseemly speed. With nauseating regularity, tubfuls of amputated limbs were ferried to the growing heap outside. Larger still were the stacks of the dead.

Necessity voided the rules that had restricted Carla's duties. Fra Lazaro set her to strip and wash the casualties before they braved the surgeon's slab. Armour still hot to the touch had to be unbuckled and levered free of its convulsing occupants. There was clotted clothing and padding to peel from gashes and blistered skin; boots to cut away from shattered feet and shins; deformed and embedded helmets to prise from skulls. Without exception, the men stretched out on the trestles were befouled with excrement and dirt. To clean them, brine by the barrel was hauled from the harbour. And the wounded screamed. They screamed as they were stripped and they screamed as they were washed and they screamed as they were portered to the slab. Carla felt like their torturer. She ground her teeth and choked on her own dry retching. She avoided their flailing hands and rolling eyes. As she scrubbed their wounds with salt, she begged their forgiveness.

There was no component or aspect of the human form, it seemed to her, that could not be punctured, slashed, crushed, burned or severed; nor was there limit to the medleys thereof. Pain and Fear and Chaos, robbed of the theatre of battle, now bestrode the stage of the hospital with glee. They danced all about her and played on her every sense, assaulting her vision with pallid, twisted faces and violated flesh, harrowing her brain with piercing pleas and shrieks, fouling her mouth and nostrils with ruptured bowels and leaked urine and sweat and rancid breath. Even her hands tormented her, for they conveyed to her gut and spine every spasm of agony and the waste-polluted seawater burned her abraded fingers like a bane.

Darkness fell early in the hospital and by the flicker of lamp and candle Death was more present and Terror more palpable than ever. Now the shadows thrown on to the walls screamed too. Carla tried. She dug deep into whatever she contained of courage and worth; but it wasn't enough. The moment came when she knew she'd have to flee. With the last of her self-command she made a promise, to herself, that she wouldn't actually run. She'd drop the bloody washcloth in the bucket and slip away. No one would see her. She'd step across the bodies to the doorway, then over those splayed supine in the vestibule, then she'd reach the archway and the piazza. And then she'd run. San Lorenzo beckoned, and the shrine of Philermo, and Our Lady's all-absolving gaze. Surely in Her embrace she would find some ease; and if not ease, at least the company of One who knew all sorrows.

She dropped the washcloth in the bucket and made her way to the door. She crossed the dusk-shadowed vestibule, where torchlight flickered on the grimacing faces of the damned. She heard her name called. Or was it a voice within? She didn't stop.

The stone arch loomed above her. The light here lingered longer. She was halted by what she saw beyond the portal.

Mutilated bodies carpeted the whole piazza. The cloisters extending to her left and right writhed with countless injured. Men; women; boys of every age. Maltese soldiers; Spaniards. Civilians of either gender. Each lying supine in the puddles that shone on the flagstones. Sisters and mothers and wives knelt among their beloved, wafting at the snarls of flies and the waning heat. Black-robed chaplains shuffled back and forth, and also the physician Jews, still not welcomed in the hospital's sacred precincts despite the many lives they'd laboured to save. The bleak red radiance of the eventide, and the murmur of prayers and lamentations, lent the whole tableau the semblance of an apocalypse foretold, as if Judgement Day was come and these war-scourged penitents had dragged themselves en masse to eternity's gate to confess their sins and petition God for mercy.

Carla stood stranded between the horrors crammed within and those without. Whatever contribution she might make to their survival seemed trivial. And to what end? Those who recovered enough of their strength to stand would only be thrown back into the fire, to inflict the same monstrous crimes on other men, for surely beyond the walls the Mohammedans languished in comparably promiscuous anguish. Her breath came too quickly and her chest tightened like a fist. Her heart pounded in her breast as if it would burst from its moorings and lay her on the ground with the rest. For a moment she desired this outcome with a passion. To lay down the burden of being the only sound body in a mob of broken and maimed. To stop rolling this stone up the mountain. To be released from duty and panic and failure and care.

Something tugged at her skirts and she looked down. A clawed hand grasped the blood-sodden linen. A youth not twenty years old lay at her feet, his shoulders trembling with the strain of raising his arm. His cheeks and eyes were hollows carved out of the dusk. Moist pinpoints of fading life gazed up at her face and a black hole moved between his lips without a sound. Her throat clenched and she tried to swallow but could not. She glimpsed purple coils, and a blue knot of flies, which bulged from a lean, ridged stomach. She clenched her eyes against a surge of tears. She turned away. She turned away from this unknown youth, who would never embrace his sweetheart, who would never again breathe the air of a bright blue morning, who in dying here in the reeking dark would rob the world of all he might have given it. She blinked. Through the blur she saw her pathway across the piazza. Through the mist of her tears it didn't seem so far. Our Lady of Philermo would forgive her, She who'd seen Her Son scourged to His end on a barren hill. The clawed hand snatched at her again and she begged him silently to release her from her pledge. She took a step towards the piazza. It wasn't so far. And what price in horror could it cost her that she'd not already paid?

She felt the hand fall away and for an instant she felt free. Then, with a crushing shame, she knew that it was not the hand that had fallen, but she. The youth had not reached out for succour, but to save her, to pull her back from the oblivion into which her soul now plunged. She turned back, desperate, dragging a sleeve across her eyes to clear her sight, and as she went down to her knees by his side, she saw that she was too late and that he was gone. The pinpoints of light had vanished from his soft brown eyes; his mouth was fixed in a silent howl; his chest, when she laid her hand upon it, was clammy and still. Even the bulging purple coils had lost their lustre. Friendless and nameless and forsaken he had died, denied so much as a stranger's parting glance. Was this how Tannhauser had died too? And Orlandu, the son she'd never known and never claimed? She wouldn't believe it. She couldn't or she could not endure. She closed the brown eyes and the gaping mouth and held his cooling face in her hands and she sobbed in the scarlet twilight and felt herself unworthy even of prayer.

Hands took her shoulders from behind and raised her to her

feet and pulled her face into a black-robed shoulder. Arms enfolded her, and she clung to a cross-emblazoned breast, and wept, with the bewilderment and abandon of a child. She wept as she'd not wept in a lifetime. A thousand sorrows coursed through her: for the nameless youth at her feet and all those like him; for Tannhauser and Orlandu, whether they lived yet or not; for her father whose heart she had broken and whose honour she'd stained; for the love she had known and had lost; for the love she'd never lived at all and missed more keenly than any.

She caught her breath and looked up. It was Lazaro, wizened, and himself sore drained, the sorrow in his own eyes no less infinite than her own; yet from the greatness of his heart he mustered a smile of boundless kindness.

'Up that staircase,' he said, nodding towards a passageway, 'is a small room and a cot. The cot is narrow and hard, but I promise you it will feel like a cloud. Go there now and rest.'

Carla stepped back and wiped her face. She stared at the dead man.

'I denied him,' she said.

Lazaro turned her face back towards his. 'Saint Peter denied Our Lord three times. It proved no barrier to his sainthood.' He essayed another smile, then his expression became stern. 'If we exhaust our spirit, we can be of no use to those we serve. And if we do not serve, our lives have no meaning. The cot is mine and I use it, believe me. Do as I say. Rest. And remember that God loves you.' He indicated the sick lying all about. 'There'll be more than enough to do when you return.'

The cot was narrow and hard and felt like a cloud. She lay on it for an hour and though she closed her eyes she was too tired and overwrought to sleep. Ribbons of thought and half-dreams entwined in her mind. She thought of Tannhauser, his scarred brawn and visionary flamboyance, the frankness of his gaze – upon her; upon a world gone mad. She imagined them married, and at peace, and concerned only with life's small hazards. She heard his voice reassure her that all things would pass. And perhaps she slumbered after all, for he stole into the tiny cell and he was naked. She'd seen him – she'd spied on him – in his tub, and memory stoked the fire of imagination. He pulled her from the cot and stripped her bloody dress to the floor. Unbidden, she knelt before him. Her fingers clung to his dense, illuminated thighs. She closed her eyes and opened them and moaned. She twisted and convulsed with an ache so intense she awoke, and the dream fled, and she found herself alone in the echoing dark. The echoes were real, from the monstrous drama below, and other images violated her fantasia. And this conjunction of war and erotism filled her with confusion and she cried and wrapped her arms tight about her chest.

She lay there thus for some time. Then her tears waned and she found herself restored. Though reason dictated otherwise, she, like Bors, refused to believe that Tannhauser was dead. Something inside her insisted on it. And if Tannhauser were alive, so was Orlandu, for Tannhauser was his shield. She loved each of them, without condition or limit. In a world of hatred ascendant, she could at least do that. Something eternal had to endure amidst so much death and only Love could. Her love; Lazaro's love; the love of the nameless soldier; the love of Jesus Christ. She rose from the hard, narrow cot that felt like a cloud and returned to the pit below and she prayed that Christ's love would heal them all.

THERE WOULD BE more assaults, and yet more, she knew, for of all the foolish and impossible hopes she entertained, the hope that the combatants might lay down their arms was most foolish of them all. Mustafa, it was said, was enraged by failure and another Turkish blow was expected soon. The walls of the Borgo and L'Isola were crumbling in half a dozen places and every human being who could lift a stone or hold a shovel now toiled alongside the slaves to repair the damage and to build new breast-works and barricades.

The hospital's supply of medicaments and drugs – of black wine, mandrake and betony, of belladonna and rose oil and opium and Saint John's wort – which had seemed inexhaustible when the siege began, had all but run out. The physic garden had long been stripped of every leaf and petal. Immense bales of bandages and lint had been exhausted, and the serving brothers went about those discharged from care to collect old dressings for washing and reuse. The fight against rampant purulence spread by miasmas had replaced the fight with raw wounds and the stench of pus was pervasive. The mass graves had been filled and fresh pits dug. Every large house in town had been seized to accommodate the less gravely ill.

In welcome counterbalance to such hardships, a man digging a shelter for his family in the basement of his house had unwittingly unearthed a freshwater spring of considerable daily yield. This miracle, for such it was and as such it was acclaimed, had resolved the waterless town's most desperate problem, and was sullied only by the violent disputation that broke out as to whether Saint Agatha, Saint Catherine or Saint Paul should get the credit.

Whatever came next, Carla would endure. She'd discovered the peace that comes with immersion in suffering. It was a strange peace, an awful peace, a peace to be wished on no one, for war's victims paid its price. In their vulnerability and helplessness they were stripped of all malice – of everything but the most primitive courage and faith – and recaptured the lost innocence of the child. Wounding revealed something of a person's core, in a way that nothing else could, and what was revealed was something marvellous, something noble; something that, despite the agony and filth and humiliation, contained more of true dignity than anything she'd ever seen. The sick were indeed closer to God and she'd learned to accept the peace that they had brought her as Christ's gift. The same gift He Himself had promised on the Cross, at the price of His own bleak Passion. Her pride had been vanquished and without regret. Her own fears and concerns had come to seem petty; and yet they remained. As she walked to the auberge she thought of Amparo, and wondered if she would be waiting.

Sometimes she found the girl curled in bed and Carla would lie beside her and they'd wake in each other's arms and the day would begin with something close to happiness. At other times Carla wouldn't see her for days and she'd hear that Amparo slept by the waterfront, or in the stables by Buraq, to whom she was devoted. With each of their intermittent meetings Amparo seemed to have retreated a little further into the untamed waif she'd found mute and bruised on a forest floor. She played with the children as if she were no older than they. She read palms and ate bread and olives with the vicious Spanish *tercios*, who seemed to count her friendship a charm against misfortune. She'd stopped going to church, except when Carla asked her to join her. Many in the town thought her daft; but none dared harm or affront her, or even speak of her unkindly abroad, for Bors had put it about that he was her champion, and had already drubbed a detractor or two with a fury that only stopped on the verge of murder. In a world turned upside down, such as this one was, Amparo was undaunted in a way that no one else could be.

Carla thought of Ludovico.

Almost a month had passed since Carla had learned of his return. Bors had seen his arrival and had warned her. Then she'd heard that Ludovico had collapsed in the hospital, a hero of Saint Michel. His comrades had taken one look at the horror contained therein and had carried him on a door to their own small infirmary by the Auberge of Italy. Carla hadn't seen him, then or since. Yet Ludovico's presence lingered in her mind. It lingered in the minds of many.

'The Inquisition isn't welcome in Malta,' said Bors, who had made a study of the matter.

They sat at the refectory table while Bors worked his way through a tray of custard tarts. Where the eggs and sugar had come from, only he knew. Thanks to his nose for spoil and his prowess as a trader – matched to that of Nicodemus as a cook – he enjoyed the distinction of being the only man on the island who'd managed to gain weight during the siege.

'Is the Inquisition welcome anywhere?' asked Carla.

Bors snorted. 'Evil always turns a profit for someone. Why else would it flourish?' The shiny pink scar that divided his tanned features lent an added grotesquerie to his expression. 'In Messina the Inquisition number in thousands – only a handful of Church officials, yes, but backed by an army of toadies, familiars and leeches. Barons and thieves, merchants and priests – as they will tell you: *all the rich, all the police, and all the criminals*. They have a hand in every pie and do as they please. At least to those who'll let them.'

He smiled at some gratifying memory and Carla remembered the priest in the carriage and how he'd died.

'The Religion wouldn't have let them into Malta, but for the deviousness of the Pope,' continued Bors. 'He appointed Domenico Cubelles as inquisitor General, and since he was already Bishop of Malta, the knights could hardly put a dagger to his throat. The knights have their bad apples. How could it be otherwise among such a band of killers? Rape, buggery, assassination, black magic, heresy – so forth – they've seen it all. And why not? But they've always settled their own affairs. The bishop made a poor fist of confronting them – some half-hearted denouncements of the knights of the French Langues, for Lutheran sympathies, but no arrests. The Inquisition only works if you have the men on the ground, and the bishop is a creature of the palace. Even so, the foot was in the door and six months ago the Pope sent Brother Ludovico.'

Carla's memory of Ludovico was of a young man bright with scholarship and spiritual ardour. Gentleness had seemed his natural state. She still couldn't match that image with the man who inspired such fear.

'Is he truly such a fiend?' she asked.

Bors paused to manoeuvre another tart into his mouth, issuing several grunts of pleasure before wiping the back of his fist across his lips.

'Ludovico is the Pope's black hand. Cardinals and counts have gone up in flames on account of him.' He considered her, as if expecting her to mirror his own view that cardinals and counts were fit for little else. 'Guzman, one of the *tercios* here, served in Calabria in '61 – in Grand inquisitor Ghisleri's campaign to exterminate the Waldensians of the high valleys. He remembers Brother Ludovico well. In order to quicken the zeal of the local marquis, Ludo arranged a red hat for his brother, just like that. Then they wiped out the village of San Sisto – to a man, woman and child. Hunted the runners through the woods with bloodhounds starved for the task. Imagine. The night, the torches, the barking of the dogs, the screams. Two thousand all told, they say. At La Guardia they tortured confessions out of seventy, then painted the survivors with pitch and set them alight on the top of a sheer cliff. Made bets on how many would jump and in what order. At Montalto, they penned up eighty-eight believers in the parish church, then took them out one at a time and cut their throats on the steps.'

Carla felt sickened to the core. She had loved this man.

'Then there was the cleansing of the Piedmont, where Ludovico first crossed paths with Mattias –'

Carla could hear no more. She said, 'Who are the Waldensians?'

Bors shrugged. 'People who worship Christ, but not in the approved fashion.'

Carla didn't reply.

'Ludovico never soils his own hands with heretic blood, but he has a long reach. Has informers and spies all over the shop, high and low, from palazzos to brothels. Familiars. They love it, intrigue, betrayal. Make a man feel important, he'll do anything. Or a woman. Tell them it's for God, Pope and Empire, that Heaven will be their reward, and throw in a pocketful of gold plus the prospect of some blackguard going up in flames, and few can resist. If they're scared witless to boot, well, so much the better.'

'Why is Ludovico here – risking his life?'

'No one knows. But since he blooded himself at Saint Michel, and bandied around a few relics, for which the brethren are notorious fools – why, if I'd known I'd have brought some splinters of the Cross myself – he's been ordained into the Order.'

'Ludovico is a Knight of Saint John?'

'He was sworn into the Convent last Sunday,' said Bors. 'And they'll be sorry, mark my words. A wolf in lion's clothing, you might say. I saw his face the night he got off the boat. Ludovico's come to hunt the big beasts, not the rabbits.'

He slaked down another custard tart in a single gulp. The ecstasy was so evident she thought he was going to cry. Instead he ate the last and smacked his lips.

'We're the little people,' he said. 'If we're lucky, we'll stay that way.'

THE STARS ABOVE the Auberge of England glimmered without number. Carla wished she could see in their disorder the archetypes and meanings that others could. That Mattias could. Was he looking at these same stars now? She wished he were here, to take her in his arms. She thought of Amparo and felt unworthy. She put such thoughts aside. The auberge, as yet undamaged, was no longer the sole preserve of what she thought of as Mattias's band, his vagrant family of wayward souls. Nicodemus would be sleeping in the kitchen, where he tended the fire, and where he would have left her a lamp to light her way up the stairs. Bors would be on the graveyard watch at the Kalkara Gate, for he favoured the cool of the night and swore that, sooner or later, Mattias would emerge from the blackness. Two other English gentlemen were now resident at the auberge and other space therein was given over to convalescents from the ward. But she still had her own room in Starkey's house adjoining and this was a treasure.

At the entrance she took her shoes off and entered in silence. She saw Nicodemus asleep on the kitchen flags and took the low-flamed lantern from its cranny by the pantry. She went up to her room and closed the door. She peeled off her blood-stiff dress, one of three in plain black linen that she'd had made, loose in the sleeves so she could roll them up and high in the throat for modesty. After a week spent restocking the water barrels from the new spring, laundry had once again been permitted, to the rejoicing of at least some, and she had one clean dress for tomorrow. Naked, she wiped herself free of dust with water from a bucket. The water was fresh and gave off the scent of oranges, and she told herself to thank Bors when next she saw him, for it was he who'd brought it.

She let the air dry and cool her. She tipped olive oil, also courtesy of Bors, from a tall bottle into her palms and she anointed it into her face and neck and arms. Her body had become leaner, but not, she hoped, hard. There was no mirror in the room nor in the whole house; monks had little use for them and she hadn't troubled to procure one. She realised that she hadn't seen her own face in weeks. She wondered what she'd find when she did so. Matters such as appearance no longer seemed important. But perhaps she was wrong; perhaps, as Mattias had suggested, her appearance was what gave men a reason to live.

She slipped into a white cotton nightgown, gone grey and near transparent by repeated launderings in brine. She let down her hair and shook it loose and indulged several minutes in the pleasure of brushing and running her fingers through its locks. Since the new springwater had been discovered, Lazaro had prepared for her a tincture made from the lees of white wine, honey and extract of bruised celandine. She'd anointed the tincture into her scalp and let it abide for twenty-four hours before washing with barley lye and rinsing with fresh water. Now, after weeks of grime, her hair felt softer than she remembered. Lazaro had let slip that he had another decoction in progress, of ox gall and cumin and wild saffron and requiring six weeks' infusion, to bring out the yellow in her hair. Perhaps she'd find a mirror after all. Bors could turn one up in a trice, she was sure, and he wouldn't hold vanity against her.

A cannon boomed in the night – Monte Corradino, she thought, her ears by now attuned to the different batteries and their locations. The target would be L'Isola. Sure enough, she heard no dull hum of an approaching ball, nor the sound of its impact. The Turks would attack tomorrow, Lazaro had said. But she'd heard that prediction for the last four days. She laid down the brush. It was time to sleep. When she turned towards the bed, there, across the dimly lit room, stood Ludovico.

THE DOOR WAS closed behind him and she hadn't heard a sound. If anyone else had so suddenly appeared she would have been startled. She wasn't. Her lack of surprise was somehow his doing; as if he had the power to materialise wherever he liked and, having done so, had so natural a claim to being there that his presence was no more surprising than the moonlight. He wore the black, high-collared habit of the Order of Saint John, with the eight-pointed cross in white silk stitched to the breast. A pair of beads were belted around his waist. His powerful skull was evenly covered in short black bristles. His face was sun-beaten, lean as a study in marble. It was over thirteen years since she'd last seen him. His prime, more so than his youth, was magnificent.

These weeks in Malta she'd been surrounded by men who carried in their bones the glamour of the outlands of experience. Mattias, Lazaro, La Valette, Bors, the many dour knights who made the earth shake as they marched down the street: men who had determined that this world was there for them to stamp their mark on. Each carried his own distinctive essence. They carried it into a room, like they carried their shadows. Ludovico carried the aura of an envoy whose masters ruled a nether realm as yet uncharted by God. Or by Satan or by Man. He'd sat at the table with popes – with kings – and had felt their hearts, not his, beating faster. He'd waded through wide rivers of innocent blood. He'd fathered her child.

He looked at her from the door without speaking, his coal-black eyes inscrutable. He could have been studying his next victim; or looking at the love of his life. With a certain dread she realised that the latter was the likelier reading. She wondered how long he'd been standing there, watching her toilet. He watched her now without expression. As, perhaps, he'd watched the heretics flaming with pitch and screaming to God, as they flung themselves in agony from the cliff top.

She found that she wasn't afraid of him. Not yet. She felt, rather, a strange and unexpected affection, a tenderness tinged with sadness. A pity. How beautiful he'd been, and how beautiful he was, and how terrible was the path he'd walked in the meanwhile. Perhaps affection always lingered, come what may, for a man one had loved to the brink of youth's madness. A man who'd not only broken her heart but had scorched the structure of her life to its blackened cornerstones.

Ludovico had seemed to her then a wild creature, wilfully self-imprisoned in the chains of his calling. Chains that she'd possessed the power to break. In breaking his bonds she'd believed she would escape from her own, for was not freedom love's first and brightest promise? They'd made love in the shade of steep valleys, the rough grass chafing the bones of her back red raw. They'd made love in the caves and temples of the long-vanished tribes, and by the pagan statue of the great stone mother at Hal Saflieni. By the Blue Grotto's sparkling phosphorescence, and to the amorous whisper of the sea, he'd woven early morning flowers into her hair. Yet the promise had been broken and all the while she'd been forging a cage, the cage that was all she'd been left with when Ludovico vanished into his own.

From the other side of the chamber, Ludovico watched her still.

Was he recalling that same heady liberty, when passion had made them immortal and immune to all fears? She closed her eyes for a moment to quell her thoughts and break his spell. This man, for all that she had loved him and had borne his son, had engineered the torment and slaughter of thousands. He was the Pope's black hand. Whatever she might have said to him, and there was so much, conversation could only draw her into a web of her own weaving. Somehow she knew this very clearly. She knew that this was what he intended, and that the web would be one about which he could scuttle at will. She yearned with an alarming intensity to open her heart, to chronicle the years of their estrangement; her heartache, her rage, her self-pity. Her quest to find her boy – their boy – and with the boy, the lost and missing pieces of her wholeness. But this was what he wanted. This was what he was counting on. She summoned the will that had empowered her to scrub the wounds of the screaming with salt. She opened her eyes. Still he watched her.

'Please,' she said. 'Leave. Leave now or I will call for Bors.'

Ludovico examined the room, as if looking for the first time at anything but her. He took in the bed, the sea chest studded with brass, the windows open to the breeze, the wash bucket and the dresser and her tiny wardrobe where it hung from a pair of hooks in the wall. His eyes lingered briefly on the bulky brown leather case of her viola da gamba, where it stood neglected in a corner. On a writing desk, which she'd been careful not to disturb, were some papers, an inkpot, a stack of manuscripts and books. Before it was a single chair. Ludovico walked over. His eyes roved briefly over the papers. He turned the chair about to face her and sat down, carefully, as if favouring unseen wounds. His rosary beads clicked in his lap.

'This is Fra Starkey's room,' he said.

His voice vibrated through her spine. Deep and unhurried, matter-of-fact, it conveyed comfort and menace in a single breath.

'It is a lady's private chamber,' she said, trying to match his imperturbable strength. 'My chamber. Your presence here, uninvited – and like a thief in the night – is at best an outrage. At worst it is a crime, even in these barbaric times.'

Ludovico tilted his head towards the viola da gamba.

'I'm happy to see that you still play.'

'You force me to be unmannerly. Get out.'

'Carla,' he said. Her name in his mouth felt like a caress. 'The years have been long, and the byways many, since last we two met together. The morrow will be bloody and this side of eternity may not grant me another chance to look on your face.'

'You've seen my face. I ask you again to leave.'

'I strove to keep a prudent distance between us. The Divine Will dictated elsewise.'

'You had me abducted at the point of a gun,' she said, 'and the Divine Will did not require you to climb my stair tonight.'

'You would have been safe at the convent of the Holy Sepulchre, in body and in spirit. In coming here to Malta, you've put both in great danger.'

She said, 'Never more so than at this moment.'

'How can you imagine I would harm you?' he asked.

'Because you are a monster.'

He lowered his head, so that she couldn't see his face, and for a moment his shoulders sagged, as if the load they carried were Herculean and suddenly too great. Then he straightened his back and looked at her from under his brow. The melancholy that she'd always sensed, deep in his nature, was for the first time undisguised.

'I am a man of God,' he said.

He said it as if this were a viler confession by far; and as if he would risk too much in saying more. Carla wanted to hear more. She wanted to hear everything. The things that he would reveal to her alone and could never in any particle reveal to any other living soul. Against that wish was stacked the fear that if she asked him to do so – and if she did, he would – she would bind him to her in an embrace that death alone could break. She turned away and walked to the paneless window and looked up at the stars. They were as enigmatic as ever and offered no counsel.

'I am told,' he said, to her back, 'that you are that rarest of creatures, a good human being. Deeply good. Without malice. Without greed. Without vanity. Full of Grace. But then I knew that already.'

She didn't turn round. With all the resolution she could muster she said, 'What do you want from me?'

Ludovico didn't answer. His silence twisted inside her and though she knew she should respond in kind, she also knew that she could never match him. Confusion stirred, as was no doubt his intention. Should she try to leave the room? Scream for help? Plead with him to go? Or should she summon the rage she didn't feel and would be hard pressed to find? She didn't turn. She spoke the truth.

'You're frightening me,' she said. 'But you must know that. It's your trade.'

'My trade?'

'Inflicting fear. On those unable to defend themselves.'

'Nothing could be further from my purpose.'

The words slipped out before she could stop them. 'Then tell me, what do you want?'

Ludovico said, 'I want you.'

Her flesh prickled and she was glad he couldn't see her face. This time it was she who stayed mute.

He said, 'Should I take your silence for surprise? Or revulsion.'

Carla didn't answer. She stiffened as she heard him rise from the chair. She felt his presence behind her, his heat, his breath on her hair. She flinched as his hands came to rest on her shoulders. Only the thin cotton shift separated her skin from his. His fingers seemed huge. He squeezed, tenderly, as if afraid of breaking her. His thumbs dug into the muscles between her shoulder blades. Her body's memory of his touch – of this exact same caress – arose as if it had been yesterday. But where was yesterday? She heard him sigh, as if a boundless yearning had at last found its fulfilment. She trembled, involuntarily, by now so distracted that she didn't know whether in fear or in pleasure.

'Forgive me if I'm too rough,' he said. 'I have not touched a woman since I last touched you.'

She believed him, completely. She felt it in his hands. They were not the hands of some lascivious priest. They were hands whose inner purpose was to touch her alone. The knowledge flattered her, frightened her. Some instinct of survival told her if she didn't elude him now, she wouldn't elude him at all. She would be his. Forever. For he'd never let her go. She ducked from his grasp, felt his fleeting impulse to tighten his grip, felt him master it. She slipped away several paces across the room but not, she realised too late, towards the door. She turned to face him.

His black eyes pierced her. He let his arms fall by his side and didn't pursue. He was too intelligent to force her; though not to be hurt by her flight. By the same token, he was too shrewd, too knowing, for her to feign what she did not feel. Any attempt to do so would only goad him. Ludovico had come to hunt the big beasts, Bors had said. She sensed that the biggest lived in Ludovico's heart, and that that beast was hunting him as well as her.

'When you last touched me I was fifteen years old,' she said. Tears, and the rage she thought she'd never find, sprang to her throat. 'I gave myself to you without reserve. I gave you all I had. I gave you everything. And you fled. I ran after you, crying, but you were gone. The hardest faces I have ever seen assured me so – gone forever – and they looked down on me as if I were a whore, and lower than a whore. As if I were the Devil's dam. I lost myself to love and I was not found.' She crammed the tears back down. 'Why did you steal my heart and then abandon it?'

'I was afraid.'

She stared at him. She felt herself shaking, her face burning, nauseated by an anger she could neither express nor contain. She whispered, 'You were afraid?'

Ludovico blinked, slowly. 'Afraid for my duty.'

'Your duty to spread terror? To torture and burn? You chose that over valleys and flowers? Over the beauty we shared? Over love?'

'Yes, Carla. I chose all that over love. Isn't that what duty requires? Isn't that what honour demands?'

Whatever emotion he felt, he kept it from view. Carla fought to stop her own from boiling over. 'I damn your honour,' she said. 'As you damned mine.'

'Now I would make a different choice.'

'The only choice to be made tonight is mine and I tell you once again: get out.'

'Hear what I have to say.'

It was all she could do not to scream in his face.

'I carried your child.'

He said, 'I know.'

'You know?'

She felt robbed of the revelation. Her privacy was more violated by this than by his outrageous visitation. 'How did you know?' she said. Before he could answer she said, 'When did you find out?'

'Since I returned with the relief I've learned many things.'

'From your spies and familiars.' Her voice reeked with contempt. He was unmoved.

'There is little in this town I am unaware of. Little in this world. Your search for an unknown boy was hardly a secret. A boy twelve years old. Born on All Hallows Eve in 1552. Who else could he have been but my own blood?'

'He was the fruit of our love. He was all I had to value. Even though you were gone, I carried him without shame.'

'From you, I would have expected nothing less.'

'I watched him stolen from my arms before I could put his tender mouth to my breast. I watched my father, whom I adored, turn into a fiend. I watched my mother broken by sorrow, by disgrace, by the ruin of every dream that she held dear.'

Ludovico said, 'I'm sorry.'

The lamp was behind him. The pale silver light from the window cast one half of his face into darkness. He said, 'I am told our son died a hero's death, at Saint Elmo's.'

Carla took a sudden, heaving breath and held on to it, afraid that if she let it go she would sob, and that he would then, in some obscure sense, have won.

'If I could quench your suffering, I'd do anything to do so,' said Ludovico. 'But these things of which you speak happened long ago and we are neither of us now who we were then.'

She said, 'Do not you – of all men – try to comfort me.'

Suddenly, all the heat drained from her anger. She let the breath out. She felt only a desperate need to be alone.

She said, 'My son died a fool's death and I failed to stop him.'

'To blame yourself for that is madness.'

'He was here, at my table, and I did not recognise him.' She recalled the evening with bitterness. It was less than two months ago, here in this house, yet seemed to have taken place in a different universe. And to a different woman. A trivial and foolish woman, blinded by prejudice and conceit. 'I was searching for something of you and I didn't find it.'

'A man's features are only half-formed at such an age. And perhaps he favoured you.'

'I searched for my own heartbeat and I didn't hear it.'

'It's difficult to see oneself in another. Perhaps in one's own flesh most of all.'

'He was vulgar. He was rude.' She felt a sour relief in her self-contempt. 'I thought him beneath me. Beneath us. Now I bathe such boys as they die in their own filth. And I count such service God's gentlest gift, to me.'

Ludovico raised his hand from his side and held it out to her – not in solace, but as if he wanted her to take it and let him lead her. 'War has worked its bitter alchemy on each of us. Perhaps we both now see our path in life more clearly.'

'Perhaps. But my path is my own.'

Ludovico said, 'With God's Grace, we could make another son.'

Carla stared at him, as if he were mad; and perhaps he was.

'If the Cross prevails, and we survive this siege, my work by then will be complete,' said Ludovico. 'No man has done more for Mother Church than I, or with greater purity of intention. You call me a monster. Yes.'

She saw again how deeply this had cut him.

'I will not deny it, nor will I offer apology. The world is monstrous – do we not stand in Hell at this moment? – and horror must be inflicted as well as endured in order to forestall greater evils. Even so, my heart is weary of the labour and would set the burden down.' He indicated the habit he wore. 'As you see, I am now a Knight of Justice of the Order of Saint John. The precedent exists in their customs that would allow me to renounce my monastic vows – and become a Knight of Devotion. That is, one who is no longer a full member of the Order, but entitled to spiritual consolation and certain privileges of rank.'

He paused as if he intended her to draw some conclusion from this. Instinct said it would be better if she did not.

Ludovico said, 'By these means, and with the blessing of certain individuals whose benevolence I may count on, I could then wed you without loss of honour.'

The statement hung in a silence that his eyes expected her to fill, and Carla felt a chill of absolute fear. A chill such as she'd not felt since her father told her she would never see her babe again.

She said, 'You talk to me of madness and then ask me to marry you?'

'Madness.' He considered the notion and nodded. 'After the battle for Saint Michel, I saw you, by chance. In the Sacred Infirmary. I glimpsed you. The work of a single moment. And I have thought of nothing else since. Nothing but you.'

His voice remained steady, the same deep, even resonance. Yet Carla felt herself step backwards. Her shoulder blades touched the wall.

He said, 'Do you know with what self-command I had until then avoided you? Every moment since I stepped on this shore I yearned to see your face. I denied myself. I saw only to my duty. Because I had some faint inkling of the power that you might wield to re-enchant my soul. But that was not to be, and, once again, enchanted I am.'

Carla realised why he would have banished her to the convent. Not for the protection of her soul, but his own. She made no answer.

Ludovico nodded again. 'The work of a single moment, and it has damned me. Just as another such glimpse, at another such moment, damned me before, on a high hill above a gold and turquoise sea. It was never my intention to devote my life to the Sacred Congregation. To the Inquisition. I was already a learned doctor twice over. A jurist. A theologian. I threw myself into the work of purging heresy to purge myself – of the malady of love. For I could find no other cure. How could love survive, I reasoned, in a man who would be the object of so much hatred? So much anguish. So much fear. I burned apostates and Anabaptists and unbelievers of every feather, in order to burn your memory from my brain.'

Carla stifled a sob. 'You blame me for your crimes?'

The look Ludovico gave her said as much, yet his answer belied it.

'Philosophical nicety bars my way to such a charge,' he said. 'As to crimes, both dogma and jurisprudence contradict you.'

'Did you feel nothing for your victims?'

'I saved their souls,' said Ludovico.

She stared at him and wondered if he believed it. Perhaps he read the question in her face, for he gave her an answer.

'And they left me something more haunting than love unfulfilled. The memory of human lives snuffed out like candle flames.'

Carla wanted to turn away, but his eyes wouldn't let her go.

He said, 'When one has seen so much light extinguished, the world becomes dark indeed. Yet it never turned dark enough to stop me from seeing your face.'

Carla understood the stab of pity that she'd felt on first seeing him at the door. It returned like hot iron stuck through her heart. 'God forgive you,' she said.

'He does,' said Ludovico. 'For I've served Him well. My question is, can you forgive me?'

'For snuffing out all that light?'

'For breaking your heart.'

Her heart almost broke again. 'Oh, Ludovico,' she said, 'I forgave you the instant I knew I was carrying your child. How could I carry a child and have room for anything but love? Especially for him who'd helped create him.'

He stared at her. For a moment the coal-black eyes shone wet. In their depths was the look of a man who found himself stranded in a bottomless pit. A pit whose fiendish design was his own work. And whose confines he was desperate to escape.

'I have never known another woman,' he said.

'Nor I another man,' she replied.

'Can we two not rekindle that amorous fire?'

Carla shook her head. 'I cannot.'

'Because of my work?'

'Because what passed between us is past.'

Later, she would not understand why she said what came next. She wanted to be rid of him. She wanted to spare him futile heartache. She wanted to tell him the truth.

She said, 'And because I love another.'

The wetness cleared from Ludovico's eyes so swiftly that she wondered if she'd seen it at all. Looking at her now was a man for whom that bottomless pit was home. With that tone of disbelief that betrays an expectation to the contrary he said, 'The German?'

Carla had left her instincts too far behind. She had wandered out too far on to the web. She didn't know how to get back. She went forward.

'Mattias Tannhauser,' she said.

'Tannhauser is dead.'

'Perhaps.'

'Only the swimmers escaped Saint Elmo's. The Turk put the rest to the sword.'

'Even if Mattias is dead, my feelings live on.' She needn't have said more, but couldn't stop. 'He and I were to be married. It was my desire. And with all my heart, I desire it still.'

And it was done. The work of a single moment. Ludovico's eyes turned hard as pebbles and he stared down into her, and she knew at once that something irrevocable had changed, and that she'd regret it more desperately than anything she could imagine. Under his gaze she felt herself dwindle into something fragile, like the last burning candle in a world already given over to impenetrable dark. She expected his hands to tear the gown from her body. She could feel that urge boil within him, a desire perpetually crushed now matched to a huge and voiceless fury and the hurt to match it. His self-command exerted itself. Nothing else could have restrained the demon that was panting and raging just beneath the surface of his calm.

'We will speak again,' he said.

He turned and walked away to the door.

Carla's relief was tainted by the uncertainty and dread he'd leave behind him. He opened the door and stopped on the threshold and turned. She could hardly see his features in the gloom.

He said, 'The men who told you I'd gone forever – who regarded you as lower than a whore? I knew them well. They were my masters. They said you'd made a charge of infamous conduct. Against me.'

'They lied.'

'Yes.'

'But you believed them.'

'I was a young priest. They were exalted dignitaries of the Church. You were a girl. With a jealous father, who had powerful friends.'

He paused. Carla didn't speak. Of the tragedy that bound them, she had no more to say.

'I didn't know until tonight, he said, 'that they'd given me my first lesson in the use of power. Their other lesson they made clear enough at the time. For the needs of the flesh, there are brothels and boys. The crime is to fall in love. And for that, the punishment is terrible.'

The gloom of the corridor swallowed him. The door closed without a sound. And Carla was left alone with the guttering lamp, and with her memories of all she had lost, and with her fears of what she yet had left to lose.

She lay on her bed without sleeping and found no consolation in prayer. She rose and put on her dress and pinned up her hair. She wrestled the big brown case from out of its corner and, taking the lantern, she stole as softly as she could down the stairs and tiptoed through the kitchen and out into the night.

She found the spot she needed on the rocks by Galley Creek.

Because the entrance to the creek was blocked by the massive iron chain, the waterfront here was one of the few unfortified stretches of the whole perimeter. There were no guards. There was a sense of peace. She unpacked her gambo violl and tightened the bow and tuned the strings. Her fingertips felt soft, their calluses faded. It was the first time she'd taken the instrument from its case since she'd played for Mattias, at the Villa Saliba, in another world and in a different age.

Across the water lay L'Isola, its windmills gay silhouettes against the stars. Beyond L'Isola – somewhere – lay the Turkish camp. If Mattias was still alive – if the whisper of hope in her heart was something more than a desperate illusion – perhaps he would hear her music and her anguish. And perhaps he would return. Carla took a deep breath. She shook the fatigue from her shoulders and she summoned her bruised spirit to find its voice and she began to play.

MONDAY 6 AUGUST 1565

The Marsa – the Pink Pavilion – Marsamxett Bay

TANNHAUSER CROSSED THE Marsa and the spoliated slopes of Monte Sciberras wearing a snow-white turban and a scarlet kaftan that made him look far more lordly than he felt. At his side was belted a dagger with a ruby pommel and a garnet sheath. His mount was a splendid chestnut mare from the personal string of Abbas bin Murad. He was on his way to find a rogue boy. As before, Orlandu had proved elusive and this was by no means Tannhauser's first foray. Today he would try his luck among the corsairs.

As he rode through the smoke-charred barbican of Saint Elmo, his costume had the desired effect on the guard on the gate, a Bulgar by the look of him, who bowed low before the sneer that Tannhauser mustered as he trotted past. He crossed the fractured courtyard where the last of the knights had been beheaded and where he'd shared Le Mas's last night. A Turkish siege battery boomed from the seaward wall overlooking the Borgo, but apart from the gun crews the fort was barely manned at all. Once it had seemed a whole world, seething with heroic madness and holy love; now it was a small, shabby ruin and its deserted aspect gave him chills. He rode into the forge unnoticed and dismounted. It was empty and cool but he spent no more time on reminiscence. With a pair of tongs he set to levering up the flagstone in the floor, to recover the five pounds of opium and the heavy gold ring he'd buried underneath. It was hardly a labour to tax an Atlas, but his forehead was rapidly filmed with a sickly sweat. He was hardly in the best of health; but at least he was back on his feet.

The ague had almost carried him away. He didn't remember the first fevered days that had followed Saint Elmo's fall, nor did he care to. They passed in a not unwelcome delirium, in which he felt little and was aware of less, including, most happily, the excision of a large abscess that swelled to the size of a fist behind the musket ball in his back and from which a pint and more of pus was ultimately drained. Had he died during this period it would have been as a shivering, mumbling bag of bones incapable of anything so refined as regret or even fear. What followed his return to consciousness was somewhat more taxing.

He found himself nursed, in as much luxury as the circumstances allowed, in the flamingo pink campaign tent of Abbas bin Murad. An Ethiopian slave fanned away the flies and sponged his brow in the deadening heat. He burned frankincense and placed heated glass cups upon his skin. He poured honeyed water, salted yoghurts and medicinal elixirs down his throat in such great quantity that Tannhauser felt he would vomit if he'd had the strength to do so. The same mute and patient fellow disposed of his stool with exquisite dignity, a humiliation Tannhauser bore with the tight-lipped fortitude of one who had no choice in the matter. In a clay jar the Ethiope collected his increasing yield of urine with great satisfaction, as if this were his primary reward for his ministrations.

For some days Tannhauser endured these episodes with embarrassment – on his nurse's part as well as his own – for it seemed to him a poor way to make a living; but then he reasoned that the Ethiope might well be the luckiest of all his brethren on the island, for if he hadn't been fanning and sponging and collecting in the shade of a tent, he would most likely have been hauling cannon and baskets of rocks around the mountains. After this, Tannhauser submitted with an easier conscience and even found himself inclined to mutter his gratitude.

When, for brief moments, he regained the power to raise his head from the pillow, he became aware that his body, and in particular his legs, were promiscuously blotched with brown and purple lesions of alarming appearance. Had he seen another man in such a state he would have granted him a wide berth, for if the Black Death were to return to smite the ungodly it would surely look like this. The thought that a blackamoor might easily be sacrificed to such a fate only increased his fear that his diagnosis might be accurate. That his penis seemed immune to this scourge brought a sense of relief that was profound, if only fleeting. However, when subsequently visited by a succession of Arab and Jewish physicians, all of whom exhibited aplomb in the face of his stigmata, he felt reassured. The consensus among his doctors was that the lesions represented the expulsion of toxic humours from his body, the detritus of his battle to stay alive. They were unanimous in their confidence that if he lived, they would disappear, a fact which the Arabs, if not the Jews, attributed to the beneficence of Allah rather than their own expertise. The numerous half-healed cuts and bruises that otherwise adorned his body aroused no comment.

The physicians had prepared a confection of red gillyflowers, deer musk and cloves infused in vinegar, which the fortunate among the high command rubbed about their nostrils thrice a day against contagion by the plague. Tannhauser enjoyed this rare protective benefit as well, and was told that it was good against nocturnal sweats and all the effects of melancholy. In this last regard, if not in the others, it proved less than effective. His care, then, was of the highest quality, and thus was he denied the chance to leave this mortal realm in a state of happy oblivion. Instead, he spent several weeks in a helplessness more complete than he imagined possible. For a man who invested a substantial portion of his pride in his physical strength, this was a singular experience.

Abbas came each night – night after night, for weeks, his face drawn gaunt by the rigours of watching good men die in the field – and he sat by Tannhauser's cushions and read passages from the Koran in a voice that called from the text a beauty so inherent that its origin in God's throat seemed quite beyond question. During these visits Tannhauser feigned an inability to speak, for Abbas's tenderness was so simple and so untarnished, that it almost broke his heart. In conditions of such debility as he was in, sentiments escape their bonds and melancholy swells the liver, and his feelings for Abbas were unbearably intricate and haunting. Friend and abductor, saviour and master, father and brother and foe. Tannhauser lay there in deceit, and perhaps in treachery. So he spoke not at all and soaked in the healing love that Abbas bestowed on him.

He lay in the great silk womb and between bouts of sleep in which horror stalked his dreams, and which followed no rhythm or pattern, he watched the changing light as it coaxed from the superbly woven fabric more shades of pink than even the painters of Suleiman's court could know existed. It was a colour for which he had never had any regard and he thought he'd sicken of it; yet he didn't. Rather, he fell ever deeper beneath its spell, as if the colour, forged as it was from silk and warp and weft, and light and dark, and the genius of the dyer's art, were a piece of music, or a woman, or a vista of high-country snow, or any such cosmic fabrication that on first acquaintance seemed one thing but on repeated study proved itself many, and each always different from the last. Many, also, were the hours of night that he spent gazing at the pinkness by the yellow light of the lamps. And when the pomegranate hues of twilight gave way to what seemed like utter blackness, the blackness too revealed itself as something more, leavened as it was by the flicker of campfires and starlight, and by the wax and wane of the moon. Pink was life. And it reminded him of what Petrus Grubenius had told him, which was that every Thing existent bears some influence on every Other, no matter how far flung from each other that they might be, for if, as is clear to any man, two events in close conjunction alter the nature of each, then each must change that of a third and fourth, for nothing is disconnected entire, much though we might sometimes wish it, and that is why the stars, most distant of all known bodies, even so exert an influence over every human destiny, a fact no intelligent man would ever dispute.

What profit or meaning could be gleaned from this study in pink, Tannhauser was unable to fathom. It was a matter that proceeded of its own accord. And he found that something similar, but more enigmatic yet, evolved with regard to the silent Ethiope, who more than any other agent was the force that restored his health and saved his life.

No one told Tannhauser that his nurse was an Ethiope, and certainly not the man himself, but he didn't doubt his judgement in this matter. No race was more distinctive, being high-boned and long-fingered, hard as ironwood and slender as reeds. He'd seen them on the block in Alexandria and Beirut, and few slaves were as highly prized, not least because they were a very fierce lot indeed, and not inclined to submit to Arab slavers without a fight. Adult males were rarely taken alive; this man had probably been abducted as a boy. Ethiopia was the land of the Queen of Sheba and Prester John and the Lost Tribes of Israel, and it was said that the Ark of the Covenant itself was hidden there, guarded by warriors wielding swords with six-foot blades, in a vast red mountain cathedral hewn from the rock. They believed in a black Jesus, and why not? And as proof of their manhood, he'd heard, they hunted wild lions in the red savannah, alone, and with no more than a simple spear, and wore the beast's hide and teeth when they went to war. No wonder, then, that the fellow who nursed him could clean another man's soil with more pride than a prince at his own coronation; who, despite being doomed to this lowly estate, walked as tall as any janissary or knight.

After Tannhauser's first attempts at conversation failed, he limited himself to bows of his head and grunts of thanks and blessings. The Ethiope slept on the ground by his bed, and when Tannhauser in his insomnia waited for the first light of dawn, and turned to study the fine ebony features in repose, the man's eyes would already be open, always, as if he never slept at all but only rested, his eyes black mirrors in which all things were reflected yet no one thing that Tannhauser could name.

Beyond the thin walls of the tent cannon thundered and whips cracked, and cruelties without number were recorded in the unread archives of Time. But here a stranger, whose name he did not know and did not ask, cared for him day and night as if he were a babe, and no matter what coercion had brought the Ethiope to this task, he performed it with a boundless kindness, in the midst of a boundless evil, and it seemed to Tannhauser that this was as close to purity as human goodness ever came.

THE DAY DAWNED when Tannhauser awoke and knew, for no particular reason, that it was over and that he was well: weak and shrivelled to a bag of sinews and bone, but free of whatever it was that had so ailed him. He looked at the Ethiope and saw that he knew too. He rose from his bed on enfeebled legs and walked out into the daylight, with the Ethiope at his side. Abbas's tent was pitched on a hill overlooking the Marsa, the broad, flat plain between Sciberras and Corradino at the landward end of Grand Harbour. The Marsa was filled by the sprawl of the Turkish camp – the bivouacs and kitchens and supply dumps; and the spreading stain of the field hospital, where those less fortunate than Tannhauser lay dying beneath scraps of canvas and the violence of the mid-summer sun. They walked the quarter-mile to the rim of the hill and from there looked down on what might have been the bore of Mount Etna.

A dense grey cloud hovered over the coastal arrangement of peninsulas and bays, and spouting smoke and muzzle blasts formed the spokes of a giant wheel that took in Gallows Point and Saint Elmo, and the heights of Sciberras, Salvatore, Margharita and Corradino, where they stood. At the centre of the holocaust's ire were the Borgo and L'Isola, themselves all acrackle and aflame with musketry and cannon fire. A howl rose through the morning and the Sultan's legions surged across the Grande Terre Plein, and over the corpse-choked ditches, to splash against the smoke-blacked bastions of either fortress. Ladders were thrown up, and fire hoops and pipkins sailed down, and hand-to-hand butchery was joined along the devastated ramparts.

After Tannhauser's sojourn in the timeless pink womb, the frenzied broil below seemed an aberrant phantasm not of this world, a devil's joke whose actors were recruited by deception.

But this was the world, and his world most of all, and the knowledge that he must soon plunge back in, for one flag or another, filled him with dread and nausea, and a yearning to retreat into the helplessness from which he'd just emerged. He glanced at the Ethiope, and for once caught him unguarded. The man had the look of a cat who sat on a window and watched two rival packs of dogs fighting in the street. He looked at Tannhauser, and saw whatever he saw, then turned and walked back towards the camp.

Tannhauser watched him go. His nausea was transformed into hunger. A bestial, raving hunger. A lust for meat. He didn't look back at the battle. If the Religion was to fall, this was as good a day as any. Clearly that was Mustafa's hope and intention. Tannhauser went to find some breakfast. At the kitchen he learned that it was 2 August, and that he'd been inside the tent for close on six weeks. When he returned from the kitchens, the Ethiope had gone, and Tannhauser never saw him there again.

The Religion did not fall on 2 August. Tannhauser watched from the hill as dusk fell and the muezzin wailed the evening call and the mauled battalions of janissaries trooped by with their tattered colours and their wounded, heading for their campfires and what comfort they could find around their cauldrons.

Abbas returned to his tent in a dark mood and Tannhauser, or as Abbas knew him, Ibrahim, joined him in prayer. Afterwards, they dined at a low table made of polished cherrywood. Abbas was now in his fifties, much admired by his peers and revered by his men, whose welfare, horses and equipment he fostered with subsidies from his own purse. His beard was steel-grey and two pale scars marked his brow and cheek. Otherwise he remained as lean and elegant as the day he'd found Mattias by his mother's corpse.

On the three-month journey they'd taken together, twenty-five years before, from the wilds of the Fâgâraš Mountains to the greatest city in the world, Abbas had taught Ibrahim the rudiments of Turkish, the rituals of daily prayer, how to conduct himself as a man when he entered the Enderun military college in Istanbul. In return, Ibrahim had proved his skill in repairing tackle and in the care and fettling of horseflesh. Though it had been the men under Abbas's command who had murdered his mother and sisters, Ibrahim had not held him to blame. Robbed of every other ally, perhaps he lacked the wit to do so. Rather, he adored the man, and in some sense his abandonment to the discipline of the Enderun had been more desolating than his departure from the village of his birth.

Since then they'd met again only once, in Iran, when the Turks had ravaged the Yerevan and razed the palace of Tahmasp Shah and in Nahjivan left no stone mortared to another. Stones that had stood since before the birth of Christ, until the janissaries came. It had been a formal occasion, an inspection of the troops and disbursement of rewards on the outskirts of the latter devastation before continuing their pursuit of the Shiites towards the Oxus. Ibrahim, as janitor of his *orta*, had accepted the bonus money due his men for their ruthlessness and bravery. Abbas had congratulated him on his distinguished career and invited him for tea, and they agreed that at some future time when circumstances allowed they should renew their special friendship. But circumstances never did.

During Tannhauser's sickness they'd talked little, Abbas being preoccupied with military matters and the intrigues of the war council, which as always on Turkish campaign were potentially lethal. Tonight they ate pilaf and roast pigeon and sugared almonds. They drank coffee. Abbas had changed into a kaftan of watered white silk, woven through with gold and silver thread. From his ear hung a perfect grey pearl the size of a hazelnut. He owned lands and shipping interests in the Golden Horn. He was a man of high refinement and great culture. He was one of those warriors to whom war was abomination. They were altogether too few, and Tannhauser found that his affection for the man had not diminished despite the years.

Tannhauser thanked him for yet again saving his life and Abbas gave thanks to Allah for the chance to do so, for Charity was a sacred obligation.

'In a time of great evils such as this one, when the wings of the Angel of Death are everywhere felt and heard, small acts of kindness are as jewels from Heaven, and more so to the giver than to he who receives them, for as the Prophet, blessed be his name, said, *Be compassionate to others, that you may be granted compassion by Allah*.' Abbas added, 'If you once save a man's life, you become his guardian forever.'

Thinking of Bors and Sabato Svi, as well as the noble *gazi* seated before him, Tannhauser said, 'In that I've known the greatest fortune, for I'm guarded by lions.'

Abbas asked him how he'd come to be taken by the Christian dogs. It was distasteful to lie into the luminous brown eyes of the man who had twice been his saviour; but it was the least of his recent crimes.

'A cavalry patrol surprised me on the road to Marsaxlokk,' Tannhauser said. 'It was a little after dawn, in early June, and they came on me like demons from Gallows Point, which I'd understood was ours.'

Abbas nodded. 'That was the morning they destroyed Torghoud's batteries. As for demons . . .' His lips twisted and he shook his head. 'These knights are the Children of Satan. Some say La Valette is a necromancer and that devils have been seen by his side.'

'He is only a man,' said Tannhauser.

'You have met him?' asked Abbas.

Tannhauser said, 'I have seen him. La Valette is one of those old men whose only true love is war. If there is necromancy at work it is that. Without war he would be shrivelled or dead, useless, decayed. But war renews his blood, lightens his step, sharpens his eyes. His own men regard him as a demigod, but there's no reason we should do the same.'

'He's proved himself a formidable adversary.'

'He plays to his strengths and our weaknesses. He has a genius for siege and defence in depth. He knows the soldier's heart, for such is his own. We're not fighting Shiites or Austrians.'

Abbas's brow rose in a weary gesture. 'Would that the Council knew it.' The reason for his earlier black mood became clear. 'Mustafa lacks the patience to let the cannon and the miners do their work. Dig, I tell him, mine their walls and destroy them from below. But mass assaults thrill his blood, like a gambler with too much gold who must risk losing all to find enjoyment. At least he's accepted my demand to construct a pair of siege towers. Two galleys at Marsaxlokk are being dismantled for the timbers.'

Abbas had once studied architecture under the famed Greek

devshirme Sinan, commander of the Sultan's war machines and builder of a thousand mosques. He added, with a muted pride, 'They'll be constructed to my own design, but will take two weeks or more to complete. In the meanwhile, the lives of our men will continue to be squandered.'

It seemed to Tannhauser that if the Turks were building war engines more suited to antiquity than the modern age, the besiegers were approaching desperation. He kept this thought to himself and said, 'And Piyale?'

'Kapudan Pasha Piyale is the wiser strategist, but his fear for our Sultan's fleet dominates his thought. He's desperate to conclude the siege before the high winds of autumn. Once the winds come, the fleet will be stranded here throughout the winter. We're a thousand miles from home. Sometimes it seems further than that.'

Words of comfort or encouragement escaped Tannhauser's effort to conjure them. He let the silence stand.

'We will conquer, if that be Allah's will,' said Abbas. 'But the cost will be high. Especially to the janissaries.'

'The cost to the janissaries is always high.'

'It is their vocation.' Abbas studied him for a moment. 'You are known in the bazaar as a trader in opium. They say that when Malta falls you plan to trade in pepper, from Alexandria.'

Abbas had kept his ears open but Tannhauser's masquerade was proven sound. He thought of Sabato Svi and inwardly smiled. Sabato would have been amused to know that his faith in the market for pepper had now spread to the heart of the Turkish high command.

He said, 'The future of the Empire lies in trade. If I may say so, more than in war.'

'Why did you leave the janissaries?'

The question was asked without either warning or threat. Tannhauser gave his stock answer. 'There are only so many times a man can march across Iran before his feet ask if there isn't another way of serving Our Sultan.'

Abbas smiled. 'The *kullar* of the Sultan's sword have little choice in such matters. You retired before the age at which it is normally permitted, and with the prospect of high advancement before you.'

Tannhauser had not expected Abbas to be so well informed. He didn't answer.

'I will tell you a story I heard,' said Abbas. 'The tragic fate of Our Sultan's eldest son, Prince Mustafa, is widely known. As a member of his personal guard, you would know it better that most.'

'Indeed,' said Tannhauser. 'I saw the Prince's body thrown on to the carpet outside Our Sultan's campaign tent.'

At the time, Suleiman had had four sons alive of the eight his two wives had borne him. Prince Mustafa's mother was Gulbahar, who had long been supplanted in the court, and in Suleiman's heart, by Roxelane, 'the Russian Woman', who was mother to the other three. Roxelane knew that if Prince Mustafa were to ascend the throne – and, since his talents were great and both the army and the aristocracy were behind him, this was likely – he would have his three half-brothers murdered. The Osmanli tradition of fratricide was hallowed by time. Suleiman himself was the only survivor of five full-blood brothers. Their father, Selim the Grim, had murdered the other four, leaving only Suleiman to rule.

By means of a series of intrigues Roxelane convinced Suleiman that his son was not only planning to dethrone him but had even established relations with the Safavid heretics of Iran, with whom Suleiman was at war. Suleiman summoned Prince Mustafa to his camp in Karamania, and with characteristic ruthlessness had him strangled by the deaf-mute eunuchs.

'If Prince Mustafa had meant to overthrow the emperor, he would never have responded to the summons,' said Tannhauser. 'I knew the Prince. The plot was a grotesque invention by the Russian Woman.'

'We will never know,' said Abbas discreetly. 'But that is not the subject of my story. The army's fury at the Prince's death was great, especially among the janissaries. If there'd been a man prepared to lead them, nothing could have stopped them from overthrowing Our Sultan on the spot, perhaps even killing him. The cauldrons would have been tipped over.'

The brass cauldron from which the janissaries ate their single daily meal was the symbol of their Order. To tip it over was the signal for revolt, an event to which at least two previous sultans owed their reigns. While the janissaries were numerically the smallest corps in the army, their political power was immense.

Tannhauser said, 'There was no such leader.'

Abbas looked at Tannhauser keenly. Tannhauser felt nothing. Whatever feeling he had harboured had been exorcised long ago. He said, 'Even if there had been such a man, and such a revolt, it would only have unleashed war between Prince Mustafa's son, Murad, and the other brothers. Better that one man die than countless thousands. Our Sultan, as always, was wise.'

'Exactly so,' agreed Abbas. 'Which brings me back to my subject. Certain powers required that all trace of the Prince's bloodline be extinguished. Forever. Murad was strangled soon afterwards. Prince Mustafa's other son was only three years old. Suleiman sent a court eunuch and a janissary captain to put the child – his grandson – to death. This captain was chosen by lot from the dead Prince's bodyguard, as a guarantee they'd renewed their loyalty to their Sultan.'

Tannhauser was suddenly bone-tired and filled with melancholy. He wanted to return to his bed. He wanted the Ethiope to watch over him. He craved his healing silence. But the Ethiope wasn't here. Only politeness prevented him from leaving Abbas's table.

'The child's elected executioner was the janissary captain,' Abbas continued. 'But when he saw the boy walk towards him –

with his little hands outstretched to offer a kiss – the janissary fainted.'

The janissary had in fact left the tent to vomit in the dust; but there seemed no merit in correcting Abbas's version of events.

Abbas concluded, 'The black eunuch performed the deed in his stead.'

'Why do you tell me this story?' asked Tannhauser.

'Is the story true?' said Abbas.

Tannhauser didn't answer.

'I can understand,' said Abbas, 'why that janissary might lose his taste for military service, and why the Sultan's gratitude might extend to permitting his honourable retirement.'

In Abbas's eyes was a look that Tannhauser recalled from the first time he'd met him, on a cold spring morning in a mountain valley whose rivers he sometimes heard in the landscapes of his dreams. A look of recognition that crossed an unbridgeable gulf for no other reason than that it was able to do so, and was therefore ordained by some higher power, be it human or Divine. Tannhauser blinked and looked away.

'At the height of your fever,' said Abbas, 'when you were insensible, and the physicians told me there was little hope, you murmured a chant, over and again. I put my ear to your lips to listen. What you repeated were the first verses of *Adh-Dhariyat*.'

The Arabic cadences rolled through Tannhauser's mind like a haunting strain. Still he didn't speak, and Abbas quoted them for him:

'By the winds that winnow with a winnowing, And those that bear the burden of the rain, And those that glide with ease upon the sea, And those Angels who scatter blessings by Allah's command, Verily that which you are promised is surely true. And verily Judgement and Justice will come to pass.'

He nodded. 'It was the first of the verses of *Al-Kitab* that you taught me, because that was the *surah* from which you chose my name.'

'God chose it, not I.'

Tannhauser nodded. He did not much dwell upon those days, but for a moment the memories caught him, and he realised that this tranquil night with Abbas was precious, and that the time comes when even dark days are remembered with something like affection.

He said, 'I learned the verses you speak now as you spoke them then, which pleased you, even though I couldn't understand them.'

'No man can wholly understand the word of God,' said Abbas.

'So you told me at the time. Would that others knew it.'

Abbas nodded, somewhat sombrely.

'You also told me,' said Tannhauser, 'that the word of Allah cannot be spoken in any other tongue, for Arabic is the tongue in which He chose to speak to the Prophet, blessed be his name. Yet you translated the name of the *Adh-Dhariyat* for me. *The Winnowing Winds*.'

Abbas laughed, surprised. 'I did?'

'It was a comfort to me, I don't know why. And a great mystery. I pressed you on its meaning. *What is a winnowing wind?* You were very patient. You considered it. *The wind that separates the wheat from the chaff*, you said. I wondered if I were one or the other – for I felt that a wind had swept me away.' He smiled. 'It sweeps me still. And I asked you, *What is the difference between the wheat and the chaff?* And you considered again, and said, *The difference between those who love life and those who love death*.'

Abbas seemed taken aback. 'I said that?'

'I forgot it for many years,' said Tannhauser. 'But the day I saw the eunuch put the bowstring round the prince-child's throat, I remembered it. I've never forgotten it since.'

'It is for the scholars to interpret the *ulema*. If I said such things, I was young, and prone to unwitting blasphemies. Forgive me.'

Abbas rose to his feet. Tannhauser followed, so weak that he had to use his hands to push up from the table. He swayed slightly and Abbas took his arm.

'Ibrahim,' said Abbas. 'When I found you at Fort Saint Elmo, you called me *Father*.'

'I have always thought of you as such,' said Tannhauser, 'though it's a presumption to which I have no right. I hope I did not offend you.'

'You could not have honoured me more highly.' Abbas turned his face away to conceal an excess of sentiment. When he turned back, his eyes were clear. 'Did you ever meet your own father again?'

'No,' said Tannhauser.

This was true and yet not true but, for this night, he'd had enough of such complexities.

'He would have been proud of the honour you've won,' said Abbas, with a smile.

Tannhauser wanted to smile back, but couldn't. 'In a world where eunuchs strangle children, and call their duty sacred, honour is hard to come by. Sometimes, so is Faith.'

'Ibrahim –'

'You see,' said Tannhauser, against all better judgement, 'it was not the stain of the child's murder that filled me with such shame – but the fact that I'd failed to fulfil my sacred duty. To the corps. To the *oçak*. To the Sultan. To God. And because I valued duty above infanticide, I knew I'd lost either my mind – or my soul.'

Abbas shook his head. 'From God we come, and to God we shall surely return. Please, tell me you are not lost.'

It was as good a moment as any to reaffirm the purity of his faith, at least in front of his patron. Tannhauser quoted the Unity. '*He is Allah, the One. Allah-us-Samad, the Eternal, Absolute. He begetteth not, nor is He begotten. And there is none like unto Him.*'

'*Allahu Akabar.*' Abbas's hand was still on his arm. He squeezed. 'Ibrahim, we must never lose our faith in Allah, even if we lose our faith in our fellow men. Even if we lose our faith in ourselves.'

Tannhauser put his hand on Abbas's. He realised, for the first time, how delicate in stature Abbas was; in his mind he had always been a giant. He said, 'It's my faith in men that I can't abandon entire, and I will tell you I've tried. Perhaps that will be my doom.'

Abbas nodded dubiously, as if fearing that fresh blasphemies might loom. 'You are far from good health, and I've taxed you by talking too long. I must check the night watch. And you must sleep.' As Abbas walked towards the exit, he stopped and turned. As if to lighten the mood of his exit he said, 'Tomorrow you will tell me more of the trade in pepper. I'm intrigued.'

'Gladly. But tell me, please, where is the Ethiope?'

Abbas looked at him. 'Gone. He belongs to Admiral Piyale.'

Tannhauser watched Abbas leave. He was grateful for the exhaustion that overcame him, for it loosened the knot of emotion in his gut. When he reached his bed he was about to throw himself down when he noticed two white silk scarves on the pillow, each with something wrapped inside. He unwrapped the first scarf and found the gold bangle that he'd hidden around his ankle.

I come to Malta not for riches or honour but to save my soul.

Perhaps the bangle had helped to save his hide. He wrapped it round his wrist. He picked up the second object and knew at once that it was a knife and his heart squeezed at a thought he dared not formulate. He unwrapped it, and for a moment his tightened nerves relaxed. It was an elegant dagger. Its hilt was worked in silver with great art and a ruby was set into its pommel. The scabbard was red leather decorated with garnets. He slid it from the sheath and his heart sprang once again into his throat. In contrast to the exquisite fittings, the blade was crude in workmanship and lacked symmetry, yet its edges gleamed sharp, and its essence was uncommonly deadly. The steel was dull and mottled with black streaks and he knew it at once. It had been forged by the voice of an angel, and quenched in the blood of a devil, by his own hand.

IN SAINT ELMO's forge, Tannhauser used the dagger to divide a one-pound slab of opium into quarters, then he packed the lot into his saddle wallet. He placed his Russian gold ring on his right-hand middle finger and reseated the stone in the floor. He tethered his horse to the anvil and made his way upstairs to the derelict solar, where he found his wheel-lock rifle and bullet pouch undisturbed in their cranny in the broken rafters. He hung the rifle's winding key round his neck. He collected the mare and rode back out of the fort, past the baffled and grovelling Bulgar, and headed over the hill to Marsamxett Bay. It was there that the bulk of the Turkish fleet, and all the Algerian corsairs, were safely harboured.

After his meal with Abbas, Tannhauser had lain on his cushions for three days and nights, and had ventured no further than the kitchen and the latrine. His liver had produced the black bile that engendered melancholy. In this sorry state, between bouts of stupefied sleep, he'd pondered what course to take next, and though this pondering exacerbated the dolorous effects of the bile, he'd found himself unable to turn his mind elsewhere. Worse still, he'd come to no firm conclusion, for no sooner had he settled on the merits of one scheme of action than he reconvinced himself of the merits of another.

Sound reason was on the side of re-embracing the Ottoman way. Malta would fall, even if later than sooner, for with their Mongol blood their stubbornness knew no bounds and for them to yield, especially in the matter of siege warfare, was almost unknown. As he'd discussed with the traders in the bazaar, conquest would leave him well placed to turn a profit, and he could count on the patronage and investment of Abbas bin Murad. In the garden of the Auberge of England a fortune in opium was buried beneath his tub. It would be easy enough in the sack to go and retrieve it. With Sabato Svi re-established in Venice, their future would be bright. More pressingly, he was confident he could avoid any further combat.

The alternative was not only bleak – and highly improbable – but would require a vigour and a passion that he seemed to have exhausted for good in the fury of Saint Elmo. He would have to return to the Borgo through both sets of hostile lines; no easy feat since the Turkish cordon thereabouts was now tight as a drumhead. Since there was no point returning merely to die like a fool for the Religion, and assuming Amparo, Carla and Bors were still alive, he'd then have to spirit all of them back out – through the same double cordon of steel – and reach the hidden boat at Zonra, whose continued existence was no real certainty either.

None of these calculations included Orlandu. When Tannhauser did so, the journey to the Borgo seemed impossible. He was willing to brass his own way out of being caught sneaking in the dark by Turkish watchmen, but with a slave boy in tow they'd be screaming under the bastinado by dawn.

Bors was his own man and as long as he died with a sword in his hand would have no complaints. The women? If they survived and were taken prisoner by the Turks – and their pale-skinned beauty would accord them considerable value, at least as far as their lives were concerned – he could probably winkle them out of their long-term fates. In Tannhauser's experience, if a bargain could be conceived, it could be made. Mustafa wouldn't put the entire population to the sword, despite his rages. Someone had to rebuild the town and plough the fields. San Lorenzo would become a mosque. The food would get better. Malta would become like Rhodes or the Balkans or any of a hundred foreign territories brought under Suleiman's fief: prosperous and peaceful. They could even go to church on Sundays. And if Carla and Amparo didn't survive he would, in time, forget them and life would go on. For life always did. He had lost women before. And at least he wouldn't have to see these die before him.

This latter, callous, sentiment, proved false, and its contrary kept him awake more than any other. He'd never forget the fair and tender ladies he'd brought across the sea. Any more than he'd forgotten his mother, or Britta or Gerta.

Next morning he'd awoken and decided that he could raise Orlandu's station – if he was alive – without either of them risking a painful death. Because Tannhauser had pointed him out in his delirium, Abbas had tried to claim the boy, on the morning Saint Elmo's fell, but the corsairs who'd taken him had been implacable. Booty had been thin on the ground that day, and after so much sacrifice they'd have held on to a three-legged goat for the sheer sake of honour.

MARSAMXETT BAY WAS choked with activity and thick with mast and sail. Ships came from Alexandria and Tripoli loaded with supplies. Others left for the same destinations with cargoes of wounded. Repairs and refitting were a perpetual chore. He spent half the day searching the waterfront, exchanging pleasantries, blessings and the occasional obscenities with the Algerian scurvies thereabouts, though nothing passed that required a resort to arms. After numerous discussions and falsely raised hopes, he eventually spotted Orlandu scraping barnacles and weed from the hull of a galley. The boy was hard at it and, from a distance, looked none the worse for wear. Tannhauser did not disturb him and made more enquiries.

He discovered that the boy was now the property of said galley's captain, a razor-featured cove named Salih Ali. He was a follower of the great Torghoud Rais, who had died the day Tannhauser had been carried from the ruins. Salih was a native Algerian, which was a relief of sorts, for the sleaziest and most vicious of the Barbary corsairs were invariably Christian renegades, like Torghoud himself. They retired to the shade of an awning and drank sweet tea and talked. Tannhauser let him glimpse the tattooed wheel on his arm, lest his finery mislead him, and they complimented each other on their valorous reputations, of which both were in fact quite ignorant. Tannhauser then intimated that he might be in the market for a Christian slave, a youth strong in back and limb, and the negotiation began.

It took two and a half hours before it was concluded. It was doubtful that any European of Tannhauser's acquaintance could have endured it; even Bors would have throttled Salih within twenty-five minutes. But to Tannhauser it was meat and drink. He loved such games – had learned them the hard way, as all loved games are learned, from masters in the bazaars of Beirut and Trebizond and the Buyuk Carsi, who'd laughed and rubbed their hands when they'd seen him coming – and he knew very quickly that he would get the better of Salih, for the corsair fell at once into the trap of coveting the wheel-lock rifle draped across his adversary's lap, a desire which Tannhauser had counted on with some confidence. Since Salih was not, of course, so vulgar as to ask for the rifle straight out, but rather made a point of admiring it, Tannhauser was only too delighted to demonstrate its accuracy, the ingenuity of its mechanism, its instantaneous discharge on pulling the trigger, and its freedom from anything so primitive as a burning length of cord. He was careful not to let the poor fellow handle it. Subsequently convincing Salih that the wheel-lock was not up for trade, at any price, despite that far a greater sum than a filthy slave boy was eventually heaped high on the table, was a masterpiece that consumed the first two hours; and Tannhauser was happy for it to do so. It was at this point, when Salih's desperation to own the gun had reduced Orlandu's value to a minor item on a lengthy list, that Tannhauser suggested they sample the opium he'd brought.

He produced a walnut-sized chunk from his kaftan and Salih's eyes slitted with covetousness. A water pipe was procured and they crumbled some of the opium with flowers of hemp and crushed raisins and tobacco, and smoked in the stifling shade, Tannhauser with the restraint of one who had himself been victim to such stratagems, Salih with the reckless gratitude of a man whose nerves, beneath his smile, were frayed raw. Salih was not the first to believe that a little relaxation would improve his trading skills. But by the time the wondrous resin had cast its spell, and the uproar and stench of the harbour had faded, and Salih started swaying on his stool within arm's reach of Paradise, Tannhauser was able to buy the boy for but two of the opium quarters. He threw in the remains of the smaller chunk as a gesture of goodwill, for it would give Salih a face-saving boast and – who knew? – the world was a small place and perhaps they would one day meet again.

Orlandu was brought up from the beach by a factotum. Tannhauser kept his face turned until the right moment and then stepped forward to place himself between Salih and the boy. He nailed Orlandu with a hard stare and in the act of stroking his beard placed a finger over his lips to tell the boy he shouldn't reveal that they were friends.

Orlandu, quick as a snake, transformed his initial gape of shock into the sullen glare of the unwillingly bought and sold. Salih's factotum, who'd caught a fragrant whiff from the hookah, was absorbed by the hope of partaking of the pipe, vain though this was, and the silent exchange went unnoticed. Salih contented himself with clubbing the boy on the ear with the heel of his fist by way of telling him to mind his manners now that he was in the service of a gentleman. By the look the Algerians exchanged, Tannhauser suspected that both assumed his purpose in buying the boy was in fact to bugger him; and Salih had repeatedly assured him that Orlandu was 'a boy of perpetual freshness'; but this was not the time to take offence at imaginary slurs. Salih Ali expressed his hope that they trade again and Tannhauser assured the corsair that indeed they would. And then they were off: Tannhauser on his mare, rifle across the pommel, and Orlandu running beside him, hanging on to the stirrup for all his life was worth.

WHEN THEY WERE out of sight of Salih's berth, Tannhauser slowed to a walk. He did not look down, as he wanted to maintain appearances. Snug beneath his thigh the wallet bulged with another four pounds of black gold. He laughed. He hadn't laughed in longer than he could remember and it improved the day no end.

'So,' he said, in Italian, 'you have reverted to your former profession as a barnacle scraper. I'm disappointed.'

'Where are we going?' said Orlandu.

'What, no gratitude?'

'I thought you were dead. I mourned for you and prayed for your soul, even though I thought you were damned.'

'Your lack of faith shames you. Did I not tell you we would meet again?'

'Why did you take so long?'

'Hold now,' said Tannhauser. 'It was not I who let himself be captured by the Sultan's sea wolves, while on a secret mission for La Valette.'

Orlandu let go of the stirrup and stopped. Tannhauser stopped too and looked down at him. The boy's eyes were filled with hurt and rage. Tannhauser had spoken lightly, without intention of cruelty; but the boy was too young to accept it as such.

'Listen,' said Tannhauser, 'you've done well to survive six weeks in the company of corsairs.' If Orlandu had been less rough hewn, and more cherubic, his perpetual freshness might well have been sullied, but he didn't say so. 'You've been resolute and brave and I'm proud of you. So much so that I've decided to make you my partner in a famous enterprise.'

Orlandu brightened. He had a mercurial nature, not given to pointless brooding; in Tannhauser's book a strength to be admired. 'Your partner?' Orlandu said.

'In the first instance, you'd be more in the way of my apprentice. After all, you know nothing of business – or of very much else. But with due diligence, and in, I should say, ten years or so, you could be a prosperous young man – a man of the world, no less – with a diamond in your turban and a ship or two at your command.'

Tannhauser was suddenly aware that these were extravagant

claims for a man wearing hand-me-down clothes, grand as they were, and who sat on a borrowed horse. But Orlandu didn't doubt his mentor for a second.

'I must wear a turban?' said Orlandu.

'You are going to become a Turk, my friend.'

'I hate the Turks.'

'Then learn to love them. They're no worse than any other kind of men, and have the advantage over most in all sorts of ways.'

'They've come here to kill us and take our land.'

'A habit they share with a good many tribes and peoples. That they've proved uncommonly good at it is not to be held against them. The Religion are invaders too.'

'But we fought the Turks,' said Orlandu. 'You fought them too.'

'For and against in my time,' said Tannhauser. 'The French fight the Italians, the Germans fight with themselves – as do Christians and Moslems both – and the Spanish fight just about anyone they can find. Fighting is a habit as naturally inborn as shitting. As you will learn, the identity of the foe hardly matters to the combatants at all. In any case, we're hardly well placed to quarrel with the Turks right now.'

Orlandu's face twisted in confusion. He was bright enough to appreciate the power of logic but, like most, he was unfamiliar with the art. He said, 'What about Jesus?'

'Worship Him if you will. The Turks won't tie you to a stake for it. But there are benefits to professing an allegiance to Allah and His Prophet, may peace be upon him, even if it be insincere.'

'How can you pretend to believe in a god?'

Tannhauser laughed. 'Mark my words, there are red-hatted scoundrels in the Vatican at this very moment who doubt that He exists at all. They're just cunning enough not to say so.'

'We'll go to the everlasting fires of Hell.'

'It's a crowded place by any account. But if you were God, would you much care by what name or means humanity grovelled before you? Indeed, would you much care what we did at all?'

'Jesus loves us. This I know.'

'Then he will forgive a petty deception designed to save us from the bastinado. And now, with your permission, we must be on our way. It's improper for a man of my standing to be seen arguing theology with his slave.'

'Your slave?'

'For the sake of appearances, certainly. And without doubt you are the Sultan's slave, as are the majority of his subjects. The Grand Viziers are slaves. The *aga* of the janissaries is a slave. The most powerful men in the Empire are slaves. Suleiman's slaves. Under the Empire only Turks are free born. But, as we've just established, when it's merely a matter of words, where is the sting? In Europe birth is all and it's a boot on every throat. But under the Ottomans, merit can take you to the highest councils of Stambouli. Piyale himself was born a Christian, found abandoned as a babe on a ploughshare outside Belgrade, when Suleiman laid that city siege. He's now the greatest admiral in the Empire, perhaps the world. Surely it's better to be a rich slave than a poor man free in name alone, scraping at the barnacles in Grand Harbour and bowing like a serf whenever a nobleman walks by.'

Orlandu considered this, not yet wholly convinced. 'Then I must pretend to be your slave, and pretend to love the Turk, and pretend to worship Allah too?'

'It's easier than it sounds,' Tannhauser assured him. 'And when your belly is full and the silks are soft against your skin, it becomes easier still.'

'And my mother?'

Tannhauser blinked, unprepared for the matter to be raised. 'She is in God's hands, as either faith would attest. You and I must see to ourselves.' Orlandu blinked at the harshness of this prescription, and, in truth, Tannhauser felt something of a fraud. He did not, however, admit it. Instead he leaned forward and squeezed the boy's shoulder. 'You've witnessed the thick of battle, boy. The madness and the waste. The sorrow, the terror, the pain. Can you tell me that there's any use to it?'

Orlandu didn't answer.

'If there is a God, he's blessed you with a keen wit,' said Tannhauser. 'You would honour Him best by employing it. And now let's away.'

TANNHAUSER TOOK ORLANDU to the bazaar and refreshed some acquaintances and exchanged two ounces of opium for silver *akçe*. He subjected Orlandu to a bath shared with two Sipahi cavalrymen, and bought him some clothes and slippers appropriate to his station, and a knife and a small iron cooking pot, which he promised would make him popular. He taught him to say the *Shahada*: *Ashhadu Alla Ilaha Illa Allah Wa Ashhadu Anna Muhammad Rasulu Allah. There is no God but Allah and Mohammed is His Messenger*. Which would endear him to the faithful in an emergency, and since Maltese and Arabic were not far distant tongues, Orlandu mastered it readily. He told him not to bow his head to any man, even a vizier, for one bows to Allah alone, and he discovered that '*Asalaamu alaykum*' was a greeting with which the boy was already familiar.

He impressed on him that they were not to appear too friendly before Abbas or his entourage. They were to believe that Tannhauser was repaying a modest debt, out of charity and reverence for Allah rather than out of affection for the boy, and no more than that. He then took him back to Abbas's camp and introduced him to the staff, and bribed the hostler to instruct him in the care of horses, a skill always in demand. Orlandu, with his street urchin's instinct to the fore, played his part with conviction and Tannhauser, his black bile purged, congratulated himself on a fair day's work.

Later, he made a gift of a pound of opium to Abbas, and told him that, with his blessing, he planned to take a ship for Tripoli the very next day. Abbas gave his blessing, and a letter of commendation, but his mood was preoccupied and dark, though he did not say why.

Tannhauser retired to his cushions to contemplate a brighter future than had recently seemed possible. He'd parlay the remaining opium into gold at the bazaar, for it was worth far more here than elsewhere. In Tripoli the gold, artfully distributed, would buy him a line of credit with the grain merchants. His knowledge of the Maltese situation, and his contacts in the army bazaar, would purchase something even more precious: their confidence. And Abbas's letter would be worth more gold than he could carry. Tannhauser had started out before with much less capital. He'd be back in Malta in a month with a cargo of goods that would make the quartermasters drool.

He'd done what he could for the boy. A place on Abbas's staff was as safe as any station on the island. He'd stood by his bargain with Carla and more. He'd paid his dues to the War God. Someone had to rise from the ashes yet to come; better he than some other. As he laid his head on the pillow and closed his eyes, what passed for his conscience was as clear as a polished mirror.

Some hours later he awoke. The light of the fires burned outside the tent. He'd been dreaming, he knew not of what. He glanced down for the Ethiope; but the Ethiope wasn't there. The dream had been haunted by a distant thread of music that had made his heart ache with sadness, that left a blurred impression of possibilities unfulfilled and paths not taken. He lay back on the pillow and scratched his privities. Then he realised that he heard the music still.

His gut clenched tight. He told himself to go back to his dreams. Come the dawn he had a ship to catch, for Tripoli. Instead, he rose from the cushions and pulled on his kaftan, and as if under the spell of some enchantment he wandered out into the night.

Watchfires speckled the vast pooled darkness of the Marsa, and he imagined the janissaries fettling their arms and binding each other's wounds by the *oçak*'s warmth, and, as was their practice, reciting heroic ballads around their *kazan*. Part of him yearned to join their hearth for an hour or two, to revisit the sacred fellowship of his youth. His tattoos would guarantee a cordial welcome. A quarter of opium would ease their dismay at events. But the past was past, and better left so, and the melody's golden thread drew him on elsewhere.

The music on the crystalline air was faint but real. It pulled him to the rim of Corradino and he overlooked the Christian harbours jumbled down below. The half-moon was in Sagittarius and a lunar beam slashed the waters of Galley Creek. He imagined she sat at the moonbeam's farther end. Wherever she sat, she sawed at her gambo violl with that same extravagant union of hope and despair that had charmed him in the rose garden, and had launched him into the core of Hell's creation. As then on that perfumed hill, so now on this one which reeked of putrefaction, he felt his eyes fill with tears and her music fill his soul where it had always been empty. Amparo was his darling. And yet. Had he chosen the wrong woman? He didn't wonder that he'd dared not choose Carla. She wielded a power to which he feared submission. But one woman or the other was hardly the present predicament. In his present predicament, all his choices were carried away on the wings of her nocturnal heartsong.

He heard steps in the dirt behind him and turned. It was Orlandu. He looked up with an unspoken question, his tongue stilled by what he saw in Tannhauser's face. Tannhauser smiled. In his mind's eye, he saw the galley for Tripoli pulling out of Marsamxett Bay without him.

'You hear that, boy?' he said.

Orlandu cocked an ear. He nodded.

'That's your mother.'

Orlandu gazed out across the bay.

Tannhauser said, 'She plays like an angel in chains.'

Orlandu looked up at him smartly, as if Tannhauser had let slip out a secret that he'd meant to keep to himself. Tannhauser scraped a thumbnail through his beard. He studied the vast terrain of darkness which enswathed the town.

'It's the Devil's bounty I'll need if I'm going to set her free. But he's always been more than happy to extend my credit.'

TUESDAY 7 AUGUST 1565

Santa Margharita – the Mdina Road – Monte San Salvatore

THE DAY DAWNED windless and still and a foetid aroma infested the air throughout the camp. As Tannhauser rose for prayer the stench told him the reason for Abbas's dour humour of the night before. The prelude to all battles included, if nothing else, a mighty swill of faeces, and faeces of a uniquely malodorous character at that. It was not a measure of cowardice, rather a fact of nature; thirty thousand men were preparing to sacrifice their lives for Allah; and even the fearless were wise to rid their bodies of the excess weight.

The battalions had manoeuvred into place in the dark and by the time he'd collected his chestnut mare and ridden across the saddle between Corradino and Margharita, the *surah* of Conquest was proclaimed over the neighbouring heights. The timpani and pipes of the *mehterhane* band struck up and the marshalling horns summoned a colossal twin-pronged offensive by the Grande Turke's legions. Admiral Piyale commanded the assault on the Borgo, Mustafa Pasha that on L'Isola.

Since the intention was to take both citadels at any cost, Tannhauser spent the morning on the Margharita ridge, in the feigned role, when necessary, of Abbas's aide-de-camp, and from there he watched the prodigies of violence and valour unfold below. After all, there was no point sneaking into the Borgo – his plan since hearing the contessa's untimely nocturne – if the Turks were already streaming in through the walls. In that event he would ride down the hill and join them, in the hope that he could salvage at least Amparo and Carla from the rampage that would follow. And a rampage it would be. Suleiman himself had failed to restrain the janissaries – at Buda, Rhodes and elsewhere – and the grudges nurtured in this war ran deeper than most. La Valette had made sure of that. The streets would run red for a day, perhaps two or three. Atrocities would abound. Men would knife each other over tawdry scraps of booty. The knights would take the brunt of the torture and execution, which was only fair. But sooner rather than later the abscess would be lanced, and once it dawned that the property, human and otherwise, being destroyed belonged to the Sultan, Mustafa would start hanging his own men in droves.

Tannhauser wondered if he'd be able to reclaim Buraq – after, he supposed, seeing the women safe – and reckoned it would take light footwork, a good deal of opium, and probably some killing.

As the opening bombardment ceased, the clearing smoke and dust revealed a huge breach in the Borgo enceinte, where a forty-foot section of the curtain wall had collapsed on to the corpses in the ditch. The banners of the Sultan surged across the Grande Terre Plein and Piyale's Tartar levies, in brilliant yellow uniforms and headdress, unleashed a whickering rain of arrows from their bows. They flung themselves at the Religion's *arquebuceros*. Scores were cut down on the gore-steeped clay of the approaches. Those who could hauled themselves up and stumbled on into the inferno, for such it became as wildfire and bubbling pig fat vomited into the breach from the enfilading crownworks. As Azebs freighted ladders in an attempt to escalade the post of Castile, a scarlet wedge of Sipahi foot drove forward in the Tartars' yellow wake.

On the hilltops more battalions, and yet more – as if Piyale could conjure them up from thin air – shunted over the rim to join the fray. The high white *borks* of the janissaries swayed like a field of giant lilies. Dervishes stomped in impatience and brandished glittering blades and cried out *Woe to the Unbelievers, on account of that Day of theirs which they have been promised.* And Iayalars delirious with hemp tore at their clothes and screamed out to Allah to grant them their right share of blood.

Above the foremost of the Catholic bastions, the seventy-fifth slave of the siege to grace the gallows on the Provençal Gate dangled over the catastrophe like a wingless and blue-tongued harpy sent by the forces of darkness to observe the day.

As the Borgo fought for existence, three hundred yards to Piyale's left, and separated by the inlet of Galley Creek, Mustafa Pasha fell on Saint Michel. A red mass of Sipahis flung their scaling irons high amidst a flaming pandemonium of fire hoops and pipkins. The stench of burning hair and fat reached Tannhauser's nose through the already dense miasma of the decomposing dead, from which latter multitudes of blowflies rose in snarling and iridescent pillars blue and green. It seemed impossible that even *gazi* could endure such demoniac treatment; yet they did; and as minutes and then hours crawled by, they climbed the bodies of the roasted and the slain, and scaled the fire-blacked walls and wormed through the embrasures, and combat at close quarters erupted high above the Ruins of Bormula.

As if to sound L'Isola's death knell, Mustafa himself appeared on that broken plain at the head of his Guards. Musket balls kicked dust spots from the sun-baked ground about him. He disdained them. Ostrich feathers surmounted his immense white turban and his pearl-grey courser was dressed in cloth of gold and red horsetail standards towered to his either side, as they'd towered over Temujin and Timur the Lame in the hecatombs of yore. Alongside the Pasha's Guard, a dozen *orta* of *solaks*, the janissary elite, accompanied by their Bektasi dervish fathers, drew themselves up, in bronze helms and ochre robes, and Mustafa rode among them, goading their pride, exhorting them with verses from the Prophet, courting their souls with the prospect of a palm-shaded Paradise and whetting their greed with that of bonuses and pillage. He and La Valette were well matched, Tannhauser thought. Both seventy years old and each still crazed with blood. The *solaks* formed up for the charge and his throat tightened, for he felt their hearts beat. If Sipahis could mount the ramparts of Saint Michel – and they had – the Lions of Islam would take them down entire.

Then a great roar – of vengeful triumph intermingled with despair – rose from the breach in the Borgo wall and Tannhauser urged his horse back along the ridge for a better view. Piyale's shock troops had cleared the fiery breach and crowded pell-mell into the vacant ground beyond. There they met the unblemished stone of the concealed interior wall – the new second wall that Tannhauser himself had suggested and which La Valette had killed slaves by the hundreds to construct. Instead of finding themselves in the town, Piyale's invaders were trapped in a couloir of slaughter, penned up in front by the wall and crushed together from behind by the scarlet wedge of *gazi* seeking glory.

The killing floor was superbly conceived. At either end of the corridor casemates and oilettes accommodated cannon charged with grape, and these ploughed the frantic press with tempests of gore. From above, *arquebuceros* and archers fired at will, and Maltese women in pairs poured cauldrons of boiling lard and dropped blocks of masonry, and the incendiary crews plied their baneful wares, all of them conspiring in the infinite ruin of the caterwauling mortals below.

The entrapped wheeled this way and that, like a herd of panicked cattle set about by predators, and as they finally understood that their only chance of salvation lay in rout, a convulsive migration exploded towards the breach, and sally gates creaked open in the new-wrought works, and grim squads of knights ventured forth to hack their prey to pieces with axes and swords. And as the quarry rose waist high in bloody stacks, and the refugees on the Grand Terre Plein were shot in the back as they ran, the knights raised their weapons skyward and praised God.

The Borgo would stand. At least for today.

Tannhauser rode back to view the progress of the fight for Saint Michel. Howling columns of *solaks* were mounting the ladders and had already pitched their Star and Crescent banner alongside the Cross. The knights and the Maltese were contesting every inch, but with immediate support unlikely from the Borgo, and Mustafa's reserves effectively unlimited, the forecast for Saint Michel seemed bleak indeed. If Saint Michel fell, the Borgo would follow within a week. Mustafa would fill L'Isola with his siege train, blast the city's undefended flank from a distance of a few hundred feet, and traverse Galley Creek with his longboats while the enceinte was being stormed from the Grand Terre Plein.

Tannhauser didn't know the byways of the island well enough to make his way into the Borgo under darkness, at least not from here; nor did he know the disposition of the Turkish lines to the east. He needed one of the Religion's Maltese scouts to get him through. They knew every nook and cranny of the rugged terrain and ferried messages to and from Mdina at the Grand Master's will. As far as he knew not one of them had been caught. Mdina was four miles away. If he wanted to return to the Borgo, Mdina was where he'd have to start.

TANNHAUSER WHEELED HIS horse and rode across the heights with as much haste as he dared. He climbed the flank of Corradino and swung past Abbas's tent and found Orlandu shovelling horse manure into a barrow. Orlandu abandoned his shovel as Tannhauser dismounted.

'We'll not be seeing each other for a while,' Tannhauser said.

The boy was at once crestfallen but squared his narrow shoulders.

'You'll stay with the entourage of General Abbas. He's wise and fair, and will see you come to no harm. Tell him nothing of our fellowship. Tell him, if you must, what I've told him myself: that you did me a kindness when I was enslaved at Fort Saint Elmo. I was dying of thirst and you gave me a drink from a goatskin water bag. That's all. In ransoming you from the Algerian, I've repaid that boon, as Allah commands. Do you understand?'

Orlandu nodded. 'A goatskin water bag.'

'Remember, you're now a man – and a Maltese at that, and I know no tougher of the species – and as Saint Paul wrote, you must put boyish manners behind you. Work hard, pray with the heathen, learn their tongue. You survived the captivity of Salih Ali; in this berth you'll live like a duke.'

He took a step nearer and stooped over, hands on thighs.

'Now listen to me close, Orlandu. If Malta falls, and I've not returned, and Abbas takes ship for Old Stambouli – as sooner or later he will – you must go with him.'

Orlandu blinked. 'Across the sea?'

'Look on it as an education, for it will certainly be that. Give me your word, now. On the Tears of the Virgin.'

'I give you my word, on the Tears of the Virgin.'

'Good. As long as you're with Abbas, I'll be able to find you again, be that it takes months or even years.'

This was rather harder to accept, but Orlandu swallowed his fear and did not demur.

'Do you have faith in me?' pressed Tannhauser.

'That's the only thing I do not need to fake,' said the boy.

At this Tannhauser almost wavered himself, but he swallowed too, and contented himself with a solemn nod of approval. He slipped the heavy gold ring from his finger and pressed it into Orlandu's palm.

'Keep this as a memento of our friendship. While you carry it, you shall not come to harm.' This was a piece of nonsense, no doubt, but Orlandu looked at the ring as if it were the Grail, and Tannhauser knew it would give him heart in the trials that lay before him. 'Let no one see it or you'll have to defend it with your life. Hide it up your arse.'

Orlandu said, 'My arse?'

'I've known men carry knives up there, and no end of contraband besides. If Abbas ever seeks to abandon you, or sell you, show him the ring, and him alone. Tell him it is my pledge – he will recognise it – and that you beg him to honour it until I return.'

Orlandu nodded. 'Where are you going?'

'As far as you – and Abbas – are concerned, I've gone to Tripoli.'

Orlando looked to the sound of guns across the bay. He looked back at Tannhauser, who saw him hover on the verge of begging to go with him. To his credit, Orlandu kept his peace, and from this Tannhauser took confidence.

'Now embrace me,' he said. 'And let us bid each other luck until we meet again.'

He lifted his hands from his thighs as the boy, for in truth a boy he still was, plunged his head into Tannhauser's chest and held tight. Tannhauser squeezed his shoulders, which for a moment felt pitifully frail in his big freckled hands. Should he take him along after all? Reason's answer was unequivocal: Orlandu was safer by far with Abbas bin Murad. Orlandu was reluctant to let go, and truth to tell he wasn't alone, but Tannhauser pushed him back and turned to his horse. He mounted. He gave the forlorn boy a salute. And then he rode away.

On the fringe of the commanders' encampment he passed a squad of musketeers without being challenged. He dropped down the western slope of Corradino on to the wide, flat apron of the Marsa and trotted south through the bazaar, where he bought a half-sack of coffee to store in his wallets. He popped a handful of beans in his mouth and chewed and the bitter tang braced him. He crossed the eerie quiet of the soldiers' encampment. Almost every fighting man had been mustered for the assault and of the lowly levies who'd been left behind to renovate the latrines none extended more than a sullen glance.

Beyond the camp proper, originally at a sanitary distance but now spreading back to meet it like leakage from a huge and pungent bog, was the Turkish field hospital. It was a primitive aggregation of tatty canvas awnings, under which lay a multitude of flux-stricken wretches. The poisoned wells had fulfilled their atrocious expectations. The burning sun and noxious miasmas from the numberless puddles of filth had done the rest. Alongside the plagued lay uncounted wounded, who swiftly succumbed to the pest. The listless, demoralised orderlies, who shuffled about the squalor with the bleak resignation of farmers in a blighted field, were outnumbered by hundreds to one. The delirious murmurs of the afflicted, their groans and prayers, their cries for water, for mercy, for deliverance, set up a chorale of desperation that harrowed Tannhauser to the gut. He covered his mouth and nostrils with the hem of his kaftan and whispered a blessing on Abbas for denying him such a fate. He skirted the sea of horror with all due speed.

The outer perimeter of the sprawling camp was picketed by a dozen or so mounted lookouts patrolling in pairs. He headed towards the nearest and nodded imperiously without slowing down, counting once again, and with the desired result, on the ostentatious splendour of his trappings to forestall delay. Once in open country and beyond their sight, he swung sharply west, set his mount to a brisk pace and put the din of the continuing battle behind him.

De Lugny's outriders captured him on the open ground, at the foot of the rocky ascent to the city of Mdina. They formed a circle of menace about him on their slaver-toothed chargers –

Lusitanos and Andalucians crossed with Swedish warmbloods for size. The knights' visors were down, their blood was up, and without their standing orders to take all prisoners in for torture they'd have been glad to hack his head off on the spot. They swapped ribald comments on his kaftan, which, it seemed, they found womanly. Despite this none of them laughed, an indignity Tannhauser would have welcomed to lighten the mood. After all, the severed head of a Turk would bring them at worst a mild rebuke, and cooped up in Mdina – far from the unhinged slaughter they craved – the pickings were slim.

He was relieved then when the Chevalier De Lugny arrived with the Religion's entire complement of two hundred cavalry. Over their armour they wore red surcoats with a large white cross. The garment had looked much better on Amparo. De Lugny at once recognised him as 'the spy' who had guided the raid on Gallows Point.

'I asked for your services a month ago, Captain,' he said. 'I was told you were dead.'

'False rumours abound in such times,' Tannhauser replied.

'May we know how you have spent this interlude?'

'Recovering from my wounds.'

'Among the Moslem devils?'

'In the tent of one of their generals.'

Sometimes the boldest answer is the best, and so it proved. De Lugny's face was for a moment a portrait in perplexity. The knight to his left – one of the outriders who'd caught him – raised his visor: he had a youthful but poisonous countenance and that air of inbred superiority that no failures in this world would ever undermine.

'Then you have much to report to our Grand Master,' said De Lugny.

'That's why I go to Mdina. I need a Maltese to take me to the Borgo.'

The popinjay spoke up and confirmed Tannhauser's impressions. 'Perhaps you had much to report to the Grande Turke too.'

Tannhauser looked at him. He briefly considered ignoring this slur, but the jibes about his kaftan may have rankled deeper than he'd thought. He said, 'I spent thirteen days at Saint Elmo's. The final thirteen days.'

Glances were exchanged and some crossed themselves in honour of that legendary stand.

Tannhauser continued, 'When the janissaries came down the hill we often thought of you lot, polishing your armour and swilling wine in the safety of Mdina.'

Several swords cleared their sheaths, including the popinjay's. Oaths were sworn. Warhorses stomped their hooves in sympathy with their riders.

Tannhauser canted his rifle against his hip. Their bloated sense of honour suddenly offended him. Perhaps he was still unbalanced in mind from the ague or from yesterday's opium. Perhaps he had just had enough of belligerent folly. He'd lately borne a great deal with the phlegmatic good humour that he prized, but the popinjay struck a spark too close to the powder keg. An uncommon if once familiar rage flooded Tannhauser's brain.

'Strip that armour,' said Tannhauser to the popinjay, 'and I'll take any three of you. On foot, any five.'

He kicked his mount forward a step. The popinjay turned white about the lips. Had he lifted his sword, Tannhauser would have shot him in the face. Beyond that, despite his boast, he made no predictions. De Lugny, who knew men better than did his young comrade, raised his hand. 'Enough!' commanded De Lugny. 'Before things are said that can never be unsaid.'

Tannhauser's gaze didn't waver. The popinjay's eyelids fluttered and he looked away. Tannhauser turned to De Lugny with a bland smile. 'Then I can count on one of your Maltese.'

'I dare say you can,' said De Lugny, relieved. He inclined his head towards the grumble of guns beyond the hills. 'How goes the battle? We heard the commotion and decided we'd had our fill of polishing and swilling.'

'Borgo will hold,' said Tannhauser. 'I doubt Saint Michel will last out the hour.'

'They held out before.'

'The pennants of the janissaries already fly from the walls.'

'Could we take them from the flank?'

Tannhauser suppressed a pitying glance. 'Mustafa has twenty thousand reserves on the heights.'

De Lugny's brow furrowed. 'How well defended is their camp?'

'Their camp?' It was a foolish question, which Tannhauser would not normally have let slip. His stomach told him that the day – which had already overtaxed his enfeebled health – was about to take a turn for the worse.

'The Turkish camp,' said De Lugny. 'The hospital, if you could call it that. Their supply train and supports. The cooks, the drovers, the blackamoors. That market of theirs.'

By the time De Lugny had completed his list of the damned, Tannhauser knew that they would go and see for themselves no matter what he said. He told the truth.

'Even Gallows Point was better protected. They've a score or so mounted pickets, thinly spread. A company of Thracian levies digging latrines. And as you say, cooks, drovers, unarmed slaves, the sick. No earthworks or palisades. Every line battalion is up on the heights.'

De Lugny did not strike him as the most cunning of fellows, but all Frenchmen of his acquaintance enjoyed an inborn duplicity that served them well, at least at moments like this. De Lugny leaned forward in the saddle.

'You'll ride into the camp ahead of us,' he said. 'At the gallop. Feign injury. Raise the alarum. Tell them that the Christian relief force from Sicily has arrived and are advancing on their rear and that Mustafa must be informed with all speed. He'll have no choice but to call off the assault on Saint Michel.'

'If he believes the false report.'

'Oh, he'll believe it,' said De Lugny.

He smiled and Tannhauser saw what was in his mind. He felt sick.

'And after that?' he said.

'After that, just stay out of our way.'

Tannhauser doubted that this latter would be as easy at it sounded. He said, 'With your permission, I'll take one of those red surcoats.'

De Lugny grinned, like one knave affirming another, and with a jerk of his head told the popinjay to give up his garment. With ill grace, the youth pulled the sleeveless war coat over his head and threw it at Tannhauser. Tannhauser bundled it into a roll, shoved it into his saddle wallet. Then he paused as if struck by a thought.

'If you're looking for booty,' he said, 'the tents of the commanders and their general staff are separate from the rest, up on the hills. But they're much more stiffly protected – by a company of musketeers – and they stand a good mile closer to any relief that Mustafa will send.'

This was an overstatement of the truth; but he wanted to dissuade them from putting Orlandu, and for that matter the Ethiope, to the edge of their swords.

'We know Mustafa's gaudy settlement,' said De Lugny, 'and their day will come, but this morning we're not out for booty. We're out for blood.'

Tannhauser retraced his route to the Turkish perimeter. The sounds of the battle grew louder again. At a quarter-mile's distance he glimpsed the first pair of pickets and glanced over his shoulder. De Lugny's cavalry were not to be seen. He roused his depleted brawn and coaxed the mare into a gallop. As he approached the pickets he sagged across the mare's neck and raised his arm in desperation. By the time he reached them, feigning injury was easy enough, as he felt more than ready to fall from the saddle before them. A picket took his horse by the bridle.

'The Hounds of Hell are here,' said Tannhauser. 'Christian dogs, from Sicily. Thousands of them.'

He waved his arm vaguely behind him and saw the expression on the pickets' faces as they turned to look. He felt a tremor in the ground and the mare whickered nervously beneath him. Then he heard the thunder of iron-shod hooves at the charge. Still hunched forward, he turned to look himself and felt animalistic terror claw his gut.

He'd never seen a charge by heavy cavalry from the victim's perspective. This was how a stag felt when it spotted the hunter's dogs. De Lugny's riders fronted a rising cloud of ochre dust and were fanned out in a broad red line which grew broader and broader until it seemed that, if one watched for long enough, it would span the horizon whole. They were picking up speed; and they showed no sign of turning back. Tannhauser looked at the pickets. They were agape with terror. He picked the more panic-stricken of the two.

'Ride to the front and warn our Pasha,' said Tannhauser, 'or the army will be lost. Ride for your life.'

Grateful for this unexpected reprieve, the man hauled his horse about and lashed it into movement. His gladness would be short-lived, for when the deception was discovered Mustafa would flog him to death; but his would be but one of many such sorry tales to be told today.

To the other man, for the sake of dismissing him, Tannhauser said, 'Rally the levies to protect the stores.'

As the second sentry fled on his futile mission, Tannhauser realised that he had yet to complete the most important element of De Lugny's order: to stay out of their way. He glanced rearward and saw that there was no chance of outflanking the line before it engulfed him. The chestnut needed little encouragement to sink her rear to the ground and hit a flat-out run. She carried him back into the camp a bare fifty feet ahead of the clanking Behemoths at her heels.

The cavalry's approach spread a wave of fear that travelled even faster than the mare. Tannhauser glanced at the field of wounded to his left and saw the figures of the orderlies fleeing from their charges. Bakers fled their ovens and cooks their fires and launderers their cauldrons and tubs, running for the shores of Grand Harbour and the boats, and knowing in their roiling bowels that most would never get there. The levies at the latrine pits, leaderless and bewildered, struggled to solve the riddle to which there was only one solution, which was to die without meaning and in vain. Some clutched their shovels like powerless talismans and clustered to make a vain stand against the onrush. Some took off with the cooks. Some dived headlong into the humming trenches of excrement, where they wallowed in the hope of remaining hidden.

Tannhauser glanced back and saw the pickets take a valiant fling at De Lugny's cataphracts. They vanished like seeds of thistle before a high wind. As the killers roared into the tents of the tattered hospital, the thunder of their hooves and the distant racket of the siege were both drowned out by a vast and heaven-flung wail of amorphous anguish. The charge slowed, and the massacre began, and Tannhauser swerved east towards the bazaar.

He wasn't sure why he did so. Perhaps it was simple fellowship; perhaps it was panic. He pulled the mare up short amid the chaos already crowned in the bazaar. He marked a couple of faces from his dealings and urged them to abandon their wares and take to the heights. This small duty done, he headed back out of the bazaar and stripped and stowed his turban as he rode. He missed its protection, but a bare head would draw fewer blows; or so at least he hoped. He unpacked the red surcoat and pulled it over his head. At once he felt the Cross to be as protective as an inch of steel. He murmured to himself in rehearsal, *For Christ and the Baptist*, then he rode back into the blood purge that presently lathered the face of the heat-twisted plain.

The labour that faces two hundred who have set themselves

the task of butchering thousands with cold steel is very great, even if the latter be defenceless, but De Lugny's corps set to like wolves in a chicken run. Their steeds proved enthusiastic colleagues, their plate-sized hooves of sharpened iron pounding the sick and recumbent into tangled and lifeless heaps of pulverised offal. The wounded clambered from the ground like wraiths resurrected, only to be lanced or hacked and trampled in the swill from which they'd risen. Some knights dismounted and waded through the sea of unfortunates afoot, braining them with axe or mace, and competing with the horses to stomp the prostrate, and shouting prayers in Latin as if to sanctify their gore-crazed ardour.

The knights next harvested the cringing bevies of Thracians as they scattered about the field. A blow in the chest from the shoulder of a riled warhorse was enough to stove in the breastbone and ribs. The vicious rear hooves snapped out and landed with a sound like breaking clayware. The knights leaned from their saddles and slaughtered the migrant levies in mewling droves. The bakers, farriers and drovers, the blackamoors, the butchers, the cooks, fled like chivvied deer and gibbered in alien tongues as they heard the sound of the riders bearing down. They were herded into docile, bleating flocks and put to the sword, and they fouled themselves as the lances pierced their bowels, and they begged on their knees for quarter as they were hewed and gutted and dismembered and left to die.

Explosions bloomed yellow and orange, and black pillars climbed the azure, as provender stores, magazines, tents, wagons and grain bins were sacked and fired. Whole herds of horses and mules bawled and milled and slithered about the corrals, their rolling eyes whited and protuberant with fear, as clanking creatures sliced their hamstrings and bellies, and waded through the steaming spillage like children hunting cockles on a blood-foamed shore. The Christian vanguard finally reached the bazaar, and Tannhauser heard the hollering of the greedy and unwise, and there too much murder followed, and billows of flame soon sullied the noontide sky.

As he travelled the scourged plain, like an Argonaut granted free passage through the empire of Dis, Tannhauser kept his eyes peeled for berserks and the coatless popinjay; but the Cross on his breast went unquestioned and he once more reached the perimeter without dispute. The Mdina road lay open and the mare seemed to understand, for she was eager to take it despite that she was blown with effort and fright. Tannhauser calmed her for the journey, then snatched one last look at the holocaust to their rear. If ever there was a moment to doubt a benevolent God, it was this one; yet, with that paradox to which the human heart is prone, Tannhauser hoped sincerely that He existed.

Acrid clouds scudded the lowlands and the despoliation groaned with the throes of men and beasts alike. The haze-warped limbs of the knights still rose and fell like marionettes commanded by the crazed. Intermingled vapours seeped forth, of burning grain and silk and flesh, and excrement and powder and overbaked bread, as if Despair had distilled its own perfume and sprinkled it from on high. On the hills he saw the puffs of Turkish muskets, which, for all the effect they wrought, might as well have been fired in salute of this massacre so incomparably achieved. From the city beyond the hills, and the other fest of carnage thither celebrant, he heard the frenetic hallooing of the Turkish horns as they marshalled an urgent retreat.

De Lugny's ruse had worked. Saint Michel would endure another day.

The cavalry heard the horns too. They regrouped and began their withdrawal across the scorched earth, extinguishing what cowering pockets of life they found on their way. The destruction of all the Turkish livestock must have been beyond them, for they drove before them a throng of frighted horseflesh. And as on Gallows Point, De Lugny had lost not a single man or war mount.

Tannhauser rubbed at the miasma stinging his eyes. His back ached and he was famished. He flexed his shoulders. Though it wasn't yet far past noon his energy was bankrupt and he'd far to go before the sun rose on the morrow. He pulled the mare about and threaded his way up the rock-strewn trail to Mdina.

The food Tannhauser ate when he got there was plentiful but poor; or maybe his appetite was soured. Marshal Copier quizzed him about Turkish losses and morale. The Maltese scout to the Borgo was provided, or, rather, Tannhauser was invited to accompany the scout already assigned: the latest message from Viceroy Garcia de Toledo, in Messina, required dispatching. They would leave after dark, on foot. Tannhauser discarded his clothes, for they stank so high of smoke as to betray him to a sentry in the night. Then he retired to a palliasse to sleep and he dreamed of the enormities in which he'd played his part.

The nap proved too brief for rejuvenation. By the time he and his Maltese guide had covered a fraction of the distance to the Borgo, Tannhauser was staggering and felt close to the utter ignominy of collapse.

THE MALTESE GUIDE went by the name of Gullu Cakie. He was a good thirty years Tannhauser's senior and looked hewn from the rock over which they travelled, in his own case with the agility of a monkey. Gullu observed his companion's pallid face, and his sweaty, reeling gait, with a mixture of disgust and awe. Since Gullu spoke only Maltese, and the effort required would have been considerable, Tannhauser didn't explain that he'd just survived a near-fatal ague, plus a nauseating day of slaughter, and suffered on in silence. The frequent swigs he took from Gullu's skin of water garnered further grunts of contempt. His yellow Turkish riding boots – which were a poor match for his Brigantine and breeches, but for which no substitutes of the necessary size had been found – earned him Gullu's suspicion. This was eased when Tannhauser asked him by way of signs to carry his rifle, which had grown heavier by the yard and for the last mile had felt like a culverin. Gullu slung it from his right shoulder. Over his left he draped the wallets containing the coffee and three pounds and a quarter of opium – contents that Tannhauser felt ever closer to plundering. Thus laden, Gullu Cakie sprang onward and within a few more paces of pursuit, Tannhauser felt his lot but little improved.

Gullu carried the dispatches in a brass cylinder, and on his belt was a firepot with a glowing coal. The cylinder also contained a charge of gunpowder: if capture looked imminent, Gullu would cram the coal inside and resign himself to torture. The wiry Maltese took a wide sweep to the south and west of the Marsa, down steep valleys and over jagged rims, and through terrain that seemed more rugged than any Tannhauser had seen since he had marched across Iran. Had he had the strength to look upward through the sweat stinging his eyes, he might have guessed their location from the stars. The Turkish guns were silent and offered no guide. Instead, he stared at his feet and stumbled onward in the wake of Gullu Cakie, who, though he vanished time and again into the blackness, always waited up ahead as if for a backward child.

They were climbing bare rock towards a ridge cut sharp against the indigo when Tannhauser caught a whiff of decomposition. Without the hope it offered he might not have made it up the ridge, but he did, and with a whimper of relief looked down upon the watchfires of the Borgo. They were on some spur of San Salvatore and the enemy lines couldn't be far, yet they hadn't seen a Turk all night and Tannhauser couldn't see one now. He considered himself a fair hand at field craft and stealth, but Gullu was a master of the art. His elation faded as Gullu pointed down to Kalkara Bay and made a froglike motion with his arms. He was suggesting they swim. Tannhauser shook his head and performed a mime, based on close experience, of a man drowning. Gullu's disgust, which had gradually abated, returned in full; nevertheless he seemed little deterred. He again vanished into the dark and Tannhauser lurched after him.

Monte San Salvatore, which Tannhauser had conceived as a glorified hill and had indeed ridden over more than once, was, away from the trails, as wrinkled as an elephant's hide. The wrinkles were deep enough to conceal a man. They crawled back and forth among them for, by his own estimate, an hour, again without a sign of human life. When next they raised their heads, they were among rocks at the southernmost lobe of Kalkara Bay. The Bastion of Castile stood not five hundred feet distant from where they lay. A hundred feet to Castile's left, overlooking the next lobe of water and sealing the enceinte, stood the Bastion of Germany and England. At its base was the Kalkara Gate.

To their left the narrow tail of the Grand Terre Plein, which separated the city walls from the saddle between Salvatore and Margharita, was thick with Moslem corpses, already bloating in the decline of the moon and casting elongate shadows across the silvered clay. The Turkish-held heights above them were silent, as if in mourning for the disaster that had befallen them that day, and here and there he caught the glimmer of campfires among the mute emplacements of siege guns. To their right, he saw that the Turkish trench works extended all the way down San Salvatore to the Kalkara shore. Fires winked there too, and their flames struck from the night the occasional turbaned silhouette with a canted musket. It was from these earthworks that they could count on receiving fire.

Gullu Cakie offered Tannhauser his rifle, and Tannhauser took it. Gullu indicated that he intended to crawl across the intervening ground, a feat he would no doubt accomplish with the speed of a cobra. Gullu further indicated that he would get the gates to open, a potentially dangerous moment even for him, and that it was then that Tannhauser should follow. This would give Tannhauser a free run to the interior, and would also give the dispatches from Sicily the greatest chance of safe delivery, a goal which Gullu valued higher than Tannhauser's life. However, the wily old dog was not entirely indifferent to his fate, for he thrust a bony finger towards the sky.

Tannhauser followed it, and for a moment was baffled. The finger pointed at Scorpius. What did he mean? Then Gullu opened his hand and moved it slowly towards the waxing three-quarter moon, now low to the south-east, and Tannhauser belatedly noted that at some considerable distance a blue-grey cloud was doing just the same. It was a small, solitary cloud, and Tannhauser would not have bet a ducat on it masking the moon, and thereby darkening the land below. Instead he was going to bet his life. Gullu mimed a sprint and stuck a finger into Tannhauser's chest. Then Gullu gave him a nod and squirmed out from the rocks towards the walls.

Tannhauser looked up at the cloud. Now that he was alone it appeared smaller than before, and its course more erratic, and the likelihood of it giving him any cover more remote. He watched Gullu work his way across the open ground. In the event he moved more like a crab than a snake, but no less swiftly than predicted, skittering this way and that on his palms and tiptoes, stopping at random to flatten himself to the ground, then breaking back into movement as abruptly as he'd stopped. Even if he'd been spotted he would've looked more like a nocturnal creature than a man.

Tannhauser watched the cloud again. It looked hardly to have moved at all and the more he stared at it the more clearly static it became. There was no wind down here, and up there the case seemed the same. When he looked back from the relative brightness of the heavens to the ground, Gullu Cakie had disappeared.

His solitude was complete. He was armed only with the wheellock and his dagger, and neither was any great comfort. His powder flask and ball pouch, he belatedly recalled, were in the wallets on Gullu's back. He gave up watching anything but the cloud and he watched for twenty minutes before he was convinced that it still moved at all. Indeed, it seemed suddenly to bear down on the moon with considerable speed, but such are the tricks that the heavens play. He levered himself into a crouch, grabbed his rifle and watched the cloud skim Sagittarius. It would cover the ice-white moon but it would pass quickly. He considered crawling to the gate, but his elbows and knees were raw and his chest was a bed of coals. Thirty seconds' exposure was better than ten minutes on his belly with his arse in the air. The cloud's foremost edge cut into the whiteness, and then covered it, and darkness fell across no-man's-land. Tannhauser lurched to his feet and ran.

In the service of Suleiman Shah he must have run fifteen thousand miles – a janissary spent his life running – and the technique hadn't left him, breathing deep and steady in the putrefying air, elbows in, rifle held firm across his chest. His stride was long and fast, weight tilted forward at the waist, the fatigue of the journey banished by the prospect of its end. Straight ahead the water of the bay loomed black as ink; to his right impenetrable shadows and the Turkish lines. The musket blasts started when he was seventy feet out, shocking in sound and brightness. He didn't slow but he threw a few zigzags. One of the blasts caught the glitter of a double-curved sword and he saw a fleet silhouette as it sped along the shore to cut him off at the bulge of Castile. Tannhauser pulled more speed from his hams. The distance closed. But a thin strip of silver light widened across the clay and unrolled towards him as the cloud drew its curtain from the moon.

The *gazi* was revealed, his robes hissing round him and his lips peeled back in effort or perhaps in rage. He'd intercept Tannhauser just short of Castile, and if the musket fire didn't take him down, the blade of the yataghan would. Tannhauser's rifle pointed across his body to the left. He could reverse the gun for a left-handed shot, which was cumbersome, or he could stop and turn and fire, which would squander his hard-won impetus and give the edge to the Turkish marksmen in the trench. Another muzzle bloomed and he felt the wind of the ball. Then the *gazi* was before him, his arms stretched like a discus thrower, the blade cocked back to strike him on the run.

On the verge of their collision, Tannhauser spun clockwise in a backward sprint. The rifle came round with him. The *gazi*'s yataghan flashed towards his skull and Tannhauser fired a six-inch flame and a half-inch ball point-blank into his chest.

At least he'd thought he'd done so. But at the same instant the *gazi*'s turbaned head flew apart in a shower of gleaming gobbets, and before the airborne corpse hit the ground Tannhauser spun back round, the whole manoeuvre complete in a single pace, a single turn, and he sprinted, head down, to cover the last hundred feet to the Kalkara Gate.

He rounded the wall of the mantlet with bullets drilling dust spouts from the bricks. Entrance to the sally port beyond was through a wicket in the large main gates. It wasn't much wider than his shoulders. A torch flickered within. The first thing Tannhauser saw on barging inside was Bors, who stood measuring powder down the still-smoking bore of his black and silver musket. Bors looked up and sniffed.

'What was the pirouette in aid of?' he said. 'I was leading that devil from the moment he left his trench.'

Tannhauser caught his breath. 'Then why didn't you shoot him sooner?'

'Why,' said Bors, 'then you might have slowed down, and that would not have done at all. You were already flagging under the weight of all that gold.' He indicated the bangle on Tannhauser's right arm. 'Glittered like a tabernacle the instant you rose up. No wonder they almost had you.'

Tannhauser declined to respond. A pair of guards sealed the wicket with an iron-shod door, which they reinforced with a complexity of buttresses and bolts, a process he watched with an eye to getting back out again, and as soon as circumstance allowed. Bors stooped and handed Tannhauser his saddle wallets.

'Gullu Cakie told me to give you these, with his thanks.'

'Gullu doesn't speak Italian.'

'He speaks Spanish as well as King Philip and Italian better than you. In his trade he needed to. You should be honoured to have such a guide.'

The wallets felt distinctly light to Tannhauser's hand. He opened them. Only a single wax-paper package remained inside: the one containing the miserly quarter of opium. More woundingly, in a way, his package of coffee had vanished too.

'The old bugger has robbed me.'

Bors clapped him on the back and a grin distorted his hugely scarred face. 'By the Rod, it's good to have you back,' he said, 'for mirth has been in very short supply.'

'In his trade?' said Tannhauser. 'What trade?'

'In his day, Gullu Cakie was the most notorious thief and smuggler of these islands. Dodged the gallows a score of times and never once was caught. It looks like you've put him back in business.'

The sally port corridor turned at an obtuse angle. Above the angle a murder hole gaped in the ceiling. Intruders could be waylaid at this junction while incendiaries and gunfire were showered from above. At the inner end was a portcullis and beyond that, to provide another killing floor in the event that the port was breached, was a small, roofless blockhouse furnished with oilettes. As Tannhauser headed through the blockhouse, Bors took his arm.

'Come and see this,' said Bors.

Tannhauser followed him up the wall stair. They reached the top and turned and Tannhauser stopped dead, and blinked, as the prospect from this vantage was revealed.

It was nearly two months since he'd left the town, at which time hardly a shot had been fired against it. Now it was a formless wasteland dense with rubble – paved with rubble, stacked with rubble, and by yet more rubble surrounded. Holes and fractures scarred the masonry of San Lorenzo, the Sacred Infirmary, the Arsenal and the Courts of Law. Whole streets had been levelled down to the cobbles. Iron balls and gun stones littered the ruins. Countless roofless houses gaped to the sky. Castel Sant' Angelo brooded like the seat of a vanquished kingdom and apart from a flicker of watchfires nothing in that wide desolation stirred, as if the place had been sacked and forsaken when history was young, and its denizens were savages yet dressed in the skins of beasts.

'The women,' said Tannhauser. 'Carla, Amparo, are they alive?'

'They're sound enough,' said Bors. 'At least in body.'

'And otherwise?'

'There are few in this benighted burg aren't heartsick to the core. Even I have moments of weariness, and I wouldn't miss all this for a palace on the Lido.'

Tannhauser's eyes sought out the Auberge of England on Majistral Street. It was one of few buildings that appeared to be undamaged. Bors caught the look and as Tannhauser started down the stair he said, 'The women don't live at the auberge any more.'

Tannhauser looked at him.

'Carla moved out with her belongings just short of a week since. Left as if she'd found that the place was haunted, but wouldn't say why. She says she has a cot in the infirmary, where she can sleep as she will and always be on hand for the sick.'

'And Amparo?'

'Amparo lives in the stables on the straw, with Buraq. Don't worry; I've kept one eye on both of them. Both women, that is, and the horse too.' He shrugged at Tannhauser's frown. 'They're a wilful pair. What else could I do?'

When they reached the foot of the stairs, La Valette's page, Andreas, who'd survived a bullet in the throat on the first day of the siege, informed them that Gullu Cakie had presented his dispatches to the Grand Master, who was now awaiting an immediate report from Tannhauser on the standing of the Turk. To the youth's shock, Tannhauser replied that he had no intelligence that would prolong the city's resistance beyond the morning, and that, with all appropriate homage and salutations, the Grand Master could wait until then to learn what he knew.

Tannhauser left Andreas stranded in the street and struck for the hospital. He did so on instinct, on a whim he was too tired to question or resist. He wanted to see Carla. He wanted to see what was in her face when she saw him. Perhaps it was the boy. He wanted to tell her Orlandu was alive. Perhaps it was something more.

When they reached the piazza that fronted the Sacred Infirmary, they found it wholly covered with the bodies of wounded men, the harvest of that day's battle laid out in bloodstained rows. They languished under the stars, their sundry mutilations and truncated limbs swaddled in blankets made threadbare by launderings and use. Brother monks and chaplains and Jews and Maltese women gave what comfort they could to their charges and loved ones. After what Tannhauser had seen that afternoon in the Turkish camp, he had no reason to be unduly moved; these men, at the least, enjoyed more succour than the lances and hooves of fiends; and yet moved he was, and didn't know why.

Then he heard a thread of music wind a sinuous path through the night. It was fainter than that he'd heard upon the hill and he looked at Bors to be sure it wasn't his fancy. Bors tossed his head towards Galley Creek.

'They make the music by the water.'

'Both of them?'

'Every night since Carla abandoned the auberge.'

Bors held out his hand and Tannhauser gave him the rifle and the empty wallets, then he turned to go.

'Mattias.'

Tannhauser stopped.

'Brother Ludovico is back.'

Tannhauser's hand gripped the hilt of his dagger.

'My thought also,' said Bors, 'but killing him would be no easy matter. Brother Ludo is now a Knight of Justice. The Italian Langue.'

'Ludovico has joined the Religion?' said Tannhauser.

'Courted them with relics and done his share of slaughter.'

'I didn't think La Valette was such a fool.'

'Ludovico's respected by all and the Italians love him.'

Tannhauser passed a hand over his face. 'This is more a madhouse than I expected.'

'The fortunes of war,' shrugged Bors. He added, 'He's caused no trouble to date, so far as I know, but his spies have their noses to the ground, so beware.'

'Beware?' said Tannhauser.

The very notion was folly. As were all his strivings. He'd waded in folly more deeply than he'd waded in blood, and he'd wade on yet in both till one or the other drowned him. The evils of the day had almost broken him and for a moment he found himself teetering, between a fit of rage too vast to admit of any object, and a fit of mirth from which he might not return. Then the music once more drifted down the evening, and the moment passed.

'You look like a man not long for this world,' said Bors. 'Come and take some brandy with me. We'll get drunk, and talk of better times.'

'Bors,' said Tannhauser, 'embrace me, my friend.'

Tannhauser clasped his arms about the immense shoulders as a drowning man might clasp the trunk of a tree. The tree was so bewildered it staggered but it did not fall. Then Tannhauser turned away and walked through the crumbling streets towards Galley Creek.

He found the women in a nest of rocks at the water's edge. At closer range the sound of Amparo's lute was delicate and clear, the notes of its many strings lifting the boldness of Carla's violl like the wings of so many hummingbirds. Both women seemed lost within the sphere of infinite beauty that they spun, their eyes closed to this world, their faces thrust up to the firmament at moments of ecstatic flight, their chins tucked into their shoulders as they dived the depths of their hearts for pearls of truth. And if the scales of the cosmic balance could ever be righted, if that calamitous measure of woe in one tray heaped could ever be countered and made to tip back from its nadir, then it was here and now, and by the power of this magic invisible that filled the air.

Tannhauser found a perch and sat down to listen. He wasn't alone. There must have been two score people gathered there and about, as one might find them drawn on a market day by a jongleur or a fool. Soldiers and peasants and women; knots of grubby boys; and tatterdemalion girls holding hands, these latter with the vacant faces and haunted eyes of children who had witnessed all that perdition allows. Some had brought candles or lamps, and these threw small arcs of light that were quickly lost in the uneven ground. All kept their distance. They sat or stood or squatted with no great fuss. Some had the glister of tears running down their cheeks. Some were merely curious. Others seemed dazed or befuddled, as if the gulf between the beauty of the music and the catastrophe around them were too vast to bridge.

The musicians themselves were oblivious to all but the Divine. The realm they were exploring lay far from this one; and perhaps its charting was the noblest gift they made, for this realm here was so dark, so caged by dolour and death, and so far stranded from all imaginable others, that to illuminate, even for a moment, a dominion where harmony reigned was to pluck the stars from the heavens above and place one in every hand.

Bors tiptoed up and sat down. He proffered a leather flask. Tannhauser rifled a drink and stifled a gasp. By its kick the brandy had been rectified in a helmet; but it spread a glow, and he drank again and handed it back. Bors tilted his head at the performers and puckered his lips in pride, as if he'd tutored them himself. While they listened, the tyranny of Time seemed overthrown forever; but forever too is another of Time's satraps, and at last the musicians stopped and they sat in a circle of silence, a silence near as exquisite as the music now long vanished on the wind.

A girl in the crowd clapped with rapture and someone shushed her, as if they were in church. Then bit by bit the crowd broke up and drifted towards the ruins like spectres called to their tombs by the onset of day, and the creek front became deserted and Tannhauser and Bors alone were left behind. The retiring crowd took their lamps and as the last yellow orbs disappeared into the streets, Tannhauser glimpsed a long face caught by the glow. A face striking for its aquiline beauty and beardless cheeks. He grabbed Bors's arm and pointed but it was gone, and he wondered if he'd seen it there at all.

Tannhauser said, 'Anacleto?'

'He's about,' agreed Bors. 'He lurks out of sight. Like the spider never seen upon the web until the fly is trapped. He too has taken holy orders, as a Knight of Magistral Grace. Want me to roust him?'

'Until it's time to kill him and Ludovico both, there's no good sense in it.'

Tannhauser turned to watch Carla and Amparo pack their instruments. How splendid it was to see them both together again. They were a little thin, yes. There were new lines carved on their features that would never be erased. But their fettle looked fine enough to him. Indeed, each in her way was so fair of form and face that his heart almost stopped as the moment of reunion loomed. He loved them both without let or doubt and in that conundrum, for once, he found neither contradiction nor anguish. That knot could be unravelled on some other occasion. As they clambered back up the rocks, toting their cases, Tannhauser rose from his seat and they saw him.

Both women stopped for a moment, as if confronted by an

apparition, or perhaps a troll escaped from some northern tale. It was true he didn't look his best. His breeches hung in shreds about his knees. His shirtless arms were streaked with sweat and dirt. And the Brigantine was the kind of garment sported by a *bravo* of the lower sort. These defects were beyond mending for the moment. At least he'd had his beard oiled in the bazaar the day before and was wearing a respectable amount of gold. But while he entertained these vain and risible frets, the women dropped their cases and rushed towards him, arms outstretched, with a gratifying display of tearful joy.

He embraced them both at once, an arm to each, as on that long-ago day of the first clash when he'd solicited their blessing for the fight. He held their heads to his chest, as if they were his children, or as if he was theirs. If they hadn't wept so hard he might have done so himself, and thus was their sentiment welcome. His chest swelled with a marvellous sense of warmth, engendered in part by the pressure of their breasts against his ribs, and when Carla raised her face to meet his eyes, Tannhauser grinned.

'You called,' he said. 'How could I not come running?'

This garnered a smile from each of them and he looked from one pair of shining eyes to the other – Amparo's irregular face yet again exerting its lethal charm, and Carla's soulful elegance knifing his soul – until affection threatened to undermine his poise and he glanced away over their heads.

'Bors,' he said, 'bring their accoutrements, if you will. We're going back to the auberge. And there, when we are snug, I will tell you all a tale you won't forget.'

PART IV

BY DENS OF LIONS ENCOMPASSED

WEDNESDAY 15 AUGUST 1565 – THE ASSUMPTION

Post of Italy – Fortress of Saint Michel

THE GIBBOUS MOON stood, by Anacleto's reckoning, in Aquarius. Siege guns boomed at disparate intervals and the walls beneath Ludovico's feet would occasionally shudder as a ball struck home. In the trenches cut into the hills, and on the Marsa plain beyond, the Turks rested to restore their strength after recent reverses. Ludovico watched the shadows in the Ruins of Bormula and brooded on those shadows that lay across his own affairs.

Ludovico had seen Tannhauser on the night of his arrival in the Borgo. That the German was still alive didn't alarm him. The Grand Master valued his military skills and in this respect Ludovico was as grateful as the next man for all the help they could get. But why had the man returned at such risk and to such a high likelihood of death? Tannhauser was sexually embroiled with the Spanish girl, Amparo. Carla had claimed she and he intended to marry. It was an odd arrangement, yet by no means without precedent, and in love all things were possible. Ludovico's own return to Malta had at least in part been influenced by the knowledge that Carla was here. Yet surely the barbarous German was beyond such chivalry. Tannhauser might fancy he could save the women should the Turks overwhelm them. Or he might plan to take them away, out of the Borgo. How this might be possible, Ludovico couldn't imagine; but he didn't underestimate the German's guile. He'd seen, too, the way that Tannhauser had taken both women to his breast, and how they'd sobbed with relief to see his face.

The day now ending was a Holy Day, the feast of the Assumption of the Blessed Virgin Mary into Heaven. Its celebration comforted the townsfolk, not least because so many had joined Her and so many more expected to do so. A chaplain from Valencia, with help of some *tercios*, and a boy to play the role of *Nuestra Señora*, had crudely staged a mystery play, which portrayed the death of the Virgin and – after a struggle between the Apostles and the Jews for Her mortal remains – the transportation of Her soul to the Gates of Paradise on the wings of five angels. There She was crowned Queen of Heaven, to a fanfare of bells, trumpets and firecrackers. That grizzled Spanish soldiers played the angels did nothing to diminish the awe and enjoyment of the crowd. This peasant devotional, of which he'd seen many, would've had little effect on Ludovico had not Carla provided a musical accompaniment on her viola da gamba. Carla had played with extravagant passion and had transformed the primitive ritual into something he would never forget.

Ludovico rested his arms on the stones of the ramparts and his head on his arms. He was exhausted. So was every man in the garrison, except, perhaps, La Valette. Physical fatigue was natural; Ludovico had courted it for years. But he'd found the mechanisms of his brain slowing too and this for him was something new. Thoughts came with difficulty and proved banal when they arrived. He went about his recruitment of political allies, within the Religion, with the enthusiasm of a man consulting the surgeon for the lancing of a boil. He slept poorly. Despair lurked about the darker labyrinths of his mind. Where his wit had always skipped, it now crawled. He could have put all this down to war, for many were affected in this fashion; but he was victim to much more potent a malady. He ruminated helplessly on Carla. His yearning for her ate at his spirit. Even his appetite for prayer was dulled and the solace it provided thin. Her sublime performance in the mystery play had triggered his present melancholy. He missed the music she and her Spaniard had played down by the rocks. He'd gone to listen to them every night and their harmonies had transported him and he'd read into Carla's performance a poem of love. So extreme – so contemptible – was his folly that, at moments, he'd allowed himself to imagine that she played for him.

Despite such absurdities, discipline had kept his passion – and his presence – invisible to Carla. Invisible to all but Anacleto. Ludovico was no expert in the field of love but knew that it was the ultimate realm of intrigue, the most intricate of human games. Like any expert in one realm, he recognised his weakness in those in which he had scant experience. Logic and instinct both assured him that he wouldn't win Carla while the siege endured. He would have to wait on peace. The love poem of her music had, for a while, given him strength; the strength to endure, to fight, to husband the fire of his own love into a glowing bed of inextinguishable coals, rather than a fiery blaze. Then Tannhauser had returned, and she'd embraced him by the rocks, and a great draught of rage and pain had blown through his heart, for he'd known that in fact she'd played for him.

Carla played still, he'd been told, but now at the Auberge of England, and still for Tannhauser. For him and his criminal companions. Ludovico raised his face and stood tall and turned away from the vacant battlefield.

'Anacleto,' he said.

Anacleto turned at once. His face in the moonlight seemed sculpted from ivory. Ludovico's association with the Spaniard was the closest and most lasting of his life. They'd shared a thousand roadside camps. Together they'd watched thousands die, in the Waldensian purges. Here, on the ramparts of Saint Michel, they'd fought shoulder to shoulder. Their relationship endured because it was without perceptible warmth. It was untrammelled by sentiment and was therefore free of lies. In a world of ceaseless perfidy, Anacleto's fealty was precious. Ludovico loved him. Like a son. Yet now Ludovico knew that he had his own son. Orlandu. The boy was alive, among Moslem devils. Tannhauser had usurped that role too. Ludovico counselled himself to patience. In time he would reclaim son and mother both.

'You have known love,' said Ludovico.

Anacleto had stabbed his father and strangled his mother. His sister, Filomena, had been hanged for the crime of incest. The lands to which he'd been heir had been confiscated. Before Ludovico had found him, he'd been put to the torture by the zealous and still had refused to repent. Anacleto nodded, his eyes wary.

'It cost you a great deal,' Ludovico went on.

Anacleto looked at him for some time. He had as true a heart as any Ludovico had known and he was moved by the turbulence in his eyes.

Anacleto said, 'To not have known it would have cost me more.'

Ludovico understood. He wished his own courage had been as great. He nodded.

'And Filomena and I will meet again,' said Anacleto. 'Be it in Heaven or the Whirlwind of Lovers.'

That Anacleto would endure Hell for his passion, Ludovico understood too. He said, 'You have my assurance it shall be the former. The Church has forgiven you your sins, as it belatedly forgave Filomena's, and Christ is all-merciful.'

As if reading his thoughts, Anacleto said, 'Do you want me to kill the German?'

Ludovico's mood suddenly lifted. The younger man's fortitude had stirred his own. He'd mope like a girl no more. He smiled.

'You're a pillar to my strength,' said Ludovico. 'To answer your question, no. The time is not right. And Tannhauser may yet serve us.'

'How so?' asked Anacleto.

Ludovico kept his own counsel. 'God will answer that question in good time.'

SATURDAY 18 AUGUST 1565

Bastion of Germany – the Tub – Bastion of Castile

Of the many trials and riddles that had vexed him since his return, one had preoccupied Tannhauser above all others: how to get back out again – with Carla, Amparo and Bors in tow. His pleasure in being reunited with his companions would be short-lived if their destination, as seemed likely, were a mass grave. Yet a thing does not come about just because one ardently desires it, and even a man as intrepid as he could find himself victim to circumstance.

The mild euphoria that had attended his return had been banished by the state of enfeeblement which the ague had bequeathed him, and which had been revived with a vengeance by the rigours of his journey from Mdina. To provide acceptable accommodation, Bors had evicted several injured troopers from Starkey's rooms, and Tannhauser had set himself to eating well, reading the works of Roger Bacon, of which Starkey had a fine edition in Italian, and – armed against the bombardment with beeswax earplugs – to sleeping as much as possible during daylight. This enlightened and restorative programme had been interrupted by calls to a series of tedious conferences with Grand Master La Valette.

These were held at La Valette's headquarters, which had been relocated from the fastness of Sant' Angelo to the town's central piazza. Although this had been widely interpreted as a gesture of camaraderie with the ravaged population, it soon became clear to Tannhauser that La Valette simply wanted to be closer to the action. Almost alone of the entire garrison his vitality was undiminished – if anything he looked like he'd shed ten years – and he subjected Tannhauser to long discussions about the Turkish losses, their morale, supplies of ammunition and provender, the condition of their cannon, the techniques of the Mameluke engineers at that very moment burrowing mines towards the city walls, and Mustafa's tactical intentions. These last seemed fairly clear to Tannhauser: Mustafa would continue to fling shot and bodies at the walls until either he ran out of both or the walls came down. The dispatches that Gullu Cakie had carried included a letter from Garcia de Toledo in Sicily. In it Toledo promised to send ten thousand men by the end of August; but since a similar promise concerning the end of June remained unfulfilled, neither La Valette nor anyone else believed a word of it.

'Toledo's prestige would survive the loss of Malta,' said La Valette, 'but not the loss of Spain's Mediterranean fleet.' He added, without discernible regret, 'We are alone.'

On 12 August La Valette had revealed to the public the papal Bull promulgated for their benefit by His Holiness Pius IV. This document assured one and all of forgiveness of their sins and immediate transit to Paradise should they die in this Holy War. The vellum was on display in San Lorenzo, where the faithful could stare in wonder at the gorgeous Latin script and the silk-veiled red wax seal with its imprint of the Fisherman's Ring. The results had been quite remarkable; but Tannhauser didn't intend to be buried in this mausoleum with the faithful.

He could think of no good reason why the boat he'd stolen and concealed at the hamlet of Zonra two months before should not still be where he'd left it. The problem lay in reaching it.

The circle of Turkish steel around the enceinte was tighter than he'd foreseen. He still hadn't worked out how to get through the Kalkara Gate; and no other route was feasible. A guard was usually on duty at the inner blockhouse; a night watchman stood on the Bastions of England and Germany high above; and though his willingness to serve the Religion was reaching its limit, he didn't want to leave the wicket gate open to the Turks when they left. These conundrums he hoped to solve by the wane of the moon.

Bors alone was privy to these affairs. Tannhauser was by no means certain that Carla would be willing to leave at all. She was devoted to her work. There was no trade more compelling than that of heroism – not even debauchery – and Carla had proved herself heroic. Many regarded her as not far short of a saint. They lit candles to her deliverance in the church of the Annunciation and blessed her when she passed in the street and kissed the hem of her dress. Knights pledged their lives to her protection. Men without number attributed their survival to her care; even more had passed into the hereafter with lighter hearts and gentled minds.

Tannhauser had seen these things with his own eyes and they had done little to diminish his regard for her or to leaven his own yearning. The other day Brother Lazaro had sought him out to thank him for introducing her, and had made a rueful joke at the expense of his own initial reluctance to employ her. But the joke might fall on Tannhauser too. Heroism and saintliness led all too easily to martyrdom; and neither her death nor his own played a part in his plans.

Time would tell.

Amparo, he was sure, would agree to go. As far as he could tell she maintained the indifference of a holy fool to the chaos around her. She'd taken him to the stables to visit Buraq, who was in finer fettle than he could have hoped, and who threw such a fit of equine happiness on their arrival that the other war-frayed beasts almost staged a riot. Buraq would not be leaving with them.

With luck a Turkish general would claim him and he'd live like a king. Perhaps even Abbas. Leaving Malta was an irksome business. There was no sense in alerting either woman before it was necessary.

He often dwelt on Orlandu. The boy had lodged himself deep in Tannhauser's heart. Yet Orlandu enjoyed a safer haven than any of them here, and that was a source of contentment. Nicodemus, fine fellow and excellent cook though he was, would have to take his chances with the garrison.

'A posset of brandy and opium,' said Bors, as they handed over the watch on the Kalkara Gate. 'That would give the blockhouse sentry a fine night's sleep.'

'I don't know how to extract the quintessence of opium and bind it to a tincture,' said Tannhauser. 'Petrus Grubenius went to the stake before he could teach me the method, which is intricate. But brandy in the posset and the opium in a cake – a honey cake, say – would give as good a result. If we feed him such delicacies every second night, but without the poppy, he won't suspect when the right moment comes.'

Bors said, with callous curiosity, 'I wonder if they'll hang the fellow for it.'

For a moment Tannhauser wondered if he were the one deranged; if his godlessness, his contempt for mindless sacrifice and blind loyalty both, his determination to care only for those he cared about, and by whatever treacherous and sordid means necessary, were not indeed as wicked as they sometimes seemed. It was not a form of nobility anyone hereabouts would easily recognise.

He said, 'It's a queer thing to be the Devil's man, when all else about are for God.'

Bors said, 'I've told you many times but you never listen: philosophy is bad for your health. But this talk of cakes has whetted my hunger. Let's to breakfast.'

Along the Bastion of Germany they passed two Scandinavian

brethren from the last Baltic priory to survive Lutheranism. Bors waved cheerily. Neither waved back.

'Swedes,' he said. 'A shy lot. They and the rest of the German Langue feel affronted that they haven't seen serious action yet. A downright gallimaufry they are – all manner of Poles, a Norwegian, two Danes, and one strange cove from Muscovy who claims to know Ivan the Terrible. My God, imagine what he had to do to earn that nickname – and we think ourselves men to be reckoned with. But when the Northmen do go in, it will be a sight, mark my words.'

'The sight I'll be happy with,' said Tannhauser. 'Just don't drag us in with them.'

As they made their way down the wall stair, the stones vibrated around them as a sudden huge barrage thundered from the hills. They emerged in daylight to see black specks arcing through the sky towards L'Isola, where their impact raised clouds of splinters. The fishing village of L'Isola no longer existed. Not a house remained undamaged and few remained standing. The windmills were long demolished and their ragged sails stood canted and forlorn. The fort of Saint Michel resembled Saint Elmo's in its last days. Members of the garrison stationed there rarely crossed the boat bridge to the Borgo any more, as if they feared that having once done so the prospect of going back would be too much to bear. Instead they abided in the havoc, with the blowflies and corpses and rats. To the best of Tannhauser's knowledge, Ludovico was among them. The bombardment this morning was dense and presaged the first major assault in over a week.

'Let's hope they're bent only on Saint Michel,' said Bors.

'Losing your taste for the broil, then,' said Tannhauser.

'I'll allow its appeal is diminished when I've had no sleep or food.'

As they reached the auberge a slave was herded by with a knotted rope in his mouth and the point of a glaive pricking notches in the scars bunched on his back. The route to the gallows had never been changed, it seemed, and Tannhauser was seized by the conviction that nor would anything else. He would never leave this island. None of them would. And not in the morbid sense that they would all die here, but that they were trapped in an endless loop of Time where neither the fighting nor his part in it would ever end.

'Did you know,' said Bors, 'that they use that very same rope gag every day – take it from the corpse before they cut him down and cram in the mouth of the next?'

'How many days has it been?'

Bors called out to the Spaniard escorting the prisoner. 'Hey, Guzman, what's this wretch's number? Eighty-eight or eighty-nine?'

'Eighty-nine,' replied Guzman.

'My thanks.' Bors turned back to Tannhauser. 'They scratch the count on the wall of the gaol, by fives. There's been a lottery on the final tally for some time, though they closed the book at fifty. I'm still in with a shout.'

'Who collected the Saint Elmo's purse?'

'You're looking at him,' said Bors. 'At thirty-one days you fellows exceeded even my wager – by a hair – but I was closest.'

'Eighty-nine days,' said Tannhauser. 'Sometimes I can't remember why we came here.'

'As I recall, it had something to do with your women.'

'Yes, the women,' he said. 'They're driving me mad still.'

'I'm all ears.'

'I've been trying to remain faithful to my future bride,' began Tannhauser.

Bors brayed with laughter. 'Why? Has Amparo contracted the pox?' He grounded the butt of his musket and leaned on the muzzle. 'Forgive me,' he said between breaths, 'but you are a sight. Please, go on.'

'Amparo's in fine health. She'll survive thee and me come what may. And it's with regret I tell you that I don't expect to see a more exquisite pair of breasts as long as I live.'

'So the charm of the contessa has triumphed, despite such splendid obstacles.'

Tannhauser couldn't bring himself to confess that he'd been captured, then and now, by the way she played a piece of music. 'Charms or my own folly, it's much of a muchness.'

'Love,' said Bors. 'I warned you.'

'And I paid heed, hence my intention to clear my mind for the trials ahead. Rutting addles matters, you'll agree –'

'Without a doubt.'

'– and when sentiment is confused, not least by the lunacy abroad, it provokes headaches, excess bile and other ills best avoided until we're on safer ground. We'll be several days at sea, and while one paramour in a boat is hazard enough, paramour plus betrothed is to court disaster.'

'You've kept your hands off the splendid breasts since your return?' said Bors, in awe.

'Since the sun rose on the following day, La Valette himself has not been more chaste.'

'Are you willing to place a wager on the outcome?'

Tannhauser ignored this impertinence with a scowl. They entered the auberge, which Carla had converted into an adjunct to the hospital and which, to Tannhauser's exasperation, groaned with recovering wounded. He kicked a pair of loafers in the ribs.

'Have these idlers sent back to the ramparts,' he said. 'I'm for the tub.' He tossed his rifle to Bors. 'Tell Nicodemus to double our rations.'

'That would be easier said if you hadn't dragged us down to Gullu Cakie's.'

THEY'D LOCATED THE lair of Gullu Cakie the day before, among the dense press of dwellings that crowded the angle between Galley Creek and the Bastion of France. They meant the fellow no serious harm – they weren't *bravi* after all – but he had to be called to account for thieving the opium, and the coffee, lest Tannhauser come to be seen as an easy mark or, worse, a laughing stock. On the way Bors paid a visit to his man inside the army commissary, where all supplies of food were now impounded, and came away with a bulging sack and his basket filled with eggs, a crock of butter and a loaf of white cane sugar. Cakie's door was opened by a young woman, whose skin, Tannhauser couldn't help but notice, was luscious, and they were welcomed inside.

All beauty and refinement ended with the woman at the door as the hovel was revealed. Two hovels in fact, each a single large room, for part of the roof and the wall that had once separated them had been destroyed. There were upwards of a dozen souls crammed inside, sheltering, he supposed, from the sun. Several dark-eyed children swatted at the flies on their cheeks. Three thickset swarthies rose from a parley at the rear of the first room and glanced at their short swords stacked by the wall. One of them was missing an arm at the elbow. It was Orlandu's friend, Tomaso. Uncertainty crossed his face, and he said nothing. In a niche in the remains of the wall a votive light burned before a small stone figure of the Virgin. The farther room hummed with flies in greater ubiquity, which plagued five badly wounded men stretched out on straw pallets. Two more women knelt among them, waving fans plaited from straw, and they looked at the visitors over their shoulders. Tannhauser's resolve to be stern wavered at once.

He glanced at Bors. 'Was this your notion?' he said.

'I told you we'd not see your goods again.'

'Then you should have dissuaded me.'

Gullu Cakie appeared, as if from nowhere. The beady eyes above the beaky nose were cautious. He extended a bony hand, and Tannhauser shook it.

'Welcome,' said Cakie, in Italian. 'You bring honour on our house.'

Tannhauser shuffled. 'These are your children?' he asked.

'Children, grandchildren, nephews.'

Tannhauser smiled, with what he hoped was warmth, at two of the youngsters. He trawled his mind for something intelligent to say. 'A handsome brood. God has blessed you.'

Gullu Cakie nodded, still wary. One of the little girls asked him a question in Maltese. Cakie answered her, indicating Tannhauser, and the girl asked him something else, and received a nod, whereupon a titter of amazed laughter spread among the children. The women smiled too, but not the three men. Cakie looked at Tannhauser and noted his curiosity.

'She asked who you were, and I told her I had guided you from Mdina,' said Cakie. 'She wanted to know if you were the one I carried over Monte Salvatore on my shoulders.'

Bors augmented the rising mirth with a guffaw.

'He hauled my rifle and pack is all,' corrected Tannhauser.

'He had to carry your rifle?' said Bors.

Bors chortled again and triggered another round of giggles, which now drew in the men along the wall. Tannhauser looked at Cakie, who'd allowed himself a smile. The fact was that in Cakie's shoes, Tannhauser would have reckoned some opium no less than fair payment for seeing him home. His resolve suffered a further collapse. But three pounds? He pressed on.

'That very occasion is the reason for my visit,' said Tannhauser. 'I hear tell you've been selling my opium.'

The laughter abated somewhat, at least among the adults.

'I've sold a little to the knights,' said Cakie, unabashed.

'Three pounds would throw the entire Order into a stupor for a week.'

'Was it three?' Cakie shrugged. 'The rest is for my blood – my family, my friends.'

Tannhauser took in the misery in the far room.

'If you were in need,' said Cakie, 'I could sell a little to you.'

Whatever exception Tannhauser might have taken to this gall

was forestalled when Bors set down his basket to slap him on the back with another rude guffaw.

'What did I tell you, Mattias? The man is a prince of thieves.'

Tannhauser found himself bested. He sought a dignified solution.

'It's true,' he said to Cakie, 'that I mightn't have made it across the mountains alone.'

He ignored Bors's snort and gestured that Cakie translate, and he did, the children listening with awe as they took in the vastly disproportionate statures of the two men.

'For I was sick – indeed close to death – and sorely weakened by the ague,' continued Tannhauser, with what he hoped was stoic gravitas.

He waited for Cakie to make this public too, but the old Maltese smuggler merely smiled and bobbed his head and said not a word. The children stared at Tannhauser with brown-eyed fascination, as if he were a friendly giant come to ease their woes. Tannhauser coughed.

'And so,' he said, 'it is to thank you for that boon that I've come here today, with these small tokens of my gratitude.'

He stooped and took the basket of luxuries and, as Bors's jaw dropped, presented it to the young woman. She hesitated and looked at Cakie. Cakie nodded and she took it with a most alluring curtsey. Tannhauser looked at Bors, whose mirth had evaporated, and slapped him on the back with a laugh of his own.

'Come, Bors, the knights are feeding these people on sea biscuit and salted fish. And didn't I hear some clinking from that sack? Hand it over to your prince.'

With a scowl for Tannhauser, and a smile and bow for the woman, Bors did so. Cakie looked at Tannhauser. He was too hard to be moved and too seasoned not to know that the visit could have climaxed in a far less cordial fashion, but he inclined his head in a salute which conveyed that the message, nevertheless, had been received. He put the sack down and indeed it clinked.

'And now we have pressing business,' said Tannhauser. He bowed to the pretty girl. 'So, with your permission, if you will excuse us.'

'Stay,' said Cakie. 'We'll make a feast and you'll share in it.'

Tannhauser looked in his eyes and saw that a thieves' bond had just been sealed between them. Such alliances were to be treasured more than gold. Or even opium.

'We'll drink a brandy to your health and enjoy your company,' said Tannhauser. 'But I warn you, a feast shared with Bors would leave precious little for the rest.'

Cakie laughed. Bors glowered. Tannhauser indicated the children, who had followed these exchanges with amazement.

'For Bors's benefit, please, would you translate?'

In such dire straits as all were adrift, the value of small comforts was hugely multiplied and in this vein Tannhauser had resorted to his morning habit of a soak in the big double-hogshead at the rear of the auberge. It had remained undisturbed during his absence, which news was welcome as it concealed his hoard of opium, but a thick skein of dust, bird dung and slime had coated its surface. It had been the work of a day to empty, scour and replenish it, but he'd seconded a pair of slaves from the endless breachworks to perform the task. And a happy pair they'd been to discover so generous a master for so light a labour. He'd let them stop to pray, had fed them salted fish and weevil-free bread, and didn't know the use of a lash. They wept and kissed his feet and clutched his knees when he sent them back, and he'd felt a deeper stab of guilt in so doing than for all the many recent murders that were stacked upon his soul. The tub was covered with a sheet of canvas, for dust was now a constant nuisance, and this he stripped off, along with his clothes, and sank into the bracing cool.

He was dozing on his haunches, arms folded, head back against the rim, and happily thinking of nothing in particular when the water splashed over his face and he opened his eyes to see Amparo climb in.

Her nipples disappeared beneath the surface before he could study them, leaving two buoyant and glistening meridians to mock his resolution to be celibate. Her face and throat were tanned dark gold by the sun and he found the stark contrast with the milk-white paleness below a powerful intoxicant. The tub was not so roomy that he could avoid contact, even if he'd been so inclined. Her smooth, serpentine legs slid around his thighs, and her arse – a feature so indistinguishable in splendour from her bosom that only a churl would think to rank one above the other – nestled down into his lap. He felt the unseen nipples brush his chest. He was afflicted at once by a burgeoning tumescence that nothing in Creation could forefend, and by which Amparo appeared to be scandalised not at all.

'Did Bors put you up to this?' he asked.

'Bors?' she said, innocent as a spring morning.

He shook his head to dismiss the notion. He groped without success for something to say. She put her hands on his shoulders and jiggled with impatience. He held her around the waist. Marvellous. In his experience women were deft enough at eluding congress when it suited them; but woe betide a man who attempted the same, no matter how enlightened his reasons.

'In Spain,' she said, 'men fight bulls with spears, did you know?'

The question took him unawares, but no more so than her self-invited entry into his tub. Perhaps it was provoked by his flagrant state of arousal.

'Of course,' he said. 'I heard that Charles Quintus himself lanced bulls, in Valladolid.'

Such pedantry impressed Amparo not a bit.

She said, 'Do you know by what means they find a fighting bull?'

His hands wandered beneath the brine. 'I do not. But I should love to know. Tell me.'

'They gather the bulls from the *finca* in great herds – fifty bulls, a hundred, an enormous mass of enormous beasts – then the herdsmen drive them along, whipping them, shouting, goading, until they form one heart, one mind, one soul – one wild and headlong creature rushing forward, rushing on. If a gorge lay before them, they would run into the gorge and die as one. If the sea was before them, they would run into the sea, and drown as one.'

Despite other powerful distractions, Tannhauser found himself captivated. She paused and watched him, until she was satisfied that this was so. She went on.

'But from that great herd – that single wild creature hurtling into nowhere across the sunset crimson plain – one bull will at last break free from the rest. One bull who will not run with the others – into nowhere, or into the gorge, or into the sea. He does not fear the herdsmen or their whips. He reclaims his heart, his mind, his soul, from the headlong rush of the many. He runs apart, he runs alone, in a direction of his own choosing.'

Tannhauser felt breathless at the thought of such a sight, and of such a beast.

'Magnificent,' he said. 'And so this is the fighting bull.'

Amparo shook her head. She leaned closer and fixed him with her twin-hued eyes, and he realised she was no mean teller of tales.

'This *might* be the fighting bull,' she said. 'For the herdsmen take him far away, far into the mountains, far away from his brothers, far away from anything the bull has ever known. There they leave him, lost and alone in a strange new land, and they go.' She threw her hand towards some far-flung horizon.

Again she paused, looking at him. Then she leaned back again.

'One week later they go back to find the bull. If he has turned thin and dull and crazy, and runs away because he is afraid, or towards them because he is lonely, then they kill him at once with their spears and eat his meat for supper.' She smiled. 'But, if he is strong and shining and proud, and eating much grass, and he stands without motion and stares at them, and snorts and kicks the dust with anger, as if they have entered a kingdom where they don't belong, and are not welcome, then they know.' She nodded. 'Then they know that *this* is the fighting bull.'

Tannhauser didn't know whether to burst into tears or into laughter, in either case as expression of an inexpressible joy. He found that he loved this extraordinary beast, unknown yet present in his inmost heart, and looming large before him in his mind's eye, as if, even there – as a phantasm – it might bear down and gore him if he looked at it too long.

'It's a rum tale,' he said. 'The bull has the largeness of spirit not to live – or die – with the common mass. Yet by that act he marks himself out as the one who must be sacrificed by Fate.'

Amparo reached out her hand and wiped one corner of his eye.

'This brine is pungent,' he said, abashed. She smiled a cat-like smile and he sniffed. 'So tell me, how do they get this magnificent fellow to the *plaza de toros*?'

'The herdsmen have their ways. They say the only one who knows the bull better than the herdsman, is the *rejoneador* at the moment that he slays him.'

'By the Rod,' he said, with sudden insight. 'You've witnessed this very manner of finding the bull with your own eyes.'

'My papa was a herdsman.'

'Was?'

'He found one bull who chose to fight in the mountains, rather than the *plaza*.'

Tannhauser took this in in silence. He wondered if it was a bull that had left the indentation in her face. He preferred to think it was so, rather than – as he'd assumed before – the fist of some brute. He didn't ask.

'So you're a nomad too,' he said.

'A nomad?'

'One who wanders, always, and claims no home.'

She touched her left breast and said, 'Here is home.' She touched Tannhauser's chest and said, 'And here.' While Tannhauser debated whether this was an erotic invitation, she said, 'Where is your father?'

'Very far away, in the northern mountains,' he replied.

'Do you love him?'

'He taught me how to forge steel,' he said. 'And how to make fires burn hot, and the meaning of the colours in iron, and the care of horses, and how to be honest, and no end of other fine things, the best of which I've forgotten and which he has not.'

'Then he is alive.'

'I've no reason to think otherwise. He was always strong as an ox. Or as one of your bulls. I haven't seen him in ten years,' said Tannhauser. 'And he hasn't seen me in almost three times that long.'

'I don't understand.'

Tannhauser stretched his shoulders and looked up into the turquoise sky. Abbas had provoked the memory too, and he'd resisted. Not so now.

AFTER RETIRING FROM the janissary corps he'd taken the decade's wages that he'd hardly had the chance to spend and bought a horse and a fur-lined kaftan, and travelled north – through the Sultan's Christian fiefdoms, to the East Hungarian marches and the Fâgâraš Mountains, and finally to the village of his birth.

Tannhauser, or as he was in those days, Ibrahim the Red, had gone at once to the smithy, and there had found a new first-born son, who shoed his horse with skill and with the deference accorded to a lord. It was then that he realised how far above these remote mountain people his finery placed him. And Ottoman finery at that. He glimpsed the boy's mother in the yard, a pretty thing not yet too hard-worn. The boy had a younger brother. Their father would be back at sundown and, yes, his name was Kristofer. It was clear from the boy's warmth that his father was greatly loved and respected.

Ibrahim returned the next morning and Kristofer was there: his father too.

Ibrahim had last seen his face when the world was young, when he was Mattias the blacksmith's son, and his mother's hair was bronze, and Britta sang of the Raven while she played with Gerta in the yard. Kristofer had clapped young Mattias on the back, as he left on his circuit of the manors, and had told him to look out for the womenfolk. And Mattias had not done so, though he'd tried.

Ibrahim found Kristofer in the forge, bent over glowing charcoal with his son, revealing some fascinating intricacy of his art. He wore a long leather apron. His hair had turned grey without thinning. For his fifty years he looked more than hale, his build as solid as ever, his forearms thickly thewed and his hands huge. His back was half-turned and Ibrahim stood in the doorway – and he watched, with the forge taste of powdered goat horn and tallow in his mouth, and his ear readjusting to the dialect long unheard, and to the voice that stirred so many echoes.

'There!' said Kristofer, as if spotting a bird of rare plumage. 'That is the blue, like the early morning sky on New Year's Day. Remember it. Always. Quickly now.'

The boy took a length of steel from the fire with his tongs and quenched it in a bucket and recited an Ave Maria. The steel looked like a mason's chisel. As steam rose from the bucket, Ibrahim sniffed distilled vinegar and liquor of quicklime. Yes: the quench for a stone chisel. The long unremembered instructions flashed through his mind.

'Not so hard that it will shatter from the blows of the hammer, nor so soft that it will bend at its holy task, for until the cutting of stone men lived in the wilderness – like Cain in the land of Nod – and without right tools, the wilderness is where we will return.'

Ibrahim almost stepped forward to grab an apron, but he

caught the expression – the smile – on Kristofer's face as he looked down at his boy and glowed with a primal sentiment and pride. They were feelings unknown to Ibrahim, for he had no son. But that look – that smile – those he'd known, and the face of God could not have been more benevolent.

And in this moment Ibrahim – who'd faced Death a score of times and called him honest – conceived a fear far greater than any he had known. Kristofer had built his family anew. He had endured, and flourished, and from the ashes of desolation rekindled his fire of family and love and peace, and by its light he taught magic and beauty and the mysteries of creation to his son. He'd borne the slaughter and sorrow that devils had wrought upon him, and upon those he'd loved more than life. Devils like Ibrahim. Whose trade was murder – and the strangling of babes – and not the cutting of stone but its razing to the ground.

Why revisit such terrible grief upon this gentle man? Why reveal what his first-born son had become in the meanwhile: a bloodstained servant of the Power that had massacred his children? Why cast a shadow too black to own a name across the radiance of his forge?

Kristofer sensed him at the door and turned, and saw Ibrahim's Turkish garb but not his face, backlit as he was by morning sunshine from the yard. The smile of God vanished from his face. He bowed, coldly, with a civility that excluded any deference.

'Good day, sir,' he said. 'How may I serve you?'

Ibrahim remembered that instruction too: the greeting, the poise, the graciousness. His throat tightened and he cleared it.

He said, 'Your boy, here, he shoed and fettled my horse, just yesterday.'

Kristofer had spoken in the German that Ibrahim thought he had lost. The blacksmith hadn't expected a reply in the same. Not from this Turk.

Kristofer blinked. 'You have a grievance?'

The boy stiffened. Ibrahim upraised his palm.

'Not at all. To the contrary, the beast has never taken better to a new set of shoes, and he and I had travelled many hard leagues.' He stopped, for fear of revealing too much. 'I felt I'd paid too little for such expert labour, and wanted to give the boy a bonus.'

The boy coloured with pleasure.

'This is not necessary,' said Kristofer. 'Your satisfaction is reward enough. Thank the gentleman, Mattie.'

The revelation of the boy's name further thickened Ibrahim's throat and intensified his confusion. 'Even so,' said Ibrahim, 'if I could do so without offence, it would please me.'

Mattie looked at his father and received a nod, and while the boy walked across the forge, Kristofer regarded the shadowed figure in the door with an odd curiosity. Ibrahim fumbled for his purse, which contained the better part of all his silver and gold. He hadn't planned this circumstance. By the time Mattie reached him, the impulse could not be debated or resisted. He pulled his purse free and crammed it in the boy's hands, shielding it, he hoped, from Kristofer's view. Mattie felt its weight and opened his mouth to protest.

'Mind your manners, boy,' said Ibrahim, under his breath. 'And don't open this until I'm gone.'

He glanced once more at Kristofer. Could the man see him or not? Go now, he thought, before it's too late. He raised his hand.

'Peace be upon you and all your household,' he said.

He turned out of the door, where his horse stood waiting.

'Stay awhile,' said Kristofer's voice behind him. 'Share some breakfast with us.'

Ibrahim paused on the threshold. An exquisite pain knifed his heart. An abyss gaped at his feet, as another had gaped on that very same threshold so many lifetimes before. Should he reclaim some small portion of that which had been taken? Or was it already gone forever and would he, in the attempt, lose even more? A familiar voice in his head, in a familiar tongue – the tongue he now thought in, the tongue in which he'd issued commands at the sack of Nahjivan – cut through the anguish.

It is over. It is done. They are not your people any more. Leave them to their peace.

Ibrahim spoke over his shoulder. 'You are very gentle, sir, but urgent affairs await me on the Stambouli Shore.'

He mounted his horse and left without looking back. In doing so he realised that he couldn't return to Stambouli. That was done too. The Turks were not his people either. If there were one man in the world who had no people at all, it was he. He was alone. And he was free.

'INSTEAD OF HEADING south I rode west,' he told Amparo, 'towards Vienna and the lands of the Franks, and to wars and follies and wonders of a different character. But that's another tale.'

Amparo watched him with wet eyes and seemed even more besotted than before.

He turned away. 'So you see,' he said, 'I saw my father, but I didn't let him see me.'

Amparo said, 'Where was the sense in that? He loved you. He would have given anything to see you.'

This observation was hardly what he wanted to hear. Tannhauser almost said, *I was ashamed. And I could not dare the chance that I'd shame him too*. But he'd had enough of such weighty matters. He said, 'There is little in the way of sense in much of what I do. Why else would I have returned to this sorry hell-hole?'

'You don't love me any more,' she said.

This charge so took him by surprise that he blurted, 'Nonsense.'

She cocked her head to one side and stared at him, with her air of a wild bird examining an earthbound creature far larger, more cumbersome and more stupid than she. Clearly his reply was inadequate. Yet be that as it may, he'd been tricked into an admission of love. She waited for him to blunder even deeper within her trap and like a fool he did so.

He said, 'I've never adored a woman more entirely in all my days.'

The truth with which this statement rang was enough to satisfy her for the moment. She said, 'Then why won't you take me to your bed?'

Her eyes bored through him. They seemed illuminated from within. How and in what fashion he couldn't say, but it was so. Illuminated. It had been so from the start, when he saw her spinning about in the gloom of his tavern. But looking into her eyes made further thought strenuous; combined with the other contents she brought to the tub, thought was impossible. He battled to keep his hands anchored to her waist; rather, he slid them a little further around the small of her back, a harmless enough manoeuvre, to be sure. His fingertips encountered the apex of the cleft between her hams. His head swam.

'Are you listening?' she said.

'Of course,' he said, his mind quite blank.

'Then why?'

'Why?'

Her mouth was the colour of crushed violets, a small mouth, the lips less than full, but of a wonderful symmetry, swelling at the centre with a pertness that matched her nose.

'Yes, why?'

Words arrived from he knew not where. They were of paltry value and, he belatedly realised, probably best unsaid. 'Sundry ailments and wounds,' he mumbled. 'Fierce agues, a touch of plague, fatiguing night duties. All manner of afflictions and woes . . .'

'I can cure all manner of woes.'

She kissed him and he surrendered his virtue without further ado. He discovered afresh her nimble, flickering tongue. Her black hair had grown longer and fell about her neck in uncultivated curls. He slid a hand beneath her arse and guided the tip of his organ between the folds of her matrix. The first half-inch was cold, and moist only with brine, and he encountered stiff resistance which, while not without appeal, made him fear for a moment that he might do her an injury if he pressed on with excess zeal. Amparo grabbed the edge of the tub behind him and anchored her heels around his thighs and launched herself down. She cried out with a passion that stoked his own as he gained another crucial inch of entry and paused. She hovered suspended, her limbs as taut as bowstrings, catching her breath. She opened her eyes and looked at him. He took her weight in his hands and straightened his legs, the barrel rim chafing the skin on his back as he stood upright and invaded her to her core. She cried out again, but from somewhere much deeper within, and her eyes rolled back under fluttering lids. He kissed her throat, the salt tart on his tongue, and realised he had more to give, and that it would not be unwelcome, and he grabbed her by the nape of the neck and held her tight as he shunted the last inch home. Her bones banged into his hips and he kissed her full on the mouth and he heard her yowling echo through his skull as he pierced her, long and slow, with lubricious strokes. In the pit of his stomach a cauldron boiled and some seething and nameless brew rose up through his spine and filled his brain with the Devil's Fire. He was deaf to the rage of the siege guns and the frenzied tintamarre of the alarum horns. He was oblivious, for once, to the foaming spate of rancour from the circle of barbarity beyond. He was aware only of Amparo clinging to his bulk, her nails clenched deep into his loins, her body at once frail and indestructible, her teeth bared in a rapture that looked like pain, his drenched hair plastered to her skin as he sucked her teats.

The ground beneath the hogshead trembled and lurched, as if some subterranean beast of mythical proportion had rammed it from below. This hardly seemed fantastic in the circumstance, nor did the stupendous percussive blast whose force drew the air from their lungs. She let go of him and lay back and gripped the iron-shod rim, half-floating, splayed and convulsing, and whimpering 'Yes', over and over and again, as if her only fear was that he'd stop. He suppressed his own explosive wave, gentleman that he was, and she felt this and it incited her to spasms more frantic yet. He stood stalwart and immobile while she helped herself to her fill, or at least until she arched her back and shuddered and began to slide back down into the water. It was a spectacle to behold, and fortunate he considered himself to witness it. He withdrew and she squirmed. He turned her about to face the parched garden and he entered her from behind and below. Her ardour was far from exhausted. With a sigh he felt the welcome gust of his second wind and, the proprieties duly observed, no obligation to hold back further. In the distance the bells of San Lorenzo began to jangle, with a fury whose significance presently eluded him. Shortly thereafter, or so it seemed, he looked up above Amparo's brine-slicked hair to find the less than agreeable spectacle of Bors as he lumbered from the rear of the auberge.

To his credit, Bors's first instinct was to perform a swift and discreet about-turn; then some higher sense of duty made him turn about again.

'The Bastion of Castile is down!' he called. His head bobbed cannily as he sought a peek at the fabled breasts in the hogshead. 'The Turks are inside the town!'

'What would you have me do about it?' roared Tannhauser.

Bors waved a vague hand, head bobbing with increased desperation, 'I supposed you'd want to know.'

'Thank you, but as you can see, I'm *in flagrante*.'

Bors retreated, thwarted by the hogshead's brim. Tannhauser held his own frustration to be rather more properly justified, but was damned if he'd let the situation best him. He withdrew and she protested loudly, and he scooped her up in his arms and hoisted her from the tub. She stood dripping and unmindful of both her nudity and the havoc sweeping the town. Tannhauser clambered out. He picked up her threadbare green dress and handed it to her and she clutched it about her with small enthusiasm. Tannhauser, with fewer concessions to decorum, loaded one arm with his dagger, breeches and boots, and with the other escorted Amparo back inside.

'It's as well,' he said, 'if we conclude within easy reach of some decent weapons.'

By the time Tannhauser reached the front some half-hour, or maybe twice that interlude, later – and in neither fit state nor mood for anything more demanding than a nap in Amparo's arms – the siege appeared to have reached its expected denouement. The streets en route were choked with staggering fugitives and fallen wounded. That sense of mass panic that commanders fear above all other calamities crackled in the air like the prelude to some meteorological cataclysm. The victim of the huge mine, which the Mamelukes had burrowed out of solid rock and crammed with tons of powder, had been the impregnable Bastion of Castile towards the eastern end of the enceinte.

The bastion was now a shapeless talus spanning the outer ditch, at the top of which flew a number of bright silk banners sporting the *surah* of Conquest, and where an array of janissary marksmen knelt or lay prone. The exploding mine had brought down with it a wide swathe of the curtain wall to either side. Worse still, the second, interior, wall was also massively breached and Turkish shock troops, having mopped up a desperate resistance, now spilled towards it, around and over the shoulders of the devastated bastion like lava round an outcropping of rock. Many good Christian knights had no doubt been buried in the eruption, and amid the still-smoking rubble a thin line of beleaguered brethren held the Turkish vanguard to a standstill, their armour dripping red in the morning light.

On this side of the breached wall was an apron of open ground where La Valette's engineers had cleared a section of dwellings two blocks deep to give an open field of fire. A pair of sixteen-pounders had been hauled up and even as the mules were unlimbered, their sweating crews were charging the barrels with grape. From the barricades and breastworks sealing the cross streets, *arquebuceros* swapped fire with the musketeers on the brow of the talus, to little effect. The air pulsated with Arabic and invocations of the Prophet and his beard. The whole arena was fogged with drifts of gunsmoke. The bells of San Lorenzo tolled as if they might do some earthly good. At a forward command post La Valette, armourless and bareheaded, observed the unfolding struggle with Oliver Starkey and a band of Provençals at his side. Several squads of pikemen trotted uncertainly across the open ground towards the melee.

'Mattias!'

He found Bors priming the pan of his Damascus matchlock behind the wall of a roofless hovel. 'Ready for glory, my friend, now that your appetites are slaked?'

'I missed breakfast,' Tannhauser replied. 'Did you think to bring me some?'

'I did not, though your portion wasn't wasted. Where's the girl?'

'I told her to find Carla and stick close by her, in case we need to improvise an exit.'

'We'll see,' said Bors. 'Seems Mustafa has Saint Michel on its knees, again. Piyale's lot are yonder. They've got ladders and ropes up all the way to the Bastion of France, but that's just to soak up our reserves. The sharp end is here.'

As Bors ploughed a ball into the Turks massed on the slope, Tannhauser settled beside him to bench his rifle on the wall and choose a mark. He saw a young chaplain of the Order stumble from the smoke, his arms cartwheeling and his habit filthy and torn, as if he'd recently burrowed out from the rubble of Castile. His face was bloodied and contorted with the absolute conviction that only extreme fear, and states of religious ecstasy, may confer. In his case perhaps both ingredients were at work for he stopped a hundred feet away, framed by the gaudy Moslem pageant just behind him, and raised his hands aloft to deliver a crazed jeremiad, fragments of which reached Tannhauser's ears through the din.

'Lost! We are all of us lost! God has turned his face against us! The harvest is over, the summer has ended, and we are not saved! Retreat and make your peace with Christ!'

Such claptrap coming from a priest was worth a fresh battalion of Sipahis to Piyale. The morale of the Spanish soldiery and the peasant militia had been fragile ever since their *maestro de campo*, Don Melchior De Robles, had been shot in the head on the 12th. Sure enough the advancing pikemen stopped and wavered in confusion. They stole looks at each other, deaf to the provost sergeant's roars, and found little comfort in what they saw. They found even less in the bloody duel for the breach or in the ululating horde trampling over the corpses of their comrades just beyond. They shifted about like leaves in a wind and teetered on the verge of rout.

Tannhauser scowled and threw down on the raving chaplain and shot him square through the Cross spanning his chest. The chaplain's fingers almost touched his toes as he left the ground and he vanished back into the fog from whence he'd emerged.

'Well,' said Bors, 'someone had to do it.'

Tannhauser crammed his powder flask into the bore. The pikemen didn't continue their advance, but at least they were thinking twice about running away. Some of them jerked and fell under gunfire from the slope. The chaplain's execution provided no more than a hiatus. Someone had to seize the hour and at this most desperate pass only one man had the stature for the job. Tannhauser glanced over to the knot of armoured men around La Valette, and found the Grand Master looking in his direction.

'Come on, you old dog,' shouted Tannhauser. 'It's time to show us what you're made of.'

He didn't know if La Valette heard him; but if not the Grand Master had come to the same conclusion. La Valette grabbed a morion and a half-pike from a startled soldier nearby and, to the consternation of his Myrmidons, the old man mounted the breastworks alone and strode across the bullet-scourged ground towards the broil.

'God's bread,' said Bors. 'He's taking them on single-handed.'

The effect could not have been more dramatic if John the Baptist himself had appeared on the field. The pikemen at once formed up in order. The Provençals fought with each other to follow in his wake. As the old man broke into a shambling run, the Christian battle cries rose above the din, and the disheartened felt their blood boil, and knights and militiamen appeared from the ruins where before there'd seemed to be none, and hundreds charged pell-mell for the smouldering slopes where the foemen in their thousands grimly waited.

Bors grounded his musket and drew his sword. He looked at Tannhauser, who was winding the key of his wheel-lock with every intention of sticking to the wall.

'Come now,' said Bors. 'The girl can't have drained all that much sap from your balls.'

Tannhauser canted his rifle against the wall and donned his gauntlets. He said, 'Because you'll never let me hear the last of it if you live.'

They joined the rush to perdition and, as if it sprang from some poisonous wellhead whose source would never run dry, the evil bliss of combat surged once more through Tannhauser's veins. He wore a salet and half-armour, cadged from the growing stockpile, and as he ran the sweat ran down his flanks like a swarm of lice. His sword was a Running Wolf blade from Passau. He hurdled fellows groaning in their own spilled bowels. He waded into the line with cut and thrust, treading on the dying and the dead. He avoided the flailing elbows and blocked the hissing blades. He carved out a space at the foot of the talus and a figure loomed in green and he doled out a backhand below the knees, felt the woody double clunk through his wrist as the shins gave way, then stabbed the man through the gut as he slithered down the scree. Uphill assaults were damnable, but it was how the janissaries earned their daily bread. Just ignore the sweat and breathe. His arm moved, in part, of its own accord, pulling out strokes that his mind was too slow to foresee, like a player contesting tennis balls on the courts of the Pallacorda, and this was a satisfaction most profound. There was joy in a throat gaping wide. There was something of beauty in the union of action and intent, as your sword clove a skull below the turban and vented brains and eyes in a single blow. It shouldn't have been so, but it was, and this was the world and this was the day and this was the way to write your name in the book of Life.

An hour or so's hard grind passed by in the scorch of the August sun, the air alive with screaming and the drone of the Paternoster. Tannhauser's armour was caked in indigo mud and the weight was tiresome. The fight was a stiff one, but he and Bors had cleared their share of the talus with reasonable dispatch, and as far as he could see – which wasn't twenty feet in any direction – the Turks were falling back and the tide had turned. Then a few yards to their right and down the incline, commotion arose.

'The Grand Master is down!'

The word spread like a pox along the widely extended line and the news got worse as it did so. Within a hundred yards, by Tannhauser's reckoning, La Valette would be being buggered by Mustafa's horse. Besides the resurgent stench of incipient panic, disaster loomed because soldiers and knights rushed to protect their Prince. In the general state of chaos, few in fact knew where he was, and the result was akin to a riot. If the Turks had the wit to take advantage, the tide would turn again, and likely for good.

Bors was making a meal of finishing a janissary half his size. Tannhauser stabbed the Turk through the back of the neck with his blood-quenched dagger and shoved him down, then jerked his head at Bors to indicate he follow him.

They encountered a hedge of fighting as savage as any that Tannhauser had yet seen, as a mob of Gauls turned berserk to shield their Warlord. The janissaries, sensing that victory itself was only inches beyond their swords, committed themselves with no lesser courage and furore. Tannhauser and Bors circumvented the melee and jostled their way to the ring of knights round La Valette.

Peering over their heads without much trouble, Tannhauser discovered the kind of squabble that only the French know how to muster, most especially in the middle of a battlefield. The exchanges were too florid and swift for Tannhauser to follow in detail, but he gathered that the Myrmidons wanted La Valette to withdraw to safety, while the old man, who seemed fairly sprightly, despite being held upright by Oliver Starkey, was having none of it. The skirt of his habit was sodden, and torn apart at the thigh, but if he looked a little pale it was more likely with rage than with blood loss, for tempers were running high enough to boil. Starkey was far too English to advance his master's cause in the face of such emotion. Gallic obstinacy looked set to triumph where Turkish valour had failed.

Tannhauser hadn't inched this far up the bloody talus to be shoved back down. With a loud clang he smacked the nearest helm with the flat of his sword. The victim dropped to his knees and Bors threw in a snigger to rub the point home. In the outraged pause that ensued, Tannhauser spoke in Italian.

'The soldiers believe their Grand Master is dead. Clear him a way to the top where they can see him and take fresh heart.'

Bors added, 'If you Gauls have the mettle to get up there.'

Before the Provençals could hack them both apart, La Valette shoved his way forward and limped up the slope. Oliver Starkey was the first to reach his side, he too hobbled by wounds. Pride and bellicosity triumphed over pique and the French knights roared like men deranged and drove in a gore-boltered wedge for the infidel banners. So furious were the Gauls in the violence they unleashed that Tannhauser revised his opinion of them on the spot. Bors made to follow. Tannhauser held him back.

'Enough's enough,' he said. 'I need to move my bowels and have some food.'

They trudged back through the reeking sewage of the fray, too hot and fatigued to spare the wounded a glance, and they crossed the open ground and collected their long guns. When they turned to look back, La Valette's attack had taken him and his men to the ruined bastion's summit, where the Turkish banners were thrown down amid a rabid orgy of killing.

The second rout of the day was thus avoided and the whole uneven embankment of blood-slaked debris was back in Christian hands. The eight-pointed cross of Saint John was wafted aloft; and taunts and obscene gestures were exchanged; and God Almighty was praised for their deliverance from evil.

THROUGHOUT THE AFTERNOON the decimated slave battalions, and the mass of the town's population, toiled to fling Turkish corpses into the ditch and to erect rough breastworks along the devastated walls. Fireworks crews set up shop in sulphurous redoubts. The cannon were entrenched and resighted. The ramparts were braced and remanned. And Gullu Cakie's confederates trawled the crippled and the slain, to slit the throats of the dying and strip the Moslem bodies of their plunder.

The long day waned and the dragon-mouthed siege guns rattled again on their chains. As cannonballs and gun stones bounced back from the walls, they raised reeking spouts of filth from the putrefying pudding of dead that clogged the ditch, and the foul vapours thereby expelled kindled a yellow-green *ignis fatuus*, which glowed like evil in the twilight and necklaced the

Borgo's throat, as if the spirits of the Moslem dead had awakened in protest, and were calling on their co-religionists to rise and avenge them.

And that spectral call to arms was heeded, despite the horror and the squanderment of the day, for, shortly after sundown, the Grande Turke attacked again across the whole enceinte. The darkness blazed as bright as day, and Satan's chorus sang, and the Gods of East and West alike concealed their faces in shame as Their benighted devotees flocked back to the slaughter.

SUNDAY 19 AUGUST 1565

The Post of Castile – a Fire in the Ruins

THE CHAOS OF the midnight broil transgressed all human codes and circumscriptions, as if every fool on earth had been there assembled and given leave to rave in the dark unfettered. Men hacked each other asunder in the sweltering darkness. Corrosive drifts of smoke nourished the confusion. Arquebuses crackled and cannon crashed. Flares and spouts of flame and spinning wildfire hoops lit up the tumult.

By these intermittent flashes of incandescence, Carla stuffed handfuls of coils back through the slit in the Spaniard's belly. It wouldn't prolong his life but it spared him indecency; and at such a grievous extremity even small dignities were precious. She'd gained some practice in this manoeuvre, and with the entrails reseated inside him she tucked the lap of his shirt into the wound to keep them in place. If he stood up, or moved overmuch, they'd spill out again; but of this the risk was slight. He lay without movement or demur, his face yellowed and shining in the waver of the flames, his eyes no longer animate with fear but fixed on his eternal destination. A smudge of chrism gleamed on his forehead. On his lips clung some fragments of Communion bread. He was in the arms of Christ. She smiled at him and he nodded with curious contentment. She shouldered her poke and stood up and left him to die.

She found Mattias watching her, his helmet under one arm, his weight slung over one hip like a piece of statuary. His cuirass was daubed with muck and a rifle hung from his shoulder. His features were in shadow and she wondered what they might have shown her of his thoughts. He came closer, into the light. Powder had blacked his face like a sweep's and was gathered like ink in the creases round his eyes. He tossed back his filth-matted hair and sweat flew, and he craned his neck to one side to reveal a congealing gash an inch or two in length.

'I'm sore afflicted with wounds,' he said. 'I need your ministrations.'

She gave the gash a glance. 'A scratch,' she said.

'A scratch?'

He feigned chagrin, with such conviction that she felt obliged to examine the gash again. He'd been close to death but the wound was superficial. His teeth appeared in a grin, and the creases round his eyes grew blacker.

'How else can I win the pleasure of your society?'

She laughed, taken by surprise, and was amazed at the sudden joy the laughter brought her. She smiled often enough, at the mutilated and doomed, but laughter was a habit unpractised. The last time, she realised, had been on the night of his return from exile, when he'd made his adventures among the heathen sound like farce. She hadn't seen him since. In one big fist he brandished a goatskin and a scorched wicker basket.

'Water and wine from God,' he said. 'And some bread, pickled eggs, olives, and a sheep's cheese, perfectly aged.' He jerked his chin at the field. 'The dying can wait, and the dead won't mind. Come, you must take something, I insist.'

He swapped his booty to the hand that cradled his helm and with his free hand took her arm and led her to a breastwork improvised from the ruins. He set down his load in the lee. He gathered chunks of burning timber from the wrack nearby and threw them together for a fire.

'Not much of a hearth,' he said, 'but better than none.'

She watched him lay out his wares.

'I brought enough for three,' he said. 'Where's Amparo?'

'She's keeping Buraq company,' she said. 'The sight of wounds upsets her, and out here I'd fret for her safety.'

'But not for your own,' he said.

'The infirmary is filled twice over, as is the piazza and every house still standing and even the tunnels and cellars underground. The wounded aren't to be taken to the hospital any more. Fra Lazaro has decreed that we now come to them.'

Mattias cast his gaze about the diabolic nightscape. Oily jets of flame gouted from the mouths of trumps along the outermost breastworks and the glare of the ochre inferno they created beyond – in which numbers unknown of Turkish souls were consumed – threw the jagged rim into sharp relief. The defenders of the Roman Faith strung out thereon lunged into the nether-realm at their feet with pikes and glaives, like shadow puppet demons on a mutinous bank of the Styx. Incendiary hoops skirred sparking into the void and the glowing barrels of muskets bucked and slammed. A hot wind keened from the deserts across the sea and sent ragged leaves of flame flying up at the stars, like pages torn from a burning book of prayer condemned and unread. And from shallow pits in the rubble men squalled like abandoned children in a dozen foreign tongues, foreign to each other and foreign to God, for He seemed unwilling to hear their cries for mercy.

'One would have thought such suffering beyond the design of men,' said Mattias. He looked at her. 'Yet that is our Genius.'

Carla didn't reply.

He brushed the dust from a block of stone, and invited her to sit, which she did. Stifling a groan, as if every joint voiced its own bitter complaint, he sat down too. She said Grace and to her surprise he joined in. They crossed themselves.

'You'll convert me yet,' he said, and offered her the wineskin. His hand was scabbed and bruised. Two fingers, one swollen as a spindle, were bound together with a length of twine. 'Your pardon,' he said, 'I neglected to bring beakers.'

She took the skin and drank. The wine was warm and sweet, and not watered as much as she was used to. Perhaps not watered at all. She handed the skin back.

'Take more,' he said, 'your throat must be dry as clay, and you'll need your strength tonight.'

She took another mouthful and wiped her lips. Mattias poured half a pint down his throat and swallowed once. He plugged the skin and set it aside and she watched him pare the rind from a wedge of cheese with a garnet-dudgeoned dagger. He did it with great precision, then cut a delicate slice and proffered it by the dagger's tip, conspicuous not to touch it with his filth-rimed fingers.

'Taste it,' he said. 'It's like a poem melting on your tongue.'

The cheese was pungent and as good as promised. Her stomach stirred with a hunger she'd been unaware of. They ate.

'When I left for Saint Elmo,' he said, 'your complaint was that the world had little use for you. I return to find you all but a subject for balladry. And justly so.'

Coming from him, the compliment touched her and she coloured. She asked, 'What have you accomplished since your return, aside from mischief?'

'Little of merit, I admit,' he said. 'My keenest ambition I haven't advanced at all.'

Carla said, 'You've brought Amparo happiness.'

Mattias coughed on a crumb of cheese. He recovered. 'Well, as is commonly known, lovemaking is vital to good health and in my current state all cures are heartily welcomed.'

Carla shifted. Her jealousy of Amparo, which she'd laboured so hard to contain, flooded her stomach. At the same time, she felt her blood rise to her head. Her eyes roved over his hands, beautiful in their strength for all that they were damaged, and to his face whose contours and crags she could have studied forever despite being mantled in grime. She recalled her dream in the cot and was discomfited. She looked away.

Mattias continued unabashed as he slathered oil from the crock of olives over his bread. 'I'm reliably informed, on the authority of Petrus Grubenius, that abstention causes noxious humours to accumulate, especially in the spleen. It's this that accounts for the ferocity of these knights, for instance, and the crabbiness and malignity of so many priests. Of its effects on women I'm less certain, but while the gentler sex are indeed a creation apart, I'd hazard that, in this respect, their natures are not far different from those of men.'

'I wasn't speaking of lovemaking' – he looked at her as if he knew this wasn't quite true, but she pressed on, – 'but rather of love.'

'The difference is often moot – for women, almost always, I should say. But you, as a woman, would know that better than me.'

Carla was lost for a reply. She was sure he could see right through her fraudulent piety. She who in her dream had taken his cock into her mouth with such vivid bliss. The tension between her erotic and religious natures, both so potent, erased her thoughts. She stared at the cheese in her hands, for which she'd lost all appetite.

'If I offend you,' he said, 'it's not my intention. But we sit bare inches from our deaths. If we can't speak openly here, then you must tell me where we can.'

The challenge and its logic lit her courage. 'Do I appear crabby, ferocious or malign?'

He arched his brow. 'Malign, never. Crabby? Once, perhaps, but not any longer. You now have a vocation and this too drains the stagnant humours, though, if I may say so, to a less efficacious degree.' He grinned, she realised, at the look on her face.

'As to ferocity,' he went on, 'well, that quality, as before, flows into that damnable gambo violl of yours.'

'Why damnable?'

'Because twice it's lured me into Hades and this time I can't see my way out.'

'Why did you abandon your Turkish friends? You were safe.'

'As I just said, your siren song called me in the night.'

'You also said we could speak openly, which I take to mean without fear. You say my music moved you, and I'm honoured, but the music alone can't stand as a reason or an end, much less as your keenest ambition.'

'You have me there,' said Mattias. He considered her. She waited for him to confess an infatuation to match her own. He said, 'My ambition remains to see you reunited with your son. All the more so since I now know him to be a most splendid boy and, I dare say, a good friend and comrade in arms.'

He spoke from the heart and she was moved. And yet. She felt remiss that she felt more for the man than the boy. She envied the depth of his relationship with Orlandu, whom she yet barely knew. She swallowed these feelings, along with her disappointment, and said nothing.

'This errand has proved more formidable than I imagined, to say the least,' he said. 'And things look set to get knottier still, but obstinacy has its uses and I'm loath to yield to despair. As you know, Orlandu is safe with my patron, Abbas bin Murad, commander of the Yellow Banners and a man of rare kindness and wisdom. Sooner or later Orlandu will be taken to Stambouli, and there I'll find him again – and a good deal more easily than I did here.' He waved a hand at Bedlam. 'The problem we face is how to escape this madness.'

For a moment Carla was bewildered. The very idea had no meaning. 'Escape?'

'If I can find the means, will you come with me?'

'Abandon Malta?'

'Abandon, forsake, flee – as you will,' he said. 'You, me, Amparo, Bors.'

'And the others?'

'The others are perfectly able to die without us, and they have the Pope's promise of Heaven to give them solace.'

He appeared quite serious. She said, 'I can hardly believe I hear you say this.'

'You've harnessed your fate to that of the Religion. More than that, your heart, your mind, perhaps even your soul. I understand. There's comfort in belonging. And no mortar binds more strongly than the threat of death. But do not imagine there's some higher principle at stake. This is just another scabby little war. It will end. A line will change on a map, or not. And then there will be other wars. And others still. And yet more after those. Men like Suleiman Shah and La Valette will fight such wars until the end of human time – it's a craving inherent to the species – and they'll never lack for disciples or reasons to do so. And I'll admit there's no finer sport. But now I have my eye on other pastimes. Will you join me? Or has the craving bitten you too?'

'This is no sport to me, but rather an abomination. Yet to run away seems wrong.'

'Your courage in the face of death begs no further proof. Perhaps it's your courage to face life that's yet to be tested.'

'What if the Religion win?'

'Win?' He snorted. 'Time renders all such victories null, without exception. Who cares now that Hannibal won at Cannae? Or Timur the Lame at Ankara? Or Alexander at Gaugamela? They're all dust now, and their mighty empires too, and so it will be with the Ottomans and the Spanish, and all the others yet to come who'll one day rise and one day just as surely fall. My notion of victory is to grow old and fat, to witness some things of beauty – perhaps even to bring some such into being – to eat some fine meals, to feel the wind on my face and the tender flesh of a lover in my hands.'

'I have a duty to the sick. A sacred trust.'

'Your boy means nothing to you, then.' Carla flinched at what she feared might hold some truth. 'And Amparo and Bors and I can join the chaff in the ditch – we who came to Hell at your behest.'

Confusion struck her dumb. She felt a burning shame. She avoided his eyes.

He said, 'I was fair set for Tripoli until I heard you play.'

'Then why didn't you leave us to our madness and go?'

'Because I conceived the foolish notion that I love you.'

She stared at him. Her heart pounded in her throat. He returned her gaze.

'Bors tells me that, in war, love is not to be trusted. For war makes men mad, and love makes them madder still, and therefore to speak on such matters is folly, for we say things we may not mean. Even so.'

He reached out his hand across the space between them and touched her cheek and she pushed her face against his palm and a shiver ran through her. He slid his fingers into her hair and she craned back her neck. She felt his breath on her face and looked at him. His eyes were fiery blue, even in the dim yellow light. Her mind swam, her body melted. With elation, with sorrow, with fear. With the spectre of guilt. Her lips parted and she closed her eyes and he kissed her. His beard was rough on her skin. He smelled of powder smoke and sweat, and the sweat stirred the memory of her original longing for him, in the garden on the hill. His lips shocked her with the delicacy of their touch. He sighed into her throat. His lips pressed harder. She wanted to throw herself against him, to hold him and be held, to slake her thirst, to fall and surrender and forget and vanish forever into his arms. But her limbs wouldn't move and instead she lay cradled by his hand as if afloat on an ocean of bliss. His mouth pulled away, and his hand too, and she didn't move and didn't want to move, for she didn't want it to be over.

'You're weeping,' he said.

She opened her eyes and her hands flew to her cheeks in distraction. They were wet. She wiped them. She felt foolish. Her rapture was banished.

Mattias leaned back on his stone. He was bone-tired, yet seemed oppressed by something deeper than exhaustion. In the gun black masking his face his eyes appeared huge. He'd always seemed a man who knew his own mind at every moment; yet now she saw a confusion that pained him and which mirrored her own. He blinked and it was gone.

'Forgive me,' he said. 'Today I've slain many men whose names I'll never know, and my brain is addled by gunfire and unjust blood.'

He reached for the wineskin. A sense of panic fluttered in her belly. She didn't want an apology. She wanted something so basic she couldn't even name it. Bors was right. Love and war and madness. Havoc, pestilence, blood. Mothers and sons and men. The sexual hunger that tormented her even now with its revelations. She knew so much she knew nothing. She blinked at the remnant tears that fogged her vision. The tears of bliss that Mattias had misconstrued. She snatched at his last phrase without thinking.

'Unjust blood?' she said.

The wrong phrase. A phrase cared nothing for. She felt the moment slipping from her grasp, the conversation, the kiss, his ardour, all sucked down the wind into the murderous night.

Mattias shrugged, his eyes on the wine stopper in his hand, and she saw that he'd retreated into himself. 'It's rare to spill any other kind,' he said, 'much though all hereabouts are convinced otherwise. Soldiers of Islam. Soldiers of Christ. Each are devils to the other, and Satan sniggers in his sleeve.'

He offered the wineskin and she shook her head. He drank and wiped his mouth. She flinched, as if it were the kiss he were wiping away. As if the kiss had never existed. As if she'd dreamed it as she'd dreamed of so much else. But the beat of her heart was quickened still and the taste of him lingered on her lips. She didn't want to talk about killing and war. She wanted to talk of love. She wanted to hear him talk of love. But she had no art in these matters. Her voice felt plugged in her throat and her shoulders were stiff. She'd retreated as much as he. And yet he had not, for retreat was not in his nature. He took a scarf from his sleeve and leaned over and wiped her face. The scarf was filthy and soaked in sweat, yet it felt exquisite.

'Better by far to spill tears,' he said. He smiled to cheer her. He put the scarf away. 'Petrus Grubenius speculated that tears are in fact blood from which the potency has been extracted by the membranes of the brain. He could not prove this, but it's true that to the taste they are similar: saltier than urine, but not so salty as brine. He believed that weeping was most healthful – nature's substitute for the bloodletting that surgeons foist upon us with such glee. And many will agree that weeping can restore a jaded spirit.'

Carla smiled too, her panic banished by his warmth, and she was curious for he'd invoked the name before. 'Tell me, who is Petrus Grubenius?'

'Petrus was a physician, an astronomer, an alchemist, a Philosopher of Natural Magick in as many of its infinite forms as he could study – cosmology, physic, the distillation of medicines and elixirs, the transmutation of metals, the design of ciphers, the secrets of lodestones and lenses.' He threw up his hands. 'In short, a scholar of all that is Marvellous. Malice and anger were unknown to him, as was that fear of the Other that turns most of us into beasts. More than all that, he was a good friend to me. In him the Quintessence – whose mysteries were his grail – was embodied in its highest form.'

His passion, and the sadness that shimmered beneath it, moved her.

'Tell me more,' she said.

'Well,' said Mattias, rubbing his palms, 'the Greeks – of the lost age, before they became the sorry race we know now – identified four fundamental elements of the Universe. Fire, Earth, Water and Air, as you know. Pythagoras recognised a fifth and higher essence – the Quintessence – which, he said, flew upwards at creation, and from which the stars themselves were formed, along with all other things, living or dead. It is the power not merely of life, but of Being.'

'I meant more about your friendship with Grubenius.'

For a moment he was crestfallen, as if her interest in the mundane over the infinite were to be expected.

She said, 'I may seem coarse of mind, or perhaps too feminine, but you intrigue me far more than Pythagoras.'

Mattias took a breath through his nostrils, as if the labour daunted him.

'I'd not been long in the land of the Franks,' he said. 'I fought for Alva against the French in the Piedmont, and had just been mustered out. Since I'd known little else since boyhood, I was just another soldier, waiting for another war. Petrus was already then an old man, of strange demeanour and habits, for he lived in solitude and cared little for appearances and manners. His earholes and nostrils and brows were monstrous hairy, his hands were scurfy and blotched from his wondrous experiments, and an ailment of the hipbone caused him to hobble. I brushed away some *bravi* who were taunting him in the street and he took me to his home for supper. What he saw in me that night I can't say, but I went on to share his roof for two years. Years whose like I'll never know again.'

She saw that some alternative destiny had been torn from his grasp, but his regrets were swept aside by fond memories.

'His workshop was a lode of hermetic arts. Every room in the house was crammed with lore, much of it written in his own hand, and scattered willy-nilly, for his mind was ever roving through pastures new. He enjoyed my curiosity, crude as it was, and since age had robbed him of dexterity, my basic skill as a metalsmith was of value. Thus I became his pupil and assistant.'

At this Mattias glowed with a private pride. He took another draught of wine.

'All this was well and good, but then Petrus found out that I was able to read Arabic script. Such excitement as he expressed I'll never forget – you'd think he'd discovered the Philosopher's Stone itself – for his wonder at Arab learning was unconfined. And it happened that he had in his library a rare tractate in their language, by Abu Musa Jabir, a sage of Baghdad, and whose secrets he'd never unlocked. In me he found his key. It was a strenuous labour, even so. Many were the words I didn't recognise, but such was his genius with ciphers that Petrus would unearth meanings where I could not.' He looked at her. 'Those were happy days. In Mondovi.'

'What brought those days to an end?' asked Carla.

Mattias pleated his brow. 'There were rumours of the Lutheran heresy taking root in that town, and of Waldensians moving down from the high valleys – matters of which Petrus and I were contentedly ignorant. Michele Ghisleri, may his soul be cursed, sent the Roman Inquisition to investigate.'

Carla suddenly felt ill.

'The worms crawled out from the wood, as they will, and Petrus was summoned to appear before the tribunal. They accused him of practising witchcraft and necromantic arts, and other crimes too vile to merit repetition. He refused to abandon his home, for it was all he knew, but with the eloquence that he owned in great abundance he persuaded me to flee. To my shame, I did. I made a league before disgust prevailed and I turned back.'

Carla watched his features darken further.

'Night had fallen and I could see the glow of the flames from up the road. I thought the pyre was for Petrus and it was over, but his torment was to be more fiendish and prolonged. The fire was built from his library. Hundreds of books and manuscripts, a life's work in the assemblage alone, for to acquire a single volume he'd travel a thousand miles – to Frankfurt, to Amsterdam, to Prague. Texts by Theophrastus, Trithemius of Sponheim, Ramon Lull, Albertus Magnus, Agrippa, Paracelsus, many more. The knowledge of two millennia turned to smoke. Worse still, Petrus's own papers were tossed into the flames – a corpus without any peer – and of which no copy exists.'

Mattias swallowed and his eyes gleamed liquid, though whether with fury or sadness she couldn't tell.

'A mob of those same *bravi* I have mentioned fed the fire, their faces shining with righteousness and evil. Petrus witnessed it all, seated backwards on a donkey and stripped to the buff. And in that moment I believe he was already broken, for his mettle was delicate, like crystal, and despite all his wisdom, such swinish rage was quite beyond his ken.'

He didn't speak for a moment. Carla said, 'What did you do?'

'You've spoken to me of helplessness, and of the odium that attends it in one's gut.'

It seemed almost a question; and was the last bond in the world she expected to share with him. She knew how hard a confession it was to make, especially for him. She nodded.

He said, 'What did I do? Why, I stood and watched the bonfire among the crowd. And I did nothing.'

His eyes were like slots, unreadable in the flicker of shadow and light. She felt chilled. She felt closer to him than ever.

'Of burning and swinish rage I'd indulged my own share and much more. In Iran we torched whole cities, one after another, and undid monuments older than the Temple in Jerusalem. And it came to me, as I stood there, that I was closer in feather to these here jeering *bravi* than I was to Petrus, and that the dream was over, and that the world is as it is, and not as men like Petrus Grubenius would make it.'

He passed a hand over his face and she almost reached out her own to take it as it fell; but he wasn't finished.

'I took food and wine to the prison, for Petrus, and found him mute and bedazed, like the children who stand by the road while a town is sacked.' She must have given some reaction, for he looked at her and nodded. 'Yes. I have seen their faces too. In terrible number.'

She said, 'Go on.'

He shrugged. 'I may as well have been one of Petrus's gaolers for all that he knew me. Each day thereafter was the same. He never spoke a word to me again. They burned him in the piazza a week later, and by then it was an act of mercy. I was able, at least, to buy the executioner's mercy. He strung a bag of gunpowder, which I gave him, round Petrus's neck.'

There was a clank in the darkness nearby and Mattias looked up. There was a homicidal flash in his eyes, and Carla felt that had she not been there he would have drawn his sword and set to. She looked over her shoulder and her stomach quailed.

Ludovico stood on the rubble in full black armour, the latter pocked with divots and matte with filth. His casque hung by a strap from his left hand. Two bright pinpricks of light shone from the sockets of his eyes. His face was drawn with fatigue, but revealed little more.

Ludovico said, 'Have you refreshment to spare a fellow Christian?'

His eyes were on Carla and she turned away. She was afraid. Afraid with a serpentine fear more unsettling than anything she'd met in the field. Mattias glanced at her. She felt him on the verge of explosive violence, and hoped he would contain it, though she didn't know why. He stood up and called to Ludovico.

'If the fellow has cheek enough to ask, then let him sit down, and welcome.'

Ludovico walked over. He limped, but so did every man in the garrison short of Bors. He bowed to Carla and sat. He set down his casque and pulled off his gauntlets, which were gummed and sticky with gore. He crossed himself and murmured Grace in Latin. Mattias gave him the wineskin and watched him drink, then took it back and drank himself. Ludovico ate in small bites, which he chewed at length with an ascetic's deliberation. He stared out at some vacant spot known only to himself.

Mattias stared at Ludovico.

Neither spoke.

Carla felt more and more disconcerted. It seemed like a contest, the rules of which she was ignorant and whose conditions of victory might include sudden death. She didn't know what to say and so said nothing. She didn't know whether to leave or to stay, and so she sat, immobile and tense. She cast furtive eyes from one man to the other but neither returned her glance. She clenched her hands in her lap and looked at her knees. A vague nausea coated her tongue. The silence that surrounded the fire became immense, until it was larger than the dark itself, until even the din of the battle seemed muffled and far. When at last she could take it no more, she started to rise to her feet.

Both men stood up at once.

'Thank you for the food and companionship,' she said to Mattias. 'Now I should return to my work.'

'No,' said Mattias. 'Our conversation isn't done. Stay.' He added, 'That is, if it should please you.'

Ludovico bowed to her again. 'I did not mean to be boorish,' he said. 'If you wish, I will leave at once.'

She saw Mattias contain a sneer. 'Finish your supper, monk,' he said. 'When you've filled your belly you may crawl back into the night.'

Ludovico regarded him without expression.

'Sit,' said Mattias. 'Our paths were bound to cross again and this is as good a place as any.' As if not to be outdone in etiquette, he bowed to Carla and added, 'That is, if the good monk's company is not too unpleasant a prospect. If it is, he will understand as well as I.'

She wondered why Mattias wanted Ludovico to stay. She found

herself nodding and they all three sat once again on their chunks of stone. She couldn't help be aware that both men were killers, for their harness was caked in gore. More disquieting still, both were in contention for her affection, and she sensed the strings of their virility drawn taut. It was like sitting between rival hunting dogs. But at least she'd broken the silence. Whatever else followed, she hoped she wouldn't have to drag them from each other's throat.

Ludovico inclined his head towards the clamour. 'You're deemed an expert in the manners of the infidel, Captain Tannhauser. How many more of these devils will we have to kill before they pack up for home?'

'Bold words for a priest, who's in the habit of sending vipers to do his killing.'

Ludovico looked at him with a bland smile. 'The question was put in earnest.'

Mattias replied in kind, yet beneath the veil of cordiality lay a cold rage. 'Suleiman's armies haven't turned their back on a siege since Vienna, in '29. And it was snow that thwarted him there, an ally we can hardly count on helping us here.'

'We can count on the mercy of Our Lord Jesus Christ.'

'Merely by passing through your lips His name is defiled,' said Mattias. 'You couldn't soil it more foully if you voiced it from your arse.'

Carla was shocked but didn't speak. Why was he provoking him so?

But Ludovico was unperturbed. 'I'm moved to hear you defend Our Saviour's dignity.'

'I'm more familiar with the words and deeds of Christ than most of your flock,' Mattias replied. 'For I've read the gospels and the letters of Paul and the Acts of the Apostles for myself.' He glanced at Carla. 'Though to do so is a crime that carries a penalty of death. Ludovico's masters have banned their own Holy Book in the common tongues – a novel idea, we all may agree, but it helps to keep the Inquisition working to capacity.'

'Without Mother Church's guidance,' explained Ludovico, 'the common man can't be expected to understand the sacred texts. Thus he may fall into error.' He looked at Carla. 'Surely no more proof is needed than the wrongs of the Protestants.'

'Christ was a common man,' countered Mattias. 'And if He'd foreseen the wrongs that you've committed in His name, He'd never have laid down His tools and left His father's workshop.'

'If you've turned your face against the One True Church,' said Ludovico, 'why make your stand here, with the soldiers of the Faith?'

'The true soldier's faith resides in the fight alone, not in the cause.'

'It's said all men believe in God on the field of battle.'

'Maybe so, for they're quick to shout His name. But if I were God I'd not be flattered, much less reassured. As Petrus Grubenius would say, their belated cries for His mercy hardly provide sound proof of His existence.'

'Ah,' said Ludovico. 'Grubenius again.'

'Carla asked to know how Petrus met his end.'

'And you told her,' said Ludovico, without expression.

Mattias nodded. 'I told her all but the name of his torturer. But I had no need, for her heart supplied that intelligence without my prompting.'

Ludovico looked at Carla and she felt sick.

'Grubenius was a brilliant man,' said Ludovico. 'His eternal soul was saved that day, for if he'd been set at liberty he'd have surely recanted and damned himself for all eternity. Mattias and I watched him go to the flames.' He looked at Mattias. 'The Captain here stood a good head and shoulders over every other man in the piazza, though he made no conspicuous protest that I can remember.'

Carla tensed in anticipation of the violence that now seemed a certainty.

Mattias moved not a muscle.

Ludovico turned back to her. 'He cut a figure too splendid to miss, as I'm sure you can imagine.' Ludovico's demeanour was serene as ever; but his black eyes gleamed with jealousy. He took the last piece of bread from the basket, but didn't eat. 'You seem distressed, Carla,' he said. 'And you must be exhausted. Surely you should take some rest.'

He was right, and she wanted nothing more than to leave, but she sensed that if she did so it would mark a subtle shift in her loyalties. She sensed also that this was his intention. She shook her head. 'Mattias and I have much to discuss,' she said.

She deliberately used his forename, and Ludovico marked it.

'No doubt you have,' he said. He turned to Mattias. 'Carla told me that you and she are to wed.'

Carla glanced at Mattias in alarm. She'd told him nothing of the visit Ludovico had paid her, for fear of what he might do. Mattias nodded as if their bargain was common knowledge.

'It's true, we are betrothed.' He smiled at Carla and his warmth banished her anxiety. 'And a love match it is, too.' He turned back to Ludovico. 'I trust we enjoy your blessing and good wishes.'

'As you told me when we first met, you're a fortunate man.'

'A reputation I cherish,' Mattias replied. 'I hear that your own has received a much-needed polish, and that you're now a Knight of Justice.'

Ludovico inclined his head in acknowledgement. As the insults and barbs accumulated Carla wondered when he would rise to the goad.

'I never expected to pity La Valette,' said Mattias, 'but at the news of your ordination I admit I did so.'

'Why pity?'

'Because you will ruin him. And his beloved Order too.'

Ludovico blinked. 'Why would I want to do that?'

'Why else would you come back to Malta? Ruin is your profession, is it not?'

Ludovico toyed with the bread in his hands. 'Even if I owned to so fantastic an ambition, what power would a lowly knight have to achieve it?'

'Ah, yes,' said Mattias. 'The lowly knight. The humble priest. As regards the art of war, La Valette may be touched by genius, but in the art of politics, he's as naïve as a choirboy invited to a bishop's bedroom.'

'You underestimate the Grand Master.'

'I hope so. But I don't underestimate you. La Valette hasn't left the island in years, and before that rarely set foot on dry land, let alone in the snake pit of Rome where the likes of you ply their slimy trade. Even Oliver Starkey is as straight as a string, and he's as skilled a diplomat as the Religion can boast. These are men who keep their word, who pay their debts, who are bound by their oaths.' Mattias leaned forward, 'Men who cleave to their holy vows. They don't bring shame on their Redeemer. They don't conceal their evil behind the smoke of burning flesh. They don't abandon young girls to pay the price of their incontinence.'

At this litany of slurs Carla saw Ludovico's head crane back and his eyes narrow to slits. It was the first and only crack in his façade, and quickly repaired. Yet he didn't dare look at her.

'Fra Starkey, I'm sure, would find these conspiracies fascinating,' he said. 'Why not enlighten him?'

'Honest men are hard pressed to understand duplicity,' said Mattias, 'especially on so extravagant a scale. I flatter myself that I'm almost as sly as you, but I've not the advantage of the fraudulent robes and lofty doctorates, and the trick bag of relics and Bulls.'

'It's as well, then,' said Ludovico, 'that our interests don't conflict.'

He tossed the heel of bread back into the basket and picked up his helm. He rose to his feet, as did Mattias, and bowed to Carla.

'I'm happy to learn that our son is alive after all,' he said, 'albeit in the hands of Moslem demons.'

'He could do much worse,' said Mattias. 'He could be within the ambit of his father.'

A movement of the wide blue jaw told her that even Ludovico's patience had worn thin.

He turned to Mattias. 'Nevertheless, I pray for his safe return to the fold of Christ. He's occupied my thoughts a great deal. And he's filled my heart with a substance I'd not known existed, thanks be to God.' His eyes were sincere, and for a moment Carla felt for him. 'Tell me, truly now, what kind of fellow is my son?'

Ludovico had opened his heart. Mattias shoved his hand in and squeezed.

'An account of his virtues would detain you until dawn,' Mattias replied. 'Suffice to say that it's damnable hard to believe that he sprang from your seed.'

Ludovico's face closed like a bear trap.

Mattias tipped him a salute. '*Asalaamu alaykum.*'

'*Pax vobiscum.*'

As she watched Ludovico limp away into the fiery night, she couldn't suppress her pity. She'd never seen a man so lost in his own darkness; except, perhaps, her father.

Mattias peered out into the murk. 'Anacleto is out there somewhere. I wonder he didn't shoot me. Without you so near, perhaps he'd have done so.'

'Anacleto?'

'Ludovico's factotum, his shadow, his knife in the back. A man of striking beauty and virulent character. He puts me in mind of the Sultan's assassins, the deaf-mutes of the seraglio – his footsteps make no sound.' He took her arm. 'Let's back to the hospital. I'll feel easier knowing you're there, at least for tonight.'

She acquiesced without argument and they walked back through the town.

'You treated him so roughly I feared you'd provoke a duel,' she said. 'Was that what you wanted?'

'I'd not contest a duel with a man I don't honour. Rather, I'd cut his throat while he slept. But he endured enough insolence for half a dozen mortal disputes and swallowed the lot. And Ludovico is no coward. This tells me that, in his mind, I'm already dead. And that you're already his chattel. He's just biding his time until the moment suits him.' He frowned. 'Tell me, Carla, what passed between you and he while I was gone?'

'I kept it to myself because –'

'That's not material.'

'He came to my room in the auberge at the dead of night.' She saw a look flit across his face that justified her fear of telling him sooner.

'What of Bors and Nicodemus?'

'Bors was on duty, Nicodemus asleep.'

Mattias scowled.

She said, 'Ludovico's footsteps also make no sound.'

'What did he say?'

'He's lost his senses. He said he wanted to marry me, and to have another child to replace Orlandu.'

'Mad with war and mad with love. In his case, mad with power too.'

'His whole life stands before him as a dreadful error, and he seeks to repair it through me. To hold him at bay I told him I loved another, and he knew at once that I spoke of you.'

'I hope that wasn't purely a ruse.' He grinned. 'Dwell no further on Ludovico. He'll bother you no more. Think only on our escape, and if you might be persuaded.'

'I'm already persuaded.'

'Good. Say nothing of all this to anyone else, not even Amparo.'

She feared that some betrayal was afoot and stopped. The street was narrow and dark. She stood close to look at his face. She said, 'Amparo must come with us.'

He looked so affronted she felt an instant of fear.

'What manner of man do you take me for?'

Before she could apologise, he waved it aside.

'I'd leave my corpse behind before I'd leave Amparo.' He grimaced with perplexity. 'But let me grasp this nettle now. I love Amparo dearly, but not as I love you. Not less. Perhaps even more. Bear with me now, for who can measure these things? Man or woman? I mean no deceit and confess myself beleaguered in this matter. The heart and loins won't always accept a harness. And you and she are a sublime pair. What else can I say? In the catalogue of my present tribulations, this vexation doesn't rate high for urgency, though it's the root of all the others, true enough, for if not for the two of you I wouldn't be here. And if I've sinned, it's a trifle compared to my other felonies. Withal, if we survive these hardships and perils, and I bring Orlandu home, and if you're still willing, we'll marry, you and I, and Amparo will endure, and what will be will be.'

He waited and Carla nodded.

'Until then, I'm prone to let things stand as they are. The sea is already stormy, so why rock the boat? Can you accept this?'

What he gave with one hand he took with the other; yet he dared to be who he was and his forthrightness stirred her. If she was a fool, then let that be so too. Her body ached and without knowing it she raised her mouth and he kissed her. He scooped her against him and lifted her on to tiptoe and she felt his own ache against her belly. The urge to surrender, there, in the alley, seized her. Some counterinstinct fought it but his mouth was hot on her throat and his hands encircled her waist and her breath was taken away. She felt her skirt rustle on her skin as he pulled it up and gathered it in, and his calloused palms caressed her thighs, and her insides convulsed and she felt dizzy. A war broke out within her. She thought, *I will not deny this out of fear or false piety*. But she didn't find either in her heart, and this itself was victory. She had other reasons – fine reasons – for not wanting to consummate her passion in an alley, like a drab. And if he was willing to fail Amparo – and he was a man just walked off a field of blood, and she would not judge him – she was not. His fingers slid between her legs and caressed her wetness – *Oh God, my Lord God* – and she clenched them hard against him and pulled away. In defiance of her every natural instinct she put her hand against his chest. He understood at once, and though his eyes drooped with lust, he didn't press her. He stood back and swiped his hair from his face.

She said, 'Until then, let things stand as they are.'

'Forgive me,' he said, his voice gruff. 'Madness rides the wind tonight. And more than one wild beast is yoked to his wagon.' His eyes cleared. He gave her a rueful smile. 'On this occasion, at least, you're wiser than I.' He glanced to the end of the alley and the hospital piazza beyond. 'It's as well you're almost home,' he said. 'And I have urgent matters that need my direct attention. So I'll bid you farewell.'

She felt a suspicion without clear substance. 'What urgent matters?'

'Military matters.'

She sensed that same cold-blooded absence in his psyche that she'd felt on the Syracuse road, before he had killed the priest. She saw he had no intention of telling her more. Without warning he whipped his sweat-drenched scarf from out his sleeve and dabbed at her neck.

'I've sullied you,' he said.

His crooked teeth flashed bright in his sooty face.

Then she watched him lope away towards the front.

CARLA FOUND AMPARO asleep in the cot. She lay down beside her and the girl shifted without waking and Carla wrapped her in her arms. She felt no self-reproach for her heart was too full of love. Love for all of her beloved. She thanked God for the companionship in which she was rich. She prayed to Jesus to understand, and to forgive her, though what, exactly, it was that required absolution she wasn't certain. Surely, amid so much cruelty, love in any form was good. Mattias's for both women; even Ludovico's for her. She prayed for Mattias and Amparo. She prayed for Orlandu. She prayed for Ludovico that his madness and pain might be healed.

She fell into a deep and exhausted slumber. She dreamed in vivid, fantastical spasms in which her spirit flew through uncharted astral realms and through mystic vortices unknowable to waking sense, and which left her breathless and in awe and yearning for worlds whose discovery prohibited return. And of these worlds, when she woke, she remembered little, except that they contained nothing of horror and fear.

And as well that was, for the new day dawning brought more of both in plenty.

The night assault on the wall had given out at first light. Casualties were heavy. Carla woke to find Amparo gone, and she ventured out with her poke of bandages and needles and twine to do what she could. Burnt timbers subsided in sparking gusts. Children watched her walk by with the stunned and vacant expressions evoked by Mattias. Knights and soldiers – and lamenting widows searching for the source of their grief – staggered about the calamity amazed, like the Angels expelled from Paradise to their smoking and infernal fiefdom newly arrived. The sun crawled up as if loath to illuminate such squalor. And vultures descended from their gyres on silent wings and roosted on the ricks of carrion unperturbed, like hunched and black-robed arbiters of some dispute on the essence of woe.

From Lazaro she heard in passing that, during the night, Fra Ludovico, of the Italian Langue, and his shield-bearer, Anacleto of Crato, had both been shot down during the battle by a volley of musketry. Both were still alive in the Italian hospital, though Lazaro was uncertain of their condition.

Carla's intuition, by contrast, was in no doubt. While she'd travelled to distant worlds on a chimera of Peace, Mattias had attended – directly – to his military matters. But she had no chance to ponder this news any further, for as the sun cleared

Monte San Salvatore the Turks attacked again along the whole of the front.

Siege guns bellowed from the heights. Tambours rolled and pipes and imams shrilled. And with ominous creaks and groans, and to the snapping of whips and a chorus of anguish from the numberless blackamoor slaves straining at the ropes, the Moslems hauled up with them from the Marsaxlokk road a siege tower of gigantic proportion. As this cyclopean engine shunted across the Grand Terre Plein, the slaves laid greased planks beneath its wheels, laying a roadway towards the Bastion of Provence. In the monster's train came a winding column of musketmen.

Carla watched the tower's progress with a giddy sense of lunacy. If her lost dreams that night had seemed fantastical, the outlandish spectacle unfolding in the arid dust made them seem banal. She looked at the faces of the defenders. The approach of the Leviathan sowed a crop of despair in every Christian breast. Yet to a man and a woman they rose from the ruins when the alarum trumpet called, and they unlimbered their arms and unfurled the colours of the Baptist, and stepped up once more to the gore-boltered rim to defend the Holy Religion against the heathen.

SUNDAY 19 AUGUST 1565

Auberge of England – Bastion of Provence

TANNHAUSER AWOKE TO the squeeze of a thick-fingered hand upon his shoulder. As he emerged from a world free of pain and erotic limitation, and in which he'd hoped to abide for ever and a day, he opened his eyes and saw Bors.

'No,' grunted Tannhauser.

'Yes,' said Bors.

Bors proffered a bowl from which arose the smell of coffee. Over previous weeks he'd broken all of Tannhauser's Izmit cups. Somewhere in the distance the sound of gunfire was general. Tannhauser hoisted himself on one elbow and took the thick-rimmed bowl and drank. Despite the rim, the taste afforded him bliss, but he didn't let on.

'You skimped on the sugar,' he said.

'I don't know how you can drink that swill.'

'Its properties are medicinal and I'm in need.'

Bors disappeared. With luck he would never return. Tannhauser glanced sideways and found Amparo peering at him from beneath the sheet. In a state of reckless arousal he'd stolen her from the hospital while Carla slept. His bargain with the latter, after all, had been to maintain the status quo. Amparo's eyes were bright and saucy. He felt her hand slide across his belly to locate what he realised was an especially splendid erection. He realised also, with dismay, that it would be wasted, for a harsh clatter drew his attention. Bors had returned with Tannhauser's harness and rattled it before him.

'We're summoned before the Grand Master,' said Bors.

'I'm sick of the sight and sound of the Grand Master,' said Tannhauser. 'I'm sick of the war. I'm sick of the Turks. Most of all, I'm sick of you interrupting my connubials.'

A snort. 'So that's what you call them.' With an even more disagreeable racket Bors dropped the armour by the bed and left by the door.

With a deal of unmanly groans and foul blasphemies, Tannhauser clambered to his feet and got into his clothes. With every bone and joint proclaiming its anguish, he felt close on a hundred years old. Amparo pranced around him and helped where she could, but undermined her efforts, not to say his own, by virtue of being quite nude. As he contemplated the armour and its evil weight, and being still in possession of the means, his spirit rebelled against the Grand Master's authority and he wrestled Amparo to her knees on the mattress's edge. Still standing, he entered her from behind. She made no protest, though the manoeuvre was accompanied by screams of delectation that might have been mistaken for such. He heard Bors cough violently outside the door and as a concession to public seemliness he clapped one hand round Amparo's mouth. She bit the web of his thumb and the screams were muffled to whimpers. Both the bite and the sounds served further to fan his abandon. His other hand he cupped around her breast and with the leverage thus provided he swived her with gusto until his seed erupted inside her. In the normal run he wouldn't have been quite so brisk, for in indulging his pleasures he inclined towards the leisurely rather than the frantic, but if the Grand Master was kept waiting overlong, agents less delicate than Bors might happen along, and that wouldn't do.

To Amparo's strident chagrin he withdrew, his sweat dripping on to her arse. He smothered her mouth with a compensatory kiss.

'You're a treasure,' he said, and disengaged her hand from his wilting member.

Overwhelmed though he now was by the urge to go back to sleep, he struggled into his armour and she buckled the straps. Unwholesome scabs of congealed filth flaked from the metal and tumbled about the floor. He resolved to recruit a slave – if he could find one alive – to give it a burnish.

He said, 'Will you visit Buraq today?'

'I visit him every day,' she said. 'He misses you.'

'Convey my affection. And mind you stick to the backstreets, there are snipers about.'

He grabbed his sword and baldric and went to the door.

'Don't die,' she said.

'I'll do my best.'

'If you were killed, I don't think I should want to live.'

He looked at her face, which was an error for his heart began to melt. He ran his fingers through her hair. Memories of doing something similar to Carla only scant hours before stirred in his mind, and he felt like a swine. It was all too much for a simple soldier.

'I won't tolerate such morbid nonsense,' he said. 'The sun is shining, the sea is blue and you're the picture of health and beauty.'

She hugged herself with woe and unwittingly created a stunning cleavage with her arms. From the crook of her elbow peaked the umber rim of one nipple. His own woes multiplied on the spot. Couldn't La Valette and the Turks wait another hour or so? The short respite notwithstanding, he was more than game to give her another seeing to. From beyond the door came a gruff voice.

'Mattias! If you don't want to share her with an Algerian, put it away.'

Tannhauser resolved to be cheerful.

He smiled and Amparo smiled too. Carla had told him that, to her knowledge, Amparo never smiled for anyone else, and this flattered his vanity hugely. 'Kiss me,' he said.

She did so, careless of the foul matter caking his breastplate. He squeezed her hams in farewell and tore himself away. In the corridor Bors detached himself from the wall and followed him towards the stair.

'Do you think this concerns Ludovico?' Bors asked.

'I thought the Algerians were hammering at the door.'

'I'm serious.'

'Has La Valette sent a page or the serjeants at arms?'

'Andreas, his page.'

'Then there's your answer. If I'm wrong we'll brass it out. Amparo will vouch for our whereabouts, and in any event, who can trust any witness from yesternight's havoc? Turkish marksmen shot him, and there's an end to it.'

'They're still alive,' said Bors.

Tannhauser stopped on the steps and turned to look at him.

'Ludo and his lyme hound too,' said Bors. 'We missed both of them.'

'We missed both of them? I saw them go down.'

'You caught Ludo square between the shoulders, but he was wearing Negroli plate. Cracked ribs and a bad back is all you gave him.'

Tannhauser cursed the Milanese. 'And Anacleto?'

'He turned in alarm as his master fell, took my ball in the face. I'm told he lost an eye – and his gorgeous looks – but will likely survive.'

Tannhauser scowled. 'I should've knifed him by the fireside.' He'd feared swordplay with Carla so close. He recalled the aplomb with which she'd witnessed his murder of the priest and cursed his timidity. But it was done. 'Don't fret,' he said. 'La Valette values our swords too much to hang us on a rumour, if rumours there be.'

'None that I've heard.'

'Then Ludo will play the hand himself. Or throw it in. In any event, he now has more reason to fear us than vice versa.' Tannhauser continued down the stairs. 'Let's find out why we're wanted.'

THEY FOUND La Valette with Oliver Starkey at his command post in the square: some chairs and a table, his famous maps and charts, all shaded from the sun by a red lateen sail strung from ships' spars sunk into the ground. From the enceinte came the din of battle, now no less familiar, and hardly more distracting, than the splash of the waves on the shore. For the first time the Grand Master looked careworn. His skin was sallow, his hair wispy, his shoulders frail, the veins and tendons in his hands prominent and fragile. The wounds sustained to his leg the previous day had left him lame, and when he rose from his chair to greet them, he almost had to sit down again. Tannhauser made the most of his own limp, both to mitigate the fact that he'd been loafing in bed and to minimise the extravagance of La Valette's expectations. He bowed.

'Your Excellency,' he said.

'Captain.' La Valette dipped his head. 'The siege tower you promised has arrived.'

Tannhauser cursed the noble Abbas; it was his infernal machine that had robbed him of a morning in bed. He wondered what his old patron's genius had inspired.

'Come,' said La Valette. 'I would have you advise me.'

THE FOUR OF them made their way through the ruins towards the Bastion of Provence. The wall that had appeared so impenetrable a few weeks before now had more gaps than a beggar's smile. Its height varied from the original forty feet to huge banks of rubble not much taller than a man. Holes yawned between broken stumps of masonry, and cracks and sags and subsidence caused by the

Turkish sappers gave the entire curtain an air of ramshackle debility. Whole sections of the rampart had been blown away at erratic intervals and it was no longer possible to walk the allure for more than a hundred-foot stretch in one go. The Bastion of Castile wasn't much more than a glorified barricade, and the breach to its either side, though still the focus of frenzied rebuilding, invited fresh invasion at any moment.

The Turkish strategy on this, the second day of their sustained assault, was to launch a tide of skirmishes, whose aim seemed not to break through but to exhaust the thin line of defenders. Instead of fighting to the death, the *gazi* would retreat in good order, and with minimal loss, to make way for a new detachment, and then another, and so on and so forth, like waves grinding down the shale of an embankment. Alongside the Christian soldiers, wherever the wall gaped open, women and children in tattered raiment, and naked slaves chained in pairs, toiled to collect and restack the broken masonry. This work on the fortifications never stopped and labour gangs worked through the night. Musket fire by daylight exacted a brutal toll, but no one was permitted to stop working. Of groans and lamentations there were plenty and, in counterpoint, the chaplains labouring with the rest conducted decades of the rosary in an endless chant and refrain, the voices weaving an elegy through the toil like a golden thread in a tapestry of despair.

'*Ave Maria, gratia plena, Dominus tecum, benedicta tu in mulieribus, et benedictus fructus ventris tui Jesus.*'

'*Sancta Maria, Mater Dei, ora pro nobis peccatoribus, nunc et in hora mortis nostrae. Amen.*'

'*Ave Maria, gratia plena, Dominus tecum, benedicta tu in mulieribus, et benedictus fructus ventris tui Jesus.*'

'*Sancta Maria, Mater Dei, ora pro nobis peccatoribus, nunc et in hora mortis nostrae. Amen.*'

La Valette made no comment on the spectacle. As they climbed the external wall stair to Provence, he stopped and pointed west and Tannhauser turned to look. Across the bridge of boats spanning Galley Creek, L'Isola smouldered in a desolation all its own.

'Del Monte inspires the defenders of Saint Michel to prodigies of valour,' said La Valette. 'But if they collapse, they can expect no assistance from us.'

They'd paused below the rim of the circular bastion. The wall shook beneath them as a cannonball slammed into the batter on the other side. Along the allure above, *arquebuceros* and knights huddled under the parapet, not daring to raise their heads. The price for doing so was displayed by bodies laid low by slags of lead. From beyond the rim came volleys of musketry, so close the smoke from their muzzles wafted overhead. A *humbara* lofted down to explode on the scorched wall walk, and a Maltese waddled on his haunches like a cumbersome toad to empty a bucket of sand on the blaze. The whole sorry portrait was one of men waiting to die. La Valette pointed at the embrasure to the east of the bastion.

'Take a look,' he said. 'And beware.'

Tannhauser crept along the allure and peered around the merlon. Although the presence of the siege tower was no surprise, the sight at close range filled him with a bowel-watering terror. It was at most twenty feet away and he could see the upper third, which tapered to an open-topped platform that permitted four musketmen abreast to squat behind an iron-sheathed gate. From here they fired directly down into the fort. Behind the first four men waited a second rank of four, and behind those a third. The front rank had just discharged their guns and Tannhauser watched as these men peeled off, two to each side, and scurried past the rear ranks and down ladders at the back to a lower gallery, where they could reload in safety. The second rank now moved to the fore and scoured the Borgo for prey. He reckoned that from that vantage their range took in a good third of the town, the workers on the breaches of Castile and anyone exposed on the wall walk as far as the Bastion of Germany. Plus anyone else, such as himself, fool enough to show their face any closer. He saw the bore of a musket seek him out and pulled back as the match fell. A moment later the ball carved a groove from the merlon and threw splinters of sandstone in his hair.

He shuffled along the allure to the next embrasure and took another look. The whole tower was proofed against bullets by layers of raw ox hides and sheets of chain mail. Here and there the hides were scorched and smouldering and the smell of burnt hair mixed with the gunsmoke. Voices within shouted orders and praised Allah. Fresh marksmen clambered the rearward ladders to refill the third rank. They were eager and well drilled, the alliance of men and machine as smooth as it was ingenious. The tower creaked and swayed with the antics of the snipers and the recoil of the nine-palm muskets, but taut ship's cables ran from stanchions at each upper corner and were anchored to stakes in the ground to provide stability. The whole conception, for all its demented appearance, bore the signature of Abbas's intelligence.

From this angle Tannhauser saw that the front gate protecting the marksmen was hinged two storeys below and could be lowered outward on chains to form a footbridge to the ramparts. But of that, as yet, there was no need. At something over a thousand shots per hour – and, more to the point, at close range – the siege engine had paralysed the defenders and was grinding them away for negligible Turkish loss.

Tannhauser rejoined La Valette, Starkey and Bors on the stair.

'She's a beauty,' said Tannhauser.

La Valette grimaced in agreement. 'And cunningly placed too. None of our cannon can mark it and we can't locate a new battery under their fire. We tried. The lower galleries of the tower are also loaded with musketmen. When Sieur Polastron launched a sally from the gate they were cut down on the threshold. Not a man reached the end of the drawbridge. If I committed, we could overwhelm it, but Mustafa would launch his cavalry from the heights. The cost in lives would be ruinous and, unlike Mustafa, lives is the one resource we can't afford.'

'Wildfire?' asked Bors.

'The hides won't burn,' said Starkey. 'They keep them watered with brine. They're pouring aimed shots into the fort for no reply. If they have the patience, they can whittle us to the bone before launching their next assault.'

'You told me they were building two engines,' said La Valette.

'So I believe,' said Tannhauser. 'If I were Mustafa, on the evidence of this one I'd be building a third.' He rasped his beard with a thumbnail. 'I couldn't see the foot of the tower.'

'It rolls on six spokeless wheels,' said Starkey. 'The lowest platform is twice the area of the uppermost. The four main stanchions are galley masts. Spars, rigging, cross-bracing, stones for ballast. The lower gallery is open and unarmoured, to allow them to mass their fire against a ground assault – as they did earlier.'

Tannhauser hadn't encountered such machines before. He rifled his mind for lore, the ten thousand tales of a thousand battles that he'd heard swapped and embroidered over the years. Despite such an archive he could dredge up no memory of towers or how to thwart them. Yet something else stirred. He leaned over the edge of the stair to look at the foot of the inner wall forty feet below. It was composed of massy limestone blocks of various sizes, up to three feet by two, and laid in an ashlar bond.

'How thick is the wall at the base?' he asked.

'Through the batter?' said Starkey. 'About twelve feet.'

The idea in Tannhauser's mind almost withered there and then; but La Valette looked at him and Tannhauser could see that he got it and was already making calculations for the task.

'When Suleiman invaded Hungary in '32,' said Tannhauser, 'the stiffest fight was for a little town of such paltry importance I can't recall its name. Guntz? No matter. Eight hundred defenders held off thirty thousand Tartars and Rumelians for over a week. At one point, as I heard it told, the Magyars knocked a hole through their own wall so as to train their cannon point-blank on the enemy charge.'

Bors and Starkey peered down simultaneously at the huge blocks below, and then upward at the titanic weight of masonry stacked above.

'It was no doubt a puny wall,' added Tannhauser, 'and I'm no engineer. But if it were possible to cut a passage through twelve feet of stone without giving notice, and run out a sixteen-pounder, you could blow the legs from that engine and watch it fall.'

'Aye,' snorted Bors, 'if we haven't watched the wall fall first and the bastion with it.'

Starkey appeared about to voice his own objections when La Valette hobbled back down the stair with that bigotry of purpose that characterised his happiest moods. He paused and turned back to Tannhauser.

'Captain, about Father Guillaume,' he said.

'I'm afraid I don't know the man, Your Excellency.'

'You denied yourself the opportunity. You shot him down, yesterday. The chaplain at the Post of Castile.'

Tannhauser recalled the near-rout and the panic-stricken priest. It seemed like weeks ago, but was less than twenty-four hours. He was about to deliver an exculpatory discourse on the chaos of battle, the fog of war and the unreliability of firearms when La Valette raised his palm.

'I'm sure your conscience is troubled –' he said.

'Most sorely, Your Excellency, most sorely.'

Both men knew that this was a bald-faced lie.

'Then set it at rest,' said La Valette. 'Father Guillaume lost his senses, rest his soul. The shot was well advised.'

'Thank you, sire.'

'But don't be overzealous. We need every man, including our priests.'

Tannhauser studied his eyes. Was this a coded reference to his attempt to murder Ludovico? It was impossible to tell. La Valette turned to Starkey and the matter was over.

'Send for the master mason and his crew.'

SINCE HE FELT he'd earned it, and since it was a shady and comfortable perch with a fine old view of the afternoon's frolics, Tannhauser sat on the top step and watched events unfold.

Leather-aproned Maltese masons armed with chisels, crowbars and lump hammers collected round La Valette at the base of the wall and a brief discussion ensued as to how best to excavate a passage to the foot of the tower. The master mason sized up the arrangement of stones in the ashlar bond and, on an instinct that he made no attempt to explain, quickly marked them with chalk in a numbered sequence. They then went at it with a phlegmatic proficiency that astounded all who watched. The mortar and stones were cut out as if the wall was made of biscuit, and within half an hour a crude arch yawned through the batter, wide enough for two men to enter abreast. Beyond was a mass of tight-packed rubble, the average rock the size of a goat's head. Timbers, crowbars and shovels were plied and, as the rubble was prised free and stacked aside, carpenters braced the roof of the emerging cavern.

The cannon was wheeled up – a bow chaser stripped from a galley and mounted on a carriage – and the gunners charged and primed it. The bow chaser could take a forty-eight-pound iron ball. La Valette's choice for the first load was that exact weight of musket balls at twelve to the pound. He ordered the balls commingled with a shovelful of lard. The carpenters laid and trued a gangway of planks over the rough floor of the cavern and within an hour of the rubble's first exposure two masons toting sledgehammers went inside to dislodge the outer stones of the batter.

Tannhauser nudged Bors and they took their long guns up to the embrasures. A peek revealed the Turkish marksmen on the platform just as one of them pointed groundward and alarm flared among them, and as one they angled their muskets down towards the hole now erupting from the wall. Tannhauser and Bors rose up and benched their guns on the merlon and fired. Twin gouts of brain matter showered the platform's occupants and the dead were flung in a tangle among their comrades. As the Turks fought to master their confusion, a dozen *arquebuceros* rose up along the Bastion of Provence and ploughed a raft of lead into the tangle.

Tannhauser craned his head over the battlement.

From the hole in the wall half a thousand musket balls and a torrent of flaming pork fat vomited point-blank into the unlucky mass of men exposed inside the tower's lowermost gallery. A vortex of smoke befouled the engine's base and within its reeking coils seethed a gruesome *microcosmos* best not imagined. Powder stores and fire grenades ignited in deafening bursts and burning and mutilated bodies tumbled forth to writhe and flail the dirt in anonymous anguish. The captains and overseers screamed at the mass of blackamoors huddled in the lee of the wall and they rushed to unfasten the guy ropes that anchored the tower. With spear point and lash, others were driven into the choking smog to breast the hauling-spars and stanchions, and the Christian marksmen took to gunning them down from their embrasures. As the engine creaked into retreat along the roadway of larded planks, slaves slipped in the blood and grease beneath the enormous spokeless wheels and were there dismembered, their screams and the crunch of their bones hardly noticed in the commotion.

The overloaded tower had crawled but five yards when the bow chaser roared again from its tunnel in the wall. The Religion's gunners had honed their skills through firing at enemy shipping from the rise and fall of a galley deck. The tower thirty-odd feet distant was the easiest mark they'd ever had. The ball smashed into the right main corner stanchion where it was crossed-braced by the lower gallery roof. A whirlwind of splinters blew through hapless flesh, and the blinded and eviscerate donated their portion of sorrow to the howling carnage. The tower lurched out of true with a loud groan. Men began leaping from the upper tiers, aiming to cushion their landing on their squirming comrades below. Two *gazi* drew swords and charged into the hole to take out the bow chaser and its crew.

Tannhauser stepped back from the wall to swab and reload his rifle.

As he measured powder down the bore he looked down into the fort where the gunners were repriming their cannon. When the two invading *gazi* emerged from the smoking archway, the Maltese masons set about them with their hammers, and with aprons swiftly besmeared like those of meatcutters they dragged the pulverised remnants aside so the cannon could trundle down its gangway once again.

It was a testament to the tower's construction that five more blasts were required before it buckled and toppled to the clay. The draught of its fall stoked the burning base and a column of flame shot skyward, and a triumphant roar from the defenders drowned the wails of the last living wretches trapped inside. The surviving blackamoors and soldiers fled for the high ground, while the *arquebuceros* had sport in shooting them down. Tannhauser studied the surrounding hills and took no part in the merriment. It wouldn't last long. Despite the thousands decomposing in the moat of human decay around the walls, the heights were still alive with the Sultan's hordes and their horsetail standards stood tall. To Mustafa their blood was but rain for the irrigation of the Padishah's soil. A fragment of a *surah* wailed by an imam drifted out across the field.

'*Has Allah not caused the earth to contain the living and the dead?*'

The stench of smouldering hides and burning flesh turned Tannhauser's stomach. He'd eaten nothing all that day. More than that, he was tired of this monstrous game. The strength drained from his limbs and his feet felt heavy; a black humour throbbed up the nape of his neck and settled behind the sockets of his eyes. He shouldered his rifle and climbed down the stair. He saw the masons go back into the cavern to restore the wall, and the artillerymen swapped jests and felicitations as they swabbed out the cannon. La Valette watched Tannhauser leave. He proffered neither word nor gesture, and Tannhauser was glad that it was so.

His heart yearned for the women, Amparo and Carla; for the softness in their glances and their voices; for that absence within them of anything cruel; for their tenderness; for their love. These were the things he fought to protect. The siege was sustained by blind faith. Only faith could endure such horror. The love that had come to bind him was the only faith he had.

Bors caught up with him and saw his face.

'Why so glum? It was well done and the Religion are in your debt yet again.'

'Let them keep their religion,' said Tannhauser. 'Leave me to tend mine.'

THE FIGHTING HAD been continuous for all of thirty-six hours, but that night the guns at last fell into silence. A pall of exhaustion seemed to cover all Creation. An obscure presentiment of doom clung to Tannhauser's mind and he couldn't sleep. He rose and went to the Kalkara Gate and sensed the shuffle of the Turkish watchmen in the gloom. In moods such as he was in it was easy to act rashly, to cast the dice and be damned out of dejection rather than wit. But escape would better wait on Turkish dejection, not his own. Their morale was on the wane. He'd heard it in the frenzy of the imams as they exhorted the Faithful to die. He'd heard it that evening in the tone of the muezzin's call. But how many more repulses would it take before their spirit was truly broken? And could the Religion effect them? To his certain knowledge, the Turkish spirit in war had never been broken before.

The constellations turned above him, aloof to mortal cares, and he wished he could hear the melody that kept them aloft. But perhaps he could best them.

He woke Amparo and she dressed and he grabbed the instrument cases. Amparo roused Carla from the infirmary and he took them down to Galley Creek, and there they played for him by the shore, with the crescent moon yet unrisen and Scorpius wheeling over the southern rim of the World. He wept in the dark to their music, and his heart was filled, and his spirit was restored. Such moments were fragments of eternity, like pearls on the bed of an ocean unexplored. Let the morrow bring on what it would, he thought, for it didn't exist. Only now could lay any claim to forever and in this forever he was indeed a fortunate man. After all, he was encompassed by ravishing Beauty.

MONDAY
20 AUGUST 1565

The Corradino Heights

Orlandu grabbed his chickpeas and flatbread and ran to the crest of the hill to watch the battle. He wasn't alone in this habit for the spectacle was not to be resisted and he stood among a collection of fellow grooms. The Sanjak Cheder, one of Suleiman's most famous fighting generals, had led eight thousand janissaries in an all-out assault against the Fortress of Saint Michel, and, as Orlandu arrived to watch, the ramparts were awash yet again with Turkish colours. There was a great deal of fire and smoke and among the silks and fog he saw flashes of the sun on Christian armour. The valour of the knights and his own Maltese brothers brought tears to his eyes. Yet he was also moved by the resolution of the janissaries. Tannhauser had been a janissary. Now Tannhauser stood somewhere on those Christian battlements.

Each Sipahi cavalryman had at least two spare horses. In the tradition of Genghis Khan, Abbas had five. Orlandu was not permitted near these latter, as they were the finest mounts in the army; but he tended those of the lower ranks and found the labour a pleasure. Compared to careening galleys it was a frolic. He'd lately been shown how to clean and trim a horse's feet and now believed himself skilled in all aspects of grooming. There'd been no role for the cavalry so far, and he was glad, for he knew what the spares were for. The beasts would suffer as horribly as the men. He wished Tannhauser were here. Before opening his bowels he'd pop out the big gold ring from his arse – it was a simpler matter than he'd imagined – and he'd clean it and slip it over his thumb until he was done, and Tannhauser would feel close.

The Turks, he'd discovered, were fine men, almost as brave as the knights themselves. Abbas radiated majesty. Those Anatolian troopers whose mounts he tended brought him almond cakes, if he'd done good work. There was the occasional kick or cuffing, but nothing near the casual violence of the dockyards. Another groom, a Rumelian older than he, had one day tried to take his cakes and Orlandu had almost brained him with a horseshoe. He'd not been bothered thereafter and had even earned a wink from the chief hostler, who was a Serb. He heard the word *devshirme* uttered and wondered what it meant. As Tannhauser had instructed, he struck a manly bearing and took pride in his manners. He joined the Moslems for their prayers and mimicked their various postures. He even grew to feel comfort in the muezzin's call. At night, he prayed to Jesus and John the Baptist, and begged them not to damn him as an infidel. Yet, strangely, at the moment of prayer, he didn't feel dishonest in either practice.

His new life, then, was tolerable and in living it he felt more than ever that he walked in the footsteps of his master. He was becoming 'a man of the world'. The thought of the Stambouli Shore now gave him excitement rather than dread. If he felt pain or sorrow it was watching the latest slaughter down below – now three days and two nights with hardly a pause. The other grooms, like Orlandu, observed the carnage with mixed feelings. None of them were ethnic Turks. Albanians, Thracians, Bulgars, Hungarians and Serbs. All nursed some hatred of the Turk in their inner hearts and hoped for the Religion to win, though, like him, not one of them said so. A Serb pointed out a big banner on which a red hand was painted. The banner bobbed up a scaling ladder thrown against Saint Michel's wall.

'Sanjak Cheder,' said the youth.

The Sanjak had vowed to take Saint Michel or die in the attempt. Orlandu said a silent prayer for Admiral Del Monte. There was a rough shout from behind and Orlandu turned. The hostler was calling them back to work. Orlandu took one last look at the distant battle. The Turks occupied the wall in fantastic numbers.

MONDAY
20 AUGUST 1565

Grand Master's Stables – Auberge of England

THE SPANISH GIRL was comely. Few men of refinement would have called her pretty; indeed, she was strange in looks and manner both. Yet she evinced her own wayward aura, an unpredictability of temper, a sensuality in movement, an inborn lasciviousness primal as an unmapped forest. He knew that the German had chosen her and this incited the voluptuary within himself. Tannhauser was everything he was not, the antithesis of everything he'd set himself to be and represent. An apostate, a criminal, a libertine; a consort of atheists, Moslems and Jews; a man proud to be steeped in cupidity and sin. Despite that, Ludovico felt that they were bound together, twinned in contrariety, mirrored as in a glass darkly.

Amparo worked in the broad central passageway that ran between the facing rows of box stalls. In the shafts of light that fell from the high windows, motes of straw and dirt danced about her. She was brushing scurf from the flank and stifle of Tannhauser's golden horse. She wore a leaf-green dress, faded by the sun to the colour of early autumn and worn ragged and thin by use. She wore nothing beneath it, like a street whore. At first glance she was all bone and sinew, lean as a greyhound, but as she brandished the dandy-brush the fullness of her buttocks and breasts was revealed, and the cloth clung to her loins in patches of sweat and her hair swayed in luxuriant curls, and Ludovico was persuaded of her beauty.

He stood inside in the stable doorway, out of the sun, and watched her for a long time. The raw smells of the place were a tonic, for he'd come direct from the fouler stench of the battle renewed that day for Saint Michel. It was strange that the shit of horses should be so much less noxious than the shit of men, but so it was. War generated shit in even greater abundance than blood and Ludovico was sick of both.

The janissaries had attacked that morning for the third day running and had almost overwhelmed the crumbling fortress. Ludovico, his newly cracked ribs robbing him of breath, had been dispatched with a contingent of Italians and Aragonese across the boat bridge. After hours of rabid killing amid rivers of fire, their counterattack had left the Sanjak dead on the field and his ravaged corps in retreat. There'd been no pursuit. Saint Michel had started the day with fewer than seven hundred men, none of them lacking for wounds, and they hadn't the numbers. More than that, those still standing by the finish hadn't the heart.

After such an episode it was sweet to watch a pretty girl as she groomed a horse, and reason enough to be here of itself; but he had another purpose. Sweeping a patch of the stable floor that was already quite spotless was a wrinkled Sicilian crone inches shorter than her broomstick. As Ludovico entered he glanced at her and she bent in a servile curtsey and shook her head. He motioned to the door. She scurried out. He walked on down the passageway and Amparo looked over her shoulder and saw him and stopped and straightened up. She put a protective hand on the horse's flaxen mane and continued to stroke his shoulder with the brush. She looked Ludovico in the chest, rather than the face, but without alarm. Her odd, asymmetrical face was untouched by either weariness or fear, and it occurred to him that no one in Malta looked this way; not any more. He wondered what power had allowed her to sustain such serenity. The mere sight of it lifted his spirit. His insight deepened into Tannhauser and his choice. He smiled and bowed his head.

'Greetings, my child,' he said, in Spanish.

She curtseyed, as if she found the practice unnatural, one hand still steadying the horse. Ludovico held his hand out to the horse's muzzle and it licked the salt from his fingers. His tongue was at once rough and soft.

'This conflict is hard on the animals,' he said. 'The noise, the confinement. They also sense death and sorrow.'

She watched the horse lick him without replying.

'Amparo, is it not?' She nodded. 'Does the horse have a name?'

'*Buraq*,' she said.

'Ah,' said Ludovico, 'the horse of the Prophet Mohammed, which was said to have wings. The Arabs love such fanciful myths. But this beast looks fleet enough to deserve the honour. He belongs to Captain Tannhauser?'

She nodded. Still she didn't look at his face.

'And you are Tannhauser's sweetheart.'

She shuffled, a little uneasy.

'Forgive my discourtesy, I'm Fra Ludovico.' He dipped his head, and realised his armour was freshly badged with blood and other unsavoury fluids violently spilled. 'Forgive also my foul appearance, which you and Buraq both must find quite repugnant.'

She turned away and set to brushing Buraq's neck.

He was entitled to take offence at this, but didn't. 'I'm told by some of the soldiers that you read palms,' he said. 'They place great store in your skill.'

She continued brushing.

'Will you read mine?' he asked. 'I'll pay you.'

'I don't take pay,' she said. 'It isn't something to be sold.'

'It's something sacred, then.'

She didn't turn. 'It's something that comes not from me, and so is not mine to sell.'

'From a world beyond this one?' he said.

'If the power speaks in this world, how can it be beyond it?'

He hadn't expected dialectics. Yet she appeared to state what to her seemed utter simplicity.

He said, 'Is it the power of God?'

She paused, as if she'd not considered this before, then said, 'The power of God speaks through all things.'

'All things? Ravens, choughs, cats?'

'And stones and trees and the sea and the sky above. Of course.'

'And the Church?' he said.

She shrugged, as if she reckoned it by far the poorest of such vehicles. 'That too.'

Ludovico held out his palm. As if it were a chore to be quickly dismissed Amparo stuck the brush beneath her arm and took his hand. She stroked its lines and calluses with her fingertips. Her touch pleased him. Her face revealed nothing.

'Some hands speak, some do not,' she said. She let go of his hand. 'Your hand does not.'

She said it not as a rebuff, but as a matter of fact. Nevertheless, and even though he set no store by such black mischief, he was disappointed. He also found that he despised her. The feeling came to him suddenly, like nausea. Her manner offended him. This slip of a girl, this exotic slut, whose contribution to the siege was what? Or to anything else of value on this earth? She groomed her master's horse and spread her legs for him. She traded augury and superstition with the vulgar soldiery. She flaunted her breasts in her flimsy wanton's dress. He'd seen her like before, in every stratum high and low. Women who justified their existence by the hole between their legs and nothing more. Who traded their flesh for a living; for vanity and a smattering of power; for this abomination falsely labelled Love. They were a disease. He noticed for the first time that her eyes were of different colours. One brown, one grey. As plain a stigma of witchery as any catalogued or known, as authorities as diverse as Appollonides and Kramer and Sprenger had attested. The efflux of beams from such eyes, being the conveyers of evil spirits, were able to strike through the eyes of those they met and thence fly to the heart, from whence they rose to condense in the blood and infect the inward parts. Aristotle himself had averred that a mirror dreads the eyes of an unclean woman, for its sheen grows cloudy and dull at her gaze.

He said, 'Is it God who speaks in so curious a manner? Or the Devil?'

'I know nothing of the Devil,' she said. 'And if he exists, what help needs he from me? Most of all here?'

A cunning reply, again innocently framed. He considered exploring this subject more; but she'd said more than enough of a necromantic character to condemn her should the need arise, and witnesses to that effect were plentiful. He didn't doubt the actuality of witchcraft. Who did? It was overdiagnosed to be sure: warts and bristles on an old haggard's chin and a cow whose milk had gone sour were grounds enough for the peasantry; lurid accounts of flying through the air and the ritual devouring of children were crude fantasies; and the Inquisition was sceptical of supernatural forces, as was he. Yet commerce with Satan took place. On this the Church was unequivocal. Amparo took up her brush and continued her work on the horse.

'I would have you do me a service,' he said.

She turned back towards him, her fraudulent mask of innocence replaced by a feral wariness. He realised that she hadn't once looked him in the face, let alone the eye, as if she knew that if she did so he'd see her true nature. He was more than ever convinced that her soul was polluted and her character pernicious. How easily he'd been fooled into ignoring the facts. How insidious was the fascination cast by a woman's erotic allure. Was

Carla really any better? Perhaps she was worse. Time would tell. He could have matched the divot in Amparo's face with another, and dragged her to the bales in the feed room and torn the threadbare linen from her skin, and profaned himself upon her flesh. It would have been no more than his right, earned and sanctified by the blood he'd spilled in battle. But he didn't. He contained himself.

'Come with me,' he said.

He stared at her until she understood that refusal wasn't a choice. She followed him outside where Castel Sant' Angelo loomed above them. Anacleto rose from a bench. His whole body was rigid with the effort of containing the agony that racked him. His right cheekbone was gone; Ludovico had held him down while the surgeons extracted the fragments, along with his eye. He'd wept at his friend's valour, for Anacleto had clenched the gag between his jaws and made not a sound. What skin was left had been sutured together like a purse string and pus oozed yellow from the puckered mass. His eye socket was a moist black hole, painted with a poultice brayed from moss found growing on a human skull.

'This is Anacleto,' said Ludovico. 'He is my friend. Mark his deformities well.'

Amparo wouldn't look at him. Ludovico grabbed her by the hair and jerked her face upwards. She gasped as she saw Anacleto's wounds and closed her eyes. Anacleto flinched.

'Mark his deformities well,' Ludovico repeated, 'for your captain was likely the perpetrator.'

Amparo squirmed away and he let go.

'Anacleto needs opium to heal his wounds and help allay his anguish.' At great cost Ludovico had purchased a thimbleful from the Maltese scoundrel, Gullu Cakie. The time had come where gold had little value, for no one expected ever to be able to spend it. Cakie had told him, under menace, where he might get more. 'Tannhauser possesses this medicine, which is in rare supply,' said

Ludovico. 'You will bring some to me, tonight, at the Auberge of Italy.'

'You'd have me steal?' she asked.

'The means of obtaining it are your concern. I'll be in your debt, which is something you'd be wise to value. See that it's done.'

'And if I do not?'

Ludovico took her arm, in a kindly fashion, and walked her away from Anacleto. He leaned towards her ear and spoke softly. 'Tannhauser intends to marry your mistress.'

Amparo blinked but seemed unperturbed. 'It's their bargain,' she said. 'It's been their bargain from the start.'

'The marriage is by way of payment?'

Amparo nodded, her eyes turned down.

Carla had deceived him, then. Fresh hope flourished in his breast.

'Nevertheless,' he said, 'Tannhauser is in love with Carla now.'

'He loves her,' she corrected, 'as I love her.'

'He is a man. As you know better than any.' He saw the seed of doubt take hold. 'He told me himself that he loved her. And they were seen in the throes of a tryst. You are betrayed.'

The words pierced her heart. She put both hands to her mouth and shook her head.

'Ask poor Anacleto – and tell that he lies.'

She tried to pull away but he held on to her. 'Look for yourself and you will see.' He let go. 'Now, do as I bid. Regard my request as the errand of mercy which it is, and God will guide you in this, as in all things.'

Tannhauser sat in his tub and watched the sun go down behind Sciberras. The solar disc was a dark and violent red, and was wreathed with tendrils of smoke that rose from the corpse-choked no-man's-land below. He tried, briefly, to read some significance beyond the obvious into the spectacle, but his mind was too blunted for such conceits, and he gave in to a stupefied awe that left no space for Philosophy.

His body was a mass of pain, lacerations and swellings. His skin was a mottled patchwork of yellow and blue. Sheepgut stitches protruded here and there, some of his own insertion. The climb into the water had almost defeated him. The brine exacerbated the bite of his wounds. His eyes were gritty with powder black and dust. His hands felt bloated and club-like, his fingers swollen as tubers. If a stone from a Turkish culverin had landed on his head, he wouldn't have found it cause for great regret; but the likelihood was remote for the siege guns were silent, and their Topchu crews no doubt as weary as he.

That morning, after launching a number of skirmishes to cover its advance, Mustafa had deployed Abbas's second siege tower. This time the Turks had reinforced its lower half against cannon shot with gabions full of earth and stone, and sections of iron plate riveted to the stanchions and joists. They'd wheeled it up to the remains of the Bastion of Castile and the overtopping janissary marksmen aloft had driven the garrison and workforce thereabouts to cower in the ruins and pray. After some hours languishing in this sorry state, and seeing a massing of troops on the heights that boded a major assault, La Valette had played a variation on the previous day's tactic.

They opened a hole through the undamaged wall some distance to the east of the breach, at a spot invisible to the musketmen in the tower. A raiding party went out under Knight Commander Claramont and Don Guevarez de Pereira. A dozen knights of the German Langue had thrust themselves to the forefront of the volunteers and the raiders charged the tower like lathered fiends, a belated Turkish volley from the muskets high above striking sheets of sparks from their armour as they ran.

The detachment of Azeb infantrymen who guarded the ladders to the rear were hacked apart in seconds by the unhinged Northmen, who then clambered up the rungs and swarmed into the galleries and cleansed the tower of Turks one floor at a time. The whole colossal edifice swayed on its squealing guy ropes at the furious violence vented inside its frame. The bellows of rage and cries of agony were hardly distinguishable, and severed limbs and gutted bodies tumbled forth in crimson cascades, as if the structure were an entertainment at a carnival barbarous and wild. When the slaughter was done, the German brethren stood triumphant on the summit and waved blood-splashed *borks* on the points of their swords, and brandished severed heads and steaming fistfuls of viscera, and stomped the slithering boards with a maniac glee, the still-venting cataracts of gore swilling from the tiered platforms as if from a temple of the Mexica in the wake of atrocious rites. They hurled curses and taunts at the legions of Islam gathered on yonder hills, then they raised their faces to Heaven and sang praises to Jesus Christ for letting them know a moment of such rapture uncontained.

As preparations were made to burn the tower to ashes, Tannhauser suggested that the engine be rather commandeered, and stationed near the wall, and used to the advantage of their own marksmen. His motive in this was to get a better view of the Turkish lines crisscrossing Monte San Salvatore, but La Valette adopted the plan with relish. The tower was emptied of corpses and rotated and repositioned, and a pair of cannon were installed on the lower tier, while *arquebuceros* were dispatched to occupy the rest. Tannhauser was among them.

The prospect from the top was of a sun-parched hellscape blackened by corpses and flies. The Turkish trenches to the east were many and interlaced. How Gullu Cakie had guided him through them he couldn't imagine. And the Turkish numbers were still huge. Any flight to the boat would have to wait on further decimation. But by now La Valette could muster barely fifteen hundred men still able to walk. Tannhauser squatted in the trodden and reeking offal behind the upper gate, deafened and choked in the brutalising heat until his powder and ball were exhausted and his arm felt blue to the elbow, and at that he had taken leave of the tower of blood.

All this he was happy to forget as he lay in his tub. He congratulated himself on its institution. He'd had no idea at that time how vital to his sanity it would prove to be. Perhaps he would lie in the tub all night and watch the stars. Perhaps he would fall asleep and drown, and be found in the morning with a grin of contentment on his face. Then he recalled that Nicodemus had procured some loin chops of mutton for supper and he put all thoughts of dying to one side. He stirred as he became aware of a human presence. Amparo's face loomed over the tub's iron rim and his heart sank. Her eyes were swollen with shed tears and they looked at him with reproach. He knew at once that the little tranquillity he'd gleaned from the war-stunned evening was about to be stolen. He mustered a grimace of welcome.

'Amparo,' he said, 'why so sad?'

She turned her face away to the sky, the very picture of sorrow. With an effort he considered heroic he reached out to stroke her hair. She pulled her head away. He hadn't seen this aspect of her before, but it had only been a matter of time, since she was female.

'You have something to tell me,' he said.

She didn't look at him. 'You are in love with Carla, it's true?'

Tannhauser sighed windily. As with most of his tribulations, he had only himself to blame. He was amazed that in the midst of so much turmoil matters so trifling could weigh this heavy. 'Let's talk of this some other time,' he said.

'Then it is true.'

'Amparo, I've been three days mired in slaughter. A man could be forgiven for thinking that the world was come to its end. Have pity, then, on this poor soldier and leave him to his moment of peace.'

She looked at him and her eyes filled. It had been too much

to hope that his own woes might outweigh hers. She reached out to him like a child and he hauled himself up on his stiff and quavering legs and put a wet arm around her shoulders.

'He made me afraid,' she said.

Tannhauser's sense of aggrievement vanished. 'Who did?' he asked.

'Fra Ludovico.'

His aches and pains were vanquished by a gust of rage. He felt his jaws and scalp tighten and the blood rush through his brain. 'Did he hurt you?'

She shook her head, without conviction. He lifted her chin towards him with his hand. The memory of the fright Ludovico had provoked was replaced by the fear of whatever it was she saw in Tannhauser's eyes. He strove for an equanimity he didn't feel. He ran his fingers through her hair again and wiped the tears from her cheeks.

'You're my darling,' he said.

'I am?' In an instant, her face was again aglow.

'You'll always be my darling. Now, tell me what Ludovico did. Tell me everything.'

Ludovico sat in the office of Del Monte, in the Auberge of Italy, the admiral having granted him its use. On the walls hung portraits of past heroes of the langue and Ottoman banners captured in battles at sea. The Red Hand standard of the Sanjak Cheder, taken that day, enjoyed the place of honour. The admiral's chair was a good one from which to conduct his impending conference with the Bailiffs of the French Langue.

He'd yet to complete the commission entrusted him by Ghisleri. The succession of Del Monte to the Grand Master's throne wasn't yet secure. Yet of all the challenges he'd faced this one had proved simpler than he'd dared hope. He'd rehearsed the argument for Del Monte's candidacy with the heads of the other langues. The Castilians, the Aragonese, the Germans and the Auvergnoise had already pledged their support. Replete with heroes though the Religion was, Del Monte's leadership of the defence of Saint Michel had been peerless. No one could match the respect in which he was held. More to the point, after ninety days of brutal attrition no one had the stomach for political manoeuvring. He anticipated no problem in recruiting the French, though temperament would oblige them to give that appearance.

He wore the black robe and the freedom from his armour was a relief. His back and ribs pained him and he shifted in his chair. The bullet that had struck him two nights before had punched a divot the size of a hen's egg in his backplate and for several moments he'd believed himself killed. The experience had been disturbing. He'd felt no fear, no regret. He'd willed into his mind's eye an image of Our Lord on the Cross. He'd murmured the Act of Contrition. He'd felt at peace. Then Carla's face had filled his brain, and his love for her had filled his heart, and then he'd felt fear. Fear that his love would never find expression. Such was the craven emotion he thought he would carry into eternity – until loyal Anacleto had crawled towards him, with his perfect face torn away, and he'd understood that death had not come calling after all.

The thought of Carla burned his entrails like a fire whose embers never cooled. But patience in this matter, as in most, would bear ripe fruit. The German wouldn't have the advantage for much longer. And Carla hadn't yet soiled herself in his bed. He heard footsteps pound down the corridor and knew at once to whom they belonged. He opened a ledger on the desk and feigned to study it. The door irrupted open. He stared at the page a moment longer, then raised his head.

'Captain,' he said. 'You're earlier than expected.'

Tannhauser's face was stony. A long-barrelled pistol was threaded though his belt, plus a dagger with Turkish jewelwork on the hilt and sheath. There was murder in his eyes.

Ludovico said, 'Amparo must place great faith in you, to spill her tale so promptly.'

Anacleto appeared behind Tannhauser, his hand on the pommel of his sword.

Without turning, Tannhauser said, 'If your boy would hang on to the one eye he still owns, he should make himself scarce.'

Ludovico gestured with his head and Anacleto disappeared.

Tannhauser reached into his Brigantine and pulled out a package wrapped with waxed paper. He tossed it and it bounced on the desk. 'A quarter of opium, with my compliments,' he said. 'A more than decent wage for bullying a girl.'

'You have my gratitude.'

'If you speak to either woman again – if you pass them in the street, if you espy them from afar, if one of them wakens from a dream and utters your name – then I'll make you dearly rue the day you left Rome.'

'With better luck, we must hope, than your last attempt.'

Tannhauser leaned across the desk. Ludovico felt his guts shift inside him.

'That would've been mere murder. Next time you will watch me as I bathe in your blood.'

Tannhauser stared for a period of time that seemed longer than the battle that morning.

Ludovico held his gaze without a blink.

Tannhauser straightened and turned and walked for the door.

'Captain,' said Ludovico.

Tannhauser stopped and turned.

'I'd rather not be your enemy.'

Tannhauser emitted a short grunt of laughter.

'Carla's one woman among many,' said Ludovico. 'At least for you. If it's a title you seek, I can raise you to a rank of nobility that would make hers seem like fishmonger's. Many a duke started out as a soldier and the Holy Father is generous to those who please him. Throw your hand in with me, man, and upon my promise you will prosper.'

'Become one of your familiars?' said Tannhauser. 'I'd rather swallow one of your turds.'

'You'd be in august company, believe me.'

'Then they have riper palates than I.'

'Do you doubt my sincerity?' said Ludovico.

'No. I piss on it.' Tannhauser pointed a finger straight at his face. The gesture was more offensive than his words. 'But take my advice, and do not be so vain as to doubt mine.'

Then Tannhauser turned and left, without shutting the door.

Ludovico picked up the opium. Not a common villain, after all. The man had his own intrigues up his sleeve. Ludovico could smell it, as a sailor smells the gathering storm. Anacleto entered. His eye fell on the package in his hand. Ludovico tossed it to him.

'Go and find the Greek,' said Ludovico. 'Bring him to me here, after the French have left.' Anacleto looked at him. Ludovico nodded. 'Nicodemus.'

THURSDAY 23 AUGUST 1565

The Sacred Council, Castel Sant' Angelo

Oliver Starkey looked about the great council table and in the wavering light of the candles saw a black-robed company of noble old men, each mutilated by battle and resigned to death. Fresh scars disfigured their faces. Some were missing fingers; three of them a hand or an arm. Despair was not in their temper, despite their bleak situation, but no one among the Piliers, Bailiffs and Knights Grand Cross of the Sacred Council expected the Holy Religion to prevail. Even La Valette, at whose right hand Starkey sat, seemed to share their gloom. The sense that this would be the last supreme assembly in the Order's history was palpable, and with it, like a threnody played but unheard, a poignant melancholy hung about the room. Never again would the world know men such as these, thought Starkey, for the world that had forged them was gone. They were the last of the true.

That day the Grande Turke had launched another all-out attack. No one present could remember how many such assaults they'd now endured and repulsed. The days of slaughter and exhaustion and anguish stretched back in every mind into a fiery infinity, as if war were the prime condition of all creation, and privation was all that ever there had been. By dint of the Divine

Will – for events had rendered military logic vain – the Moslem throng had once more been driven back across the blood-rutted wastes of the Grande Terre Plein. The Council had been called in the aftermath by a majority of the Knights Grand Cross, who'd conceived a radical stratagem they wished to propose. It fell to Claramont, Knight Commander of the Langue of Aragon and at forty-seven the youngest of the grandees, to press the argument.

'Fra Starkey,' said Claramont, 'what do the latest roll calls tell us?'

Starkey didn't need to glance at the muster roll among the documents before him. 'Two hundred and twenty of our brethren remain capable of bearing arms. Of the Spanish troops, gentlemen adventurers and Maltese militia, perhaps nine hundred. All are wounded, some gravely. There are almost three thousand wounded unable to man the walls.'

'And the dead?'

'Two hundred and seventeen brother knights. Of the Spanish and Maltese soldiery, something over six thousand have perished. Of the slaves, nearly two thousand. Of the non combatants, seventeen hundred or so.'

'My own estimate of the infidel army,' said Claramont, 'is that they can still field fifteen thousand trained men, perhaps more.'

Starkey did not contest this figure. After ninety-four days of killing Turks, with steel, shot, plague, stone and fire, and in greater numbers than any living general would have dared dream possible, the enemy force remained overwhelming.

'And the news from Sicily and Garcia de Toledo?' asked Claramont.

'None,' said Starkey. 'In his last dispatch he promised ten thousand men by the end of this month.'

'Yes. As he promised them in June, and as he promised them in July,' countered Claramont, to an angry murmur from the rest.

Starkey tried to leaven their pessimism. 'The Turkish siege guns are breaking apart from overuse and their stores of powder run low,' he said. 'Captain Tannhauser tells us that their morale is waning. Their imams chant different verses, of a woeful character. They begin to believe that it's not Allah's will that Malta be theirs.'

'Allah's will be damned,' said Claramont. 'We are an army of ghosts. Our walls are little more than a heap of stones. The very ground beneath us is a honeycomb of Turkish mines. There's no question here of want of courage. Every man would rather die than submit their shoulders to the Turkish yoke. If the foe must inherit this island they'll inherit a graveyard. The question is the price we make them pay. How much longer can we defend the Borgo and Saint Michel with a thousand men? A thousand crippled men. Can we survive another mass offensive such as today's? Another two? Another five? Another week like the last? And does anyone doubt that such onslaughts will soon come?'

Starkey didn't answer and he glanced at the Grand Master.

La Valette sat in silence, his gaunt face unreadable, his grey eyes focused on some point infinitely distant, as if communing with spiritual powers known to him alone.

Claramont continued his brief. 'This fortress in which we sit, Castel Sant' Angelo, is barely scratched. It is moated by a broad canal on the landward side and surrounded on all others by the sea. The stores are still half-full with grain and pickled meats. We can charge forty thousand casks with fresh water. We have plenty of powder and ball. We may bring here our Holy Relics – the Hand of the Baptist, Our Lady of Philermo, the Madonna of Damascus – and our archives and standards, where they'll be safe from Moslem desecration. Strung out on the walls like a murder of crows we'll be destroyed, be it piece by piece or in one fell swoop. But if we pull all our fighting men back to Sant' Angelo, and blow the bridge to the Borgo, a thousand of us fastened up here could last out the Turk the whole winter long. Will anyone gainsay me?'

No one did.

Admiral Del Monte exchanged a glance with Ludovico, who sat beside him, but neither spoke. Starkey looked at La Valette. La Valette did not blink.

Claramont said, 'Sound military reason therefore demands a single conclusion.' He hesitated. 'We must abandon the Borgo. And Saint Michel and L'Isola too. In this I can speak for the Sacred Council, for we are all of us agreed.'

Claramont sat down. A long silence followed, notable for the absence of dissension from any of the supreme assembly's members, and for the intensity with which all studied their Grand Master and awaited his decree. They knew that in abandoning the outer fortifications, they would be abandoning the surviving population – twelve thousand or more Maltese, largely women and children, all virtually helpless – to their immediate doom. La Valette at last rose to his feet, one hand on the table to favour his wounds.

'My beloved and honourable brethren,' he said, 'I've listened to your counsel with the greatest care, and the highest respect. But I reject it.'

The council members stiffened in their chairs. Some leaned forward.

'The military case for abandoning the town is powerful, and you make it well. Perhaps, as you suggest, it is incontrovertible. But we are not here for a military purpose alone.'

A head nodded once, discreetly. Starkey noted that it was Ludovico.

La Valette continued. 'God has willed that we face this moment for a reason. Our Faith now meets its sternest test and we must ask ourselves: what does our Holy Religion mean?'

He looked about the table.

'What is its justification? Its essence? What is its reason for being?'

No one answered, for they knew he would.

'We are not mere soldiers, noble though that calling may be.

We are the Knights of the Hospital of Saint John the Baptist of Jerusalem. We are the Hospitallers. The defence of the faithful pilgrims to Jerusalem was our original calling. *Tuitio Fidei et Obsequium Pauperum*. It is the first and last rule of our Order: Protect the Faith and Serve the Poor. We defend the Faith most truly not by feats of arms, but through our service to the poor. And in return, our service to the poor strengthens and protects our Faith. You all will recall that on our profession as knights we made a solemn promise: to be servants – slaves – to the poor of Jesus Christ. To the Blessed, to Our Lords the Sick. Do they not belong to Our Lord Jesus Christ? And are they not to be treated – and protected – as we would treat and protect Our Lord Jesus Christ Himself?'

He spoke with a quiet but intense passion.

Among the old knights, Starkey saw some with tears rolling into their beards.

'We are by dens of lions encompassed,' said La Valette. 'Is this, then, the time to abandon Our Lords the Sick? To fling our numberless wounded upon the mercy of Moslem fiends? To condemn our brave Maltese brothers in arms, and their women and their children too, to the chains of the Turkish galleys? Are we to forsake our most Sacred Infirmary in its hour of greatest peril?'

He looked about the table. Many were too ashamed to meet his gaze.

'This fortress will not accommodate more than a thousand, you are right. But outside its walls are many thousands more. It may well be the Divine Will that our Holy Religion be buried in these ruins, and that our Order will be no more. That in itself is not something to be feared, for God and his Angels and Saints await our coming. But if we leave our sick and our poor to die without us, the Religion will have perished already – and for Nothing. For without our sick and poor, we are Nothing. The Religion is Nothing. And even should it then endure, its honour would be stained in the eyes of God, if not the eyes of men, until the End of Time.'

La Valette sat down.

That every man had been persuaded was not in doubt, but an awkward pause succeeded in which the council lacked a spokesman.

Admiral Del Monte finally stood up. Had Ludovico pressed him to do so? Starkey hadn't noticed. The rise of Ludovico's prestige within the Order had amazed Starkey, not least because the man remained impeccably modest in manner. So had his valour on the field. That no one resented his presence was more amazing still.

'As always,' said Del Monte, 'His Excellency shows us where our duty lies. If we fall into error, we beg his forgiveness and pray that he remember we are but his children. We will defend the Borgo, and the people of Malta, to the last drop of our blood. Whatever their fate shall be, we will share it. The choice between Defeat and Damnation is no choice at all.'

With relief, the rest affirmed their support one by one, Claramont, the last, displaying particular penitence, which La Valette forestalled with a raised hand. La Valette gave Starkey a familiar glance, which indicated he resume the chair.

'Are there any other matters for the council to consider?' asked Starkey.

Ludovico rose. His sonorous baritone seemed too soft to carry the length of the table; yet it filled the room. 'With Your Excellency's permission, two matters,' he said. 'The first of a delicate nature that I pray gives no offence.'

'Speak freely, Fra Ludovico,' said La Valette. 'The Holy Father's guidance is always esteemed and you are his voice.'

The barb in this encomium was not lost on Starkey nor, he was sure, on Ludovico, but the inquisitor merely proffered a gracious bow. 'In last Saturday's battle, Your Excellency was valiantly wounded, and the carelessness in which he holds his own life is both well known and an inspiration to all.'

Grunts of approval for the Grand Master's valour rippled round the table.

'It is also a source of concern,' continued Ludovico, to more of the same. 'In these dire days, death may visit any in the blink of an eye. As events that day proved, the loss of Your Excellency would leave a void which, if not immediately filled, would prove catastrophic.'

He paused, his eyes rock-steady on La Valette's.

La Valette, with equal poise, gestured that he continue.

'If I may be so bold, I suggest that the Sacred Council nominate and approve Your Excellency's successor, so that if that dreadful disaster should indeed befall us, our army would not be robbed of that leadership so vital to its courage and morale.'

The tension about the table was evident. Every man had considered this possibility; none other would have dared speak of it.

'I realise that this would mean waiving the formal electoral process,' Ludovico went on. 'But in such circumstances as we've considered, three days of uncertainty would be calamitous.'

La Valette replied without hesitation. 'You have the council's gratitude for introducing this matter, Fra Ludovico. I have been remiss in not doing so myself. Your argument enjoys my full support, and I hope that of our fellow brethren.'

He cast about the table for disputants, and found none. He looked at Ludovico. 'I trust you have a nominee in mind.'

Ludovico said, 'Admiral Pietro Del Monte of the Italian Langue.'

No one stirred. Every eye was on La Valette. La Valette looked at Del Monte.

'Fra Pietro and I have sailed on the same deck,' said La Valette. The warmth and relief in his voice at once allayed the tension abroad. 'In brilliance and gallantry, his defence of Saint Michel can only be compared to that of Saint Elmo's – which epic, we will agree, can be compared to none. If there is any man in

Christendom better suited to the task, I should like to know his name.'

One by one the council members added their eulogies and Del Monte was anointed La Valette's successor to the throne.

As the admiral accepted, with characteristic humility and no more words than were necessary, Starkey reflected on Ludovico's subtlety. Such unanimity in the matter of an election was unprecedented. Even La Valette's elevation, though also ultimately unanimous, had been attended by a frenzy of machination, bribery and coercion in which Starkey himself had played a key role. If, as now seemed evident, Ludovico had been at work on Del Monte's behalf, he'd managed to keep Starkey in ignorance, a fact he found unsettling. That Ludovico had picked a candidate who was not only superb but would also, presumably, delight his masters in Rome, was further testament to his ingenuity.

'Fra Ludovico, what is the second, less delicate, matter you would raise?' asked La Valette.

Ludovico stooped by his chair and produced a stout leather valise. He opened it and removed a silver reliquary ornamented with precious stones. He carried the reliquary the length of the table and set it down before La Valette.

'I hope I've not betrayed the trust of our Holy Father in Rome, which was to delay the conveyance of this sacred instrument until the hour of greatest peril.'

La Valette indicated that Starkey open the casket, and he did so. He took a sudden breath. The casket was lined with crimson velvet. Nestled in a sculpted recess and held in place by golden cords was the hilt of a sword and two inches of snapped-off blade. The tang and blade were rusted and eaten away by the passage of time. Of what would have been the wooden dudgeon a single fragment, held by a rivet, remained. The style was that of the Roman *gladius* of antiquity. His heart raced with emotion. He dared not presume its origin. He looked at Ludovico.

Ludovico nodded. 'Its existence is a great secret,' he said. He looked at La Valette. 'This is the sword which Peter used to protect Our Lord, when he cut off the ear of the Roman soldier in the Garden of Gethsemane.'

La Valette pushed back his chair and sank to one knee and made the sign of the Cross. The other council members followed. La Valette rose and pored over the casket. He stood back as the other knights filed past the relic in awe, their eyes brimming, prayers on their lips. Starkey saw La Valette study Fra Ludovico. Each man's expression was as impenetrable as that of the other.

'His Holiness has once again demonstrated his wisdom,' said La Valette. 'And you have proved yourself his perfect servant.'

Ludovico bowed his head and said nothing.

'This relic shall lie in San Lorenzo with the Hand of the Baptist,' announced La Valette.

'With respect, Your Excellency,' said Claramont, 'should we not consider removing at least our Holy relics to the safety of Sant' Angelo?'

La Valette shook his head. 'To do so would be a signal to our soldiers that we expect to be defeated. And despite all that's been said, defeat I will not countenance. With the help of God we will yet drive the Turk back into the sea. The Hand of John the Baptist, the Sword of Saint Peter, the icon of Our Lady of Philermo are the root of our strength. They will remain in their rightful place until there is no one left to defend them.'

He had the attention of the whole assembly.

'And to return to the matter which brought us here, I have one last order. Tomorrow, Castel Sant' Angelo will be evacuated of all except the crews required to supply and man the batteries on the roof. Then the bridge to the Borgo shall be destroyed.'

A stunned silence greeted this command. Even Ludovico arched a black brow.

'There will be no retreat,' said La Valette. 'Let every man understand – and the Grande Turke too – that we will fight and die where we now stand.'

FRIDAY 31 AUGUST 1565

The Borgo – Monte San Salvatore

If there was any virtue in sustaining a multiplicity of wounds, fractures and abrasions it was that the global discomfort thus produced diverted one's attention from any given pang in particular. The last major assault, of 23 August, had left Tannhauser with two new cuts to his left cheek, a knee which felt as if it was filled with gravel, another broken finger, some cracked ribs over the liver, sundry gashes to the thighs which he doctored himself and a twisted ankle. He had also been twice stunned insensible and had awoken half-drowned in pools of human filth whose least offensive ingredient was vomit. In all this he considered himself fortunate to have escaped unscathed, for the majority of those still left alive sported wounds and deformities of hideous dimension. Even so, the inability to move without pain made him feel like a man twice his age. Having resisted both logic and the urge of his body for longer than honour required, he'd concocted a batch of the Stones of Immortality and spent the last week in a state of heady indifference to the apocalyptic events unfolding around him.

The stones also fended off the bouts of black melancholia that had started to afflict him. In such moments he knew he'd never see Orlandu again. Reason always reaffirmed that, in leaving him with Abbas, Tannhauser had done what was best. Yet he missed Orlandu. And he was punished by a strange fear: that he'd doomed the boy to a life of shedding blood.

He was far from alone in suffering troubles of the spleen and brain. Throughout the skeletal remnants of the town he often came upon stunned and mutilated men who gibbered to themselves as they cowered in the rubble, or stared mute into nothingness, or wept over the detritus of their families, their homes, their lives. The battered churches were crammed with such folk and lamentation there was ceaseless. The women of the town seemed made of sterner stuff. With most men dead or wounded, and the slave battalions reduced – in part by the violent suppression of a mutiny – to a few stupefied gangs of hollow-eyed wraiths, the women toiled to rebuild the walls and carry corpses to the rear. Yet they too were spiritless and gaunt, going through the motions of collecting food from the depot and water from the well – and of trying to impose order on their ragamuffin offspring – with the listlessness of the condemned.

When the alarums rang, provost marshals stalked the wreckage with knotted ropes to drive the laggards to the front. While dead knights were accorded all the honours and obsequies due to martyrs, less valued corpses lay unburied in the streets, or were tossed into the sea, for there was no spare strength left to bury them and the mass graves had long been glutted and filled back in. The whole town stank of putrefaction. Rats swarmed in daylight, the scuttling black mobs catching one's eye unawares and turning one's stomach with an antediluvian disgust. Emboldened vultures colonised whole city sections and flapped and squawked in outrage when dislodged, as if this were now their realm by right and humans the impudent interlopers. Flies plagued every moment of every day and earned themselves a hatred that exceeded even that reserved for the Turks. The Catholics had a horror of cremation, for it precluded resurrection, but

Tannhauser reckoned they'd soon have to change their tune and light some pyres.

Bors alone maintained an admirable buoyancy and proved a tonic to all, for he was never short of a story, a jest or a ripe observation on the nature of men and things. He, too, partook of the Stones of Immortality, which he swallowed like nuts when given the chance, and perhaps this, in some degree, accounted for his pluck. The news of the marvellous pills spread wide, and Bors suggested they make hay while this grim sun shone. So coveted were the stones, and so great was the price that the market would bear, that even gold would not suffice to buy them, for it would have proved too heavy to lug away. Instead they were exchanged for emeralds and diamonds and other precious stones, which had been culled in plenty by the Spaniards and Maltese from the extravagant raiment and gear of the Turkish dead.

When Carla discovered this lucrative trade she shamed Tannhauser into donating ten pounds of opium to Fra Lazaro, a gift he accepted as miraculous and which he believed was Turkish booty. The gift caused Bors much anguish, but Tannhauser argued it would stop the confiscation of their stock; for such had been Carla's icy and uncompromising threat. Bors kept the kitchen well supplied with foodstuffs, brandies and wines, which if anything had been more easily procured as the population fell, and the denizens of the Auberge of England ate well.

Indeed, for the gentlemen adventurers from Italy and England, the Spanish *tercios* and those of the German Langue not overly committed to austerity, the auberge became a much-loved haven. Holes yawned in the walls and the roof, and the refectory had been partly demolished, but if open gaiety was uncommon, hearty company was always to be found. Tomaso brought Gullu Cakie and his bunch, and conspiracies of smuggling and tax evasion were spun. A handful of the braver town girls chanced their luck and frantic romances flourished in catastrophe's shadow.

The best nights, unforgettable to all those present, were when

Carla and Amparo were cajoled into dusting off their instruments. They played for the gathered and, as Tannhauser had predicted, their music was more precious than rubies. Even the hardiest among them shed tears at their melodies sublime, and sometimes there was dancing, and sometimes there was song, for the Asturian Andreas de Munatones displayed an exquisite tenor voice when in his cups. And sometimes – in defiance of rowdy jeers and if need be discharging a pistol to enforce silence – Tannhauser would recite laments and erotic *gazels* in the Turkish style, for he insisted that poetry in any tongue be honoured, and never more so than in a time and place such this.

As Bors pointed out, the ghost of the Oracle had followed them down to Hades.

After the repulse of the 23rd the Turks licked their wounds for eight days and launched no major offensives. The war continued underground, however, as the Mameluke sappers redoubled their efforts to undermine the bastions of the knights. While they tunnelled though the limestone of no-man's-land, La Valette's engineers crawled about with basins of water and probes festooned with tiny bells, in an attempt to detect the vibrations caused by their tools. When they did so, the Maltese sappers sank countermines to intercept the enemy diggings, and to burn the underground galleries before they reached the walls. If successful, these measures resulted in subterranean duels – with shovels, picks and knives – of such dark and heinous savagery that even Tannhauser's blood ran cold to hear them related. The half-dozen mines that the Turks did explode further reduced the enceinte to a jagged-toothed ruin.

The knights made their own contribution to the chaos when they blew up the bridge that connected the Borgo to Sant' Angelo. This eccentric act baffled many of the garrison for days, it being deemed either an accident or an act of sabotage, for which latter crime the slaves who'd helped to haul the explosive charges were drowned in the canal. When it later emerged that the bridge's destruction was a stratagem to raise morale, the logic of denying this last redoubt was lost on all but the most sophisticated, for it also meant that tons of supplies had to be freighted daily by barge across to the Borgo. But the knights, as everyone knew, were strange folk, and none stranger than the Reverend Grand Master whose order it was.

Tannhauser continued to worry the problem of their escape to the boat at Zonra. In darker moments his plan seemed an infantile fantasy, designed only to prevent him from going mad. Bors never raised the matter. Neither did Carla. Both, he knew, thought the plan wanted for honour. That they no longer took it seriously was plain. Yet they hadn't seen that sleek little boat, as he had in his mind's eye a thousand times, nor felt the sea breeze in their hair as they flew back to Italy.

On the 29th a collective fast had been ordered to commemorate the beheading of John the Baptist. In contrast, and perhaps as compensation, Friday the 31st brought an evening of revelry that exceeded in abandon anything the auberge had seen before. Since Bors was master of ceremonies, it probably exceeded anything seen theretofore on Malta itself. The occasion developed of its own accord, perhaps stoked by some sense of premonition. They'd survived one hundred days in the teeth of Hell and that was reason enough for the mad frivolity. The women played. Wine and brandy flowed. Ballads and airs were sung. Carla essayed a jig with Munatones, and a fine pair they made, and envy and arousal provoked Tannhauser to steal an assignation with Amparo in the tub, and though he loved Amparo more dearly than ever he did not say so, and again did not know why. Stones of Immortality were consumed. Yet as the evening wore on, and despite such revels, Tannhauser could not scratch the itch in the back of his mind. The boat at Zonra called him.

And so as midnight beckoned, the waxing crescent moon having long set in the west, and despite being the worse for opium and drink, Tannhauser decided on a reconnaissance and he donned the red robes and yellow boots of a Sipahi sergeant, purloined from a corpse.

Tannhauser's inebriation proved a boon. Without such narcotic aid the three-hundred-yard crawl to the slope of San Salvatore would have been too arduous by far. Nor would he have thought to take the frequent rests in which he lay on his back and stared, deranged by wonder, at the wheeling stars. To the north the Great Bear was in flight; Orion bestrode the tail of the Milky Way out in the east; Scorpius disappeared below the horizon. Yet who now was the hunter, and whom his prey? And what did it matter? For all things would pass and, as Grubenius averred, even the stars themselves would one day fall. Philosophy added its glow to that of opium and liquor. When he reached the Turkish lines his confidence and bonhomie were such that he found himself within minutes at one of their watchfires, sharing bowls of lentil broth and bread.

They were Anatolians, four simple men, not much more than boys, brave and bewildered as most boy soldiers are, and he listened to their doleful accounts of this cursed campaign, to their memories of families and sweethearts they might never see again, to their gloomy opinions of Allah's will and the brute indifference of their commanders. They were cast away in a bleak and hostile land, and while for Tannhauser the teeming sky above brought a measure of succour, these poor levies stared only at their paltry fire, as if by looking at the alien void they'd be robbed of what little remained of their souls and their sanity.

There was talk of the fiends who inhabited the Christian fortress, manifestly in league with Satan one and all – for what human beings could fight as they fought without diabolic aid? The name of the Christian sorcerer, La Valette, was invoked with superstitious awe. He'd been seen, they said, communing with demons on the walls at the dead of night. He'd conjured up the plague that thinned their ranks. His knights were demoniac phantoms, resurrected from the dead by his spells and incantations. He could fly with the vultures and crows. He could not be killed, for he'd sold his soul to the Devil, and the Devil protected his own.

Tannhauser reassured them, for they moved him with their easy friendship and were stranded not by necromantic powers but – as were they all – by the greed of emperors and kings, and because – in this company and in this tongue – he was by experience a leader of men and to raise their quaking spirits was his instinct and duty.

'La Valette is only a man,' he said. 'A great and terrible man, perhaps, but a man just the same. So too his knights. The men and women of the town fight like devils because this is their home, the soil of their forefathers, and we have come to take it by conquest. Would not any of us fight as fiercely for hearth and kin?'

They nodded and stared at the fire, and rags of flame flew up into the measureless night and vanished just as swiftly as they were realised, as if to show that by the reckoning of a Cosmos so implacable and so huge, the passage of human life was hardly more important.

'Ibrahim,' said the one named Davud, looking up. 'Will the morrow see an end to them? Or to us?'

'The morrow?' asked Tannhauser.

'The great attack,' said Davud. 'The last battle.'

This revelation sobered Tannhauser. He fished for more. 'We've been promised many last battles.'

Davud grimaced in agreement.

Tannhauser pointed into the dark, across the saddle towards Santa Margharita. 'I'm with the Kirmizi Bayrak,' he said. He'd seen the Red Banners deployed there on many days. 'We'll support the Lions of Islam, in the second wave.'

Davud glanced at Tannhauser's scarred face and splinted fingers. 'You've seen the worst, my friend.'

'The worst?' replied Tannhauser. He shook his head. 'As long as one is alive, the worst lies waiting. What are your orders?'

'So far Allah the merciful has been kind to us here, up above the bay,' said Davud. 'Even those devils can't walk on water. But tomorrow we are in the first wave.'

The Anatolians exchanged grim glances. Tannhauser frowned in sympathy.

'All of you?'

Davud waved a hand across the invisible bulk of Monte San Salvatore.

'All except the gunners.'

Tannhauser's heart quickened. He leaned forward and in a display of indifference pushed a half-charred stick of wood into the embers. He watched the flames catch and said, 'They tell us nothing, of course. But you say our Pasha intends to commit the reserve? The entire reserve?'

'The time has come,' confirmed Davud.

The reserve regiments stationed on San Salvatore, besides protecting its siege batteries, had acted to block any repeat of the Christian relief force that had marched across its slopes to Kalkara Bay – with Ludovico – back in July. But the Turks couldn't walk on water either. To attack the Borgo the reserves would have to deploy to the south and with only the artillery crews left behind, the route to Zonra – and his boat – would be open. Even for a band of four. Tannhauser marked the North Star and just above the rim of the hill in the north-east, towards Zonra, the horns of Taurus. The Bull would guide them home. He thought of Amparo and reckoned it a strong omen. He stretched his arms.

'The time has come, also, for me to go,' he said.

The look of a child flitted across Davud's face.

A fragment of the Koran floated up through Tannhauser's brain.

He said, '*With Allah lies the knowledge of the end of the world. He is the One who sends the rain and who knows the contents of the womb. No soul knows what he will earn tomorrow, and no soul knows in what land he will die. Only Allah is all-knowing, wholly aware.*'

The four youths made reverent gestures, but were no less frightened.

'Have you been in battle before?' asked Tannhauser.

He glanced around the fire. All four shook their heads.

'In the charge,' said Tannhauser, 'stick close together and watch for each other's safety.'

They all four stared at him intently.

'In the noise, the smoke, the terror, you'll think only of yourself – and Allah, most exalted is He. It's natural but also fatal. Eight eyes are better than two, four swords better than one. Pool your courage and your skill. Where goes one, go all, but do not group tight in the open or you'll give them a target.'

He waited so that this sank in, and they nodded.

'Watch for their Greek fire – the flying hoops. And the cannon-balls too – they'll rise from the clay like cobras, but if you're sharp, you can straddle them. And avoid the Christians wearing full armour; they may not be devils but they're devilish hard to kill.'

They looked at him as if he were Solomon. Their earnest faces moved him. He reached into his robe and took out his box and fingered two stones of opium. Why not? He drew his dagger, its stained blade black and wicked in the flames, and they watched him carve the gold-flecked pills in half.

'The advantages of being in the first wave are few,' he continued, 'but remember this one. Your role is to engage the enemy – on the whole by dying – so that the second wave might overwhelm them. If you survive until the second wave arrives, pull back – but do so slyly, like a cutpurse from a crowd. Don't panic. Don't run. Keep your war face. Grab a wounded comrade, and carry him back to the lines. Carry him proudly. If you make it, at worst you'll earn a flogging, at best a bonus for valour. Now, show me your right palms.'

They held out their hands. By now, if he'd told them to stick them in the fire, they would've obeyed him. He placed a half-pill in each palm.

'Swallow these as you draw up on the hill, when your heart begins to knock against your ribs. Not before. They are a taste of Paradise and will help to banish your fear. And if Paradise is where you're bound, they will make the journey easier.'

He wondered if he should ask about Orlandu, for the boy's health was often on his mind, but here at the opposite end of the front the likelihood that they'd know him was remote. In any case, he knew that the *silahadar* cavalry hadn't been committed since the first day. There was no point sending horses to scale walls. He stood up.

They reached their feet before him and showered him with blessings.

'Say nothing of what has passed between us to anyone else,' he said. They nodded. '*Asalaamu alaykum*,' said Tannhauser. He added, '*May Allah keep you safe*.'

As he walked away he saw the watchfires on Corradino and was tempted to go and find Orlandu, and perhaps share his fire too. But he'd pushed his luck far enough, and it wasn't long until sunrise. Let the boy sleep. He needed some rest himself. His return to the Kalkara Gate was without incident. Bors covered his approach and opened the wicket. Before he went to give Starkey the latest intelligence, Tannhauser explained his findings. Bors was sceptical.

'The road to Zonra will be open?'

'The boat is ours for the taking,' Tannhauser assured him. 'It's time to pack our opium and jewels. We sail tomorrow night.'

'All that stands in our way is Mustafa's last battle.'

'I've fought more last battles than I can count on this bloody island. Have some faith, man, and it will be our last, even if no one else's.'

SATURDAY 1 SEPTEMBER 1565

Bastion of Germany – Sacred Infirmary – Post of Castile

At dawn, timed as always to the muezzin's call, the one hundred and third Moslem captive of the siege was strung from a greasy rope above the Provençal Gate. It had been many weeks since anyone on either side had paid much attention to this ritual – the victims excepted – yet had it failed to take place the consternation would have been as great as if a flag of surrender, not a body, had been hung above the gate. This morning, as the garrison prepared to meet their end, the genius of this macabre practice was reaffirmed in Tannhauser's mind, for as the rope snapped tight the garrison raised a hoarse and defiant cheer.

The gallows thus replenished, a Mass for the island's deliverance was held in the church of San Lorenzo. At the same time, chaplains stationed at intervals along the enceinte said Mass for the ragtag soldiery. In the infirmary, and the pain-choked piazza outside, other chaplains did the same for the afflicted. The service was solemn and yet, as on the last day at Fort Saint Elmo, a curious calm pervaded the population. There was nothing left to fear. The only task remaining was to die. As the last Amen rose heavenwards, La Valette pulled off another brilliant stroke.

The Order's silver processional Cross was carried down the aisle of San Lorenzo and behind it came the holy icon of Our Lady of Philermo. As the icon passed by, there were many who saw real tears stream down the Madonna's pale cheeks. Some fainted away with ecstasy. Next came the Sword of Saint Peter, the lid of its silver casket open so that the fortunate might glimpse the heroic relic therein. Finally came the Religion's most sacred possession, the Right Hand of John the Baptist, sealed in a jewelled reliquary. An honour guard of knights drawn from each of the eight langues brought up the rear, led by La Valette himself.

The procession left the church and toured the blasted streets, wending by the infirmary and the fragile line of defenders strung out along the bastions and walls. All genuflected and crossed themselves as the Holy Relics passed by, and everyone felt the power of Jesus Christ and Our Lady and Saint Peter and the Baptist surge through their hearts. The thought of Moslem dogs desecrating the Hand of Saint John fuelled the rage and redoubled the strength of every Christian soldier on the ramparts. By the time the procession repaired back to San Lorenzo, the spirit of the depleted garrison was as undaunted as at any time during the siege.

Tannhauser missed the Eucharistic rites due to his indulgence in baser forms of worship; but while searching for Carla, with Amparo at his side, he caught a portion of the grand procession marching by, and marvelled that a piece of theatre could have so profound an effect. By any reckoning the parade of relics was worth an extra thousand men, and maybe more than that, for to fight for oneself is one thing, but to fight for the right hand of the man who baptised Jesus is quite another. The hand that lowered His head beneath the Waters of Jordan, no less. Even Tannhauser felt his blood rise, and wondered if the Way of Christ were not after all the path to Transcendence.

He found Carla in the hospital piazza, looking not far short of Blessedness herself. She held a cup of wine to the lips of a man both of whose foreshortened arms were swathed in clotted lint. She was haggard and worn, her hair tangled with filth, and her faded black dress was tattered, but when she turned to him and smiled he swore she'd never looked so lovely. He realised that appearing with his mistress on his arm was poor form, but Carla took this in her stride. He wondered if the arrangement might be continued beyond their union, and decided that, even if that were so, it would create a new touchstone for folly. Compared to the complexities of loving two women at once, war was a mere bagatelle. He let go of Amparo and assumed a military demeanour.

Before he could open his mouth, Carla said, 'I trust you slept well.'

Tannhauser thought the remark rather cutting, and perhaps her smile too. He took an added step away from Amparo and resorted to bluster. 'Since you ask I was up the better part of the night,' he said, 'risking life and limb behind enemy lines in pursuit of our shared ambitions.'

'Our keenest ambition?'

'The very same.'

Carla looked about the serried wounded, and he saw the doubts resurface in her mind.

'Of every ten men who took up arms in this city's defence, nine are dead or very close to it,' said Tannhauser. 'You've served them with more heart than honour or valour – or even God – can demand. If we can see out this day, we'll have a chance to serve Orlandu. And ourselves.'

She looked at him. He smiled. She nodded. He motioned to Amparo to join her.

'Stay here and stick together,' he said. 'No wandering. I'll be back after dark. Be ready.'

TANNHAUSER LEARNED THAT there had been other nocturnal actions besides his own. During the pre-dawn hours, Andreas de

Munatones, the singer, dancer and Asturian knight of Santiago, had led an underground foray through the Christian countermines. After savage fighting by torchlight the Mamelukes and Laghimji sappers had been vanquished, and two of the timbered Turkish galleries snaking under no-man's-land had been set ablaze with incendiary pipkins. The Maltese sappers dragged Andreas back from the second with a pickaxe through his chest and carried him to San Lorenzo, where he died during dawn Mass.

These sorties, though brave, had failed to detect several other mines packed with gunpowder that the Turks had built beneath the enceinte. Three of these mines exploded with great destruction as a prelude to the attack.

Tannhauser and Bors, who'd decided to throw their lot in with the Northmen, saw the mines blow as they reached the Bastion of Germany on the far Christian left. The painstaking weeks of repairs to the inner wall of Castile were demolished in an instant. Between the Bastions of Italy and Provence a thirty-foot section of curtain collapsed into the ditch. A score of defenders were buried beneath the stones. On the summit of Santa Margharita the *Sanjak i-sherif* was unfurled. A rippling barrage from the Turkish siege guns illumined the rim of the heights. And as the smoke rolled down on to the flatlands and *jihad* was once more rejoined, thousands of *gazi* reeled across the Grande Terre Plein to determine the judgement of Allah.

'*Allahu Akabar!*'

The plain had the look of a lake of reeking mud glazed hard by the sun, but no rain had fallen all summer and the native clay was pale. The encrusted black pan across which the heathen charged was baked from spilled gore and the last evacuations of the dying. The dust kicked up by the *gazi*'s feet wasn't dirt, but the desiccated blood of their dead comrades. Iridescent swarms of blowflies spiralled skyward green and blue and some men fell as they sank up to the ankles in seething nests of maggots invisible to the eye. When the Religion's cannon opened up, scores more were mowed down with atrocious wounds and they writhed in the foetid corruption like creatures primeval. Yet still they came. At three hundred feet a volley of musketry raked them and the carnage was redoubled.

Tannhauser rammed a fresh ball down the barrel of his rifle and wiped his brow. The army labouring towards them was no longer the implacable force that had landed at Marsaxlokk. The tenor of the Moslem battle cries was reedy, their fervour scraped from the dregs of a harrowed spirit. They no longer stormed the ramparts for their Sultan, or for booty or for honour, nor to slake the hatred of Christ that had animated previous assaults. They came not even to see the Face of God. They charged forward now out of that blind collective impulse which is the curse and doom of mankind. Each man went forward because the next man did, and with the same purposeless courage. Tannhauser cranked the wheel-lock's key and primed the pan.

As he rose up to fire again a cluster of four young levies caught his eye as they stumbled for the gap in the Post of Castile. They moved as if they'd have held each other's hands if they could, like children wandering lost through a degenerate bazaar. He lowered his gun. A brass cannonball bounced across the field and a futile pity clawed his heart as he foresaw its intersection with their path. The youths saw the cannon shot too and exchanged frantic yells, and if one hadn't grabbed at the others they might have eluded its calamitous arc. But he did and panic froze them. They watched, as did Tannhauser, as the ball skipped up from the clay at knee height and chopped them down one and all before bounding on. A figure struggled free from the limbless and tangled melee, screaming as much as his friends though he appeared unharmed. He looked down on the dismembered mass. He threw up his guts. Then he raised both arms and his mouth gaped soundlessly at the bastions above, as if surrendering not to the enemy but to a Power more vicious and unfeeling than them all.

Tannhauser recognised Davud.

Bors's Syrian long gun bucked across the merlon and Davud's head was shrouded in crimson mist. When the mist cleared, his body stood erect for a moment, his skull a half-sheared nubbin, bubbling and obscene, then he keeled over into the still-convulsing bodies of his mates, his impact exacerbating their agony.

Tannhauser turned away.

From the escarpment a thousand feet distant he watched the second wave of Turkish infantry hazard the anguished plain. He looked along the enceinte. Beyond Galley Creek flames and smoke marked embattled Saint Michel. Before the breach in the ruins of Castile, the sacrificial remnant of the first Turkish wave had faltered as the wildfire bloomed. Those few who scrabbled up the talus were speared and hacked to pieces by the knights. The *arquebuceros* on the ramparts recharged their pieces and unleashed a volley into the charge renewed. The tumbling bodies were trampled into the filth by the oncoming tide. On the left flank of the advance, an *orta* of Tüfekchi marksmen drew up at the limit of arquebus range and laid down a blanket of fire with their nine-palm muskets. A blare of horns released a third torrential wave that rolled in hard on the second. The Grande Terre Plein now seethed with martial finery and with fluttering pennants of red and yellow and green. Iayalars, dervishes, Mamelukes, Azebs. Their blood was up and their cries had gained conviction and so numerous they were, and so quickly did they close ranks, that the cannon shot scything through them now left hardly a wake.

Oliver Starkey joined Tannhauser at the Bastion of Germany and brought the English Langue with him, all two of them, the Catholic adventurers John Smith and Edward Stanley. They each unloaded a musket into the advance. Then Starkey grounded his gun against a crenel and drew his sword. He evinced an adamantine ruthlessness, made the more unnerving by his scholarly mien.

Tannhauser noted, with chagrin, that the Germans, Swedes and Poles were unlimbering axes and swords.

'With me,' said Starkey to the brethren. 'To the Post of Castile.'

They were more than ready. Starkey glanced at Tannhauser, as if for comment. Tannhauser pointed to the rubble of the Post of Castile, where Turkish lassoes whirred above the fray and barbed spears and melee arms glinted in the rising sun. From the second wave a formation of chain-armoured janissaries braved the wildfire and came up short against the thin and wavering echelon of Christian knights. Another fight boiled about the foot of the captured siege tower, from the top of which a crew of Maltese and *tercios* poured gunfire and incendiary pipkins into the mob.

'If Mustafa's sent in the Zirhli Nefer at this early stage,' said Tannhauser, 'he's gambling on a rapid victory.'

'Then we'll deny him,' said Starkey. 'Close quarters it is.' He addressed the score or so knights of the German Langue. 'Our brothers won't hold the line without us. Form up in a wedge to their rear and keep your order. Drive through on my word. And remember, when the Turk breaks, we are not to pursue.'

Tannhauser hefted his rifle. With bullets he could reliably drop a man every five or six minutes, a better rate than was likely at close quarters. 'I can lay more to rest from up here.'

Starkey did not quarrel. 'As you will,' he said.

'God's wounds!' said Bors, staring over the parapet.

A dull subterranean rumble reached Tannhauser's ears and he turned.

Before his eyes two broad, deep trenches unravelled across the Grande Terre Plein and palisades of orange flame, stoked high by the sudden draught, erupted through the advancing Moslem ranks. The horde swerved in confusion and, as if Satan had drawn the bolts on Hell's roof, droves of men vanished wholesale into the fire-choked chasms underfoot.

Tannhauser understood at once that the underground galleries Munatones had set ablaze earlier that morning had collapsed under the weight of the charge. No doubt Starkey understood it too, but that did not dissuade him from a deft invocation of Divine favour.

'There is our sign!' said Starkey. 'God is with us yet.'

Bors roared, 'For Christ and the Baptist!'

Tannhauser looked at him with horror. The German Langue echoed the cry with zeal. With Starkey and his Englishmen in the van they clanked along the wall walk towards the stair. Tannhauser grabbed Bors's arm. Bors unslung a two-hander and shook his head.

'Prithee peace,' said Bors. 'The English Langue will not go in without me.'

Bors stumped off after his compatriots. Tannhauser quelled a sudden uprising in his belly. The sweat running down his back and chest in pints turned icy cold and he shivered in his armour. He threw the rifle to his shoulder and aimed at the tall white bonnets pressing the breach and fired. Without marking the result he stacked the rifle with the rest and pulled his gauntlets from his belt. His heart sank. He dreaded the grinding toil that lay in store. He looked out to the east across Monte San Salvatore. The Turkish tents and trenches were deserted. Only the Topchu artillery crews remained. Come nightfall, freedom was a brisk stroll hence; but the sun had only just cleared Salvatore's rim. As he was about to don his gauntlets he saw the gold bangle on his wrist. The mouths of the lions still roared. On a superstitious impulse he slipped it off and read the Arabic graving on its inner face.

I come to Malta not for riches or honour but to save my soul.

That prospect seemed as unlikely as ever, yet the motto gave him comfort. He replaced the bangle and pulled on his armoured gloves. He drew his sword and headed for the stair. Moments later he joined Bors and the other Northmen in the wedge of steel, and Bors laughed at him, and Tannhauser devil-damned him back. On Starkey's command they mounted the talus and, to the dismay of the Zirhli Nefer who crowded the breach, the langues of Germany and England ploughed into the delirium.

SHORTLY AFTER MIDDAY, and with a hushed urgency, the staff of the Sacred Infirmary were assembled in the laundry room and Carla listened to Fra Lazaro impart the Grand Master's command that every wounded man who could make the journey was to join the defenders on the ramparts, and with all possible speed.

Since patients no longer qualified for admission without losing a limb, or sustaining the most heinous mutilations, a moment of incredulity greeted this decree. The look in Lazaro's eyes, and the greyness of his pallor, suggested that he shared their confusion, but he had had more time, and the benefit of La Valette's presence, to accept that the order was in earnest. There was no great expectation that the wounded plunge into combat, but they were to dress in helmets and red surcoats – this was most important – and display themselves at the battlements to give the Grande Turke the impression of a strength they no longer possessed. Hundreds of women and boys were already wielding spears alongside the soldiers. To fight to the last drop of blood was no longer rhetoric. It fell to the assembled to prepare the volunteers and help to convey them to their posts.

Lazaro asked Carla to stand by him while he harangued the casualties in the great ward, for her presence, he said, would stir them more than his words. The alacrity with which the sick tried to rise from their beds moved them both to near tears, and when they repeated La Valette's plea to those carpeting the piazza and choking the nearby streets, the response was just as valiant. Lazaro calmed their fervour while gear was collected and some form of order imposed, for chaos threatened to overwhelm the endeavour before it could begin. Carla and Amparo were in the crew sent to gather up helmets and it was here, more than during the harangue, that Carla's emotions overcame her.

They rounded the rear of the Arsenal and she found herself

confronted by a mountain of discarded steel helms. Thousands of them, banked up against the wall to thrice her height like some profane and careless monument to the slain. Many were dented and tarnished with blood, and fat blue flies took flight and buzzed around the pile in swarms, as if to defend their squalid treasure trove. The hospital had inured her to a stream of afflicted individuals; but not to loss represented on this huge scale. Beyond the mountain of helms lay stacks of pikes and short swords in similar abundance. A pair of monks pulled up a two-wheeled handcart and they helped them fill it to the brim with clattering refuse. The monks hauled the cart back to the piazza. As Amparo, mute and dispirited, made to follow, Carla took her hand and held her back.

'Amparo, Mattias plans to leave the island – tonight.' It didn't seem likely to her that there would be a tonight, but now was the time to broach the matter of escape.

Amparo looked at her. 'How?'

'He has a boat hidden up the coast and will guide us through the Turkish lines. Are you happy to come with us, back to Italy and home?'

'With Tannhauser? And with you? But of course.' She started to smile, then stopped in a frown. 'What will become of Buraq?'

'You must ask Mattias.'

'Buraq can't come with us?'

Carla didn't have the heart to shake her head. 'You must ask Mattias.'

Amparo turned and hurried towards the stables. Carla almost called after her, then reasoned that it was safer to leave her at the stables than to drag her about the battlefield. At least she'd know where the girl was. Carla returned to the infirmary to prepare La Valette's brigade of the infirm and lame.

Despite their willingness, most of the casualties would never reach the front, short of being portered there on wattles and laid along the breach flat on their backs. Several had already died from the effort they'd made in standing, as fragile membranes ruptured inside and dropped them on the spot. Others were defeated by lungs so ravaged by smoke that they couldn't rise. Those with severe burns, and they were many, couldn't move at all. Nevertheless, three hundred or so volunteers were deemed fit enough to make their march plausible. They helped each other into the surcoats and swapped helms to find their right size. They bound sashes and belts around newly sutured wounds. They improvised crutches out of pike shafts and shovels and timbers from demolished homes. They hung on to each other and to the monks and surgeons who accompanied them. They did these things without ado, with the practical stolidity of peasants and common soldiers. In their bloodstained and battered casques and their crimson surcoats splashed with the white Latin cross, they seemed like a ramshackle army of lost crusaders resurrected from the tombs of Outremer. That or a cruel allegory of Folly Unbound. A young Maltese rendered sightless by burns grabbed Carla's arm. He recoiled and begged forgiveness as he realised she was a woman. She was reminded of her first charge in the hospital, Angelu, the man with no face and no hands. She took the youth's arm in hers.

The battalion of the maimed set out from the piazza and Lazaro led them forth towards the roar of the guns. He began to chant a Psalm of David in plainsong, with a high, clear, wavering voice that pierced her heart. Another monk joined in, accompanying Lazaro's cantus an octave below, then others joined in counterpoint at the fourth tone and the fifth, and a sound as if of cherubim lifted their spirits and carried them forward to the final encounter.

Their city crumbled around them as they marched. Here and there a wall collapsed as a ball from a Turkish culverin hurtled home. The debris entombed a handful of the men stumbling by, but no one dithered. Carla saw groups of old women sink to their knees and they wept and lamented and pressed crosses and beads and icons of the saints to their cracked and wrinkled lips as they passed by. Occasionally one of the valiant would stumble and fall as his wounds took their toll, and sometimes he would get up again and sometimes not, but the monks of the hospital – now, like their brethren, monks of war – did not pause in their march or in their singing, and nor did their legion, for they marched and sang to save the Holy Religion.

They reached an apron of broken ground at the limit of what passed muster for the city and a screaming pandemonium there unfolded before her eyes.

Turbid drifts of powder smoke roiled the contested brim – from the siege tower's roof, from artillery mounted on the crown-works, from whirling incendiary hoops and the volleys of the musketeers. Yellow sheets of wildfire leapt skyward and danced above the ditch beyond the massive breaches in the wall. Against this incandescence she saw the twisted silhouettes of the fighting knights, warped and quaking in the heat like the nightmares of the crazed as they harvested heads and limbs from the gaudy throng. Among the soldiers lurked the shapes of the Maltese women, scattering sweat from the long hair dangling beneath their helms and brandishing short swords and pikes, and crawling along the line dragging tubs of gruel, and squatting to slay the Moslem wounded with their knives, like Viragos reincarnate from some bleak and ancient saga of retribution.

Somewhere within this hallucination fought Mattias too. There, on the Post of Castile, where sprays of blood arced hither and sizzled on plated armour like frying fat. Where wounded mauled wounded to a finish with bare hands and teeth, squirming one atop the other like mutant creatures mating in swill. Where men flapped wings of flame in a fiery epilepsis. Where the air clamoured with gun blasts and clashing steel and with screams of dying and screams of rage and with curses and entreaties and mad laughter. Where above the deafening lunacy of Holy War, the magisterial calm of Lazaro's choir swooped and soared. Where – Carla prayed – Mattias might yet live.

Havoc unconstrained was master of the field and Carla could make no sense of it, nor see with whom the battle's advantage lay. She followed with the rest as Lazaro conducted the ragtags up the wall stair. They filed along the ramparts to left and right, filling the allure to the Post of France and the Posts of Auvergne and Italy. Some retrieved arquebuses, powder and ball. Those with the means declined the stair and muddled into the fray where she saw them slain. The remainder breasted the crenels with their warcoats and let the implacable sun wink from their casques. They drew a hail of Turkish musket fire, and though many of them fell those still standing didn't flinch. If they could take a bullet meant for a man in the line, they would die justified.

Carla left the blind youth in his place and descended the stair. If she returned to the hospital, or went to find Amparo, no one would have stopped her. Yet the tumult called and she had to take part. She didn't want to kill; yet, perhaps for the first time, she had some inkling of the bewitchment cast by war. She saw a bucket by a butt of water and ran towards it.

THE MOURNFUL NOTES of the Moslem trumpets quavered through the smoke-dimmed gloaming and died. The vermilion decline of the sun cast doleful and elongate shadows on the Grande Terre Plein. The shadows were thrown by the dregs of the Turkish retreat as they trudged through the black and flyblown blood-dust like hobbled refugees from some conclave of the deranged. They dared not turn to look hinder. Left unclaimed behind them were vast moaning piles of abandoned and slain, which shifted and heaved like fantastic multilimbed beasts brought down by disease. Women clogged with gore from hair to skirts rooted through the charnel in the dying light, whispering vengeful maledictions and slitting throats. On the fractured ramparts above them no celebrants were found, but only human scarecrows yet too stunned to realise they were alive.

A chaplain rang the Angelus bell. It echoed across the desecration like the tocsin that will summon forth the guilty on the Last Day of Time. The haggard remnants of the garrison sank to their knees in the puddled gore. Scuds of acrid fog from the pools of wildfire drifted about them. They removed their helms and grounded them and made the sign of the Cross. And in that hushed and haunted penumbra of rank enormity their hoarsened voices took up the chant and refrain.

'*Angelus Domini, nuntiavit Mariae.*'

'*Et concepit de Spiritu Sancto.*'

'*Hail Mary, full of grace, the Lord is with thee.*
Blessed are thou amongst women, and blessed is the fruit of thy womb, Jesus.
Holy Mary, Mother of God, pray for us sinners,
Now and at the hour of our death.'

'*Behold the handmaid of the Lord.*'

'*Be it done unto me according to Thy word.*'

'*Ave Maria, gratia plena, Dominus tecum.*
Benedicta tu in mulieribus . . .'

Favouring his bad knee, Tannhauser leaned on his sword and genuflected beside Bors, more from exhaustion than piety, though he guessed he wasn't quite alone in that. Bors prayed with closed eyes and Tannhauser held his peace as the Angelus proceeded.

'*And the Word was made Flesh.*'

'*And dwelt among us.*'

Tannhauser murmured with the rest, '*Ave Maria, gratia plena, Dominus tecum. Benedicta tu in mulieribus, et benedictus fructus ventris tui, Iesus. Sancta Maria, Mater Dei, ora pro nobis peccatoribus, nunc, et in hora mortis nostrae.*'

'*Pray for us, O holy Mother of God.*'

'*That we may be made worthy of the promises of Christ.*'

The prayer brought him comfort and for a moment he was glad to belong to something larger than himself. Yet he reminded himself that there was no virtue in belonging to a row of corpses;

or to a community of the insane. His sojourn with the Religion was over. Tonight the Turks would sit by their watchfires and ponder without enquiry the inscrutability of Allah's Will. They'd see to their hurting compatriots as best they could. They'd eat and shun the darkness, as all men sorely dismayed are prone to do. And in that darkness would Tannhauser make his escape. The thought gave some sinew to his aching limbs. The Angelus concluded.

'*. . . Pour forth, we beseech Thee, O Lord, Thy grace into our hearts, that we to whom the Incarnation of Christ Thy Son was made known by the message of an angel, may by His Passion and Cross be brought to the glory of His Resurrection. Through the same Christ Our Lord.*'

'*Amen.*'

Bors opened his eyes and looked at him with a glazed bemusement, as if the rules of the Universe had changed in order to permit his continuing existence. He looked like he'd bathed in the run-off from a butcher's yard, but sported no mortal injuries. Tannhauser nodded.

Bors put a hand on Tannhauser's shoulder and levered his own armoured bulk to his feet. Then he took Tannhauser's hand and hoisted him upright. He looked up and down along the dire and smoking battlefront. A dazed air attended the survivors as they rose from their knees, as if with no more killing to be done they were denuded of purpose. Some looked about for officers, in search of instruction. Some stared mute into the wasteland as if waiting for night to rob them of what they could see. Others stayed on their knees and wept, though whether from shame or relief, Tannhauser could not say.

'By God,' said Bors. 'By God. If there are more than four hundred men left standing I'll devote myself to Islam, circumcision and all. Heaven help us if they come again tomorrow.'

Tannhauser looked over at the hills to the south, where the Banner of the Prophet still waved above his broken legions. In the purpling sky overhead a crescent moon shone, as if the Cosmos sought to mock the symbol of Osman. He turned away and shook his head.

'I don't think they will,' he said. 'Sooner or later, yes, but not tomorrow.'

'Why not? Look at them. They'd surely take the town by breakfast.'

'They interpret blows of Fate such as this one in a singular fashion. It's not just a defeat. It's a message from Allah. They won't throw it back in His face.' He peeled his gauntlets and strolled towards a water butt and Bors followed. 'Besides, by tomorrow we'll be long gone, with no more daunting a fear than of getting seasick.'

He shouldered his way through the crowd that had gathered at the butt and filled his helmet and emptied it over his head. His armour steamed. He'd shortly jettison the cursed plate for good and the thought cheered him. He made a note to find the time for a dip in his tub. He filled the helmet again and emptied several pints down his throat. It was warm enough to brew tea but it was wet. He handed the remnant to Bors, who drank too.

'You're still for the road?' asked Tannhauser.

Bors returned the helmet and wiped his lips. 'I never thought to say this, but I've had my fill. I'm with you in earnest.'

'Good. Say no farewells. We'll collect our gear and our women and be gone. The moon will be down by midnight and the Bull's horns point the way. But first some food for I'm famished.'

'There's a tub of slop yonder,' said Bors.

'Thank you, I will eat at the auberge.'

'If Nicodemus is alive and has claim to all his fingers.'

'If not,' said Tannhauser, 'you can cook.'

He glanced again at the slop tub and saw Carla. She was kneeling with her face in her hands, but it could be no other. She seemed unhurt. He hoped so. He hurried over and sank to his haunches beside her.

'Carla?'

She dropped her hands and looked up. Her face was smeared with grime. Her eyes were clear. Her hands were raw from the ropes. Tannhauser nodded at the tub.

'So this is a family occupation,' he said.

She glanced at the tub with bewilderment and his quip went unappreciated. Tears welled in her eyes. She said, 'You're alive.'

'I've too many obligations to die just yet.'

The tears spilled forth and she threw her arms round his neck. Pain lanced through his knee and he steadied himself on the tub to avoid collapse. He gritted his teeth and rose to his feet with her weight around his shoulder. He rubbed her back to comfort her. Her living flesh was such a rapture to his touch he almost shed a tear himself.

'There now,' he said, somewhat beflummoxed. 'We're all of us amazed by this day.'

She heaved out a few more sobs and he waited. He gestured with his head to Bors, who retreated to a discreet distance. Carla regained her composure and wiped the tears across the dirt on her cheeks. Tannhauser pulled the red silk scarf from the cheek flaps of his morion. He squeezed out the sweat and wiped her face. She raised no protest.

'I see you ignored my advice,' he said. 'As I've come to expect. Did you accompany the wounded to the ramparts?'

She nodded. 'Most of them are dead.'

'Then we're in their debt and all the more reason not to mope. Where's Amparo?'

'The last I saw her she was going to the stables, to see to Buraq.'

'Must I use shackles to keep you together?'

She managed a pale smile.

'I'll track her down,' he said. 'Meanwhile, Bors will return you to the auberge. We've a stiff walk ahead and you must recruit your strength.'

'We still leave tonight?'

On whim he said, 'Wear your red dress for the journey.'

She blinked and looked at him as if he'd asked her to go naked, which wasn't far from the case. To ameliorate the eccentricity of his request, he added, 'And a cloak against the chill of night, and some stout shoes, if you have them.' He took her hand and led her towards the town. 'I may not be worthy of the promises of Christ, but my promise to you and your son I've a mind to keep.'

SUNDAY
2 SEPTEMBER 1565

The Kalkara Gate – the Guva

THE EASTERN SECTION of the wall overlooking Kalkara Bay was the least vulnerable of the whole enceinte and the garrison was so depleted by the day that their route to freedom lay unguarded. The blockhouse was empty and boasted no sentinel. By dint of accepting sentry duty on the Bastion of England above, and then abandoning it, they ensured themselves a clear run at the hills. Midnight had passed – only a little later than Tannhauser had planned – and two hours' sleep had fortified the women and had given him the chance to advise La Valette of his expectations of the foe and thus diminish the chance of being summoned again before morning. Bors slipped into the chamber housing the winch and hoisted the iron portcullis aloft.

The stickiest aspect of their preparations had been persuading Amparo to abandon Buraq. Tannhauser had assured her that no living beast was safer. His manifest splendour and Mongol blood would ensure that no one of right mind would harm him, least of all the Turks, who would prize him far above any human being, Christian or Moslem. With a few last tearful hysterics, he'd prised Amparo loose and carried her back to the auberge. She evidenced little interest in his own sorely mauled condition; but he'd learned by now that the tenderness of women was a patchy, if not entirely random, phenomenon.

They now passed into the gatehouse beneath the portcullis and Bors winched it down behind them, Tannhauser propping it aloft with his rifle until Bors ducked underneath. When he pulled the rifle away, there was a rumble of cogs and counterweights and the spiked feet of the grill crashed into the stones. It seemed loud to them, but the sound wouldn't carry far. Closing the portcullis relieved them of securing the wicket once they were outside. They looked at each other: there was no going back.

'*Alea jacta est*,' whispered Bors.

This uncharacteristic flourish of classical learning provoked an anxious glance from Carla. She looked gaunt in the torchlight, but was making a firm fist of controlling her fear. Tannhauser gave her a nod of reassurance. Amparo, reconciled to Buraq's fate, might have been on a Sunday promenade. He raised the torch, which they'd need to solve the riddle of the wicket, and flaring iotas of naphtha and pitch drifted down towards the flags. The broad passageway glimmered towards the bloody angle, where intruders could be pinned beneath the murder hole in the roof. Tannhauser led them on.

Despite all the hazard and slaughter that had marked his career, and not least the bloody japes of the long day ended, Tannhauser couldn't recall when his heart had beaten so like a drum. He was surprised the others didn't hear it. He could think of no sound reason for this portent and so it vexed him all the more. He checked on Bors to see if his sixth sense was tickled, but he appeared unperturbed. As they passed beneath the murder hole he couldn't help sniffing for wildfire or oil, matchcords or men, but the passage above seemed deserted and the drumbeat eased. Apart from two goatskins of water and the satchels on Bors's back, which were crammed with opium and enough precious stones to ransom an emperor's son, they travelled light. Carla, as a concession to his request, carried her red dress in her poke, or so she assured him. Tannhauser, if no one else, had considered lugging the gambo violl, but had reluctantly left it behind. They reached the outer sally port. The Kalkara Gate stood before them.

Tannhauser held the torch and helped Bors dismantle the profusion of bolts and buttresses securing the wicket. They were half done when Tannhauser grabbed Bors's shoulder to stop him and cocked an ear down the passageway. The portcullis winch was well greased; they'd seen to it themselves that evening; but there was no doubt: he could hear the faint creak as it was cranked back open.

'Can you finish this in the dark?' said Tannhauser.

Bors took in the remaining bolts. 'Count on it,' he said, and set to.

There was a sentry's alcove built into one side of the sally ports. Without ceremony Tannhauser herded Carla and Amparo inside it and mimed sealing his lips. He turned and threw the torch. It flew in a guttering arc and landed in a fountain of sparks beneath the murder hole. He returned and took up his rifle and went down on one knee. With the pistol in his belt and Bors's long gun they had three rounds. He didn't relish shooting some poor watchman blundered in on them by chance; if the fellow kept his wits they could merely subdue him. Bolts clanked behind him. Bors grunted and the wicket creaked. A gust of brash sea air drifted in from the bay.

'It's done,' said Bors.

'Hold,' said Tannhauser.

He heard footsteps beyond the angle and saw the flicker of a second torch.

Nicodemus stepped into the light. He was unarmed.

Tannhauser lowered his rifle with relief. Nicodemus they could take with them. Perhaps they should have done so in the first place. Had he followed them or had someone told him of their flight? He looked at Bors, who cradled his gun in the shadows.

Bors shrugged, 'I said not a word.'

There was no point quizzing the women.

Nicodemus stopped by the torch. He peered into the gloom. 'Mattias?'

'Nicodemus,' said Tannhauser. He spoke in Turkish. 'What news?'

'You are betrayed,' said Nicodemus.

Tannhauser's bowels shifted. 'Not by you, I hope.'

'No.'

'Then who?'

'I don't know.'

'Why do we tarry?' said Bors, from the open wicket.

'Peace,' said Tannhauser. He turned back to Nicodemus. 'Explain.'

Nicodemus waved his torch towards the Kalkara Gate. 'There are men on the wall above the mantlet, with muskets and *humbaras*. You must surrender.'

The gesture must have been a signal, conveyed via someone at the portcullis to the blockhouse and thence to the outer wall above, for a moment later a fire pipkin exploded in the mantlet outside the wicket door. Bors cursed and ducked back inside. He shouldered the iron door closed against the flames.

'Surrender to whom?' asked Tannhauser.

Nicodemus said, 'Fra Ludovico.'

Tannhauser glanced at Carla in the alcove. Her eyes were wide with dread.

Bors unlimbered his satchels and let them drop. 'Ludovico? How many allies can he boast? Let's go and take them. Ten minutes and we're on our way.'

They heard more footsteps and Nicodemus turned to watch their approach. He was terrified. The steps stopped just short of the shallow turn in the wall. Ludovico's bass voice rolled down the passageway.

'If you choose to fight,' said Ludovico, 'the women will not be spared.'

'We'll surrender to Oliver Starkey or the Grand Master,' said Tannhauser. 'No one else.'

'The Grand Master is ignorant of your treachery,' replied Ludovico. 'For which fact you should be grateful. In his hands you would face the gallows.'

'And in yours?'

'A chance to keep the riches you've extorted and to earn the freedom you crave.'

'How so?' said Tannhauser.

'The Holy Office does not bargain. You stand in my power.'

Tannhauser sensed a gesture. The barrel of a musket protruded from the murder hole in the roof. Flame lanced from the bore with a deafening roar and Nicodemus was thrown to the flags with a shattered leg. He lay stunned with pain. The blood gouting from his wound hissed with a sudden pungent odour as it pooled around the fallen torches.

'The Greek had the chance to choose his friends wisely, and was foolish,' said Ludovico. 'I urge you to be more prudent.'

'Show your face, you filthy blackguard,' roared Bors.

Carla emerged from the alcove. She called down the passageway.

'Ludovico,' she said. 'Give me your word you will let them go, and I'll willingly stay here, with you.'

Tannhauser raised no objection. If Ludovico accepted, Tannhauser would be back before dawn to cut his throat; but the monk had no reason to do so.

'Do I hear no demurrer from the gallant bridegroom?' asked Ludovico.

'She wastes her breath but I will not,' Tannhauser replied. 'Give us leave to share counsel.'

'As you will, but hurry. Poor Nicodemus ails.'

Tannhauser looked at Bors and spoke in a low voice. 'Any fight is suicide. While we're alive, all things are possible.'

'And if the snake cuts us down?' growled Bors.

'If that was his purpose he'd have done so already. He has other uses for us, wherein lies our chance.'

Bors grimaced, the pink diagonal scar twisting in ire. 'After all this it would gall me to die in a torture chamber.'

'It's a poor time to ask you to trust me, I know,' said Tannhauser. 'But will you?'

Bors nodded. 'When did I not?'

Tannhauser took Carla's wrists and pulled her close. Her face was pale in the gloom.

'To find out what hand he holds, we must play ours one card at a time,' he said. 'But don't despair. If we have only one advantage, it's a singular one. Ludovico loves you.'

Carla blinked, uncertain of his meaning.

'Do not play false. Don't try to outwit him or to counter his intrigues and games. You'll lose. Simply be true to yourself, no matter what threats he flaunts against the rest of us, no matter how cruelly he may treat us.' He saw her heart quail and squeezed her wrists. 'The outcome depends on you, do you understand?'

Carla nodded, still uncertain, but he knew she would rise to circumstance.

He let go of her and turned to Amparo. Of the four of them, she was the least afraid. As during their night at Saint Elmo's by the light of the forge, he sensed that the violence she'd suffered in her youth – whatever it was – had been so terrible that she'd been left immune to its threat. Her liquid eyes looked up into his and, as before, he had the sense that she saw only him, and not what he represented, or what he might appear to be, or what the world imagined that he was. And he knew that no one else would ever look at him so, and that he'd never know such love again, and that she was the woman of his life and that he'd not dared know it. He took her in his arms in a tight embrace, for he knew she'd need the memory of its comfort.

'Amparo,' he said, 'they will use you as their bluntest weapon.' Carla made a muffled sound of dismay. He ignored it. The next words caught in his craw, for none could have shamed him more. 'And I cannot protect you. Tell me you will endure.'

She looked into his eyes for a moment, and even in the shadows her own were bright and clear, and full of an infinite love that he didn't deserve.

Amparo said, 'The nightingale is happy.'

His throat constricted and he stifled a surge of emotion that rose from he knew not where. He kissed her on the lips and she melted against him. Then he let her go and turned at once away, lest he lose his resolve and draw his sword and charge down the passage to doom them all. He called out to Ludovico, hoping his voice was steady.

'We'll surrender our weapons in the blockhouse, not before.'

'Very well,' Ludovico agreed.

Tannhauser looked to his companions. 'Courage,' he said.

THEY STARTED DOWN the corridor and they covered the murder hole with their guns while the omen passed by. Ludovico was gone. They hauled Nicodemus to his feet between them, the youth's head lolling in a faint, and carried him through the portcullis and into the blockhouse.

From oilettes on the three external sides of the roofless structure, five arquebus muzzles pointed at them. If massacre was to occur it would be here, but better than in the dark passage, for at least they could see the stars as they passed on. But the villains held their fire. Tannhauser and Bors laid their guns and blades on the floor. Nicodemus came to from his faint and Bors took his arm across his shoulders. They walked back into the town they'd so recently vacated.

Ludovico and his cohort of familiars circled them about. The monk was in the robes of the Religion and, true to the grandiose madness that lurked in his eyes, he was unarmed. To the shame of their Order, three half-armoured knights flanked him. One was Bruno Marra, of whom Tannhauser was distantly aware; the second also looked to be of the Italian Langue. The third was Escobar de Corro, whom Tannhauser had crossed on Gallows Point.

Of the remaining four, two were gentlemen adventurers from Messina, Tasso and Ponti; one was a Spanish *tercio* named Remigio; and the last was Ludovico's factotum, Anacleto.

Anacleto's gaze was fixed on Amparo and Tannhauser's blood ran cold, and again he suppressed the rage that would have killed the one-eyed bastard on the spot. He thought to ask who'd betrayed them; but it would serve no purpose here. The monk would no doubt let him know in good time. From his pocket Tannhauser took the letter that Starkey had provided weeks before, and which he'd preserved in the auberge for such a moment as this. With a flourish that belied his lack of faith in its utility, he held it out towards Ludovico.

'This is our *passe porte* to Mdina, authorised by Brother Starkey. It proves we are no deserters.'

Ludovico took the letter. Without breaking the seal he passed it to Anacleto. 'I will give it close study in due course,' said Ludovico.

'Do you place yourself beyond the Grand Master's authority?' said Carla.

Ludovico looked at her and bowed his head. 'In the affairs of the Inquisition, the Grand Master has no authority.'

Tannhauser gave Carla a glance, for this was futile, but she ignored him. Her lips were pale and her scorn was unrestrained. Tannhauser looked at her with new eyes. He'd not known her capable of such anger.

'Then tell me,' she said, 'are we arrested as deserters or as heretics? Or will you admit that any treachery here belongs to you alone?'

Ludovico said, 'These matters too will be addressed in their right time and place. For now it would be better if no more is said.'

Carla seemed about to defy him further.

Tannhauser said, 'Carla.'

Carla looked at him and bit her tongue. Ludovico inclined his head to Escobar de Corro, who prodded Tannhauser aside from the rest. Tannhauser found himself surrounded by the three knights. He exchanged a look with Bors to calm him. Nicodemus had passed out again and the Spaniard, Remigio, took his other arm. The two Italian adventurers, who'd collected the surrendered firearms, corralled Carla and Amparo together. Ludovico motioned to Anacleto, who led the entourage down the street.

Escobar de Corro pushed Tannhauser in the opposite direction.

Amparo looked back at him and stopped. She broke away to run towards him.

Anacleto grabbed her wrist and dragged her back, and Amparo stumbled, and whatever rage Carla contained exploded. She slapped Anacleto hard across his mutilated face. He reeled back with a cry, and Bors looked at Tannhauser, urging him to give the signal to go. Tannhauser shook his head. Anacleto's mouth twisted in agony. He started to draw his sword and he took a step towards Carla and Tannhauser shouldered Bruno Marra, shoving him aside. As he did so he palmed a dagger from the knight's belt and started forward.

'Anacleto!'

Ludovico's voice, always so even, stunned Anacleto with its force. Anacleto froze, staring at Carla with murder in his eye. Tannhauser stopped too, but close enough to take Anacleto down if needs be. Anacleto returned the sword to its sheath. Amparo, mute with shock at what she'd almost unleashed, grasped Carla's hand. Ludovico looked at Tannhauser, at the knife in his hand. Tannhauser was close enough to kill him. He gave it some thought.

Ludovico's voice levelled again. 'What will it be, Captain?'

Tannhauser said, 'Where are you taking them?'

'They'll be held under my jurisdiction at the Courts of Law. You need not fear for their wellbeing.'

'And your dogs – can you control them?'

'You have my word.'

'Ludovico, please,' said Carla. 'Let Mattias keep our company.'

'I will come,' said Tannhauser, fearing more ado. 'Be strong and don't lose heart.'

Tannhauser turned to Ludovico. 'Where do these villains take me?'

'A man like you can't abandon Hell without sounding its nethermost circle.'

'That would be a pity,' Tannhauser agreed. The monk's face was inscrutable. Yet somewhere behind it lay a purpose. Tannhauser said, 'And there you and I will meet?'

Ludovico nodded. 'And there we will meet.'

'Good enough.' Tannhauser tossed the dagger at Marra without looking at him.

Then he turned his back on Ludovico and walked away.

The three knights escorted Tannhauser through the broken heart of the town. The younger knight, when asked, gave his name as Pandolfo of Siena, and earned a glare from Escobar de Corro for the courtesy. In the exhausted aftermath of the battle, and with the population so generally reduced, the town had never been so quiet. Squeaking swarms of rats, heedless of their feet, disturbed the tranquillity of their passage, but nothing else. Apart from a hollow-eyed mother, watching over her children in the ruins, they met no other humans. Had Tannhauser been alone in this misfortune the walk would have afforded opportunity to escape, for the trio too were exhausted and therefore careless. He could have butchered all three with their own weapons within a quarter of a mile. Would La Valette have backed him? He thought not. Killing brethren would unlikely endear him and the inquisitor's behaviour, legally speaking, was impeccable. Sense dictated he submit to events and wait.

They reached the bridge lately destroyed and which had formerly crossed the moat, and where the canal and waterfront both were wholly deserted. A crewless barge sat waiting. They climbed aboard and the knights punted Tannhauser across the still black water to Castel Sant' Angelo.

The water slid by and he dipped his hand and his cuts stung sharp in the brine. Pandolfo and Marra on the poles he could've pitched into the drink in a trice, where their armour would have seen them drowned. De Corro he could take by hand. He contained himself to the fantasy alone. The barge docked and they disembarked.

By torchlight they led him through the dark and abandoned precincts of the castle. Emptied of all pomp and hurly-burly, the fortress felt like a monumental tomb. They traversed a maze of hallways that sucked the sound of their footfalls into an oblivion brute and huge and shorn of echo, as if their destination were nowhere and none would reach it. Peculiar whispers, ambiguous and occult, rustled beyond the limit of their torches, and Marra and Pandolfo exchanged glances rank with fear. Tannhauser quelled his own fear, for it was useless. They descended a stair, and then another, and a third, and again Tannhauser fancied loping off into the uttermost blackness, then tracking them down and murdering them in these catacombs without name. He realised that wherever they were taking him a darkness without equal would form his world, and he resolved to make it his own, for if he didn't it would devour him. They reached a wide door studded with iron and a key was produced and the door was opened and he walked ahead of them, unprompted, into the gloom.

The air was dank and cool and redolent of urine and desiccated shit, as one would expect of a dungeon as deep and dreadful as this one was. Inside the door, de Corro told him to strip his clothes and he complied without a qualm. As he did so he palmed his last three Stones of Immortality. He stood there nude as an egg in the flicker of the flames. He did not remove his lion's head bangle and he looked at his gaolers and they let that be. He could see that his calm unnerved the two Italians, and fanned de Corro's hatred, and since it came at no great cost he gave the latter a smile.

By gesture they provoked him deeper into that subterranean cave, until a stark black hole gaped before him in the floor. They stopped, and his gaolers held out their torches so he might examine it in the flames.

The hole was nine feet across and eleven feet deep. It was in the shape of an inverted bell, carved from the base rock of the island on which Castel Sant' Angelo was built. The smooth perfection of its symmetry and the flawless circularity of its maw won Tannhauser's amazement. Not even the largest and most athletic of men could get out of this pit unaided. And in this geometric punctiliousness lay the source of its power to terrify. Tannhauser might almost have applauded, for it was, without doubt, the most exquisite prison in Creation. It could only have been conceived and built by the Religion.

Then in the flickering yellow light he saw that its integrity had been blemished in its lower reaches by a screed of markings, as primitive in execution as those left in caves by the vanquished races. The bald walls below were gouged by . . . he knew not what. Rings, fingernails, bones or teeth, perhaps. The carvings were scattered in confusion random and wild, as if authored by a blind man gone insane: numerous crosses, often eccentric in dimension; the words 'Iesus' and 'God' and 'mercy' in various tongues; scratches to mark the days, yet too higgledy-piggledy to serve; representations of tombstones; most artful of all, a portrait of a gallows, complete with a dangling man. They were the last marks left upon this world by the pit's former occupants.

De Corro looked at Tannhauser, and Tannhauser looked at him.

'This is the Guva,' said Escobar de Corro. 'It is the dungeon reserved for false and wicked knights. Once delivered into its keeping, the only destination hence is the place of execution.'

Tannhauser spat in his face.

So shocked was de Corro by this insult that he reeled back and lost his footing and almost tumbled into the pit. Had he done so, Tannhauser's restraint would have been in vain, and Pandolfo and Marra would have had to die right there. With a determination that could only be rooted in the strictest possible orders from one they feared, Marra and Pandolfo restrained the trembling Castilian from hacking Tannhauser apart. All then was fair and proper: for if it was Ludovico who forestalled their rage, and it could be no other, then it was this proof – that Ludovico wanted him alive – that prevented Tannhauser from slaying them.

'Next time we meet,' said de Corro, 'it will be to the death.'

Marra dropped a goatskin of water over the edge and de Corro moved to push Tannhauser after it. Tannhauser denied him the satisfaction. He vaulted into the pit of his own accord, one hand clasping its edge to gentle his fall. He landed without fresh injury, sliding on to his arse in the pit's nadir. Tannhauser stood up and looked at the wall and he saw once more by the evanescing flames the gallows carved therein. The torches retreated from the rim of his desolate habitat and with them the light.

Tannhauser resolved to be cheerful.

And for a while, at least, he had the means. He popped a Stone of Immortality under his tongue. He moulded the other two pills into cones and crammed them into his ear holes to keep them safe and at hand. The bitter flavours of opium and citrus and gold filled his mouth. The bitterness reassured him, he knew not why. Then the door to the Guva crashed shut and darkness absolute descended and with it an enormous silence that was scarcely less profound.

PART V

BLOOD-RED ROSES

THURSDAY 6 SEPTEMBER 1565

The Courts of Law – the Oubliette

Ludovico sat on the Grand inquisitor's throne, in the tribunal chamber of the Courts of Law. Here were souls cleansed and the temporal fates of guilty and innocent alike determined and fixed. The beauty of Law lay in its purity, its clarity of instruction and purpose, its absolute exclusion of feeling. Within its halls all confusion and doubt were vanquished in favour of Decision, right or wrong. And as long as that purity, that process, was honoured, any error in regard to Justice was the province of eternity. Yet what Law could root out his own doubt, his own confusion and guilt?

He was alone. Shafts of light from the south-facing windows fell on the empty benches and bounced in random flares from the varnished oak. Dust milled through the yellow beams, disturbed by the draught from the shot hole in one wall. Here, in the seat of power, he brooded on his powerlessness. His body ached from wounds. His heart ached from wounds more obscure and less readily healed and more heavily borne. Carla's face, her eyes, haunted him. Were the theories of Appollonides true? Had those eyes bewitched him? Should he relax her to the flames and have done? Certainly no poison or ague could make him suffer so evil a malaise. He had neither counsellor nor confessor. In this he was friendless. The only one whose wisdom, he sensed, might best guide him was confined to the darkest pit in Christendom. If there was such a thing as a Guva of the mind, Ludovico was immured within it.

The staff of the Courts of Law had been either evacuated or conscripted, and its precincts were Ludovico's to do with as he pleased. He'd kept his prisoners segregated, each woman in a more or less comfortable room; the grotesque English brute in a basement dungeon. He'd seen none of them since their arrest. In the whirlwind of debate that consumed his mind there remained an eye of tranquillity. It contained two words. Patience and Time. He had waited weeks. He had waited years. A few days more he could endure.

The Turks had maintained an attrition of musket fire, bombardment, mining and sluggish raids. After the great repulse of the 2nd a mood of low-grade despair had settled over the city, as another famous victory became just another reprieve won at tragic cost. The question in the minds of the high command was: *Where was Garcia de Toledo?* The promised relief force was over two months late. Where were the knights from the far-flung priories of the Order, who must have gathered in Sicily throughout the summer? Was the Viceroy really content to let Malta fall?

Since the Grand Master's pleas had had little evident effect, Ludovico had sent his own Maltese messenger, a cousin of Gullu Cakie, to Messina some weeks before. He carried two letters to a trusted familiar in the high Sicilian nobility. One letter was to be opened only in the event that Malta fell without Toledo's aid. It contained material and instructions that would ensure the Viceroy's downfall and disgrace. The second was delivered to Toledo in person.

This letter was prefaced by an account of the sufferings endured by the besieged, the valour of the Christian defenders and the heroic death, in the fight for the first siege tower, of Toledo's own son, Federico. Only the direct intervention of Divine Will could justify their survival to date, for it defied all human and military explanation. If Toledo intended to set himself against that Will, his eternal destiny would be a matter for God to decide. In the temporal realm, however, there were those, such as Michele Ghisleri, who would feel obliged to honour the dead by chastising those who had so dishonourably failed them. It would be a very great sadness if a soldier of Toledo's reputation were to end his days as the basest coward in Europe.

Threatening a Spanish Viceroy was unexampled, but Ludovico knew Toledo. The letter would inspire a fury awesome to contemplate; and fury would provoke him into action.

Despite Ludovico's faith in Providence and his own diplomatic ploys, there was yet no sign of reprieve. Until there was, he did not dare execute the final stroke that his intrigue required. More than ever the Grand Master's leadership was vital to the garrison's spirit. The miracle required to withstand the next Turkish assault would, as had the last, hinge on La Valette's person. When the relief landed, Ludovico would advance his cause. If it did not, he'd die with the rest. Death caused him no great anxiety. If he feared Death at all, it was because it would deny him the consummation with Carla that he craved. Thither did his mind turn yet again. Her proximity troubled him. She was here, waiting, in this very building. Waiting for his visit, as were they all, for on his appearance hinged their futures. Yet he didn't know what to say to her. He didn't know how to bend her to his will. All others, always, yes; but not her. And if he could not bend her, how could he cut her from his brain?

Anacleto entered the chamber. A scabbed mass distorted his eye socket and cheek: the purulence had resolved but not yet the pain. The deformity to his beauty never would. The sight filled Ludovico with pity. Tannhauser's English brute, Bors, had fired the bullet. The man had boasted as much as they'd thrown him in the cell. Anacleto walked towards the throne. His gait was odd: not unsteady, yet less nimble than usual. He bowed.

'The English screams your name,' said Anacleto. 'He's banging the door of his cell, the turnkey says with his head. His own head.'

'He's emptied the keg already?'

Anacleto shrugged. 'It seems so.'

'Let him bang. What news of the women?'

'All is quiet.'

Anacleto's single eye focused on him. It oscillated minutely from side to side, as if unhinged by the loss of its fellow. The pupil was tiny. Opium. Hence his gait. Yet there was something else amiss.

'What more?' asked Ludovico. 'Tell me what troubles you?'

Anacleto shook his head. 'Nothing.'

'The pain?' said Ludovico.

Anacleto didn't answer. Tolerance of pain was a matter of honour.

'You have enough opium?' asked Ludovico. Tannhauser's packs had been crammed with slabs of the stuff. And with gunnysacks stuffed with jewels. Anacleto nodded.

'The relief will come.' Ludovico took his arm. 'I believe it. So should you. The war will soon be over. Our work is almost done. There will be less of horror and, by God's grace, our lives will change.'

'Life will always change,' said Anacleto. 'And of horror there is always an abundance. Why would I wish it otherwise?'

'You were lost when I found you,' said Ludovico. 'In some ways you are lost still. Let me be your guide.'

Anacleto took his hand and kissed it. 'Always,' he said.

'Good,' said Ludovico, but his mind was already elsewhere. A revelation so bright he'd been blind to it. The boy lost. His own boy.

'I will see the English after all,' he said. 'Have him taken to the *oubliette* and restrained.'

Bors did not dare open his eyes, for they'd left it on a stool right in front of him, and of that fell vision he could take no more. God had abandoned him. And why not? He was the bad thief. He too would have taunted Christ to call down His Father's vengeance on the rabble. It had taken only four of them to drag him from one cell to another and chain him to this wall, and only two had been carried out insensible; hopefully dead. Thus had his strength abandoned him too. Was that any surprise? Gallons of brandy he'd poured down his throat. Gallons. Gallons of poisoned brandy. And worse than poisoned. Defiled. Polluted. A decoction of evil, the squeezed juice of madness. He retched but there was nothing left in his stomach. His beard and chest hair were matted with old puke. Nothing could cleanse his blood now. Or his brain. Nothing short of death, and that they would not allow him. Not yet. He felt the tendrils of insanity growing inside his skull, strangling his reason, cracking the container of his fears and undermining the walls of his courage. All was lost. But what of it? Losing had never broken him before. Nor hardship nor poverty nor pain. Bring on pain. Bring on the hot irons and the lash. Rope him to the rack and heave away. He craved pain. At least it would fill his mind with something he could embrace, something he understood and knew, something more tolerable than this crawling venom in his veins, his gut, his spine. Something to uproot these weeds of delirium. He'd never greatly warmed to the Jew, it was true. But he'd admired him, had stood by him, had never shied from admitting their association. And woe betide any man who whispered an insult within his earshot. Even so. An act of madness to sow madness. There was blood in his mouth for he'd bitten off the turnkey's nose. Human flesh he could stomach; it was a bite he'd enjoyed before, a time or two. But this? This – this what? Was it a phantasm born of liquor and the evil of his heart? He opened his eyes. And there it was. Pale and wrinkled as a maggot. The hair curled into obscene clumps and spikes. The dead eyes gelid and opaque. And it was no phantasm. He'd felt its monstrous weight with his own hands. They'd brought it all the way from Messina. Imagine. Shipped it across the sea, and lugged it through the Turkish lines and stored it, through the grimmest siege in the books, for just such a moment as this. A moment such as he'd now inherited and somehow deserved. He closed his eyes.

The lock rattled in the door and a bolt was thrown back. He retched again. He spat bile.

He heard Ludovico's voice. 'Take it away.'

Tasso, the Sicilian *bravo*, shuffled in. He walked half-bent, his arm wrapped round his side. Bors had fed a fist into his liver and had felt the ribs crackle like burnt pork. Tasso balked before the stool, halted by revulsion. All that was left to Bors was his bestiality. He lunged to the limit of the chain around his neck and roared, and though the chain held Bors well short, Tasso reeled back in terror and Bors laughed at him, and at himself and at his fate, and at the puckered and pickled head of Sabato Svi, which sat before him on the stool.

There was a comfort in madness too. An annulment. A soaring as on wings of eagles.

They'd left him in the dungeon with a box of candles and a spiled keg on the sleeping bench, and for a night and a day he'd stared at that keg, for though he was no fox, as was Mattias, he knew there had to be some object behind these particulars. He'd finally turned the spigot and discovered the brandy inside. And object and particulars be damned in the light of such joy. He'd drunk himself blind while hours and days without reckoning slipped him by, and he'd dozed through reveries long, of glory and comradeship and blood, and had drunk again, and had plunged, as a man decided on drunkenness will, into an oblivion reckless and without imaginable end, until that end had come, and like a mother's teat the spigot at the last had given no more, and the keg sat empty as his belly and his soul. And yet not empty, for as he'd raised the keg above his mouth, and tilted it to liberate the dregs, something had shifted inside. Something solid and substantial, that bumped against the wood like a seed in a gourd, which in his blurred mind he recalled was the sound of folly. He'd set the keg down, with a sickness in his gut, and let it be. But curiosity is a torment as keen as any and it bested him. He'd smashed the keg apart upon the flagstones, and from inside rolled the head of Sabato Svi. Severed at the neck and pickled like an onion in the brandy. And with that all his notions of what was vile had been dwarfed, and his own cruelty humbled, and the thread that connected his mind to his soul had snapped, and with that he had howled to a God he no longer had faith in.

Tasso found a lice-raddled blanket on the floor and netted the severed head inside it and disappeared, with Bors still laughing all the while. Then Ludovico walked in, and Bors's laughter stopped. The monk halted and looked at the floor at Bors's feet, as if noticing something striking for the first time. Bors followed his gaze. A trap door was set into the flagstones. In the wood was set a hoop and an inch-thick bolt.

'Do you speak French?' asked Ludovico.

Bors didn't answer.

'This is an *oubliette*,' said Ludovico. 'It's a place where one is forgotten.'

Ludovico stooped and threw the bolt and lifted the door by its hoop. A foul miasma gusted forth and Bors grimaced and looked down. Beyond the trap door's maw was a space as cramped as a coffin. Inside lay Nicodemus. His face was the colour of a jellyfish. Wormlike grubs crawled over his half-closed eyes and his motionless lips.

Bors's throat convulsed with rage and sorrow. No more rounds of backgammon. No more custard tarts, the most delicious he'd ever eaten. Bors closed his eyes. His mind reeled with sudden vertigo. He leaned back against the wall. The urge to vomit assailed him afresh. He swallowed. He clung to the thought of Mattias. *Hold on to the rage and sorrow both*, he heard him counsel, *for while we breathe, we may yet prevail.*

Ludovico let the trap door fall and sat down on the stool without a qualm and rested his hands on his thighs, and it was strange, for Bors didn't fear him, nor anything else Ludovico might do, for somehow, in pickling the head of a man he had not liked but whose side he had taken – in pickling the head of Sabato Svi, the Jew – Ludovico had done all that he might, and so much more.

'Bors of Carlisle,' said Ludovico, as cordial as you please. 'So tell me, where is Carlisle?'

And Bors thought: *Forgive me, Mattias, my friend, for this is a game I cannot win.*

A CRONE BROUGHT her food and wine while Anacleto lingered at the door, but neither had responded to her questions. When Ludovico finally came to visit her, Carla found that a primitive gratitude for company overwhelmed all other sentiments. She turned away from him to conceal it. She despised her weakness. She despised him for knowing that such would be her reaction. She turned back to face him. His eye sockets receded into his skull as if into endless night and they returned no light from the window high in the wall. Yet their shadows did not conceal the torment therein. In some ways he looked like the man she had once fallen in love with. In others he was quite unknown to her.

'Where is Amparo?' she said.

'Nearby,' Ludovico replied. 'The comforts you've enjoyed, though mean, are better than most in this city. Amparo enjoys the same. You seem in good health. I'm assured that so is she.'

'You've seen her?'

'No.'

'I wish to see her.'

'Soon,' he said.

'At once,' said Carla.

'May I sit down?'

He advanced into the room. It was furnished with a bed and two chairs and was otherwise bare. Its original function she hadn't been able to deduce. He limped, though it was no attempt to win her sympathy. Her request would not be met, she knew. She remembered Mattias's advice not to cross swords with the inquisitor. She nodded and Ludovico sat down.

'I regret these circumstances,' said Ludovico. 'But you must understand that I'm committed to a certain course and will not be swayed. Some aspects of my design concern you, others do not.'

'And Tannhauser?'

'His quarters are less opulent, but he's not been ill-treated. Your companions can survive this ordeal unscathed. In part that depends upon them, in part upon you.'

'So you've come with threats against the lives of those I love.'

'I've come to illuminate the nature of things as they are. How they will be is contingent on the role we each play.'

'Is the role required of me still that of your lover? Your wife?'

'I've prayed upon this matter, as I'm sure you have too.'

She let silence stand as her reply.

He said, 'I believe it's God's Will that we be joined. I believe it always was.'

'You presume to speak for God, as do many who are wedded to evil. I'd rather you spoke for your own will and desire.'

'I desire your happiness. I know you regard me with loathing, at this moment, and view my proposal with revulsion. But in time you will appreciate that your happiness is indivisible from mine.'

'So you presume to speak for me too.'

'Scorn ill becomes you and will profit no one.'

Anger crushed her chest like a heavy stone. 'Scorn?'

Ludovico blinked.

'Can you imagine how much I despise you?'

'I have tried,' he said. 'And failed. But there is another face to that coin. You cannot imagine what torment your presence has inflicted upon me.'

'You accuse me of tormenting you?'

'I merely state a fact. I didn't ask you to return to Malta. I tried to prevent it.'

A too-familiar guilt twisted inside her. She'd brought disaster in her train.

'I've sought to rid myself of this malaise,' said Ludovico. 'I've mortified the flesh. I've contemplated acts so atrocious they would place me forever beyond redemption in your eyes. In that result, at least, there would be a resolution, and some kind of peace.'

Fear uncoiled in her belly. On this matter of atrocious acts she didn't doubt his word.

He said, 'If I've refrained from committing them, it was out of horror at inflicting further grief, on you.'

A shudder ran through her. She clenched her shoulders to suppress another.

He stood and pulled the second chair closer to his own. 'Come, sit down, please.'

She walked to the second chair and sat down. He returned to his seat. He sat for a moment with his elbows on his thighs and his fingers laced into a fist and his head held down. His knuckles turned white. She took a deep breath. He looked up at her. The deep-seated eyes were like tunnels bored into something abominable beyond.

'I've asked myself,' he said, 'how do I win back the affection of a woman I've injured so gravely, and in such a multiplicity of ways? A woman whose pride I have trampled. Whose liberty I have stolen. Whose most beloved friends I have consigned to darkness and chains.'

Carla felt tears rise in her throat. She swallowed.

'To these questions I've found no answers,' he said. 'For I am chained in a darkness thicker than any. If I've cut the knot of many riddles, and unravelled many more, this one is beyond my genius, for its most tangled threads are those of my own emotions. Their strength exceeds all ligatures and compulsions. War and its rapture have drawn them even tighter. Anger, pity and lust have throttled me each in turn. Love has suffocated me, so that I've woken in the night and believed that my last hour was come. Aye, and as oft as not wished that it were so. But it was not so. Even on the field of battle, even when your German fired an assassin's bullet in my back, death eluded me. And so things are not as I might wish them, but as they are. Thus I come to throw myself upon your compassion.'

Carla looked away from his eyes to find her own thoughts. She had prayed, yes. Mattias had told her to be true to herself, no matter what the cost. She'd wrestled with that conundrum night and day, for what did it mean? That under no circumstance was she to submit to Ludovico's demands? That all were to be consumed on the pyre of her honour – and in a world that reeked already of sacrifice and death? She'd decided that it did not mean that, but that that was only one choice among many, and that Mattias, as always, had meant only what he said: that she should be true to her highest conception of herself, not to some conception held by others. She looked back at Ludovico.

'Can you not let us live our lives and find your consolation in God?'

'Did you find such consolation?'

'Yes,' she said. 'I did.'

'And yet you came back to Malta.'

'Despite your accusations, I didn't come back to cause you harm.'

'Even so.'

'You haven't answered me.'

He said, 'You haven't slept with Tannhauser. Yet.'

How did he know this?

Ludovico nodded. 'There's little I don't know. There's less that I won't do. I will not leave you to the German, even though I be damned for it. My sin is already mortal. I cannot root it out. God sees the truth in my heart, and my lack of contrition. And so, if I must, I'll be damned for my deeds rather than my thoughts.'

If she'd ever doubted his resoluteness, she did so no longer.

He said, 'Hear me, Carla. Abhorrence, though it stalks me, need not find its prey. What we once had can never die. Resurrection is the heart of our Faith, and so is Love, and the one is at the heart of the other. I love you. More than I love God. Together we'll find peace. Amparo will remain your companion. We will be reunited with our child. And, in time, you will rediscover the tenderness you felt for me before.'

'Our child?' she said.

'Orlandu is in the entourage of Abbas bin Murad, Aga of the Yellow Banners. When the relief arrives from Sicily, and the Turk is thrown into confusion, my knights and I will pluck Orlandu from their grasp.'

'So you seek to steal Tannhauser's part in more ways than one.'

He flinched. 'I'll not let my son be shipped to Constantinople and turned into an infidel. I would rather he perished before he thus lost his soul.'

This last she didn't want to dwell on. She said, 'The relief is on its way?'

'When Toledo's army arrives, you and I will go to Mdina. From there I will join the relief and effect Orlandu's rescue.'

'And Mattias?'

'I will free him to rejoin the Turks and among them he will prosper and thrive. He will forget you, as you will forget him. And unless you give me reason to do so, I will bear him no more injury or malice. His life then – like Amparo's – is in your hands.'

He stood up.

'You have my answer,' he said. 'Now give me yours, for I won't come to ask you again.'

Carla stood up too. She'd made her decision. She'd made it before he'd entered the room, for his demands in general terms were hardly unforeseen.

'If my surrender spares Mattias and Amparo, it's a price I will pay free and full, and glad to do so.'

Ludovico took a breath.

'When the relief arrives,' she said, 'we will go to Mdina. And all shall be as you wish it.'

SATURDAY 8 SEPTEMBER 1565

The Courts of Law

HE'D VISITED SEVERAL times a day for more days than she'd counted, and each time he stripped his breeches and splayed her legs and raped her on the mattress. The rapes were brutal and prolonged, for Anacleto struggled to climax and seemed to hold this against her. He was possessed by something she knew was evil, something which gave his single eye a peculiar light. His half-face gasped and contorted above hers, his breath sour, his fingers hard and full of rage. When at last he exploded inside her, he cried out, '*Filomena.*' Then he would crawl from on top of her, as if extricating himself from a hill of dung, and he would dress with his back turned to her and leave. The mysterious name was the only word he uttered.

Amparo bore these assaults as she'd borne others far in her past. Tannhauser had told her to endure and that was all the strength she needed. She'd been prepared for worse. She'd known worse. Anacleto was of unremarkable dimensions. When she heard him at the door she would spit on her fingers and moisten her parts. She closed her eyes and submitted. She squeezed the comb of ivory and silver in her hand until her palm bled. And while Anacleto thrashed between her thighs, she thought of

Tannhauser, her blood-red rose. Though his thorns had pierced her heart, he had made her sing. And how she'd sung. And how she sang still. Teeth clenched tight, Amparo made not a sound. Yet in that Realm within her which was wider and more intricate than the mighty Cosmos without, and over which nothing held sway except her soul, she sang with Love. She sang. She sang. She sang. After Anacleto left, his seed leaked out between her legs and this humiliation upset her more than the pain in her belly and the bruises on her arms. But as she washed she reminded herself that Tannhauser would come.

He would come and take her away. And she would sing for him.

In between the rapes she lay naked on the bed and retreated into herself and far away. The Sicilian crone brought her food. The same dried out and spider-fingered hag who had haunted the stables for weeks. She looked at Amparo with disgust, her rheumy gaze as possessed in its way as Anacleto's. She would mutter beneath her breath and spit with words that sounded like curses. She gave her the evil eye. Then the key would twist in the lock and the crone would be gone.

Amparo ate little. In the days she waited for the light from the high window to fade, for Anacleto never came in the dark. In the nights she watched stars maunder across the tiny patch of sky that she could see. She thought little of her ordeal. Cruelty was part of Nature, like a winter frost; something to be survived and then forgotten. She didn't let it reach her inmost heart. She thought of Nicodemus and Bors, who'd befriended her and cared for her for no reason she could imagine. She thought of Carla and the last – horrifying – image revealed in her shew stone: of the woman hanged, in the red silk dress. And she thought again of Tannhauser, who had made her feel so beautiful when no one else ever had. She brushed her hair with the ivory comb. She watched the play of light on its silver arabesques. She relived their hours together. She conjured the feel of his skin and the blue of his eyes and the sound of his voice. She smiled at the memory of his tomfoolery. She thought of the tale he'd told her, of the nightingale and the rose.

She cried.

She started in the mortuary darkness before dawn as the door to her prison creaked open. A lamp illuminated Anacleto's face. Her stomach turned with nausea. She prepared herself. She turned to face him so he would not twist her by her arms. Anacleto raised his hand. He held a length of dark fabric. It shimmered like something alive where the lamplight caught it. It possessed an unmistakable gorgeousness. And it was red. It was Carla's dress.

Carla's beautiful red dress.

Amparo's mouth went dry and for the first time she felt terror.

Anacleto threw it at her.

The dress landed on her thighs and slithered over her skin. She knew the dress signalled her end, yet its touch was lovely. She looked at Anacleto. The rope she expected to find in his hand wasn't there; but in his face was a black, childish fury that she hadn't seen before. A fury instilled by some other but directed at her. Anacleto pointed to the dress in her lap.

Amparo shook her head.

'Wear it,' he said.

Amparo squeezed on her ivory comb. Its teeth dug into her palm.

'No,' said Amparo. 'Never.'

SATURDAY 8 SEPTEMBER 1565

The Guva

Silence. Darkness. Stone.

Time without days. Time without nights.

Without sun. Without stars. Without wind.

A purity of absence designed to strike despair into the dishonoured.

Those ignominious wretches who had suffered the unscalable geometry of the Guva had withered for want of hope. Like the knotted tails of rat kings, the contents of their brains had tangled and drawn tight. Like castaways driven to feast on human flesh, their thoughts and nightmares and fears had consumed their minds.

Not so the brain or thoughts of Mattias Tannhauser.

Of the Guva's many occupants, Tannhauser was the first to enjoy his dark sojourn.

Suffused by a heady elixir decocted from exhaustion, solitude, opium and peace, he wandered through far-flung dreams, where faces smiled and wine flowed in rivers from the rocks, and where all women were comely and all men mild, and where many a strange beast prowled without offering harm. The relief from battle, from the clamour of war, from the anxious burden of companions – from the need to ponder, determine and act at the turbulent core of Chaos – was as profound a tonic as the drug. He pissed often, and in small quantities, distributing his urine around the inverted cone's surface where it would dry rather than puddle at his feet. He pitched his infrequent stool into the void beyond the rim. He braced his hands and feet against the curved interior for hours, and strengthened and refurbished his sinews. He dwelt upon the mysteries of Quintessence, for from Nothingness Absolute sprang All Things, and so it might be again, and he recalled the deeds and teachings of Jesus Christ, in which not dissimilar philosophies were contained, and he found them noble, and here, in the Guva, where the boundary between the Infinity without and the Infinity inside his mind seemed at moments to dissolve, he sought the Grace of God. He sensed It in the near distance, as forest creatures sense the approach of spring, but he didn't find It, and he concluded that the Devil's lien on his soul was yet to be paid. He did not dwell upon the fate of his loved ones, for it served no useful purpose. He did not dwell on the plots of the inquisitor, for he was powerless to affect them. Thus he made the Guva his fastness, and he used his desolation to refortify body and mind. He slept in prolonged bouts, curled around the Guva's bell-shaped bilge, and he coaxed himself back into oblivion when consciousness summoned. The stone was cold against his skin yet after the months of crippling heat this too was not unwelcome. He awoke cramped and with his spine chafed raw, but such discomforts hardly compared to those of the battle front. While sleeping, he was woken twice by someone unknown, when a light that could only have been dim but which dazzled his senses appeared above the Guva's edge and a cloth-wrapped bundle of bread and dried fish was thrown down. Ludovico did not want him starved, but only broken by isolation and uncertainty. The inquisitor would be disappointed, though Tannhauser made a note not to let him know it.

When the black monk at last came calling, it was with that peculiar faculty for theatre that was the Inquisition's own.

TANNHAUSER HEARD THE door unlocked and opened. The sound and the footfalls and the clank of armour that followed were strident in the stillness to which he was inured. One man or two? Two, yes. A torch flame emerged from the formless blackness and circled half-about the Guva's maw. The torch stopped and guttered, suspended in thin air, and Tannhauser realised its shaft had been slotted through a bracket on the chamber wall. While his eyes adapted to the shock of its incandescence, the footsteps hurried back and forth. A figure passed by the torch. A ladder was lowered down the side of the Guva farthest from the door. He glimpsed a flash of steel helmet. Then the shadowy figure skirted the pit and his footsteps retreated and the door opened, and closed, and silence fell once more.

Tannhauser waited, for it struck him as unseemly to show too ardent a desire to escape his prison. With his ears sharpened by quiet he could hear the gutter of the flames. And he could hear a man's breathing. The breaths were slow, and calm, as were his own. In the light bouncing down from above he was aware of his nakedness, the heathen tattoos on his arms and thighs, the lustre of the golden lions around his wrist. Yet to his gilded nakedness too he was now accustomed. He climbed the ladder, aware of eyes on his back, and stepped out of the Guva on to the rim. He turned.

Across the diameter bisecting the pit between them stood Ludovico. Though the darkness beyond was impenetrable, Tannhauser sensed no one else inside the chamber. Ludovico was resplendent in his black Negroli harness. Its newly fettled plate glimmered, as if the origin of the flames were not the torch but the enamelled steel. His head was bare. He appeared unarmed. The illumination from the wall torch threw one half of his face into shadow. His eyes were Stygian pools. If he was surprised at Tannhauser's vigour, he gave no signal. Ludovico inclined his head in greeting. Tannhauser sat himself cross-legged on the Guva's edge, and rested a palm on either knee. He nodded in return and the two men studied each other across the void.

Some minutes passed. Perhaps many. After the timeless silence of the pit it seemed natural enough. Then Tannhauser realised that some act of submission was in order.

Tannhauser said, 'What day might this be?'

'The Feast of the Nativity of the Virgin. Saturday the eighth.'

Six days. It had seemed both longer and shorter.

'Day or night?'

'We have two hours until sunrise.'

'And the city still stands.'

'Not only does the city stand,' said Ludovico, 'but the siege is broken.'

Tannhauser stared at him. No news could have been more unlikely; yet Ludovico could have no reason to deceive him.

'Yesterday morning, close on ten thousand soldiers came ashore at Mellieha Bay,' said Ludovico. 'They're encamped out on the high ground of Naxxar Ridge.'

'And the Turks?' asked Tannhauser.

'They've dismantled their siege guns and are retreating to their ships as we speak.'

'Mustafa runs from ten thousand?'

'Our Grand Master released a Moslem prisoner, and gave him to understand that the relief was twice that number.'

Tannhauser took this in. The Religion had won. And he had tried to escape the island at a moment when, in the event, it had no longer been necessary. As Ludovico shifted, and the light caught his eyes, Tannhauser saw that this irony was not lost on him either.

'It's true, upon my word,' said Ludovico. 'The timing of your flight could hardly have been worse.'

Tannhauser said, 'I trust you didn't come here simply to share these glad tidings.'

Ludovico glanced down behind him, then sat on a chair placed at the Guva's edge.

'If I've understood your history, you're a man more than able to abandon the past when circumstance requires it. Family, country, religion, emperor, cause. Even your beloved Oracle.'

Tannhauser knew no solid ground on which to contest this.

Ludovico smiled. 'Even Sabato Svi.'

The ominous ring of this slur almost provoked Tannhauser to take exception. But his purpose was better served by letting Ludovico believe him a knave.

'So Sabato didn't make it back to Venice.'

'He never left Messina, for which credit belongs, I'm told, to one Dimitrianos.' Ludovico's mouth twisted in distaste. 'The denunciation of Jews is ever a popular sport.'

Tannhauser had thought himself by now immune to horror and pity. He closed his eyes. Had he not, he might have circled the pit and torn the black monk limb from limb. Or revealed the depths of his grief. Neither would have served him well.

For a moment Ludovico left him to his mute and silent mourning.

Then he said, 'The Jew you will forget. As, too, you must forget the Lady Carla.'

Tannhauser mustered the necessary callousness. 'My contract to marry Carla was payment for services rendered. I fancied myself a count. It was never an affair of the heart.'

'For her, it became so.'

'Women are prone to infatuation, especially with their protector. The protector of a woman's child exerts a charm more potent still.'

'I'm reassured to hear you say that,' said Ludovico. 'It reflects my own observations; but in these respects you are more seasoned than I.'

'I was a monk of sorts, too.'

'But you never fell in love.'

'That abyss I was never able to bridge. My weakness inclines to the flesh, not the spirit.'

'The Spanish girl, Amparo, dotes on you.'

'Is she well?'

'Like Carla, she's enjoyed every courtesy and comfort.'

'I'd be loath to see her come to any harm,' said Tannhauser.

'Use your wits and no hand will touch her but your own.'

It occurred to Tannhauser that there was a serpentine vagueness to these answers; yet he did not sense any lies. Lies or not, the inquisitor held the trumps.

'Why did you return to the Borgo?' said Ludovico.

Ludovico intended the query to discomfit him. Tannhauser shrugged. 'I left a small fortune here in opium and precious stone. Enough to mount a healthy enterprise, be that in Italy or Tunis or back on the Stambouli Shore. Besides, the thought of my companions in Turkish chains did not sit well, and I fancied I could save them from that end.'

Ludovico leaned forward. 'Does Carla hate me?'

The question escaped as if he'd held it captive for a lifetime.

'She's never said so to me,' replied Tannhauser, 'and not for want of opportunity. Or encouragement. Her soul provides no ground in which hate might take root. She's bewildered by your cruelty. Women in general find barbarity an insoluble puzzle. I doubt she'd appreciate you tying me to a stake. But I would say in respect of you that her sentiments are more in the way of sorrow, at the spectacle of a man she once loved given over to evil.'

Ludovico nodded, as if for the moment sorrow would do. 'During all the years I dealt with death, I never wanted anyone to die. Duty and the safety of the Church demanded otherwise. But at times, I will admit, I've desired your death with a very great passion indeed.'

'I'll admit a similar hankering for yours,' said Tannhauser.

'Nevertheless, when now we meet face to face, I find my anger drained.'

'As the Arabs say, better a wise man for an enemy than a fool for a friend.'

'I've come to offer you a bargain.'

'I find myself with precious little to trade.'

Ludovico said, 'I want you to kill La Valette.'

Tannhauser managed not to blink. That this might be Ludovico's purpose had escaped his every speculation; yet an instant's reflection made it almost banal. Treachery of the highest order; yet he knew better than most that no instrument of State was more hallowed than murder.

He said, 'When?'

Ludovico said, 'At once,'

'So Admiral Del Monte is the Pope's man.'

'He will be Ghisleri's man, though as yet he is unaware of it. No stain attaches to the admiral's character, except, perhaps, an insufficiency of guile.'

'I can see Del Monte bending to a Pope, but not to an inquisitor.'

'Before the year is out, the Fisherman's Ring will shine on Ghisleri's finger.'

Tannhauser shrugged one brow. 'If you plan a pope's murder too, I expect the Prince of the Religion is small game.'

'The business must be concluded quickly – while the outcome of the war is yet uncertain and passions are high. As a final act to the drama it will play nicely. The valiant Grand Master, slain in the moment of victory by a nameless Turkish assassin. A role you are more than fit to play. In the vulgar outpouring of grief, as well as of triumph, no one will dare dispute La Valette's chosen successor. Del Monte will ascend the throne. And La Valette's name will live forever.'

'Superb,' said Tannhauser.

In a rare show of vanity, Ludovico inclined his head.

'And the bargain?' asked Tannhauser.

'If you decline,' said Ludovico, 'your throat will be cut in this room and your body consigned to the sea by first light.'

'I've struck less compelling deals,' said Tannhauser. 'But as this will be concluded on a handshake – perhaps not even that – and will require you to set me at liberty, your proposition requires a healthy degree of good faith – on your part.'

'Then you have no qualms?'

'La Valette is no innocent. The Turks would hail me as the slayer of a vicious demon, and with good reason. But what chance will I have to survive this escapade?'

'Your survival is my earnest desire. If you are killed in the attempt, your identity would tarnish the stratagem's perfection. There would be a mystery, and questions – an investigation – and while such obstacles could be surmounted, I'd rather they didn't arise.'

'By what means shall I perform this assassination?'

'Your rifle has been fettled, the finest powder and solid steel shot provided.'

'My pistol?'

'As you wish. Your horse will be saddled and at your disposal. The Kalkara Gate will be open and the bastion unmanned. These things I pledge on my honour. As always, La Valette is careless of his person. He is armourless and in plain view at the shrine of Philermo. He will remain in San Lorenzo until lauds are concluded. Place yourself while it's dark. When he leaves the church at dawn, you can kill him from a hundred feet and be beyond the walls before the hue and cry is up. From the look of him your Buraq can outpace any other mount in the city. After that the choice is yours: the Turkish fleet at Marsamxett or your little boat at Zonra.'

This deliberate mention of the boat disturbed him. It must have gone hard with Bors. For the moment he let it lie.

'I recommend the Mohammedans,' continued Ludovico, 'who, as you point out, will treat you as a hero.'

'These pledges,' said Tannhauser. 'My horse, the open gate.'

'Trust them. I'm able to rise above malice, especially in success. Your future among the infidel is of no consequence to me. But if you're captured alive, the torturers will have their day. While my word would prevail over yours, it's not a complication I relish and might provide grounds to dispute Del Monte's succession. In the event of your capture my men have orders to slaughter you, as if in a fit of rage, but as you've proved yourself hard to kill, uncertainties abound. Your clean escape is in my interest as much as it's in yours.'

'My sword, dagger and cuirass, in case I must fight my way out?'

'Ready and waiting. Along with Turkish garb.'

'My opium and precious stones?'

Something shifted in Ludovico's expression, as if this were a request he'd hoped for. 'Already packed in your saddle wallets. Wages may not guarantee fidelity, but they help.'

'The prospect of prosperity will lend me wings,' said Tannhauser. He added, 'I want Bors with me.'

'No,' said Ludovico. His tone brooked no negotiation.

'He's alive?'

'Sound in body but addled in mind.'

'Then give me your pledge that you'll free him when I'm gone.'

'The English only lives as a possible, though inferior, assassin should you have refused. I will grant him a quick death, but no more.' Ludovico spread his hands. 'If I make one false promise, you'd have reason to doubt those which are sincere, and you know that Bors must die. He'd spill this tale, somewhere, over the first jug of wine.'

Tannhauser made a show of considering this. He said, 'I don't want Bors to suffer damnation. Will he have a chance to make his peace with God?'

Ludovico took this as proof of hardheaded acquiescence. 'Confession and Holy Communion from my own hand,' he said.

'What of the women?'

'When I leave this chamber, Carla will ride with me to Mdina. Since I treasure her favour, and enjoy her consent to our marriage, Amparo will enjoy every luxury and protection in our household. You will never see either again.'

'And Orlandu?'

Ludovico looked at him for what seemed like a long time.

'My son is dear to me. To Carla, dearer still. Bors told me you left him in the care of the Yellow Banners. One General Abbas bin Murad.'

He waited for confirmation. Tannhauser nodded.

'Mustafa's cavalry protect the retreat to the ships. The Yellow Banners will be among the last to embark. I will secure Orlandu's release.'

'The boy works with hostlers,' said Tannhauser. 'If it comes to battle, the regiment will take spare horses into the field to replace those killed. If he's there, that's where you'll find him.'

'Thank you for that.'

'Orlandu's a fine boy. I wish him all good fortune.'

Ludovico nodded. 'Therein lies another reason why I wish for your escape to the Turk. If I should fail to find my son, I would pay a healthy ransom for his return from Constantinople.' He added, 'He is my flesh.'

Tannhauser nodded. 'Then we seal a twofold bargain in this pit.'

'Good.' Ludovico stood up. 'Is any part of this stratagem unclear?'

Tannhauser hoisted himself to his feet. 'What if I reveal your plot to La Valette?'

'Then Del Monte would not succeed, a disappointing outcome, and wounding to my pride, but hardly disastrous. You, however, would have to defend your charge of an absurd conspiracy against the word of four heroic knights in good standing – you who would be proven guilty of desertion by the testimony of Carla alone. The torturers would be called, you would confess to a vile slander, and by sundown you'd be swinging from the gallows.'

'And if I just ride out of the Kalkara Gate and away?'

'My agents in the Courts of Law must have news of La Valette's death before the sun clears Monte San Salvatore. If not, Amparo will die in his place. She will die unpleasantly, and in terror. If La Valette lives, Amparo dies. The choice is yours.'

'You'd risk Carla's abhorrence?'

'Carla would never know. She'd be given to understand that I'd allowed Amparo to leave the island with you.'

Tannhauser ignored the lurch in his gut. He nodded. 'Again, I congratulate you.'

'I have a man close to La Valette in the church,' added Ludovico. 'Any treachery on your part and he will expedite the girl's death.'

'This is yet a tricky chore,' said Tannhauser. 'Its essence is stealth. If I find some knight clanking after me in the dark, or one of your familiars on my tail, I won't answer for their lives.'

'The degree of trust you ask for is yours. I agree you need it. My man will watch La Valette, not you. You'll find your gear and clothing outside the door. A barge waits at the wharf. Buraq is tethered by the ruined bridge.'

'When first we met you absolved me of my sins,' said Tannhauser.

Ludovico studied him, as if for mockery. He found none. He raised his hand.

'*Ego te absolvo a peccatis tuis in nomine Patris et Filii et Spiritus Sancti, Amen.*'

Ludovico turned and started away into the dark.

'At the Kalkara Gate,' said Tannhauser. 'Who betrayed us?'

Ludovico stopped and turned, now a faceless black silhouette against the gloom.

'Your girl, Amparo,' he said.

'I don't believe you,' said Tannhauser.

'Her abandonment of Buraq so broke her heart, she told the horse everything she knew.'

Did Ludovico smile in the dark? Tannhauser couldn't tell.

'The Sicilian crone overheard her.'

SATURDAY 8 SEPTEMBER 1565 – THE NATIVITY OF THE BLESSED VIRGIN MARY

Church of the Annunciation – San Lorenzo – the Courts of Law

By the time he'd located Gullu Cakie, in the church of the Annunciation, Tannhauser's temper had risen to a boil. The tearful rapture that crammed the church cooled his fury back down, and this was good, for he wanted the blood in his veins to run cold as snow.

Though it was still dark, the parish church overflowed and he guessed it would overflow until the feast of the evening to come. That deliverance from the Moslem peril should come on so holy a day of obligation was taken by all as a sign of Divine compassion. And if, this year, the people had no harvest to celebrate, they'd reaped their freedom on the field of battle, and it was for this that they gave their heartfelt thanks to Christ and the Virgin. The summer was over, and they were saved.

The Annunciation's interior flickered yellow and black with hundreds of candles and votive lights. Lamp wicks smoked in the brackets below the Stations of the Cross. A child-sized statue of the Madonna was festooned with silk flowers. A fistful of dried wheat stalks and a bunch of grapes from some garden vineyard on L'Isola lay at her feet. Goats bedecked with ribbons trembled here and there among the crowd. Baskets of shrivelled vegetables and eggs lay at the foot of the altar. After a struggle through the congregation, Tannhauser found Gullu Cakie against one wall, below a plaster relief of Christ being scourged at the pillar. When he saw the look on Tannhauser's face, he genuflected to the altar and crossed himself, and without a word being said he followed him back outside. Buraq stood with hanging reins in the shadows.

'I didn't expect to see you again,' said Gullu Cakie. 'Many believe you deserted.'

'And you?' asked Tannhauser.

Gullu shook his head. 'Your boat was still at Zonra.'

Tannhauser's surprise lasted only an instant. Cakie knew of more intrigues and goings on than anyone in Malta. He'd probably known about the boat since the day Tannhauser stole it.

Gullu added, 'And the inquisitor's Sicilian hag decamped to the Courts of Law.'

'Is Starkey aware of this?'

Gullu shook his head. 'He believes you gone, with the women.'

Tannhauser felt vaguely wounded. 'Starkey believes me a deserter?'

Gullu shrugged, too gnarled to point out that Tannhauser was just that.

Tannhauser said, 'I need you to deliver him a message.'

Gullu Cakie was one of very few outside the Order with immediate access to the high command. He pleated his bald brow. 'To Starkey?'

'I need to speak with Starkey at once, on a matter of the greatest urgency.'

'He'll be in San Lorenzo, at lauds. They're all there. Why not go yourself?'

'I can't reveal my hand. He and I must meet in secrecy. Tell him so. Do you know Ludovico's familiars?'

Gullu gave him a look, as if offended by the suggestion he might not.

'He has a man on La Valette's staff,' said Tannhauser. 'Who might that be?'

'The Sienese, Pandolfo, is a snake in the grass.'

'Pandolfo it is. Neither he nor La Valette must suspect anything is amiss.'

Gullu Cakie said, 'Only a fool tangles with the Inquisition.'

'A fool stands before you, sure enough, but you'll earn the Grand Master's gratitude.'

'I've earned myself an abundance of his gratitude,' Gullu scowled. 'And it won't put a single loaf of bread on my kitchen table.'

'La Valette's life is at stake.'

Gullu pursed his lips, both unmoved and unimpressed. 'Grand Masters? They come, they go, we shovel up their shit. And now that the war is over?' He shrugged again.

'You'll earn my gratitude too. I'll be in your debt as deep as you want to call it.'

'But both of us will have to live if I'm to collect.'

Tannhauser couldn't help a grin. 'You're a man after my own heart.' His grin faded. 'Amparo's life is in danger, too. Ludovico has her in his lair.'

Gullu's expression changed. 'Amparo is one of us.'

'I'd say so.'

Gullu looked at his shiny, calloused palm. 'Amparo told me I'd live to see my great grandson born.' He looked up at Tannhauser. There was no hesitation in the beady eyes. 'That's a prophecy I will not see cursed.'

Torchlight made the crypt of San Lorenzo seem eerie. The vaults set into the floor stretched back with geometric ingenuity until lost in the haunted darkness. Some of the burial chambers lay open, their stone lids stacked aside, and the white folds of recently shrouded corpses could be seen within. Flies snarled in the gloom. A lingering tang of incense was swamped by the stench of putrefaction, for embalmment was a luxury long abandoned. The chancel of San Lorenzo lay directly above and Tannhauser heard the faint sound of singing. The monks' celebration of the Dawn was underway. And time was running out. He heard a set of footsteps and returned to the crypt's entrance. Starkey stepped into the torchlight. His expression was guarded, yet not unfriendly.

'Tannhauser. You've been missed.'

'I've been taking my ease,' said Tannhauser. 'In the Guva.'

'The Guva?' Starkey was shocked. A rare sight. 'On whose authority?'

Tannhauser waved this aside. 'There's a plot afoot against the Grand Master's life. I am his appointed assassin.'

Starkey was unarmed. His eyes reaffirmed the fact that Tannhauser was festooned with weapons; but whatever alarm he felt didn't show on his face. 'Appointed by whom?' he asked.

'Brother Ludovico.'

Starkey didn't seem surprised, but was ever difficult to read. 'Fra Ludovico,' he mused. 'Ghisleri's man to the knife.'

Tannhauser summarised his arrest and confinement – relocating their capture to the Auberge of England. He outlined Ludovico's proposition and plan.

'You have proof of this intrigue?' Starkey asked.

'Give me a free hand with young Pandolfo and you'll hear it for yourself.'

'Pandolfo too?' Starkey's mouth twisted. 'Ludovico's scheming to promote Del Monte was brazen enough, but I did not imagine he'd be so bold as this.'

'Time presses,' said Tannhauser.

'Is Del Monte party to this conspiracy?'

'No.'

'Thank God.'

'Amparo and Bors are in the inquisitor's gaol,' said Tannhauser. 'They'll be murdered at sunrise – sooner if Pandolfo gets wind of this parley.'

Starkey tented his fingers against his lips. He pondered the lawful scenario.

'Serjeants at arms invading the Courts of Law. Arrests. Trials. Executions. The Italian Langue disgraced, with much bad blood. Our victory sullied. Open conflict with the Roman Inquisition – perhaps the Vatican too.'

He shook his head in distaste. He looked at Tannhauser.

'This ugly matter would be best buried deep.'

Tannhauser said, 'Give me your warrant and I'll bury them all.'

'Warrant?' said Starkey. 'If Ludovico survives – and you're taken alive – this conversation never took place. You'll almost certainly be hanged.'

Tannhauser felt a flicker of surprise; then amazement that he should have expected loyalty. He knew these creatures. He was, after all, the man who'd been sent to murder the Sultan's grandchild. By the Sultan. Sultan, Vatican, Religion. Islam or Rome. All these cults sought only power and the submission of peoples. The people themselves, the little people, like him, like Gullu Cakie, like Amparo, were no more than grist to their mill. La Valette, Ludovico, Pope, Mustafa, Suleiman – what scum they were, one and all. Swathed in pomp and orchestrating carnage to coddle their unreckonable vanity. In his heart he'd have killed them all without a qualm, and counted it a service to mankind. Yet there'd never be a shortage of candidates to fill their shoes and to deplore this fact was an errand only fit for a fool.

Tannhauser nodded. He said, 'Of course.'

'Ludovico left for Mdina with a troop of cavalry,' said Starkey.

'They intend to join the attack on the Turkish withdrawal. If he should die on the battlefield, this scandal would die with him.'

Tannhauser and his rifle had a new employer. 'And Bruno Marra? Escobar de Corro?'

'Foul and rotten limbs to be severed from the Order's tree,' said Starkey. 'They accompanied their new master to Mdina.'

'Was the Lady Carla with them?'

'I don't know.'

Tannhauser handed him the torch. 'Keep Pandolfo in your sights.'

'He'll be escorted from the church doors directly to the Guva.'

Tannhauser slid back the pan cover on his rifle to freshen the priming. He slung the wheel lock across his back. He pulled out the pistol and rechecked it. He'd wiped the bores and loaded each gun himself with a double charge of powder.

'Why did Ludovico trust you?' asked Starkey.

'He had a need to make me his dog.' The cold rage stirred. His limbs felt light; his head clear. He belted the pistol. He thought of Gullu Cakie and looked at Starkey. 'And he failed to take the measure of my allegiances.'

Starkey said, 'Perhaps of your character too.'

'No,' said Tannhauser. 'My character he weighed with precision. For if Gullu Cakie hadn't agreed to help me, your Grand Master would be dead.'

To THE WEST the sky was indigo. Cassiopeia sat on her throne above Saint Elmo. To the south the Dog Star was bright. Above San Lorenzo the night had already faded to a lilac blue. Where the blunted ridge of Salvatore distinguished the eastern horizon, a nimbus of palest gold crowned the dawn. Tannhauser walked down the street towards the Courts of Law.

The building was two storeys of sandstone, with a stab at juridical grandeur in the portico. Turkish cannon had left their mark as elsewhere. Tannhauser reckoned up the likely opposition:

the two familiars from Messina, Tasso and Ponti; the Spaniard Remigio. Seasoned fighters – there was no one left in the city who was not so – but they didn't expect him. He drew his Running Wolf sword and the Devil-bladed dagger, right and left. He ascended the stairs. The twin doors of the entrance stood wide open. Something like a ship's lantern hung on a chain from the roof of the lobby. By its light he saw no one. He'd expected some kind of sentry – someone to signal Amparo's murder, should it be required – and this disturbed him. He walked inside.

Passageways led off to his either side. A flight of stairs led into darkness straight ahead. A search might take more minutes than he had left. He decided to stir the rats from their nest directly. He raised his voice by an octave to disguise it and shouted as if in alarm.

'The Grand Master is dead!'

He waited. Seconds later he heard rapid footsteps from the passageway to his left. He concealed himself by its mouth. He heard a muffled exchange. A laugh. Remigio emerged from the passage. Behind him, two abreast, came Tasso and Ponti. Only Ponti wore a cuirass. They carried sheathed swords in their hands. Remigio was chewing and Tasso wore a bib, as if they'd been interrupted eating breakfast.

Tannhauser shoved twelve inches of Passau steel through Remigio's belly and cranked the hilt. Remigio's hands flew to the blade but it was gone and Tannhauser slashed his throat backhand and opened his neck to the spine and sidestepped as he fell. He lunged at Tasso's face and the sword slid clean through Tasso's forearm as he threw it up as a guard and the point split the arm bones and stuck him through the lip below the nose. Tannhauser cleared his sword smartly and closed and stabbed Tasso in the privities with the dagger and took out his legs with a footsweep. He landed a shallow slash to his chest as he hit the stones. Then he stepped back.

Ponti had retreated to jettison his scabbard but came back

into the fray as Tasso fell. Tannhauser parried blows, the attack bold and fierce, head, thigh, arm, head, thigh, and he gave ground towards the centre of the lobby to leave Tasso out of range, to give Ponti headlong momentum, then he opened Ponti's guard up high, quillions locked to blade, and lunged forward and braced him, their breastplates clashing, swords aloft, Tannhauser's weight gaining the vantage and Ponti winded, his left hand grappling for the throat as Tannhauser dropped a head-butt into his nose. The tip of his dagger sought the armhole in Ponti's cuirass, and Ponti clenched his elbow to his side and forced the dagger away and abandoned the throat grab, for Tannhauser's neck was too thick, and he grabbed instead for his balls and Tannhauser stuck the dagger through Ponti's hand and pricked his own thigh as Ponti jerked back. He threaded his leg between Ponti's knees and hooked his calf and shoved from the hip and Ponti toppled backwards, sword flailing – and here was Tasso charging back in – and as Ponti hit the flagstones Tannhauser stabbed him in the groin and Ponti rolled and Tannhauser sliced him again at the back of the knee, but could find no killing blow. He warded Tasso's charge with a slash and a turn and he retreated, hacking Ponti a good, deep bite through the elbow of his sword arm as he clambered to his knees, then two, three steps across the lobby and Tannhauser turned again and stopped and sucked for breath.

Tannhauser stared at the two Italians while they all three caught their wind. He sheathed the dagger, drew the pistol left-handed and heeled back the dog. He'd wanted to avoid a shot, as the sound might alert unknown others and endanger Amparo. Ponti swayed in the aftershock of his wounds, his right arm broken, his sword swapped over to his injured left hand. His eyes were hooded with rage. Tasso was more unhinged. He stared at the black stain spreading from his crotch. Blood tumbled from his beard from his half-severed lip.

'He's cut my bollocks off,' he said, with disbelief.

'I want Bors and the girl,' said Tannhauser.

'The English is down below,' said Ponti. 'The turnkey watches him. The girl is locked upstairs. We don't know where. The women were tended by the Sicilian hag.'

Tannhauser said, 'Then who was to kill Amparo?'

The Italians swapped a glance to confirm each other's ignorance.

'We know not of what you speak.'

'You had no such orders?'

Their faces answered and Tannhauser felt sick. 'Where's the crone?'

Ponti said, 'We don't know.'

'Is it true the Grand Master's dead?' blurted Tasso.

'No,' said Tannhauser. 'He prepares your gallows. Ludovico's too.'

Their shoulders sagged with the resignation of those who've gambled all and lost.

'Yield,' said Tannhauser, 'and at least you'll see a priest before you die.'

The thought of hellfire was enough for Tasso. He threw down his sword.

'I'll not go to the Devil,' he said. 'God will forgive us yet.'

Ponti howled and lumbered at Tannhauser, his sword upraised. Tannhauser parried and stepped aside and severed Ponti's hand through the root of his thumb. He clubbed him to his knees with a blow from the pommel. He stepped back and set his stance firm. Then he rotated his hips and swung and hacked Ponti's head from his shoulders with a single stroke.

Tannhauser waded through the spew of blood towards Tasso and Tasso darted for the outer doors. Tannhauser moved to cut him off. Both stopped as Gullu Cakie mounted the threshold. He held the Sicilian crone before him with her arm cranked up between her shoulders. The crone looked at the slain and at the great puddles of gore that befouled the lobby. She let out a terrible wail. As well she might. Tasso turned back to Tannhauser and spread his empty hands.

'Mercy and a priest for a fellow soldier,' he begged.

Tannhauser stabbed him up beneath the basket of his ribs and through the liver. The man gave him a woeful look. Tannhauser unseamed him to the belt buckle and let him fall at the old hag's feet. He sheathed his sword and grabbed the hag by her knot of white hair.

'Take me to Amparo.'

Her toothless mouth clamped shut. Her face incarnated that peculiar malice unique to the withered female in the winter of her days. Her eyes were tiny and quavered from side to side with blind fear. Tannhauser dragged her screaming and threw her face down in the merging burgundy pools of Ponti's and Remigio's blood. She shrieked and slithered in the gore like a newly happened member of the Damned. She tried to regain her feet and failed and swashed back into the welter and rolled about in the waste like a panicked dog.

Tannhauser turned away and handed the pistol to Gullu Cakie.

'Bors is somewhere below. There's a turnkey on guard.'

Gullu took the gun and nodded. As he circled the lobby he picked up Tasso's sword. Tannhauser grabbed the hag from the cooling swill and shoved her towards the stairs. She clambered up them like a frantic black spider, shuddering with sobs of horror and retching gobs of bile down her reeking dress, and Tannhauser heard from his conscience not a whisper of pity. At the top of the stair a lamp burned on a stand and Tannhauser took it and prodded the hag in the back. She stumbled away and stopped at the heavy door. She fumbled at her throat and produced a key on the end of a string. She turned it in the lock and pushed the door open, then fell to her knees at his feet and threw her arms about his ankles and babbled. And he knew by then that Ludovico had lied and that he was already too late by far.

He looked down at the crone. Her face was a mask of crimson wrinkles.

He said, 'Who?'

'Anacleto,' she wailed.

He kicked the old crone into the room and she left a slimy trail as she crawled into a corner and chewed on her knuckles with her gums.

Tannhauser walked inside.

A lemony first light streamed through a high window and fell across the bed where Amparo lay. He set down the lamp and walked over. She was nude and cold and the fabric with which she'd been strangled was still drawn tight about her neck. He peeled the garrotte away. It was silk, and the dark red of a pomegranate, and had left no mark on her throat. He realised it was Carla's dress. The dress she'd packed on his word. He threw it to the floor. He saw the bruises on Amparo's arms, days old, and he knew she'd been raped – over and again – for at least that long. These observations struck him mute and numb. He sat on the mattress and lifted her head in his hands. Her hair was still soft and smooth. Her skin was as white as a pearl. Her lips were drained of colour. Her eyes were open, one brown, one grey, and each was filmed with death. He couldn't bring himself to close them. He stroked her left cheek and traced the flawed bone that had somehow revealed her strange and incomparable beauty. He touched her mouth. Of all the many thousands who had died on this scourged shore, she had been the purest in heart. She'd died alone and violate and without a defender to count on, and his numbness broke and an awesome grief overwhelmed him, and this time there was no Abbas to stay his tears. He'd failed to protect her, and worse. He'd failed in the courage to love her as she'd deserved. To love her as she'd loved him, despite that he'd not earned it. To love her as in fact he had, which was beyond his power to voice, then and now. He hadn't dared to meet such love on the square. He'd hidden from it like a cur. And he realised how mean a vision of courage he had owned, and how true and indomitable the courage of Amparo had been. He tried to recall the last thing he'd heard her say to him, and he could not, and his heart was cleaved apart inside him. Through that wound the Grace of God flowed into him. He was filled with a sorrow too enormous to contain and he groaned and squeezed her to his chest and buried his face in her hair and grunted with pain. And he begged Jesus Christ for His Mercy and he implored Amparo's spirit to forgive him.

THUS AND so did Gullu Cakie find him. Tannhauser felt the old rogue's hand on his shoulder and looked up. In the deep clefts scored in Gullu's cheeks, in the sun-creased eyes, he saw a smoky mirror of himself, for Gullu too had lost many he had loved, and though in loss all felt alone, all here had a deal of fellowship. Tannhauser lowered Amparo to the bed. Her eyes were still open. Even in death they seemed luminous with some essence that refused extinction. He closed them. He stood up.

'See,' said Gullu Cakie.

He pointed to Amparo's hand. It clutched the ivory and silver comb that he'd bought in the bazaar. Tannhauser worked it loose. The teeth were crusted with blood.

'Jesus triumphed over Death, and so will she, for that is His promise,' said Cakie. 'She'll be forever with you if you so want it. But life goes on. And you have work to do.'

Tannhauser's heart sank. He was sickened and weary. He'd had enough. Sorrow was no fit baggage for the killing fields. He wanted to nurture his tears. He wanted to run. To the boat at Zonra. To the Turkish ships. To a bottle and a wedge of opium. But Carla was still out there. And Orlandu. And Ludovico and his foul and rotten limbs. Tannhauser stuck the ivory comb in his own hair. He laid Amparo out straight and folded her arms across her chest. He saw once again the bruises yellow and blue on her slender arms and the bite marks profaning her breasts. The sorrow retreated to some hidden haven within, and with good reason, for something terrible rose in his chest to take its place. And this was as well, for he'd terrible things to do. He took the crumpled sheet from the bed and unfurled it and it fell across her body like a caress. And it was done and Amparo was gone.

With the onset of day, the bells of San Lorenzo broke into peals of victory.

Tannhauser crossed the room and hauled the trembling crone from her corner.

He turned to Gullu Cakie. 'I'm going to find the boy, Orlandu. Will you ride with us?'

He followed Gullu Cakie down to the dungeons and he dragged the squalling crone along by her hair. Bors had been confined in a hole in the floor, and on his release had set about the turnkey with such outrageous violence that Gullu had skipped from the cell and locked the door. As they approached down the dank corridor they heard Bors bellowing, and they heard the blood-muffled whimpers of his victim. Gullu opened the door and Bors turned to face them with clawed hands. On the floor behind him sprawled the turnkey, his limbs twisted about at unnatural angles and the sockets of his eyes gouged clean. The trap door of an *oubliette* lay open.

'Bors,' said Tannhauser. 'Are you steady?'

Bors's eyes cleared. For a moment Tannhauser got a glimpse of something gentle, something young that pre-dated all the violent roads he'd travelled. Then Bors, without even knowing it, banished it for good. 'Steady as a rock,' he said.

'Throw him in the hole and let's go.'

Bors wiped his mouth and picked up the wretched turnkey like a sack. He pitched him headfirst underground and stomped him from sight. He reached for the trap door to close it.

'This hag was Amparo's keeper,' Tannhauser said. 'Amparo is dead.'

Bors blinked and his viciousness was tempered by grief, for he'd considered Amparo his friend, and he too had failed to protect her. Tannhauser shoved the crone across the dungeon floor and she gibbered with fear as Bors seized her by the neck. Tannhauser pointed to the *oubliette* and the broken and caterwauling turnkey crammed within.

'Let the hag keep him company.'

SATURDAY 8 SEPTEMBER 1565 – THE NATIVITY OF THE BLESSED VIRGIN MARY

The Grande Terre Plein – Naxxar Ridge – Saint Paul's Bay

With their reprieve from certain doom the townsfolk had succumbed to a festive frenzy. So crowded were the churches that the Te Deum was sung in the streets while chaplains celebrated Mass in the piazza and the market square. Icons of the Virgin were brandished and bells of salvation pealed. People embraced in the rubble and wept. The Hand of Saint John the Baptist was taken from the conventual sacristy and paraded for adoration. Their prayers had been answered and their stoical heroism rewarded. The Will of God had been determined. The Knights of the Holy Religion stood vindicated before eternity and the world.

Yet through this joy three riders rode whose hearts were closed to rapture.

Their mounts stepped over the shot that littered the cobbles as they threaded the abandoned barricades and wended to the Provençal Gate. Tannhauser looked up. On the bastion above he saw the launch from the gallows of the last, the unlucky, the one hundred and tenth Moslem sacrifice of the siege. As if the stones themselves protested at this enormity a section of the breached wall moaned and crumbled with a sigh of dust into the ditch. But if anyone heard, none cared. No more would the call of the muezzin echo from the hills.

The gates stood open and they passed through and out and over the Grande Terre Plein. Thousands of forsaken corpses lay bloated and liquefying in the sun, and if the Turks had been vanquished, the blowflies in their multitudes had not, and they revelled about the black and stinking wasteland in whirling vortices of blue. Vultures hopped about the putrefaction and ravens and seagulls and crows cawed and squawked as they wheeled and swooped in their own grim ovation to victory.

Tannhauser, Bors and Gullu Cakie rode fanned out and abreast, crossing this scourged estate like three apocalyptic horsemen who were missing only Famine from their rank. None spoke for there was nothing to say, nor words to do the job even if there had been. To the outer limit of sight in every direction was a land laid desolate by war. The collapsed galleries of the mines, some smoking still, split the flatland's surface like the evidence of some vast geological rupture. The hacked entrenchments that gutted the slopes lay vacant, as if their aim had only ever been to violate the hills. The gullies running from the heights were contaminate with gun waste and cannon swabs and mounds of human faeces. To their right the broken façade of Saint Michel was striped with an impasto of blood and soot and lard. Its ditch heaved and stank with a charred human humus infested with worms. As they crossed the Ruins of Bormula, across which so many charges had been launched only to be broken, weapons and bones and fragments of rotting gear, and the fleshless skulls of horses and men, and stacks of yellowed carrion half-consumed, were heaped and scattered in profusion. The horses shied as affronted vultures flapped and waddled about them, and Buraq in particular trembled with an equine horror, as if the beast's great soul could not incorporate such ugliness into its ken.

They climbed the slopes of Corradino and took in the Marsa.

The once fertile plain was pocked with dead campfires by the thousand and mottled with poisoned wells and humming latrines. A sirocco had begun its laggardly rise from Africa, and on its desert breath smoke in numberless tendrils spiralled aloft from dumps of provender torched and abandoned by the Turk. It drifted in filthy scuds through tattered tents, flapping empty and forlorn, and wove notes that were bitter and harsh through the sweet and yellow stench of decomposition. Out by one far rim hundreds of clay brick bread kilns stood in geometric clusters, like villages built by dwarves who feared the sunlight. And where once the wretched hospital had sprawled across the landscape like disease, pyramids of corpses drew colonies of hunchbacked birds, and the sordid awnings thrown together from poles and canvas shifted like boneless scarecrows in the wind. And in all that bleak and godforsaken detritus, nothing human stirred except they three.

Beyond the scarred back of Monte Sciberras to the north, the white-on-scarlet banner of the knights flew above the shell of Fort Saint Elmo's. In Marsamxett Bay, the tail of the Turkish fleet pulled out into the offing and struck north for Saint Paul's Bay. They left behind them scores of galleys in flames, for they'd neither mariners to crew them nor passengers to bear away. The harbour smouldered black as if the sea were brewed from brimstone, and as this ghost fleet burned and sank beneath the blue, huge white plumes of steam erupted skyward and shreds of fiery sail feathered the beach, and though no living man had seen such sights before, they three said naught, nor felt any wonder, for Hell held no more marvels for such as they.

They rode on and left this *terra damnata* behind them and Gullu Cakie led them north towards the rim of Naxxar Ridge. There they heard the sounds of battle joined: the final battle, one more needless even than the rest, and which would choke the waters of Saint Paul's Bay with its slain.

AT THE CREST of the ridge they found the Knight Commander of the relief, Ascanio de la Corna. From an excited aide-de-camp Tannhauser gleaned the news.

The Turkish army – still near thirty thousand strong including supports, but in fear of twenty thousand fresh Christian combat troops – had spent most of the previous twenty-four hours boarding the ships and galleys of Piyale's fleet. In the early hours of that morning, Sipahi scouts of the Sari Bayrak had confirmed that the relief was in fact less than half that number, and Mustafa's notorious rage had consumed him. Determined to reclaim some honour from impending disaster, he'd at once disembarked nine thousand of his best remaining men at Marsamxett and at their head had marched to Naxxar Ridge to offer battle. Rage or not, a famous victory would so restore the Turks' morale that the conquest of Malta might even now be achieved. Piyale's fleet had sailed up the coast and anchored in Saint Paul's Bay, where the army could evacuate from the beach in the event of catastrophe.

Catastrophe was where Mustafa had led his men.

Between Naxxar and the Wardija Ridge, under a mile further north, the Bingemma Basin opened out from the defile and rolled down to the bay. At dawn de la Corna's Spanish infantry and the knights of the Order newly arrived from Sicily had charged down the hill to meet the Turkish sally head-on. At the same time, De Lugny's cavalry had debouched from Mdina along the high road to Mgarr, and had swept down from the west to take Mustafa's column in the flank. After an hour of ferocious fighting, the weary Moslem army had broken and fled for the bay.

Tannhauser took in the prospect. Neglected all summer long, the Bingemma Basin was a broad vale of parched grass and fields. Once the island's breadbasket, it was now a bloody circus bepopulate with half a thousand dead and the totter of walking wounded and the thrashing forms of scores of dying horses. It shimmered in the rising heat like a melancholiac's fantasy of Gehenna and Tannhauser wondered if Orlandu had managed to cross it.

If he'd done so, then he'd reached Saint Paul's Bay, which was hardly a more appealing location. It was dark with galleys and transports and its waters foamed with the oars of the longboats that desperately ferried the soldiers back to the ships. The beaches milled with thousands of disorganised men. On the apron of flat-land that guarded the approach, and along the low hills that commanded the southern foreshore, a valiant rearguard braced the Christian onslaught to buy their comrades time. Along this line, amid dense thickets of musket smoke, the battle raged hand to hand. Among the Turkish pennants there planted, Tannhauser recognised the *Sanjak i-sherif* and Mustafa's standard in the centre. The stubborn old general and his *garibs* – the guardians of the Prophet's Banner – would be the last to board the ships. To his right were the mailed janissaries of the Zirhli Nefer. Hassem's Algerian musketmen occupied the hillocks. And at the opposite extremity of the line, to Mustafa's left and hard against Salina Bay, flew the yellow banners of the Sari Bayrak. Abbas's cavalry regiment.

'Look at them,' said Bors. The brawny Cumbrian sat on his horse with his Damascus musket laid across his thighs. He seemed to speak for the Turk. 'So much valour has been squandered on this rock it's obscene.'

'Today we're not here for the Turk,' said Tannhauser.

Bors said, 'I know whose blood we're here for.' He blinked and looked away, as if he felt less than the man he once had been. Then he turned back to Tannhauser. 'I told him everything.'

'I would have told him too,' said Tannhauser. He'd heard the tale of Sabato Svi's head. 'But there's no harm done, for it gave him the rope he needed to tie his own noose.'

Bors took no comfort from this. He looked down the bloody vale to the seething swathe of violence that truncated the basin. 'Where will we find him?'

Tannhauser turned to Gullu Cakie, who was observing the destruction of Turkish pride with greater relish than either of his companions. Tannhauser pointed.

'The Yellow Banners,' he said. Gullu nodded. 'Can we reach them quickly, without daring the front? If Orlandu's down there, that's where he'll be.'

Gullu started his horse down the ridge. Tannhauser turned to Bors.

'That's where we'll find Ludovico, too.'

Bors nudged his horse after Gullu Cakie.

'Bors,' said Tannhauser.

Bors stopped. Tannhauser motioned Buraq closer. He said, '*Usque Ad Finem.*'

He held out his hand. Bors took it and squeezed.

They followed Gullu north down the ridge's sloping spine towards Salina Bay. To their right the sea was white with reflected light. Piyale's squadrons patrolled just off the coast. As the ridge narrowed to a low saddle, and then unfolded into an easy decline of undulating hills, the clamour of the fight grew louder and drifts of burnt powder stung their eyes. They passed by men with hideous wounds and amputated limbs and arrows protruding from their bellies in the gullies where they'd dragged themselves to die. They pulled their mounts up two hundred feet short of the melee and Tannhauser studied the chaos there unleashed.

A full squadron of *tercios* – there must have been fifteen hundred – harried the Turkish line with halberds and pikes while five *mangas* of black-lipped *arquebuceros* – two hundred men in each and well protected by the hedged fortress of polearms – tore cartridges with their teeth and fumbled in their pouches for shot, rotating the front rank and keeping up an intermittent volley fire that inflicted dire carnage on the luckless Turks. Panicked and riderless horses reared and plunged as they fled the field, trampling wailing wounded under their hooves. As far as Tannhauser could tell, the Turkish cavalry, thwarted by the Christian pikemen, were fighting for the most part on foot.

On the gentle slope of the basin two hundred yards removed from the battle line, several hundred mounted knights had reformed in a wedge, and these now lowered their lances and rode at the hinge of the Turkish left. The Spanish infantry felt their thunder through the ground and the *sargento mayor* roared an order, which was taken up at once by the *abanderados*. The genius of the *tercio* squadron was in the strict cooperation between pikemen and gunmen in the same formation. To the blue and green signals of the flag bearers they now peeled back from the battlefront like a huge pair of gates swinging open, volleys still raking the gap, and through this widening aperture the charging knights roared. They ploughed the Turkish ranks with cold steel and burst through into their rear. As the horsemen hacked a swathe of the basin clear of life, a block of pikemen – six deep and a hundred wide – wheeled through the breach and commenced to roll the Sari Bayrak into the sea.

Tannhauser turned to Gullu Cakie and held out his hand for the dog-lock pistol.

'Wait here, for the sake of your great grandson.'

With this spectacle of Turkish misery to entertain him, Gullu seemed content to do so. Tannhauser belted the pistol and drew his sword and Bors blew on the match of his Damascus musket. They rode down from the escarpment and into the widening gap in the battle line. The ground was thick with Turkish slain and the horses picked their way among them with the fastidiousness of dancers. As Tannhauser and Bors circled the rear of the pikemen, the outflanked Moslems abandoned the neck of the basin. With the iron courage of Mustafa himself holding their centre, the rearguard pulled back towards the foreshore of Saint Paul's Bay.

In a desperate attempt to join them the remains of the Sari Bayrak – now cut off – remounted and fought their way through the closing gap between the basin and Salina Bay. While the pikemen relentlessly narrowed their window of escape, the *mangas* of *arquebuceros* sloshed them with shot and the mounted knights attacked with the vengeance of the righteous. The ground was boggy with blood, the air a throat-stripping haze of gunsmoke and dust. The pipes, the war cries, the gunfire and the braying of horses hamstrung and disembowelled sent tremors through Buraq's withers, and Tannhauser whispered a *gazel* in his ear to calm him. He scanned the fog-dimmed melee and recognised no one. He urged Buraq closer and stood high in the stirrups as he traversed the rear of the line. Where, in all this havoc, was Orlandu?

HAVING ENDURED THE snarling madness of Saint Elmo's final days, Orlandu had kept his head throughout the retreat. Even so, the fight for Saint Elmo's had been confined to a strip of stones and the capricious spasms of battle on open ground demanded all his wits. He'd been charged with the care of three spare war mounts and he'd dragged them by their bridles since dark. With so much noise and violence, and trained to such though they were, the horses took frequent fright and the greater part of his effort was consumed in calming them. He murmured the *Shahada* over and over, in the belief that the Arabic sounds would be familiar. For the most part it worked, but he was bruised from head to toe with kicks and had forgotten the number of times he'd escaped being brained.

Other grooms were not so lucky. He saw two trampled insensible and a third struck down by a musket ball in the face. From their abandoned strings he replenished his own, for time after time cavalrymen would stagger over on foot and snatch a fresh set of reins from his hands. Some rode away bareback, others hauled their saddles with them. The suffering of the horses felled by the battle was atrocious and moved him more than the screams of the men. The beasts floundered in wallows of blood, crippled and bewildered, or charged about blinded and insane, or hauled great unravelling sacs of yellow intestines between their hind legs as they stumbled for the plain.

Orlandu considered fleeing to the Borgo many times, but the moment never came and he was borne along like a stick on a crimson tide. Most of the time he couldn't tell where was the front and where the rear, and desertion carried a high chance of death. The Sari Bayrak fought like demons unchained, but the toll from the banks of musket fire was high. He tried to keep Abbas's standard in sight, but it disappeared for what seemed like hours at a time as the valiant general led charge after charge into the heart of the Christian ranks.

The regiment now seemed trapped against the shores of Salina Bay. A broad arc of smoke and mounted combatants was the limit of Orlandu's horizon and he tried to ignore the confusion and control his fear and clear his mind. As Tannhauser would. Orlandu had but one mount left in his keeping, and he covered its eyes with a discarded pennant and murmured the *Shahada* into its ear. *There is no God but Allah and Mohammed is His Messenger*. The knights were giving no quarter that he could see. If they broke through, they'd as likely cut him down as any other Turk. He glanced at the water a hundred feet distant and came up with a plan. He stopped and dragged off his boots, the grass clean and cool between his toes. He wouldn't abandon the horse, not yet. But if this one was claimed, or the battle drew too close, he'd sprint for the sea and swim away. No one would follow him into the water, and if needs be he could hold his own there for hours.

No sooner had he conceived this strategy than a knot of ferocious knights hacked their way through the Turkish line and rode directly towards him. They were led by a man wearing striking black armour that glimmered like liquid obsidian in the sun. Despite no shortage of targets, the whole band bore down on

Orlandu as if he were the only Turk whose blood was worthy of spilling. He ditched his helm and dropped the horse's reins and ducked under its neck and sprinted for his life towards the bay. He stripped his shirt as he ran and threw it aside. He heard the pounding of hooves and the snort of the animals. He picked up his knees as his feet hit the sand and he threw his weight forward with his arms cartwheeling for balance. As the waves loomed closer, he heard a deep voice roar out behind him.

'Orlandu!'

The name bounced round his brain as his feet hit the water. He didn't stop. He slowed as the waves hit his knees and waded on.

'Orlandu!'

He chanced a look over his shoulder without stopping.

The Black Knight had hauled up at the water's edge. He held his sword inverted by its blade, the hilt aloft like a crucifix. With his free hand he beckoned. The face that stared out from the visor was gaunt and brave, the eyes as black as his armour and just as bright. Orlandu didn't know the man, but he was a knight of the Religion. Orlandu turned but continued walking backwards. Three other knights fanned out behind the first in a defensive arc. The Black Knight called again and nudged his mount into the shallows.

'Orlandu! I am Fra Ludovico, of the Langue of Italy! We've come for you! For you, my boy! To return you to your mother!'

Orlandu stopped, the sea waist-deep and splashing over his chest. The Black Knight dismounted. He seemed huge. He waded towards him. Then stopped. Orlandu saw that there were tears in his eyes. He raised his inverted sword up to the heavens.

'All praises be to You, my Lord Jesus Christ.' Ludovico lowered the sword and looked at Orlandu. Again, his emotion seemed almost to overwhelm him and now the tears rolled freely down his cheeks. He held out his arm.

'Come here, my boy, and let me embrace you.'

Orlandu was too bewildered not to comply. He waded back towards the shore and stood before his rescuer. He was indeed gigantic. As tall and broad as Tannhauser. A steel arm circled Orlandu's shoulders and he was clasped to the man's breast. The armour against his skin was hot and smeared with gore. He looked up into the liquid eyes and again he saw something he had only seen before in the eyes of Tannhauser. It was love.

'Come,' said Ludovico, and let him go. 'We must to horse and away from this broil. Our part in it is done. Our part in ventures more glorious we've yet to play.'

Ludovico caught up his reins and they climbed back up the beach. A young knight with only one eye handed him the reins of the Arabian Orlandu had guarded, and Ludovico held the beast steady while he leapt up bareback. Ludovico mounted too. The four knights drew up in a box around Orlandu. He felt a tingle down his spine. He was no less bewildered than before but this was a marvel. More marvellous yet, Ludovico drew a spare sword from a sheath buckled on to his saddle. He gave it to Orlandu.

'To Mdina,' said Ludovico.

Orlandu clenched the Arabian's sides with his knees and rode towards the battle line, the four noble knights packed tight around him.

TANNHAUSER SCANNED THE calamity without success. As always the field of battle was a shifting patchwork of exertion and sudden stasis. Fit as the fighting men were, and they were the fittest men alive, none could wield their arms for more than moments at a burst without catching their wind. Mounts as well as men stood with nostrils flared and forefeet splayed as they wheezed for air, and here and there knights murdered by the heat lay prostrate in their kiln-hot armour. A triangular spit of land separated the waters of Salina from those of Saint Paul's Bay, and as the disordered press of combatants shunted yard by relentless yard towards the beachhead, ruptures broke apart in the contention. Through one of these gaps, Tannhauser saw Abbas bin Murad as he was blown from his saddle.

Abbas's horse went down with him, then struggled to its feet, its hooves treading its master as it scrambled away. At Abbas's either side, the regimental standard-bearer and two other officers were felled by the same volley. Tannhauser pulled Buraq's head about.

'Mattias!'

Tannhauser turned. Bors pointed down the line with the barrel of his musket. From another breach, two hundred feet down the ever-changing front, a knot of five riders spilled out on to the open plain to the rear of the fighting. Their horses were lathered, almost blown. The group started back across the basin towards the defile. The knight at their head wore a peerless black carapace of Negroli armour. The three knights behind him completed a diamond-shaped square and in the square's centre rode Orlandu.

He was naked to the waist and looked as proud as a gamecock.

Tannhauser looked back at Abbas. He stood swaying on his feet among the knot of dead, leaning on the shaft of the yellow standard in his hands. A knight rode down on him and Abbas tilted the shaft and wedged its butt against his foot and speared the horse through the chest on its spiked finial. He stumbled aside from the collapse of man and beast and dropped to one knee, and came up with a scarlet sword, and fell on the downed knight with the last of his strength. Thirty yards behind him, another knight wheeled about and made to charge him down.

Tannhauser sheathed his sword and turned back to Bors.

'Follow them but don't engage. I'll join you.'

Bors nodded and set forth. Tannhauser crunched back the dog of his pistol and shortened his grip on the reins and Buraq kicked into a gallop from a standing start. He rose forward in the stirrups as they bolted through the gap towards Abbas, closing the distance between them as the knight with lowered lance did just the same from the farther side. Abbas rose from his victim and with a flick of his head saw both his seeming executioners bearing down. He raised his sword to meet Tannhauser's charge, and Tannhauser thumbed the strap of his helmet from under his chin and threw it aside. At thirty feet Abbas blinked with recognition and Tannhauser pointed past him with the pistol. With the halting gait of one badly hurt, Abbas turned to meet the oncoming lance. Tannhauser gave Buraq a free head and leaned forward into the jump. Buraq cleared the mound of dead to Abbas's left and landed without breaking stride. The head of the onrushing knight flicked towards him in surprise. At ten-feet range Tannhauser aimed and shot him through the chest.

The steel ball punched through the breastplate and the knight reeled back against the cantle, the lance flying wide and falling as his mount carried on. Tannhauser pulled Buraq to a sliding stop and wheeled. The knight was slumped forward. Abbas flashed the point of his blade at the horse's face and it swung aside, and as its rider toppled to the ground, his hand tangled in the reins and pulled the beast to a halt. Abbas fell to his knees and leaned on his sword.

Tannhauser dismounted beside him. Abbas was covered with so much blood it was futile to seek out the wounds. He looked up.

'Ibrahim.'

'Father,' said Tannhauser. 'Have faith.'

He hauled Abbas to his feet and manhandled him against Buraq's flank. He stooped and laced his hands under Abbas's foot. 'With me now.' He heaved and Abbas threw his leg and made the saddle and lay with his arms round Buraq's neck. Tannhauser took the bridle.

'Pray,' he said. '*Adh-Dhariyat*.'

As Tannhauser led Abbas towards the stranded horse, they sang the verses together:

'By the winds that winnow with a winnowing, And those that bear the burden of the rain, And those that glide with ease upon the sea, And those Angels who scatter blessings by Allah's command, Verily that which you are promised is surely true. And verily Judgement and Justice will come to pass.'

Tannhauser stooped over the fallen knight. A red froth bubbled from his nostrils and his beard gleamed with gore. He clung on to the reins of his mount and Tannhauser stomped on his arm and ripped them free. He mounted the warhorse, and it reared beneath him and he dug in his knees and mastered it, and Buraq pulled up close and his presence seemed to gentle the other. Abbas hung on to the short flaxen mane, his lips now moving without sound. Tannhauser took Buraq's rein and led them back through the gap into the open basin.

He glanced south and saw the knot of Ludovico's band, now halfway up the vale towards the defile. Orlandu was safe. Some way behind them and to their left another pair of riders followed: Gullu Cakie and Bors. Since the vale was randomly populated with the to and fro of de la Corna's messengers, a trickle of knights from the Borgo newly arrived, and with stumbling coveys of wounded, mounted and afoot, neither group drew attention. To the north, the battle had shifted to the grassy slopes and sandstone shelves that rimmed Saint Paul's Bay. Beyond it lay the turmoil of boats, and the long voyage home to the Golden Horn.

Tannhauser worked the horses to a trot and skirted the Christian rear where the Sari Bayrak continued their fighting retreat. Between this action and the main engagement lay a section where the tumult was less fierce, and Tannhauser set towards it. They rode within the great arc of killing like beings transported by sorcery into someone else's dream, for none appeared able to see them and no one barred their way. The horses high-stepped the carcasses littering their path and among these latter no Moslem wounded were seen, for the succedent waves of Christians had butchered them all. They passed through a hiatus in the line and reached the foreshore, where fifteen thousand men fought hand to hand across a mile of sand.

The beaches teemed with Turks struggling to embark. In places the contest had spilled into the shallows and the surf crested red about the soldiers' knees. From the longboats pulling for the transports janissaries exchanged fire with the *mangas* on the slopes, and the cannon of the galleys ploughed shot into the Christian pikemen. The battle had hours yet to go, but the only question was how many dead the Turks would leave behind them. Tannhauser no longer cared. He pushed his mount through the press, the warhorse shouldering the crowd aside and treading with imperious scorn on those who fell.

'*Agasi sari bayrak*,' Tannhauser barked, and the ranks parted as they saw the bloodied general he led behind him.

At the water's edge three longboats were loading. Tannhauser swung down and went to Abbas. Abbas's eyes were slitted with pain. He let himself slide from the saddle into Tannhauser's arms. Tannhauser carried him to the shallows, the child now the father of the man. In the stern of the second longboat he saw Salih Ali, who seemed to be in charge of the loading for he brandished a pistol at the refugees crowding the water, desperate to board.

'Salih!' Tannhauser called.

The corsair knew him at once. His eyes widened at the panoplied general in his arms. Tannhauser waded to the gunwale.

'Staunch the Aga's wounds,' said Tannhauser. 'To you he's worth a fortune if he lives.'

Despite the anarchy abounding thereabouts, Salih recognised a rich source of profit – and no little glory to boot – when it was dumped in his lap. He tapped his forehead in salute and helped Tannhauser lower Abbas into the boat. Salih screamed at the oarsmen to push off at once and they ran out their looms into the water.

Tannhauser slipped off his treasured gold bangle and wrapped the lions' heads around Abbas's arm. Abbas opened his eyes and Tannhauser took his hand and squeezed it.

Tannhauser said, '*I came to Malta not for wealth or honour but to save my soul.*'

Abbas squeezed back, his fingers feeble. He raised his head and stared into Tannhauser's eyes. Tannhauser saw his unvoiced agony. Beyond the agony, there was concern: for him.

'My son,' said Abbas. 'Have you found salvation among the infidel?'

'I found you,' said Tannhauser. 'And I found Love. That is salvation enough.'

Abbas said, 'Then you're not coming with me.'

Tannhauser felt pain lance his heart. He smiled and shook his head.

'No, Father. Not this time.'

Abbas smiled back. 'This time I travel to the Golden Horn without you.'

'Only in body. In spirit I am by your side. As you have always been by mine.'

Abbas squeezed his hand for the last time. He said, '*Astowda Okomallah*.'

'*Asalaamu alaykum*,' said Tannhauser. '*Fee iman Allah*.'

Tannhauser let go his hand and Abbas sank into Salih's lap. Tannhauser stepped back. He watched the boat pull away through the blood-crested foam, with Abbas bin Murad in its prow. Then he turned and remounted Buraq, and he rode back through the crowd and up the foreshore, and he left the final slaughter to its disputants, for he'd yet to settle one last quarrel of his own.

SATURDAY 8 SEPTEMBER 1565 – THE NATIVITY OF THE BLESSED VIRGIN MARY

Naxxar Gap – the Heights of Corradino

At its narrowest point the road between the mountains was almost throttled with bodies. Those Turkish wounded who'd crawled this way had been butchered where they lay, and a dozen or so Spanish foot were stripping the bodies of ornaments and gold. They looked up as Tannhauser rode by and their faces were as bright children caught at play. As he debouched from the defile and on to the plain, he saw three riderless warhorses cropping the browned grass in the haze up ahead, and a sense of desolation swept through his chest. The sirocco stirred whorls of dust from the trail and in the warping heat thrown up from the sun-flayed earth the mounts appeared towering and misshapen, like imaginary monsters compounded of incongruous parts. A fourth horse was tethered by the roadside, in the shade of a withered tree, and two human figures appeared seated against its trunk. Tannhauser coaxed a canter out of Buraq and as he got closer his heart sank yet further.

A pair of armoured hulks lay cooking and spreadeagled in the noontide sun. The first was Bruno Marra. Blood poured from his ears and from out of the rims of his eyeballs, and his helm was creviced so deep into the underlying skull that tools would have been required to lever it off. The breastplate of the second knight still rose and fell. Among other wounds the shaft of a broken lance jutted from his groin. It was Escobar de Corro. Tannhauser swung down and drew his sword and de Corro looked up at him. The Castilian's features trembled with the effort of containing his screams, for he was unwilling to give his enemy that satisfaction. Beyond that, his face wrote nothing that could be read and Tannhauser cut his throat and walked to the tree.

Gullu Cakie held a Turkish water flask to Bors's lips, and Bors drank with a vengeance, then spat a stream into his hand and mopped his face. Gullu seemed unharmed and for that Tannhauser gave thanks. Bors was bareheaded, his hair curled and matted with sweat, and he boasted multiple gashes to the scalp and face. His left arm was half-detached at the tip of the shoulder and bone and tendril-like sinews gleamed in the gap. From beneath his cuirass, blood had pooled and curdled in his lap. His silver and ebony musket was cradled upright by his ear, as if he'd carry it as his staff in the afterworld to come.

Tannhauser squatted beside him and Bors smiled.

'Only one dead out of four?' said Tannhauser. 'Those days in the hole must have left you weak in the arm as well as in the head.'

'Time would have given me claim on three but for you showing up,' growled Bors.

'Three?'

'The Black Hand shouldn't overtrouble you. I finally put one through that cursed Negroli plate. Steel shot, double load, at a hundred and fifty feet.'

'That will get the job done,' said Tannhauser.

'Anacleto I left for you.'

Tannhauser looked at Gullu Cakie.

'I tracked them as far as the Mdina road,' Gullu said. 'Ludovico wasn't fit to make the climb. They turned towards the Borgo instead.'

'And the boy?'

'In fine fettle,' said Bors. 'I think I surprised him.' He grinned. 'I surprised them all, the bastards. Better make haste or Ludovico may make the town and blacken your name.'

Tannhauser asked, 'Am I going to see you again?'

Bors shook his head. 'Not this side of perdition.' He pointed up at the shadeless tree. Three fat ravens perched on the same bare branch and watched with curious motions of their heads. 'They've come to accompany my spirit to the other side. But do not mourn, for I've slaked my pride and made my peace with God. The road was long and its end a sight more glorious than I deserved.'

Tannhauser put a hand to the nape of Bors's neck and squeezed. He'd imagined this moment many times. The death of his most beloved friend. Now it was here, his sadness was more than he could bear and he couldn't speak. He swallowed on a plug of emotion and smiled.

'When you get back to Venice,' said Bors, 'and you cash in our goods and count our gold, give my share to the family of Sabato Svi. He was a damnable Jew, to be sure, and if I'm bound for Hell, he and I will toast you through Eternity, but his kin will have more use for my spoils than you will.'

Bors contained a spasm from below. He wiped his mouth and raised his hand and took Tannhauser's arm. Despite the extremity of his condition, his grip was still like a vice.

'Gullu will see my carcass back to the Borgo,' he said. 'Will you see me buried proper?'

Tannhauser nodded. He squeezed the great ox neck again, for his tongue was still tied.

'Now kiss me, my friend, and be gone,' said Bors, 'for I don't enjoy lengthy farewells.'

Tannhauser cradled his massive head in both hands. He kissed him on the lips.

'Until the end,' said Tannhauser.

'The very end,' said Bors.

Tannhauser swallowed and stood up and walked to Buraq.

'Mattias,' called Bors.

Tannhauser turned. He looked into the wild grey northern eyes.

'Stand by the Lady Carla and don't be a fool,' said Bors. He grinned. 'You'll make the liveliest pair of nobles since Solomon and Sheba.' He took a mighty breath, as if to laugh at his own wit, as was his habit, and something gave way inside him, and he didn't let the breath back out again. His head fell back against the tree trunk. Thus Bors of Carlisle did die.

Tannhauser mounted Buraq. He rode on through the wind-raised dust of the defile.

THE TWO KNIGHTS and the half-naked boy left the polluted plain and rode up the trail to Corradino at a pace so slow they might have crawled it on their hands and knees. At the summit they stopped. Around them here and there lay the quitted Turkish trenches, and in them bones and improvised hovels and forsaken gear and ruptured cannon, and racks of ribs both animal and human stretched with stiffened hide and mottled skin. Spread out below was the landscape Orlandu had thought he would never see again.

Grand Harbour sparkled sapphire-blue. The twinned peninsulas of L'Isola and the Borgo were as familiar as his hand, and yet seemed changed forever. The great enceinte was shattered from Saint Michel to the Kalkara Gate and moated by incalculable numbers of dead. Whole sections of either town looked stomped into the ground by a titan's rage. The shot-tattered sails of L'Isola's windmills turned no more, despite the rising sirocco. Yet from this seeming necropolis the church bells pealed without cease, and somewhere within the wrack they celebrated life and hope and the future to come.

Orlandu's throat tightened. The Moslems had been driven from their shores, and to these shores they never should have come; yet he'd witnessed their massacre in Saint Paul's Bay with an anguish scarcely less rending than that which he had felt for the men of Saint Elmo's. He wondered what Tannhauser would say, and Tannhauser would say that it didn't matter, for it was done, and what mattered was the things they'd do next. Orlandu turned to study Ludovico.

The Black Knight with his mortal wound was a mystery. Ludovico of Naples. He'd never heard of him, yet he thought he'd known all the most gallant brethren of the Order. Still with them was the haunted, one-eyed youth, whom Escobar de Corro had called Anacleto. Orlandu had assumed that these men were allies of Tannhauser. Then Bors had bearded them at the defile and had almost slain them all. Ludovico now hunched forward in his saddle. He breathed in short, shallow breaths. His agony was great. He saw Orlandu watching him and raised his head.

'Are you pleased to be home, boy?' he said.

His voice was gentle. The obsidian eyes still radiated something like love.

'Yes, sir,' replied Orlandu. 'I'll be in your debt forever.'

Ludovico managed a smile. 'You have the manners and the bearing of a man. From whom did a boy like you learn such?'

'The great captain, Mattias Tannhauser,' said Orlandu.

Ludovico nodded, as if he'd thought as much. 'You could've wished for no better mentor.'

Orlandu's confusion multiplied. 'Then you do know him?'

'He and I are bound together by God's Will. As to your debt, consider it discharged already, and more than generously repaid.'

Ludovico's smile became a grimace as pain lanced through his bowels and he doubled over. He made no sound and the spasm passed and he raised his head again. 'I wanted to reunite you with your mother, the Lady Carla, in Mdina, but the mountain would have finished me off.'

He doubled forward yet again.

Questions filled Orlandu's mind. Anacleto urged his horse up and took the reins from Ludovico's slack grasp and handed them to Orlandu.

'Take him to the hospital,' said Anacleto. 'Find Father Lazaro.'

Orlandu nodded and Anacleto wheeled and whipped his horse back down the hill. Orlandu glanced after him. Out of the spoliated plain of the Marsa below, a horseman galloped towards them tailing dust. The horse was the colour of a new gold coin and its tail was as pale as wheat. The rider's hair flowed wild and glinted a fiery bronze in the westering sun.

Orlandu said, 'Tannhauser.'

Ludovico saw him too. He called out to his comrade as if he'd stop him. 'Anacleto!'

The effort clenched him up again. Anacleto did not heed him. Orlandu sensed the dark wrath hurtling across the barrens; and he craved nothing more than to see Tannhauser hale. But whatever riddles were here to be resolved, this brave knight needed the surgeon and he wanted to help him. He started forward with Ludovico's reins.

'Hold,' ordered Ludovico.

Orlandu said, 'Father Lazaro –'

'No,' said Ludovico. 'I am beyond the surgeon's art. But not, perhaps, beyond honour.'

Ludovico took the reins back. He turned his horse round to face the plain, and tossed his chin to indicate that Orlandu do the same. They watched Tannhauser bear down on his golden horse. Anacleto rode out to meet him with drawn sword.

'God knows All,' said Ludovico. 'All things that are, and all things that have been, and all things that ever there will be. Even so, Divine Election cannot be approached, and each man graves the chart of Life with his own free hand.'

Ludovico looked at Orlandu, and Orlandu looked back into the fathomless eyes, and the sorrow there enshrined was so immense it encompassed, or so it seemed, all the wasted heartache there heaped on the destitute island around them.

Ludovico took a breath and continued. 'The scholars call this paradox "the Hidden Mystery" and to such questions as these, Augustine answers, *Inscrutabilia sunt judicia Dei*.'

'Sir?'

'The Judgements of God are inscrutable.'

Ludovico turned back to the plain and so did Orlandu.

They saw Tannhauser rein the golden horse to a halt. Anacleto charged towards him. They saw Tannhauser circle his arms round about his head and saw the blue wink of the sun on the barrel of his rifle. They saw smoke and flame plume from the muzzle and Anacleto keeled backwards from his saddle. Then they heard the shot and its echo from the bone-strewn scarp. They saw Tannhauser hold the barrel upright in his fist and saw him cram a flask into its bore. They saw Anacleto roll on to his belly and clamber to his knees. They saw Tannhauser drive home a ball and lay the loaded rifle on his thighs and draw his sword. He walked the golden horse forward. They saw the gleam of the sword's rise and fall, and Anacleto fell forward, and something rolled from his shoulders and came to a halt in the dust.

With a strange sense of contentment that chilled Orlandu's spine, Ludovico said, 'This is where my own chart ends. Yet even in writing his end, a man may become one thing and not another. Perhaps in writing his end most of all.'

WHEN TANNHAUSER SAW Anacleto ride down the hill he realised he was drained of hatred and rage. He'd imagined taking the youth apart piece by piece, prolonging his suffering, humiliating him, leaving him certain to die but not yet dead. Now he wanted only to have it done. He unlimbered his wheel-lock and shot him and the rifleball cracked loud as it breached the chest plate. He recharged the gun and wound the lock tight with the key and primed and closed the pan. He drew his sword and as he passed the kneeling villain, he cut him down without deigning to look him in the face. He scabbarded the sword, then looked up to the shoulder of the scarp and saw their silhouettes against the azure. The man and the boy. The father and his son. Tannhauser canted the rifle against his hip. He rode up the slope to kill the one in front of the other.

When he got there, he saw that there would be no contest of arms.

It wasn't the sight of the bullet hole in the belly of the monk's armour, or of the glistening matt of blood that coated Ludovico's thighs and saddle and which clung in sticky swathes to the flank of his horse. It was the expression on the monk's pallid face and the glimmer from the sockets of his eyes, a glimmer such as thrown by certain stars, so that when you look at them direct they disappear.

'I've asked Orlandu to wait for us in the Borgo,' said Ludovico. 'But he was reluctant to leave without greeting you.'

Tannhauser looked at Orlandu. For the first time in what seemed like an eternity, he felt something close to happiness flicker through his chest. He said, 'You look to have put some flesh on your bones in your exile among the heathen.'

'After working in Galley Creek,' said Orlandu, 'working for Abbas was like a *festa*.'

Tannhauser smiled and Orlandu beamed. The boy's expression faded as he looked at Ludovico. It occurred to Tannhauser that the boy had no inkling of his enmity for the monk; or at least had not, until Bors had shot the latter through the gut.

Tannhauser said, 'Brother Ludovico is right. Wait at the Borgo.'

He threw his rifle to Orlandu and the boy caught it with both hands and swayed on the bareback horse. Tannhauser dismounted and looped his canteen around his neck and handed Buraq's reins to the boy.

'Take Buraq to the Grand Master's stables. Blanket him and walk him and see he's watered when he's cool. No feed until I get there.' He pointed to the bulging pouches slung behind the saddle. 'And don't let my wallets out of your sight.'

'After such a day as he's had, Buraq should have his feet picked,' said Orlandu. 'And his eyes and nostrils wiped, for the dust and smoke were something fierce.'

'Excellent,' said Tannhauser. He looked at Ludovico. 'The boy is a fiend for learning and hard work. When first we met he'd hardly touched a horse in his life.'

Ludovico mastered a spasm and nodded his admiration.

'The boy is all you said he was and more. Brave, proud, tall.'

Orlandu glowed. But Tannhauser could see that his awareness that Death was the fourth member of their circle remained keen. Tannhauser said, 'Now say goodbye to your saviour. And thank him.'

'He's already thanked me,' said Ludovico.

Tannhauser said, 'Then goodbye will do.'

Ludovico stripped a bloody gauntlet and held up his hand. 'Come closer,' he said to Orlandu. Orlandu did so and bent his head to receive the blessing. Ludovico placed his hand on the boy's skull. The contact seemed to fill the black monk with a transcendental joy.

'*Ego te absolvo a peccatis tuis*,' Ludovico raised the hand and made the Cross, '*in nomine Patris et Filii et Spiritus Sancti, Amen.*'

Orlandu crossed himself. Ludovico held out the hand. Orlandu was surprised, for knights never offered such courtesies to such as him. He shook it.

'Honour your mother, always,' said Ludovico. 'There is no wiser commandment.'

'Yes, sir. Thank you, sir,' said Orlandu.

He glanced at Tannhauser. Tannhauser nodded.

'Goodbye,' said Orlandu.

'Godspeed,' said Ludovico. He let go of Orlandu's hand.

Tannhauser and Ludovico watched the boy's descent down the trail. They watched him through the Ruins of Bormula, and across the Grande Terre Plein, and through the Provençal Gate. Then they stood in a silence of their own, for a while, and took in the harbour, and the derelict fortresses, and the half-razed town, and the shambles of ashes and blood for which so many folk, from so many corners of the Earth, had fought and died. The bells of victory pealed. And Tannhauser remembered that it was from a spot very close to this one that he'd heard Carla play her gambo violl in the night. And he thought of the two women playing their music together, and of the moments of rapture and beauty they'd wrought between them, and he thought of Amparo as she swam the moonlit bay, and the wind in his hair evoked her wayward spirit passing by. For Gullu was right, and she would always be with him, and he tried again to recall the last words she'd said to him, and, again, he could not.

From the Provençal Gate a fresh pair of riders appeared, and the hooves of their mounts raised blood dust from the Grande Terre Plain. Tannhauser turned to Ludovico. The man was teetering in the saddle, as pale and gaunt and fragile as the spectre of night.

'Let me help you down,' said Tannhauser.

Ludovico nodded and leaned across his mount's neck. He swung one leg across its back, and as he threw his weight on to its mate his strength failed him complete and Tannhauser took his bulk around the waist and the armour scraped his neck as he lowered him to the stones by the edge of the trail.

'You're the second man I've helped from his horse today.'

'I hope the first was not so frail as I.'

'I too. That's a vicious hole Bors drilled into your gut.'

Tannhauser drew the Devil's blade, which he'd forged three decades before, and Ludovico braced himself without a word. Tannhauser cut the straps of his Negroli armour and Ludovico watched him at it. Here on the ridge, the breeze came in torrid gusts.

'The wind is hot,' said Tannhauser. 'The sirocco, from the deserts of Libya and beyond. But after cooking inside this steel, it will feel like spring.'

He opened the vambraces like the shells of clams, and uncapped the pauldrons from the shoulders. He lifted free the great black breastplate and set it to one aside. He peeled away the bloody padding underneath, and though Ludovico's ruptured belly was as tight as a drumskin, and the bowels inside were dissolving in their own filth, not once did the monk make a sound. Against his skin he wore the plain black habit of Saint John, with the white eight-pointed cross stitched on the breast.

'Better?' asked Tannhauser.

'I'm grateful.'

Tannhauser uncorked the canteen and held it to Ludovico's lips. Ludovico took two swallows and nodded. Tannhauser drank himself.

'Does the Grand Master live?' asked Ludovico.

'La Valette lives.'

'Good,' said Ludovico. 'At least I don't have that upon my soul.'

Tannhauser studied him. 'You're not the man I last saw in the Guva.'

Ludovico looked at him. 'Perhaps I had a wise man for an enemy.'

'I'd hazard it took more than that.'

'When I saw Orlandu on the field,' said Ludovico. 'When I called his name and he turned waist-deep in the water, and for the first time I saw his face. So brave, so –' He struggled for words, and his shoulders lapsed back against the rock and he rolled his great head and looked up at the sky. The black eyes filmed with emotion. 'Oh God,' he said. 'Oh My Lord God.'

In those words was a regret too monumental to be compassed.

Tannhauser wondered it didn't kill him. He said, 'That's answer enough. Does Orlandu know who you are?'

'No.'

'Why didn't you tell him?'

'I leave that choice to Carla.'

'Do you think she'd lie?'

Ludovico's lips were parted, and he panted in short gasps. His mouth didn't move, but some glancing of the light in his eyes suggested a smile.

'Perhaps she has a wise man for a friend,' he said.

'I'd thought to tell the boy you were a coward and a traitor,' said Tannhauser. 'But the one would be a falsehood, and in a world as degenerate as this one, what man is not a traitor to his own best promise?'

'Tell Carla I'm sorry.'

'I know,' said Tannhauser. 'I will.'

Ludovico blinked. 'I didn't intend for Amparo to die.'

Tannhauser studied him. Then said, 'I know that too.'

'I wonder if God will forgive me.'

'Christ will.'

'You speak of Christ, at last?'

Tannhauser smiled. 'A religion that makes room for the good thief has much to recommend it to the likes of me.'

Ludovico's eyes bored into him and for a moment he was the inquisitor of old, the man in search of other men's hidden truths. He said, 'Then much else has changed since the Guva.'

'You told me in Messina that Sorrow opens the gate to the Grace of God. And you asked, if such were the case, what right man might shun it.'

Ludovico's eyes shifted, as if recalling that conversation far away.

'Those were merely words,' he said. 'Scholarly words.'

'Life inclines to making such words flesh,' Tannhauser replied.

Ludovico nodded. He put the palms of his hands to his chest, and breathed deeply of the rank and dusty air. He let it out through his mouth. He essayed a smile. He looked up. Their eyes locked across the mighty gulf that had divided them. Ludovico had made his Peace.

'You were right,' said Ludovico. 'It feels like spring.'

Tannhauser stabbed him through the heart and Ludovico died on the instant.

The blade forged in a devil's blood had found its destined home. And there it rested.

TANNHAUSER LET GO of the precious garnet hilt. His throat was thick with emotions he couldn't name and he swallowed them down. He picked up Ludovico in his arms. Burned down to the sinew by the siege as he was – as were they all – he remained a big man. He carried him into a chest-deep Turkish entrenchment and laid him down. He rolled him in a length of canvas scavenged from an abandoned magazine. He covered him with timbers and gun stones and pieces of rock. He left no marker but the dagger lodged in his heart. He climbed back up on to the trail. He baled the Negroli armour and tied it to the saddle of Ludovico's horse. As he was about to mount up, the Grand Master, Jean Parisot de La Valette, and his distinguished Latin Secretary, Oliver Starkey, emerged from beneath the hill's rim. They both saw the monk's black armour.

'Captain Tannhauser,' said La Valette. 'How goes the day?'

'The day is yours.'

La Valette nodded and dismounted. He favoured his injured leg but his vigour remained a wonderment. He drew his sword. Tannhauser looked at him.

'Would you be rid of me too?' Tannhauser asked.

La Valette laughed. Tannhauser had never heard him laugh before. It was a pirate's laugh. And something more. The laugh of one able to send everyone he loved to their deaths; and, at that, for a monstrous ideal. La Valette shook his head.

'There's no better place than a battlefield,' he said, 'on which to be dubbed a knight.'

Tannhauser stared at him.

'I know there are few you would kneel for,' said La Valette. 'Will you kneel for the Prince of the Religion?'

Still Tannhauser stared.

'Do you doubt that such a gift is in my power?' asked La Valette.

'No,' said Tannhauser, at last arousing his mind from out of its stupor. 'I doubt only what it might commit me to. I'm not about to make vows I cannot keep. I've made such mistakes before.'

La Valette seemed impressed by such integrity. 'When the Order sees fit to honour a man of singular service, it may confer upon him the habit of Magistral Grace. The usual requirements of nobility are waived – clearly a necessity in this case – the probationary period is dispensed with, and you're not obliged to make a full profession of our vows. Nevertheless, you belong to the Religion, and wherever the brethren gather you may claim your right of allowance and canteen.'

Tannhauser considered this. 'May I indulge in commerce?'

'Only the Vatican itself is richer than the Religion,' said Starkey. 'With this victory, our donations may well outstrip theirs, though the Holy Father will never know by just how much.'

'And may I style myself "Chevalier" or some other such worthy appellation?'

'Of course,' said La Valette. The pirate's smile creased his eyes. 'You will also be immune to the arm of the Civil Law.'

Tannhauser caught his jaw before it dropped. What brotherhood of criminals was ever more ingeniously conceived? 'The law has no jurisdiction over the brethren?'

'You will answer only to our laws,' said La Valette. 'Since you're the only man alive who's outlasted the Guva, I trust you will keep them.'

At the risk of appearing unappreciative, Tannhauser said, ' Is celibacy a requirement?'

'No, it is not. Though I might say I recommend it if you'd live a long life.'

Tannhauser sank to one knee and squared his shoulders.

'In that case, Your Excellency, you may wield your sword with gladness.'

SATURDAY 8 SEPTEMBER 1565 – THE NATIVITY OF THE BLESSED VIRGIN MARY

Mdina

WITHOUT WALLS AND entrenchments and gunfire – and the homicidal patrols of either flag – Tannhauser realised how tiny Malta was. The journey from the Borgo to Mdina, which at times had seemed a trip to tax Odysseus, was a mere eight miles. With the horses recruited, and some food and wine in their bellies, he and Orlandu rode up the mountain to the sound of numberless bells. They passed a deal of jubilant traffic on the way, for it was as if the gates of an enormous gaol had been opened and its prisoners released to revel as they would. But Tannhauser was sombre, and ignored the gay halloos, and Orlandu riding beside him caught his mood.

'You're angry with me?' he asked.

Tannhauser considered him. The boy looked as lively as a slaughterhouse dog. If any could be said to have come through all this madness unscathed, it was he. He was sound in limb, sharp of mind, and had – as far as Tannhauser knew – no murders or cruelties to tarnish his immortal soul. And it occurred to

Tannhauser, as if out of the blue, that he himself could claim no small share of credit in this triumph, and with this thought his disposition improved.

'Let me put it this way,' he said. 'If I'd known what your existence was going to cost me – in more blood, sweat and tears than I knew I had to shed – I'd have made my way to Malta twelve years ago and strangled you in your crib.'

Orlandu recoiled as if slapped and Tannhauser grinned. 'If we're going to walk the road ahead together,' he said, 'you must acquaint yourself with my drollery, which tends to the grim.'

'Then you're not angry.'

'Have you given me reason to be so?'

'Then why do you wish you had strangled me in my crib?'

'When we met on the woeful gantlet at Saint Elmo's, I told you that you'd led me a merry dance. I didn't know then that the jig had hardly begun. But now that it's almost over, I would say that the sight of you makes every bloody step worthwhile.'

He thought of Amparo. And Bors. Not every step, then. But the boy was not accountable for that. If Orlandu could not make head nor tail of this, it was not for want of acumen. He struck, instead, right to the essence.

'So we are still friends.'

'Yes, lad,' said Tannhauser. 'You may be the only true friend I have left.'

'I'm sorry for the dead English, Bors of Carlisle. He said he was my friend too.'

'Indeed he was. His last sally must have been a spectacle.'

'Oh my God,' said Orlandu, wide-eyed. 'Four against one? Four *knights*? It was terrible. Fantastic. But why?'

'Because they were false knights – foul and rotten limbs, no less – and enemies of La Valette as well as ourselves.'

'How so, false and foul?'

'That's a tale for another time.' He gave him a solemn look. 'You must keep everything you saw a tight secret. Few men are capable of such a challenge, simple though it seems, but it's a skill that will stand you in good stead.'

'Like pretending,' said Orlandu.

'Exactly so, exactly so.'

'But, to each other, friends should not pretend,' said Orlandu.

'No, they should not,' said Tannhauser.

'You say Fra Ludovico was a false knight.'

Tannhauser sighed. 'Within the bigger tent, his allegiances were divided. Such rivalries thrive in all big tents, for men are seldom content with the way things are and in striving to better them are intolerant of ideas contrary – or merely different – to their own. Life is often a puzzle in that respect and I'm the last man in the world to cast that stone. Certainly Ludovico was brave, and a man possessed by powerful convictions. But in my experience, any conviction strongly held is a sword with two edges, both of them sharp.'

'He told me to honour my mother.'

Tannhauser felt the tightrope sway beneath his feet. 'A splendid notion.'

'He wanted to take me to Mdina, to be reunited with her.'

'He bequeathed that happy duty to me.'

Orlandu said, 'Was Fra Ludovico my father?'

And there it was. Tannhauser pulled Buraq in, and they stopped, and he feigned some business with the bridle. It was odd, but until he'd done the deed he hadn't considered the business of telling Orlandu that the father the boy so craved had died by his hand. Nor perhaps had he realised how much he valued the boy's affection. He turned to look at him and Orlandu's brown eyes bored into his, and in them that affection was so naked that Tannhauser faltered. Ludovico, after all, had decided to leave this to Carla, and had even given his blessing to the telling of a lie. But Ludovico's shame was not Tannhauser's. Tannhauser's soul was his own.

He said, 'Yes. Brother Ludovico was your father.'

Orlandu's lips clenched.

Tannhauser said, 'I killed him.'

Orlandu blinked, twice. He said, 'Because he was false?'

'At the last he was as true as any man may find it in himself to be.'

'Then why?'

In Tannhauser's reckoning this was not the time to list Ludovico's crimes. The boy would know them in time, but not today. He said, 'I killed him because Fate ordained it.'

Orlandu took this in and perhaps Tannhauser had underestimated him, for the answer seemed adequate, at least for now. In any case, the statement was true enough. Orlandu said, 'If my father was a foul and rotten limb, and I am his blood, will I too be foul and rotten?'

'I told you once before, it isn't blood that matters but the way we walk through life. We've walked a mile or two together, you and I, and believe me, there's nothing foul or rotten in your soul.'

Again Orlandu absorbed this. Then he said, 'Will we walk a few miles more?'

Tannhauser felt his heart squeeze, for he wanted to say, '*Until the End*'. Yet he couldn't make a promise that he wasn't certain he could keep. He said, 'We'll see.'

Then he grinned and the boy grinned too. And so all was well.

Above the rim of the hill, rockets exploded in the sky and church bells rang. Tannhauser tossed his head yonder. 'Let's to Mdina, for Carla is waiting.' A thought struck him. 'By the way, do you still have my ring? My gold ring?'

Orlandu nodded. 'Of course.'

Tannhauser held out his hand. 'Then let's have it. Without gold I feel half-naked.'

CARLA SAT IN the gloom of the Casa Manduca. Despite the celebrations in the streets, she felt alone. Don Ignacio was dead. He'd been buried in the Manduca crypt in Saint Paul's Cathedral. A single mourner, the old steward, Ruggiero, had attended; as he now attended her. Ruggiero had begged her forgiveness for deeds and sins committed long ago, and she gave it free and full, for too much horror in the present was born from the horror of the past, and he fell to his knees and kissed her hands, and she sent him away. She forgave her father too and sadness filled her, for he'd died friendless and alone, and need not have done so. Ruggiero had told her that the house, and her father's farmland in the Pawles Valley, and his shipping interests and gold, now belonged to her. The news had surprised her but left her unmoved.

The house oppressed her. The ghosts who'd squandered their lives in loveless misery stalked its halls. In the wane of the day she went to the walled garden and stood beneath the lengthening shade of the orange trees. It was the feast of the Madonna's Nativity, and a Saturday, and during the first decade of the rosary she would meditate on the mystery of the Annunciation, when the Archangel Gabriel appeared to Mary and told her she was to bear God's child. It was one of the joyful mysteries, and perhaps it would help. She knelt on the grass and kissed the crucifix on her rosary. She made the sign of the Cross and began the Credo.

'I believe in God, the Father Almighty, Maker of heaven and earth. And in Jesus Christ, his only Son, our Lord, who was conceived by the Holy Ghost, born of the Virgin Mary, suffered under Pontius Pilate, was crucified, dead, and was buried. He descended into hell. The third day He rose again from the dead. He ascended into heaven, and sitteth on the right hand of God, the Father Almighty. From thence he shall come again to judge the quick and the dead.'

She heard the door of the casa creak open. Then footsteps. And a cough from the garden behind her. She crossed herself and looked over her shoulder. She expected Ruggiero.

Mattias stood framed in the arbour.

Carla's heart almost stopped. She rose to her feet. His cheeks were scored with exhaustion. Something nameless, something anguished, haunted his eyes. He started down the path and – as when first she saw him, in another garden long ago and far away – she was put in mind of a wolf. She hastened towards him and he opened his arms and she fell into them. He held her while she caught her breath, her mind so full of questions that her tongue was stilled.

'Ludovico and his cohorts are dead,' Mattias said.

She felt nothing but a wave of relief. Then she saw Mattias's eyes.

He said, 'Bors too. And Nicodemus.' He hesitated. 'And Amparo.'

Pain knifed her soul and her eyes welled with tears. Mattias put a finger to her lips.

'Please,' he said. 'There will be time enough for mourning. And in that we'll not be alone. Speaking for myself, a moment of joy would be most welcome. And despite that much has been taken, much endures, and we've reason to smile.'

On instinct she looked past his shoulder. Beyond the threshold of the casa doorway she sensed a presence. Mattias turned in that direction, and Carla's tears began to fall, and in them joy and hope and grief were intermingled. She wiped her face.

'Orlandu,' he called.

Orlandu emerged from the door. He walked towards her stiffly, with his shoulders back and his head held high, as if under instruction to put his best foot forward. His skin glowed, and his eyes were deep and honest, and Carla knew she'd never seen a being more beautiful in her life. He stopped before her and bowed, his face as serious as a judge. Her tears welled again, with sentiments too complex and numerous to name, and this time she couldn't contain them.

'Smile, boy,' said Mattias. 'And watch your manners.'

He smiled himself.

'For this is your mother.'

Carla threw her arms around Orlandu and held him tight.

SUNDAY 9 SEPTEMBER 1565

Hal Saflieni

The tombs of Hal Saflieni had been carved from the living rock before iron was known, before bronze was known. Perhaps, for no one could know, before Prometheus stole fire from the gods. Carved, then, with bones and flints when the world of men was young, when the Creator of the universe was Woman, when these ancient masons worshipped a goddess alone: a goddess whose belly swelled with perpetual fecundity. Carved in an age when War was but a dream and waited for the sleepers to awaken. Here at Hal Saflieni, in the chambers and the side chambers, and in the serried niches and vaults beneath ceilings spiralled and honeycombed with red ochre, skeletons by the thousand lay at rest.

To Carla, Hal Saflieni had been a refuge whose solace was mysterious but profound. Though its precincts had been forbidden, her girl's heart had been drawn here. When her soul was troubled she'd kneel before the Great Stone Mother and feel the wisdom of Time. The priests said this was a pagan place, and as such to be shunned. But young Carla had felt no sense of sin. She'd prayed here to the Virgin, in the city of the dead, and Virgin and Stone Mother both had given her peace. She hadn't been to this site for many years. Today, in need of solace, in need of peace, she determined to take her friend there and commit her to eternity.

In the Borgo, in the darkness before dawn, Vespers and Matins for the Dead were performed at the church of the Annunciation. Although the fighting was over, many had died the day before, and many would die yet among the gravely wounded. Psalms were sung, and nocturnes from the Book of Job were recited. *O Lord, grant them eternal rest, and let everlasting light shine upon them.* Among those mourned were Amparo and Nicodemus and Bors. *Deliver me, O Lord, from eternal death in that awful day, when the heavens and the earth shall be shaken, and Thou shalt come to judge the world by fire.* Lauds followed, and the Miserere was sung, and the Canticle of Ezechias, and the Antiphon of John. *I am the resurrection and the life: he that believeth in Me, though he were dead, yet shall he live: and whosoever liveth and believeth in Me shall never die.* Then the sins of those souls dead to this world, but not to the next, were absolved, and the mourners emerged into the dawn.

At Carla's bidding, Tannhauser and Orlandu loaded the bodies of Bors and Amparo into a two-wheeled cart. That of Nicodemus could not be found. As a pale white sun ascended above the rim of Monte San Salvatore, they hauled them up to the necropolis at Hal Saflieni, and there they laid them to rest among ancient companions. At Carla's bidding too came Lazaro, and though he quailed at that pagan landscape she was one he could not refuse, and he consecrated the niches that they chose, for according to the canon law each man may choose for himself the ground of his burial. He sprinkled the bodies with holy water, and the Kyrie and the Canticle Benedictus were recited, and Lazaro performed with all fidelity the rites of the Catholic faith. Then Lazaro left, reciting the De Profundis as they watched him go, and they three and their departed friends were left in the catacombs, in a silence painful to bear.

From the cart Tannhauser took out the gambo violl. And Carla played.

She played until she thought her heart would break. And looking at Tannhauser, it seemed to her that his had already done so, and she realised that she'd lost him to grief. When Carla knew she could play no more, she looked at Orlandu, and he looked back, his eyes strong and warm and steady, and he smiled, a little shyly, and she played on from the flame of happiness he kindled.

THEY RODE BACK to the Borgo and Mattias told her that he'd determined to sail for Venice on the earliest ship. Carla's love for him had not dwindled; rather, its heat and her yearning were all the more intense. But Amparo's death lay as heavily upon him as it did on her, perhaps much more so, and a grief mutually shared made poor soil for passion to grow in. He made no mention of their bargain, and neither did she. He asked if she would stay in Malta, and she said she would not. She would settle her father's affairs and return to the Aquitaine, with Orlandu, and Mattias understood, for the knights now claimed the island by right of blood, and not merely residence, and they would turn it into a shrine consecrate to War. As they approached the Kalkara Gate, they dismounted and Tannhauser turned to Carla.

'The night we were taken in the gatehouse,' he said. 'Do you remember the last words Amparo said to me?'

'Yes, of course,' replied Carla. 'What did they mean?'

She saw the pain in his face. 'I cannot recall them,' he said. 'It has brought me considerable torment.'

'*The nightingale is happy*,' said Carla.

Tannhauser nodded. 'Of course.' He smiled; yet his eyes filmed with sadness.

Carla said, 'What did she mean?'

'She meant that I was her blood-red rose,' said Tannhauser.

Carla looked at him, intrigued, and waited for more.

'It is a tale the Arabs tell,' he said. 'Amparo admired it.'

'Will you tell me?'

Tannhauser took her in his arms and squeezed until she feared that he would crush away her life. She felt him make some decision that tore him in two and his arms relaxed. He looked at her and in the fierce blue coals of his eyes she saw a sorrow too deep to fathom, and she felt a sudden dread. Her voice wavered.

'Will you tell me the tale?' she asked, again.

'Yes,' said Tannhauser. 'Some day.'

EPILOGUE

THE GRACE OF GOD

1566

The Spanish Viceroy of Sicily, Garcia de Toledo, arrived on Malta a week after the siege was lifted, and so overcome he was by the extremities of suffering he found there that some said he wept tears of pity, and some said of shame. Toledo was taken on a tour of the blood-soaked ground, and he heard of the valiant deeds thereon enacted, and he claimed from the crypt the body of his son, Federico, who had died in the battle for the first of the Turkish siege towers. Three days later, Toledo left. He never returned to Malta and passed thereafter into obscurity.

Obscurity did not wait for La Valette or the Holy Religion. The Grand Master was acclaimed the bravest man in Christendom, its most brilliant soldier and statesman, the bulwark of the Church Militant. La Valette himself was indifferent to the honours heaped upon him. He did not go to Rome despite the promise of a Triumph. Indeed, he never left the island again, despite invitations from every palace in Europe, and he appreciated glorification only because it brought a colossal influx of gold and eager new recruits to replenish the Order. With characteristic vigour, he at once set about the design and construction of a massive new stronghold on the slopes of Monte Sciberras, a citadel that would be the most impregnable ever built, and which would be christened Valletta in honour of his fame. His distinguished Latin Secretary, Oliver Starkey, worked alongside him night and day, for the labour and its complexities were fantastic, and, absorbed in this task for their Holy Religion, both men found contentment for the rest of their days.

Mustafa Pasha and his commanders left forty thousand *gazi* in the dust of Malta and with those unburied dead their reputations too. After sixty bleak days at sea they returned to the Golden Horn to face their Sultan's scorn. To their own surprise most of all, they were spared the eunuch's bowstring, and Suleiman bowed his head to Allah's Will. He then ordered preparations for a second assault on the island the following year, one that he himself would lead to a famous victory. But this was not to be. Late in the summer of 1566, at the age of seventy-two, the mighty Shah died in Hungary while conducting the siege of Szeged. He died as he had lived, making war, and so stunning was this catastrophe that his doctors were strangled in his tent and his death kept a secret from his Agas for forty-three days, until his embalmed corpse was buried in the tomb Sinan had built for him, by the Suleimanye mosque in Old Stambouli.

Suleiman the Magnificent was succeeded by his last surviving son, Selim, known, for excellent reasons, as 'The Sot'. Thus did the Ottoman sun begin its slow descent, for in the passing of God's Shadow On Earth, so too passed its zenith and meridian.

In Rome an attempt was made on the life of Pope Pius IV, Giovanni Medici. His would-be murderer was one of those lone, mad assassins well known to historians of every age, and the villain died in custody before he could betray his phantom co-conspirators. The Will of God, however, was not so easily thwarted. Medici succumbed to a crueller hand, that of Roman fever, in December of 1565. Michele Ghisleri stepped into the Shoes of the Fisherman, as long planned, and provoked much callous mirth among his inner circle by taking the pontifical name of Pius V. Under his reign the Inquisition flourished anew. Ghisleri fomented further wars against the Mohammedans, and against Protestants throughout the rest of Europe. Intellectual darkness benighted the Catholic world and a long and needless decline was blindly embraced. For these egregious crimes, the inquisitor Pope would one day be canonised a saint.

To the heroic natives of Malta fell the task of rebuilding the island in Hell's wake. Out of a total population of some twenty-odd thousand, seven thousand adult males had perished in the siege. Their fields lay scorched and barren, their houses smashed to rubble, and many of those spared death remained crippled for life. They endured in the shadows thrown by the Religion's radiance and their feelings about what had passed were never recorded, for while the knights were '*i nostri*', the Maltese remained '*la basse plebe*', and all that needed to be known of the lower orders was that they'd done what was required of them by their betters.

In August of 1566, the granddaughter of Gullu Cakie gave birth to a son. On taking the patriarch's counsel, she had the newborn babe christened Matheu.

The Chevalier Mattias Tannhauser, Magistral Knight of the Order of Saint John of Jerusalem, remained unaware that he'd been honoured by a second namesake. For all his lifelong intimacy with the evils and fortunes of war, the Maltese Iliad left him in a deep melancholia, one for which he knew no balm, and he departed from the island on the first galley bound for Sicily.

Before he set sail, he submitted to the rituals of the Order and received the Habit of Magistral Grace. In a bout of generosity he later had cause to regret, he donated most of his opium to the Sacred Infirmary, which remained in dire need. He secured Starkey's promise that when Carla left for France she'd be accompanied by a pair of guardian knights of the soundest possible character. Then, on the brink of his departure, a boon befell him, and it was something to shine a light through the night of his gloom.

Among the few men taken alive in the slaughter at Saint Paul's Bay was the silent Ethiope, the man who'd restored him to life in the pink pavilion of Abbas bin Murad. Tannhauser found him in chains and knee-deep in human swill, hauling disintegrating corpses from the ditch around the town. Tannhauser purchased his freedom. He washed him and bought him some clothes. And throughout all this the Ethiope remained quite mute. They sat at the refectory table in the Auberge of England, and while they ate Tannhauser studied him at length.

'I will be damned if I know what to do with you,' he said.

The Ethiope seemed to grasp the essence of this for he upped from the table and went outside. Tannhauser followed him. The Ethiope pointed to the far blue fastness to the south.

In Arabic, he said, '*Home*.'

Tannhauser talked his way into an hour with La Valette's secret library of maps and with his broken fingers he copied as best he could what was known of Egypt and the African Horn. He showed it to the Ethiope, who recognised the Red Sea. If he could cross Egypt and reach the sea's northern shore, the Ethiope believed, he could sail to its southernmost tip and from there cross what he said was called the Danakil and make his way to the mountains of his far distant origin. It would be a most daring and singular journey, Tannhauser thought, and for a moment the epic vision of it leapt from one man's mind to the other, and the urge to accompany the Ethiope blazed through Tannhauser's breast. But only for a moment. That would be another journey, for another time, and another life, and not for this one.

Tannhauser loaded a mule with supplies and he and the Ethiope rode over Monte San Salvatore to the ruins of Zonra, where Tannhauser's fabled boat yet lay concealed. They reassembled and launched it and Tannhauser instructed the Ethiope, as best he could, on the route to Alexandria and by which heavenly constellations he might be guided. He gave him a pound of opium and some hooks and line, and a Turkish sword and some Turkish specie in silver to pay his way, and he told him when he reached Alexandria to seek out Moshe Mosseri and ask for his counsel, and to invoke to him the name of Sabato Svi.

And all this the Ethiope accepted like a man who knew that his prow would be guided by God. Finally, Tannhauser made him custodian of the ebony and silver musket that Bors had so treasured.

'If you fail,' said Tannhauser, 'it won't be for want of fine tackle.'

The Ethiope smiled. And this smile was a jewel to be treasured always.

Tannhauser never knew his name, and to the last he did not ask it, for he knew he'd never see the man again. The Ethiope embraced him and climbed in his felucca and ran up the lateen.

Tannhauser stood and watched until the red sail was lost in the haze.

When Tannhauser sailed away himself, he watched Carla and Orlandu salute him from the wharf. This parting tore rents in the fabric of his heart and he knew not if he'd see these two again. Or even if he'd want to. There was no sense in this, it was true; for he felt a terrible love for Carla and harboured for the boy an uncommon affection for which the word 'love' seemed trite. But so it was. And he had to go. Orlandu couldn't comprehend his leaving, and raised 'the famous enterprise', in which Tannhauser had suggested they'd engage.

'If you honour your mother, and learn something useful, then perhaps one day it shall be so,' Tannhauser told him. 'Meanwhile our ways must part, for I've business in the north.'

Carla didn't make his parting more painful by trying to dissuade him. She contained the many emotions that battled within her. She tried to understand his need to journey alone. Her own needs would wait on Hope, and as she embraced him in farewell, she gave it voice.

'On the main road from Bordeaux to Perpignan is a church with a bell tower in the Norman style, the only one of that character in those parts. Beyond it is a fork in the road. The southern fork leads to a *manoire* on a hill, whose roof has a single turret tiled in red.'

Tannhauser took this in without making any answer.

Carla said, 'If a certain bargain is – some day – to be concluded, that's where you will find the appropriate partner.'

In answer to this, Tannhauser kissed her.

And letting that stand as his promise, he was gone.

In Messina, Tannhauser paid a visit to Dimitrianos.

In Venice he settled the affairs of Sabato Svi.

Then on an instinct too primal to refuse, he continued north – far north, and east – and on this journey he learned to treasure solitude above all things. He slept in monasteries where silence was the rule, and the company of women he abjured, and as he and the winter closed fast upon each other, he reached the village of his birth, and threw himself upon the kindness of his father.

Tannhauser spent the winter and spring at work in Kristofer's forge and the bond that war had long broken was spliced anew. In the frosty dawns he wrestled with fire and steel. He became a great favourite with his new-found sisters and brother. He accompanied his father on his circuits and they talked of simple things. They shared memories – at first with pain, but then with a bittersweet joy – of the kin they'd so loved and had lost. They prayed together at the graves – which Kristofer had dug from the earth with his own hands – of Tannhauser's mother and Gerta and dear Britta. And Tannhauser sometimes wondered, did Kristofer remember the mysterious Ottoman stranger who'd called at his forge? And sometimes he sensed that he did, and that the stranger was no stranger at all; and sometimes not. And neither ever mentioned the stranger, and this was fitting, for the man was a ghost, and a ghost to Tannhauser himself most of all.

Thus he regained his strength in heart and limb. And through winter's slow retreat and the burgeoning of spring he believed that he would never leave again. And perhaps it was from that conviction that the healing came, for these people cared little for his past or his deeds or his glory. They cared only for him. And this put him in mind of Amparo and he thought of her in the nights when he watched the stars traverse the sky. And he thought, too, of Carla and Orlandu. And he thought of Ludovico Ludovici, the tragic monk who lost his mind in the gulf between Power and Love, and who told him that Sorrow was the route to Grace and spoke true.

In these mountains far from everywhere, Tannhauser came to understand that sadness was the thread that wove his life into a single piece, and that in this there was no reason for regret, much less surrender. And this his father taught him: that in spite of sadness, in spite of loss without measure, Life beckoned yet, like a billet of base iron awaiting transformation. Since Tannhauser had last raised a fire in that pale stone temple, where his father brought things into being that had not been before, Emperors and Popes had fallen and the lines on the maps had been changed. Flags had been brandished and armies had marched and multitudes had killed and died for their tribes and their gods. But the Earth yet turned, for the Spheres danced to a music of their own, and the Cosmos was indifferent to the vanity and genius of Men. The human spirit eternal, if such a thing there was, was here, in an old man with his hammer and his hearth, and with a woman and fine children whom he loved.

Tannhauser realised, at last, that it was in the gap between Desolation and Love, between Sorrow and Faith, that Christ and the Grace of God were to be found.

As summer kissed the Alps and melted all but the highest snows, Tannhauser packed his gear and saddled Buraq and bade farewell. And though many tears were shed, this parting didn't rend his heart as had others before, for it was only a parting of flesh and not of spirit. He headed back across a continent, through the dominions of many different kings, and in the shortening days of summer, Tannhauser entered once again the land of the Franks.

THUS, ON AN auburn autumn day, the Chevalier Mattias Tannhauser rode from the city of Bordeaux and down the Perpignan road into the Aquitaine. Horse and rider together had covered a thousand miles in the year by now gone by. It had taken that long and that far for the wounds to his spirit to heal. Buraq was in fine fettle and ate up the sunlit miles with equine joy. Tannhauser had found the city greatly to his liking. It was a splendid port, a start that could not be bettered, and a town committed to commerce rather than war. He would have to improve his French, a chore he didn't relish, but it could be done. As a Chevalier de Malte, and a veteran of the greatest siege in history, all doors were open to him there as they'd been elsewhere. More than all this, he'd seen the Atlantic Ocean, a grey and turbulent immensity that entranced his imagination, and which set him to wondering what lay on its farther shores.

He saw in the distance the Norman church tower that marked the road he was seeking. He took the southern fork, and half a league later saw a small *manoire* on a hill. And suddenly he was aware of the beating of his heart, for from its roof rose a turret tiled in red.

In a cobbled yard beside a barn he found two youths brawling in the horse manure and straw. Rather, one youth lay curled in a ball while the second kicked him – without any great appearance of mercy – in the back and skull. Since the one prostrate and whining for quarter was somewhat the elder and larger of the two, Tannhauser felt a distinct glow of pride.

'Orlandu,' he said. 'Let the oaf get up and send him on his way.'

Orlandu turned in mid-kick and saw the golden horse. He raised his eyes, as if to an apparition, and stared at its rider. He swallowed his shock and said, 'Tannhauser?'

By God the boy looked well. And what a power of good it was to see him. Tannhauser suppressed his inclination to smile, which required a considerable effort, and assumed a stern expression. 'I'd hoped to find you studying Latin, or Geometry, or some other such higher enterprise,' he said. 'Instead I find you brawling in the dung like a common serf.'

Orlandu continued to gape, now torn between rapture and shame. His mouth opened and closed. The oaf scrambled to his feet and stumbled off. Tannhauser dismounted. He could contain the smile no longer.

'Come here, boy.' He opened his arms. 'And tell me how you've been keeping.'

When Orlandu's excitement was at last contained to the degree that he could carry out an order, Tannhauser said, 'I think it's time you announced my presence to the Lady of the manor.' He added, 'Then recruit Buraq and leave us in peace until I call you.'

Tannhauser chose to take a seat in the chateau's garden, where he enjoyed the wane of the day and took in the scents of the fruit trees and flowers, and reflected on the lushness that abounded thereabouts. He felt the presence of Carla – that strange aura of control and impending abandon that she cast about her. A woman of property and taste. He re-examined his gear for stains and found himself presentable. Time passed and he grew a mite perturbed. He'd been certain of a warm welcome from the boy; but from Carla he was less sure. She'd had time and tranquillity in plenty to reflect on the folly of falling in league with such as him. Carla's allure may have drawn him across a continent, but the potency of his own was wide open to doubt.

Music drifted from the manor house at his back. A gambo violl. It started with great delicacy, perhaps hesitation, then it found its wings and soared and swooped and plunged with majestic freedom. And Tannhauser felt a great happiness, as great as any he'd known, for the music was the voice of Carla's inmost heart, and she played for him.

When the music stopped he collected himself and stood up and Carla walked down the garden path to greet him. She was every bit as elegant, if not as erotically attired, as when they'd first met, yet, in compensation, her hair fell unrestrained about her shoulders and there was an exuberance in her carriage that he'd never seen before. Her beauty was not just undimmed; it had bloomed. She smiled, as if she'd believed in a moment like this, but hadn't expected it.

'You haven't lost your touch,' he said. 'Sublime. If I may say so, in art and appearance both.'

Carla inclined her head in appreciation.

For a moment they took each other in.

'As you see,' he said, at last, 'I'm powerless, once again, to resist your call.'

She said, 'I hope it will ever be thus.'

Her green eyes shone. She smiled. She tossed her hair. He was lost for words. What had he meant to say to her? So much. But where to begin? They stood looking at each other. The silence lengthened. He reached out and she gave him her hand. The loveliness of its touch sent a tremor through his spine. Her fingers squeezed and he saw her swallow the emotion that rose in her throat. His impulse was to pull her against him, and to crush her lips to his, and submit to long-dormant instincts that now roared to life. Yet he resisted. Their last kiss had been stolen from a world replete with horror. And though horror and fire and madness would forever be mixed in the mortar that bound them together, he wanted their first kiss here, in a gentler world, to be free of shadows. And there was a shadow – of an unforgettable passion, and of a spirit who had to be honoured before they were free. The spirit of one they'd both loved and who loved them still.

He said, 'I made you a promise that I want to keep.'

In the garden lay a bed of roses, white and red, which Tannhauser had marked as soon as Orlandu had left him there. He led her down the path and stopped by the flowers.

'I'd hoped to find these here,' he said.

Carla said, 'So you're going to tell me a tale.'

She smiled. Her green and black eyes brimmed. And Tannhauser knew she understood, and he knew why he loved her, and why he always would. They both were blood-red roses. They all of them were. He pointed out a tall white bloom.

'In Araby,' he said, 'they say that, once upon a time, all roses were white.'

Mattias Tannhauser returns to the fray in *The Twelve Children of Paris*, published on 23rd May 2013 by Jonathan Cape. Here is a little something to whet your appetite. . .

SWINE

ARNAULD DE TORCY led them through a sequence of corridors, salons and halls whose extravagance left Grégoire agape and filled Tannhauser with contempt. He was not immune to architectural beauty, but of late he'd seen too much scorched earth; and the Italians did it better.

Statuary inspired by the Romans abounded, along with ornamented masonry, delicate friezes, and allegories in relief that portrayed the fantasy of Valois genius. Each gallery and ceiling sang the praises of its patrons and recast historic acts of violence and greed as grand myths. All was newly built and on a scale so lavish that Tannhauser did not wonder that Italian cash, at excruciating interest, was paying the bills. He foresaw years of fresh taxes with every step he took. Household officials scuttled back and forth to assuage the whims of the lordly, who were as numerous as they were repellent. As Arnauld strutted towards each new room, footmen bowed and opened twin gilt doors.

'Note that most courtiers merit the opening of only one door,' explained Arnauld.

'Did you hear that, Grégoire? For such as we, you must open both doors.'

'Very amusing. But here, in the jewel box of civilisation, such distinctions are not inconsequential, nor are they empty ceremony. Each detail helps to define one's rank in the court hierarchy. If such details are neglected or ignored, then how can we tell who – or indeed what – a given individual truly is?'

In the salons of the pavilion, as on the streets, an undertow of disquiet was general, but this did not prevent a determined display of the decadence for which the court was famed. Women of outstanding beauty and high station, perhaps in an attempt to raise morale, displayed their tits for the languid gentlemen who sprawled about the furniture, several of whom wore silver cages hung about their necks in which they carried miniature dogs. While a handsome young footman served a reviving cordial, one of the gentlemen stroked the former's crotch bulge with a tongue-moistened forefinger, to a chorus of titters and squeals. The footman bore this ordeal with admirable stoicism and of the cordial he did not spill a drop. The smell of urine lingered everywhere.

'To a provincial this must seem a paradise,' said Arnauld, 'but what you are seeing is an intense struggle to conquer the pyramid of precedence. The ambitious are constantly developing elaborate manoeuvres, either to establish superiority or to undermine rivals, which latter are in endless supply. It may look gay but there is little real enjoyment, rather a perpetual commerce in suspicion, jealousy and spite. I doubt you would do very well here, but that you may take as a compliment.'

As they passed from one wing to another, Tannhauser saw a woman topped with a mass of golden curls hoist up the skirts of her blue silk dress, the pearls on which alone must have cost the price of a modest farm. She squatted over a mound of human faeces piled beneath a staircase.

'What am I seeing now?' he asked. 'An elaborate manoeuvre to establish her superiority? Or her intense struggle to conquer the pyramid of precedence?'

'That is why the court has to move every month from one

palace to another,' tutted Arnauld. 'The stench becomes intolerable and the building has to be aired for fear of the plague.'

'And what do the midget dogs in cages signify?'

'One expects the centre of power to attract the dishonest, the greedy, the venal, the vain and even the wicked,' admitted Arnauld. 'It would be a shabby little court that did not. The elite must be allowed their privileges or what is the point? What is so dispiriting is that nine out of ten courtiers are also stupid, ignorant, talentless and scared. In every respect, except perhaps physical beauty, they are mediocrities. Yet they prosper.'

Swiss and French Guard were stationed so that every room and corridor was watched. Ranks of Swiss steel walled off certain stairways and entrances all together. The apartments of the royal family stood above. They left the *Pavillon du Roi* through a grandiose portico.

A huge courtyard opened out before them, perhaps a hundred paces square. It was walled in by buildings old, new, demolished and half-complete. The north and east wings were ancient, and unlike the new to the south and west, which were created to satisfy the vices of degenerates, the old Louvre was built to be a fortress. Its three conical towers rose above the courtyard's angles at all but the south-west corner. The courtyard swarmed with armed Huguenots.

Most of them were young and milled in truculent cliques. Some affected a silence suggesting righteous anger straining at the end of its tether. Others held vehement debates. Some, probably drunk, yelled insults and threats at the windows of the royal apartments. A handful wore armour. The white cross on Tannhauser's chest marked him out as someone worthy of their scorn. Some had already noticed him and were pointing him out to their fellows.

Tannhauser said, 'Where are the Swiss Guard?'

'His Majesty has posted them indoors, for fear of further inflaming high passions.'

'Where do we go next?'

'The office of the *Plaisirs du Roi*, where we'll find Picart, is in the North Wing.' Arnauld stared across the courtyard as if wishing for an underground tunnel. 'Unless this fury passes we will witness some terrible madness. Don't these fanatics understand? The King is the best friend they've got.'

'Perhaps not for much longer.'

Tannhauser studied the armed cliques. He wondered if he could reach the other side without shedding blood and decided he didn't much care. He set out across the courtyard with Grégoire behind him. He realised that Arnauld had not budged from the portico. He turned and looked at him. Arnauld pointed to a narrow gateway at the centre of the North Wing.

'Today the duty captain of the military household is Dominic Le Tellier, of the Scots Guard.'

'Vicious, dour and intemperate, and given to drink?'

'I doubt the Guard have a real Scotsman left. I was in the Guard for a year. It's a prestige posting, the senior company of the King's Life Guard. We swear to protect His Majesty wherever he goes – that is, to banquets, on hunting trips, to take the waters, and so on. The Life Guard only take to the field of battle when the King himself does so in person.'

'Not exactly veterans then.'

'That does not stop us having a high opinion of ourselves. I'm sure Captain Le Tellier will gladly take you to find Monsieur Picart.'

'Retz said anything I need. You will take me yourself, gladly or not.'

'We could adopt a different route,' offered Arnauld.

'You should've thought of that sooner. I'll walk where I choose.'

'You're as much a fanatic as they are.'

'If we turn tail now, they'll know why. We can't do it, can we, Grégoire?'

Grégoire hoisted the waist of his new red pants. In hindsight, they ended too far short of his knees, but the boy seemed not to mind. Under his arm the package for Carla was a sodden mass.

'No, sire,' he said.

'Then let this creature be your guide.'

'I could drag you across the yard,' said Tannhauser.

Arnauld stepped from the portico as if into a pool of vomit.

'Walk beside me, on my left,' said Tannhauser. 'Imagine you're still a Scots Guard. Head high. Eyes on the gatehouse yonder. If it comes to swordplay, grab Grégoire and run.'

They started across the courtyard, Arnauld almost trotting to match Tannhauser's stride. Though it galled him to do so, Tannhauser navigated the cliques in a series of straight lines designed to avoid a petty confrontation. If any of them moved to block his way, he'd take the man's measure. They skirted several bands without encountering anything worse than stares. When they reached the halfway mark, at the centre of the square, the catcalls began.

'Who's that fat swine?'

'His arse is bigger than the Queen's.'

'I bet it's seen a lot more cock.'

Laughter. To distract Arnauld, Tannhauser struck up a conversation.

'I've been getting about the city on foot but I'm hoping to find a horse.'

'Shit, shit, shit,' said Arnauld.

'Can I get a mount here at the palace?'

'Not without an authorisation.'

'You seem lordly enough to provide one.'

'I'd rather provide a warrant for your arrest.'

Twenty feet ahead, a Huguenot detached himself from the bunch. He stepped into Tannhauser's line of march and crossed his arms over his barrel chest. He was sturdy enough to try such a manoeuvre and angry enough to want to. He had sufficient lumps and scars on his face to prove himself a brawler but men who indulged such ploys as this drew half their courage from their fellows. Tannhauser checked the group to see if the brawler was a decoy deployed to set him up for someone more dangerous. He saw no candidates.

Arnauld quailed. 'What shall we do?'

'Give me some room but don't stop walking.'

Arnauld put his hand on his sword hilt and loosened it in its scabbard.

'Take your hand from your sword and do as I say.'

As they approached the burly Huguenot, Tannhauser did him the favour of altering course so that a confrontation was not inevitable. But the brawler was not to be denied. As he stepped once more into their path, he pointed a finger at Arnauld's face but spoke to Tannhauser.

'What does his arsehole taste like?'

Tannhauser grabbed the extended finger and cranked it backwards. The brawler howled with pain. Tannhauser stepped past him and the brawler, his strength rendered useless, was forced to bend backwards from the waist to avoid the dislocation of his knuckle. With the back of his right leg Tannhauser swept him behind the knee. As the hulk crashed into the flagstones Tannhauser felt the finger snap at the second joint and let go. Tannhauser had barely altered pace. He didn't stop walking nor did he look back. He didn't need to. The fallen brute – and not them – now formed the focus of the courtyard's attention. Arnauld craned his head back over his shoulder.

'Eyes front,' said Tannhauser. 'It'll take him a minute to get to his feet, another to get over his shame. By then we'll be inside. By the time the buffoon gets angry, he'll be a problem for the Guard, not for us.'

They reached the gateway without further incident. On the steps a pair of guards stood grinning from behind their halberds. They nodded to Tannhauser but avoided looking at Arnauld, who was further incensed.

'This kind of insolence is the cross I bear for being so close to Anjou.'

Henri, Duc d'Anjou – a man who by all accounts preferred wearing women's jewellery to wearing a sword – was the King's younger brother and no friend to the Huguenots. He made amends for his decadence with periodic bouts of self-flagellation.

'Ignore it,' said Tannhauser. 'You did well.'

'Really?'

'You didn't lose your head and you were ready to fight.'

Arnauld gained a couple of inches in height and strode on into the lobby. He looked back and forth then set off down a corridor. The windows of the old palace were hardly more than slits in the stone. Lamps and candles struggled to fend off the gloom.

'You're one of Anjou's *mignons*?' asked Tannhauser.

'I am his friend and counsellor. He's in great need of both.'

'Counsellors seem to outnumber footmen round here.'

'The palace is a stew of rivalries and plots.'

'Perhaps that's why.'

'And by the way, my lord Anjou's taste in clothes does not necessarily make him a sodomite, nor does his tolerance of masculine love among some of his favourites. I myself saw him take a maidservant from behind while she was scrubbing the floor, though, I admit, he was intent on proving himself to his mother, who was also witness.'

'Buggery's not a practice to which I've given much thought. Must I?'

Arnauld smirked. 'Tell me, why did you insist on crossing the courtyard?'

'Aren't you glad we did?'

'I do believe I am.'

'There's your answer.'

They entered a large room stacked with the detritus of diverse theatrical productions.

'Wait here,' said Arnauld. 'Christian Picart, yes?'

Tannhauser nodded. While Arnauld went to question the man in charge, Tannhauser studied the room. Artificial mountains, painted silver and topped with thrones, lined one wall. Here were sheaves of scenery designed to recreate the flames of Hell. The masks of demons and imps filled several shelves. Animal costumes and angels' wings hung from racks. A strange sequence of noises drew him deeper into the clutter.

Hidden from view was a large cube covered by a sheet of black velvet. From beneath the cover came rustlings followed by silence, then whispers and croonings, then more silence. Tannhauser lifted the velvet and was greeted by a gale of shrieks so violent he took two steps backward and dragged the cover off with him.

The cage was made of hardwood slats. Its interior teemed with scores of monkeys, each no bigger than a squirrel. Their coats were short and yellowish. Their mouths and eyes were rimmed with black fur, which gave them the look of skulls. Their tiny and perfect fingers clung to the slats, which showed the marks of their teeth. Their ribs heaved rapidly beneath their skins. When they pulled back their lips, their gums were grey. Their eyeballs were shrunken from the rims of their sockets. Some lay on the cage floor, too lethargic to move. Grégoire stared at the creatures with a sigh of pity.

'What are they?'

'They're called monkeys.'

Grégoire made a fair attempt at pronouncing the word.

'They live in trees. These are from the New World, across the ocean.'

'They're scared and hungry. And there's no water in there.'

'Well spotted. Lend me a hand.'

Tannhauser threw the velvet cover aside. With a deafening exacerbation in the violence of the shrieks, he and Grégoire manhandled the cage from its obscure location and left it at the door. Arnauld reappeared and studied the monkeys with distaste.

'What are you doing?'

'The poor creatures are dying of thirst. Here they can let their keepers know it.'

They left the monkeys to raise the roof and Arnauld led them back down the corridor.

'Why do you want to find Picart?' asked Arnauld.

'He can tell me where to find my wife.'

'His nickname is "Petit Christian" because he was born with a deformity of the genitals. He has no testicles and his penis is barely visible, or so I am reliably told. In his younger days this made him sexually desirable to those of more outlandish tastes, whom this place draws as a manure bin flies. Christian submitted to these humiliations in the belief it would advance his ambitions as a playwright. If he had trace of talent as a writer, perhaps it would have.'

'He's a writer?'

'He wrote a single play, crudely borrowed from Gringoire but lacking his wit, and outstanding only for its pretentiousness and vacuity. In some circles these qualities are highly valued but the bloom quickly faded from his buttocks and with it his career. He now pens spiteful pamphlets aimed at dramatists more gifted than he and erotic doggerel for a private clientele. He is most valued for the sexual freak shows that he stages to titillate his former abusers at the court. He can draw on a whole stable of grotesques, midgets, freaks and children, or so I am reliably told. In his official role, however, he is an administrator of court entertainments.'

'Not a man of great importance, then.'

'Who is of lesser importance than a failed playwright?'

Tannhauser said, 'I've never seen a play.'

'After spending half an hour in your company I will never watch one again.'

Arnauld investigated three further offices. Christian had been busy enough that morning but had not been seen at all that afternoon. No one knew where to find him.

'I've done my best,' said Arnauld. 'I'll order Dominic Le Tellier to send his guards to find the wretch. Then, with your permission, I'll attend to my other obligations, which are many.'

Tannhauser nodded.

They returned to the vestibule and stopped. Two men stood in the shaft of light thrown from the gateway, engaged in urgent conversation. Tannhauser could only see the face of the taller, an officer dressed in an expensive buff jerkin and matching hose. His handsome features were set off by a figure-of-eight ruff. He glanced over the other's head and his eyes stopped too suddenly on Tannhauser. Once again Tannhauser had the sensation of being recognised by someone he was certain he had never met.

'At last, there's Dominic Le Tellier,' said Arnauld.

Dominic nodded in their direction and the second man looked over his shoulder. It was the weasel in bottle-green velvet from the Grand Hall. Alarm flitted through his eyes. As in the market, he turned away.

'And that's Petit Christian,' said Arnauld. 'Do you want me to introduce you?'

Tannhauser studied him. There was nothing in Arnauld's eyes to suggest duplicity.

'No. If all goes well, our paths won't cross again. But I won't forget your generosity.'

'Then hear my counsel. Imagine a nest that is home to a family of vicious and overfed rats, all of whose members harbour secret hatreds for each other. Imagine further that the nest is festooned with webs spun from the purest lies, and that on those webs scuttle venomous spiders almost as big as the rats. Finally, imagine that this nest is located in a pit filled with vipers and poisonous toads.'

'You have there the material for a painting that would cheer the King of Spain.'

'I would not joke, because such a nest in such a web in such a pit is where we stand right now. Loyalties turn on a rumour. A sacred oath may be broken on a whim, an old friendship betrayed for a promise that will never be kept. Even an honest man, and they are few, may go to bed sworn to one faction and wake up supporting another because his master has changed allegiance while he slept. In short: leave as soon as you can.'

'I plan to quit the city with the sunrise, if not before.'

'Good.' Arnauld bowed. 'May God go with you.'

'Be careful crossing the courtyard.'

Arnauld smiled. He turned and headed for the gateway.

Tannhauser indicated Christian Picart.

'Grégoire, look at the man talking with the captain. He holds his arms like a monkey.'

Grégoire nodded.

'Have you ever seen him before?'

Grégoire nodded again.

'Where?'

'Across the street from the Red Ox. By the college gate.'

'Was it before or after we ate?'

'Just after. When the girls took us to their shop.'

'Well done. Go and stand by the gateway and watch for young Arnauld crossing the courtyard. If he chances on trouble, come and tell me.'

Tannhauser walked over to Dominic.

'I'll be having a word with this fellow Petit Christian.'

Dominic swallowed the discourtesy without comment.

'As you wish.' He left.

Christian turned with a false smile, as if seeing Tannhauser for the first time.

'Christian Picart, at your service, my lord.'

'Mattias Tannhauser, Comte de La Penautier. I understand you can tell me where my wife, Lady Carla, is lodging.'

'Lady Carla is the guest of Symonne D'Aubray.'

'I'd appreciate directions.'
'I can take you there myself, sire, if you can wait a short while.'
'Who is Symonne D'Aubray?'
'The widow of Roger D'Aubray,' said Christian.
'Both widow and husband are unknown to me.'
'Roger was a merchant and a much admired rector among the Protestants of Paris.'
Christian paused, as if waiting for Tannhauser's reaction to the fact that his wife was lodged with a prominent Huguenot. Given the state of the city, the news was hardly welcome.
Tannhauser said, 'Go on.'
'Roger was murdered last year in the Gastines riots, during the Third War. Symonne has continued his business. She imports gold braid from the Dutch, with considerable success.'
'I am delighted for her. Why does she play hostess to my wife?'
Christian flapped his hands.
'They both are wonderful musicians, as are also the four D'Aubray children. Since the underlying theme of the royal wedding was religious conciliation, a joint performance at the Queen's Ball – a musical allegory so to speak – was considered an excellent idea.'
'By whom?'
'Why, by all involved, including, we must assume, since she accepted the invitation, your good Lady Carla. Due to the recent unfortunate events, the ball, and so the allegory, were cancelled.'
'Who conceived this allegory?'
'I'm afraid I don't know,' said Christian. 'As you will appreciate, over a thousand guests were invited. I was instructed to make the arrangements for Lady Carla, just as I was for many others who had roles in the celebrations.'
'It was your decision to lodge her with Madame D'Aubray?'
'No, no, sire,' said Christian. 'I'm far too humble a servant.'
'Then who was responsible?'
'I am given lists of names and instructions. Long lists. The

means are complex and many by which a name appears on such a list. A friend, a favour, a bribe, a debt. I cannot account for the habits of the court.'

Petit Christian was lying, or, rather, he was concealing what he knew under a mass of factual generalities. Tannhauser was certain that the playwriting pimp had followed him. If he quizzed him on the matter, he would only invite more mendacity. He would not get satisfactory answers short of inflicting fear and pain, which methods were not practicable here.

'Tell me where to find the Lady Carla.'

'You don't want me to act as your guide? I could do so within the hour.'

'Are you trying to delay me?'

'Why of course not, sire.'

'I have a guide. Directions will do.'

Christian's eyes flickered about, as if hoping assistance might arrive.

'For Paris, they are simple enough. Follow the river east to the Place de Grève, which will make itself obvious by the presence of thc Hôtel de Ville and the gallows. Turn due north and you will by turns find the Rue du Temple. You will pass an old chapel and a priory on your right. A little further and you'll see the remains of the old city walls, beyond which lies the Temple itself. Just south of the old walls, on the west side of the street, you will find three fine houses in the new bourgeois style, not more than ten years old. You won't mistake them for they're dressed with an abundance of glass. The middle house is taller than the others and has a double façade. Carved in the lintel above the door are three honeybees. That is the Hôtel D'Aubray.'

'It had better be.'

'I hope the proximity of the Temple reassures you.'

'Why would I be in need of reassurance?'

'I meant only to be courteous, sire. Can I be of any further service?'

Tannhauser said, 'You can tell me where to locate the Collège d'Harcourt.'

It was hardly the subtlest of snares but Petit Christian did not expect it. In the Louvre dissembling was so habitual some didn't know when the canniest move was to be honest.

'There are scores of colleges, sire. I'm afraid I know little about them beyond that most can be found on the Left Bank.'

'I'm told it's near a tavern called the Red Ox.'

'Taverns outnumber the colleges ten to one, sire.'

Tannhauser didn't speak.

Christian shuffled, as if unsure who had outwitted whom. He knew that Tannhauser already knew the location of both buildings, for he had seen him there. Yet he dared not say so. A profession of complete ignorance must have seemed the safest course, and he stuck to it.

Christian said, 'Shall I make enquiries for you, sire?'

'I'll be making my own.'

Christian's lies confirmed he had followed Tannhauser up to the moment he met Retz. The porter must have sent a messenger while Tannhauser was eating. What had Orlandu been doing to justify this espionage? The answer would have to wait. He was eager to see Carla and the details of her location he believed.

'One last matter, but an urgent one. Your monkeys are dying of thirst.'

'My monkeys, sire?'

'See that they're watered and fed. See to it now.'

Christian bowed as he retreated to a safe distance. He turned and scuttled away.

Tannhauser heard footsteps and the rattle of weapons and tack.

'There he is, the swine.'

Tannhauser turned.

Four Huguenot nobles stood in a menacing formation. The eldest was the brawler from the yard; the youngest was a stripling. They were flanked by two Scots Guard. Dominic Le Tellier stood at the fore but off to one side. His features bore no trace of charity. One of the Huguenots held Grégoire by the scruff. A red welt from a slap marked the boy's cheek. Tannhauser took a breath to gentle the sudden urge to violence in his chest.

'So you're men enough to best a helpless boy. Let him go.'

Dominic spoke up. 'These noble gentlemen –'

'These noble gentlemen will let the boy go.'

The Huguenot shoved Grégoire forward.

Tannhauser tilted Grégoire's chin to examine the welt.

'Are you all right, lad?'

Grégoire nodded.

'Stand behind me.'

Tannhauser looked at Dominic.

'Which of these great warriors struck him? Or did the Scots Guard need practice?'

'I chastised him as he deserved,' said Dominic. 'He cheeked me.'

'Can you quote him?'

'Enough of this,' said the brawler. 'Let's get to the business.'

'Wait your turn or draw your sword,' said Tannhauser.

The sword remained untouched. Tannhauser looked back to Dominic.

'Grégoire is my lackey. I'll do the chastising.'

Dominic dipped his head. 'I was unaware, sire. I beg your pardon.'

Tannhauser said, 'Let's to the business.'

'These noble gentlemen claim you have impeached their honour.'

'All four of them? I didn't know I'd had the chance.'

'They are brothers,' said Dominic. 'A slur upon one is a slur upon all.'

Weighty texts expounded the formalities of the Code of the Duello, designed, like the laws of chivalry, and the supposed conventions of war, to preserve the illusions of those too civilised to celebrate pure savagery. Under the Code an insult might be offered by word or deed, and since the latitude extended to either category was wide, duelling was rife. Tannhauser had never taken part in a formal duel; he preferred to set to without the mummery. But unlike the violence indulged by the lower orders, the duel enjoyed the protection of the law, and this he was more than happy to accept.

Dominic indicated the brawler. 'This is Benedykt of –'

'Let him save his name for his tombstone,' said Tannhauser.

This discourtesy further inflamed the brothers. Dominic began again.

'Sieur Benedykt claims that you did injure him in an unjust, cunning and dishonourable manner. It is his right, therefore, without further debate or questioning, to challenge you to the combat – unless you decline the same by making satisfaction for the offence.'

The thought of Carla's disapproval pierced Tannhauser's conscience. If a formal apology, however insincere, would see him on his way, he owed it to her to make it.

He swallowed. 'How might I give this gentleman satisfaction?'

He managed to make the word 'gentleman' sound like 'turd'. All present noted it.

Benedykt stepped forward. 'Submit the first finger of your right hand to be severed.'

Tannhauser felt a burden lift from his shoulders. 'And if I refuse?'

'A refusal would impute me liar,' said Benedykt, 'and in such a state life is unsupportable, till death terminates either my existence or yours.'

A second brother stepped forward.

'However,' said this one, 'since the said dishonourable injury renders my brother unfit for combat, I, Octavien, as his second, claim the right to fight in his stead.'

Octavien was taller and leaner than Benedykt, younger by several years and a sight more handsome. He sported one of the long quadrate rapiers fashionable among those who had never seen a battlefield. The way he wore it said he fancied himself a swordsman. He weighed up Tannhauser's shorter, broader, cut-and-thrust sword with confidence.

Tannhauser looked at Dominic. 'Do you call this lawful?'

Dominic shrugged. 'Seconds often enter the fight.'

Octavien said, 'Consider my brother's offer. In the Duello I have slain five men.'

Tannhauser laughed at him. He turned to Benedykt.

'Let me see this crippling injury.'

Benedykt brandished his index finger in front of Tannhauser's face. It was swollen like a bobbin and mottled black beneath the skin. Tannhauser grabbed it and wrenched it sideways. The pop echoed from the walls, as did Benedykt's agony. Tannhauser felt sundry tissues and sinews snap their moorings. Benedykt fell to his knees, jaws clenched. Tannhauser looked at Octavien.

'Walk away or I will kill you. Think of the stripling.'

Tannhauser nodded at the blond-haired youngster, who was terrified.

Octavien looked at the boy. His resolve wavered.

Benedykt's malice exceeded his pain. 'Octavien! Kill him.'

Tannhauser drove a knee into his chin and splayed him on the floor.

Octavien had turned a shade paler. He put his hand on his rapier.

'Will you be known as a coward?' asked Dominic Le Tellier. 'Or does your challenge stand?'

Tannhauser stared at him.

The captain retreated to stand behind his guards.

Octavien said, 'The challenge stands.'

Tannhauser said, 'Then the choice of time, place and weapons is mine.'

No one took exception to this ordinance of the Code.

'Now is the time. In the courtyard. With those.'

Tannhauser pointed above the gateway. Mounted on the wall

was a pair of ball-and-chain maces, their iron-bound handles crossed. A murmur. Octavien turned paler still.

'I've no skill with such a weapon,' he said.

Neither had Tannhauser. He smiled.

'Then I will instruct you.'

In the courtyard the crowd formed a square in which the duellists would contest their lives. Tannhauser gave his belted sword and dagger to Grégoire.

'Grégoire, you're my second.'

He pointed out Octavien, who was in conference with his kin.

'I'm going to kill that man, do you understand?'

Grégoire passed his tongue over his sundered lip and licked mucus from his gums.

'If anyone else enters this square, you must bring me my sword. Run as fast as you can. Grip it tight by the scabbard and hold the hilt towards me. Show me, now.'

Grégoire kicked his shoes off. Blistered and bleeding toes poked from holes in his new socks. He took a breath and gripped the sword by the scabbard. He proffered the hilt.

'Like this?'

'Perfect. You will make a fine second.'

'Are you going to die, sire?'

'Not today.'

He took up the mace. The chain clanked as he examined the links to make sure they were sound. The tarnished iron sphere, the size of a large apple, was welded about its surface with blunt pyramidal spikes, designed to destroy plate armour. Tannhauser had never used one in combat. He had chosen the mace because the choice itself had defeated Octavien already. He could see the brothers clustered around him, bemoaning the injustice of it all and further undermining his spirit. Benedykt was sobbing, and this time not from pain.

The sun had dropped below the roof of the West Wing, whose new tiles and chimneys were chased in a virulent red. Tannhauser hefted the mace with his left hand and swung it and the swivel spun. He turned his back to the sunset and started forward. Silence fell on the crowd. Tannhauser went down on one knee and crossed himself and rose to his feet. He sensed that many eyes were on him. He took in the Huguenot spectators with a slow turn of his head.

'Does Octavien intend to fight in the dark?

Octavien parted from his brothers, their hands slapping his back, their last words of advice lost in the gloaming. As he approached he took an underhand swing with his mace and shifted to correct his balance as its weight arced behind him. He would aim for the legs, the best of his options. He circled to Tannhauser's right and tried some footwork and again he almost stumbled.

Tannhauser advanced head-on, his mace held limp before his chest, the haft in his left hand. In this fight he was the bigger dog and he stared Octavien full in the eyes. Had he been the underdog, and times enough it had been so, he would have stared at the mouth, for the eyes of the stronger are a dark abyss inviting one to fall. Octavien tried to match his gaze. Tannhauser bore down. Three yards. Octavien still circled, still whirled his mace, the mace still the master of the man, the man puzzled more and more by the fact that Tannhauser did not wield his weapon.

Tannhauser stopped. 'Yield,' he said.

Octavien's lips compressed and signalled his move. He struck out for Tannhauser's thigh, as expected, but he lost control of the tension in the chain, thrusting the haft too eagerly, too far in advance of the arc, and the chain clanked and the swing was slow. Tannhauser pulled his left foot back, avoiding the blow by inches, and grabbed the ball of his mace in the palm of his right hand. The momentum of Octavien's swing wrapped his right arm across his chest.

Tannhauser shifted his weight and lunged, the iron ball cocked to the crook of his neck, like an artilleryman in a wager to heave a cannon shot. With the whole of his bodyweight behind it, he shoved the ball of the mace through Octavien's face. The force of the impact shivered up his arm.

He braced his shoulder and followed through.

The sound of the iron on flesh and bone broke the silence. Blood spattered Tannhauser's chest. Octavien uttered a dull cry and hurtled to the ground. Tannhauser stood over him and looked down. The iron ball had caved in the left side of his face from the upper jaw unto the brow. His eye appeared to have vanished upward, into his skull. The blunt spikes had ploughed runnels through the muscle and skin of his cheek. Bloody teeth gaped through the rents.

'The surgeons have healed worse,' said Tannhauser. 'Yield.'

Octavien shook his head. Tannhauser looked around the square of dour men. None spoke. The brothers were in shock. Tannhauser took the haft in his right hand and raised the mace.

'I ask him a third time to yield.'

Octavien shook his head.

Tannhauser estimated the strength required to punch a hole through the vault of Octavien's skull. His muscles decided they didn't want to do it. There was no morality in the decision, just an arm that had had its fill. He had had his fill, too. He turned away, towards Grégoire.

Grégoire exploded into a sprint.

Tannhauser looked back. Benedykt was lumbering across the square, a sword in his left hand, his face crazed. He let out a roar. At the sound of the roar, the other two brothers followed him. Tannhauser turned to the slap of bare feet as Grégoire extended the sword.

'Brave boy. Get back.'

Tannhauser spun with his sword to meet Benedykt's charge. The brute was beyond reason, his rapier extended to run him through. Tannhauser let him come. As the thrust was launched he side-stepped right and parried, his heavier blade swatting the rapier aside across Benedykt's body. Benedykt's impetus carried him past a pace too far. Tannhauser followed him round, the rotation of his body at one with the rotation of the chain, and lashed the mace through the inner side of Benedykt's lower left leg. He felt the shinbone shatter like porcelain, and to that very bone was Benedykt's weight committed as he stalled his rush. Benedykt fell screaming, on his face.

Tannhauser glanced athwart his shoulder as the third brother ran at his back. Sword and dagger, right and left. He had not the fury of Benedykt, nor the skill of Octavien. Or perhaps he knew that his actions were those of a scoundrel. He hesitated. Tannhauser stepped and spun to his left, covering and parrying, and swung the mace from maximum vantage, all his might in the blow. The ball hummed through its arc and flailed the scoundrel through the ear. His skull collapsed and an eyeball burst from its hole amid bloody fragments. Groans and whistles of approval rose from the crowd and the carcass dropped. Tannhauser turned to the fourth and last of the brothers.

The stripling, for he was fourteen at most, stood with a sword in hand, agape at the speed with which his family had ceased to exist. He was fair of face. He stared at Tannhauser without any notion of what to do. Tannhauser turned to Benedykt, who sat panting like some foundered beast in a swill of gore.

'Die in the blood of your kin, for it's you that spilt it.'

Tannhauser maced him with the motion one might use to split a log and this time his arm was willing. The ball lodged so deep in the vault of Benedykt's skull that it looked as if it had grown out from within it. Blood cascaded over his shoulders in remarkable quantity. Tannhauser let go of the haft and Benedykt dragged it with him as he toppled.

Octavien was choking on the spillings of his shattered sinuses. Tannhauser stabbed him in the heart. He turned and looked at the stripling. He had no intention of harming him, but he gave the lad the respect apt to the field. He had little else to offer.

'No dishonour falls on you. Shall we two make peace?'

The stripling did not answer. He was yet too bewildered for sorrow.

'Tell me your name,' said Tannhauser.

'Justus.' His voice caught. 'They, my brothers, called me Juste. I am the last.'

'Sheath your sword, Juste. Go to your Huguenot companions.'

Juste clenched his lips to stifle his emotion. His sword clattered to the stones.

'Pick it up. Show them some pride. And go.'

Juste's shoulders trembled. He picked up the fallen sword and sheathed it. He turned and stumbled away. Tannhauser spat gall. He watched Dominic Le Tellier approach with his two Scots Guard. Dominic stopped before him.

'By the laws of the Duello the bodies are yours to do with as you please.'

'Feed them to the dogs,' said Tannhauser.

'As you wish.'

The Huguenots forming the square began to break up. Dominic nodded to his guards. Instead of tending to the corpses, they moved to take up positions surrounding Tannhauser, halberds at the ready. To their surprise and unease, Tannhauser moved backwards, at the same time circling so that one was obliged to line up behind the other. Neither of the guards looked like a master, or even a killer. From this angle he could take the first at the knees and be onto the second. He smiled.

'Hold fast,' ordered Dominic.

The guards stopped in their cramped formation.

Tannhauser continued circling, counting on the guards to hold their ground, which they did. As he stopped within range of Dominic, the latter realised his error but could hardly retreat.

'Explain this treachery or there'll be more than the dogs can stomach.'

'You are under arrest,' said Dominic.

'I've broken no law.'

'It is a measure for your own protection.'

'From whom?'

'These men will take you to your quarters, which I assure you are most civilised.'

Tannhauser flicked his sword and stippled the buff of Dominic's chest with Octavien's blood. Dominic flinched. The guards tensed. Again Dominic swallowed the insult. His master had a minion with unusual self-control. It suited Tannhauser to be seen as a man with none.

'I'll not surrender my weapons to anyone lesser in rank than Alberte Gondi.'

This gave Dominic pause. 'A gentleman can be trusted with his sword, even in confinement,' he said. 'You may take your lackey, too. You have my word there need be no more bloodshed.'

'Tell me who you serve.'

'I can't.'

Tannhauser raised the sword point to Dominic's throat.

Dominic said, 'It's enough you know I'd choose your mercy over his.'

Some intrigue was mounted. By whom? Why? He could kill these three with less trouble than the first. He doubted anyone watching would try to prevent him leaving the courtyard. Then he would be on the run, in a strange city on a hot night, where his only friends were a stable boy and two half-grown girls. Could he call on Arnauld or Retz? Both were waist-deep in their own complots, and their fealty to a man who had killed three palace guards could not be counted on. If he ran, he would have to make a fugitive of Carla, too, or she would be questioned. What that might mean was best not imagined.

He saw Petit Christian watching from the gateway.

If he killed Dominic, the deformed playwright would raise the alarm. They knew Carla's location better than Tannhauser did.

He didn't see how he could reach Carla much ahead of a pursuit, if at all. He struggled with his instincts. He had surrendered once before. But he had to do what he reckoned best for Carla. If they had him where they wanted him, at least for the moment, Carla would be safe. Or as safe as she currently was. He thought of Altan Savas and felt some comfort.

'Where am I to be confined?'

'Gentlemen prisoners are kept in the East Wing.'

The cell was a suite comprised of a parlour, a study and a bedroom. Numerous men of noble estate had given their kings reason to confine them. Some had gone from here to the block; others had been released or restored to high office. Coligny himself had once been sentenced to death before regaining favour. There was no reason to embitter a foe who might one day become an ally by shoving him in a dungeon with the rabble.

Dusk had fallen and candles lit the gloom. Tannhauser found a pitcher of water in a basin. He quenched his thirst. He washed the blood from his hands. Sooner or later whoever had concocted this riddle would make himself known. Until then there was no point dwelling on it. His worry for Carla was extreme but she'd survived this long without him; at least he hoped so. In the study he found a desk equipped with pen, paper, sealing wax and ink. He doubted Guzman could read but if Fortune would place the letter in his hand, he could have someone read it for him. Tannhauser wrote the message in both Italian and French.

Guzman, I am imprisoned on the second floor of the East Wing. Get me out, at once. I will be in your debt. Your brother from the Bastion of Castile – Mattias Tannhauser.

He sealed the letter with wax. On the front he printed: *Albert Gondi, Comte de Retz.* Few would dare break the seal, and if Retz was the reader, so much the better.

Carla's image returned to his mind. He shouldn't have made

the voyage to North Africa at such a time. But was the world to grind to a halt on account of a baby? What had Petit Christian told him of Carla's location? He couldn't remember. He turned to ask Grégoire; but the boy had not been present at that conversation. Gallows. A church. Symonne, widow of some Huguenot rabble-raiser.

'Grégoire, where are the gallows?'

'The Place de Grève, sire.'

The Place de Grève. North on the Rue du Temple. It came back to him. A fine house with a double façade. Three honeybees above the door. On the west side of the street. Symonne D'Aubray. He noted it on paper. He put down the pen.

'Grégoire, I've a labour worthy of Hercules to set you.'

'Hercules?'

'A hero of mighty strength and courage.'

'I'm not very strong,' said Grégoire.

'It's the courage that counts. Are you game?'

'Yes.'

The boy had put his shoes back on. Tannhauser tucked his shirt in and tidied up his slops. He wiped his face and hands and smoothed his hair with a wet neckerchief. The lad would not pass as a page to the Duc d'Anjou, but neither did he look like a beggar just in from the street.

'Do you remember Guzman, the Spaniard?'

Grégoire nodded.

'Find him and give him this letter. Bring Guzman back here to set me free.'

Tannhauser held out the letter.

Grégoire took it as if it were a fragment of the True Cross.

'You must walk these halls as if you walked them every day. Hold the letter out before you – just so. Perfect. If anyone stops you, show him the name on the front. Retz is a man of great importance and with luck they won't interfere. If you are asked any questions, recite an *Ave*.'

'An *Ave Maria*?'

'Exactly. Shout it as loud as you can and with passion. No one will understand a word you say. Do you remember the first grand building we entered?'

'Where the men wore dogs around their necks?'

'That's the place that Retz is most likely to be – upstairs in conference with the King – and that's where you'll find Guzman, if you find him at all.'

'I will find him.'

'If you don't, do not think you have failed me.'

'I will not fail you.'

Tannhauser summoned the guard by means of a chain by the heavy door that rang a bell.

'My page has an urgent message for the Comte de Retz.'

The guard frowned at Grégoire, who held out the letter like a talisman.

'I was with Retz this afternoon,' said Tannhauser. 'His mood is testy. Tell me your name.'

'I'll see your page through the gates at once, sire.'

Tannhauser tossed the guard a silver franc. He motioned to Grégoire.

'Good luck, lad.'

Grégoire bowed. The door closed. The key turned.

The bedroom was dark. By the candlelight from the parlour Tannhauser glimpsed a bed. His exhaustion was so deep he was almost glad to be in gaol. He stripped his weapons, his boots and his shirt, and did what good sense demanded. He lay on the bed, and thought not of his troubles, and fell into a sound sleep.

www.vintage-books.co.uk